SKETCHES BY BOZ

THE ELECTION FOR BEADLE.

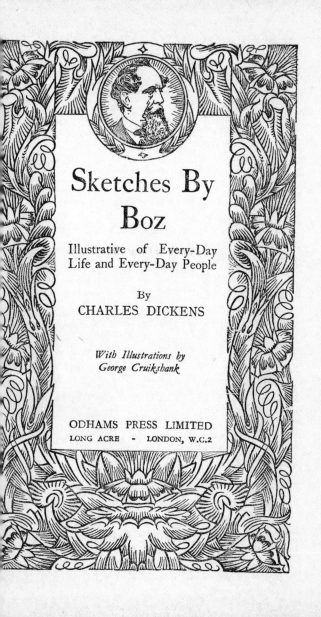

Sketches By Boz

Illustrative of Every-Day Life and Every-Day People

By
CHARLES DICKENS

*With Illustrations by
George Cruikshank*

ODHAMS PRESS LIMITED
LONG ACRE - LONDON, W.C.2

Printed in Great Britain

PREFACE

THE whole of these Sketches were written and published, one by one, when I was a very young man. They were collected and republished while I was still a very young man; and sent into the world with all their imperfections (a good many) on their heads.

They comprise my first attempt at authorship—with the exception of certain tragedies achieved at the mature age of eight or ten, and represented with great applause to overflowing nurseries. I am conscious of their often being extremely crude and ill-considered, and bearing obvious marks of haste and inexperience; particularly in that section of the present volume which is comprised under the general head of Tales.

But as this collection is not originated now, and was very leniently and favourably received when it was first made, I have not felt it right either to remodel or expunge, beyond a few words and phrases here and there.

CONTENTS

OUR PARISH

CHAPTER   PAGE

I. THE BEADLE. THE PARISH ENGINE. THE
  SCHOOLMASTER 13
II. THE CURATE. THE OLD LADY. THE HALF-
  PAY CAPTAIN 17
III. THE FOUR SISTERS 22
IV. THE ELECTION FOR BEADLE . . . 26
V. THE BROKER'S MAN 32
VI. THE LADIES' SOCIETIES 39
VII. OUR NEXT-DOOR NEIGHBOUR . . . 44

SCENES

I. THE STREETS—MORNING 50
II. THE STREETS—NIGHT 54
III. SHOPS AND THEIR TENANTS . . . 58
IV. SCOTLAND YARD 62
V. SEVEN DIALS 66
VI. MEDITATIONS IN MONMOUTH STREET . . 71
VII. HACKNEY-COACH STANDS 77
VIII. DOCTORS' COMMONS 80
IX. LONDON RECREATIONS 85
X. THE RIVER 89
XI. ASTLEY'S 95
XII. GREENWICH FAIR 100
XIII. PRIVATE THEATRES 107
XIV. VAUXHALL GARDENS BY DAY . . . 112
XV. EARLY COACHES 116
XVI. OMNIBUSES 121
XVII. THE LAST CAB-DRIVER AND THE FIRST OMNI-
  BUS CAD 124
XVIII. A PARLIAMENTARY SKETCH . . . 132
XIX. PUBLIC DINNERS 142
XX. THE FIRST OF MAY 146
XXI. BROKERS' AND MARINE-STORE SHOPS . . 153
XXII. GIN-SHOPS 156
XXIII. THE PAWNBROKER'S SHOP . . . 163
XXIV. CRIMINAL COURTS 169
XXV. A VISIT TO NEWGATE 173

12 CONTENTS

CHARACTERS

CHAPTER   PAGE
I. THOUGHTS ABOUT PEOPLE 185
II. A CHRISTMAS DINNER 189
III. THE NEW YEAR 193
IV. MISS EVANS AND THE EAGLE 197
V. THE PARLOUR ORATOR 200
VI. THE HOSPITAL PATIENT 204
VII. THE MISPLACED ATTACHMENT OF MR. JOHN
      DOUNCE 210
VIII. THE MISTAKEN MILLINER. A TALE OF AMBITION 215
IX. THE DANCING ACADEMY 220
X. SHABBY-GENTEEL PEOPLE 225
XI. MAKING A NIGHT OF IT 228
XII. THE PRISONERS' VAN 233

TALES

I. THE BOARDING-HOUSE.   CHAPTER THE FIRST 236
                                CHAPTER THE SECOND 249
II. MR. MINNS AND HIS COUSIN 267
III. SENTIMENT 276
IV. THE TUGGS'S AT RAMSGATE 285
V. HORATIO SPARKINS 302
VI. THE BLACK VEIL 317
VII. THE STEAM EXCURSION 327
VIII. THE GREAT WINGLEBURY DUEL . . . 347
IX. MRS. JOSEPH PORTER 362
X. A PASSAGE IN THE LIFE OF MR. WATKINS
     TOTTLE.   CHAPTER THE FIRST . . 370
                  CHAPTER THE SECOND . . 387
XI. THE BLOOMSBURY CHRISTENING . . . 400
XII. THE DRUNKARD'S DEATH 414

SKETCHES BY BOZ

OUR PARISH

CHAPTER I: *The Beadle. The Parish Engine. The School-master*

How much is conveyed in those two short words—"The Parish!" And with how many tales of distress and misery, of broken fortune and ruined hopes, too often of unrelieved wretchedness and successful knavery, are they associated! A poor man, with small earnings, and a large family, just manages to live on from hand to mouth, and to procure food from day to day; he has barely sufficient to satisfy the present cravings of nature, and can take no heed of the future. His taxes are in arrear, quarter-day passes by, another quarter-day arrives: he can procure no more quarter for himself, and is summoned by—the parish. His goods are distrained, his children are crying with cold and hunger, and the very bed on which his sick wife is lying, is dragged from beneath her. What can he do? To whom is he to apply for relief? To private charity? To benevolent individuals? Certainly not —there is his parish. There are the parish vestry, the parish infirmary, the parish surgeon, the parish officers, the parish beadle. Excellent institutions, and gentle, kind-hearted men. The woman dies—she is buried by the parish. The children have no protector—they are taken care of by the parish. The man first neglects, and afterwards cannot obtain, work—he is relieved by the parish; and when distress and drunkenness have done their work upon him, he is maintained, a harmless babbling idiot, in the parish asylum.

The parish beadle is one of the most, perhaps *the* most, important member of the local administration. He is not so well off as the churchwardens, certainly, nor is he so learned as the vestry-clerk, nor does he order things quite so much his own way as either of them. But his power is very great, notwithstanding; and the dignity of his office is never impaired by the absence of efforts on his part to maintain it. The beadle of our parish is a splendid fellow. It is quite delightful to hear him, as he explains the state of the existing poor laws to the deaf old women in the board-room passage on business nights; and to hear what he said to the senior churchwarden, and what the senior churchwarden said to him; and what "we" (the beadle and the other gentlemen) came to the determination of doing. A miserable-looking woman is called into the board-room, and represents a case of extreme destitution, affecting herself—a widow, with six small children. "Where do you live?" inquires one of the overseers. "I rents a two-pair back, gentlemen, at Mrs. Brown's, Number 3, Little King William's Alley, which has lived there this fifteen year, and knows me to be very hard-working and industrious, and when my poor husband was alive, gentlemen, as died in the hospital——" "Well, well," interrupts the overseer, taking a note of the address, "I'll send Simmons, the beadle, to-morrow morning, to ascertain whether your story is correct: and if so, I suppose you must have an order into the House. Simmons, go to this woman's the first thing to-morrow morning, will you?" Simmons bows assent, and ushers the woman out. Her previous admiration of "the board" (who all sit behind great books, and with their hats on) fades into nothing before her respect for her lace-trimmed conductor; and her account of what has passed inside, increases—if that be possible—the marks of respect, shown by the assembled crowd, to that solemn functionary. As to taking out a summons, it's quite a hope-less case if Simmons attends it, on behalf of the parish. He knows all the titles of the Lord Mayor by heart; states the case without a single stammer: and it is even reported that on one occasion he ventured to make a joke, which the Lord Mayor's head footman (who happened to be present) after-wards told an intimate friend, confidentially, was almost equal to one of Mr. Hobler's.

See him again on Sunday in his state-coat and cocked-hat, with a large-headed staff for show in his left hand, and a small cane for use in his right. How pompously he marshals the children into their places! and how demurely the little urchins look at him askance as he surveys them when they are all seated, with a glare of the eye peculiar to beadles! The churchwardens and overseers being duly installed in their curtained pews, he seats himself on a mahogany bracket, erected expressly for him at the top of the aisle, and divides his attention between his prayer-book and the boys. Suddenly, just at the commencement of the communion service, when the whole congregation is hushed into a profound silence, broken only by the voice of the officiating clergyman, a penny is heard to ring on the stone floor of the aisle with astounding clearness. Observe the generalship of the beadle. His involuntary look of horror is instantly changed into one of perfect indifference, as if he were the only person present who had not heard the noise. The artifice succeeds. After putting forth his right leg now and then, as a feeler, the victim who dropped the money ventures to make one or two distinct dives after it; and the beadle, gliding softly round, salutes his little round head, when it again appears above the seat, with divers double knocks, administered with the cane before noticed, to the intense delight of three young men in an adjacent pew, who cough violently at intervals until the conclusion of the sermon.

Such are a few traits of the importance and gravity of a parish-beadle—a gravity which has never been disturbed in any case that has come under our observation, except when the services of that particularly useful machine, a parish fire-engine, are required: then indeed all is bustle. Two little boys run to the beadle as fast as their legs will carry them, and report from their own personal observation that some neighbouring chimney is on fire; the engine is hastily got out, and a plentiful supply of boys being obtained, and harnessed to it with ropes, away they rattle over the pavement, the beadle, running—we do not exaggerate—running at the side, until they arrive at some house, smelling strongly of soot, at the door of which the beadle knocks with considerable gravity for half-an-hour. No attention being paid to these manual applications, and the turn-cock having turned on the water, the engine turns off amidst the shouts of the boys; it pulls up once more at the workhouse, and the beadle "pulls up" the unfortunate householder next day, for the amount of his legal reward. We never saw a parish engine at a regular fire but once. It came up in gallant style—three miles and a half an hour, at least; there was a capital supply of water, and it was first on the spot. Bang went the pumps—the people cheered—the beadle perspired profusely; but it was unfortunately discovered, just as they were going to put the fire out, that nobody understood the process by which the engine was filled with water; and that eighteen boys, and a man, had exhausted themselves in pumping for twenty minutes, without producing the slightest effect!

The personages next in importance to the beadle, are the master of the workhouse and the parish schoolmaster. The vestry-clerk, as everybody knows, is a short, pudgy little man, in black, with a thick gold watch-chain of considerable length, terminating in two large seals and a key. He is an attorney, and generally in a bustle; at no time more so, than when he is hurrying to some parochial meeting, with his gloves crumpled up in one hand, and a large red book under the other arm. As to the churchwardens and overseers, we exclude them altogether, because all we know of them is, that they are usually respectable tradesmen, who wear hats with brims inclined to flatness, and who occasionally testify in gilt letters on a blue ground, in some conspicuous part of the church, to the important fact of a gallery having been enlarged and beautified, or an organ rebuilt.

The master of the workhouse is not, in our parish—nor is he usually in any other—one of that class of men the better part of whose existence has passed away, and who drag out the remainder in some inferior situation, with just enough thought of the past, to feel degraded by, and discontented with, the present. We are unable to guess precisely to our own satisfaction what station the man can have occupied before; we should think he had been an inferior sort of attorney's clerk, or else the master of a national school— whatever he was, it is clear his present position is a change for the better. His income is small certainly, as the rusty black coat and threadbare velvet collar demonstrate: but then he lives free of house-rent, has a limited allowance of coals and candles, and an almost unlimited allowance of authority in his petty kingdom. He is a tall, thin, bony man; always wears shoes and black cotton stockings with his surtout; and eyes you, as you pass his parlour-window, as if he wished you were a pauper, just to give you a specimen of his power. He is an admirable specimen of a small tyrant: morose, brutish, and ill-tempered; bullying to his inferiors, cringing to his superiors, and jealous of the influence and authority of the beadle.

Our schoolmaster is just the very reverse of this amiable official. He has been one of those men one occasionally hears of, on whom misfortune seems to have set her mark; nothing he ever did, or was concerned in, appears to have prospered. A rich old relation who had brought him up, and openly announced his intention of providing for him, left him 10,000*l.* in his will, and revoked the bequest in a codicil. Thus unexpectedly reduced to the necessity of providing for himself, he procured a situation in a public office. The young clerks below him, died off as if there were a plague among them; but the old fellows over his head, for the reversion of whose places he was anxiously waiting, lived on and on, as if they were immortal. He speculated and lost. He speculated again, and won—but never got his money. His talents were great; his disposition, easy, generous and liberal. His friends profited by the one, and abused the other. Loss succeeded loss; misfortune crowded on misfortune; each successive day brought him nearer the verge of hopeless penury, and the quondam friends who had been warmest in their professions, grew strangely cold and indifferent. He had children whom he loved, and a wife on whom he doted. The former turned their backs on him; the latter died broken-hearted. He went with the stream—it had ever been his failing, and he had not courage sufficient to bear up against so many shocks—he had never cared for himself, and the only being who had cared for him, in his poverty and distress, was spared to him no longer. It was at this period that he applied for parochial relief. Some kind-hearted man who had known him in happier times, chanced to be churchwarden that year, and through his interest he was appointed to his present situation.

He is an old man now. Of the many who once crowded round him in all the hollow friendship of boon-companionship, some have died, some have fallen like himself, some have prospered —all have forgotten him. Time and misfortune have mercifully been permitted to impair his memory, and use has habituated him to his present condition. Meek, uncomplaining, and zealous in the discharge of his duties, he has been allowed to hold his situation long beyond the usual period; and he will no doubt continue to hold it, until infirmity renders him incapable, or death releases him. As the grey-headed old man feebly paces up and down the sunny side of the little court-yard between school hours, it would be difficult, indeed, for the most intimate of his former friends to recognise their once gay and happy associate, in the person of the Pauper Schoolmaster.

CHAPTER II: *The Curate. The Old Lady. The Half-Pay Captain*

WE commenced our last chapter with the beadle of our parish, because we are deeply sensible of the importance and dignity of his office. We will begin the present, with the clergyman. Our curate is a young gentleman of such prepossessing appearance, and fascinating manners, that within one month after his first appearance in the parish, half the young-lady inhabitants were melancholy with religion, and the other half, desponding with love. Never were so many young ladies seen in our parish-church on Sunday before; and never had the little round angels' faces on Mr. Tomkins's monument in the side aisle, beheld such devotion on earth as they all exhibited. He was about five-and-twenty when he first came to astonish the parishioners. He parted his hair on the centre of his forehead in the form of a Norman arch, wore a brilliant of the first water on the fourth finger of his left hand (which he always applied to his left cheek when he read prayers), and had a deep sepulchral voice of unusual solemnity. Innumerable were the calls made by prudent mammas on our new curate, and innumerable the invitations with which he was assailed, and which, to do him justice, he readily accepted. If his manner in the pulpit had created an impression in his favour, the sensation was increased tenfold, by his appearance in private circles. Pews in the immediate vicinity of the pulpit or reading-desk rose in value; sittings in the centre aisle were at a premium: an inch of room in the front row of the gallery could not be procured for love or money; and some people even went so far as to assert, that the three Miss Browns, who had an obscure family pew just behind the churchwardens', were detected, one Sunday, in the free seats by the communion-table, actually lying in wait for the curate as he passed to the vestry! He began to preach extempore sermons, and even grave papas caught the infection. He got out of bed at half-past twelve o'clock one winter's night, to half-baptize a washerwoman's child in a slop-basin, and the gratitude of the parishioners knew no bounds—the very churchwardens grew generous, and insisted on the parish defraying the expense of the watch-box on wheels, which the new curate had ordered for himself, to perform the funeral service in, in wet weather. He sent three pints of gruel and a quarter of a pound of tea to a poor woman who had been brought to bed of four small children, all at once—the parish were charmed. He got up a subscription for her—the woman's fortune was made. He spoke for one hour and twenty-five minutes, at an anti-slavery meeting at the Goat and Boots—the enthusiasm was at its height. A proposal was set on foot for presenting the curate with a piece of plate, as a mark of esteem for his valuable services rendered to the parish. The list of subscriptions was filled up in no time; the contest was, not who should escape the contribution, but who should be the foremost to subscribe. A splendid silver inkstand was made, and engraved with an appropriate inscription; the curate was invited to a public breakfast, at the before-mentioned Goat and Boots; the inkstand was presented in a neat speech by Mr. Gubbins, the ex-church-warden, and acknowledged by the curate in terms which drew tears into the eyes of all present—the very waiters were melted.

One would have supposed that, by this time, the theme of universal admiration was lifted to the very pinnacle of popularity. No such thing. The curate began to cough; four fits of coughing one morning between the Litany and the Epistle, and five in the afternoon service. Here was a discovery—the curate was consumptive. How interestingly melancholy! If the young ladies were energetic before, their sympathy and solicitude now knew no bounds. Such a man as the curate—such a dear—such a perfect love—to be consumptive! It was too much. Anonymous presents of black-currant jam, and lozenges, elastic waistcoats, bosom friends, and warm stockings, poured in upon the curate until he was as completely fitted out, with winter clothing, as if he were on the verge of an expedition to the North Pole: verbal bulletins of the state of his health were circulated throughout the parish half-a-dozen times a day; and the curate was in the very zenith of his popularity.

About this period, a change came over the spirit of the parish. A very quiet, respectable, dozing old gentleman, who had officiated in our chapel-of-ease for twelve years previously, died one fine morning, without having given any notice whatever of his intention. This circumstance gave rise to counter-sensation the first; and the arrival of his successor occasioned counter-sensation the second. He was a pale, thin, cadaverous man, with large black eyes, and long straggling black hair: his dress was slovenly in the extreme, his manner ungainly, his doctrines startling; in short, he was in every respect the antipodes of the curate. Crowds of our female parishioners flocked to hear him: at first, because he was *so* odd-looking, then because his face was *so* expressive, then because he preached *so* well; and at last, because they really thought that, after all, there was something about him which it was quite impossible to describe. As to the curate, he was all very well; but certainly, after all, there was no denying that—that—in short, the curate wasn't a novelty, and the other clergyman was. The inconstancy of public opinion is proverbial: the congregation migrated one by one. The curate coughed till he was black in the face—it was in vain. He respired with difficulty—it was equally ineffectual in awakening sympathy. Seats are once again to be had in any part of our parish church, and the chapel-of-ease is going to be enlarged as it is crowded to suffocation every Sunday!

The best known and most respected among our parishioners, is an old lady, who resided in our parish long before our name was registered in the list of baptisms. Our parish is a suburban one, and the old lady lives in a neat row of houses in the most airy and pleasant part of it. The house is her own; and it, and everything about it, except the old lady herself, who looks a little older than she did ten years ago, is in just the same state as when the old gentleman was living. The little front parlour, which is the old lady's ordinary sitting-room, is a perfect picture of quiet neatness: the carpet is covered with brown Holland, the glass and picture-frames are carefully enveloped in yellow muslin; the table-covers are never taken off, except when the leaves are turpentined and bees' waxed, an operation which is regularly commenced every other morning at half-past nine o'clock—and the little nicnacs are always arranged in precisely the same manner. The greater part of these are presents from little girls whose parents live in the same row; but some of them, such as the two old-fashioned watches (which never keep the same time, one being always a quarter of an hour too slow, and the other a quarter of an hour too fast), the little picture of the Princess Charlotte and Prince Leopold as they appeared in the Royal

Box at Drury Lane Theatre, and others of the same class, have been in the old lady's possession for many years. Here the old lady sits with her spectacles on, busily engaged in needle-work—near the window in summer time; and if she sees you coming up the steps, and you happen to be a favourite, she trots out to open the street-door for you before you knock, and as you must be fatigued after that hot walk, insists on your swallowing two glasses of sherry before you exert yourself by talking. If you call in the evening you will find her cheerful, but rather more serious than usual, with an open Bible on the table, before her, of which "Sarah," who is just as neat and methodical as her mistress, regularly reads two or three chapters in the parlour aloud.

The old lady sees scarcely any company, except the little girls before noticed, each of whom has always a regular fixed day for a periodical tea-drinking with her, to which the child looks forward as the greatest treat of its existence. She seldom visits at a greater distance than the next door but one on either side; and when she drinks tea here, Sarah runs out first and knocks a double-knock, to prevent the possibility of her "Missis's" catching cold by having to wait at the door. She is very scrupulous in returning these little invitations, and when she asks Mr. and Mrs. So-and-so, to meet Mr. and Mrs. Somebody-else, Sarah and she dust the urn, and the best china tea-service, and the Pope Joan board; and the visitors are received in the drawing-room in great state. She has but few relations, and they are scattered about in different parts of the country, and she seldom sees them. She has a son in India, whom she always describes to you as a fine, handsome fellow—so like the profile of his poor dear father over the sideboard, but the old lady adds, with a mournful shake of the head, that he has always been one of her greatest trials, and that indeed he once almost broke her heart; but it pleased God to enable her to get the better of it, and she would prefer your never mentioning the subject to her again. She has a great number of pensioners: and on Saturday, after she comes back from market, there is a regular levee of old men and women in the passage, waiting for their weekly gratuity. Her name always heads the list of any benevolent subscription, and hers are always the most liberal donations to the Winter Coal and Soup Distribution Society. She sub-scribed twenty pounds towards the erection of an organ in our parish church, and was so overcome the first Sunday the children sang to it, that she was obliged to be carried out by the pew-opener. Her entrance into church on Sunday is always the signal for a little bustle in the side aisle, occa-sioned by a general rise among the poor people, who bow and curtsey until the pew-opener has ushered the old lady into her accustomed seat, dropped a respectful curtsey, and shut the door: and the same ceremony is repeated on her leaving church, when she walks home with the family next door but one, and talks about the sermon all the way, invariably opening the conversation by asking the youngest boy where the text was.

Thus, with the annual variation of a trip to some quiet place on the sea-coast, passes the old lady's life. It has rolled on in the same unvarying and benevolent course for many years now, and must at no distant period be brought to its final close. She looks forward to its termination, with calmness and without apprehension. She has everything to hope and nothing to fear.

A very different personage, but one who has rendered himself very conspicuous in our parish, is one of the old lady's next-door neighbours. He is an old naval officer on half-pay, and his bluff and unceremonious behaviour disturbs the old lady's domestic economy, not a little. In the first place he *will* smoke cigars in the front court, and when he wants something to drink with them—which is by no means an uncommon circumstance—he lifts up the old lady's knocker with his walking-stick, and demands to have a glass of table ale handed over the rails. In addition to this cool proceeding, he is a bit of a Jack of all trades, or to use his own words, "a regular Robinson Crusoe;" and nothing delights him better than to experimentalise on the old lady's property. One morning he got up early, and planted three or four roots of full-grown marigolds in every bed of her front garden, to the inconceivable astonishment of the old lady, who actually thought when she got up and looked out of the window, that it was some strange eruption which had come out in the night. Another time he took to pieces the eight-day clock on the front landing, under pretence of cleaning the works, which he put together again, by some undiscovered process in so wonderful a manner, that the large hand has done nothing but trip up the little one ever since. Then he took to breeding silk-worms, which he *would* bring in two or three times a day, in little paper boxes, to show the old lady, generally dropping a worm or two at every visit. The consequence was, that one morning a very stout silk-worm was discovered in the act of walking upstairs—probably with the view of inquiring after his friends, for, on further inspection, it appeared that some of his companions had already found their way to every room in the house. The old lady went to the seaside in despair, and during her absence he completely effaced the name from her brass door-plate, in his attempts to polish it with aqua-fortis.

But all this is nothing to his seditious conduct in public life. He attends every vestry meeting that is held; always opposes the constituted authorities of the parish, denounces the profligacy of the churchwardens, contests legal points against the vestry-clerk, *will* make the tax-gatherer call for his money till he won't call any longer, and then he sends it; finds fault with the sermon every Sunday, says that the organist ought to be ashamed of himself, offers to back himself for any amount to sing the psalms better than all the children put together, male and female; and, in short, conducts himself in the most turbulent and uproarious manner. The worst of it is, that having a high regard for the old lady, he wants to make her a convert to his views, and therefore walks into her little parlour with his newspaper in his hand, and talks violent politics by the hour. He is a charitable, open-hearted old fellow at bottom, after all; so, although he puts the old lady a little out occasionally, they agree very well in the main, and she laughs as much at each feat of his handiwork when it is all over as anybody else.

CHAPTER III: *The Four Sisters*

THE row of houses in which the old lady and her troublesome neighbour reside, comprises, beyond all doubt, a greater number of characters within its circumscribed limits than all the rest of the parish put together. As we cannot, consistently with our present plan, however, extend the number of our parochial sketches beyond six, it will be better, perhaps, to select the most peculiar, and to introduce them at once without further preface.

The four Miss Willises, then, settled in our parish thirteen years ago. It is a melancholy reflection that the old adage, "time and tide wait for no man," applies with equal force to the fairer portion of the creation; and willingly would we conceal the fact, that even thirteen years ago, the Miss Willises were far from juvenile. Our duty as faithful parochial chroniclers, however, is paramount to every other consideration, and we are bound to state that thirteen years since, the authorities in matrimonial cases considered the youngest Miss Willis in a very precarious state, while the eldest sister was positively given over, as being far beyond all human hope. Well, the Miss Willises took a lease of the house; it was fresh painted and papered from top to bottom: the paint inside was all wainscoted, the marble all cleaned, the old grates taken down, and register-stoves, you could see to dress by, put up; four trees were planted in the back garden, several small baskets of gravel sprinkled over the front one, vans of elegant furniture arrived, spring blinds were fitted to the windows, carpenters who had been employed in the various preparations, alterations, and repairs, made confidential statements to the different maid-servants in the row, relative to the magnificent scale on which the Miss Willises were commencing; the maidservants told their "Missises," the Missises told their friends, and vague rumours were circulated throughout the parish, that No. 25, in Gordon Place, had been taken by four maiden ladies of immense property.

At last the Miss Willises moved in; and then the "calling" began. The house was the perfection of neatness—so were the four Miss Willises. Everything was formal, stiff and cold—so were the four Miss Willises. Not a single chair of the whole set was ever seen out of its place—not a single Miss Willis of the whole four was ever seen out of hers. There they always sat, in the same places, doing precisely the same things at the same hour. The eldest Miss Willis used to knit, the second to draw, the two others to play duets on the piano. They seemed to have no separate existence, but to have made up their minds just to winter through life together. They were three long graces in drapery, with the addition, like a school-dinner, of another long grace afterwards—the three fates with another sister—the Siamese twins multiplied by two. The eldest Miss Willis grew bilious—the four Miss Willises grew bilious immediately. The eldest Miss Willis grew ill-tempered and religious—the four Miss Willises were ill-tempered and religious directly. Whatever the eldest did, the others did, and whatever anybody else did, they all disapproved of; and thus they vegetated—living in Polar harmony among themselves, and, as they sometimes went out, or saw company "in a quiet-way" at home, occasionally iceing the neighbours. Three years passed over in this way, when an unlooked for and extraordinary phenomenon occurred. The Miss Willises showed symptoms of summer, the frost gradually broke up; a complete thaw took place. Was it possible? one of the four Miss Willises was going to be married!

Now, where on earth the husband came from, by what feelings the poor man could have been actuated, or by what process of reasoning the four Miss Willises succeeded in persuading themselves that it was possible for a man to marry one of them, without marrying them all, are questions too profound for us to resolve: certain it is, however, that the visits of Mr. Robinson (a gentleman in a public office, with a good salary and a little property of his own, beside) were received—that the four Miss Willises were courted in due form by the said Mr. Robinson—that the neighbours were perfectly frantic in their anxiety to discover which of the four Miss Willises was the fortunate fair, and that the difficulty they experienced in solving the problem was not at all lessened by the announcement of the eldest Miss Willis,—"*We* are going to marry Mr. Robinson."

It was very extraordinary. They were so completely identified, the one with the other, that the curiosity of the whole row—even of the old lady herself—was roused almost beyond endurance. The subject was discussed at every little card-table and tea-drinking. The old gentleman of silkworm notoriety did not hesitate to express his decided opinion that Mr. Robinson was of Eastern descent, and contemplated marrying the whole family at once; and the row, generally, shook their heads with considerable gravity, and declared the business to be very mysterious. They hoped it might all end well;—it certainly had a very singular appearance, but still it would be uncharitable to express any opinion without good grounds to go upon, and certainly the Miss Willises were *quite* old enough to judge for themselves, and to be sure people ought to know their own business best, and so forth.

At last, one fine morning, at a quarter before eight o'clock, A.M., two glass-coaches drove up to the Miss Willises' door, at which Mr. Robinson had arrived in a cab ten minutes before, dressed in a light-blue coat and double-milled kersey panta-loons, white neckerchief, pumps, and dress-gloves, his manner denoting, as appeared from the evidence of the housemaid at No. 23, who was sweeping the door-steps at the time, a con-siderable degree of nervous excitement. It was also hastily reported on the same testimony, that the cook who opened the door, wore a large white bow of unusual dimensions, in a much smarter headdress than the regulation cap to which the Miss Willises invariably restricted the somewhat excursive tastes of female servants in general.

The intelligence spread rapidly from house to house. It was quite clear that the eventful morning had at length arrived; the whole row stationed themselves behind their first and second-floor blinds, and waited the result in breathless expectation.

At last the Miss Willises' door opened; the door of the first glass-coach did the same. Two gentlemen, and a pair of ladies to correspond—friends of the family, no doubt; up went the steps, bang went the door, off went the first glass-coach, and up came the second.

The street door opened again; the excitement of the whole row increased—Mr. Robinson and the eldest Miss Willis. "I thought so," said the lady at No. 19; "I always said it was *Miss* Willis!"—"Well, I never!" ejaculated the young lady at No. 18 to the young lady at No. 17—"Did you ever, dear!" responded the young lady at No. 17 to the young lady at No. 18. "It's too ridiculous!" exclaimed a spinster of an *un*certain age, at No. 16, joining in the conversation. But who shall portray the astonishment of Gordon Place, when Mr. Robinson handed in *all* the Miss Willises, one after the other, and then squeezed himself into an acute angle of the glass-coach, which forthwith proceeded at a brisk pace, after the other glass-coach, which other glass-coach had itself proceeded, at a brisk pace, in the direction of the parish church. Who shall depict the perplexity of the clergyman, when *all* the Miss Willises knelt down at the communion table, and repeated the responses incidental to the marriage service in an audible voice—or who shall describe the confusion which prevailed, when—even after the difficulties thus occasioned had been adjusted—*all* the Miss Willises went into hysterics at the conclusion of the ceremony, until the sacred edifice resounded with their united wailings!

As the four sisters and Mr. Robinson continued to occupy the same house after this memorable occasion, and as the married sister, whoever she was, never appeared in public without the other three, we are not quite clear that the neighbours ever would have discovered the real Mrs. Robinson, but for a circumstance of the most gratifying description, which *will* happen occasionally in the best regulated families. Three quarter-days elapsed, and the row, on whom a new light appeared to have been bursting for some time, began to speak with a sort of implied confidence on the subject, and to wonder how Mrs. Robinson—the youngest Miss Willis that was— got on; and servants might be seen running up the steps, about nine or ten o'clock every morning, with "Missis's compliments, and wishes to know how Mrs. Robinson finds herself this morning?" And the answer always was, "Mrs. Robinson's compliments, and she's in very good spirits, and doesn't find herself any worse." The piano was heard no longer, the knitting-needles were laid aside, drawing was neglected, and mantua-making and millinery, on the smallest scale imaginable, appeared to have become the favourite amusement of the whole family. The parlour wasn't quite as tidy as it used to be, and if you called in the morning, you would see lying on a table, with an old newspaper carelessly thrown over them, two or three particularly small caps, rather larger than if they had been made for a moderate-sized doll, with a small piece of lace, in the shape of a horse-shoe, let in behind: or perhaps a white robe, not very large in circumference, but very much out of proportion in point of length, with a little tucker round the top, and a frill round the bottom; and once when we called, we saw a long white roller, with a kind of blue margin down each side, the probable use of which, we were at a loss to conjecture. Then we fancied that Mr. Dawson, the surgeon, &c., who displays a large lamp with a different colour in every pane of glass, at the corner of the row, began to be knocked up at night oftener than he used to be; and once we were very much alarmed by hearing a hackney-coach stop at Mrs. Robinson's door, at half-past two o'clock in the morning, out of which there emerged a fat old woman, in a cloak and nightcap, with a bundle in one hand, and a pair of pattens in the other, who looked as if she had been suddenly knocked up out of bed for some very special purpose.

When we got up in the morning we saw that the knocker was tied up in an old white kid glove; and we, in our innocence (we were in a state of bachelorship then), wondered what on earth it all meant, until we heard the eldest Miss Willis, *in propriâ personâ*, say, with great dignity, in answer to the next inquiry, "*My* compliments, and Mrs. Robinson's doing as well as can be expected, and the little girl thrives wonderfully." And then, in common with the rest of the row, our curiosity was satisfied, and we began to wonder it had never occurred to us what the matter was before.

CHAPTER IV: *The Election for Beadle*

A GREAT event has recently occurred in our parish. A contest of paramount interest has just terminated; a parochial convulsion has taken place. It has been succeeded by a glorious triumph, which the country—or at least the parish—it is all the same—will long remember. We have had an election; an election for beadle. The supporters of the old beadle system have been defeated in their stronghold, and the advocates of the great new beadle principles have achieved a proud victory.

Our parish, which, like all other parishes, is a little world of its own, has long been divided into two parties, whose contentions, slumbering for a while, have never failed to burst forth with unabated vigour, on any occasion on which they could by possibility be renewed. Watching-rates, lighting-rates, paving-rates, sewer's-rates, church-rates, poor's-rates—all sorts of rates, have been in their turns the subjects of a grand struggle; and as to questions of patronage, the asperity and determination with which they have been contested is scarcely credible.

The leader of the official party—the steady advocate of the churchwardens, and the unflinching supporter of the overseers—is an old gentleman who lives in our row. He owns some half-dozen houses in it, and always walks on the opposite side of the way, so that he may be able to take in a view of the whole of his property at once. He is a tall, thin, bony man, with an interrogative nose, and little restless perking eyes, which appear to have been given him for the sole purpose of peeping into other people's affairs with. He is deeply impressed with the importance of our parish business, and prides himself, not a little, on his style of addressing the parishioners in vestry assembled. His views are rather confined than extensive; his principles more narrow than liberal. He has been heard to declaim very loudly in favour of the liberty of the press, and advocates the repeal of the stamp duty on newspapers, because the daily journals who now have a monopoly of the public, never give *verbatim* reports of vestry meetings. He would not appear egotistical for the world, but at the same time he must say, that there *are* speeches—that celebrated speech of his own, on the emoluments of the sexton, and the duties of the office, for instance—which might be communicated to the public, greatly to their improvement and advantage.

His great opponent in public life is Captain Purday, the old naval officer on half-pay, to whom we have already introduced our readers. The captain being a determined opponent of the constituted authorities, whoever they may chance to be, and our other friend being their steady supporter, with an equal disregard of their individual merits, it will readily be supposed, that occasions for their coming into direct collision are neither few nor far between. They divided the vestry fourteen times on a motion for heating the church with warm water instead of coals: and made speeches about liberty and expenditure, and prodigality and hot water, which threw the whole parish into a state of excitement. Then the captain, when he was on the visiting committee, and his opponent overseer, brought forward certain distinct and specific charges relative to the management of the workhouse, boldly expressed his total want of confidence in the existing authorities, and moved for "a copy of the recipe by which the paupers' soup was prepared, together with any documents relating thereto." This the overseer steadily resisted; he fortified himself by precedent, appealed to the established usage, and declined to produce the papers, on the ground of the injury that would be done to the public service, if documents of a strictly private nature, passing between the master of the workhouse and the cook, were to be thus dragged to light on the motion of any individual member of the vestry. The motion was lost by a majority of two; and then the captain, who never allows himself to be defeated, moved for a committee of inquiry into the whole subject. The affair grew serious: the question was discussed at meeting after meeting, and vestry after vestry; speeches were made, attacks repudiated, personal defiances exchanged, explanations received, and the greatest excitement prevailed, until at last, just as the question was going to be finally decided, the vestry found that somehow or other, they had become entangled in a point of form, from which it was impossible to escape with propriety. So, the motion was dropped, and everybody looked extremely important, and seemed quite satisfied with the meritorious nature of the whole proceeding.

This was the state of affairs in our parish a week or two

since, when Simmons, the beadle, suddenly died. The
lamented deceased had over-exerted himself, a day or two
previously, in conveying an aged female, highly intoxicated,
to the strong room of the workhouse. The excitement thus
occasioned, added to a severe cold, which this indefatigable
officer had caught in his capacity of director of the parish
engine, by inadvertently playing over himself instead of a
fire, proved too much for a constitution already enfeebled
by age; and the intelligence was conveyed to the Board one
evening, that Simmons had died and left his respects.

The breath was scarcely out of the body of the deceased
functionary, when the field was filled with competitors for
the vacant office, each of whom rested his claims to public
support entirely on the number and extent of his family,
as if the office of beadle were originally instituted as an
encouragement for the propagation of the human species.
"Bung for Beadle. Five small children!"—"Hopkins for
Beadle. Seven small children!!"—"Timkins for Beadle.
Nine small children!!!" Such were the placards in large
black letters on a white ground, which were plentifully pasted
on the walls, and posted in the windows of the principal
shops. Timkins's success was considered certain: several
mothers of families half promised their votes, and the nine
small children would have run over the course, but for the
production of another placard, announcing the appearance
of a still more meritorious candidate. "Spruggins for Beadle.
Ten small children (two of them twins), and a wife!!!" There
was no resisting this; ten small children would have been
almost irresistible in themselves, without the twins, but the
touching parenthesis about that interesting production in
nature, and the still more touching allusion to Mrs. Spruggins,
must ensure success. Spruggins was the favourite at once,
and the appearance of his lady, as she went about to solicit
votes (which encouraged confident hopes of a still further
addition to the house of Spruggins at no remote period),
increased the general prepossession in his favour. The other
candidates, Bung alone excepted, resigned in despair. The
day of election was fixed; and the canvass proceeded with
briskness and perseverance on both sides.

The members of the vestry could not be supposed to escape
the contagious excitement inseparable from the occasion.
The majority of the lady inhabitants of the parish declared
at once for Spruggins; and the *quondam* overseer took the
same side, on the ground that men with large families always
had been elected to the office, and that although he must
admit, that, in other respects, Spruggins was the least
qualified candidate of the two, still it was an old practice,
and he saw no reason why an old practice should be departed
from. This was enough for the captain. He immediately

sided with Bung, canvassed for him personally in all directions, wrote squibs on Spruggins, and got his butcher to skewer them up on conspicuous joints in his shop-front; frightened his neighbour, the old lady, into a palpitation of the heart, by his awful denunciations of Spruggins's party; and bounced in and out, and up and down, and backwards and forwards, until all the sober inhabitants of the parish thought it inevitable that he must die of a brain fever, long before the election began.

The day of election arrived. It was no longer an individual struggle, but a party contest between the ins and outs. The question was, whether the withering influence of the overseers, the domination of the churchwardens, and the blighting despotism of the vestry-clerk, should be allowed to render the election of beadle a form—a nullity: whether they should impose a vestry-elected beadle on the parish, to do their bidding and forward their views, or whether the parishioners, fearlessly asserting their undoubted rights, should elect an independent beadle of their own.

The nomination was fixed to take place in the vestry, but so great was the throng of anxious spectators, that it was found necessary to adjourn to the church, where the ceremony commenced with due solemnity. The appearance of the churchwardens and overseers, and the ex-churchwardens and ex-overseers, with Spruggins in the rear, excited general attention. Spruggins was a little thin man, in rusty black, with a long pale face, and a countenance expressive of care and fatigue, which might either be attributed to the extent of his family or the anxiety of his feelings. His opponent appeared in a cast-off coat of the captain's—a blue coat with bright buttons: white trousers, and that description of shoes familiarly known by the appellation of "high-lows." There was a serenity in the open countenance of Bung—a kind of moral dignity in his confident air—an "I wish you may get it" sort of expression in his eye—which infused animation into his supporters, and evidently dispirited his opponents.

The ex-churchwarden rose to propose Thomas Spruggins for beadle. He had known him long. He had had his eye upon him closely for years; he had watched him with twofold vigilance for months. (A parishioner here suggested that this might be termed "taking a double sight," but the observation was drowned in loud cries of "Order!") He would repeat that he had had his eye upon him for years, and this he would say, that a more well-conducted, a more well-behaved, a more sober, a more quiet man, with a more well-regulated mind he had never met with. A man with a larger family he had never known (cheers). The parish required a man who could be depended on ("Hear!" from the Spruggins side, answered by ironical cheers from the Bung party). Such a man he now proposed ("No," "Yes"). He would not allude to individuals (the ex-churchwarden continued, in the celebrated negative style adopted by great speakers). He would not advert to a gentleman who had once held a high rank in the service of His Majesty; he would not say, that that gentleman was no gentleman; he would not assert, that that man was no man; he would not say, that he was a turbulent parishioner; he would not say, that he had grossly misbehaved himself, not only on this, but on all former occasions; he would not say, that he was one of those discontented and treasonable spirits, who carried confusion and disorder wherever they went; he would not say, that he harboured in his heart envy, and hatred, and malice and all uncharitableness. No! He wished to have everything comfortable and pleasant, and therefore, he would say—nothing about him (cheers).

The captain replied in a similar parliamentary style. He would not say, he was astonished at the speech they had just heard; he would not say, he was disgusted (cheers). He would not retort the epithets which had been hurled against him (renewed cheering); he would not allude to men once in office, but now happily out of it, who had mismanaged the workhouse, ground the paupers, diluted the beer, slack-baked the bread, boned the meat, heightened the work, and lowered the soup (tremendous cheers). He would not ask what such men deserved (a voice, "Nothing a-day, and find themselves!"). He would not say, that one burst of general indignation should drive them from the parish they polluted with their presence ("Give it him!"). He would not allude to the unfortunate man who had been proposed—he would not say, as the vestry's tool, but as Beadle. He would not advert to that individual's family; he would not say, that nine children, twins, and a wife, were very bad examples for pauper imitation (loud cheers). He would not advert in detail to the qualifications of Bung. The man stood before him, and he would not say in his presence, what he might be disposed to say of him, if he were absent. (Here Mr. Bung telegraphed to a friend near him, under cover of his hat, by contracting his left eye, and applying his right thumb to the tip of his nose). It had been objected to Bung that he had only five children ("Hear, hear!" from the opposition). Well; he had yet to learn that the legislature had affixed any precise amount of infantine qualification to the office of beadle; but taking it for granted that an extensive family were a great requisite, he entreated them to look to facts, and compare *data*, about which there could be no mistake. Bung was 35 years of age. Spruggins—of whom he wished to speak with all possible respect—was 50. Was it not more than possible—was it not very probable—that by the time Bung attained the latter age, he might see around him a family, even exceeding in number and extent, that to which Spruggins at present laid claim (deafening cheers and waving of handkerchiefs)? The captain concluded, amidst loud applause, by calling upon the parishioners to sound the tocsin, rush to the poll, free themselves from dictation, or be slaves for ever.

On the following day the polling began, and we never have had such a bustle in our parish since we got up our famous antislavery petition, which was such an important one, that the House of Commons ordered it to be printed, on the motion of the member for the district. The captain engaged two hackney-coaches and a cab for Bung's people—the cab for the drunken voters, and the two coaches for the old ladies, the greater portion of whom, owing to the captain's impetuosity, were driven up to the poll and home again, before they recovered from their flurry sufficiently to know, with any degree of clearness, what they had been doing. The opposite party wholly neglected these precautions, and the consequence was, that a great many ladies who were walking leisurely up to the church—for it was a very hot day—to vote for Spruggins, were artfully decoyed into the coaches, and voted for Bung. The captain's arguments, too, had produced considerable effect: the attempted influence of the vestry produced a greater. A threat of exclusive dealing was clearly established against the vestry-clerk—a case of heartless and profligate atrocity. It appeared that the delinquent had been in the habit of purchasing six penn'orth of muffins, weekly, from an old woman who rents a small house in the parish, and resides among the original settlers; on her last weekly visit, a message was conveyed to her through the medium of the cook, couched in mysterious terms, but indicating with sufficient clearness, that the vestry-clerk's appetite for muffins, in future, depended entirely on her vote on the beadleship. This was sufficient: the stream had been turning previously, and the impulse thus administered directed its final course. The Bung party ordered one shilling's-worth of muffins weekly for the remainder of the old woman's natural life; the parishioners were loud in their exclamations; and the fate of Spruggins was sealed.

It was in vain that the twins were exhibited in dresses of the same pattern, and night-caps to match, at the church door: the boy in Mrs. Spruggins's right arm, and the girl in her left—even Mrs. Spruggins herself failed to be an object of sympathy any longer. The majority attained by Bung on the gross poll was four hundred and twenty-eight, and the cause of the parishioners triumphed.

CHAPTER V: *The Broker's Man*

THE excitement of the late election has subsided, and our
parish being once again restored to a state of comparative
tranquillity, we are enabled to devote our attention to those
parishioners who take little share in our party contests or
in the turmoil and bustle of public life. And we feel sincere
pleasure in acknowledging here, that in collecting materials
for this task we have been greatly assisted by Mr. Bung
himself, who has imposed on us a debt of obligation which
we fear we can never repay. The life of this gentleman has
been one of a very chequered description: he has undergone
transitions—not from grave to gay, for he never was grave
—not from lively to severe, for severity forms no part of
his disposition; his fluctuations have been between poverty
in the extreme, and poverty modified, or, to use his own
emphatic language, "between nothing to eat and just half
enough." He is not, as he forcibly remarks, "one of those
fortunate men who, if they were to dive under one side of a
barge stark-naked, would come up on the other with a new
suit of clothes on, and a ticket for soup in the waistcoat-
pocket:" neither is he one of those, whose spirit has been broken
beyond redemption by misfortune and want. He is just one
of the careless, good-for-nothing, happy fellows, who float,
cork-like, on the surface, for the world to play at hockey
with: knocked here, and there, and everywhere: now to the
right, then to the left, again up in the air, and anon to the
bottom, but always reappearing and bounding with the
stream buoyantly and merrily along. Some few months
before he was prevailed upon to stand a contested election for
the office of beadle, necessity attached him to the service
of a broker; and on the opportunities he here acquired of
ascertaining the condition of most of the poorer inhabitants
of the parish, his patron, the captain, first grounded his
claims to public support. Chance threw the man in our way
a short time since. We were, in the first instance, attracted
by his prepossessing impudence at the election; we were not
surprised, on further acquaintance, to find him a shrewd
knowing fellow, with no inconsiderable power of observation;
and, after conversing with him a little, were somewhat struck
(as we dare say our readers have frequently been in other
cases) with the power some men seem to have, not only of
sympathising with, but to all appearance of understanding
feelings to which they themselves are entire strangers. We
had been expressing to the new functionary our surprise
that he should ever have served in the capacity to which we
have just adverted, when we gradually led him into one or
two professional anecdotes. As we are induced to think,

on reflection, that they will tell better in nearly his own words, than with any attempted embellishments of ours, we will at once entitle them MR. BUNG'S NARRATIVE.

"It's very true, as you say, sir," Mr. Bung commenced, "that a broker's man's is not a life to be envied; and in course you know as well as I do, though you don't say it, that people hate and scout 'em because they're the ministers of wretchedness, like, to poor people. But what could I do, sir? The thing was no worse because I did it, instead of somebody else; and if putting me in possession of a house would put me in possession of three and sixpence a day, and levying a distress on another man's goods would relieve my distress and that of my family, it can't be expected but what I'd take the job and go through with it. I never liked it, God knows; I always looked out for something else, and the moment I got other work to do, I left. If there is anything wrong in being the agent in such matters—not the principal, mind you—I'm sure the business, to a beginner like I was, at all events, carries its own punishment along with it. I wished again and again that the people would only blow me up, or pitch into me—that I wouldn't have minded, it's all in my way; but it's the being shut up by yourself in one room for five days, without so much as an old newspaper to look at, or anything to see out o' the winder but the roofs and chimneys at the back of the house, or anything to listen to, but the ticking, perhaps, of an old Dutch clock, the sobbing of the missis, now and then, the low talking of friends in the next room, who speak in whispers, lest 'the man' should overhear them, or perhaps the occasional opening of the door, as a child peeps in to look at you, and then runs half-frightened away—it's all this, that makes you feel sneaking somehow, and ashamed of yourself; and then, if it's winter time, they just give you fire enough to make you think you'd like more, and bring in your grub as if they wished it 'ud choke you—as I dare say they do, for the matter of that, most heartily. If they're very civil, they make you up a bed in the room at night, and if they don't your master sends one in for you; but there you are, without being washed or shaved all the time, shunned by everybody, and spoken to by no one, unless some one comes in at dinner time, and asks you whether you want any more, in a tone as much as to say 'I hope you don't,' or, in the evening, to inquire whether you wouldn't rather have a candle, after you've been sitting in the dark half the night. When I was left in this way, I used to sit, think, think, thinking, till I felt as lonesome as a kitten in a wash-house copper with the lid on; but I believe the old brokers' men who are regularly trained to it, never think at all. I have heard some on 'em say, indeed, that they don't know how!

"I put in a good many distresses in my time (continued Mr. Bung), and in course I wasn't long in finding, that some people are not as much to be pitied as others are, and that people with good incomes who get into difficulties, which they keep patching up day after day, and week after week, get so used to these sort of things in time, that at last they come scarcely to feel them at all. I remember the very first place I was put in possession of, was a gentleman's house in this parish here, that everybody would suppose couldn't help having money if he tried. I went with old Fixem, my old master, 'bout half arter eight in the morning; rang the area-bell; servant in livery opened the door: 'Governor at home?' 'Yes, he is,' says the man; 'but he's breakfasting just now.' 'Never mind,' says Fixem, 'just you tell him there's a gentleman here, as wants to speak to him partickler.' So the servant he opens his eyes, and stares about him all ways—looking for the gentleman as it struck me, for I don't think anybody but a man as was stone-blind would mistake Fixem for one; and as for me, I was as seedy as a cheap cowcumber. Hows'ever, he turns round, and goes to the breakfast-parlour, which was a little snug sort of room at the end of the passage, and Fixem (as we always did in that profession), without waiting to be announced, walks in arter him, and before the servant could get out—'Please, sir, here's a man as wants to speak to you,' looks in at the door as familiar and pleasant as may be. 'Who the devil are you, and how dare you walk into a gentleman's house without leave?' says the master, as fierce as a bull in fits. 'My name,' says Fixem, winking to the master to send the servant away, and putting the warrant into his hands folded up like a note, 'My name's Smith,' says he, 'and I called from Johnson's about that business of Thompson's.'—'Oh,' says the other, quite down on him directly, 'How *is* Thompson?' says he. 'Pray sit down, Mr. Smith: John, leave the room.' Out went the servant; and the gentleman and Fixem looked at one another till they couldn't look any longer, and then they varied the amusements by looking at me, who had been standing on the mat all this time. 'Hundred and fifty pounds, I see,' said the gentleman at last. 'Hundred and fifty pounds,' said Fixem, 'besides cost of levy, sheriff's poundage, and all other incidental expenses.'—'Um,' says the gentleman, "I sha'n't be able to settle this before to-morrow afternoon.'—'Very sorry; but I shall be obliged to leave my man here till then,' replies Fixem, pretending to look very miserable over it. 'That's very unfort'nate,' says the gentleman, 'for I have got a large party here to-night, and I'm ruined if those fellows of mine get an inkling of the matter—just step here, Mr. Smith,' says he, after a short pause. So Fixem walks with him up to the window, and after a good deal of whispering, and a little chinking of suverins, and looking at me, he comes back and says, 'Bung, you're a handy fellow, and very honest I know. This gentleman wants an assistant to clean the plate and wait at table to-day, and if you're not particularly engaged,' says old Fixem, grinning like mad, and shoving a couple of suverins into my hand, 'he'll be very glad to avail himself of your services.' Well, I laughed, and the gentleman laughed, and we all laughed; and I went home and cleaned myself, leaving Fixem there, and when I went back, Fixem went away, and I polished up the plate, and waited at table, and gammoned the servants, and nobody had the least idea I was in possession, though it very nearly came out after all; for one of the last gentlemen who remained, came down-stairs into the hall where I was sitting pretty late at night, and putting half-a-crown into my hand, says, 'Here, my man,' says he, 'run and get me a coach, will you?' I thought it was a do, to get me out of the house, and was just going to say so, sulkily enough, when the gentleman (who was up to everything) came running down-stairs, as if he was in great anxiety. 'Bung,' says he, pretending to be in a consuming passion. 'Sir,' says I. 'Why the devil ain't you looking after that plate?'—'I was just going to send him for a coach for me,' says the other gentleman. 'And I was just a-going to say,' says I—— 'Anybody else, my dear fellow,' interrupts the master of the house, pushing me down the passage to get me out of the way, 'anybody else; but I have put this man in possession of all the plate and valuables, and I cannot allow him on any consideration whatever to leave the house. Bung, you scoundrel, go and count those forks in the breakfast-parlour instantly.' You may be sure I went laughing pretty hearty when I found it was all right. The money was paid next day, with the addition of something else for myself, and that was the best job that I (and I suspect old Fixem too) ever got in that line.

"But this is the bright side of the picture, sir, after all," resumed Mr. Bung, laying aside the knowing look, and flash air, with which he had repeated the previous anecdote— "and I'm sorry to say, it's the side one sees very, very, seldom, in comparison with the dark one. The civility which money will purchase, is rarely extended to those who have none; and there's a consolation even in being able to patch up one difficulty, to make way for another, to which very poor people are strangers. I was once put into a house down George's-yard—that little dirty court at the back of the gas-works; and I never shall forget the misery of them people, dear me! It was a distress for half a year's rent—two pound ten I think. There was only two rooms in the house, and as there was no passage, the lodgers upstairs always went through the room of the people of the house, as they passed in and out; and every time they did so—which, on the average, was about four times every quarter of an hour—they blowed up quite frightful: for their things had been seized too, and included in the inventory. There was a little piece of enclosed dust in front of the house with a cinder-path leading up to the door, and an open rain-water butt on one side. A dirty striped curtain, on a very slack string, hung in the window, and a little triangular bit of broken looking-glass rested on the sill inside. I suppose it was meant for the people's use, but their appearance was so wretched, and so miserable, that I'm certain they never could have plucked up courage to look themselves in the face a second time, if they survived the fright of doing so once. There was two or three chairs, that might have been worth, in their best days, from eightpence to a shilling a-piece; a small deal table, an old corner cupboard with nothing in it, and one of those bedsteads which turn up half-way, and leave the bottom legs sticking out for you to knock your head against, or hang your hat upon; no bed, no bedding. There was an old sack, by way of rug, before the fireplace, and four or five children were grovelling about, among the sand on the floor. The execution was only put in, to get 'em out of the house, for there was nothing to take to pay the expenses; and here I stopped for three days, though that was a mere form too: for, in course, I knew, and we all knew, they could never pay the money. In one of the chairs, by the side of the place where the fire ought to have been, was an old 'ooman—the ugliest and dirtiest I ever see—who sat rocking herself backwards and forwards, backwards and forwards, without once stopping, except for an instant now and then, to clasp together the withered hands which, with these exceptions, she kept constantly rubbing upon her knees, just raising and depressing her fingers convulsively, in time to the rocking of the chair. On the other side sat the mother with an infant in her arms, which cried till it cried itself to sleep, and when it 'woke, cried till it cried itself off again. The old 'ooman's voice I never heard: she seemed completely stupefied; and as to the mother's, it would have been better if she had been so too, for misery had changed her to a devil. If you had heard how she cursed the little naked children as was rolling on the floor, and seen how savagely she struck the infant when it cried with hunger, you'd have shuddered as much as I did. There they remained all the time: the children ate a morsel of bread once or twice, and I gave 'em best part of the dinners my missis brought me, but the woman ate nothing; they never even laid on the bedstead, nor was the room swept or cleaned all the time. The neighbours were all too poor themselves to take any notice of 'em, but from what I could make out from the abuse of the woman up stairs, it seemed the husband had been transported a few weeks before. When the time was up, the landlord and old Fixem too, got rather frightened about the family, and so they made a stir about it, and had 'em taken to the workhouse. They sent the sick couch for the old 'ooman, and Simmons took the children away at night. The old 'ooman went into the infirmary, and very soon died. The children are all in the house to this day, and very comfortable they are in comparison. As to the mother, there was no taming her at all. She had been a quiet, hard-working woman, I believe, but her misery had actually drove her wild; so after she had been sent to the house of correction half a dozen times, for throwing inkstands at the overseers, blaspheming the churchwardens, and smashing everybody as come near her, she burst a blood-vessel one mornin', and died too; and a happy release it was, both for herself and the old paupers, male and female, which she used to tip over in all directions, as if they were so many skittles, and she the ball.

"Now this was bad enough," resumed Mr. Bung, taking a half-step towards the door, as if to intimate that he had nearly concluded. "This was bad enough, but there was a sort of quiet misery—if you understand what I mean by that, sir—about a lady at one house I was put into, as touched me a good deal more. It doesn't matter where it was exactly: indeed, I'd rather not say, but it was the same sort o' job. I went with Fixem in the usual way—there was a year's rent in arrear; a very small servant-girl opened the door, and three or four fine-looking little children was in the front parlour we were shown into, which was very clean, but very scantily furnished, much like the children themselves. 'Bung,' says Fixem, in a low voice, when we were left alone for a minute, 'I know something about this here family, and my opinion is, it's no go.' 'Do you think they can't settle?' says I, quite anxiously; for I liked the looks of them children. Fixem shook his head, and was just about to reply, when the door opened, and in came a lady, as white as ever I see any one in my days, except about the eyes, which were red with crying. She walked in, as firm as I could have done; shut the door carefully after her, and sat herself down with a face as composed as if it was made of stone. 'What is the matter, gentlemen?' says she, in a surprisin' steady voice. '*Is* this an execution?'—'It is, mum,' says Fixem. The lady looked at him as steady as ever: she didn't seem to have understood him. 'It is, mum,' says Fixem again; 'this is my warrant of distress, mum,' says he, handing it over as polite as if it was a newspaper which had been bespoke arter the next gentleman.

"The lady's lip trembled as she took the printed paper. She cast her eye over it, and old Fixem began to explain the

form, but I saw she wasn't reading it, plain enough, poor thing.
'Oh, my God!' says she, suddenly a-bursting out crying,
letting the warrant fall, and hiding her face in her hands.
'Oh, my God! what will become of us!' The noise she made,
brought in a young lady of about nineteen or twenty, who, I
suppose, had been a-listening at the door, and who had got
a little boy in her arms: she sat him down in the lady's lap,
without speaking, and she hugged the poor little fellow to her
bosom, and cried over him, till even old Fixem put on his
blue spectacles to hide the two tears, that was a-trickling
down, one on each side of his dirty face. 'Now, dear ma,'
says the young lady, 'you know how much you have borne.
For all our sakes—for pa's sake,' says she, 'don't give way
to this!'—'No, no, I won't!' says the lady, gathering herself
up hastily, and drying her eyes; 'I am very foolish, but I'm
better now—much better.' And then she roused herself
up, went with us into every room while we took the inventory,
opened all the drawers of her own accord, sorted the children's
little clothes to make the work easier; and, except doing
everything in a strange sort of hurry, seemed as calm and
composed as if nothing had happened. When we came
down-stairs again, she hesitated a minute or two, and at
last says, 'Gentlemen,' says she, 'I am afraid I have done
wrong, and perhaps it may bring you into trouble. I secreted
just now,' she says, 'the only trinket I have left in the world
—here it is.' So she lays down on the table, a little miniature
mounted in gold. 'It's a miniature,' she says, 'of my poor
dear father! I little thought once, that I should ever thank
God for depriving me of the original, but I do, and have done
for years back, most fervently. Take it away, sir,' she says,
'it's a face that never turned from me in sickness or distress,
and I can hardly bear to turn from it now, when, God knows,
I suffer both in no ordinary degree.' I couldn't say nothing,
but I raised my head from the inventory which I was filling
up, and looked at Fixem; the old fellow nodded to me
significantly, so I ran my pen through the '*Mini*' I had just
written, and left the miniature on the table.

"Well, sir, to make short of a long story, I was left in
possession, and in possession I remained; and though I was
an ignorant man, and the master of the house a clever one,
I saw what he never did, but what he would give worlds
now (if he had 'em) to have seen in time. I saw, sir, that
his wife was wasting away, beneath cares of which she never
complained, and griefs she never told. I saw that she was
dying before his eyes; I knew that one exertion from him
might have saved her, but he never made it. I don't blame
him: I don't think he *could* rouse himself. She had so long
anticipated all his wishes, and acted for him, that he was a
lost man when left to himself. I used to think when I caught

sight of her, in the clothes she used to wear, which looked shabby even upon her, and would have been scarcely decent on any one else, that if I was a gentleman it would wring my very heart to see the woman that was a smart and merry girl when I courted her, so altered through her love for me. Bitter cold and damp weather it was, yet, though her dress was thin, and her shoes none of the best, during the whole three days, from morning to night, she was out of doors running about to try and raise the money. The money *was* raised, and the execution was paid out. The whole family crowded into the room where I was, when the money arrived. The father was quite happy as the inconvenience was removed —I dare say he didn't know how; the children looked merry and cheerful again; the eldest girl was bustling about, making preparations for the first comfortable meal they had had since the distress was put in; and the mother looked pleased to see them all so. But if ever I saw death in a woman's face, I saw it in hers that night.

"I was right, sir," continued Mr. Bung, hurriedly passing his coat-sleeve over his face, "the family grew more prosperous, and good fortune arrived. But it was too late. Those children are motherless now, and their father would give up all he has since gained—house, home, goods, money: all that he has, or ever can have, to restore the wife he has lost."

CHAPTER VI: *The Ladies' Societies*

OUR Parish is very prolific in ladies' charitable institutions. In winter, when wet feet are common, and colds not scarce, we have the ladies' soup distribution society, the ladies' coal distribution society, and the ladies' blanket distribution society; in summer, when stone fruits flourish and stomach aches prevail, we have the ladies' dispensary, and the ladies' sick visitation committee; and all the year round we have the ladies' child examination society, the ladies' bible and prayer-book circulation society, and the ladies' childbed-linen monthly loan society. The two latter are decidedly the most important; whether they are productive of more benefit than the rest, it is not for us to say, but we can take upon ourselves to affirm, with the utmost solemnity, that they create a greater stir and more bustle, than all the others put together.

We should be disposed to affirm, on the first blush of the matter, that the bible and prayer-book society is not so popular as the childbed-linen society; the bible and prayer-book society has, however, considerably increased in importance within the last year or two, having derived some adventitious aid from the factious opposition of the child's examination society; which factious opposition originated in manner following:—When the young curate was popular, and all the unmarried ladies in the parish took a serious turn, the charity children all at once became objects of peculiar and especial interest. The three Miss Browns (enthusiastic admirers of the curate) taught, and exercised, and examined, and re-examined the unfortunate children, until the boys grew pale, and the girls consumptive, with study and fatigue. The three Miss Browns stood it out very well, because they relieved each other; but the children, having no relief at all, exhibited decided symptoms of weariness and care. The unthinking part of the parishioners laughed at all this, but the more reflective portion of the inhabitants abstained from expressing any opinion on the subject until that of the curate had been clearly ascertained.

The opportunity was not long wanting. The curate preached a charity sermon on behalf of the charity school, and in the charity sermon aforesaid, expatiated in glowing terms on the praiseworthy and indefatigable exertions of certain estimable individuals. Sobs were heard to issue from the three Miss Browns' pew; the pew-opener of the division was seen to hurry down the centre aisle to the vestry door, and to return immediately, bearing a glass of water in her hand. A low moaning ensued; two more pew-openers rushed to the spot, and the three Miss Browns, each supported by a pew-opener, were led out of the church, and led in again after the lapse of five minutes with white pocket-handkerchiefs to their eyes, as if they had been attending a funeral in the churchyard adjoining. If any doubt had for a moment existed, as to whom the allusion was intended to apply, it was at once removed. The wish to enlighten the charity children became universal, and the three Miss Browns were unanimously besought to divide the school into classes, and to assign each class to the superintendence of two young ladies.

A little learning is a dangerous thing, but a little patronage is more so; the three Miss Browns appointed all the old maids, and carefully excluded the young ones. Maiden aunts triumphed, mammas were reduced to the lowest depth of despair, and there is no telling in what act of violence the general indignation against the three Miss Browns might have vented itself, had not a perfectly providential occurrence changed the tide of public feeling. Mrs. Johnson Parker, the mother of seven extremely fine girls—all unmarried—hastily reported to several other mammas of several other unmarried families, that five old men, six old women, and children innumerable, in the free seats near her pew, were in the habit of coming to church every Sunday, without either bible or prayer-book. Was this to be borne in a civilised country?

Could such things be tolerated in a Christian land? Never! A ladies' bible and prayer-book distribution society was instantly formed: president, Mrs. Johnson Parker; treasurers, auditors, and secretary, the Misses Johnson Parker: subscriptions were entered into, books were bought, all the free-seat people provided therewith, and when the first lesson was given out, on the first Sunday succeeding these events, there was such a dropping of books, and rustling of leaves, that it was morally impossible to hear one word of the service for five minutes afterwards.

The three Miss Browns, and their party, saw the approaching danger, and endeavoured to avert it by ridicule and sarcasm. Neither the old men nor the old women could read their books, now they had got them, said the three Miss Browns. Never mind; they could learn, replied Mrs. Johnson Parker. The children couldn't read either, suggested the three Miss Browns. No matter; they could be taught, retorted Mrs. Johnson Parker. A balance of parties took place. The Miss Browns publicly examined—popular feeling inclined to the child's examination society. The Miss Johnson Parkers publicly distributed—a reaction took place in favour of the prayer-book distribution. A feather would have turned the scale, and a feather did turn it. A missionary returned from the West Indies; he was to be presented to the Dissenters' Missionary Society on his marriage with a wealthy widow. Overtures were made to the Dissenters by the Johnson Parkers. Their object was the same, and why not have a joint meeting of the two societies? The proposition was accepted. The meeting was duly heralded by public announcement, and the room was crowded to suffocation. The Missionary appeared on the platform; he was hailed with enthusiasm. He repeated a dialogue he had heard between two negroes, behind a hedge, on the subject of distribution societies; the approbation was tumultuous. He gave an imitation of the two negroes in broken English; the roof was rent with applause. From that period we date (with one trifling exception) a daily increase in the popularity of the distribution society, and an increase of popularity, which the feeble and impotent opposition of the examination party, has only tended to augment.

Now, the great points about the childbed-linen monthly loan society are, that it is less dependent on the fluctuations of public opinion than either the distribution or the child's examination; and that, come what may, there is never any lack of objects on which to exercise its benevolence. Our parish is a very populous one, and, if anything, contributes, we should be disposed to say, rather more than its due share to the aggregate amount of births in the metropolis and its environs. The consequence is, that the monthly loan society flourishes, and invests its members with a most enviable amount of bustling patronage. The society (whose only notion of dividing time, would appear to be its allotment into months) holds monthly tea-drinkings, at which the monthly report is received, a secretary elected for the month ensuing, and such of the monthly boxes as may not happen to be out on loan for the month, carefully examined.

We were never present at one of these meetings, from all of which it is scarcely necessary to say, gentlemen are carefully excluded; but Mr. Bung has been called before the board once or twice, and we have his authority for stating, that its proceedings are conducted with great order and regularity: not more than four members being allowed to speak at one time on any pretence whatever. The regular committee is composed exclusively of married ladies, but a vast number of young unmarried ladies of from eighteen to twenty-five years of age, respectively, are admitted as honorary members, partly because they are very useful in replenishing the boxes, and visiting the confined; partly because it is highly desirable that they should be initiated, at an early period, into the more serious and matronly duties of after life; and partly, because prudent mammas have not unfrequently been known to turn this circumstance to wonderfully good account in matrimonial speculations.

In addition to the loan of the monthly boxes (which are always painted blue, with the name of the society in large white letters on the lid), the society dispense occasional grants of beef-tea, and a composition of warm beer, spice, eggs, and sugar, commonly known by the name of "caudle," to its patients. And here again the services of the honorary members are called into requisition, and most cheerfully conceded. Deputations of twos or threes are sent out to visit the patients, and on these occasions there is such a tasting of caudle and beef-tea, such a stirring about of little messes in tiny saucepans on the hob, such a dressing and undressing of infants, such a tying, and folding, and pinning; such a nursing and warming of little legs and feet before the fire, such a delightful confusion of talking and cooking, bustle, importance, and officiousness, as never can be enjoyed in its full extent but on similar occasions.

In rivalry of these two institutions, and as a last expiring effort to acquire parochial popularity, the child's examination people determined, the other day, on having a grand public examination of the pupils; and the large school-room of the national seminary was, by and with the consent of the parish authorities, devoted to the purpose. Invitation circulars were forwarded to all the principal parishioners, including, of course, the heads of the other two societies, for whose especial behoof and edification the display was intended; and a large audience was confidently anticipated on the occasion. The floor was carefully scrubbed the day before, under the immediate superintendence of the three Miss Browns; forms were placed across the room for the accommodation of the visitors, specimens of writing were carefully selected, and as carefully patched and touched up, until they astonished the children who had written them, rather more than the company who read them; sums in compound addition were rehearsed and rehearsed until all the children had the totals by heart; and the preparations altogether were on the most laborious and most comprehensive scale. The morning arrived: the children were yellow-soaped and flannelled, and towelled, till their faces shone again; every pupil's hair was carefully combed into his or her eyes, as the case might be; the girls were adorned with snow-white tippets, and caps bound round the head by a single purple ribbon: the necks of the elder boys were fixed into collars of startling dimensions.

The doors were thrown open, and the Misses Brown and Co. were discovered in plain white muslin dresses, and caps of the same—the child's examination uniform. The room filled: the greetings of the company were loud and cordial. The distributionists trembled, for their popularity was at stake. The eldest boy fell forward, and delivered a propitiatory address from behind his collar. It was from the pen of Mr. Henry Brown; the applause was universal, and the Johnson Parkers were aghast. The examination proceeded with success, and terminated in triumph. The child's examination society gained a momentary victory, and the Johnson Parkers retreated in despair.

A secret council of the distributionists was held that night, with Mrs. Johnson Parker in the chair, to consider the best means of recovering the ground they had lost in the favour of the parish. What could be done? Another meeting! Alas! who was to attend it? The Missionary would not do twice; and the slaves were emancipated. A bold step must be taken. The parish must be astonished in some way or other; but no one was able to suggest what the step should be. At length, a very old lady was heard to mumble, in indistinct tones, "Exeter Hall." A sudden light broke in upon the meeting. It was unanimously resolved, that a deputation of old ladies should wait upon a celebrated orator imploring his assistance, and the favour of a speech; and the deputation should also wait on two or three other imbecile old women, not resident in the parish, and entreat their attendance. The application was successful, the meeting was held; the orator (an Irishman) came. He talked of green isles—other shores—vast Atlantic—bosom of the deep—Christian charity—blood and extermination—mercy in hearts—arms in hands—altars and homes—household gods. He wiped his eyes, he blew his nose, and he quoted Latin. The effect was tremendous—the Latin was a decided hit. Nobody knew exactly what it was about, but everybody knew it must be affecting, because even the orator was overcome. The popularity of the distribution society among the ladies of our parish is unprecedented; and the child's examination is going fast to decay.

CHAPTER VII: *Our Next-door Neighbour*

WE are very fond of speculating as we walk through a street, on the character and pursuits of the people who inhabit it; and nothing so materially assists us in these speculations as the appearance of the house doors. The various expressions of the human countenance afford a beautiful and interesting study; but there is something in the physiognomy of street-door knockers, almost as characteristic, and nearly as infallible. Whenever we visit a man for the first time, we contemplate the features of his knocker with the greatest curiosity, for we well know, that between the man and his knocker, there will inevitably be a greater or less degree of resemblance and sympathy.

For instance, there is one description of knocker that used to be common enough, but which is fast passing away—a large round one, with the jolly face of a convivial lion smiling blandly at you, as you twist the sides of your hair into a curl, or pull up your shirt-collar while you are waiting for the door to be opened; we never saw that knocker on the door of a churlish man—so far as our experience is concerned, it invariably bespoke hospitality and another bottle.

No man ever saw this knocker on the door of a small attorney or bill-broker; they always patronise the other lion; a heavy ferocious-looking fellow, with a countenance expressive of savage stupidity—a sort of grand master among the knockers, and a great favourite with the selfish and brutal.

Then there is a little pert Egyptian knocker, with a long thin face, a pinched up nose, and a very sharp chin, he is most in vogue with your government-office people, in light drabs and starched cravats; little spare priggish men, who are perfectly satisfied with their own opinions, and consider themselves of paramount importance.

We were greatly troubled a few years ago, by the innovation of a new kind of knocker, without any face at all, composed of a wreath, depending from a hand or small truncheon. A little trouble and attention, however, enabled us to overcome this difficulty, and to reconcile the new system to our favourite theory. You will invariably find this knocker on the doors of cold and formal people, who always ask you why you *don't* come, and never say *do*.

Everybody knows the brass knocker is common to suburban villas, and extensive boarding-schools; and having noticed this genus we have recapitulated all the most prominent and strongly-defined species.

Some phrenologists affirm, that the agitation of a man's brain by different passions, produces corresponding developments in the form of his skull. Do not let us be understood as pushing our theory to the length of asserting, that any alteration in a man's disposition would produce a visible effect on the feature of his knocker. Our position merely is, that in such a case, the magnetism which must exist between a man and his knocker, would induce the man to remove, and seek some knocker more congenial to his altered feelings. If you ever find a man changing his habitation without any reasonable pretext, depend upon it, that, although he may not be aware of the fact himself, it is because he and his knocker are at variance. This is a new theory, but we venture to launch it, nevertheless, as being quite as ingenious and infallible as many thousands of the learned speculations which are daily broached for public good and private fortune-making.

Entertaining these feelings on the subject of knockers, it will be readily imagined with what consternation we viewed the entire removal of the knocker from the door of the next house to the one we lived in, some time ago, and the substitution of a bell. This was a calamity we had never anticipated. The bare idea of anybody being able to exist without a knocker, appeared so wild and visionary, that it had never for one instant entered our imagination.

We sauntered moodily from the spot, and bent our steps towards Eaton Square, then just building. What was our astonishment and indignation to find that bells were fast becoming the rule, and knockers the exception! Our theory trembled beneath the shock. We hastened home; and fancying we foresaw in the swift progress of events, its entire abolition, resolved from that day forward to vent our speculations on our next-door neighbours in person. The house adjoining ours on the left hand was uninhabited, and we had, therefore, plenty of leisure to observe our next-door neighbours on the other side.

The house without the knocker was in the occupation of a city clerk, and there was a neatly-written bill in the parlour window intimating that lodgings for a single gentleman were to be let within.

It was a neat, dull little house, on the shady side of the way, with new, narrow floorcloth in the passage, and new, narrow stair-carpets up to the first floor. The paper was new, and the paint was new, and the furniture was new; and all three, paper, paint, and furniture, bespoke the limited means of the tenant. There was a little red and black carpet in the drawing-room, with a border of flooring all the way round; a few stained chairs and a pembroke table. A pink shell was displayed on each of the little sideboards, which, with the addition of a tea-tray and caddy, a few more shells on the mantelpiece, and three peacock's feathers tastefully arranged above them, completed the decorative furniture of the apartment.

This was the room destined for the reception of the single gentleman during the day, and a little back room on the same floor was assigned as his sleeping apartment by night.

The bill had not been long in the window, when a stout good-humoured looking gentleman, of about five-and-thirty, appeared as a candidate for the tenancy. Terms were soon arranged, for the bill was taken down immediately after his first visit. In a day or two the single gentleman came in, and shortly afterwards his real character came out.

First of all, he displayed a most extraordinary partiality for sitting up till three or four o'clock in the morning, drinking whiskey-and-water, and smoking cigars; then he invited friends home, who used to come at ten o'clock, and begin to get happy about the small hours, when they evinced their perfect contentment by singing songs with half a dozen verses of two lines each, and a chorus of ten, which chorus used to be shouted forth by the whole strength of the company, in the most enthusiastic and vociferous manner, to the great annoyance of the neighbours, and the special discomfort of another single gentleman overhead.

Now, this was bad enough, occurring as it did three times a week on the average, but this was not all; for when the company *did* go away, instead of walking quietly down the street, as anybody else's company would have done, they amused themselves by making alarming and frightful noises, and counterfeiting the shrieks of females in distress; and one night, a red-faced gentleman in a white hat knocked in the most urgent manner at the door of the powdered-headed old gentleman at No. 3, and when the powdered-headed old gentleman who thought one of his married daughters must have been taken ill prematurely, had groped down-stairs, and after a great deal of unbolting and key-turning, opened the street door, the red-faced man in the white hat said he hoped he'd excuse his giving him so much trouble, but he'd feel obliged if he'd favour him with a glass of cold spring water, and the loan of a shilling for a cab to take him home, on which the old gentleman slammed the door and went up-stairs and threw the contents of his water jug out of window—very straight, only it went over the wrong man; and the whole street was involved in confusion.

A joke's a joke; and even practical jests are very capital in their way, if you can only get the other party to see the fun of them; but the population of our street were so dull of apprehension, as to be quite lost to a sense of the drollery of this proceeding: and the consequence was, that our next-door neighbour was obliged to tell the single gentleman, that unless he gave up entertaining his friends at home, he really must be compelled to part with him. The single gentleman received the remonstrance with great good-humour, and promised from that time forward, to spend his evenings at a coffee-house—a determination which afforded general and unmixed satisfaction.

The next night passed off very well, everybody being delighted with the change; but on the next, the noises were renewed with greater spirit than ever. The single gentleman's friends being unable to see him in his own house every alternate night, had come to the determination of seeing him home every night; and what with the discordant greetings of the friends at parting, and the noise created by the single gentleman in his passage up-stairs, and his subsequent struggles to get his boots off, the evil was not to be borne. So, our next-door neighbour gave the single gentleman, who was a very good lodger in other respects, notice to quit; and the single gentleman went away, and entertained his friends in other lodgings.

The next applicant for the vacant first floor, was of a very different character from the troublesome single gentleman who had just quitted it. He was a tall, thin, young gentleman, with a profusion of brown hair, reddish whiskers, and very slightly developed moustaches. He wore a braided surtout, with frogs behind, light grey trousers, and wash-leather gloves, and had altogether rather a military appearance. So unlike the roystering single gentleman. Such insinuating manners, and such a delightful address! So seriously disposed, too! When he first came to look at the lodgings, he inquired most particularly whether he was sure to be able to get a seat in the parish church, and when he had agreed to take them, he requested to have a list of the different local charities, as he intended to subscribe his mite to the most deserving among them.

Our next-door neighbour was now perfectly happy. He had got a lodger at last, of just his own way of thinking— a serious, well-disposed man, who abhorred gaiety, and loved retirement. He took down the bill with a light heart, and pictured in imagination a long series of quiet Sundays, on which he and his lodger would exchange mutual civilities and Sunday papers.

The serious man arrived, and his luggage was to arrive from the country next morning. He borrowed a clean shirt, and a prayer-book, from our next-door neighbour, and retired to rest at an early hour, requesting that he might be called punctually at ten o'clock next morning—not before, as he was much fatigued.

He *was* called, and did not answer: he was called again, but there was no reply. Our next-door neighbour became alarmed and burst the door open. The serious man had left the house mysteriously; carrying with him the shirt, the prayer-book, a teaspoon, and the bedclothes.

Whether this occurrence, coupled with the irregularities of his former lodger, gave our next-door neighbour an aversion to single gentlemen, we know not; we only know that the next bill which made its appearance in the parlour window intimated generally, that there were furnished apartments to let on the first floor. The bill was soon removed. The new lodgers at first attracted our curiosity, and afterwards excited our interest.

They were a young lad of eighteen or nineteen, and his mother, a lady of about fifty, or it might be less. The mother wore a widow's weeds, and the boy was also clothed in deep mourning. They were poor—very poor; for their only means of support, arose from the pittance the boy earned, by copying writings, and translating for booksellers.

They had removed from some country place and settled in London; partly because it afforded better chances of employment for the boy, and partly, perhaps, with the natural desire to leave a place where they had been in better circumstances, and where their poverty was known. They were proud under their reverses, and above revealing their wants and privations to strangers. How bitter those privations were, and how hard the boy worked to remove them, no one ever knew but themselves. Night after night, two, three, four hours after midnight, could we hear the occasional raking up of the scanty fire, or the hollow and half-stifled cough, which indicated his being still at work; and day after day, could we see more plainly, that nature had set that unearthly light in his plaintive face, which is the beacon of her worst disease.

Actuated, we hope, by a higher feeling than mere curiosity, we contrived to establish, first an acquaintance, and then a close intimacy, with the poor strangers. Our worst fears were realised; the boy was sinking fast. Through a part of the winter, and the whole of the following spring and summer, his labours were unceasingly prolonged: and the mother attempted to procure needlework, embroidery—anything for bread.

A few shillings now and then were all she could earn. The boy worked steadily on; dying by minutes, but never once giving utterance to complaint or murmur.

One beautiful autumn evening we went to pay our customary visit to the invalid. His little remaining strength had been decreasing rapidly for two or three days preceding, and he was lying on the sofa at the open window, gazing at the setting sun. His mother had been reading the Bible to him, for she closed the book as we entered, and advanced to meet us.

"I was telling William," she said, "that we must manage to take him into the country somewhere, so that he may get quite well. He is not ill, you know, but he is not very strong, and has exerted himself too much lately." Poor thing! The tears that streamed through her fingers, as she turned aside, as if to adjust her close widow's cap, too plainly showed how fruitless was the attempt to deceive herself.

We sat down by the head of the sofa but said nothing, for we saw the breath of life was passing gently but rapidly from the young form before us. At every respiration, his heart beat more slowly.

The boy placed one hand in ours, grasped his mother's arm with the other, drew her hastily towards him, and fervently kissed her cheek. There was a pause. He sunk back upon his pillow, and looked long and earnestly in his mother's face.

"William, William!" murmured the mother after a long interval, "don't look at me so—speak to me, dear!"

The boy smiled languidly, but an instant afterwards his features resolved into the same cold, solemn gaze.

"William, dear William! rouse yourself, dear; don't look at me so, love—pray don't! Oh, my God! what shall I do!" cried the widow, clasping her hands in agony—"my dear boy! he is dying!"

The boy raised himself by a violent effort, and folded his hands together—"Mother! dear, dear mother, bury me in the open fields—anywhere but in these dreadful streets. I should like to be where you can see my grave, but not in these close crowded streets; they have killed me; kiss me again, mother; put your arm round my neck——"

He fell back, and a strange expression stole upon his features; not of pain or suffering, but an indescribable fixing of every line and muscle.

The boy was dead.

SCENES

CHAPTER I: *The Streets—Morning*

THE appearance presented by the streets of London an hour before sunrise, on a summer's morning, is most striking even to the few whose unfortunate pursuits of pleasure, or scarcely less unfortunate pursuits of business, cause them to be well acquainted with the scene. There is an air of cold, solitary desolation about the noiseless streets which we are accustomed to see thronged at other times by a busy, eager crowd, and over the quiet, closely-shut buildings, which throughout the day are swarming with life and bustle, that is very impressive.

The last drunken man, who shall find his way home before sunlight, has just staggered heavily along, roaring out the burden of the drinking song of the previous night: the last houseless vagrant whom penury and police have left in the streets, has coiled up his chilly limbs in some paved corner, to dream of food and warmth. The drunken, the dissipated, and the wretched have disappeared; the more sober and orderly part of the population have not yet awakened to the labours of the day, and the stillness of death is over the streets; its very hue seems to be imparted to them, cold and lifeless as they look in the grey, sombre light of daybreak. The coach-stands in the larger thoroughfares are deserted: the night-houses are closed; and the chosen promenades of profligate misery are empty.

An occasional policeman may alone be seen at the street corners, listlessly gazing on the deserted prospect before him; and now and then a rakish-looking cat runs stealthily across the road and descends his own area with as much caution and slyness—bounding first on the water-butt, then on the dust-hole, and then alighting on the flag-stones—as if he were conscious that his character depended on his gallantry of the preceding night escaping public observation. A partially opened bedroom-window here and there, bespeaks the heat of the weather, and the uneasy slumbers of its occupant; and the dim scanty flicker of the rushlight, through the window-blind, denotes the chamber of watching or sickness. With these few exceptions, the streets present no signs of life, nor the houses of habitation.

An hour wears away; the spires of the churches and roofs

of the principal buildings are faintly tinged with the light of the rising sun; and the streets, by almost imperceptible degrees, begin to resume their bustle and animation. Market-carts roll slowly along: the sleepy waggoner impatiently urging on his tired horses, or vainly endeavouring to awaken the boy, who, luxuriously stretched on the top of the fruit-baskets, forgets, in happy oblivion, his long-cherished curiosity to behold the wonders of London.

Rough, sleepy-looking animals of strange appearance, some-thing between ostlers and hackney-coachmen, begin to take down the shutters of early public-houses; and little deal tables, with the ordinary preparations for a street-breakfast, make their appearance at the customary stations. Numbers of men and women (principally the latter), carrying upon their heads heavy baskets of fruit, toil down the park side of Piccadilly, on their way to Covent Garden, and, following each other in rapid succession, form a long straggling line from thence to the turn of the road at Knightsbridge.

Here and there, a bricklayer's labourer, with the day's dinner tied up in a handkerchief, walks briskly to his work, and occasionally a little knot of three or four schoolboys on a stolen bathing expedition rattle merrily over the pavement, their boisterous mirth contrasting forcibly with the demeanour of the little sweep, who, having knocked and rung till his arm aches, and being interdicted by a merciful legislature from endangering his lungs by calling out, sits patiently down on the door-step until the housemaid may happen to awake.

Covent Garden market, and the avenues leading to it, are thronged with carts of all sorts, sizes, and descriptions, from the heavy lumbering waggon, with its four stout horses, to the jingling costermonger's cart, with its consumptive donkey. The pavement is already strewed with decayed cabbage-leaves, broken hay-bands, and all the indescribable litter of a vegetable market; men are shouting, carts backing, horses neighing, boys fighting, basket-women talking, piemen expatiating on the excellence of their pastry, and donkey: braying. These and a hundred other sounds form a compound discordant enough to a Londoner's ears, and remarkably disagreeable to those of country gentlemen who are sleeping at the Hummums for the first time.

Another hour passes away, and the day begins in good earnest. The servant of all work, who, under the plea of sleeping very soundly, has utterly disregarded "Missis's" ringing for half an hour previously, is warned by Master (whom Missis has sent up in his drapery to the landing-place for that purpose), that it's half-past six, whereupon she awakes all of a sudden, with well-feigned astonishment, and goes down stairs very sulkily, wishing, while she strikes a light, that the principle of spontaneous combustion would extend itself to coals and kitchen range. When the fire is lighted, she opens the street-door to take in the milk, when, by the most singular coincidence in the world, she discovers that the servant next door has just taken in her milk too, and that Mr. Todd's young man over the way, is, by an equally extraordinary chance, taking down his master's shutters. The inevitable consequence is, that she just steps, milk-jug in hand, as far as next door, just to say "good morning," to Betsy Clark, and that Mr. Todd's young man just steps over the way to say "good morning" to both of 'em; and as the aforesaid Mr. Todd's young man is almost as good-looking and fascinating as the baker himself, the conversation quickly becomes very interesting, and probably would become more so, if Betsy Clark's Missis, who always will be a-followin' her about, didn't give an angry tap at her bedroom window, on which Mr. Todd's young man tries to whistle coolly, as he goes back to his shop much faster than he came from it; and the two girls run back to their respective places, and shut their street doors with surprising softness, each of them poking their heads out of the front parlour-window, a minute afterwards, however, ostensibly with the view of looking at the mail which just then passes by, but really for the purpose of catching another glimpse of Mr. Todd's young man, who being fond of mails, but more of females, takes a short look at the mails, and a long look at the girls, much to the satisfaction of all parties concerned.

The mail itself goes on to the coach-office in due course, and the passengers who are going out by the early coach stare with astonishment at the passengers who are coming in by the early coach, who look blue and dismal, and are evidently under the influence of that odd feeling produced by travelling, which makes the events of yesterday morning seem as if they had happened at least six months ago, and induces people to wonder with considerable gravity whether the friends and relations they took leave of a fortnight before, have altered much since they left them. The coach-office is all alive, and the coaches which are just going out, are surrounded by the usual crowd of Jews and nondescripts, who seem to consider, Heaven knows why, that it is quite impossible any man can mount a coach without requiring at least sixpennyworth of oranges, a penknife, a pocket-book, a last year's annual, a pencil-case, a piece of sponge, and a small series of caricatures.

Half an hour more, and the sun darts his bright rays cheerfully down the still half-empty streets, and shines with sufficient force to rouse the dismal laziness of the apprentice, who pauses every other minute from his task of sweeping out the shop and watering the pavement in front of it, to tell another apprentice similarly employed, how hot it will be to-day, or to stand with his right hand shading his eyes, and his left resting on the broom, gazing at the "Wonder," or the "Tally-ho," or the "Nimrod," or some other fast coach, till it is out of sight, when he re-enters the shop, envying the passengers on the outside of the fast coach, and thinking of the old red brick house "down in the country," where he went to school: the miseries of the milk and water, and thick bread and scrapings, fading into nothing before the pleasant recollection of the green field the boys used to play in, and the green pond he was caned for presuming to fall into, and other schoolboy associations.

Cabs, with trunks and band-boxes between the drivers' legs and outside the apron, rattle briskly up and down the streets on their way to the coach-offices or steam-packet wharfs; and the cab-drivers and hackney-coachmen who are on the stand polish up the ornamental part of their dingy vehicles—the former wondering how people can prefer "them wild beast cariwans of homnibuses, to a riglar cab with a fast trotter," and the latter admiring how people can trust their necks into one of "them crazy cabs, when they can have a 'spectable 'ackney cotche with a pair of 'orses as von't run away with no vun;" a consolation unquestionably founded on fact, seeing that a hackney-coach horse never was known to run at all, "except" as the smart cabman in front of the rank observes, "except one, and *he* run back'ards."

The shops are now completely opened, and apprentices and shopmen are busily engaged in cleaning and decking the windows for the day. The bakers' shops in town are filled with servants and children waiting for the drawing of the first batch of rolls—an operation which was performed a full hour ago in the suburbs, for the early clerk population of Somers and Camden Towns, Islington, and Pentonville, are fast pouring into the city, or directing their steps towards Chancery Lane and the Inns of Court. Middle-aged men, whose salaries have by no means increased in the same proportion as their families, plod steadily along, apparently with no object in view but the counting-house; knowing by sight almost everybody they meet or overtake, for they have seen them every morning (Sundays excepted) during the last twenty years, but speaking to no one. If they do happen to overtake a personal acquaintance, they just exchange a hurried salutation, and keep walking on either by his side, or in front of him, as his rate of walking may chance to be. As to stopping to shake hands, or to take the friend's arm, they seem to think that as it is not included in their salary, they have no right to do it. Small office lads in large hats, who are made men before they are boys, hurry along in pairs with their first coat carefully brushed, and the white trousers of last Sunday plentifully besmeared with dust and ink. It

evidently requires a considerable mental struggle to avoid
investing part of the day's dinner-money in the purchase of
the stale tarts so temptingly exposed in dusty tins at the
pastry-cooks' doors; but a consciousness of their own
importance and the receipt of seven shillings a week, with
the prospect of an early rise to eight, comes to their aid, and
they accordingly put their hats a little more on one side,
and look under the bonnets of all the milliners' and stay-
makers' apprentices they meet—poor girls!—the hardest-
worked, the worst paid, and too often, the worst used class
of the community.

Eleven o'clock, and a new set of people fill the streets.
The goods in the shop-windows are invitingly arranged;
the shopmen in their white neckerchiefs and spruce coats,
look as if they couldn't clean a window if their lives depended
on it; the carts have disappeared from Covent Garden; the
waggoners have returned, and the costermongers repaired
to their ordinary "beats" in the suburbs; clerks are at their
offices, and gigs, cabs, omnibuses, and saddle-horses, are
conveying their masters to the same destination. The
streets are thronged with a vast concourse of people, gay and
shabby, rich and poor, idle and industrious; and we come to
the heat, bustle, and activity of NOON.

CHAPTER II: *The Streets—Night*

BUT the streets of London, to be beheld in the very height of
their glory, should be seen on a dark, dull, murky winter's
night, when there is just enough damp gently stealing down
to make the pavement greasy, without cleansing it of any
of its impurities; and when the heavy hazy mist, which hangs
over every object, makes the gas-lamps look brighter, and
the brilliantly-lighted shops more splendid, from the contrast
they present to the darkness around. All the people who are
at home on such a night as this, seem disposed to make
themselves as snug and comfortable as possible; and the
passengers in the streets have excellent reason to envy the
fortunate individuals who are seated by their own firesides.

In the larger and better kind of streets, dining parlour
curtains are closely drawn, kitchen fires blaze brightly up,
and savoury steams of hot dinners salute the nostrils of the
hungry wayfarer, as he plods wearily by the area railings. In
the suburbs, the muffin boy rings his way down the little
street, much more slowly than he is wont to do; for Mrs.
Macklin, of No. 4, has no sooner opened her little street-door,
and screamed out "Muffins!" with all her might, than Mrs.
Walker, at No. 5, puts her head out of the parlour-window,
and screams "Muffins!" too; and Mrs. Walker has scarcely

got the words out of her lips, than Mrs. Peplow, over the way, lets loose Master Peplow, who darts down the street, with a velocity which nothing but buttered muffins in perspective could possibly inspire, and drags the boy back by main force, whereupon Mrs. Macklin and Mrs. Walker, just to save the boy trouble, and to say a few neighbourly words to Mrs. Peplow at the same time, run over the way and buy their muffins at Mrs. Peplow's door, when it appears from the voluntary statement of Mrs. Walker, that her "kittle's jist a-biling, and the cups and sarsers ready laid," and that, as it was such a wretched night out o' doors, she'd made up her mind to have a nice hot comfortable cup o' tea—a determination at which, by the most singular coincidence, the other two ladies had simultaneously arrived.

After a little conversation about the wretchedness of the weather and the merits of tea, with a digression relative to the viciousness of boys as a rule, and the amiability of Master Peplow as an exception, Mrs. Walker sees her husband coming down the street; and as he must want his tea, poor man, after his dirty walk from the Docks, she instantly runs across, muffins in hand, and Mrs. Macklin does the same, and after a few words to Mrs. Walker, they all pop into their little houses, and slam their little street-doors, which are not opened again for the remainder of the evening, except to the nine o'clock "beer," who comes round with a lantern in front of his tray, and says as he lends Mrs. Walker "Yesterday's 'Tiser" that he's blessed if he can hardly hold the pot, much less feel the paper, for it's one of the bitterest nights he ever felt, 'cept the night when the man was frozen to death in the Brick-field.

After a little prophetic conversation with the policeman at the street-corner, touching a probable change in the weather, and the setting-in of a hard frost, the nine o'clock beer returns to his master's house, and employs himself for the remainder of the evening, in assiduously stirring the tap-room fire, and deferentially taking part in the conversation of the worthies assembled round it.

The streets in the vicinity of the Marsh Gate and Victoria Theatre present an appearance of dirt and discomfort on such a night, which the groups who lounge about them in no degree tend to diminish. Even the little block-tin temple sacred to baked potatoes, surmounted by a splendid design in variegated lamps, looks less gay than usual; and as to the kidney-pie stand, its glory has quite departed. The candle in the transparent lamp, manufactured of oil-paper, embellished with "characters," has been blown out fifty times, so the kidney-pie merchant, tired with running backwards and forwards to the next wine-vaults, to get a light, has given up the idea of illumination in despair, and the only signs of his "whereabouts," are the bright sparks, of which a long irregular train is whirled down the street every time he opens his portable oven to hand a hot kidney-pie to a customer.

Flat fish, oyster, and fruit venders linger hopelessly in the kennel, in vain endeavouring to attract customers; and the ragged boys who usually disport themselves about the streets, stand crouched in little knots in some projecting doorway, or under the canvas blind of the cheesemonger's, where great flaring gas-lights, unshaded by any glass, display huge piles of bright red, and pale yellow cheeses, mingled with little fivepenny dabs of dingy bacon, various tubs of weekly Dorset, and cloudy rolls of "best fresh."

Here they amuse themselves with theatrical converse, arising out of their last half-price visit to the Victoria gallery, admire the terrific combat, which is nightly encored, and expatiate on the inimitable manner in which Bill Thompson can "come the double monkey," or go through the mysterious involutions of the sailor's hornpipe.

It is nearly eleven o'clock, and the cold thin rain which has been drizzling so long, is beginning to pour down in good earnest; the baked-potato man has just departed—the kidney-pie man has just walked away with his warehouse on his arm—the cheesemonger has drawn in his blind, and the boys have dispersed. The constant clicking of pattens on the slippy and uneven pavement, and the rustling of umbrellas, as the wind blows against the shop windows, bear testimony to the inclemency of the night; and the policeman, with his oilskin cape buttoned closely round him, seems as he holds his hat on his head, and turns round to avoid the gust of wind and rain which drives against him at the street-corner, to be very far from congratulating himself on the prospect before him.

The little chandler's shop with the cracked bell behind the door, whose melancholy tinkling has been regulated by the demand for quarterns of sugar and half-ounces of coffee, is shutting up. The crowds which have been passing to and fro during the whole day, are rapidly dwindling away; and the noise of shouting and quarrelling which issues from the public-houses, is almost the only sound that breaks the melancholy stillness of the night.

There was another, but it has ceased. That wretched woman with the infant in her arms, round whose meagre form the remnant of her own scanty shawl is carefully wrapped, has been attempting to sing some popular ballad, in the hope of wringing a few pence from the compassionate passer-by. A brutal laugh at her weak voice is all she has gained. The tears fall thick and fast down her own pale face; the child is cold and hungry, and its low half-stifled wailing adds to the misery of its wretched mother, as she moans aloud, and sinks despairingly down, on a cold damp door-step.

Singing! How few of those who pass such a miserable creature as this, think of the anguish of heart, the sinking of soul and spirit, which the very effort of singing produces. Bitter mockery! Disease, neglect, and starvation, faintly articulating the words of the joyous ditty, that has enlivened your hours of feasting and merriment, God knows how often! It is no subject of jeering. The weak tremulous voice tells a fearful tale of want and famishing; and the feeble singer of this roaring song may turn away, only to die of cold and hunger.

One o'clock! Parties returning from the different theatres foot it through the muddy streets; cabs, hackney-coaches, carriages, and theatre omnibuses, roll swiftly by; watermen with dim dirty lanterns in their hands, and large brass plates upon their breasts, who have been shouting and rushing about for the last two hours, retire to their watering-houses, to solace themselves with the creature comforts of pipes and purl; the half-price pit and box frequenters of the theatres throng to the different houses of refreshment; and chops, kidneys, rabbits, oysters, stout, cigars, and "goes" innumerable, are served up amidst a noise and confusion of smoking, running, knife-clattering, and waiter-chattering, perfectly indescribable.

The more musical portion of the play-going community betake themselves to some harmonic meeting. As a matter of curiosity let us follow them thither for a few moments.

In a lofty room of spacious dimensions, are seated some eighty or a hundred guests knocking little pewter measures on the tables, and hammering away, with the handles of their knives, as if they were so many trunk-makers. They are applauding a glee, which has just been executed by the three "professional gentlemen" at the top of the centre table, one of whom is in the chair—the little pompous man with the bald head just emerging from the collar of his green coat. The others are seated on either side of him—the stout man with the small voice, and the thin-faced dark man in black. The little man in the chair is a most amusing personage,— such condescending grandeur, and such a voice!

"Bass!" as the young gentleman near us with the blue stock forcibly remarks to his companion, "bass! I b'lieve you; he can go down lower than any man: so low sometimes that you can't hear him." And so he does. To hear him growling away, gradually lower and lower down, till he can't get back again, is the most delightful thing in the world, and it is quite impossible to witness unmoved the impressive solemnity with which he pours forth his soul in "My 'art's in the 'ighlands," or "The brave old Hoak." The stout man is also addicted to sentimentality, and warbles "Fly, fly from the world, my Bessy with me," or some such song, with ladylike sweetness, and in the most seductive tones imaginable.

"Pray give your orders, gen'l'm'n—pray give your orders," says the pale-faced man with the red head; and demands for "goes" of gin and "goes" of brandy, and pints of stout, and cigars of peculiar mildness, are vociferously made from all parts of the room. The "professional gentlemen" are in the very height of their glory, and bestow condescending nods, or even a word or two of recognition, on the better-known frequenters of the room, in the most bland and patronising manner possible.

That little round-faced man, with the small brown surtout, white stockings and shoes, is in the comic line; the mixed air of self-denial, and mental consciousness of his own powers, with which he acknowledges the call of the chair, is particularly gratifying. "Gen'l'men," says the little pompous man, accompanying the word with a knock of the president's hammer on the table—"Gen'l'men, allow me to claim your attention—our friend, Mr. Smuggins will oblige."—"Bravo!" shout the company; and Smuggins, after a considerable quantity of coughing by way of symphony, and a most facetious sniff or two, which afford general delight, sings a comic song, with a fal-de-ral—tol-de-rol chorus at the end of every verse, much longer than the verse itself. It is received with unbounded applause, and after some aspiring genius has volunteered a recitation, and failed dismally therein, the little pompous man gives another knock, and says, "Gen'l'men, we will attempt a glee, if you please." This announcement calls forth tumultuous applause, and the more energetic spirits express the unqualified approbation it affords them, by knocking one or two stout glasses off their legs—a humorous device; but one which frequently occasions some slight altercation when the form of paying the damage is proposed to be gone through by the waiter.

Scenes like these are continued until three or four o'clock in the morning; and even when they close, fresh ones open to the inquisitive novice. But as a description of all of them, however slight, would require a volume, the contents of which, however instructive, would be by no means pleasing, we make our bow, and drop the curtain.

CHAPTER III: *Shops and their Tenants*

WHAT inexhaustible food for speculation, do the streets of London afford! We never were able to agree with Sterne in pitying the man who could travel from Dan to Beersheba, and say that all was barren; we have not the slightest commiseration for the man who can take up his hat and stick, and walk from Covent Garden to St. Paul's Churchyard, and back into the bargain, without deriving some amusement

—we had almost said instruction—from his perambulation. And yet there are such beings: we meet them every day. Large black stocks and light waistcoats, jet canes and discontented countenances, are the characteristics of the race; other people brush quickly by you, steadily plodding on to business, or cheerfully running after pleasure. These men linger listlessly past, looking as happy and animated as a policeman on duty. Nothing seems to make an impression on their minds: nothing short of being knocked down by a porter, or run over by a cab, will disturb their equanimity. You will meet them on a fine day in any of the leading thoroughfares: peep through the window of a West-end cigar shop in the evening, if you can manage to get a glimpse between the blue curtains which intercept the vulgar gaze, and you see them in their only enjoyment of existence. There they are lounging about, on round tubs and pipeboxes, in all the dignity of whiskers, and gilt watch-guards; whispering soft nothings to the young lady in amber, with the large earrings, who, as she sits behind the counter in a blaze of adoration and gas-light, is the admiration of all the female servants in the neighbourhood, and the envy of every milliner's apprentice within two miles round.

One of our principal amusements is to watch the gradual progress—the rise or fall—of particular shops. We have formed an intimate acquaintance with several, in different parts of town, and are perfectly acquainted with their whole history. We could name off-hand, twenty at least, which we are quite sure have paid no taxes for the last six years. They are never inhabited for more than two months consecutively, and, we verily believe, have witnessed every retail trade in the directory.

There is one, whose history is a sample of the rest, in whose fate we have taken especial interest, having had the pleasure of knowing it ever since it has been a shop. It is on the Surrey side of the water—a little distance beyond the Marsh Gate. It was originally a substantial, good-looking private house enough; the landlord got into difficulties, the house got into Chancery, the tenant went away, and the house went to ruin. At this period our acquaintance with it commenced: the paint was all worn off; the windows were broken, the area was green with neglect and the overflowings of the water-butt; the butt itself was without a lid, and the street-door was the very picture of misery. The chief pastime of the children in the vicinity had been to assemble in a body on the steps, and take it in turn to knock loud double-knocks at the door, to the great satisfaction of the neighbours generally, and especially of the nervous old lady next door but one. Numerous complaints were made, and several small basins of water discharged over the offenders, but without effect. In this state of things, the marine-store dealer at the corner of the street, in the most obliging manner took the knocker off, and sold it: and the unfortunate house looked more wretched than ever.

We deserted our friend for a few weeks. What was our surprise, on our return, to find no trace of its existence! In its place was a handsome shop, fast approaching to a state of completion, and on the shutters were large bills informing the public that it would shortly be opened with "an extensive stock of linen drapery and haberdashery." It opened in due course; there was the name of the proprietor "and Co." in gilt letters, almost too dazzling to look at. Such ribbons and shawls! and two such elegant young men behind the counter, each in a clean collar and white neckcloth, like the lover in a farce. As to the proprietor, he did nothing but walk up and down the shop, and hand seats to the ladies, and hold important conversations with the handsomest of the young men, who was shrewdly suspected by the neighbours to be the "Co." We saw all this with sorrow; we felt a fatal presentiment that the shop was doomed—and so it was. Its decay was slow, but sure. Tickets gradually appeared in the windows; then rolls of flannel, with labels on them, were stuck outside the door; then a bill was pasted on the street-door, intimating that the first floor was to let *un-furnished*; then one of the young men disappeared altogether, and the other took to a black neckerchief, and the proprietor took to drinking. The shop became dirty, broken panes of glass remained unmended, and the stock disappeared piecemeal. At last the company's man came to cut off the water, and then the linen-draper cut off himself, leaving the landlord his compliments and the key.

The next occupant was a fancy stationer. The shop was more modestly painted than before, still it was neat; but somehow we always thought, as we passed, that it looked like a poor and struggling concern. We wished the man well, but we trembled for his success. He was a widower evidently, and had employment elsewhere, for he passed us every morning on his road to the city. The business was carried on by his eldest daughter. Poor girl! she needed no assistance. We occasionally caught a glimpse of two or three children, in mourning like herself, as they sat in the little parlour behind the shop; and we never passed at night without seeing the eldest girl at work, either for them, or in making some elegant little trifle for sale. We often thought, as her pale face looked more sad and pensive in the dim candle-light, that if those thoughtless females who interfere with the miserable market of poor creatures such as these, knew but one-half of the misery they suffer, and the bitter privations they endure, in their honourable attempts to earn a scanty subsistence, they would, perhaps, resign even opportunities for the gratification of vanity, and an immodest love of self-display, rather than drive them to a last dreadful resource, which it would shock the delicate feelings of these *charitable* ladies to hear named.

But we are forgetting the shop. Well, we continued to watch it, and every day showed too clearly, the increasing poverty of its inmates. The children were clean, it is true, but their clothes were threadbare and shabby; no tenant had been procured for the upper part of the house, from the letting of which, a portion of the means of paying the rent was to have been derived, and a slow, wasting consumption prevented the eldest girl from continuing her exertions. Quarter-day arrived. The landlord had suffered from the extravagance of his last tenant, and he had no compassion for the struggles of his successor; he put in an execution. As we passed one morning, the broker's men were removing the little furniture there was in the house, and a newly-posted bill informed us it was again "To Let." What became of the last tenant we never could learn; we believe the girl is past all suffering, and beyond all sorrow. God help her! We hope she is.

We were somewhat curious to ascertain what would be the next stage—for that the place had no chance of succeeding now, was perfectly clear. The bill was soon taken down, and some alterations were being made in the interior of the shop. We were in a fever of expectation; we exhausted conjecture—we imagined all possible trades, none of which were perfectly reconcilable with our idea of the gradual decay of the tenement. It opened, and we wondered why we had not guessed at the real state of the case before. The shop—not a large one at the best of times—had been converted into two: one was a bonnet-shape maker's, the other was opened by a tobacconist, who also dealt in walking-sticks and Sunday newspapers; the two were separated by a thin partition, covered with tawdry striped paper.

The tobacconist remained in possession longer than any tenant within our recollection. He was a red-faced, impudent, good-for-nothing dog, evidently accustomed to take things as they came, and to make the best of a bad job. He sold as many cigars as he could, and smoked the rest. He occupied the shop as long as he could make peace with the landlord, and when he could no longer live in quiet, he very coolly locked the door, and bolted himself. From this period, the two little dens have undergone innumerable changes. The tobacconist was succeeded by a theatrical hair-dresser, who ornamented the window with a great variety of "characters," and terrific combats. The bonnet-shape maker gave place to a greengrocer, and the histrionic barber was succeeded, in his turn, by a tailor. So numerous have been the changes, that we have of late done little more than mark the peculiar but certain indications of a house being poorly inhabited. It has been progressing by almost imperceptible degrees. The occupiers of the shops have gradually given up room after room, until they have only reserved the little parlour for themselves. First there appeared a brass plate on the private door, with "Ladies' School" legibly engraved thereon; shortly afterwards we observed a second brass plate, then a bell, and then another bell.

When we paused in front of our old friend, and observed these signs of poverty, which are not to be mistaken, we thought, as we turned away, that the house had attained its lowest pitch of degradation. We were wrong. When we last passed it, a "dairy" was established in the area, and a party of melancholy-looking fowls were amusing themselves by running in at the front door, and out at the back one.

CHAPTER IV: *Scotland Yard*

SCOTLAND YARD is a small—a very small—tract of land, bounded on one side by the river Thames, on the other by the gardens of Northumberland House: abutting at one end on the bottom of Northumberland Street, at the other on the back of Whitehall Place. When this territory was first accidentally discovered by a country gentleman who lost his way in the Strand, some years ago, the original settlers were found to be a tailor, a publican, two eating-house keepers, and a fruit-pie maker; and it was also found to contain a race of strong and bulky men, who repaired to the wharfs in Scotland Yard regularly every morning, about five or six o'clock, to fill heavy waggons with coal, with which they proceeded to distant places up the country, and supplied the inhabitants with fuel. When they had emptied their waggons, they again returned for a fresh supply; and this trade was continued throughout the year.

As the settlers derived their subsistence from ministering to the wants of these primitive traders, the articles exposed for sale, and the places where they were sold, bore strong outward marks of being expressly adapted to their tastes and wishes. The tailor displayed in his window a Lilliputian pair of leather gaiters, and a diminutive round frock, while each doorpost was appropriately garnished with a model of a coal-sack. The two eating-house keepers exhibited joints of a magnitude, and puddings of a solidity, which coalheavers alone could appreciate; and the fruit-pie maker displayed on his well-scrubbed window-board large white compositions of flour and dripping, ornamented with pink stains, giving rich promise of the fruit within, which made their huge mouths water, as they lingered past.

But the choicest spot in all Scotland Yard was the old public-house in the corner. Here, in a dark wainscoted-room of ancient appearance, cheered by the glow of a mighty fire, and decorated with an enormous clock, whereof the face was white, and the figures black, sat the lusty coalheavers, quaffing large draughts of Barclay's best, and puffing forth volumes of smoke, which wreathed heavily above their heads, and involved the room in a thick dark cloud. From this apartment might their voices be heard on a winter's night, penetrating to the very bank of the river, as they shouted out some sturdy chorus, or roared forth the burden of a popular song; dwelling upon the last few words with a strength and length of emphasis which made the very roof tremble above them.

Here, too, would they tell old legends of what the Thames was in ancient times, when the Patent Shot Manufactory wasn't built, and Waterloo Bridge had never been thought of; and then they would shake their heads with portentous looks, to the deep edification of the rising generation of heavers, who crowded round them, and wondered where all this would end; whereat the tailor would take his pipe solemnly from his mouth, and say, how that he hoped it might end well, but he very much doubted whether it would or not, and couldn't rightly tell what to make of it—a mysterious expression of opinion, delivered with a semi-prophetic air, which never failed to elicit the fullest concurrence of the assembled company; and so they would go on drinking and wondering till ten o'clock came, and with it the tailor's wife to fetch him home, when the little party broke up, to meet again in the same room, and say and do precisely the same things, on the following evening at the same hour.

About this time the barges that came up the river began to bring vague rumours to Scotland Yard of somebody in the city having been heard to say that the Lord Mayor had threatened in so many words to pull down the old London Bridge, and build up a new one. At first these rumours were disregarded as idle tales, wholly destitute of foundation, for nobody in Scotland Yard doubted that if the Lord Mayor contemplated any such dark design, he would just be clapped up in the Tower for a week or two, and then killed off for high treason.

By degrees, however, the reports grew stronger, and more frequent, and at last a barge laden with numerous chaldrons of the best Wallsend, brought up the positive intelligence that several of the arches of the old bridge were stopped, and that preparations were actually in progress for constructing the new one. What an excitement was visible in the old tap-room on that memorable night! Each man looked into his neighbour's face, pale with alarm and astonishment and read therein an echo of the sentiments which filled his own breast. The oldest heaver present proved to demonstration, that the moment the piers were removed, all the water in the Thames would run clean off, and leave a dry gully in its place. What was to become of the coal-barges—of the trade of Scotland Yard—of the very existence of its population? The tailor shook his head more sagely than usual, and, grimly pointing to a knife on the table, bid them wait and see what happened. He said nothing—not he; but if the Lord Mayor didn't fall a victim to popular indignation, why he would be rather astonished; that was all.

They did wait; barge after barge arrived, and still no tidings of the assassination of the Lord Mayor. The first stone was laid; it was done by a Duke—the King's brother. Years passed away, and the bridge was opened by the King himself. In course of time, the piers were removed; and when the people in Scotland Yard got up next morning in the confident expectation of being able to step over to Pedlar's Acre without wetting the soles of their shoes, they found to their unspeakable astonishment that the water was just where it used to be.

A result so different from that which they had anticipated from this first improvement, produced its full effect upon the inhabitants of Scotland Yard. One of the eating-house keepers began to court public opinion, and to look for customers among a new class of people. He covered his little dining-tables with white cloths, and got a painter's apprentice to inscribe something about hot joints from twelve to two, in one of the little panes of his shop-window. Improvements began to march with rapid strides to the very threshold of Scotland Yard. A new market sprang up at Hungerford, and the Police Commissioners established their office in Whitehall Place. The traffic in Scotland Yard increased; fresh Members were added to the House of Commons, the Metropolitan Representatives found it a near cut, and many other foot-passengers followed their example.

We marked the advance of civilisation, and beheld it with a sigh. The eating-house keeper who manfully resisted the innovation of table-cloths, was losing ground every day, as his opponent gained it, and a deadly feud sprang up between them. The genteel one no longer took his evening's pint in Scotland Yard, but drank gin and water at a "parlour" in Parliament Street. The fruit-pie maker still continued to visit the old room, but he took to smoking cigars, and began to call himself a pastrycook, and to read the papers. The old heavers still assembled round the ancient fire-place, but their talk was mournful: and the loud song and the joyous shout were heard no more.

And what is Scotland Yard now? How have its old customs changed; and how has the ancient simplicity of its inhabitants faded away! The old tottering public-house is converted into a spacious and lofty "wine-vaults"; gold leaf has been used in the construction of the letters which emblazon its exterior, and the poet's art has been called into requisition, to intimate that if you drink a certain description of ale, you must hold fast by the rail. The tailor exhibits in his window the pattern of a foreign-looking brown surtout, with silk buttons, a fur collar and fur cuffs. He wears a stripe down the outside of each leg of his trousers: and we have detected his assistants (for he has assistants now) in the act of sitting on the shop-board in the same uniform.

At the other end of the little row of houses a bootmaker has established himself in a brick box, with the additional innovation of a first floor; and here he exposes for sale, boots —real Wellington boots—an article which a few years ago, none of the original inhabitants had ever seen or heard of. It was but the other day that a dressmaker opened another little box in the middle of the row; and, when we thought that the spirit of change could produce no alteration beyond that, a jeweller appeared, and not content with exposing gilt rings and copper bracelets out of number, put up an announcement, which still sticks in his window, that "ladies' ears may be pierced within." The dressmaker employs a young lady who wears pockets in her apron; and the tailor informs the public that gentlemen may have their own materials made up.

Amidst all this change, and restlessness, and innovation, there remains but one old man, who seems to mourn the downfall of this ancient place. He holds no converse with human kind, but, seated on a wooden bench at the angle of the wall which fronts the crossing from Whitehall Place, watches in silence the gambols of his sleek and well-fed dogs. He is the presiding genius of Scotland Yard. Years and years have rolled over his head; but, in fine weather or in foul, hot or cold, wet or dry, hail, rain, or snow, he is still in his accustomed spot. Misery and want are depicted in his countenance; his form is bent by age, his head is grey with length of trial, but there he sits from day to day, brooding over the past; and thither he will continue to drag his feeble limbs, until his eyes have closed upon Scotland Yard, and upon the world together.

A few years hence, and the antiquary of another generation looking into some mouldy record of the strife and passions that agitated the world in these times, may glance his eye over the pages we have just filled: and not all his knowledge

of the history of the past, not all his black-letter lore, or his
skill in book-collecting, not all the dry studies of a long life,
or the dusty volumes that have cost him a fortune, may help
him to the whereabouts, either of Scotland Yard, or of any
one of the landmarks we have mentioned in describing it.

CHAPTER V: *Seven Dials.*

WE have always been of opinion that if Tom King and the
Frenchman had not immortalised Seven Dials, Seven Dials
would have immortalised itself. Seven Dials! The region
of song and poetry—first effusions, and last dying speeches:
hallowed by the names of Catnac and of Pitts—names that
will entwine themselves with costermongers, and barrel-
organs, when penny magazines shall have superseded penny
yards of song, and capital punishment be unknown!

Look at the construction of the place. The Gordian knot
was all very well in its way: so was the maze of Hampton
Court: so is the maze at the Beulah Spa: so were the ties of
stiff white neckcloths, when the difficulty of getting one on
was only to be equalled by the apparent impossibility of
ever getting it off again. But what involutions can compare
with those of Seven Dials? Where is there such another
maze of streets, courts, lanes, and alleys? Where such a
pure mixture of Englishmen and Irishmen, as in this complicated part of London? We boldly aver that we doubt
the veracity of the legend to which we have adverted. We
can suppose a man rash enough to inquire at random—
at a house with lodgers too—for a Mr. Thompson, with all
but the certainty before his eyes, of finding at least two or
three Thompsons in any house of moderate dimensions; but
a Frenchman—a Frenchman in Seven Dials! Pooh! He
was an Irishman. Tom King's education had been neglected
in his infancy, and as he couldn't understand half the man
said, he took it for granted he was talking French.

The stranger who finds himself in "The Dials" for the first
time, and stands, Belzoni-like, at the entrance of seven
obscure passages, uncertain which to take, will see enough
around him to keep his curiosity and attention awake for
no inconsiderable time. From the irregular square into
which he has plunged, the streets and courts dart in all
directions, until they are lost in the unwholesome vapour
which hangs over the house-tops, and renders the dirty
perspective uncertain and confined; and lounging at every
corner, as if they came there to take a few gasps of such fresh
air as has found its way so far, but is too much exhausted
already, to be enabled to force itself into the narrow alleys
around, are groups of people, whose appearance and dwellings

George Cruikshank

SEVEN DIALS.

would fill any mind but a regular Londoner's with astonishment.

On one side, a little crowd has collected round a couple of ladies, who having imbibed the contents of various "threeouts" of gin and bitters in the course of the morning, have at length differed on some point of domestic arrangement, and are on the eve of settling the quarrel satisfactorily, by an appeal to blows, greatly to the interest of other ladies who live in the same house, and tenements adjoining, and who are all partisans on one side or other.

"Vy don't you pitch into her, Sarah?" exclaims one half-dressed matron, by way of encouragement. "Vy don't you? if *my* 'usband had treated her with a drain last night, unbeknown to me, I'd tear her precious eyes out—a wixen!"

"What's the matter, ma'am?" inquires another old woman, who has just bustled up to the spot.

"Matter!" replies the first speaker, talking *at* the obnoxious combatant, "matter! Here's poor dear Mrs. Sulliwin, as has five blessed children of her own, can't go out a charing for one arternoon, but what hussies must be a comin', and 'ticing avay her oun 'usband, as she's been married to twelve year come next Easter Monday, for I see the certificate ven I vas a drinkin' a cup o' tea vith her, only the werry last blessed Ven'sday as ever was sent. I 'appen'd to say promiscuously 'Mrs. Sulliwin,' says I——"

"What do you mean by hussies?" interrupts a champion of the other party, who has evinced a strong inclination throughout to get up a branch fight on her own account ("Hooroar," ejaculates a pot-boy in parenthesis, "put the kye-bosh on her, Mary!"). "What do you mean by hussies?" reiterates the champion.

"Niver mind," replies the opposition expressively, "niver mind; *you* go home, and, ven you're quite sober, mend your stockings."

This somewhat personal allusion, not only to the lady's habits of intemperance, but also to the state of her wardrobe, rouses her utmost ire, and she accordingly complies with the urgent request of the bystanders to "pitch in," with considerable alacrity. The scuffle became general, and terminates, in minor play-bill phraseology, with "arrival of the policemen, interior of the station-house, and impressive *dénouement.*"

In addition to the numerous groups who are idling about the gin-shops, and squabbling in the centre of the road, every post in the open space has its occupant, who leans against it for hours, with listless perseverance. It is odd enough that one class of men in London appear to have no enjoyment beyond leaning against posts. We never saw a regular bricklayer's labourer take any other recreation, fighting excepted. Pass through St. Giles in the evening of a week-day, there they are in their fustian dresses, spotted with brick-dust and whitewash, leaning against posts. Walk through Seven Dials on Sunday morning: there they are again, drab or light corduroy trousers, Blucher boots, blue coats, and great yellow waistcoats, leaning against posts. The idea of a man dressing himself in his best clothes, to lean against a post all day!

The peculiar character of these streets, and the close resemblance each one bears to its neighbour, by no means tends to decrease the bewilderment in which the unexperienced wayfarer through "The Dials" finds himself involved. He traverses streets of dirty, straggling houses, with now and then an unexpected court composed of buildings as ill-proportioned and deformed as the half-naked children that wallow in the kennels. Here and there, a little dark chandler's shop, with a cracked bell hung up behind the door to announce the entrance of a customer, or betray the presence of some young gentleman in whom a passion for shop tills has developed itself at an early age: others, as if for support, against some handsome lofty building, which usurps the place of a low dingy public-house; long rows of broken and patched windows expose plants that may have flourished when "The Dials" were built, in vessels as dirty as "The Dials" themselves; and shops for the purchase of rags, bones, old iron, and kitchen-stuff, vie in cleanliness with the bird-fanciers and rabbit-dealers, which one might fancy so many arks, but for the irresistible conviction that no bird in its proper senses, who was permitted to leave one of them, would ever come back again. Brokers' shops, which would seem to have been established by humane individuals, as refuges for destitute bugs, interspersed with announcements of day-schools, penny theatres, petition-writers, mangles, and music for balls or routs, complete the "still life" of the subject; and dirty men, filthy women, squalid children, fluttering shuttle-cocks, noisy battledores, reeking pipes, bad fruit, more than doubtful oysters, attenuated cats, depressed dogs, and anatomical fowls, are its cheerful accompaniments.

If the external appearance of the houses, or a glance at their inhabitants, present but few attractions, a closer acquaintance with either is little calculated to alter one's first impression. Every room has its separate tenant, and every tenant is, by the same mysterious dispensation which causes a country curate to "increase and multiply" most marvellously, generally the head of a numerous family.

The man in the shop, perhaps, is in the baked "jemmy" line, or the firewood and hearthstone line, or any other line which requires a floating capital of eighteenpence or there-abouts; and he and his family live in the shop, and the small back parlour behind it. Then there is an Irish labourer and *his* family in the back kitchen, and a jobbing man—carpet-beater and so forth—with *his* family in the front one. In the front one-pair there's another man with another wife and family, and in the back one-pair there's "a young 'oman as takes in tambour-work, and dresses quite genteel," who talks a good deal about "my friend," and can't "a-bear anything low." The second floor front, and the rest of the lodgers, are just a second edition of the people below, except a shabby-genteel man in the back attic, who has his half-pint of coffee every morning from the coffee-shop next door but one, which boasts a little front den called a coffee-room, with a fire-place, over which is an inscription, politely requesting that, "to prevent mistakes," customers will "please to pay on delivery." The shabby-genteel man is an object of some mystery, but as he leads a life of seclusion, and never was known to buy anything beyond an occasional pen, except half-pints of coffee, penny loaves, and ha'porths of ink, his fellow-lodgers very naturally suppose him to be an author; and rumours are current in the Dials, that he writes poems for Mr. Warren.

Now anybody who passed through the Dials on a hot summer's evening, and saw the different women of the house gossiping on the steps, would be apt to think that all was harmony among them, and that a more primitive set of people than the native Diallers could not be imagined. Alas! the man in the shop ill-treats his family; the carpet-beater extends his professional pursuits to his wife; the one-pair front has an undying feud with the two-pair front, in consequence of the two-pair front persisting in dancing over his (the one-pair front's) head when he and his family have retired for the night; the two-pair back *will* interfere with the front kitchen's children; the Irishman comes home drunk every other night, and attacks everybody; and the one-pair back screams at everything. Animosities spring up between floor and floor; the very cellar asserts his equality. Mrs. A. "smacks" Mrs. B.'s child for "making faces." Mrs. B. forthwith throws cold water over Mrs. A.'s child for "calling names." The husbands are embroiled—the quarrel becomes general—an assault is the consequence, and a police-officer the result.

CHAPTER VI: *Meditations in Monmouth Street*

WE have always entertained a particular attachment towards Monmouth Street, as the only true and real emporium for second-hand wearing apparel. Monmouth Street is venerable from its antiquity, and respectable from its usefulness.

Holywell Street we despise; the red-headed and red-whiskered Jews who forcibly haul you into their squalid houses, and thrust you into a suit of clothes, whether you will or not, we detest.

The inhabitants of Monmouth Street are a distinct class; a peaceable and retiring race, who immure themselves for the most part in deep cellars, or small back parlours, and who seldom come forth into the world, except in the dusk and coolness of evening, when they may be seen seated, in chairs on the pavement, smoking their pipes, or watching the gambols of their engaging children as they revel in the gutter, a happy troop of infantine scavengers. Their countenances bear a thoughtful and a dirty cast, certain indications of their love of traffic; and their habitations are distinguished by that disregard of outward appearance, and neglect of personal comfort, so common among people who are constantly immersed in profound speculations, and deeply engaged in sedentary pursuits.

We have hinted at the antiquity of our favourite spot. "A Monmouth Street laced coat" was a byword a century ago; and still we find Monmouth Street the same. Pilot great-coats with wooden buttons, have usurped the place of the ponderous laced coats with full skirts; embroidered waistcoats with large flaps have yielded to double-breasted checks with roll-collars; and three-cornered hats of quaint appearance have given place to the low crowns and broad brims of the coachman school; but it is the times that have changed, not Monmouth Street. Through every alteration and every change, Monmouth Street has still remained the burial-place of the fashions; and such, to judge from all present appearances, it will remain until there are no more fashions to bury.

We love to walk among these extensive groves of the illustrious dead, and to indulge in the speculations to which they give rise; now fitting a deceased coat, then a dead pair of trousers, and anon the mortal remains of a gaudy waistcoat, upon some being of our own conjuring up, and endeavouring, from the shape and fashion of the garment itself, to bring its former owner before our mind's eye. We have gone on speculating in this way, until whole rows of coats have started from their pegs, and buttoned up, of their own accord, round the waists of imaginary wearers; lines of trousers have jumped down to meet them; waistcoats have almost burst with anxiety to put themselves on; and half an acre of shoes have suddenly found feet to fit them, and gone stumping down the street with a noise which has fairly awakened us from our pleasant reverie, and driven us slowly away, with a bewildered stare, an object of astonishment to the good people of Monmouth Street, and of no slight suspicion to the policemen at the opposite street corner.

We were occupied in this manner the other day, endeavouring to fit a pair of lace-up half-boots on an ideal personage, for whom, to say the truth, they were full a couple of sizes too small, when our eyes happened to alight on a few suits of clothes ranged outside a shop-window, which it immediately struck us, must at different periods have all belonged to, and been worn by, the same individual, and had now by one of those strange conjunctions of circumstances which will occur sometimes, come to be exposed together for sale in the same shop. The idea seemed a fantastic one, and we looked at the clothes again, with a firm determination not to be easily led away. No, we were right; the more we looked, the more we were convinced of the accuracy of our previous impression. There was the man's whole life written as legibly on those clothes as if we had his autobiography engrossed on parchment before us.

The first was a patched and much-soiled skeleton suit; one of those straight blue cloth cases in which small boys used to be confined, before belts and tunics had come in, and old notions had gone out: an ingenious contrivance for displaying the full symmetry of a boy's figure, by fastening him into a very tight jacket, with an ornamental row of buttons over each shoulder, and then buttoning his trousers over it, so as to give his legs the appearance of being hooked on, just under the armpits. This was the boy's dress. It had belonged to a town boy, we could see; there was a shortness about the legs and arms of the suit; and a bagging at the knees, peculiar to the rising youth of London streets. A small day-school he had been at, evidently. If it had been a regular boys' school they wouldn't have let him play on the floor so much, and rub his knees so white. He had an indulgent mother too, and plenty of halfpence, as the numerous smears of some sticky substance about the pockets, and just below the chin, which even the salesman's skill could not succeed in disguising, sufficiently betokened. They were decent people, but not overburdened with riches, or he would not have so far outgrown the suit when he passed into those corduroys with the round jacket; in which he went to a boys' school, however, and learnt to write—and in ink of pretty tolerable blackness too, if the place where he used to wipe his pen might be taken as evidence.

A black suit and the jacket changed into a diminutive coat. His father had died, and the mother had got the boy a message-lad's place in some office. A long-worn suit that one; rusty and threadbare before it was laid aside, but clean and free from soil to the last. Poor woman! We could imagine her assumed cheerfulness over the scanty meal, and the refusal of her own small portion, that her hungry boy might have enough. Her constant anxiety for his welfare, her pride in his growth mingled sometimes with the thought, almost too acute to bear, that as he grew to be a man his old affection might cool, old kindnesses fade from his mind, and old promises be forgotten—the sharp pain that even then a careless word or a cold look would give her—all crowded on our thoughts as vividly as if the very scene were passing before us.

These things happen every hour, and we all know it; and yet we felt as much sorrow when we saw, or fancied we saw —it makes no difference which—the change that began to take place now, as if we had just conceived the bare possibility of such a thing for the first time. The next suit, smart but slovenly; meant to be gay, and yet not half so decent as the threadbare apparel; redolent of the idle lounge, and the blackguard companions, told us, we thought, that the widow's comfort had rapidly faded away. We could imagine that coat—imagine! we could see it; we *had* seen it a hundred times—sauntering in company with three or four other coats of the same cut, about some place of profligate resort at night.

We dressed, from the same shop-window in an instant, half a dozen boys of from fifteen to twenty; and putting cigars into their mouths, and their hands into their pockets, watched them as they sauntered down the street, and lingered at the corner, with the obscene jest, and the oft-repeated oath. We never lost sight of them, till they had cocked their hats a little more on one side, and swaggered into the public-house; and then we entered the desolate home, where the mother sat late in the night, alone; we watched her, as she paced the room in feverish anxiety, and every now and then opened the door, looked wistfully into the dark and empty street, and again returned, to be again and again disappointed. We beheld the look of patience with which she bore the brutish threat, nay, even the drunken blow; and we heard the agony of tears that gushed from her very heart, as she sank upon her knees in her solitary and wretched apartment.

A long period had elapsed, and a greater change had taken place, by the time of casting off the suit that hung above. It was that of a stout, broad-shouldered, sturdy-chested man; and we knew at once, as anybody would, who glanced at that broad-skirted green coat, with the large metal buttons, that its wearer seldom walked forth without a dog at his heels, and some idle ruffian, the very counterpart of himself, at his side. The vices of the boy had grown with the man, and we fancied his home then—if such a place deserve the name.

We saw the bare and miserable room, destitute of furniture, crowded with his wife and children, pale, hungry, and emaciated; the man cursing their lamentations, staggering to the tap-room, from whence he had just returned, followed by his wife and a sickly infant, clamouring for bread; and heard the street-wrangle and noisy recrimination that his striking her occasioned. And then imagination led us to some metropolitan workhouse, situated in the midst of crowded streets and alleys, filled with noxious vapours, and ringing with boisterous cries, where an old and feeble woman, imploring pardon for her son, lay dying in a close dark room, with no child to clasp her hand, and no pure air from heaven to fan her brow. A stranger closed the eyes that settled into a cold unmeaning glare, and strange ears received the words that murmured from the white and half-closed lips.

A coarse round frock, with a worn cotton neckerchief, and other articles of clothing of the commonest description, completed the history. A prison, and the sentence—banishment or the gallows. What would the man have given then, to be once again the contented humble drudge of his boyish years; to have restored to life, but for a week, a day, an hour, a minute, only for so long a time as would enable him to say one word of passionate regret to, and hear one sound of heartfelt forgiveness from, the cold and ghastly form that lay rotting in the pauper's grave! The children wild in the streets, the mother a destitute widow; both deeply tainted with the deep disgrace of the husband and father's name, and impelled by sheer necessity, down the precipice that had led him to a lingering death, possibly of many years' duration, thousands of miles away. We had no clue to the end of the tale; but it was easy to guess its termination.

We took a step or two further on, and by way of restoring the naturally cheerful tone of our thoughts, began fitting visionary feet and legs into a cellar-board full of boots and shoes, with a speed and accuracy that would have astonished the most expert artist in leather, living. There was one pair of boots in particular—a jolly, good-tempered, hearty-looking pair of tops, that excited our warmest regard; and we had got a fine, red-faced, jovial fellow of a market-gardener into them, before we had made their acquaintance half a minute. They were just the very thing for him. There were his huge fat legs bulging over the tops, and fitting them too tight to admit of his tucking in the loops he had pulled them on by; and his knee-cords with an interval of stocking; and his blue apron tucked up round his waist; and his red neckerchief and blue coat, and a white hat stuck on one side of his head; and there he stood with a broad grin on his great red face, whistling away, as if any other idea but that of being happy and comfortable had never entered his brain.

This was the very man after our own heart; we knew all about him; we had seen him coming up to Covent Garden in his green chaise-cart, with the fat tubby little horse, half a thousand times; and even while we cast an affectionate look upon his boots, at that instant, the form of a coquettish servant-maid suddenly sprang into a pair of Denmark satin shoes that stood beside them, and we at once recognised the very girl who accepted his offer of a ride, just on this side of the Hammersmith suspension-bridge, the very last Tuesday morning we rode into town from Richmond.

A very smart female, in a showy bonnet, stepped into a pair of grey cloth boots, with black fringe and binding, that were studiously pointing out their toes on the other side of the top-boots, and seemed very anxious to engage his attention, but we didn't observe that our friend the market-gardener appeared at all captivated with these blandishments; for beyond giving a knowing wink when they first began, as if to imply that he quite understood their end and object, he took no further notice of them. His indifference, however, was amply recompensed by the excessive gallantry of a very old gentleman with a silver-headed stick, who tottered into a pair of large list shoes, that were standing in one corner of the board, and indulged in a variety of gestures expressive of his admiration of the lady in the cloth boots, to the immeasurable amusement of a young fellow we put into a pair of long-quartered pumps, who we thought would have split the coat that slid down to meet him, with laughing.

We had been looking on at this little pantomime with great satisfaction for some time, when, to our unspeakable astonishment, we perceived that the whole of the characters, including a numerous *corps de ballet* of boots and shoes in the background, into which we had been hastily thrusting as many feet as we could press into the service, were arranging themselves in order for dancing; and some music striking up at the moment, to it they went without delay. It was perfectly delightful to witness the agility of the market-gardener. Out went the boots, first on one side, then on the other, then cutting, then shuffling, then setting to the Denmark satins, then advancing, then retreating, then going round, and then repeating the whole of the evolutions again, without appearing to suffer in the least from the violence of the exercise.

Nor were the Denmark satins a bit behindhand, for they jumped and bounded about in all directions; and though they were neither so regular, nor so true to the time as the cloth boots, still, as they seemed to do it from the heart, and to enjoy it more, we candidly confess that we preferred their style of dancing to the other. But the old gentleman in the list shoes was the most amusing object in the whole party; for, besides his grotesque attempts to appear youthful, and amorous, which were sufficiently entertaining in themselves, the young fellow in the pumps managed so artfully that every time the old gentleman advanced to salute the lady in the cloth boots, he trod with his whole weight on the old fellow's toes.

which made him roar with anguish, and rendered all the others like to die of laughing.

We were in the full enjoyment of these festivities when we heard a shrill, and by no means musical voice, exclaim, "Hope you'll know me agin, imperence!" and on looking intently forward to see from whence the sound came, we found that it proceeded, not from the young lady in the cloth boots, as we had at first been inclined to suppose, but from a bulky lady of elderly appearance, who was seated in a chair at the head of the cellar-steps, apparently for the purpose of superintending the sale of the articles arranged there.

A barrel-organ, which had been in full force close behind us, ceased playing; the people we had been fitting into the shoes and boots took flight at the interruption; and as we were conscious that in the depth of our meditations we might have been rudely staring at the old lady for half an hour without knowing it, we took to flight too, and were soon immersed in the deepest obscurity of the adjacent "Dials."

CHAPTER VII: _Hackney-coach Stands_

WE maintain that hackney-coaches, properly so called, belong solely to the metropolis. We may be told, that there are hackney-coach stands in Edinburgh; and not to go quite so far for a contradiction to our position, we may be reminded that Liverpool, Manchester, "and other large towns" (as the Parliamentary phrase goes), have _their_ hackney-coach stands. We readily concede to these places, the possession of certain vehicles, which may look almost as dirty, and even go almost as slowly, as London hackney-coaches: but that they have the slightest claim to compete with the metropolis, either in point of stands, drivers, or cattle, we indignantly deny.

Take a regular, ponderous, rickety, London hackney-coach of the old school, and let any man have the boldness to assert, if he can, that he ever beheld any object on the face of the earth which at all resembled it, unless, indeed, it were another hackney-coach of the same date. We have recently observed on certain stands, and we say it with deep regret, rather dapper green chariots, and coaches of polished yellow, with four wheels of the same colour as the coach, whereas it is perfectly notorious to every one who has studied the subject, that every wheel ought to be of a different colour, and a different size. These are innovations, and, like other miscalled improvements, awful signs of the restlessness of the public mind, and the little respect paid to our time-honoured institutions. Why should hackney-coaches be clean? Our ancestors found them dirty, and left them so. Why should we, with a feverish wish to "keep moving," desire to roll along at the rate of six miles an hour, while they were content to rumble over the stones at four? These are solemn considerations. Hackney-coaches are part and parcel of the law of the land; they were settled by the Legislature; plated and numbered by the wisdom of Parliament.

Then why have they been swamped by cabs and omnibuses? Or why should people be allowed to ride quickly for eightpence a mile, after Parliament had come to the solemn decision that they should pay a shilling a mile for riding slowly? We pause for a reply;—and, having no chance of getting one, begin a fresh paragraph.

Our acquaintance with hackney-coach stands is of long standing. We are a walking book of fares, feeling ourselves half-bound, as it were, to be always in the right on contested points. We know all the regular watermen within three miles of Covent Garden by sight, and should be almost tempted to believe that all the hackney-coach horses in that district knew us by sight too, if one-half of them were not blind. We take great interest in hackney-coaches, but we seldom drive, having a knack of turning ourselves over, when we attempt to do so. We are as great friends to horses, hackney-coach and otherwise, as the renowned Mr. Martin, of costermonger notoriety, and yet we never ride. We keep no horse, but a clothes-horse; enjoy no saddle so much as a saddle of mutton; and, following our own inclinations, have never followed the hounds. Leaving these fleeter means of getting over the ground, or of depositing oneself upon it, to those who like them, by hackney-coach stands we take our stand.

There is a hackney-coach stand under the very window at which we are writing; there is only one coach on it now, but it is a fair specimen of the class of vehicles to which we have alluded—a great, lumbering, square concern of a dingy yellow colour (like a bilious brunette), with very small glasses, but very large frames; the panels are ornamented with a faded coat of arms, in shape something like a dissected bat, the axletree is red, and the majority of the wheels are green. The box is partially covered by an old greatcoat, with a multiplicity of capes, and some extraordinary-looking clothes; and the straw, with which the canvas cushion is stuffed is sticking up in several places as if in rivalry of the hay, which is peeping through the chinks in the boot. The horses, with drooping heads, and each with a mane and tail as scanty and straggling as those of a worn-out rocking-horse, are standing patiently on some damp straw, occasionally wincing, and rattling the harness; and, now and then, one of them lifts his mouth to the ear of his companion, as if he were saying, in a whisper, that he should like to assassinate the coachman. The coachman himself is in the watering-house; and the waterman, with his hands forced into his pockets as far as they can possibly go, is dancing the "double shuffle" in front of the pump to keep his feet warm.

The servant-girl, with the pink ribbons, at No. 5, opposite, suddenly opens the street-door, and four small children forthwith rush out, and scream "Coach!" with all their might and main. The waterman darts from the pump, seizes the horses by their respective bridles, and drags them, and the coach too, round to the house, shouting all the time for the coachman at the very top, or rather very bottom of his voice, for it is a deep bass growl. A response is heard from the tap-room; the coachman, in his wooden-soled shoes, makes the street echo again as he runs across it; and then there is such a struggling, and backing, and grating of the kennel, to get the coach-door opposite the house-door, that the children are in perfect ecstasies of delight. What a commotion! The old lady, who has been stopping there for the last month, is going back to the country. Out comes box after box, and one side of the vehicle is filled with luggage in no time; the children get into everybody's way, and the youngest, who has upset himself in his attempts to carry an umbrella, is borne off wounded and kicking. The youngsters disappear, and a short pause ensues, during which the old lady is, no doubt, kissing them all round in the back parlour. She appears at last, followed by her married daughter, all the children, and both the servants, who, with the joint assistance of the coachman and waterman, manage to get her safely into the coach. A cloak is handed in, and a little basket, which we could almost swear contains a small black bottle, and a paper of sandwiches. Up go the steps, bang goes the door, "Golden Cross, Charing Cross, Tom," says the waterman; "Good-bye, grandma," cry the children, off jingles the coach at the rate of three miles an hour, and the mamma and children retire into the house, with the exception of one little villain, who runs up the street at the top of his speed, pursued by the servant; not ill-pleased to have such an opportunity of displaying her attractions. She brings him back, and, after casting two or three gracious glances across the way, which are either intended for us or the pot-boy (we are not quite certain which) shuts the door, and the hackney-coach stand is again at a standstill.

We have been frequently amused with the intense delight with which "a servant of all work," who is sent for a coach, deposits herself inside; and the unspeakable gratification which boys, who have been despatched on a similar errand, appear to derive from mounting the box. But we never recollect to have been more amused with a hackney-coach party, than one we saw early the other morning in Tottenham Court Road. It was a wedding-party, and emerged from one of the inferior streets near Fitzroy Square. There were the bride, with a thin white dress, and a great red face; and the bridesmaid, a little dumpy, good-humoured young woman, dressed, of course, in the same appropriate costume; and the bridegroom and his chosen friend, in blue coats, yellow waistcoats, white trousers, and Berlin gloves to match. They stopped at the corner of the street, and called a coach with an air of indescribable dignity. The moment they were in the bridesmaid threw a red shawl, which she had, no doubt, brought on purpose, negligently over the number on the door, evidently to delude pedestrians into the belief that the hackney-coach was a private carriage; and away they went, perfectly satisfied that the imposition was successful, and quite unconscious that there was a great staring number stuck up behind, on a plate as large as a schoolboy's slate. A shilling a mile!—the ride was worth five, at least, to them.

What an interesting book a hackney-coach might produce, if it could carry as much in its head as it does in its body! The autobiography of a broken-down hackney-coach, would surely be as amusing as the autobiography of a broken-down hackneyed dramatist; and it might tell as much of its travels *with* the pole, as others have of their expeditions *to* it. How many stories might be related of the different people it had conveyed on matters of business or profit—pleasure or pain! And how many melancholy tales of the same people at different periods! The country-girl—the showy, over-dressed woman—the drunken prostitute! The raw apprentice—the dissipated spendthrift—the thief!

Talk of cabs! Cabs are all very well in cases of expedition, when it's a matter of neck or nothing, life or death, your temporary home or your long one. But, besides a cab's lacking that gravity of deportment which so peculiarly distinguishes a hackney-coach, let it never be forgotten that a cab is a thing of yesterday, and that he never was anything better. A hackney-cab has always been a hackney-cab, from his first entry into public life; whereas a hackney-coach is a remnant of past gentility, a victim to fashion, a hanger-on of an old English family, wearing their arms, and, in days of yore, escorted by men wearing their livery, stripped of his finery, and thrown upon the world, like a once-smart footman when he is no longer sufficiently juvenile for his office, progressing lower and lower in the scale of four-wheeled degradation, until at last it comes to—*a stand!*

CHAPTER VIII: *Doctors' Commons*

WALKING, without any definite object, through St. Paul's Churchyard, a little while ago, we happened to turn down a street entitled "Paul's Chain," and keeping straight forward for a few hundred yards, found ourself, as a natural consequence, in Doctors' Commons. Now Doctors' Commons being familiar by name to everybody, as the place where they grant marriage-licenses to love-sick couples, and divorces to unfaithful ones; register the wills of people who have any property to leave, and punish hasty gentlemen who call ladies by unpleasant names, we no sooner discovered that we were really within its precincts, than we felt a laudable desire to become better acquainted therewith; and as the first object of our curiosity was the Court, whose decrees can even unloose the bonds of matrimony, we procured a direction to it; and bent our steps thither without delay.

Crossing a quiet and shady court-yard, paved with stone, and frowned upon by old red brick houses, on the doors of which were painted the names of sundry learned civilians, we paused before a small, green-baized, brass-headed-nailed door, which yielding to our gentle push, at once admitted us into an old quaint-looking apartment, with sunken windows, and black carved wainscoting, at the upper end of which, seated on a raised platform, of semicircular shape, were about a dozen solemn-looking gentlemen, in crimson gowns and wigs.

At a more elevated desk in the centre, sat a very fat and red-faced gentleman, in tortoise-shell spectacles, whose dignified appearance announced the judge; and round a long green-baized table below, something like a billiard-table without the cushions and pockets, were a number of very self-important-looking personages, in stiff neckcloths, and black gowns with white fur collars, whom we at once set down as proctors. At the lower end of the billiard-table was an individual in an arm-chair, and a wig, whom we afterwards discovered to be the registrar; and seated behind a little desk, near the door, were a respectable-looking man in black, of about twenty stone weight or thereabouts, and a fat-faced, smirking, civil-looking body, in a black gown, black kid gloves, knee shorts, and silks, with a shirt-frill in his bosom, curls on his head, and a silver staff in his hand, whom we had no difficulty in recognising as the officer of the Court. The latter, indeed, speedily set our mind at rest upon this point, for, advancing to our elbow, and opening a conversation forthwith, he had communicated to us, in less than five minutes, that he was the apparitor, and the other the court-keeper; that this was the Arches Court, and therefore the counsel wore red gowns, and the proctors fur collars; and that when the other Courts sat there they didn't wear red gowns or fur collars either; with many other scraps of intelligence equally interesting. Besides these two officers, there was a little thin old man, with long grizzly hair, crouched in a remote corner, whose duty, our communicative friend informed us, was to ring a large hand-bell when the Court opened in the morning, and who, for ought his appearance betokened to the contrary, might have been similarly employed for the last two centuries at least.

The red-faced gentleman in the tortoise-shell spectacles had got all the talk to himself just then, and very well he was doing it, too, only he spoke very fast, but that was habit; and rather thick, but that was good living. So we had plenty of time to look about us. There was one individual who amused us mightily. This was one of the bewigged gentlemen in the red robes, who was straddling before the fire in the centre of the Court, in the attitude of the brazen Colossus, to the complete exclusion of everybody else. He had gathered up his robe behind, in much the same manner as a slovenly woman would her petticoats on a very dirty day, in order that he might feel the full warmth of the fire. His wig was put on all awry, with the tail straggling about his neck, his scanty grey trousers and short black gaiters, made in the worst possible style, imparted an additionally inelegant appearance to his uncouth person; and his limp, badly-starched shirt-collar almost obscured his eyes. We shall never be able to claim any credit as a physiognomist again, for, after a careful scrutiny of this gentleman's countenance, we had come to the conclusion that it bespoke nothing but conceit and silliness, when our friend with the silver staff whispered in our ear that he was no other than a doctor of civil law, and heaven knows what besides. So, of course, we were mistaken, and he must be a very talented man. He conceals it so well though— perhaps with the merciful view of not astonishing ordinary people too much—that you would suppose him to be one of the stupidest dogs alive.

The gentleman in the spectacles having concluded his judgment, and a few minutes having been allowed to elapse, to afford time for the buzz in the Court to subside, the registrar called on the next cause, which was "the office of the Judge promoted by Bumple against Sludberry." A general movement was visible in the Court, at this announcement, and the obliging functionary with silver staff whispered us that "there would be some fun now, for this was a brawling case."

We were not rendered much the wiser by this piece of information, till we found by the opening speech of the counsel for the promoter, that, under a half-obsolete statute of one of the Edwards, the court was empowered to visit with the penalty of excommunication, any person who should be proved guilty of the crime of "brawling," or "smiting" in any church, or vestry adjoining thereto; and it appeared, by some eight-and-twenty affidavits, which were duly referred to, that on a certain night, at a certain vestry-meeting, in a certain parish particularly set forth, Thomas Sludberry, the party appeared against in that suit, had made use of, and applied to Michael Bumple, the promoter, the words "You be blowed"; and that, on the said

Michael Bumple and others remonstrating with the said Thomas Sludberry, on the impropriety of his conduct, the said Thomas Sludberry repeated the aforesaid expression, "You be blowed"; and furthermore desired and requested to know whether the said Michael Bumple "wanted anything for himself"; adding, "that if the said Michael Bumple did want anything for himself, he, the said Thomas Sludberry was the man to give it him;" at the same time making use of other heinous and sinful expressions, all of which, Bumple submitted, came within the intent and meaning of the Act; and therefore he, for the soul's health and chastening of Sludberry, prayed for sentence of excommunication against him accordingly.

Upon these facts a long argument was entered into, on both sides, to the great edification of a number of persons interested in the parochial squabbles, who crowded the court; and when some very long and grave speeches had been made *pro* and *con*, the red-faced gentleman in the tortoise-shell spectacles took a review of the case, which occupied half an hour more, and then pronounced upon Sludberry the awful sentence of excommunication for a fortnight, and payment of the costs of the suit. Upon this, Sludberry, who was a little red-faced, sly-looking, ginger-beer seller, addressed the court, and said, if they'd be good enough to take off the costs, and excommunicate him for the term of his natural life instead, it would be much more convenient to him, for he never went to church at all. To this appeal the gentleman in the spectacles made no other reply than a look of virtuous indignation; and Sludberry and his friends retired. As the man with the silver staff informed us that the court was on the point of rising, we retired too—pondering, as we walked away, upon the beautiful spirit of these ancient ecclesiastical laws, the kind and neighbourly feelings they are calculated to awaken, and the strong attachment to religious institutions which they cannot fail to engender.

We were so lost in these meditations, that we had turned into the street, and run up against a door-post, before we recollected where we were walking. On looking upwards to see what house we had stumbled upon, the words "Prerogative Office," written in large characters, met our eye; and as we were in a sight-seeing humour, and the place was a public one, we walked in.

The room into which we walked, was a long, busy-looking place, partitioned off, on either side, into a variety of little boxes, in which a few clerks were engaged in copying or examining deeds. Down the centre of the room were several desks, nearly breast high, at each of which three or four people were standing, poring over large volumes. As we knew that they were searching for wills, they attracted our attention at once.

It was curious to contrast the lazy indifference of the attorney's clerks who were making a search for some legal purpose, with the air of earnestness and interest which distinguished the strangers to the place, who were looking up the will of some deceased relative; the former pausing every now and then with an impatient yawn, or raising their heads to look at the people who passed up and down the room; the latter stooping over the book, and running down column after column of names in the deepest abstraction.

There was one little dirty-faced man in a blue apron, who after a whole morning's search, extending some fifty years back, had just found the will to which he wished to refer, which one of the officials was reading to him in a low hurried voice from a thick vellum book with large clasps. It was perfectly evident that the more the clerk read, the less the man with the blue apron understood about the matter. When the volume was first brought down, he took off his hat, smoothed down his hair, smiled with great self-satisfaction, and looked up in the reader's face with the air of a man who had made up his mind to recollect every word he heard. The first two or three lines were intelligible enough; but then the technicalities began, and the little man began to look rather dubious. Then came a whole string of complicated trusts, and he was regularly at sea. As the reader proceeded, it was quite apparent that it was a hopeless case, and the little man, with his mouth open and his eyes fixed upon his face, looked on with an expression of bewilderment and perplexity irresistibly ludicrous.

A little further on, a hard-featured old man with a deeply-wrinkled face was intently perusing a lengthy will with the aid of a pair of horn spectacles: occasionally pausing from his task, and slyly noting down some brief memorandum of the bequests contained in it. Every wrinkle about his toothless mouth, and sharp keen eyes, told of avarice and cunning. His clothes were nearly threadbare, but it was easy to see that he wore them from choice and not from necessity; all his looks and gestures down to the very small pinches of snuff which he every now and then took from a little tin canister, told of wealth, and penury, and avarice.

As he leisurely closed the register, put up his spectacles, and folded his scraps of paper in a large leathern pocket-book, we thought what a nice hard bargain he was driving with some poverty-stricken legatee, who, tired of waiting year after year, until some life-interest should fall in, was selling his chance, just as it began to grow most valuable, for a twelfth part of its worth. It was a good speculation—a very safe one. The old man stowed his pocket-book carefully in the breast of his great-coat, and hobbled away with a leer of triumph. That will had made him ten years younger at the lowest computation.

Having commenced our observations, we should certainly

have extended them to another dozen of people at least, had not a sudden shutting up and putting away of the worm-eaten old books, warned us that the time for closing the office had arrived; and thus deprived us of a pleasure, and spared our readers an infliction.

We naturally fell into a train of reflection as we walked homewards, upon the curious old records of likings and dislikings; of jealousies and revenges; of affection defying the power of death, and hatred pursued beyond the grave, which these depositories contain; silent but striking tokens, some of them, of excellence of heart, and nobleness of soul; melancholy examples, others, of the worst passions of human nature. How many men as they lay speechless and helpless on the bed of death, would have given worlds but for the strength and power to blot out the silent evidence of animosity and bitterness, which now stands registered against them in Doctors' Commons!

CHAPTER IX: *London Recreations*

THE wish of persons in the humbler classes of life, to ape the manners and customs of those whom fortune has placed above them, is often the subject of remark, and not unfrequently of complaint. The inclination may, and no doubt does, exist to a great extent, among the small gentility—the would-be aristocrats—of the middle classes. Tradesmen and clerks, with fashionable novel-reading families, and circulating-library-subscribing daughters, get up small assemblies in humble imitation of Almack's, and promenade the dingy "large room" of some second-rate hotel with as much complacency as the enviable few who are privileged to exhibit their magnificence in that exclusive haunt of fashion and foolery. Aspiring young ladies, who read flaming accounts of some "fancy fair in high life," suddenly grow desperately charitable; visions of admiration and matrimony float before their eyes; some wonderfully meritorious institution, which, by the strangest accident in the world, has never been heard of before, is discovered to be in a languishing condition: Thomson's great room, or Johnson's nursery-ground is forthwith engaged, and the aforesaid young ladies, from mere charity, exhibit themselves for three days, from twelve to four, for the small charge of one shilling per head! With the exception of these classes of society, however, and a few weak and insignificant persons, we do not think the attempt at imitation to which we have alluded, prevails in any great degree. The different character of the recreations of different classes has often afforded us amusement; and we have chosen it for the subject of our present sketch, in the hope that it may possess some amusement for our readers.

If the regular City man, who leaves Lloyd's at five o'clock, and drives home to Hackney, Clapton, Stamford Hill, or elsewhere, can be said to have any daily recreation beyond his dinner, it is his garden. He never does anything to it with his own hands; but he takes pride in it notwithstanding; and if you are desirous of paying your addresses to the youngest daughter, be sure to be in raptures with every flower and shrub it contains. If your poverty of expression compel you to make any distinction between the two, we would certainly recommend your bestowing more admiration on his garden than his wine. He always takes a walk round it, before he starts for town in the morning, and is particularly anxious that the fish-pond should be kept specially neat. If you call on him on Sunday in summer-time, about an hour before dinner, you will find him sitting in an arm-chair, on the lawn behind the house, with a straw hat on, reading a Sunday paper. A short distance from him you will most likely observe a handsome paroquet in a large brass-wire cage; ten to one but the two eldest girls are loitering in one of the side-walks accompanied by a couple of young gentlemen, who are holding parasols over them—of course only to keep the sun off—while the younger children, with the under-nursery-maid, are strolling listlessly about, in the shade. Beyond these occasions, his delight in his garden appears to arise more from the consciousness of possession than actual enjoyment of it. When he drives you down to dinner on a week-day, he is rather fatigued with the occupations of the morning, and tolerably cross into the bargain; but when the cloth is removed, and he has drunk three or four glasses of his favourite port, he orders the French windows of his dining-room (which of course look into the garden) to be opened, and throwing a silk handkerchief over his head, and leaning back in his arm-chair, descants at considerable length upon its beauty, and the cost of maintaining it. This is to impress you—who are a young friend of the family—with a due sense of the excellence of the garden, and the wealth of its owner; and when he has exhausted the subject, he goes to sleep.

There is another and a very different class of men, whose recreation is their garden. An individual of this class, resides some short distance from town—say in the Hampstead Road, or the Kilburn Road, or any other road where the houses are small and neat, and have little slips of back garden. He and his wife—who is as clean and compact a little body as himself—have occupied the same house ever since he retired from business twenty years ago. They have no family. They once had a son, who died at about five years old. The child's portrait hangs over the mantelpiece in the best sitting-room, and a little cart he used to draw about is carefully preserved as a relic.

In fine weather the old gentleman is almost constantly in the garden; and when it is too wet to go into it, he will look out of the window at it, by the hour together. He has always something to do there, and you will see him digging, and sweeping, and cutting, and planting, with manifest delight. In spring time, there is no end to the sowing of seeds, and sticking little bits of wood over them, with labels, which look like epitaphs to their memory; and in the evening, when the sun has gone down, the perseverance with which he lugs a great watering-pot about is perfectly astonishing. The only other recreation he has is the newspaper, which he peruses every day, from beginning to end, generally reading the most interesting pieces of intelligence to his wife, during breakfast. The old lady is very fond of flowers, as the hyacinth-glasses in the parlour-window, and geranium-pots in the little front court testify. She takes great pride in the garden too: and when one of the four fruit-trees produces rather a larger gooseberry than usual, it is carefully preserved under a wine-glass on the sideboard, for the edification of visitors, who are duly informed that Mr. So-and-so planted the tree which produced it, with his own hands. On a summer's evening, when the large watering-pot has been filled and emptied some fourteen times, and the old couple have quite exhausted themselves by trotting about, you will see them sitting happily together in the little summer-house, enjoying the calm and peace of the twilight, and watching the shadows as they fall upon the garden, and gradually growing thicker and more sombre, obscure the tints of their gayest flowers—no bad emblem of the years that have silently rolled over their heads, deadening in their course the brightest hues of early hopes and feelings which have long since faded away. These are their only recreations, and they require no more. They have within themselves the materials of comfort and content; and the only anxiety of each, is to die before the other.

This is no ideal sketch. There *used* to be many old people of this description; their numbers may have diminished, and may decrease still more. Whether the course female education has taken of late days—whether the pursuit of giddy frivolities, and empty nothings, has tended to unfit women for that quiet domestic life, in which they show far more beautifully than in the most crowded assembly, is a question we should feel little gratification in discussing: we hope not.

Let us turn now, to another portion of the London population, whose recreations present about as strong a contrast as can well be conceived—we mean the Sunday pleasurers; and let us beg our readers to imagine themselves stationed by our side in some well-known rural "Tea-gardens."

The heat is intense this afternoon, and the people, of whom

there are additional parties arriving every moment, look as warm as the tables which have been recently painted, and have the appearance of being red-hot. What a dust and noise! Men and women—boys and girls—sweethearts and married people—babies in arms, and children in chaises—pipes and shrimps—cigars and periwinkles—tea and tobacco. Gentlemen, in alarming waistcoats, and steel watch-guards, promenading about, three abreast, with surprising dignity (or as the gentleman in the next box facetiously observes, "cutting it uncommon fat!")—ladies, with great, long, white pocket-handkerchiefs like small table-cloths in their hands, chasing one another on the grass in the most playful and interesting manner, with the view of attracting the attention of the aforesaid gentlemen—husbands in perspective ordering bottles of ginger-beer for the objects of their affections, with a lavish disregard of expense; and the said objects washing down huge quantities of "shrimps" and "winkles," with an equal disregard of their own bodily health and subsequent comfort—boys, with great silk hats just balanced on the top of their heads, smoking cigars, and trying to look as if they liked them—gentlemen in pink shirts and blue waistcoats, occasionally upsetting either themselves, or somebody else, with their own canes.

Some of the finery of these people provokes a smile, but they are all clean, and happy, and disposed to be good-natured and sociable. Those two motherly-looking women in the smart pelisses, who are chatting so confidentially, inserting a "ma'am" at every fourth word, scraped an acquaintance about a quarter of an hour ago; it originated in admiration of the little boy who belongs to one of them—that diminutive specimen of mortality in the three-cornered pink satin hat with black feathers. The two men in the blue coats and drab trousers, who are walking up and down, smoking their pipes, are their husbands. The party in the opposite box are a pretty fair specimen of the generality of the visitors. These are the father and mother, and old grandmother: a young man and woman, and an individual addressed by the euphonious title of "Uncle Bill," who is evidently the wit of the party. They have some half-dozen children with them, but it is scarcely necessary to notice the fact, for that is a matter of course here. Every woman in "the gardens," who has been married for any length of time, must have had twins on two or three occasions; it is impossible to account for the extent of juvenile population in any other way.

Observe the inexpressible delight of the old grandmother, at Uncle Bill's splendid joke of "tea for four: bread-and-butter for forty;" and the loud explosion of mirth which follows his wafering a paper "pigtail" on the waiter's collar. The young man is evidently "keeping company" with

Uncle Bill's niece: and Uncle Bill's hints—such as "Don't forget me at the dinner, you know," "I shall look out for the cake, Sally," "I'll be godfather to your first, wager it's a boy," and so forth, are equally embarrassing to the young people, and delightful to the elder ones. As to the old grandmother, she is in perfect ecstasies, and does nothing but laugh herself into fits of coughing, until they have finished the "gin-and-water warm with," of which Uncle Bill ordered "glasses round" after tea, "just to keep the night air out, and do it up comfortable and riglar arter sitch an as-tonishing hot day!"

It is getting dark, and the people begin to move. The field leading to town is quite full of them; the little hand-chaises are dragged wearily along, the children are tired, and amuse themselves and the company generally by crying, or resort to the much more pleasant expedient of going to sleep—the mothers begin to wish they were at home again—sweethearts grow more sentimental than ever, as the time for parting arrives—the gardens look mournful enough, by the light of the two lanterns which hang against the trees for the convenience of smokers—and the waiters, who have been running about incessantly for the last six hours, think they feel a little tired, as they count their glasses and their gains.

CHAPTER X: *The River*

"ARE you fond of the water?" is a question very frequently asked, in hot summer weather, by amphibious-looking young men. "Very," is the general reply, "ain't you?"— "Hardly ever off it," is the response, accompanied by sundry adjectives, expressive of the speaker's heartfelt admiration of that element. Now, with all respect for the opinion of society in general, and cutter clubs in particular, we humbly suggest that some of the most painful reminiscences in the mind of every individual who has occasionally disported himself on the Thames, must be connected with his aquatic recreations. Who ever heard of a successful water-party? —or to put the question in a still more intelligible form, who ever saw one? We have been on water excursions out of number, but we solemnly declare that we cannot call to mind one single occasion of the kind which was not marked by more miseries than any one would suppose could reasonably be crowded into the space of some eight or nine hours. Something has always gone wrong. Either the cork of the salad-dressing has come out, or the most anxiously expected member of the party has not come out, or the most disagreeable man in company would come out, or a child or two have fallen into the water, or the gentleman who undertook

to steer has endangered everybody's life all the way, or the
gentlemen who volunteered to row have been "out of practice,"
and performed very alarming evolutions, putting their oars
down into the water and not being able to get them up again,
or taking terrific pulls without putting them in at all; in
either case, pitching over on the backs of their heads with
startling violence, and exhibiting the soles of their pumps
to the "sitters" in the boat, in a very humiliating manner.

We grant that the banks of the Thames are very beautiful
at Richmond and Twickenham, and other distant havens,
often sought though seldom reached: but from the "Red-us"
back to Blackfriars Bridge, the scene is wonderfully changed.
The Penitentiary is a noble building, no doubt, and the
sportive youths who "go in" at that particular part of the
river, on a summer's evening, may be all very well in perspective; but when you are obliged to keep in shore coming
home, and the young ladies will colour up, and look perseveringly the other way, while the married dittoes cough slightly,
and stare very hard at the water, you feel awkward—especially
if you happen to have been attempting the most distant
approach to sentimentality, for an hour or two previously.

Although experience and suffering have produced in our
minds the result we have just stated, we are by no means
blind to a proper sense of the fun which a looker-on may
extract from the amateurs of boating. What can be more
amusing than Searle's yard on a fine Sunday morning? It's
a Richmond tide, and some dozen boats are preparing for
the reception of the parties who have engaged them. Two
or three fellows in great rough trousers and Guernsey shirts
are getting them ready by easy stages; now coming down the
yard with a pair of sculls and a cushion—then having a chat
with the "jack," who, like all his tribe, seems to be wholly
incapable of doing anything but lounging about—then
going back again, and returning with a rudder-line and a
stretcher—then solacing themselves with another chat—and
then wondering, with their hands in their capacious pockets,
"where them gentlemen's got to as ordered the six." One
of these, the head man, with the legs of his trousers carefully
tucked up at the bottom, to admit the water, we presume—
for it is an element in which he is infinitely more at home
than on land—is quite a character, and shares with the
defunct oyster-swallower the celebrated name of "Dando."
Watch him, as taking a few minutes' respite from his toils,
he negligently seats himself on the edge of a boat, and fans
his broad bushy chest with a cap scarcely half so furry.
Look at his magnificent, though reddish whiskers, and mark
the somewhat native humour with which he "chaffs" the
boys and 'prentices, or cunningly gammons the gen'lm'n into
the gift of a glass of gin, of which we verily believe he swallows

in one day as much as any six ordinary men, without ever being one atom the worse for it.

But the party arrives, and Dando relieved from his state of uncertainty starts up into activity. They approach in full aquatic costume, with round blue jackets, striped shirts, and caps of all sizes and patterns, from the velvet skull-cap of French manufacture, to the easy head-dress familiar to the students of the old spelling-books, as having, on the authority of the portrait, formed part of the costume of the Reverend Mr. Dilworth.

This is the most amusing time to observe a regular Sunday water-party. There has evidently been up to this period no inconsiderable degree of boasting on everybody's part relative to his knowledge of navigation; the sight of the water rapidly cools their courage, and the air of self-denial with which each of them insists on somebody else's taking an oar, is perfectly delightful. At length, after a great deal of changing and fidgeting, consequent upon the election of a stroke-oar: the inability of one gentleman to pull on this side, of another to pull on that, and of a third to pull at all, the boat's crew are seated. "Shove her off!" cries the coxswain, who looks as easy and comfortable as if he were steering in the Bay of Biscay. The order is obeyed; the boat is immediately turned completely round, and proceeds towards Westminster Bridge, amidst such a splashing and struggling as never was seen before, except when the Royal George went down. "Back wa'ater, sir," shouts Dando, "Back wa'ater, you sir, aft;" upon which everybody thinking he must be the individual referred to, they all back water, and back comes the boat, stern first, to the spot whence it started. "Back water, you sir, aft; pull round, you sir, for'ad, can't you?" shouts Dando, in a frenzy of excitement. "Pull round, Tom, can't you?" re-echoes one of the party. "Tom ain't for'ad," replies another. "Yes, he is," cries a third; and the unfortunate young man, at the imminent risk of breaking a blood-vessel, pulls and pulls, until the head of the boat fairly lies in the direction of Vauxhall Bridge. "That's right—now pull all on you!" shouts Dando again, adding, in an undertone, to somebody by him, "Blowed if hever I see sich a set of muffs!" and away jogs the boat in a zigzag direction, every one of the six oars dipping into the water at a different time; and the yard is once more clear, until the arrival of the next party.

A well-contested rowing match on the Thames, is a very lively and interesting scene. The water is studded with boats of all sorts, kinds, and descriptions; places in the coal-barges at the different wharfs are let to crowds of spectators, beer and tobacco flow freely about; men, women, and children wait for the start in breathless expectation, cutters of six and eight oars glide gently up and down, waiting to accompany their *protégés* during the race; bands of music add to the animation, if not to the harmony of the scene, groups of watermen are assembled at the different stairs, discussing the merits of the respective candidates: and the prize wherry which is rowed slowly about by a pair of sculls, is an object of general interest.

Two o'clock strikes, and everybody looks anxiously in the direction of the bridge, through which the candidates for the prize will come—half-past two, and the general attention which has been preserved so long begins to flag, when suddenly a gun is heard, and a noise of distant hurra'ing along each bank of the river—every head is bent forward—the noise draws nearer and nearer—the boats which have been waiting at the bridge start briskly up the river, and a well-manned galley shoots through the arch, the sitters cheering on the boats behind them, which are not yet visible.

"Here they are," is the general cry—and through darts the first boat, the men in her, stripped to the skin, and exerting every muscle to preserve the advantage they have gained—four other boats follow close astern; there are not two boats' length between them—the shouting is tremendous, and the interest intense. "Go on, Pink"—"Give it her, Red"—"Sulliwin for ever"—"Bravo! George"—"Now, Tom, now —now—now—why don't your partner stretch out?"—"Two pots to a pint on Yellow," &c., &c. Every little public-house fires its gun, and hoists its flag; and the men who win the heat, come in, amidst a splashing and shouting, and banging and confusion, which no one can imagine who has not witnessed it, and of which any description would convey a very faint idea.

One of the most amusing places we know, is the steam-wharf of the London Bridge, or St. Katherine's Dock Company, on a Saturday morning in summer, when the Gravesend and Margate steamers are usually crowded to excess; and as we have just taken a glance at the river above bridge, we hope our readers will not object to accompany us on board a Gravesend packet.

Coaches are every moment setting down at the entrance to the wharf, and the stare of bewildered astonishment with which the "fares" resign themselves and their luggage into the hands of the porters, who seize all the packages at once as a matter of course, and run away with them, heaven knows where, is laughable in the extreme. A Margate boat lies alongside the wharf, the Gravesend boat (which starts first) lies alongside that again; and as a temporary communication is formed between the two, by means of a plank and hand-rail, the natural confusion of the scene is by no means diminished.

"Gravesend?" inquires a stout father of a stout family, who follow him under the guidance of their mother, and a servant, at the no small risk of two or three of them being left behind in the confusion. "Gravesend?"

"Pass on, if you please, sir," replies the attendant—"other boat, sir."

Hereupon the stout father, being rather mystified, and the stout mother rather distracted by maternal anxiety, the whole party deposit themselves in the Margate boat, and after having congratulated himself on having secured very comfortable seats, the stout father sallies to the chimney to look for his luggage, which he has a faint recollection of having given some man, something, to take somewhere. No luggage, however, bearing the most remote resemblance to his own, in shape or form, is to be discovered; on which the stout father calls very loudly for an officer, to whom he states the case, in the presence of another father of another family—a little thin man—who entirely concurs with him (the stout father) in thinking that it's high time something was done with these steam companies, and that as the Corporation Bill failed to do it, something else must; for really people's property is not to be sacrificed in this way; and that if the luggage isn't restored without delay, he will take care it shall be put in the papers, for the public is not to be the victim of these great monopolies. To this, the officer, in his turn, replies, that that company, ever since it has been St. Kat'rine's Dock Company, has protected life and property; that if it had been the London Bridge Wharf Company, indeed, he shouldn't have wondered, seeing that the morality of that company (they being the opposition) can't be answered for, by no one; but as it is, he's convinced there must be some mistake, and he wouldn't mind making a solemn oath afore a magistrate that the gentleman'll find his luggage afore he gets to Margate.

Here the stout father, thinking he is making a capital point, replies, that as it happens he is not going to Margate at all, and that "Passenger to Gravesend" was on the luggage, in letters of full two inches long; on which the officer rapidly explains the mistake, and the stout mother, and the stout children, and the servant, are hurried with all possible despatch on board the Gravesend boat, which they reach just in time to discover that their luggage is there, and that their comfortable seats are not. Then the bell, which is the signal for the Gravesend boat starting, begins to ring most furiously: and people keep time to the bell, by running in and out of our boat at a double-quick pace. The bell stops; the boat starts; people who have been taking leave of their friends on board, are carried away against their will; and people who have been taking leave of their friends on shore, find that they have performed a very needless ceremony, in consequence of their not being carried away at all. The regular passengers, who have season tickets, go below to breakfast; people who have purchased morning papers, compose themselves to read them; and people who have not been down the river before, think that both the shipping and the water, look a great deal better at a distance.

When we get down about as far as Blackwall, and begin to move at a quicker rate, the spirits of the passengers appear to rise in proportion. Old women who have brought large wicker hand-baskets with them, set seriously to work at the demolition of heavy sandwiches, and pass round a wine-glass, which is frequently replenished from a flat bottle like a stomach-warmer, with considerable glee: handing it first to the gentleman in the foraging-cap, who plays the harp—partly as an expression of satisfaction with his previous exertions, and partly to induce him to play "Dumble-dumb-deary," for "Alick" to dance to; which being done, Alick, who is a damp earthy child in red worsted socks, takes certain small jumps upon the deck, to the unspeakable satisfaction of his family circle. Girls who have brought the first volume of some new novel in their reticule become extremely plaintive, and expatiate to Mr. Brown, or young Mr. O'Brien, who has been looking over them, on the blueness of the sky, and bright-ness of the water; on which Mr. Brown or Mr. O'Brien, as the case may be, remarks in a low voice that he has been quite insensible of late to the beauties of nature—that his whole thoughts and wishes have centred in one object alone —whereupon the young lady looks up, and failing in her attempt to appear unconscious, looks down again; and turns over the next leaf with great difficulty, in order to afford opportunity for a lengthened pressure of the hand.

Telescopes, sandwiches, and glasses of brandy-and-water cold without, begin to be in great requisition; and bashful men who have been looking down the hatchway at the engine, find, to their great relief, a subject on which they can converse with one another—and a copious one too—Steam.

"Wonderful thing steam, sir." "Ah! (a deep-drawn sigh) it is indeed, sir." "Great power, sir." "Immense— immense!" "Great deal done by steam, sir." "Ah! (another sigh at the immensity of the subject, and a knowing shake of the head) you may say that, sir." "Still in its infancy they say, sir." Novel remarks of this kind, are generally the commencement of a conversation which is prolonged until the conclusion of the trip, and, perhaps, lays the foundation of a speaking acquaintance between half a dozen gentlemen, who, having their families at Gravesend, take season-tickets for the boat, and dine on board regularly every afternoon.

CHAPTER XI: *Astley's*

WE never see any very large, staring, black Roman capitals, in a book, or shop-window, or placarded on a wall, without their immediately recalling to our mind an indistinct and confused recollection of the time when we were first initiated in the mysteries of the alphabet. We almost fancy we see the pin's point following the letter, to impress its form more strongly on our bewildered imagination; and wince involuntarily, as we remember the hard knuckles with which the reverend old lady who instilled into our mind the first principles of education for ninepence per week, or ten and sixpence per quarter, was wont to poke our juvenile head occasionally, by way of adjusting the confusion of ideas in which we were generally involved. The same kind of feeling pursues us in many other instances, but there is no place which recalls so strongly our recollections of childhood as Astley's. It was not a "Royal Amphitheatre" in those days, nor had Ducrow arisen to shed the light of classic taste and portable gas over the sawdust of the circus; but the whole character of the place was the same, the pieces were the same, the clown's jokes were the same, the riding-masters were equally grand, the comic performers equally witty, the tragedians equally hoarse, and the "highly-trained chargers" equally spirited. Astley's has altered for the better—we have changed for the worse. Our histrionic taste is gone, and with shame we confess, that we are far more delighted and amused with the audience, than with the pageantry we once so highly appreciated.

We like to watch a regular Astley's party in the Easter or Midsummer holidays—pa and ma, and nine or ten children, varying from five foot six to two foot eleven: from fourteen years of age to four. We had just taken our seats in one of the boxes, in the centre of the house, the other night, when the next was occupied by just such a party as we should have attempted to describe, had we depicted our *beau ideal* of a group of Astley's visitors.

First of all, there came three little boys and a little girl, who, in pursuance of pa's directions, issued in a very audible voice from the box-door, occupied the front row; then two more little girls were ushered in by a young lady, evidently the governess. Then came three more little boys, dressed like the first, in blue jackets and trousers, with lay-down shirt-collars: then a child in a braided frock and high state of astonishment, with very large round eyes, opened to their utmost width, was lifted over the seats—a process which occasioned a considerable display of little pink legs—then came ma and pa, and then the eldest son, a boy of fourteen years old, who was evidently trying to look as if he did not belong to the family.

The first five minutes were occupied in taking the shawls off the little girls, and adjusting the bows which ornamented their hair; then it was providentially discovered that one of the little boys was seated behind a pillar and could not see, so the governess was stuck behind the pillar, and the boy lifted into her place. Then pa drilled the boys, and directed the stowing away of their pocket-handkerchiefs; and ma having first nodded and winked to the governess to pull the girls' frocks a little more off their shoulders, stood up to review the little troop—an inspection which appeared to terminate much to her own satisfaction, for she looked with a complacent air at pa, who was standing up at the further end of the seat. Pa returned the glance, and blew his nose very emphatically; and the poor governess peeped out from behind the pillar, and timidly tried to catch ma's eye, with a look expressive of her high admiration of the whole family. Then two of the little boys who had been discussing the point whether Astley's was more than twice as large as Drury Lane, agreed to refer it to "George" for his decision; at which "George," who was no other than the young gentleman before noticed, waxed indignant, and remonstrated in no very gentle terms on the gross impropriety of having his name repeated in so loud a voice at a public place, on which all the children laughed very heartily, and one of the little boys wound up by expressing his opinion that "George began to think himself quite a man now," whereupon both pa and ma laughed too; and George (who carried a dress cane, and was cultivating whiskers) muttered that "William always was encouraged in his impertinence;" and assumed a look of profound contempt, which lasted the whole evening.

The play began, and the interest of the little boys knew no bounds. Pa was clearly interested too, although he very unsuccessfully endeavoured to look as if he wasn't. As for ma, she was perfectly overcome by the drollery of the principal comedian, and laughed till every one of the immense bows on her ample cap trembled, at which the governess peeped out from behind the pillar again, and whenever she could catch ma's eye, put her handkerchief to her mouth, and appeared, as in duty bound, to be in convulsions of laughter also. Then when the man in the splendid armour vowed to rescue the lady or perish in the attempt, the little boys applauded vehemently, especially one little fellow who was apparently on a visit to the family, and had been carrying on a child's flirtation, the whole evening, with a small coquette of twelve years old, who looked like a model of her mamma on a reduced scale; and who in common with the other little girls (who generally speaking have even more coquettishness about them than much older ones) looked very properly shocked, when the knight's squire kissed the princess's confidential chambermaid.

When the scenes in the circle commenced, the children were more delighted than ever; and the wish to see what was going forward, completely conquering pa's dignity, he stood up in the box, and applauded as loudly as any of them. Between each feat of horsemanship, the governess leant across to ma, and retailed the clever remarks of the children on that which had preceded: and ma, in the openness of her heart, offered the governess an acidulated drop, and the governess, gratified to be taken notice of, retired behind her pillar again with a brighter countenance: and the whole party seemed quite happy, except the exquisite in the back of the box, who, being too grand to take any interest in the children, and too insignificant to be taken notice of by anybody else, occupied himself, from time to time, in rubbing the place where the whiskers ought to be, and was completely alone in his glory.

We defy any one who has been to Astley's two or three times, and is consequently capable of appreciating the perseverance with which precisely the same jokes are repeated night after night, and season after season, not to be amused with one part of the performances at least—we mean the scenes in the circle. For ourself, we know that when the hoop, composed of jets of gas, is let down, the curtain drawn up for the convenience of the half-price on their ejectment from the ring, the orange-peel cleared away, and the sawdust shaken, with mathematical precision, into a complete circle, we feel as much enlivened as the youngest child present; and actually join in the laugh which follows the clown's shrill shout of "Here we are!" just for old acquaintance' sake. Nor can we quite divest ourself of our old feeling of reverence for the riding-master, who follows the clown with a long whip in his hand, and bows to the audience with graceful dignity. He is none of your second-rate riding masters in nankeen dressing-gowns, with brown frogs, but the regular gentleman-attendant on the principal riders, who always wears a military uniform with a table-cloth inside the breast of the coat, in which costume he forcibly reminds one of a fowl trussed for roasting. He is—but why should we attempt to describe that of which no description can convey an adequate idea? Everybody knows the man, and everybody remembers his polished boots, his graceful demeanour, stiff, as some misjudging persons have in their jealousy considered it, and the splendid head of black hair parted high on the forehead, to impart to the countenance an appearance of deep thought and poetic melancholy. His soft and pleasing voice, too, is in perfect unison with his noble bearing, as he humours the clown by indulging in a little badinage; and the striking recollection of his own dignity, with which he exclaims, "Now, sir, if you

please, inquire for Miss Woolford, sir," can never be forgotten.
The graceful air, too, with which he introduces Miss Woolford
into the arena, and, after assisting her to the saddle, follows
her fairy courser round the circle, can never fail to create a
deep impression in the bosom of every female servant present.

When Miss Woolford, and the horse, and the orchestra, all
stop together to take breath, he urbanely takes part in some
such dialogue as the following (commenced by the clown):
"I say, sir!"—"Well, sir?" (it's always conducted in the
politest manner).—"Did you ever happen to hear I was in the
army, sir?"—"No, sir."—"Oh, yes, sir; I can go through my
exercise, sir."—"Indeed, sir!"—"Shall I do it now, sir?"—
"If you please, sir; come, sir, make haste" (a cut with the long
whip, and "Ha' done now—I don't like it," from the clown).
Here the clown throws himself on the ground, and goes through
a variety of gymnastic convulsions, doubling himself up, and
untying himself again, and making himself look very like a man
in the most hopeless extreme of human agony, to the vociferous delight of the gallery, until he is interrupted by a second
cut from the long whip, and a request to see "what Miss Woolford's stopping for?" On which, to the inexpressible mirth
of the gallery, he exclaims, "Now, Miss Woolford, what can I
come for to go, for to fetch, for to bring, for to carry, for to do,
for you, ma'am?" On the lady's announcing with a sweet
smile that she wants the two flags, they are with sundry
grimaces, procured and handed up; the clown facetiously
observing after the performance of the latter ceremony—
"He, he, oh! I say, sir, Miss Woolford knows me; she smiled
at me." Another cut from the whip, a burst from the
orchestra, a start from the horse, and round goes Miss Woolford again on her graceful performance, to the delight of every
member of the audience, young or old. The next pause
affords an opportunity for similar witticisms, the only additional fun being that of the clown making ludicrous grimaces
at the riding-master every time his back is turned; and finally
quitting the circle by jumping over his head, having previously
directed his attention another way.

Did any of our readers ever notice the class of people who
hang about the stage-doors of our minor theatres in the daytime? You will rarely pass one of these entrances without
seeing a group of three or four men conversing on the pavement
with an indescribable public-house-parlour swagger, and a kind
of conscious air, peculiar to people of this description. They
always seem to think they are exhibiting; the lamps are ever
before them. That young fellow in the faded brown coat,
and very full light green trousers, pulls down the wrist-bands
of his check shirt, as ostentatiously as if it were of the finest
linen, and cocks the white hat of the summer-before-last as
knowingly over his right eye, as if it were a purchase of yester-

day. Look at the dirty white Berlin gloves, and the cheap silk-handkerchief stuck in the bosom of his threadbare coat. Is it possible to see him for an instant, and not come to the conclusion that he is the walking gentleman who wears a blue surtout, clean collar, and white trousers, for half an hour, and then shrinks into his worn-out scanty clothes: who has to boast night after night of his splendid fortune, with the painful consciousness of a pound a week and his boots to find; to talk of his father's mansion in the country, with a dreary recollection of his own two-pair back, in the New Cut; and to be envied and flattered as the favoured lover of a rich heiress, remembering all the while that the ex-dancer at home is in the family way, and out of an engagement?

Next to him, perhaps, you will see a thin pale man, with a very long face, in a suit of shining black, thoughtfully knocking that part of his boot which once had a heel, with an ash stick. He is the man who does the heavy business, such as prosy fathers, virtuous servants, curates, landlords, and so forth.

By the way, talking of fathers, we should very much like to see some piece in which all the dramatis personæ were orphans. Fathers are invariably great nuisances on the stage, and always have to give the hero or heroine a long explanation of what was done before the curtain rose, usually commencing with "It is now nineteen years, my dear child, since your blessed mother (here the old villain's voice falters) confided you to my charge. You were then an infant," &c., &c. Or else they have to discover, all of a sudden, that somebody whom they have been in constant communication with, during three long acts, without the slightest suspicion, is their own child: in which case they exclaim, "Ah! what do I see? This bracelet! That smile! These documents! Those eyes! Can I believe my senses?—It must be!—Yes—it is, it is my child!"—"My father!" exclaims the child; and they fall into each other's arms, and look over each other's shoulders, and the audience give three rounds of applause.

To return from this digression, we were about to say, that these are the sort of people whom you see talking, and atti-tudinising, outside the stage-doors of our minor theatres. At Astley's they are always more numerous than at any other place. There is generally a groom or two, sitting on the win-dow-sill, and two or three dirty shabby-genteel men in checked neckerchiefs, and sallow linen, lounging about, and carrying, perhaps, under one arm, a pair of stage shoes badly wrapped up in a piece of old newspaper. Some years ago we used to stand looking, open-mouthed, at these men, with a feeling of mysteri-ous curiosity, the very recollection of which provokes a smile at the moment we are writing. We could not believe, that the beings of light and elegance, in milk-white tunics, salmon-coloured legs, and blue scarfs, who flitted on sleek cream-coloured horses before our eyes at night, with all the aid of lights, music, and artificial flowers, could be the pale, dissipated looking creatures we beheld by day.

We can hardly believe it now. Of the lower class of actors we have seen something, and it requires no great exercise of imagination to identify the walking gentleman with the "dirty swell," the comic singer with the public-house chairman, or the leading tragedian with drunkenness and distress; but these other men are mysterious beings, never seen out of the ring, never beheld but in the costume of gods and sylphs. With the exception of Ducrow, who can scarcely be classed among them, who ever knew a rider at Astley's, or saw him but on horseback? Can our friend in the military uniform ever appear in threadbare attire, or descend to the comparatively unwadded costume of every-day life? Impossible! We cannot—we will not—believe it.

CHAPTER XII: *Greenwich Fair*

IF the Parks be "the lungs of London," we wonder what Greenwich Fair is—a periodical breaking out, we suppose, a sort of spring-rash: a three days' fever, which cools the blood for six months afterwards, and at the expiration of which, London is restored to its old habits of plodding industry, as suddenly and completely as if nothing had ever happened to disturb them.

In our earlier days, we were a constant frequenter of Greenwich Fair for years. We have proceeded to, and returned from it, in almost every description of vehicle. We cannot conscientiously deny the charge of having once made the passage in a spring-van, accompanied by thirteen gentlemen, fourteen ladies, an unlimited number of children, and a barrel of beer; and we have a vague recollection of having, in later days, found ourself the eighth outside, on the top of a hackney-coach, at something past four o'clock in the morning, with a rather confused idea of our own name, or place of residence. We have grown older since then, and quiet, and steady: liking nothing better than to spend our Easter, and all our other holidays, in some quiet nook, with people of whom we shall never tire; but we think we still remember something of Greenwich Fair, and of those who resort to it. At all events we will try.

The road to Greenwich during the whole of Easter Monday, is in a state of perpetual bustle and noise. Cabs, hackney-coaches, "shay" carts, coal-waggons, stages, omnibuses, sociables, gigs, donkey-chaises—all crammed with people (for the question never is, what the horse can draw, but what the vehicle will hold), roll along at their utmost speed; the dust flies in clouds, ginger-beer corks go off in volleys, the balcony of every public-house is crowded with people, smoking and drinking, half the private houses are turned into tea-shops, fiddles are in great request, every little fruit-shop displays its stall of gilt gingerbread and penny toys; turnpike men are in despair; horses won't go on, and wheels will come off; ladies in "carawans" scream with fright at every fresh concussion, and their admirers find it necessary to sit remarkably close to them, by way of encouragement; servants of all-work, who are not allowed to have followers, and have got a holiday for the day, make the most of their time with the faithful admirer who waits for a stolen interview at the corner of the street every night, when they go to fetch the beer—apprentices grow sentimental, and straw-bonnet makers kind. Everybody is anxious to get on, and actuated by the common wish to be at the fair, or in the park, as soon as possible.

Pedestrians linger in groups at the roadside, unable to resist the allurements of the stout proprietress of the "Jack-in-the-box—three shies a penny," or the more splendid offers of the man with three thimbles and a pea on a little round board, who astonishes the bewildered crowd with some such address as, "Here's the sort o' game to make you laugh seven years arter you're dead, and turn ev'ry air on your ed gray vith delight! Three thimbles and vun little pea—with a vun, two, three, and a two, three, vun: catch him who can, look on, keep your eyes open, and niver say die! niver mind the change, and the expense: all fair and above board: them as don't play can't vin, and luck attend the ryal sportsman! Bet any gen'l'm'n any sum of money, from harf-a-crown up to a suverin, as he doesn't name the thimble as kivers the pea!" Here some greenhorn whispers his friend, that he distinctly saw the pea roll under the middle thimble— an impression which is immediately confirmed by a gentleman in top-boots, who is standing by, and who, in a low tone, regrets his own inability to bet in consequence of having unfortunately left his purse at home, but strongly urges the stranger not to neglect such a golden opportunity. The "plant" is successful, the bet is made, the stranger of course loses: and the gentleman with the thimbles consoles him, as he pockets the money, with an assurance that it's "all the fortin of war! this time I vin, next time you vin: niver mind the loss of two bob and a bender! Do it up in a small parcel, and break out in a fresh place. Here's the sort o' game," &c.—and the eloquent harangue, with such variations as the speaker's exuberant fancy suggests, is again repeated to the gaping crowd, reinforced by the accession of several new-comers.

The chief place of resort in the daytime, after the public-houses, is the park, in which the principal amusement is to drag young ladies up the steep hill which leads to the observatory, and then drag them down again, at the very top of their speed, greatly to the derangement of their curls and bonnet-caps, and much to the edification of lookers-on from below. "Kiss in the Ring," and "Threading my Grandmother's Needle," too, are sports which receive their full share of patronage. Love-sick swains, under the influence of gin-and-water, and the tender passion, become violently affectionate: and the fair objects of their regard enhance the value of stolen kisses, by a vast deal of struggling, and holding down of heads, and cries of "Oh! Ha' done, then, George—Oh, do tickle him for me, Mary—Well, I never!" and similar Lucretian ejaculations. Little old men and women, with a small basket under one arm, and a wine-glass, without a foot, in the other hand, tender "a drop o' the right sort" to the different groups; and young ladies, who are persuaded to indulge in a drop of the aforesaid right sort, display a pleasing degree of reluctance to taste it, and cough afterwards with great propriety.

The old pensioners, who, for the moderate charge of a penny, exhibit the mast-house, the Thames and shipping, the place where the men used to hang in chains, and other interesting sights, through a telescope, are asked questions about objects within the range of the glass, which it would puzzle a Solomon to answer; and requested to find out particular houses in particular streets, which it would have been a task of some difficulty for Mr. Horner (not the young gentleman who ate mince-pies with his thumb, but the man of Colosseum notoriety) to discover. Here and there, where some three or four couples are sitting on the grass together, you will see a sunburnt woman in a red cloak "telling fortunes" and prophesying husbands, which it requires no extraordinary observation to describe, for the originals are before her. Thereupon the lady concerned laughs and blushes, and ultimately buries her face in an imitation cambric handkerchief, and the gentleman described looks extremely foolish, and squeezes her hand, and fees the gipsy liberally; and the gipsy goes away, perfectly satisfied herself, and leaving those behind her perfectly satisfied also: and the prophecy, like many other prophecies of greater importance, fulfils itself in time.

But it grows dark: the crowd has gradually dispersed, and only a few stragglers are left behind. The light in the direction of the church shows that the fair is illuminated; and the distant noise proves it to be filling fast. The spot which half an hour ago was ringing with the shouts of boisterous mirth, is as calm and quiet as if nothing could ever disturb its serenity; the fine old trees, the majestic building at their feet, with the noble river beyond, glistening in the moonlight, appear in all their beauty, and under their most favourable aspect; the voices of the boys, singing their evening hymn, are borne gently on the air; and the humblest mechanic who has been lingering on the grass so pleasant to the feet that beat the same dull round from week to week in the paved streets of London, feels proud to think as he surveys the scene before him, that he belongs to the country which has selected such a spot as a retreat for its oldest and best defenders in the decline of their lives.

Five minutes' walking brings you to the fair; a scene calculated to awaken very different feelings. The entrance is occupied on either side by the vendors of gingerbread and toys: the stalls are gaily lighted up, the most attractive goods profusely disposed, and unbonneted young ladies, in their zeal for the interest of their employers, seize you by the coat, and use all the blandishments of "Do dear"—"There's a love"—"Don't be cross now," &c., to induce you to purchase half a pound of the real spice nuts, of which the majority of the regular fair-goers carry a pound or two as a present supply, tied up in a cotton pocket-handkerchief. Occasionally you pass a deal table, on which are exposed pen'orths of pickled salmon (fennel included), in little white saucers: oysters, with shells as large as cheese-plates and divers specimens of a species of snail (wilks, we think they are called) floating, in a somewhat bilious-looking green liquid. Cigars, too, are in great demand; gentlemen must smoke, of course, and here they are, two a penny, in a regular authentic cigar-box, with a lighted tallow candle in the centre.

Imagine yourself in an extremely dense crowd, which swings you to and fro, and in and out, and every way but the right one; add to this the screams of women, the shouts of boys, the clanging of gongs, the firing of pistols, the ringing of bells, the bellowings of speaking-trumpets, the squeaking of penny dittoes, the noise of a dozen bands, with three drums in each, all playing different tunes at the same time, the hallooing of showmen, and an occasional roar from the wild-beast shows; and you are in the very centre and heart of the fair.

This immense booth, with the large stage in front, so brightly illuminated with variegated lamps, and pots of burning fat, is "Richardson's," where you have a melodrama (with three murders and a ghost), a pantomime, a comic song, an overture, and some incidental music, all done in five-and-twenty minutes.

The company are now promenading outside in all the dignity of wigs, spangles, red-ochre, and whitening. See with what a ferocious air the gentleman who personates the Mexican chief, paces up and down, and with what an eye of calm dignity the principal tragedian gazes on the crowd below, or converses confidentially with the harlequin! The four clowns, who are engaged in a mock broadsword combat, may be all very well or the low-minded holiday-makers; but these are the people for the reflective portion of the community. They look so noble in those Roman dresses, with their yellow legs and arms, long black curly heads, bushy eyebrows, and scowl expressive of assassination, and vengeance, and everything else that is grand and solemn. Then, the ladies—were there ever such innocent and awful-looking beings; as they walk up and down the platform in twos and threes, with their arms round each others' waists, or leaning for support on one of those majestic men! Their spangled muslin dresses and blue satin shoes and sandals (a *leetle* the worse for wear) are the admiration of all beholders; and the playful manner in which they check the advances of the clown is perfectly enchanting.

"Just a-going to begin! Pray come for'erd, come for'erd," exclaims the man in the countryman's dress, for the seventieth time: and people force their way up the steps in crowds. The band suddenly strikes up, the harlequin and columbine set the example, reels are formed in less than no time, the Roman heroes place their arms a-kimbo, and dance with considerable agility; and the leading tragic actress, and the gentleman who enacts the "swell" in the pantomime, foot it to perfection. "All in to begin," shouts the manager, when no more people can be induced to "come for'erd," and away rush the leading members of the company to do the dreadful in the first piece.

A change of performance takes place every day during the fair, but the story of the tragedy is always pretty much the same. There is a rightful heir, who loves a young lady, and is beloved by her; and a wrongful heir, who loves her too, and isn't beloved by her; and the wrongful heir gets hold of the rightful heir, and throws him into a dungeon, just to kill him off when convenient, for which purpose he hires a couple of assassins—a good one and a bad one—who, the moment they are left alone, get up a little murder on their own account, the good one killing the bad one, and the bad one wounding the good one. Then the rightful heir is discovered in prison, carefully holding a long chain in his hands, and seated despondingly in a large arm-chair; and the young lady comes in to two bars of soft music, and embraces the rightful heir; and then the wrongful heir comes in to two bars of quick music (technically called "a hurry"), and goes on in the most shocking manner, throwing the young lady about, as if she was nobody, and calling the rightful heir "Ar-recreant—ar-wretch!" in a very loud voice, which answers the double purpose of displaying his passion, and preventing the sound being deadened by the sawdust. The interest becomes intense; the wrongful heir draws his sword, and rushes on the rightful heir; a blue smoke is seen, a gong is heard, and a tall white figure (who has been all this time, behind the arm-chair, covered over with a table-cloth), slowly rises to the tune of "Oft in the stilly night." This is no other than the ghost of the rightful heir's father, who was killed by the wrongful heir's father, at sight of which the wrongful heir becomes apoplectic, and is literally "struck all of a heap," the stage not being large enough to admit of his falling down at full length. Then the good assassin staggers in, and says he was hired in conjunction with the bad assassin, by the wrongful heir to kill the rightful heir; and he's killed a good many people in his time, but he's very sorry for it, and won't do so any more—a promise which he immediately redeems, by dying off hand, without any nonsense about it. Then the rightful heir throws down his chain; and then two men, a sailor, and a young woman (the tenantry of the rightful heir) come in, and the ghost makes dumb motions to them, which they, by supernatural interference, understand—for no one else can; and the ghost (who can't do anything without blue fire) blesses the rightful heir and the young lady, by half suffocating them with smoke: and then a muffin-bell rings, and the curtain drops.

The exhibitions next in popularity to these itinerant theatres are the travelling menageries, or, to speak more intelligibly, the "Wild-beast shows," where a military band in beef-eater's costume, with leopard-skin caps, play incessantly; and where large highly-coloured representations of tigers tearing men's heads open, and a lion being burnt with red-hot irons to induce him to drop his victim, are hung up outside, by way of attracting visitors.

The principal officer at these places is generally a very tall, hoarse man, in a scarlet coat, with a cane in his hand, with which he occasionally raps the pictures we have just noticed, by way of illustrating his description—something in this way. "Here, here, here; the lion, the lion (tap), exactly as he is represented on the canvas outside (three taps): no waiting, remember; no deception. The fe-ro-cious lion (tap, tap) who bit off the gentleman's head last Cambervel vos a twelvemonth, and has killed on the awerage three keepers a-year ever since he arrived at matoority. No extra charge on this account recollect; the price of admission is only sixpence." This address never fails to produce a considerable sensation, and sixpences flow into the treasury with wonderful rapidity.

The dwarfs are also objects of great curiosity, and as a dwarf, a giantess, a living skeleton, a wild Indian, "a young lady of singular beauty, with perfectly white hair and pink eyes," and two or three other natural curiosities, are usually exhibited together for the small charge of a penny, they attract very numerous audiences. The best thing about a dwarf is, that he has always a little box, about two feet six inches high, into which, by long practice, he can just manage to get, by doubling himself up like a boot-jack; this box is painted outside like a six-roomed house, and as the crowd see him ring a bell, or fire a pistol out of the first-floor window, they verily believe that it is his ordinary town residence, divided like other mansions into drawing-rooms, dining-parlour, and bed-chambers. Shut up in this case, the unfortunate little object is brought out to delight the throng by holding a facetious dialogue with the proprietor: in the course of which, the dwarf (who is always particularly drunk) pledges himself to sing a comic song inside, and plays various compliments to the ladies, which induce them to "come for'erd" with great alacrity. As a giant is not so easily moved, a pair of indescribables of most capacious dimensions, and a huge shoe, are usually brought out, into which two or three stout men get all at once, to the enthusiastic delight of the crowd, who are quite satisfied with the solemn assurance that these habiliments form part of the giant's everyday costume.

The grandest and most numerously-frequented booth in the whole fair, however, is "The Crown and Anchor"—a temporary ball-room—we forget how many hundred feet long, the price of admission to which is one shilling. Immediately on your right hand as you enter, after paying your money, is a refreshment place, at which cold beef, roast and boiled, French rolls, stout, wine, tongue, ham, even fowls, if we recollect right, are displayed in tempting array. There is a raised orchestra, and the place is boarded all the way down, in patches, just wide enough for a country dance.

There is no master of the ceremonies in this artificial Eden —all is primitive, unreserved, and unstudied. The dust is blinding, the heat insupportable, the company somewhat noisy, and in the highest spirits possible: the ladies, in the height of their innocent animation, dancing in the gentlemen's hats, and the gentlemen promenading "the gay and festive scene" in the ladies' bonnets, or with the more expensive ornaments of false noses, and low-crowned, tinder-box-looking hats: playing children's drums, and accompanied by ladies on the penny trumpet.

The noise of these various instruments, the orchestra, the shouting, the "scratchers," and the dancing, is perfectly bewildering. The dancing, itself, beggars description—every figure lasts about an hour, and the ladies bounce up and down the middle, with a degree of spirit which is quite indescribable. As to the gentlemen, they stamp their feet against the ground, every time "hands four round" begins, go down the middle and up again, with cigars in their mouths, and silk handkerchiefs in their hands, and whirl their partners round, nothing loath, scrambling and falling, and embracing, and knocking up against the other couples, until they are fairly tired out, and can move no longer. The same scene is repeated again and again (slightly varied by an occasional "row") until a late hour at night: and a great many clerks and 'prentices find themselves next morning with aching heads, empty pockets, damaged hats, and a very imperfect recollection of how it was they did *not* get home.

CHAPTER XIII: *Private Theatres*

"RICHARD THE THIRD.—DUKE OF GLO'STER, 2*l*.; EARL OF RICHMOND, 1*l*.; DUKE OF BUCKINGHAM, 15*s*.; CATESBY, 12*s*.; TRESSEL, 10*s*. 6*d*.; LORD STANLEY, 5*s*.; LORD MAYOR OF LONDON, 2*s*. 6*d*."

Such are the written placards wafered up in the gentlemen's dressing-room, or the green-room (where there is any), at a private theatre; and such are the sums extracted from the shop-till, or overcharged in the office expenditure by the donkeys who are prevailed upon to pay for permission to exhibit their lamentable ignorance and boobyism on the stage of a private theatre. This they do, in proportion to the scope afforded by the character for the display of their imbecility. For instance, the Duke of Glo'ster is well worth two pounds, because he has it all to himself; he must wear a real sword, and what is better still, he must draw it, several times in the course of the piece. The soliloquies alone are well worth fifteen shillings; then there is the stabbing King Henry—decidedly cheap at three-and-sixpence, that's eighteen-and-sixpence; bullying the coffin-bearers—say eighteen-pence, though it's worth much more—that's a pound. Then the love scene with Lady Ann, and the bustle of the fourth act, can't be dear at ten shillings more—that's only one pound ten, including the "off with his head!"—which is sure to bring down the applause, and it is very easy to do— "Orf with his ed" (very quick and loud; then slow and sneeringly)—"So much for Bu-u-u-u-uckingham!" Lay the emphasis on the "uck"; get yourself gradually into a corner, and work with your right hand, while you're saying it, as if you were feeling your way, and it's sure to do. The tent scene is confessedly worth half-a-sovereign, and so you have the fight in, gratis, and everybody knows what an effect may be produced by a good combat. One—two—three—four— over; then one—two—three—four—under; then thrust, then dodge and slide about; then fall down on one knee; then fight upon it, and then get up again and stagger. You may keep on doing this, as long as it seems to take—say ten minutes— and then fall down (backwards, if you can manage it without hurting yourself), and die game: nothing like it for producing an effect. They always do it at Astley's and Sadlers' Wells, and if they don't know how to do this sort of thing, who in the world does? A small child, or a female in white, increases the interest of a combat materially—indeed, we are not aware that a regular legitimate terrific broadsword combat could be done without; but it would be rather difficult, and somewhat unusual, to introduce this effect in the last scene of Richard the Third, so the only thing to be done, is, just to make the best of a bad bargain, and be as long as possible fighting it out.

The principal patrons of private theatres are dirty boys, low copying-clerks in attorneys' offices, capacious-headed youths from city counting-houses, Jews whose business, as lenders of fancy dresses, is a sure passport to the amateur stage, shop-boys who now and then mistake their masters' money for their own; and a choice miscellany of idle vagabonds. The proprietor of a private theatre may be an ex-scene-painter, a low coffee-house-keeper, a disappointed eighth-rate actor, a retired smuggler, or uncertificated bankrupt. The theatre itself may be in Catherine Street, Strand, the purlieus of the City, the neighbourhood of Gray's Inn Lane, or the vicinity of Sadlers' Wells; or it may, perhaps, form the chief nuisance of some shabby street on the Surrey side of Waterloo Bridge.

The lady performers pay nothing for their characters, and it is needless to add, are usually selected from one class of society; the audiences are necessarily of much the same character as the performers, who receive, in return for their contributions to the management, tickets to the amount of the money they pay.

All the minor theatres in London, especially the lowest, constitute the centre of a little stage-struck neighbourhood. Each of them has an audience exclusively its own; and at any you will see dropping into the pit at half-price, or swaggering into the back of a box, if the price of admission be a reduced one, divers boys of from fifteen to twenty-one years of age, who throw back their coat and turn up their wristbands, after the portraits of Count D'Orsay, hum tunes and whistle when the curtain is down, by way of persuading the people near them that they are not at all anxious to have it up again, and speak familiarly of the inferior performers as Bill Such-a-one, and Ned So-and-so, or tell each other how a new piece called *The Unknown Bandit of the Invisible Cavern*, is in rehearsal; how Mister Palmer is to play *The Unknown Bandit ;* how Charley Scarton is to take the part of an English sailor, and fight a broadsword combat with six unknown bandits, at one and the same time (one theatrical sailor is always equal to half a dozen men at least); how Mister Palmer and Charley. Scarton are to go through a double hornpipe in fetters in the second act; how the interior of the invisible cavern is to occupy the whole extent of the stage; and other town-surprising theatrical announcements. These gentlemen are the amateurs—the *Richards, Shylocks, Beverleys,* and *Othellos*—the *Young Dorntons, Rovers, Captain Absolutes,* and *Charles Surfaces*—of a private theatre.

See them at the neighbouring public-houses or the theatrical coffee-shop! They are the kings of the place, supposing no real performers to be present; and roll about, hats on one side, and arms a-kimbo, as if they had actually come into possession of eighteen shillings a-week, and a share of a ticket night. If one of them does but know an Astley's supernumerary he is a happy fellow. The mingled air of envy and admiration with which his companions will regard him, as he converses familiarly with some mouldy-looking man in a fancy neckerchief, whose partially corked eyebrows, and half-rouged face, testify to the fact of his having just left the stage or the circle, sufficiently shows in what high admiration these public characters are held.

With the double view of guarding against the discovery of friends or employers, and enhancing the interest of an assumed character, by attaching a high-sounding name to its representative, these geniuses assume fictitious names, which are not the least amusing part of the play-bill of a private theatre. Belville, Melville, Treville, Berkeley, Randolph, Byron, St. Clair, and so forth, are among the humblest; and the less imposing titles of Jenkins, Walker, Thomson, Barker, Solomons, &c., are completely laid aside. There is something imposing in this, and it is an excellent apology for shabbiness into the bargain. A shrunken, faded coat, a decayed hat, a patched and soiled pair of trousers—nay, even a very dirty shirt (and none of these appearances are very uncommon among the members of the *corps dramatique*), may be worn for the purpose of disguise, and to prevent the remotest chance of recognition. Then it prevents any troublesome inquiries or explanations about employment and pursuits; everybody is a gentleman at large, for the occasion, and there are none of those unpleasant and unnecessary distinctions to which even genius must occasionally succumb elsewhere. As to the ladies (God bless them), they are quite above any formal absurdities; the mere circumstance of your being behind the scenes is a sufficient introduction to their society—for of course they know that none but strictly respectable persons would be admitted into that close fellowship with them, which acting engenders. They place implicit reliance on the manager, no doubt; and as to the manager, he is all affability when he knows you well—or, in other words, when he has pocketed your money once, and entertains confident hopes of doing so again.

A quarter before eight—there will be a full house to-night —six parties in the boxes, already; four little boys and a woman in the pit: and two fiddles and a flute in the orchestra, who have got through five overtures since seven o'clock (the hour fixed for the commencement of the performances), and have just begun the sixth. There will be plenty of it, though, when it does begin, for there is enough in the bill to last six hours at least.

That gentleman in the white hat and checked shirt, brown coat and brass buttons, lounging behind the stage-box on the O. P. side, is Mr. Horatio St. Julien, alias Jem Larkins. His line is genteel comedy—his father's, coal and potato. He *does* Alfred Highflier in the last piece, and very well he'll do it—at the price. The party of gentlemen in the opposite box, to whom he has just nodded, are friends and supporters of Mr. Beverley (otherwise Loggins), the *Macbeth* of the night. You observe their attempts to appear easy and gentlemanly, each member of the party, with his feet cocked upon the cushion in front of the box! They let them do these things here, upon the same humane principle which permits poor people's children to knock double-knocks at the door of an empty house—because they can't do it anywhere else. The two stout men in the centre box, with an opera-glass ostentatiously placed before them, are friends of the proprietor—opulent country managers, as he confidentially informs every individual among the crew behind the curtain—opulent country managers looking out for recruits; a representation which Mr. Nathan, the dresser, who is in the manager's interest, and has just arrived, with the costumes, offers to confirm upon oath if required—corroborative evidence, however, is quite unnecessary, for the gulls believe it at once.

The stout Jewess, who has just entered, is the mother of the pale bony little girl, with the necklace of blue glass beads, sitting by her; she is being brought up to "the profession." Pantomime is to be her line, and she is coming out to-night, in a hornpipe after the tragedy. The short thin man beside Mr. St. Julien, whose white face is so deeply scared with the small-pox, and whose dirty shirt-front is inlaid with open work, and embossed with coral studs like lady-birds, is the low comedian and comic singer of the establishment. The remainder of the audience—a tolerably numerous one by this time—are a motley group of dupes and blackguards.

The foot-lights have just made their appearance: the wicks of the six little oil lamps round the only tier of boxes, are being turned up, and the additional light thus afforded serves to show the presence of dirt, and absence of paint, which forms a prominent feature in the audience part of the house. As these preparations, however, announce the speedy commencement of the play, let us take a peep "behind," previous to the ringing-up.

The little narrow passages beneath the stage are neither

especially clean nor too brilliantly lighted; and the absence
of any flooring, together with the damp mildewy smell
which pervades the place, does not conduce in any great
degree to their comfortable appearance. Don't fall over
this plate basket—it's one of the "properties"—the caldron
for the witches' cave; and the three uncouth-looking figures,
with broken clothes-props in their hands, who are drinking
gin-and-water out of a pint pot, are the weird sisters. This
miserable room, lighted by candles in sconces placed at
lengthened intervals round the wall, is the dressing-room,
common to the gentlemen performers, and the square hole
in the ceiling is *the* trap-door of the stage above. You will
observe that the ceiling is ornamented with the beams that
support the boards, and tastefully hung with cobwebs.

The characters in the tragedy are all dressed, and their
own clothes are scattered in hurried confusion over the
wooden dresser which surrounds the room. That snuffshop-
looking figure, in front of the glass, is *Banquo :* and the young
lady with the liberal display of legs, who is kindly painting
his face with a hare's foot, is dressed for *Fleance.* The large
woman, who is consulting the stage directions in Cumberland's
edition of *Macbeth,* is the *Lady Macbeth* of the night; she is
always selected to play the part, because she is tall and
stout, and *looks* a little like Mrs. Siddons—at a considerable
distance. That stupid-looking milksop, with light hair and
bow legs—a kind of man whom you can warrant town-made
—is fresh caught; he plays *Malcolm* to-night, just to accustom
himself to an audience. He will get on better by degrees;
he will play *Othello* in a month, and in a month more, will
very probably be apprehended on a charge of embezzlement.
The black-eyed female with whom he is talking so earnestly,
is dressed for the "gentlewoman." It is *her* first appearance,
too—in that character. The boy of fourteen, who is having
his eyebrows smeared with soap and whitening, is *Duncan,*
King of Scotland; and the two dirty men with the corked
countenances, in very old green tunics, and dirty drab boots,
are the "army."

"Look sharp below there, gents," exclaims the dresser, a
red-headed and red-whiskered Jew, calling through the
trap, "they're a-going to ring up. The flute says he'll be
blowed if he plays any more, and they're getting precious
noisy in front." A general rush immediately takes place to
the half-dozen little steep steps leading to the stage, and the
heterogeneous group are soon assembled at the side scenes,
in breathless anxiety and motley confusion.

"Now," cries the manager, consulting the written list
which hangs behind the first P.S. wing, "Scene 1, open country
—lamps down—thunder and lightning—all ready, White?"
[This is addressed to one of the army.]   "All ready."—"Very

well. Scene 2, front chamber. Is the front chamber down?"
—"Yes."—"Very well."—"Jones" [to the other army who
is up in the flies]. "Hallo!"—"Wind up the open country
when we ring up."—"I'll take care."—"Scene 3, back perspective with practical bridge. Bridge ready, White? Got
the trestles there?"—"All right."

"Very well. Clear the stage," cries the manager, hastily
packing every member of the company into the little space
there is between the wings and the wall, and one wing and
another. "Places, places. Now then, Witches—Duncan—
Malcolm—bleeding officer—where's the bleeding officer?"—
"Here!" replies the officer, who has been rose-pinking for
the character. "Get ready, then; now, White, ring the
second music-bell." The actors who are to be discovered, are
hastily arranged, and the actors who are not to be discovered
place themselves, in their anxiety to peep at the house, just
where the whole audience can see them. The bell rings, and
the orchestra, in acknowledgment of the call, play three
distinct chords. The bell rings—the tragedy (!) opens—and
our description closes.

CHAPTER XIV: *Vauxhall Gardens by Day*

THERE was a time when if a man ventured to wonder how
Vauxhall Gardens would look by day, he was hailed with a
shout of derision at the absurdity of the idea. Vauxhall by
daylight! A porter-pot without porter, the House of Commons without the Speaker, a gas-lamp without the gas—
pooh, nonsense, the thing was not to be thought of. It was
rumoured, too, in those times, that Vauxhall Gardens by day,
were the scene of secret and hidden experiments; that there,
carvers were exercised in the mystic art of cutting a moderate-
sized ham into slices thin enough to pave the whole of the
grounds; that beneath the shade of the tall trees, studious
men were constantly engaged in chemical experiments, with
the view of discovering how much water a bowl of negus
could possibly bear; and that in some retired nooks, appropriated to the study of ornithology, other sage and learned
men were, by a process known only to themselves, incessantly
employed in reducing fowls to a mere combination of skin and
bone.

Vague rumours of this kind, together with many others of
a similar nature, cast over Vauxhall Gardens an air of deep
mystery; and as there is a great deal in the mysterious, there
is no doubt that to a good many people, at all events, the
pleasure they afforded was not a little enhanced by this very
circumstance.

Of this class of people we confess to having made one. We

loved to wander among these illuminated groves, thinking of the patient and laborious researches which had been carried on there during the day, and witnessing their results in the suppers which were served up beneath the light of lamps, and to the sound of music, at night. The temples and saloons and cosmoramas and fountains glittered and sparkled before our eyes; the beauty of the lady singers and the elegant deportment of the gentlemen, captivated our hearts; a few hundred thousand of additional lamps dazzled our senses; a bowl or two of reeking punch bewildered our brain; and we were happy.

In an evil hour, the proprietors of Vauxhall Gardens took to opening them by day. We regretted this, as rudely and harshly disturbing that veil of mystery which had hung about the property for many years, and which none but the noonday sun, and the late Mr. Simpson, had ever penetrated. We shrank from going; at this moment we scarcely know why. Perhaps a morbid consciousness of approaching disappointment—perhaps a fatal presentiment—perhaps the weather; whatever it was, we did *not* go until the second or third announcement of a race between two balloons tempted us, and we went.

We paid our shilling at the gate, and then we saw for the first time, that the entrance, if there had ever been any magic about it at all, was now decidedly disenchanted, being, in fact, nothing more nor less than a combination of very roughly-painted boards and sawdust. We glanced at the orchestra and supper-room as we hurried past—we just recognised them, and that was all. We bent our steps to the firework-ground; there, at least, we should not be disappointed. We reached it, and stood rooted to the spot with mortification and astonishment. *That* the Moorish tower—that wooden shed with a door in the centre, and daubs of crimson and yellow all round, like a gigantic watch-case! *That* the place where night after night we had beheld the undaunted Mr. Blackmore make his terrific ascent, surrounded by flames of fire, and peals of artillery, and where the white garments of Madame Somebody (we forget even her name now), who nobly devoted her life to the manufacture of fireworks, had so often been seen fluttering in the wind, as she called up a red, blue, or party-coloured light to illumine her temple! *That* the——but at this moment the bell rang; the people scampered away, pell-mell, to the spot from whence the sound proceeded; and we, from the mere force of habit, found ourself running among the first, as if for very life.

It was for the concert in the orchestra. A small party of dismal men in cocked hats were "executing" the overture to *Tancredi*, and a numerous assemblage of ladies and gentlemen, with their families, had rushed from their half-emptied stout mugs in the supper-boxes, and crowded to the spot. Intense was the low murmur of admiration when a particularly small gentleman, in a dress coat, led on a particularly tall lady in a blue sarcenet pelisse and bonnet of the same, ornamented with large white feathers, and forthwith commenced a plaintive duet.

We knew the small gentleman well; we had seen a lithographed semblance of him, on many a piece of music, with his mouth wide open as if in the act of singing; a wineglass in his hand; and a table with two decanters and four pineapples on it in the back-ground. The tall lady, too, we had gazed on, lost in raptures of admiration, many and many a time—how different people *do* look by daylight, and without punch, to be sure! It was a beautiful duet: first the small gentleman asked a question, and then the tall lady answered it; then the small gentleman and the tall lady sang together most melodiously; then the small gentleman went through a little piece of vehemence by himself, and got very tenor indeed, in the excitement of his feelings, to which the tall lady responded in a similar manner; then the small gentleman had a shake or two, after which the tall lady had the same, and then they both merged imperceptibly into the original air: and the band wound themselves up to a pitch of fury, and the small gentleman handed the tall lady out, and the applause was rapturous.

The comic singer, however, was the especial favourite; we really thought that a gentleman, with his dinner in a pocket-handkerchief, who stood near us, would have fainted with excess of joy. A marvellously facetious gentleman that comic singer is; his distinguishing characteristics are, a wig approaching to the flaxen, and an aged countenance, and he bears the name of one of the English counties, if we recollect right. He sang a very good song about the seven ages, the first half-hour of which afforded the assembly the purest delight; of the rest we can make no report, as we did not stay to hear any more.

We walked about, and met with a disappointment at every turn; our favourite views were mere patches of paint; the fountain that had sparkled so showily by lamp-light, presented very much the appearance of a water-pipe that had burst; all the ornaments were dingy, and all the walks gloomy. There was a spectral attempt at rope-dancing in the little open theatre. The sun shone upon the spangled dresses of the performers, and their evolutions were about as inspiriting and appropriate as a country dance in a family vault. So we retraced our steps to the firework-ground, and mingled with the little crowd of people who were contemplating Mr. Green.

Some half-dozen men were restraining the impetuosity of one of the balloons, which was completely filled, and had the car already attached; and as rumours had gone abroad that a Lord was "going up," the crowd were more than usually anxious and talkative. There was one little man in faded black, with a dirty face and a rusty black neckerchief with a red border, tied in a narrow wisp round his neck, who entered into conversation with everybody, and had something to say upon every remark that was made within his hearing. He was standing with his arms folded, staring up at the balloon, and every now and then vented his feelings of reverence for the aëronaut, by saying, as he looked round to catch somebody's eye, "He's a rum 'un is Green; think o' this here being up'ards of his two hundredth ascent; ecod, the man as is ekal to Green never had the toothache yet, nor won't have within this hundred year, and that's all about it. When you meets with real talent, and native, too, encourage it, that's what I say;" and when he had delivered himself to this effect, he would fold his arms with more determination than ever, and stare at the balloon with a sort of admiring defiance of any other man alive, beyond himself and Green, that impressed the crowd with the opinion that he was an oracle.

"Ah, you're very right, sir," said another gentleman, with his wife, and children, and mother, and wife's sister, and a host of female friends, in all the gentility of white pocket-handkerchiefs, frills, and spencers, "Mr. Green is a steady hand, sir, and there's no fear about him."

"Fear!" said the little man: "isn't it a lovely thing to see him and his wife a going up in one balloon, and his own son and *his* wife a jostling up against them in another, and all of them going twenty or thirty mile in three hours or so and then coming back in pochayses? I don't know where this here science is to stop, mind you; that's what bothers me."

Here there was a considerable talking among the females in the spencers.

"What's the ladies a laughing at, sir?" inquired the little man, condescendingly.

"It's only my sister Mary," said one of the girls, "as says she hopes his lordship won't be frightened when he's in the car, and want to come out again."

"Make yourself easy about that there, my dear," replied the little man. "If he was so much as to move an inch without leave, Green would jist fetch him a crack over the head with the telescope, as would send him into the bottom of the basket in no time, and stun him till they come down again."

"Would he, though?" inquired the other man.

"Yes, would he," replied the little one, "and think nothing of it, neither, if he was the king himself. Green's presence of mind is wonderful."

Just at this moment all eyes were directed to the preparations which were being made for starting. The car was attached to the second balloon, the two were brought pretty close together, and a military band commenced playing, with a zeal and fervour which would render the most timid man in existence but too happy to accept any means of quitting that particular spot of earth on which they were stationed. Then Mr. Green, sen., and his noble companion entered one car, and Mr. Green, jun., and *his* companion the other; and then the balloons went up, and the aërial travellers stood up, and the crowd outside roared with delight, and the two gentlemen who had never ascended before, tried to wave their flags, as if they were not nervous, but held on very fast all the while; and the balloons were wafted gently away, our little friend solemnly protesting, long after they were reduced to mere specks in the air, that he could still distinguish the white hat of Mr. Green. The gardens disgorged their multitudes, boys ran up and down screaming "bal-loon!" and in all the crowded thoroughfares people rushed out of their shops into the middle of the road, and having stared up in the air at two little black objects till they almost dislocated their necks, walked slowly in again, perfectly satisfied.

The next day there was a grand account of the ascent in the morning papers, and the public were informed how it was the finest day but four in Mr. Green's remembrance; how they retained sight of the earth till they lost it behind the clouds; and how the reflection of the balloon on the undulating masses of vapour was gorgeously picturesque; together with a little science about the refraction of the sun's rays, and some mysterious hints respecting atmospheric heat and eddying currents of air.

There was also an interesting account how a man in a boat was distinctly heard by Mr. Green, jun., to exclaim, "My eye!" which Mr Green, jun., attributed to his voice rising to the balloon, and the sound being thrown back from its surface into the car; and the whole concluded with a slight allusion to another ascent next Wednesday, all of which was very instructive and very amusing, as our readers will see if they look to the papers. If we have forgotten to mention the date, they have only to wait till next summer, and take the account of the first ascent, and it will answer the purpose equally well.

CHAPTER XV: *Early Coaches*

WE have often wondered how many months' incessant travelling in a postchaise, it would take to kill a man; and wondering by analogy, we should very much like to know

how many months of constant travelling in a succession of
early coaches, an unfortunate mortal could endure. Breaking
a man alive upon the wheel, would be nothing to breaking
his rest, his peace, his heart—everything but his fast—upon
four; and the punishment of Ixion (the only practical person,
by-the-by, who has discovered the secret of the perpetual
motion) would sink into utter insignificance before the one
we have suggested. If we had been a powerful churchman
in those good times when blood was shed as freely as water
and men were mowed down like grass, in the sacred cause of
religion, we would have lain by very quietly till we got hold
of some especially obstinate miscreant, who positively refused
to be converted to our faith, and then we would have booked
him for an inside place in a small coach, which travelled
day and night: and securing the remainder of the places for
stout men with a slight tendency to coughing and spitting,
we would have started him forth on his last travels: leaving
him mercilessly to all the tortures which the waiters, landlords,
coachmen, guards, boots, chambermaids, and other familiars
on his line of road, might think proper to inflict.

Who has not experienced the miseries inevitably consequent
upon a summons to undertake a hasty journey? You
receive an intimation from your place of business—wherever
that may be, or whatever you may be—that it will be necessary to leave town without delay. You and your family
are forthwith thrown into a state of tremendous excitement;
an express is immediately despatched to the washerwoman's;
everybody is in a bustle; and you, yourself, with a feeling of
dignity which you cannot altogether conceal, sally forth to
the booking-office to secure your place. Here a painful
consciousness of your own unimportance first rushes on your
mind—the people are as cool and collected as if nobody were
going out of town, or as if a journey of a hundred odd miles
were a mere nothing. You enter a mouldy-looking room,
ornamented with large posting-bills; the greater part of the
place enclosed behind a huge, lumbering rough counter, and
fitted up with recesses that look like the dens of the smaller
animals in a travelling menagerie, without the bars. Some
half-dozen people are "booking" brown-paper parcels, which
one of the clerks flings into the aforesaid recesses with an air
of recklessness which you, remembering the new carpet-bag
you bought in the morning, feel considerably annoyed at;
porters, looking like so many Atlases, keep rushing in and
out, with large packages on their shoulders; and while you
are waiting to make the necessary inquiries, you wonder
what on earth the booking-office clerks can have been before
they were booking-office clerks; one of them with his pen
behind his ear, and his hands behind him, is standing in
front of the fire, like a full-length portrait of Napoleon; the

other with his hat half off his head, enters the passengers' names in the books with a coolness which is inexpressibly provoking; and the villain whistles—actually whistles— while a man asks him what the fare is outside, all the way to Holyhead!—in frosty weather too! They are clearly an isolated race, evidently possessing no sympathies or feelings in common with the rest of mankind. Your turn comes at last, and having paid the fare, you tremblingly inquire— "What time will it be necessary for me to be here in the morning?"—"Six o'clock," replies the whistler, carelessly pitching the sovereign you have just parted with, into a wooden bowl on the desk. "Rather before than arter," adds the man with the semi-roasted unmentionables, with just as much ease and complacency as if the whole world got out of bed at five. You turn into the street, ruminating as you bend your steps homewards on the extent to which men become hardened in cruelty, by custom.

If there be one thing in existence more miserable than another, it most unquestionably is the being compelled to rise by candle-light. If you ever doubted the fact, you are painfully convinced of your error, on the morning of your departure. You left strict orders, overnight, to be called at half-past four, and you have done nothing all night but doze for five minutes at a time, and start up suddenly from a terrific dream of a large church-clock with the small hand running round with astonishing rapidity, to every figure on the dial-plate. At last, completely exhausted, you fall gradually into a refreshing sleep—your thoughts grow confused—the stage-coaches, which have been "going off" before your eyes all night, become less and less distinct, until they go off altogether; one moment you are driving with all the skill and smartness of an experienced whip—the next you are exhibiting, *à la* Ducrow, on the off-leader; anon you are closely muffled up, inside, and have just recognised in the person of the guard an old schoolfellow, whose funeral, even in your dream, you remember to have attended eighteen years ago. At last you fall into a state of complete oblivion, from which you are aroused, as if into a new state of existence, by a singular illusion. You are apprenticed to a trunk maker; how, or why, or when, or wherefore, you don't take the trouble to inquire; but there you are, pasting the lining in the lid of a portmanteau. Confound that other apprentice in the back shop, how he is hammering!—rap, rap, rap—what an industrious fellow he must be! you have heard him at work for half an hour past, and he has been hammering incessantly the whole time. Rap, rap, rap, again—he's talking now—what's that he said? Five o'clock! You make a violent exertion, and start up in bed. The vision is at once dispelled; the trunk-maker's shop is your own bedroom, and the other apprentice your shivering servant, who has been vainly endeavouring to wake you for the last quarter of an hour, at the imminent risk of breaking either his own knuckles, or the panels of the door.

You proceed to dress yourself with all possible despatch. The flaring flat candle with the long snuff, gives light enough to show that the things you want, are not where they ought to be, and you undergo a trifling delay in consequence of having carefully packed up one of your boots in your over-anxiety of the preceding night. You soon complete your toilet, however, for you are not particular on such an occasion, and you shaved yesterday evening; so mounting your Peter-sham greatcoat, and green travelling shawl, and grasping your carpet-bag in your right hand, you walk lightly down-stairs, lest you should awaken any of the family, and after pausing in the common sitting-room for one moment, just to have a cup of coffee (the said common sitting-room looking remarkably comfortable, with everything out of its place, and strewed with the crumbs of last night's supper). you undo the chain and bolts of the street-door, and find yourself fairly in the street.

A thaw, by all that is miserable! The frost is completely broken up. You look down the long perspective of Oxford Street, the gas-lights mournfully reflected on the wet pave-ment, and can discern no speck in the road to encourage the belief that there is a cab or a coach to be had—the very coachmen have gone home in despair. The cold sleet is drizzling down with that gentle regularity, which betokens a duration of four-and-twenty hours at least; the damp hangs upon the house-tops and lamp-posts, and clings to you like an invisible cloak. The water is "coming in" in every area, the pipes have burst, the water butts are running over; the kennels seem to be doing matches against time, pump-handles descend of their own accord, horses in market-carts fall down, and there's no one to help them up again, policemen look as if they had been carefully sprinkled with powdered glass; here and there a milk-woman trudges slowly along, with a bit of list round each foot to keep her from slipping; boys who "don't sleep in the house," and are not allowed much sleep out of it, can't wake their masters by thundering at the shop-door, and cry with the cold—the compound of ice, snow, and water on the pavement, is a couple of inches thick—nobody ventures to walk fast to keep himself warm, and nobody could succeed in keeping himself warm if he did.

It strikes a quarter past five as you trudge down Waterloo Place on your way to the Golden Cross, and you discover, for the first time, that you were called about an hour too early. You have not time to go back; there is no place open to go into, and you have, therefore, no resource but to go forward, which you do, feeling remarkably satisfied with yourself, and everything about you. You arrive at the office, and look wistfully up the yard for the Birmingham Highflier, which, for aught you can see, may have flown away altogether, for no preparations appear to be on foot for the departure of any vehicle in the shape of a coach. You wander into the booking-office, which with the gas-lights and blazing fire, looks quite comfortable by contrast—that is to say, if any place *can* look comfortable at half-past five on a winter's morning. There stands the identical book-keeper in the same position as if he had not moved since you saw him yesterday. As he informs you, that the coach is up the yard, and will be brought round in about a quarter of an hour, you leave your bag, and repair to "The Tap"— not with any absurd idea of warming yourself, because you feel such a result to be utterly hopeless, but for the purpose of procuring some hot brandy-and-water, which you do,— when the kettle boils! an event which occurs exactly two minutes and a half before the time fixed for the starting of the coach.

The first stroke of six, peals from St. Martin's church steeple, just as you take the first sip of the boiling liquid. You find yourself at the booking-office in two seconds, and the tap-waiter finds himself much comforted by your brandy-and-water, in about the same period. The coach is out; the horses are in, and the guard and two or three porters, are stowing the luggage away, and running up the steps of the booking-office, and down the steps of the booking-office, with breathless rapidity. The place, which a few minutes ago was so still and quiet, is now all bustle; the early vendors of the morning papers have arrived, and you are assailed on all sides with shouts of "*Times*, gen'lm'n, *Times*," "Here's Chron—Chron—Chron," "*Herald*, ma'am," "Highly interesting murder, gen'lm'n," "Curious case o' breach o' promise, ladies." The inside passengers are already in their dens, and the outsides with the exception of yourself, are pacing up and down the pavement to keep themselves warm; they consist of two young men with very long hair, to which the sleet has communicated the appearance of crystallized rats' tails; one thin young woman cold and peevish, one old gentleman ditto, ditto, and something in a cloak and cap, intended to represent a military officer; every member of the party, with a large stiff shawl over his chin, looking exactly as if he were playing a set of Pan's pipes.

"Take off the cloths, Bob," says the coachman, who now appears for the first time, in a rough blue greatcoat, of which the buttons behind are so far apart, that you can't see them both at the same time. "Now, gen'lm'n," cries the guard,

with the way-bill in his hand. "Five minutes behind time
already!" Up jump the passengers—the two young men
smoking like lime-kilns, and the old gentleman grumbling
audibly. The thin young woman is got upon the roof, by dint
of a great deal of pulling, and pushing, and helping and
trouble, and she repays it by expressing her solemn conviction
that she will never be able to get down again.

"All right," sings out the guard at last, jumping up as the
coach starts, and blowing his horn directly afterwards, in
proof of the soundness of his wind. "Let 'em go, Harry,
give 'em their heads," cries the coachman—and off we start
as briskly as if the morning were "all right," as well as the
coach: and looking forward as anxiously to the termination
of our journey, as we fear our readers will have done, long
since, to the conclusion of our paper.

CHAPTER XVI: *Omnibuses*

IT is very generally allowed that public conveyances afford
an extensive field for amusement and observation. Of all
the public conveyances that have been constructed since the
days of the Ark—we think that is the earliest on record—
to the present time, commend us to an omnibus. A long
stage is not to be despised, but there you have only six
insides, and the chances are, that the same people go all the
way with you—there is no change, no variety. Besides,
after the first twelve hours or so, people get cross and sleepy,
and when you have seen a man in his nightcap, you lose all
respect for him; at least, that is the case with us. Then on
smooth roads people frequently get prosy, and tell long
stories, and even those who don't talk, may have very
unpleasant predilections. We once travelled four hundred
miles, inside a stage-coach, with a stout man, who had a
glass of rum-and-water, warm, handed in at the window at
every place where we changed horses. This was decidedly
unpleasant. We have also travelled occasionally, with a
small boy of a pale aspect, with light hair, and no perceptible
neck, coming up to town from school under the protection of
the guard, and directed to be left at the Cross Keys till called
for. This is, perhaps, even worse than rum-and-water in a
close atmosphere. Then there is the whole train of evils
consequent on a change of the coachman; and the misery of
the discovery—which the guard is sure to make the moment
you begin to doze—that he wants a brown-paper parcel, which
he distinctly remembers to have deposited under the seat
on which you are reposing. A great deal of bustle and groping
takes place, and when you are thoroughly awakened, and
severely cramped, by holding your legs up by an almost

supernatural exertion, while he is looking behind them, it suddenly occurs to him that he put it in the fore-boot. Bang goes the door, the parcel is immediately found: off starts the coach again, and the guard plays the key-bugle as loud as he can play it, as if in mockery of your wretchedness.

Now you meet with none of these afflictions in an omnibus; sameness there can never be. The passengers change as often in the course of one journey as the figures in a kaleidoscope, and though not so glittering, are far more amusing. We believe there is no instance upon record of a man's having gone to sleep in one of these vehicles. As to long stories, would any man venture to tell a long story in an omnibus? and even if he did, where would be the harm? nobody could possibly hear what he was talking about. Again; children, though occasionally, are not often to be found in an omnibus; and even when they are, if the vehicle be full, as is generally the case, somebody sits upon them, and we are unconscious of their presence. Yes, after mature reflection, and considerable experience, we are decidedly of opinion, that of all known vehicles, from the glass-coach in which we were taken to be christened, to that sombre caravan in which we must one day make our last earthly journey, there is nothing like an omnibus.

We will back the machine in which we make our daily peregrination from the top of Oxford Street to the city, against any "buss" on the road, whether it be for the gaudiness of its exterior, the perfect simplicity of its interior, or the native coolness of its cad. This young gentleman is a singular instance of self-devotion; his somewhat intemperate zeal on behalf of his employers, is constantly getting him into trouble, and occasionally into the house of correction. He is no sooner emancipated, however, than he resumes the duties of his profession with unabated ardour. His principal distinction is his activity. His great boast is "that he can chuck an old gen'lm'n into the buss, shut him in, and rattle off, afore he knows where it's a-going to"—a feat which he frequently performs, to the infinite amusement of every one but the old gentleman concerned, who, somehow or other, never can see the joke of the thing.

We are not aware that it has ever been precisely ascertained how many passengers our omnibus will contain. The impression on the cad's mind, evidently is, that it is amply sufficient for the accommodation of any number of persons that can be enticed into it. "Any room?" cries a very hot pedestrian. "Plenty o' room, sir," replies the conductor, gradually opening the door, and not disclosing the real state of the case, till the wretched man is on the steps. "Where?" inquires the entrapped individual, with an attempt to back out again. "Either side, sir," rejoins the cad, shoving him in, and slamming the door. "All right, Bill." Retreat is impossible; the new-comer rolls about, till he falls down somewhere, and there he stops.

As we get into the city a little before ten, four or five of our party are regular passengers. We always take them up at the same places, and they generally occupy the same seats; they are always dressed in the same manner, and invariably discuss the same topics—the increasing rapidity of cabs, and the disregard of moral obligations evinced by omnibus men. There is a little testy old man, with a powdered head, who always sits on the right-hand side of the door as you enter, with his hands folded on the top of his umbrella. He is extremely impatient, and sits there for the purpose of keeping a sharp eye on the cad, with whom he generally holds a running dialogue. He is very officious in helping people in and out, and always volunteers to give the cad a poke with his umbrella, when any one wants to alight. He usually recommends ladies to have sixpence ready to prevent delay; and if anybody puts a window down, that he can reach, he immediately puts it up again.

"Now, what are you stopping for?" says the little old man every morning, the moment there is the slightest indication of "pulling up" at the corner of Regent Street, when some such dialogue as the following takes place between him and the cad:

"What are you stopping for?"

Here the cad whistles, and affects not to hear the question.

"I say [a poke], what are you stopping for?"

"For passengers, sir. Ba—nk.—Ty."

"I know you're stopping for passengers; but you've no business to do so. *Why* are you stopping?"

"Vy, sir, that's a difficult question. I think it is because we prefer stopping here to going on."

"Now mind," exclaims the little old man, with great vehemence, "I'll pull you up to-morrow; I've often threatened to do it; now I will."

"Thankee, sir," replies the cad, touching his hat with a mock expression of gratitude;—"werry much obliged to you indeed, sir." Here the young men in the omnibus laugh very heartily, and the old gentleman gets very red in the face, and seems highly exasperated.

The stout gentleman in the white neckcloth, at the other end of the vehicle, looks very prophetic, and says that something must shortly be done with these fellows, or there's no saying where all this will end; and the shabby-genteel man with the green bag, expresses his entire concurrence in the opinion, as he has done regularly every morning for the last six months.

A second omnibus now comes up, and stops immediately

behind us. Another old gentleman elevates his cane in the air, and runs with all his might towards our omnibus; we watch his progress with great interest; the door is opened to receive him, he suddenly disappears—he has been spirited away by the opposition. Hereupon the driver of the opposition taunts our people with his having "regularly done 'em out of that old swell" and the voice of the "old swell" is heard, vainly protesting against this unlawful detention. We rattle off, the other omnibus rattles after us, and every time we stop to take up a passenger, they stop to take him too; sometimes we get him; sometimes they get him; but whoever don't get him, say they ought to have had him, and the cads of the respective vehicles abuse one another accordingly.

As we arrive in the vicinity of Lincoln's Inn Fields, Bedford Row, and other legal haunts, we drop a great many of our original passengers, and take up fresh ones, who meet with a very sulky reception. It is rather remarkable, that the people already in an omnibus, always look at new-comers as if they entertained some undefined idea that they have no business to come in at all. We are quite persuaded the little old man has some notion of this kind and that he considers their entry as a sort of negative impertinence.

Conversation is now entirely dropped; each person gazes vacantly through the window in front of him, and everybody thinks that his opposite neighbour is staring at him. If one man gets out at Shoe Lane, and another at the corner of Farringdon Street, the little old gentleman grumbles, and suggests to the latter, that if he had got out at Shoe Lane too, he would have saved them the delay of another stoppage; whereupon the young men laugh again, and the old gentleman looks very solemn, and says nothing more till he gets to the Bank, when he trots off as fast as he can, leaving us to do the same, and to wish, as we walk away, that we could impart to others any portion of the amusement we have gained for ourselves.

CHAPTER XVII: *The Last Cab-driver and the First Omnibus Cad*

OF all the cabriolet-drivers whom we have ever had the honour and gratification of knowing by sight—and our acquaintance in this way has been most extensive—there is one who made an impression on our mind which can never be effaced, and who awakened in our bosom a feeling of admiration and respect, which we entertain a fatal presentiment will never be called forth again by any human being. He was a man of most simple and prepossessing appearance.

He was a brown-whiskered, white-hatted, no-coated cabman; his nose was generally red, and his bright blue eye not unfrequently stood out in bold relief against a black border of artificial workmanship; his boots were of the Wellington form, pulled up to meet his corduroy knee-smalls, or at least to approach as near them as their dimensions would admit of; and his neck was usually garnished with a bright yellow handkerchief. In summer he carried in his mouth a flower; in winter, a straw—slight, but to a contemplative mind, certain indications of a love of nature, and a taste for botany.

His cabriolet was gorgeously painted—a bright red; and wherever we went, City or West End, Paddington or Holloway, North, East, West, or South, there was the red cab, bumping up against the posts at the street corners, and turning in and out, among hackney-coaches, and drays, and carts, and waggons, and omnibuses, and contriving by some strange means or other, to get out of places which no other vehicle but the red cab could ever by any possibility have contrived to get into at all. Our fondness for that red cab was unbounded. How we should have liked to see it in the circle at Astley's! Our life upon it, that it should have performed such evolutions as would have put the whole company to shame—Indian chiefs, knights, Swiss peasants, and all.

Some people object to the exertion of getting into cabs, and others object to the difficulty of getting out of them; we think both these are objections which take their rise in perverse and ill-conditioned minds. The getting into a cab is a very pretty and graceful process, which, when well-performed, is essentially melodramatic. First, there is the expressive pantomime of every one of the eighteen cabmen on the stand, the moment you raise your eyes from the ground. Then there is your own pantomime in reply—quite a little ballet. Four cabs immediately leave the stand, for your especial accommodation; and the evolutions of the animals who draw them are beautiful in the extreme, as they grate the wheels of the cabs against the curb-stones, and sport playfully in the kennel. You single out a particular cab, and dart swiftly towards it. One bound, and you are on the first step; turn your body lightly round to the right, and you are on the second; bend gracefully beneath the reins, working round to the left at the same time, and you are in the cab. There is no difficulty in finding a seat; the apron knocks you comfortably into it at once, and off you go.

The getting out of a cab is, perhaps, rather more complicated in its theory, and a shade more difficult in its execution. We have studied the subject a great deal, and we think the best way is, to throw yourself out, and trust to chance for alighting on your feet. If you make the driver alight first, and then throw yourself upon him, you will find that he breaks your fall materially. In the event of your contemplating an offer of eightpence, on no account make the tender, or show the money, until you are safely on the pavement. It is very bad policy attempting to save the fourpence. You are very much in the power of a cabman, and he considers it a kind of fee not to do you any wilful damage. Any instruction, however, in the art of getting out of a cab, is wholly unnecessary if you are going any distance, because the probability is, that you will be shot lightly out before you have completed the third mile.

We are not aware of any instance on record in which a cab-horse has performed three consecutive miles without going down once. What of that? It is all excitement. And in these days of derangement of the nervous system and universal lassitude, people are content to pay handsomely for excitement; where can it be procured at a cheaper rate?

But to return to the red cab; it was omnipresent. You had but to walk down Holborn, or Fleet Street, or any of the principal thoroughfares in which there is a great deal of traffic, and judge for yourself. You had hardly turned into the street, when you saw a trunk or two, lying on the ground: an uprooted post, a hat-box, a portmanteau, and a carpet-bag, strewed about in a very picturesque manner: a horse in a cab standing by, looking about him with great unconcern; and a crowd, shouting and screaming with delight, cooling their flushed faces against the glass windows of a chemist's shop.—"What's the matter here, can you tell me?"—"On'y a cab, sir."—"Anybody hurt, do you know?"—"On'y the fare, sir. I see him a turnin' the corner, and I ses to another gen'lm'n 'that's a reg'lar little oss that, and he's a comin' along rayther sweet, ain't he?'—'He just is,' ses the other gen'lm'n, ven bump they cums agin the post, and out flies the fare like bricks." Need we say it was the red cab; or that the gentleman with the straw in his mouth, who emerged so coolly from the chemist's shop, and philosophically climbing into the little dickey, started off at full gallop, was the red cab's licensed driver?

The ubiquity of this red cab, and the influence it exercised over the risible muscles of justice itself, was perfectly astonishing. You walked into the justice-room of the Mansion House; the whole court resounded with merriment. The Lord Mayor threw himself back in his chair, in a state of frantic delight at his own joke, every vein in Mr. Hobler's countenance was swollen with laughter, partly at the Lord Mayor's facetiousness, but more at his own, the constables and police-officers were (as in duty bound) in ecstasies at Mr. Hobler and the Lord Mayor combined; and the very paupers, glancing respectfully at the beadle's countenance, tried to smile, as even he relaxed. A tall, weazen-faced man, with an impediment in his speech, would be endeavouring to state a case of imposition against the red cab's driver; and the red cab's driver, and the Lord Mayor, and Mr. Hobler, would be having a little fun among themselves, to the inordinate delight of everybody but the complainant. In the end, justice would be so tickled with the red cab driver's native humour, that the fine would be mitigated, and he would go away full gallop, in the red cab, to impose on somebody else without loss of time.

The driver of the red cab, confident in the strength of his own moral principles, like many other philosophers, was wont to set the feelings and opinions of society at complete defiance. Generally speaking, perhaps, he would as soon carry a fare safely to his destination, as he would upset him—sooner, perhaps, because in that case he not only got the money, but had the additional amusement of running a longer heat against some smart rival. But society made war upon him in the shape of penalties, and he must make war upon society in his own way. This was the reasoning of the red cab driver. So, he bestowed a searching look upon the fare, as he put his hand in his waistcoat pocket, when he had gone half the mile, to get the money ready; and if he brought forth eightpence, out he went.

The last time we saw our friend was one wet evening in Tottenham Court Road, when he was engaged in a very warm and somewhat personal altercation with a loquacious little gentleman in a green coat. Poor fellow! there were great excuses to be made for him: he had not received above eighteenpence more than his fare, and consequently laboured under a great deal of very natural indignation. The dispute had attained a pretty considerable height, when at last the loquacious little gentleman, making a mental calculation of the distance, and finding that he had already paid more than he ought, avowed his unalterable determination to "pull up" the cabman in the morning.

"Now, just mark this, young man," said the little gentleman, "I'll pull you up to-morrow morning."

"No! will you though?" said our friend, with a sneer.

"I will," replied the little gentleman, "mark my words, that's all. If I live till to-morrow morning, you shall repent this."

There was a steadiness of purpose, and indignation of speech, about the little gentleman, as he took an angry pinch of snuff, after this last declaration, which made a visible impression on the mind of the red cab driver. He appeared to hesitate for an instant. It was only for an instant; his resolve was soon taken.

"You'll pull me up, will you?" said our friend.

"I will," rejoined the little gentleman, with even greater vehemence than before.

"Very well," said our friend, tucking up his shirt sleeves very calmly. "There'll be three veeks for that. Wery good; that'll bring me up to the middle o' next month. Three veeks more would carry me on to my birthday, and then I've got ten pound to draw. I may as well get board, lodgin', and washin', till then, out of the country, as pay for it myself; consequently here goes!"

So, without more ado, the red cab driver knocked the little gentleman down and then called the police to take himself into custody, with all the civility in the world.

A story is nothing without the sequel; and therefore, we may state, that to our certain knowledge, the board, lodging, and washing, were all provided in due course. We happen to know the fact, for it came to our knowledge thus: We went over the House of Correction for the county of Middlesex shortly after, to witness the operation of the silent system; and looked on all the "wheels" with the greatest anxiety, in search of our long-lost friend. He was nowhere to be seen, however, and we began to think that the little gentleman in the green coat must have relented, when, as we were traversing the kitchen-garden, which lies in a sequestered part of the prison, we were startled by hearing a voice, which apparently proceeded from the wall, pouring forth its soul in the plaintive air of "All round my hat," which was then just beginning to form a recognised portion of our national music.

We started.—"What voice is that?" said we.

The Governor shook his head.

"Sad fellow," he replied, "very sad. He positively refused to work on the wheel; so, after many trials, I was compelled to order him into solitary confinement. He says he likes it very much though, and I am afraid he does, for he lies on his back on the floor, and sings comic songs all day."

Shall we add, that our heart had not deceived us; and that the comic singer was no other than our eagerly-sought friend, the red cab driver?

We have never seen him since, but we have strong reason to suspect that this noble individual was a distant relative of a waterman of our acquaintance, who, on one occasion, when we were passing the coach-stand over which he presides, after standing very quietly to see a tall man struggle into a cab, run up very briskly when it was all over (as his brethren invariably do), and, touching his hat, asked, as a matter of course, for "a copper for the waterman." Now, the fare was by no means a handsome man; and, waxing very indignant at the demand, he replied: "Money! What for? Coming up and looking at me, I suppose?": "Vell, sir!" rejoined the waterman with a smile of immovable complacency, "*That's* worth twopence, at least."

This identical waterman afterwards attained a very prominent station in society; and as we know something of his life, and have often thought of telling what we *do* know, perhaps we shall never have a better opportunity than the present.

Mr. William Barker, then, for that was the gentleman's name, Mr. William Barker was born—But why need we relate where Mr. William Barker was born, or when? Why scrutinise the entries in parochial ledgers, or seek to penetrate the Lucinian mysteries of lying-in hospitals? Mr. William Barker *was* born, or he had never been. There is a son—there was a father. There is an effect—there was a cause. Surely this is sufficient information for the most Fatima-like curiosity; and, if it be not, we regret our inability to supply any further evidence on the point. Can there be a more satisfactory, or more strictly parliamentary course? Impossible.

We at once avow a similar inability to record at what precise period, or by what particular process, this gentleman's patronymic, of William Barker, became corrupted into "Bill Boorker." Mr. Barker acquired a high standing, and no inconsiderable reputation, among the members of that profession to which he more peculiarly devoted his energies; and to them he was generally known, either by the familiar appellation of "Bill Boorker," or the flattering designation of "Aggerawatin' Bill," the latter being a playful and expressive *sobriquet*, illustrative of Mr. Barker's great talent in "aggerawatin'" and rendering wild such subjects of her Majesty as are conveyed from place to place, through the instrumentality of omnibuses. Of the early life of Mr. Barker little is known, and even that little is involved in considerable doubt and obscurity. A want of application, a restlessness of purpose, a thirsting after porter, a love of all that is roving and cadger-like in nature, shared in common with many other great geniuses, appear to have been his leading characteristics. The busy hum of a parochial free-school, and the shady repose of a county gaol, were alike inefficacious in producing the slightest alteration in Mr. Barker's disposition. His feverish attachment to change and variety nothing could repress; his native daring no punishment could subdue.

If Mr. Barker can be fairly said to have had any weakness in his earlier years, it was an amiable one—love; love in its most comprehensive form—a love of ladies, liquids, and pocket-handkerchiefs. It was no selfish feeling; it was not confined to his own possessions, which but too many men regard with exclusive complacency. No; it was a nobler love—a general principle. It extended itself with equal force to the property of other people.

There is something very affecting in this. It is still more

affecting to know, that such philanthropy is but imperfectly rewarded. Bow Street, Newgate, and Millbank, are a poor return for general benevolence, evincing itself in an irrepressible love for all created objects. Mr. Barker felt it so. After a lengthened interview with the highest legal authorities, he quitted his ungrateful country, with the consent, and at the expense, of its Government; proceeded to a distant shore; and there employed himself, like another Cincinnatus, in clearing and cultivating the soil—a peaceful pursuit, in which a term of seven years glided almost imperceptibly away.

Whether, at the expiration of the period we have just mentioned, the British Government required Mr. Barker's presence here, or did not require his residence abroad, we have no distinct means of ascertaining. We should be inclined, however, to favour the latter position, inasmuch as we do not find that he was advanced to any other public post on his return, than the post at the corner of the Haymarket, where he officiated as assistant-waterman to the hackney-coach-stand. Seated, in this capacity, on a couple of tubs near the curb-stone, with a brass plate and number suspended round his neck by a massive chain, and his ankles curiously enveloped in haybands, he is supposed to have made those observations on human nature which exercised so material an influence over all his proceedings in later life.

Mr. Barker had not officiated for many months in this capacity, when the appearance of the first omnibus caused the public mind to go in a new direction, and prevented a great many hackney-coaches from going in any direction at all. The genius of Mr. Barker at once perceived the whole extent of the injury that would be eventually inflicted on cab and coach-stands, and, by consequence, on watermen also, by the progress of the system of which the first omnibus was a part. He saw, too, the necessity of adopting some more profitable profession; and his active mind at once perceived how much might be done in the way of enticing the youthful and unwary, and shoving the old and helpless, into the wrong buss, and carrying them off, until, reduced to despair, they ransomed themselves by the payment of sixpence a-head, or, to adopt his own figurative expression in all its native beauty, "till they was rig'larly done over, and forked our the stumpy."

An opportunity for realising his fondest anticipations, soon presented itself. Rumours were rife on the hackney-coach-stands, that a buss was building, to run from Lisson Grove to the Bank, down Oxford Street and Holborn; and the rapid increase of busses on the Paddington Road, encouraged the idea. Mr. Barker secretly and cautiously inquired in the proper quarters. The report was correct; the "Royal William" was to make its first journey on the following Monday. It was a crack affair altogether. An enterprising young cabman, of established reputation as a dashing whip—for he had compromised with the parents of three scrunched children, and just "worked out" his fine, for knocking down an old lady—was the driver; and the spirited proprietor, knowing Mr. Barker's qualifications, appointed him to the vacant office of cad on the very first application. The buss began to run, and Mr. Barker entered into a new suit of clothes, and on a new sphere of action.

To recapitulate all the improvements introduced by this extraordinary man, into the omnibus system—gradually, indeed, but surely—would occupy a far greater space than we are enabled to devote to this imperfect memoir. To him is universally assigned the original suggestion of the practice which afterwards became so general—of the driver of the second buss keeping constantly behind the first one, and driving the pole of his vehicle either into the door of the other, every time it was opened, or through the body of any lady or gentleman who might make an attempt to get into it; a humorous and pleasant invention, exhibiting all that originality of idea, and fine bold flow of spirits, so conspicuous in every action of this great man.

Mr. Barker had opponents of course; what man in public life has not? But even his worst enemies cannot deny that he has taken more old ladies and gentlemen to Paddington who wanted to go to the Bank, and more old ladies and gentlemen to the Bank who wanted to go to Paddington, than any six men on the road; and however much malevolent spirits may pretend to doubt the accuracy of the statement, they well know it to be an established fact, that he has forcibly conveyed a variety of ancient persons of either sex, to both places, who had not the slightest or most distant intention of going anywhere at all.

Mr. Barker was the identical cad who nobly distinguished himself, some time since, by keeping a tradesman on the step—the omnibus going at full speed all the time—till he had thrashed him to his entire satisfaction, and finally throwing him away, when he had quite done with him. Mr. Barker it *ought* to have been, who, honestly indignant at being ignominiously ejected from a house of public entertainment, kicked the landlord in the knee, and thereby caused his death. We say it *ought* to have been Mr. Barker, because the action was not a common one, and could have emanated from no ordinary mind.

It has now become matter of history; it is recorded in the Newgate Calendar; and we wish we could attribute this piece of daring heroism to Mr. Barker. We regret being compelled to state that it was not performed by him. Would, for the family credit we could add, that it was achieved by his brother!

It was in the exercise of the nicer details of his profession, that Mr. Barker's knowledge of human nature was beautifully displayed. He could tell at a glance where a passenger wanted to go to, and would shout the name of the place accordingly, without the slightest reference to the real destination of the vehicle. He knew exactly the kind of old lady that would be too much flurried by the process of pushing in, and pulling out of the caravan, to discover where she had been put down, until too late; had an intuitive perception of what was passing in a passenger's mind when he inwardly resolved to "pull that cad up to-morrow morning;" and never failed to make himself agreeable to female servants, whom he would place next the door, and talk to all the way.

Human judgment is never infallible, and it would occasionally happen that Mr. Barker experimentalised with the timidity or forbearance of the wrong person, in which case a summons to a Police-office, was, on more than one occasion, followed by a committal to prison. It was not in the power of trifles such as these, however, to subdue the freedom of his spirit. As soon as they passed away, he resumed the duties of his profession with unabated ardour.

We have spoken of Mr. Barker and of the red cab driver, in the past tense. Alas! Mr. Barker has again become an absentee; and the class of men to which they both belonged are fast disappearing. Improvement has peered beneath the aprons of our cabs, and penetrated to the very innermost recesses of our omnibuses. Dirt and fustian will vanish before cleanliness and livery. Slang will be forgotten when civility becomes general: and that enlightened, eloquent, sage, and profound body, the Magistracy of London, will be deprived of half their amusement, and half their occupation.

CHAPTER XVIII: *A Parliamentary Sketch*

WE hope our readers will not be alarmed at this rather ominous title. We assure them that we are not about to become political, neither have we the slightest intention of being more prosy than usual—if we can help it. It has occurred to us that a slight sketch of the general aspect of "the House," and the crowds that resort to it on the night of an important debate, would be productive of some amusement; and as we have made some few calls at the aforesaid house in our time—have visited it quite often enough for our purpose, and a great deal too often for our own personal peace and comfort—we have determined to attempt the description. Dismissing from our minds, therefore, all that feeling of awe, which vague ideas of breaches of privilege, Serjeant-at-Arms, heavy denunciations, and still heavier fees, are calculated to awaken, we enter at once into the building, and upon our subject.

Half-past four o'clock—and at five the mover of the Address will be "on his legs," as the newspapers announce sometimes by way of novelty, as if speakers were occasionally in the habit of standing on their heads. The members are pouring in, one after the other, in shoals. The few spectators who can obtain standing-room in the passages, scrutinise them as they pass, with the utmost interest, and the man who can identify a member occasionally, becomes a person of great importance. Every now and then you hear earnest whispers of "That's Sir John Thomson." "Which? him with the gilt order round his neck?" "No, no; that's one of the messengers—that other with the yellow gloves, is Sir John Thomson." "Here's Mr. Smith." "Lor!" "Yes, how d'ye do, sir?—(He is our new member)—How do you do, sir?" Mr. Smith stops: turns round with an air of enchanting urbanity (for the rumour of an intended dissolution has been very extensively circulated this morning); seizes both the hands of his gratified constituent, and, after greeting him with the most enthusiastic warmth, darts into the lobby with an extraordinary display of ardour in the public cause, leaving an immense impression in his favour on the mind of his "fellow-townsman."

The arrivals increase in number, and the heat and noise increase in very unpleasant proportion. The livery servants form a complete lane on either side of the passage, and you reduce yourself into the smallest possible space to avoid being turned out. You see that stout man with the hoarse voice, in the blue coat, queer crowned, broad brimmed hat, white corduroy breeches, and great boots, who has been talking incessantly for half an hour past, and whose importance has occasioned no small quantity of mirth among the strangers. That is the great conservator of the peace of Westminster. You cannot fail to have remarked the grace with which he saluted the noble Lord who passed just now, or the excessive dignity of his air, as he expostulates with the crowd. He is rather out of temper now, in consequence of the very irreverent behaviour of those two young fellows behind him, who have done nothing but laugh all the time they have been here.

"Will they divide to-night, do you think, Mr. ——?" timidly inquires a little thin man in the crowd, hoping to conciliate the man of office.

"How *can* you ask such questions, sir?" replies the functionary, in an incredibly loud key, and pettishly grasping the thick stick he carries in his right hand. "Pray do not, sir, I beg of you; pray do not, sir." The little man looks remarkably out of his element, and the uninitiated part of the throng are in positive convulsions of laughter.

Just at this moment some unfortunate individual appears, with a very smirking air, at the bottom of the long passage.

He has managed to elude the vigilance of the special constable down-stairs, and is evidently congratulating himself on having made his way so far.

"Go back, sir—you must *not* come here," shouts the hoarse one, with tremendous emphasis of voice and gesture, the moment the offender catches his eye.

The stranger pauses.

"Do you hear, sir—will you go back?" continues the official dignitary, gently pushing the intruder some half dozen yards.

"Come, don't push me," replies the stranger, turning angrily round.

"I will, sir."

"You won't, sir."

"Go out, sir."

"Take your hands off me, sir."

"Go out of the passage, sir."

"You're a Jack-in-office, sir."

"A what?" ejaculates he of the boots.

"A Jack-in-office, sir, and a very insolent fellow," reiterates the stranger, now completely in a passion.

"Pray do not force me to put you out, sir," retorts the other —"pray do not—my instructions are to keep this passage clear—it's the Speaker's orders, sir."

"D—n the Speaker, sir!" shouts the intruder.

"Here, Wilson!—Collins!" gasps the officer, actually paralysed at this insulting expression, which in his mind is all but high treason; "take this man out—take him out, I say! How dare you, sir?" and down goes the unfortunate man five stairs at a time, turning round at every stoppage, to come back again, and denouncing bitter vengeance against the commander-in-chief, and all his supernumeraries.

"Make way, gentlemen,—pray make way for the Members, I beg of you;" shouts the zealous officer, turning back, and preceding a whole string of the liberal and independent.

You see this ferocious-looking gentleman, with a complexion almost as sallow as his linen, and whose large black moustache would give him the appearance of a figure in a hairdresser's window, if his countenance possessed the thought which is communicated to those waxen caricatures of the human face divine. He is a militia-officer, and the most amusing person in the House. Can anything be more exquisitely absurd than the burlesque grandeur of his air, as he strides up to the lobby, his eyes rolling like those of a Turk's head in a cheap Dutch clock? He never appears without that bundle of dirty papers which he carries under his left arm, and which are generally supposed to be the miscellaneous estimates for 1804, or some equally important documents. He is very punctual in his attendance at the House, and his self satisfied "He-ar-He-ar," is not unfrequently the signal for a general titter.

This is the gentleman who once actually sent a messenger up to the Strangers' Gallery in the Old House of Commons, to inquire the name of an individual who was using an eye-glass, in order that he might complain to the Speaker that the person in question was quizzing him! On another occasion, he is reported to have repaired to Bellamy's kitchen—a refreshment-room, where persons who are not Members are admitted on sufferance, as it were—and perceiving two or three gentlemen at supper, who he was aware were not Members, and could not, in that place, very well resent his behaviour, he indulged in the pleasantry of sitting with his booted leg on the table at which they were supping! He is generally harmless, though, and always exceedingly amusing.

By dint of patience, and some little interest with our friend the constable, we have contrived to make our way to the Lobby, and you can just manage to catch an occasional glimpse of the House, as the door is opened for the admission of Members. It is tolerably full already, and little groups of Members are congregated here, discussing the interesting topics of the day.

That smart-looking fellow in the black coat with velvet facings and cuffs, who wears his *D'Orsay* hat so rakishly, is "Honest Tom," a metropolitan representative; and the large man in the cloak with the white lining—not the man by the pillar; the other with the light hair hanging over his coat collar behind,—is his colleague. The quiet gentlemanly-looking man in the blue surtout, gray trousers, white necker-chief, and gloves, whose closely-buttoned coat displays his manly figure and broad chest to great advantage, is a very well-known character. He has fought a great many battles in his time, and conquered like the heroes of old, with no other arms than those the gods gave him. The old hard-featured man who is standing near him, is really a good specimen of a class of men, now nearly extinct. He is a county Member, and has been from time whereof the memory of man is not to the contrary. Look at his loose, wide, brown coat, with capacious pockets on each side; the knee-breeches and boots, the immensely long waistcoat, and silver watch-chain dangling below it, the wide-brimmed brown hat, and the white handkerchief tied in a great bow, with straggling ends sticking out beyond his shirt-frill. It is a costume one seldom sees nowadays, and when the few who wear it have died off, it will be quite extinct. He can tell you long stories of Fox, Pitt, Sheridan, and Canning, and how much better the House was managed in those times, when they used to get up at eight or nine o'clock, except on regular field-days, of which everybody was apprised beforehand. He has a great contempt for all young Members of Parliament, and

thinks it quite impossible that a man can say anything worth
hearing, unless he has sat in the House for fifteen years at least
without saying anything at all. He is of opinion that "that
young Macaulay" was a regular impostor; he allows, that Lord
Stanley may do something one of these days, but "he's too
young, sir—too young." He is an excellent authority on
points of precedent, and when he grows talkative, after his
wine, will tell you how Sir Somebody Something, when he was
whipper-in for the Government, brought four men out of their
beds to vote in the majority, three of whom died on their way
home again; how the House once divided on the question, that
fresh candles be now brought in; how the Speaker was once
upon a time left in the chair by accident, at the conclusion of
business, and was obliged to sit in the House by himself for
three hours, till some Member could be knocked up and
brought back again, to move the adjournment, and a great
many other anecdotes of a similar description.

There he stands, leaning on his stick; looking at the throng
of Exquisites around him with most profound contempt; and
conjuring up, before his mind's eye, the scenes he beheld in
the old House in days gone by, when his own feelings were
fresher and brighter, and when, as he imagines, wit, talent,
and patriotism flourished more brightly too.

You are curious to know who that young man in the rough
greatcoat is, who has accosted every member who has entered
the House since we have been standing here. He is not a
Member; he is only an "hereditary bondsman," or, in other
words, an Irish correspondent of an Irish newspaper, who
has just procured his forty-second frank from a Member
whom he never saw in his life before. There he goes again
—another! Bless the man, he has his hat and pockets full
already.

We will try our fortune at the Strangers' Gallery, though
the nature of the debate encourages very little hope of success.
What on earth are you about? Holding up your order as if it
were a talisman at whose command the wicket would fly open?
Nonsense. Just preserve the order for an autograph, if it be
worth keeping at all, and make your appearance at the door
with your thumb and fore-finger expressively inserted in your
waistcoat-pocket. This tall stout man in black is the door-
keeper. "Any room?" "Not an inch—two or three dozen
gentlemen waiting down-stairs on the chance of somebody's
going out." Pull out your purse—"Are you *quite* sure there's
no room?"—"I'll go and look," replies the door-keeper, with
a wistful glance at your purse, "but I'm afraid there's not."
He returns, and with real feeling assures you that it is morally
impossible to get near the gallery. It is of no use waiting.
When you are refused admission into the Strangers' Gallery
at the House of Commons, under such circumstances, you may

return home thoroughly satisfied that the place must be remarkably full indeed.*

Retracing our steps through the long passage, descending the stairs, and crossing Palace Yard, we halt at a small temporary doorway adjoining the King's entrance to the House of Lords. The order of the serjeant-at-arms will admit you into the Reporters' Gallery, from whence you can obtain a tolerably good view of the House. Take care of the stairs, they are none of the best; through this little wicket—there. As soon as your eyes become a little used to the mist of the place, and the glare of the chandeliers below you, you will see that some unimportant personage on the Ministerial side of the House (to your right hand) is speaking, amidst a hum of voices and confusion which would rival Babel, but for the circumstance of its being all in one language.

The "hear, hear," which occasioned that laugh, proceeded from our warlike friend with the moustache; he is sitting on the back seat against the wall, behind the Member who is speaking, looking as ferocious and intellectual as usual. Take one look around you, and retire: the body of the House and the side galleries are full of Members, some with their legs on the back of the opposite seat; some with theirs stretched out to their utmost length on the floor; some going out, others coming in; all of them talking, laughing, lounging, coughing, o-ing, questioning, or groaning; presenting a conglomeration of noise and confusion, to be met with in no other place in existence, not even excepting Smithfield on a market-day, or a cock-pit in its glory.

But let us not omit to notice Bellamy's kitchen, or, in other words, the refreshment-room, common to both Houses of Parliament, where Ministerialists and Oppositionists, Whigs and Tories, Radicals, Peers, and Destructives, strangers from the gallery, and the more favoured strangers from below the bar, are alike at liberty to resort; where divers honourable Members prove their perfect independence by remaining during the whole of a heavy debate, solacing themselves with the creature comforts; and whence they are summoned by whippers-in, when the House is on the point of dividing; either to give their "conscientious votes" on questions of which they are conscientiously innocent of knowing anything whatever, or to find a vent for the playful exuberance of their wine-inspired fancies, in boisterous shouts of "Divide," occasionally varied with a little howling, barking and crowing, or other ebullitions of senatorial pleasantry.

When you have ascended the narrow staircase which, in the present temporary House of Commons, leads to the

* This paper was written before the practice of exhibiting Members of Parliament, like other curiosities, for the small charge of half-a-crown, was abolished.

place we are describing, you will probably observe a couple of rooms on your right hand, with tables spread for dining. Neither of these is the kitchen, although they are both devoted to the same purpose; the kitchen is further on to our left, up these half-dozen stairs. Before we ascend the staircase, however, we must request you to pause in front of this little bar-place with the sash-windows; and beg your particular attention to the steady honest-looking old fellow in black, who is its sole occupant. Nicholas (we do not mind mentioning the old fellow's name, for if Nicholas be not a public man, who is?—and public men's names are public property) —Nicholas is the butler of Bellamy's, and has held the same place, dressed exactly in the same manner, and said precisely the same things, ever since the oldest of its present visitors can remember. An excellent servant Nicholas is—an unrivalled compounder of salad dressing—an admirable preparer of soda-water and lemon—a special mixer of cold grog and punch, and, above all, an unequalled judge of cheese. If the old man have such a thing as vanity in his composition, this is certainly his pride; and if it be possible to imagine that anything in this world could disturb his impenetrable calmness, we should say it would be the doubting his judgment on this important point.

We needn't tell you all this, however, for if you have an atom of observation, one glance at his sleek knowing-looking head and face—his prim white neckerchief, with the wooden tie into which it has been regularly folded for twenty years past, merging by imperceptible degrees into a small-plaited shirt-frill; and his comfortable-looking form encased in a well-brushed suit of black—would give you a better idea of his real character than a column of our poor description could convey.

Nicholas is rather out of his element now; he cannot see the kitchen as he used to in the old House; there, one window of his glass-case opened into the room, and then for the edification and behoof of more juvenile questioners, he would stand for an hour together, answering deferential questions about Sheridan, and Percival, and Castlereagh, and Heaven knows who beside, with manifest delight, always inserting a "Mister" before every name.

Nicholas, like all men of his age and standing, has a great idea of the degeneracy of the times. He seldom expresses any political opinions, but we managed to ascertain, just before the passing of the Reform Bill, that Nicholas was a thorough Reformer. What was our astonishment to discover shortly after the meeting of the first reformed Parliament, that he was a most inveterate and decided Tory! It was very odd: some men change their opinions from necessity, others from expediency, others from inspiration; but that

Nicholas should undergo any change in any respect, was an event we had never contemplated, and should have considered impossible. His strong opinion against the clause which empowered the metropolitan districts to return Members of Parliament, too, was perfectly unaccountable.

We discovered the secret at last; the metropolitan Members always dined at home. The rascals! As for giving additional Members to Ireland, it was even worse—decidedly unconstitutional. Why, sir, an Irish Member would go up there, and eat more dinner than three English Members put together. He took no wine; drank table-beer by the half-gallon; and went home to Manchester Buildings or Millbank Street, for his whiskey-and-water, and what was the consequence? Why the concern lost—actually lost—by their patronage. A queer old fellow is Nicholas, and as completely a part of the building as the House itself. We wonder he ever left the old place, and fully expected to see in the papers, the morning after the fire, a pathetic account of an old gentleman in black, of decent appearance, who was seen at one of the upper windows when the flames were at their height, and declared his resolute intention of falling with the floor. He must have been got out by force. However, he was got out —here he is again, looking as he always does, as if he had been in a bandbox ever since the last session. There he is, at his old post every night, just as we have described him: and, as characters are scarce, and faithful servants scarcer, long may he be there say we.

Now, when you have taken your seat in the kitchen, and duly noticed the large fire and roasting-jack at one end of the room—the little table for washing glasses and draining jugs at the other—the clock over the window opposite St. Margaret's Church—the deal tables and wax candles—the damask table-cloths and bare floor—the plate and china on the tables, and the gridiron on the fire; and a few other anomalies peculiar to the place—we will point out to your notice two or three of the people present, whose station or absurdities render them the most worthy of remark.

It is half-past twelve o'clock, and as the division is not expected for an hour or two, a few Members are lounging away the time here, in preference to standing at the bar of the House, or sleeping in one of the side galleries. That singularly awkward and ungainly-looking man, in the brownish-white hat, with the straggling black trousers, which reach about half-way down the leg of his boots, who is leaning against the meat-screen, apparently deluding himself into the belief that he is thinking about something, is a splendid sample of a Member of the House of Commons concentrating in his own person the wisdom of a constituency. Observe the wig, of a dark hue but indescribable colour, for if it be naturally brown, it has acquired a black tint by long service, and if it be naturally black, the same cause has imparted to it a tinge of rusty brown; and remark how very materially the great blinker-like spectacles assist the expression of that most intelligent face. Seriously speaking, did you ever see a countenance so expressive of the most hopeless extreme of heavy dulness, or behold a form so strangely put together? He is no great speaker: but when he *does* address the House the effect is absolutely irresistible.

The small gentleman with the sharp nose, who has just saluted him, is a Member of Parliament, an ex-Alderman, and a sort of amateur fireman. He, and the celebrated fireman's dog, were observed to be remarkably active at the conflagration of the two Houses of Parliament—they both ran up and down, and in and out, getting under people's feet, and into everybody's way, fully impressed with the belief that they were doing a great deal of good, and barking tremendously. The dog went quietly back to his kennel with the engine, but the other gentleman kept up such an incessant noise for some weeks after the occurrence, that he became a positive nuisance. As no more parliamentary fires have occurred, however, and he has consequently had no more opportunities of writing to the newspapers to relate how by way of preserving pictures he cut them out of their frames, and performed other great national services, he has gradually relapsed into his old state of calmness.

That female in black—not the one whom the Lord's-Day-Bill Baronet has just chucked under the chin; the shorter of the two—is "Jane:" the Hebe of Bellamy's. Jane is as great a character as Nicholas in her way. Her leading features are a thorough contempt for the great majority of her visitors; her predominant quality, love of admiration, as you cannot fail to observe, if you mark the glee with which she listens to something the young Member near her mutters somewhat unintelligibly in her ear (for his speech is rather thick from some cause or other) and how playfully she digs the handle of a fork into the arm with which he detains her, by way of reply.

Jane is no bad hand at repartees, and showers them about, with a degree of liberality and total absence of reserve or constraint, which, occasionally, excites no small amazement in the minds of strangers. She cuts jokes with Nicholas, too, but evidently looks up to him with a great deal of respect; and the immovable stolidity with which Nicholas receives the aforesaid jokes, and looks on, at certain pastoral friskings and rompings (Jane's only recreations) which occasionally take place in the passage, is not the least amusing part of his character.

The two persons who are seated at the table in the corner,

at the further end of the room, have been constant guests here, for many years past; and one of them has feasted within these walls, many a time, with the most brilliant characters of a brilliant period. He has gone up to the other House since then; the greater part of his boon companions have shared Yorick's fate, and his visits to Bellamy's are comparatively few.

If he really be eating his supper now, at what hour can he possibly have dined? A second solid mass of rump-steak has disappeared, and he ate the first in four minutes and three quarters, by the clock over the window. Was there ever such a personification of Falstaff! Mark the air with which he gloats over that Stilton as he removes the napkin which had been placed beneath his chin to catch the superfluous gravy of the steak, and with what gusto he imbibes the porter which has been fetched expressly for him in the pewter pot. Listen to the hoarse sound of that voice, kept down as it is by layers of solids, and deep draughts of rich wine, and tell us if you ever saw such a perfect picture of a regular *gourmand ;* and whether he is not exactly the man whom you would pitch upon, as having been the partner of Sheridan's parliamentary carouses, the volunteer driver of the hackney-coach that took him home, and the involuntary upsetter of the whole party?

What an amusing contrast between his voice and appearance, and that of the spare, squeaking old man, who sits at the same table, and who elevating a little cracked bantam sort of voice to its highest pitch, invokes damnation upon his own eyes or somebody else's at the commencement of every sentence he utters. "The Captain," as they call him, is a very old frequenter of Bellamy's; much addicted to stopping "after the House is up" (an inexpiable crime in Jane's eyes), and a complete walking reservoir of spirits and water.

The old Peer—or rather, the old man—for his peerage is of comparatively recent date—has a huge tumbler of hot punch brought him; and the other damns and drinks, and drinks and damns, and smokes. Members arrive every moment in a great bustle to report that "The Chancellor of the Exchequer's up," and to get glasses of brandy-and-water to sustain them during the division; people who have ordered supper, countermand it, and prepare to go down-stairs, when suddenly a bell is heard to ring with tremendous violence, and a cry of "Di-vi-sion" is heard in the passage. This is enough; away rush the Members pell-mell. The room is cleared in an instant; the noise rapidly dies away; you hear the creaking of the last boot on the last stair, and are left alone with the leviathan of rump-steaks.

CHAPTER XIX: *Public Dinners*

ALL public dinners in London, from the Lord Mayor's annual banquet at Guildhall, to the Chimney-sweepers' anniversary at White Conduit House; from the Goldsmiths' to the Butchers', from the Sheriffs' to the Licensed Victuallers', are amusing scenes. Of all entertainments of this description, however, we think the annual dinner of some public charity is the most amusing. At a Company's dinner, the people are nearly all alike—regular old stagers who make it a matter of business, and a thing not to be laughed at. At a political dinner, everybody is disagreeable, and inclined to speechify—much the same thing, by-the-by; but at a charity dinner you see people of all sorts, kinds, and descriptions. The wine may not be remarkably special, to be sure, and we have heard some hard-hearted monsters grumble at the collection; but we really think the amusement to be derived from the occasion, sufficient to counterbalance, even these disadvantages.

Let us suppose you are induced to attend a dinner of this description—"Indigent Orphans' Friends' Benevolent Institution," we think it is. The name of the charity is a line or two longer, but never mind the rest. You have a distinct recollection, however, that you purchased a ticket at the solicitation of some charitable friend: and you deposit yourself in a hackney-coach, the driver of which—no doubt that you may do the thing in style—turns a deaf ear to your earnest entreaties to be set down at the corner of Great Queen Street, and persists in carrying you to the very door of the Freemasons, round which a crowd of people are assembled to witness the entrance of the indigent orphans' friends. You hear great speculations as you pay the fare, on the possibility of your being the noble Lord who is announced to fill the chair on the occasion, and are highly gratified to hear it eventually decided that you are only a "wocalist."

The first thing that strikes you, on your entrance, is the astonishing importance of the committee. You observe a door on the first landing, carefully guarded by two waiters, in and out of which stout gentlemen with very red faces keep running, with a degree of speed highly unbecoming the gravity of persons of their years and corpulency. You pause, quite alarmed at the bustle, and thinking, in your innocence, that two or three people must have been carried out of the dining-room in fits, at the very least. You are immediately undeceived by the waiter—"Up-stairs, if you please, sir; this is the committee-room." Up-stairs, you go, accordingly; wondering as you mount, what the duties of the committee can be, and whether they ever do anything beyond confusing each other, and running over the waiters.

Having deposited your hat and cloak, and received a remarkably small scrap of pasteboard in exchange (which, as a matter of course, you lose, before you require it again), you enter the hall, down which there are three long tables for the less distinguished guests, with a cross table on a raised platform at the upper end for the reception of the very particular friends of the indigent orphans. Being fortunate enough to find a plate without anybody's card in it, you wisely seat yourself at once, and have a little leisure to look about you. Waiters, with wine-baskets in their hands, are placing decanters of sherry down the tables, at very respectable distances; melancholy-looking salt-cellars, and decayed vinegar cruets, which might have belonged to the parents of the indigent orphans in their time, are scattered at distant intervals on the cloth; and the knives and forks look as if they had done duty at every public dinner in London since the accession of George the First. The musicians are scraping and grating and screwing tremendously—playing no notes but notes of preparation; and several gentlemen are gliding along the sides of the tables, looking into plate after plate with frantic eagerness, the expression of their countenances growing more and more dismal as they meet with everybody's card but their own.

You turn round to take a look at the table behind you, and —not being in the habit of attending public dinners—are somewhat struck by the appearance of the party on which your eyes rest. One of its principal members appears to be a little man, with a long and rather inflamed face, and gray hair brushed bolt upright in front; he wears a wisp of black silk round his neck, without any stiffener, as an apology for a neckerchief, and is addressed by his companions by the familiar appellation of "Fitz." Near him is a stout man in a white neckerchief and buff waist-coat, with shining dark hair cut very short in front, and a great round healthy-looking face, on which he studiously preserves a half-sentimental simper. Next him again, is a large-headed man, with black hair and bushy whiskers; and opposite them are two or three others, one of whom is a little round-faced person, in a dress-stock and blue under-waistcoat. There is something peculiar in their air and manner, though you could hardly describe what it is; and you cannot divest yourself of the idea that they have come for some other purpose than mere eating and drinking. You have no time to debate the matter, however, for the waiters (who have been arranged in lines down the room, placing the dishes on table) retire to the lower end; the dark man in the blue coat and bright buttons, who has the direction of the music, looks up to the gallery, and calls out "band" in a very loud voice, out burst the orchestra, up rise the visitors, in march fourteen stewards, each with a long wand in his hand like the evil genius in a pantomime; then the chairman, then the titled visitors; they all make their way up the room, as fast as they can, bowing, and smiling, and smirking, and looking remarkably amiable. The applause ceases, grace is said, the clatter of plates and dishes begins; and every one appears highly gratified, either with the presence of the distinguished visitors, or the commencement of the anxiously-expected dinner.

As to the dinner itself—the mere dinner—it goes off much the same everywhere. Tureens of soup are emptied with awful rapidity—waiters take plates of turbot away, to get lobster-sauce, and bring back plates of lobster-sauce, without turbot; people who can carve poultry are great fools if they own it, and people who can't have no wish to learn—the knives and forks form a pleasing accompaniment to Auber's music, and Auber's music would form a pleasing accompaniment to the dinner, if you could hear anything besides the cymbals. The substantials disappear—moulds of jelly vanish like lightning—hearty eaters wipe their foreheads, and appear rather overcome by their recent exertions—people who have looked very cross hitherto, become remarkably bland, and ask you to take wine in the most friendly manner possible—old gentlemen direct your attention to the ladies' gallery, and take great pains to impress you with the fact that the charity is always peculiarly favoured in this respect—every one appears disposed to become talkative—and the hum of conversation is loud and general.

"Pray, silence, gentlemen, if you please, for *Non nobis*," shouts the toast-master with stentorian lungs—a toast-master's shirt-front, waistcoat, and neckerchief, by-the-by, always exhibit three distinct shades of cloudy-white.— "Pray, silence, gentlemen, for *Non nobis*." The singers, whom you discover to be no other than the very party that excited your curiosity at first, after "pitching" their voices immediately begin *too-too*ing most dismally, on which the regular old stagers burst into occasional cries of "Sh—Sh—waiters!—Silence, waiters—stand still, waiters—keep back, waiters," and other exorcisms, delivered in a tone of indignant remonstrance. The grace is soon concluded, and the company resume their seats. The uninitiated portion of the guests applaud *Non nobis* as vehemently as if it were a capital comic song, greatly to the scandal and indignation of the regular diners, who immediately attempt to quell this sacrilegious approbation, by cries of "Hush, hush!" whereupon the others, mistaking these sounds for hisses, applaud more tumultuously than before, and, by way of placing their approval beyond the possibility of doubt, shout "*Encore!*" most vociferously.

The moment the noise ceases, up starts the toast-master:—"Gentlemen, charge your glasses, if you please." Decanters having been handed about, and glasses filled, the toast-master proceeds, in a regular ascending scale:—"Gentlemen —*air*—you—all—charged? Pray—silence—gentlemen—for —the cha—i—r!" The chairman rises, and, after stating that he feels it quite unnecessary to preface the toast he is about to propose, with any observations whatever, wanders into a maze of sentences, and flounders about in the most extraordinary manner, presenting a lamentable spectacle of mystified humanity, until he arrives at the words, "constitutional sovereign of these realms," at which elderly gentlemen exclaim "Bravo!" and hammer the table tremendously with their knife-handles. "Under any circumstances, it would give him the greatest pride, it would give him the greatest pleasure—he might almost say, it would afford him satisfaction [cheers] to propose that toast. What must be his feelings, then, when he has the gratification of announcing, that he has received her Majesty's commands to apply to the Treasurer of her Majesty's Household, for her Majesty's annual donation of 25*l.* in aid of the funds of this charity!" This announcement (which has been regularly made by every chairman, since the first foundation of the charity, forty-two years ago) calls forth the most vociferous applause; the toast is drunk with a great deal of cheering and knocking, and "God save the Queen" is sung by the "professional gentlemen"; the unprofessional gentlemen joining in the chorus, and giving the national anthem an effect which the newspapers, with great justice, describe as "perfectly electrical."

The other "loyal and patriotic" toasts having been drunk with all due enthusiasm, a comic song having been well sung by the gentleman with the small neckerchief, and a sentimental one by the second of the party, we come to the most important toast of the evening—"Prosperity to the charity." Here again we are compelled to adopt newspaper phraseology, and to express our regret at being "precluded from giving even the substance of the noble lord's observations." Suffice it to say, that the speech, which is somewhat of the longest, is rapturously received; and the toast having been drunk, the stewards (looking more important than ever) leave the room, and presently return, heading a procession of indigent orphans, boys and girls, who walk round the room, curtseying, and bowing, and treading on each other's heels, and looking very much as if they should like a glass of wine apiece, to the high gratification of the company generally, and especially of the lady patronesses in the gallery. *Exeunt* children, and re-enter stewards, each with a blue plate in his hand. The band plays a lively air; the majority of the company put their hands in their pockets and look rather serious; and the noise of sovereigns, rattling on crockery, is heard from all parts of the room.

After a short interval, occupied in singing and toasting, the secretary puts on his spectacles, and proceeds to read the report and list of subscriptions, the latter being listened to with great attention. "Mr. Smith, one guinea—Mr. Tompkins, one guinea—Mr. Wilson, one guinea—Mr. Hickson, one guinea—Mr. Nixon, one guinea—Mr. Charles Nixon, one guinea—[hear, hear!]—Mr. James Nixon, one guinea—Mr. Thomas Nixon, one pound one [tremendous applause]. Lord Fitz Binkle, the chairman of the day, in addition to an annual donation of fifteen pounds—thirty guineas [prolonged knocking: several gentlemen knock the stems off their wine-glasses, in the vehemence of their approbation]. Lady Fitz Binkle, in addition to an annual donation of ten pound—twenty pound" [protracted knocking and shouts of "Bravo!"] The list being at length concluded, the chairman rises and proposes the health of the secretary, than whom he knows no more zealous or estimable individual. The secretary, in returning thanks, observes that *he* knows no more excellent individual than the chairman —except the senior officer of the charity, whose health *he* begs to propose. The senior officer, in returning thanks, observes that *he* knows no more worthy man than the secretary— except Mr. Walker, the auditor, whose health *he* begs to propose. Mr. Walker, in returning thanks, discovers some other estimable individual, to whom alone the senior officer is inferior—and so they go on toasting and lauding and thanking: the only other toast of importance being "The Lady Patronesses now present," on which all the gentlemen turn their faces towards the ladies' gallery, shouting tremendously, and little priggish men, who have imbibed more wine than usual, kiss their hands and exhibit very distressing contortions of visage supposed to be intended for ogling.

We have protracted our dinner to so great a length, that we have hardly time to add one word by way of grace. We can only entreat our readers not to imagine, because we have attempted to extract some amusement from a charity dinner, that we are at all disposed to underrate, either the excellence of the benevolent institutions with which London abounds, or the estimable motives of those who support them.

CHAPTER XX: *The First of May*

"Now ladies, up in the sky-parlour: only once a year, if you please."
YOUNG LADY WITH BRASS LADLE.

"Sweep—sweep—sw-e-ep!"
ILLEGAL WATCHWORD.

THE first of May! There is a merry freshness in the sound, calling to our minds a thousand thoughts of all that is pleasant and beautiful in nature, in her sweetest and most delightful form. What man is there, over whose mind a bright spring morning does not exercise a magic influence—carrying him back to the days of his childish sports, and conjuring up before him the old green field with its gently-waving trees, where the birds sang as he has never heard them since—where the butter-fly fluttered far more gaily than he ever sees him now, in all his ramblings—where the sky seemed bluer, and the sun shone more brightly—where the air blew more freshly over greener grass, and sweeter-smelling flowers—where everything wore a richer and more brilliant hue than it is ever dressed in now! Such are the deep feelings of childhood, and such are the impressions which every lovely object stamps upon its heart. The hardy traveller wanders through the maze of thick and pathless woods, where the sun's rays never shone, and heaven's pure air never played; he stands on the brink of the roaring waterfall, and, giddy and bewildered, watches the foaming mass as it leaps from stone to stone, and from crag to crag; he lingers in the fertile plains of a land of perpetual sunshine, and revels in the luxury of their balmy breath. But what are the deep forests, or the thundering waters, or the richest land-scapes that bounteous nature ever spread, to charm the eyes, and captivate the senses of man, compared with the recollection of the old scenes of his early youth?—Magic scenes indeed; for the fairy thoughts of infancy dressed them in colours brighter than the rainbow, and almost as fleeting; colours which are the reflection only of the sparkling sunbeams of childhood, and can never be called into existence in the dark and cloudy days of after-life!

In former times, spring brought with it not only such associations as these, connected with the past, but sports and games for the present—merry dances round rustic pillars, adorned with emblems of the season, and reared in honour of its coming. Where are they now! Pillars we have, but they are no longer rustic ones; and as to dancers, they are used to rooms, and lights, and would not show well in the open air. Think of the immorality, too! What would your sabbath enthusiasts say, to an aristocratic ring encircling the Duke of York's column in Carlton Terrace—a grand *poussette* of the middle classes, round Alderman Waithman's monument in Fleet Street,—or a general hands-four-round of ten-pound householders, at the foot of the Obelisk in St. George's Fields? Alas! romance can make no head against the Riot Act; and pastoral simplicity is not understood by the police.

Well; many years ago we began to be a steady and matter-of-fact sort of people, and dancing in spring being beneath our dignity, we gave it up, and in course of time it descended to the sweeps—a fall certainly, because, though sweeps are very good fellows in their way, and moreover very useful in a civilised community, they are not exactly the sort of people to give the tone to the little elegances of society. The sweeps, however, got the dancing to themselves, and they kept it up, and handed it down. This was a severe blow to the romance of spring-time, but it did not entirely destroy it either; for a portion of it descended to the sweeps with the dancing, and rendered them objects of great interest. A mystery hung over the sweeps in those days. Legends were in existence of wealthy gentlemen who had lost children, and who, after many years of sorrow and suffering, had found them in the character of sweeps. Stories were related of a young boy who, having been stolen from his parents in his infancy, and devoted to the occupation of chimney-sweeping, was sent, in the course of his professional career, to sweep the chimney of his mother's bed-room; and how, being hot and tired when he came out of the chimney, he got into the bed he had so often slept in as an infant, and was discovered and recognised therein by his mother, who once every year of her life, thereafter, requested the pleasure of the company of every London sweep, at half-past one o'clock, to roast beef, plum-pudding, porter, and sixpence.

Such stories as these, and there were many such, threw an air of mystery round the sweeps, and produced for them some of those good effects which animals derive from the doctrine of the transmigration of souls. No one except the masters thought of ill-treating a sweep, because no one knew who he might be, or what nobleman's or gentleman's son he might turn out. Chimney-sweeping was, by many believers in the marvellous, considered as a sort of probationary term, at an earlier or later period of which, divers young noblemen were to come into possession of their rank and titles: and the profession was held by them in great respect accordingly.

We remember, in our young days, a little sweep about our own age, with curly hair and white teeth, whom we devoutly and sincerely believed to be the lost son and heir of some illustrious personage—an impression which was resolved into an unchangeable conviction on our infant mind, by the subject of our speculations informing us, one day, in reply to our question, propounded a few moments before his ascent to the summit of the kitchen chimney, "that he believed he'd been born in the vurkis, but he'd never know'd his father." We felt certain from that time forth that he would one day be owned by a lord; and we never heard the church-bells ring, or saw a flag hoisted in the neighbourhood, without thinking that the happy event had at last occurred, and that his long-lost parent had arrived in a coach and six, to take him home to Grosvenor Square. He never came, however; and, at the present moment, the young gentleman in question is settled down as a master sweep in the neighbourhood of Battle Bridge, his distinguishing characteristics being a decided antipathy to washing himself, and the possession of a pair of legs very inadequate to the support of his somewhat unwieldy and corpulent body.

The romance of spring having gone out before our time, we were fain to console ourselves as we best could with the uncertainty that enveloped the birth and parentage of its attendant dancers, the sweeps; and we *did* console ourselves with it, for many years. But even this wretched source of comfort received a shock, from which it has never recovered—a shock, which has been, in reality, its death-blow. We could not disguise from ourselves the fact that whole families of sweeps were regularly born of sweeps, in the rural districts of Somers Town and Camden Town—that the eldest son succeeded to the father's business, that the other branches assisted him therein, and commenced on their own account; that their children again were educated to the profession; and that about their identity there could be no mistake whatever. We could not be blind, we say, to this melancholy truth, but we could not bring ourselves to admit it, nevertheless, and we lived on for some years in a state of voluntary ignorance. We were roused from our pleasant slumber by certain dark insinuations thrown out by a friend of ours, to the effect that children in the lower ranks of life were beginning to *choose* chimney-sweeping as their particular walk; that applications had been made by various boys to the constituted authorities, to allow them to pursue the object of their ambition with the full concurrence and sanction of the law; that the affair, in short, was becoming one of mere legal contract. We turned a deaf ear to these rumours at first, but slowly and surely they stole upon us. Month after month, week after week, nay, day after day, at last, did we meet with accounts of similar applications. The veil was removed, all mystery was at an end, and chimney-sweeping had become a favourite and chosen pursuit. There is no longer any occasion to steal boys; for boys flock in crowds to bind themselves. The romance of the trade has fled, and the chimney-sweeper of the present day, is no more like unto him of thirty years ago, than is a Fleet Street pickpocket to a Spanish brigand, or Paul Pry to Caleb Williams.

This gradual decay and disuse of the practice of leading noble youths into captivity, and compelling them to ascend chimneys, was a severe blow, if we may so speak, to the romance of chimney-sweeping, and to the romance of spring at the same time. But even this was not all, for some few years ago the dancing on May-day began to decline; small sweeps were observed to congregate in twos or threes, unsupported by a "green," with no "My Lord" to act as master of the ceremonies, and no "My Lady" to preside over the exchequer. Even in companies where there was a "green" it was an absolute nothing—a mere sprout; and the instrumental accompaniments rarely extended beyond the shovels and a set of Panpipes, better known to the many, as a "mouth-organ."

These were signs of the times, portentous omens of a coming change; and what was the result which they shadowed forth? Why, the master sweeps, influenced by a restless spirit of innovation, actually interposed their authority, in opposition to the dancing, and substituted a dinner—an anniversary dinner at White Conduit House—where clean faces appeared in lieu of black ones smeared with rose pink; and knee cords and tops superseded nankeen drawers and rosetted shoes.

Gentlemen who were in the habit of riding shy horses; and steady-going people, who have no vagrancy in their souls, lauded this alteration to the skies, and the conduct of the master sweeps was described as beyond the reach of praise. But how stands the real fact? Let any man deny, if he can, that when the cloth had been removed, fresh pots and pipes laid upon the table, and the customary loyal and patriotic toasts proposed, the celebrated Mr. Sluffen, of Adam and Eve Court, whose authority not the most malignant of our opponents can call in question, expressed himself in a manner following: "That now he'd cotcht the cheerman's hi, he vished he might be jolly vell blessed, if he worn't a goin' to have his innings, vich he vould say these here obserwashuns—that how some mischeevus coves as know'd nuffin about the consarn, had tried to sit people agin the mas'r swips, and take the shine out o' their bis'nes, and the bread out o' the traps o' their preshus kids, by a makin' o' this here remark, as chimblies could be as vell svept by 'sheenery as by boys; and that the makin' use o' boys for that theer purpuss vos babareous; vereas, he 'ad been a chummy—he begged the cheerman's parding for usin' such a wulgar hexpression—more nor thirty year—he might say he'd been born in a chimbley, and he know'd uncommon vell as 'sheenery vos vus nor o' no use; and as to kerhewelty to the boys, everybody in the chimbley line know'd as vell as he did, that they liked the climbin' better nor nuffin as vos." From this day, we date the total fall of the last lingering remnant of May-day dancing, among the *élite* of the profession: and from this period we commence a new era in that portion of our spring associations which relates to the 1st of May.

We are aware that the unthinking part of the population will meet us here, with the assertion, that dancing on May-day still continues—that "greens" are annually seen to roll along the streets—that youths in the garb of clowns precede them, giving vent to the ebullitions of their sportive fancies; and that lords and ladies follow in their wake.

Granted. We are ready to acknowledge that in outward

show, these processions have greatly improved: we do not deny the introduction of solos on the drum; we will even go so far as to admit an occasional fantasia on the triangle, but here our admissions end. We positively deny that the sweeps have art or part in these proceedings. We distinctly charge the dustmen with throwing what they ought to clear away, into the eyes of the public. We accuse scavengers, brickmakers, and gentlemen who devote their energies to the coster-mongering line, with obtaining money once a year, under false pretences. We cling with peculiar fondness to the custom of days gone by, and have shut out conviction as long as we could, but it has forced itself upon us; and we now proclaim to a deluded public, that the May-day dancers are *not* sweeps. The size of them, alone, is sufficient to repudiate the idea. It is a notorious fact that the widely-spread taste for register-stoves has materially increased the demand for small boys; whereas the men, who, under a fictitious character, dance about the streets on the first of May nowadays, would be a tight fit in a kitchen flue, to say nothing of the parlour. This is strong presumptive evidence, but we have positive proof—the evidence of our own senses. And here is our testimony.

Upon the morning of the second of the merry month of May, in the year of our Lord one thousand eight hundred and thirty-six, we went out for a stroll, with a kind of forlorn hope of seeing something or other which might induce us to believe that it was really spring, and not Christmas; and after wandering as far as Copenhagen House, without meeting anything calculated to dispel our impression that there was a mistake in the almanacs, we turned back down Maiden Lane, with the intention of passing through the extensive colony lying between it and Battle Bridge, which is inhabited by proprietors of donkey-carts, boilers of horseflesh, makers of tiles, and sifters of cinders; and through this colony we should have passed, without stoppage or interruption, if a little crowd gathered round a shed had not attracted our attention, and induced us to pause.

When we say a "shed," we do not mean the conservatory sort of building, which, according to the old song, Love tenanted when he was a young man, but a wooden house with windows stuffed with rags and paper, and a small yard at the side, with one dust-cart, two baskets, a few shovels, and little heaps of cinders, and fragments of china and tiles scattered about it. Before this inviting spot we paused; and the longer we looked, the more we wondered what exciting circumstance it could be, that induced the foremost members of the crowd to flatten their noses against the parlour window, in the vain hope of catching a glimpse of what was going on inside. After staring vacantly about us for some minutes, we appealed, touching the cause of this assemblage, to a gentleman in a suit of tarpauling, who was smoking his pipe on our right hand; but as the only answer we obtained was a playful inquiry whether our maternal parent had disposed of her mangle, we determined to wait the issue in silence.

Judge of our virtuous indignation, when the street-door of the shed opened, and a party emerged therefrom, clad in the costume and emulating the appearance of May-day sweeps!

The first person who appeared was "my lord," habited in a blue coat and bright buttons, with gilt paper tacked over the seams, yellow knee-breeches, pink cotton stockings, and shoes; a cocked hat, ornamented with shreds of various-coloured paper, on his head, a *bouquet* the size of a prize cauliflower in his button-hole, a long Belcher handkerchief in his right hand, and a thin cane in his left. A murmur of applause ran through the crowd (which was chiefly composed of his lordship's personal friends), when this graceful figure made his appearance, which swelled into a burst of applause as his fair partner in the dance bounded forth to join him. Her ladyship was attired in pink crape over bed-furniture, with a low body and short sleeves. The symmetry of her ankles was partially concealed by a very perceptible pair of frilled trousers; and the inconvenience which might have resulted from the circumstances of her white satin shoes being a few sizes too large, was obviated by their being firmly attached to her legs with strong tape sandals.

Her head was ornamented with a profusion of artificial flowers; and in her hand she bore a large brass ladle, wherein to receive what she figuratively denominated "the tin." The other characters were a young gentleman in girl's clothes and a widow's cap: two clowns who walked upon their hands in the mud, to the immeasurable delight of all the spectators; a man with a drum; another man with a flageolet; a dirty woman in a large shawl, with a box under her arm for the money,—and last, though not least, the "green," animated by no less a personage than our identical friend in the tarpauling suit.

The man hammered away at the drum, the flageolet squeaked, the shovels rattled, the "green" rolled about, pitching first on one side and then on the other—my lady threw her right foot over her left ankle, and her left foot over her right ankle, alternately; my lord ran a few paces forward, and butted at the "green," and then a few paces backward upon the toes of the crowd, and then went to the right, and then to the left, and then dodged my lady round the "green;" and finally drew her arm through his, and called upon the boys to shout, which they did lustily—for this was the dancing.

We passed the same group accidentally in the evening. We never saw a "green" so drunk, a lord so quarrelsome (no: not even in the House of Peers after dinner), a pair of clowns so melancholy, a lady so muddy, or a party so miserable.

How has May-day decayed! How many merry sports, such as dancing round the Maypole, have fallen into desuetude! And, apparently trifling as their loss may appear, with how many profligate and vicious customs have they been replaced! How much of cheerfulness, and simplicity of character, have they carried away with them, and how much of degradation and discontent have they left behind!

CHAPTER XXI: Brokers' and Marine-Store Shops

WHEN we affirm that brokers' shops are strange places, and that if an authentic history of their contents could be procured, it would furnish many a page of amusement, and many a melancholy tale, it is necessary to explain the class of shops to which we allude.—Perhaps when we make use of the term "Broker's Shop," the minds of our readers will at once picture large, handsome warehouses, exhibiting a long perspective of French-polished dining-tables, rosewood chiffoniers, and mahogany washhand-stands, with an occasional vista of a four-post bedstead and hangings, and an appropriate foreground of dining-room chairs. Perhaps they will imagine that we mean an humble class of second-hand furniture repositories. Their imagination will then naturally lead them to that street at the back of Long Acre, which is composed almost entirely of brokers' shops: where you walk through groves of deceitful, showy-looking furniture, and where the prospect is occasionally enlivened by a bright red, blue, and yellow hearth-rug, embellished with the pleasing device of a mail-coach at full-speed, or a strange animal, supposed to have been originally intended for a dog, with a mass of worsted-work in his mouth, which conjecture has likened to a basket of flowers.

This, by-the-by, is a tempting article to young wives in the humbler ranks of life, who have got a first-floor front to furnish —they are lost in admiration, and hardly know which to admire most. The dog is very beautiful, but they have got a dog already on the best tea-tray, and two more on the mantelpiece. Then there is something so genteel about that mail-coach, and the passengers outside (who are all hat) give it such an air of reality!

The goods here are adapted to the taste, or rather to the means, of cheap purchasers. There are some of the most beautiful *looking* Pembroke tables that were ever beheld: the wood as green as the trees in the Park, and the leaves almost as certain to fall off in the course of a year. There is also a most extensive assortment of tent and turn-up bedsteads, made of stained wood, and innumerable specimens of that base imposition on society—a sofa bedstead.

A turn-up bedstead is a blunt, honest piece of furniture; it may be slightly disguised with a sham drawer, and sometimes a mad attempt is even made to pass it off for a bookcase: ornament it as you will, however, the turn-up bedstead seems to defy disguise, and to insist on having it distinctly understood that he is a turn-up bedstead, and nothing else; that he is indispensably necessary, and that being so useful, he disdains to be ornamental.

How different is the demeanour of a sofa bedstead! Ashamed of its real use, it strives to appear an article of luxury and gentility—an attempt in which it miserably fails. It has neither the respectability of a sofa, nor the virtues of a bed; every man who keeps a sofa bedstead in his house, becomes a party to a wilful and designing fraud—we question whether you could insult him more, than by insinuating that you entertain the least suspicion of its real use.

To return from this digression, we beg to say, that neither of these classes of brokers' shops forms the subject of this sketch. The shops to which we advert, are immeasurably inferior to those on whose outward appearance we have slightly touched. Our readers must often have observed in some by-street, in a poor neighbourhood, a small dirty shop exposing for sale the most extraordinary and confused jumble of old, worn-out, wretched articles, that can well be imagined. Our wonder at their ever having been bought, is only to be equalled by our astonishment at the idea of their ever being sold again. On a board, at the side of the door, are placed about twenty books—all odd volumes, and as many wine-glasses—all different patterns; several locks, an old earthenware pan, full of rusty keys; two or three gaudy chimney-ornaments—cracked of course; the remains of a lustre, without any drops, a round frame like a capital O, which has once held a mirror; a flute, complete with the exception of the middle joint; a pair of curling-irons, and a tinder-box. In front of the shop-window, are ranged some half-dozen high-backed chairs, with spinal complaints and wasted legs; a corner cupboard, two or three very dark mahogany tables with flaps like mathematical problems; some pickle-jars, some surgeons' ditto, with gilt labels and without stoppers; an unframed portrait of some lady who flourished about the beginning of the thirteenth century, by an artist who never flourished at all; an incalculable host of etceteras of every description, including bottles and cabinets, rags and bones, fenders and street-door knockers, fire-irons, wearing apparel and bedding, a hall-lamp, and a room-door. Imagine, in addition to this incongruous mass, a black doll in a white frock, with two faces—one looking up the street, and the other looking down, swinging over the door: a board with the squeezed-up inscription "Dealer in marine stores," in lanky white letters, whose height is strangely out of proportion to their width; and you have before you precisely the kind of shop to which we wish to direct your attention.

Although the heterogeneous mixture of things which we have attempted to describe, will be found at all these places, it is curious to observe how truly and accurately some of the minor articles which are exposed for sale—articles of wearing apparel, for instance—mark the character of the neighbourhood. Take Drury Lane and Covent Garden for example.

This is essentially a theatrical neighbourhood. There is not a potboy in the vicinity who is not, to a greater or less extent, a dramatic character. The errand-boys and chandler's-shop-keepers' sons, are all stage-struck: they "get up" plays in back kitchens hired for the purpose, and will stand before a shop-window for hours, contemplating a great staring portrait of Mr. Somebody or other, of the Royal Coburg Theatre, "as he appeared in the character of Tongo the Denounced." The consequence is, that there is not a marine-store shop in the neighbourhood which does not exhibit for sale some faded articles of dramatic finery, such as three or four pairs of soiled buff boots with turn-over red tops, heretofore worn by a "fourth robber," or "fifth mob"; a pair of rusty broadswords, a few gauntlets, and certain resplendent ornaments, which, if they were yellow instead of white, might be taken for insurance plates of the Sun Fire-office. There are several of these shops in the narrow streets and dirty courts, of which there are so many near the national theatres, and they all have tempting goods of this description, with the addition, perhaps, of a lady's pink dress covered with spangles, white wreaths, stage shoes, and a tiara like a tin lamp reflector. They have been purchased of some wretched supernumeraries, or sixth-rate actors, and are now offered for the benefit of the rising generation, who, on condition of their making certain weekly payments, amounting in the whole to about ten times their value, may avail themselves of such desirable bargains.

Let us take a very different quarter, and apply it to the same test. Look at a marine-store dealer's, in that reservoir of dirt, drunkenness, and drabs: thieves, oysters, baked potatoes, and pickled salmon—Ratcliff Highway. Here the wearing apparel is all nautical. Rough blue jackets, with mother-of-pearl buttons, oil-skin hats, coarse checked shirts, and large canvas trousers that look as if they were made for a pair of bodies instead of a pair of legs, are the staple commodities. Then there are large bunches of cotton pocket-handkerchiefs, in colour and pattern unlike any one ever saw before, with the exception of those on the backs of three young ladies without bonnets who passed us just now. The furniture is much the same as elsewhere, with the addition of one or two models of ships, and some old prints of naval engagements in still older frames. In the window are a few compasses, a small tray containing silver watches, in clumsy thick cases; and tobacco-boxes, the lid of each ornamented with a ship or an anchor, or some such trophy. A sailor generally pawns or sells all he has before he has been long ashore, and if he does not, some favoured companion kindly saves him the trouble. In either case, it is an even chance that he afterwards unconsciously repurchases the same things at a higher price than he gave for them at first.

Again: pay a visit with a similar object, to a part of London, as unlike both of these as they are to each other. Cross over to the Surrey side, and look at such shops of this description as are to be found near the King's Bench prison, and in "the Rules." How different, and how strikingly illustrative of the decay of some of the unfortunate residents in this part of the metropolis! Imprisonment and neglect have done their work. There is contamination in the profligate denizens of a debtor's prison; old friends have fallen off; the recollection of former prosperity has passed away, and with it all thoughts for the past, all care for the future. First, watches and rings, then cloaks, coats, and all the more expensive articles of dress have found their way to the pawnbroker's. That miserable resource has failed at last, and the sale of some trifling article at one of these shops has been the only mode left of raising a shilling or two, to meet the urgent demands of the moment.— Dressing-cases and writing-desks, too old to pawn but too good to keep: guns, fishing-rods, musical instruments, all in the same condition, have first been sold, and the sacrifice has been but slightly felt. But hunger must be allayed, and what has already become a habit, is easily resorted to, when an emergency arises. Light articles of clothing, first of the ruined man, then of his wife, and at last of their children, even of the youngest, have been parted with piecemeal. There they are, thrown carelessly together until a purchaser presents himself —old, and patched and repaired, it is true, but the make and materials tell of better days; and the older they are, the greater the misery and destitution of those whom they once adorned.

CHAPTER XXII: Gin-Shops

IT is a very remarkable circumstance, that different trades appear to partake of the disease to which elephants and dogs are especially liable, and to run stark, staring, raving mad, periodically. The great distinction between the animals and the trades, is, that the former run mad with a certain degree of propriety—they are very regular in their irregularities. We know the period at which the emergency will arise, and provide against it accordingly. If an elephant run mad, we are all ready for him—kill or cure—pills or bullets—calomel in conserve of roses, or lead in a musket-barrel. If a dog happen to look unpleasantly warm in the summer months, and to trot about the shady side of the streets with a quarter of a yard of tongue hanging out of his mouth, a thick leather muzzle, which has been previously prepared in compliance with the thoughtful injunctions of the Legislature, is instantly clapped over his head by way of making him cooler, and he either looks remarkably unhappy for the next six weeks, or becomes legally insane, and goes mad as it were, by Act of Parliament. But these trades are as eccentric as comets; nay, worse, for no one can calculate on the recurrence of the strange appearances which betoken the disease. Moreover, the contagion is general, and the quickness with which it diffuses itself, almost incredible.

We will cite two or three cases in illustration of our meaning. Six or eight years ago, the epidemic began to display itself among the linen-drapers and haberdashers. The primary symptoms were an inordinate love of plate-glass, and a passion for gas-lights and gilding. The disease gradually progressed, and at last attained a fearful height. Quiet dusty old shops in different parts of town were pulled down; spacious premises with stuccoed fronts and gold letters were erected instead; floors were covered with Turkey carpets; roofs supported by massive pillars; doors knocked into windows, a dozen squares of glass into one, one shopman into a dozen, and there is no knowing what would have been done, if it had not been fortunately discovered, just in time, that the Commissioners of Bankrupts were as competent to decide such cases as the Commissioners of Lunacy, and that a little confinement and gentle examination did wonders. The disease abated. It died away; and a year or two of comparative tranquillity ensued. Suddenly it burst out again among the chemists; the symptoms were the same, with the addition of a strong desire to stick the royal arms over the shop-door, and a great rage for mahogany, varnish, and expensive floor-cloth. Then the hosiers were infected, and began to pull down their shop-fronts with frantic recklessness. The mania again died away, and the public began to congratulate themselves upon its entire disappearance, when it burst forth with ten-fold violence among the publicans and keepers of "wine vaults." From that moment it has spread among them with unprecedented rapidity, exhibiting a concatenation of all the previous symptoms; and onward it has rushed to every part of town, knocking down all the old public-houses, and depositing splendid mansions, stone balustrades, rosewood fittings, immense lamps, and illuminated clocks, at the corner of every street

The extensive scale on which these places are established, and the ostentatious manner in which the business of even the smallest among them is divided into branches, is most amusing. A handsome plate of ground glass in one door directs you "To the Counting-house;" another to the "Bottle Department;" a third to the "Wholesale Department;" a fourth, to "The Wine Promenade;" and so forth, until we are in daily expectation of meeting with a "Brandy Bell," or a "Whiskey Entrance." Then ingenuity is exhausted in devising attractive titles for the different descriptions of gin; and the dram-drinking portion of the community as they gaze upon the gigantic black and white announcements, which are only to be equalled in size by the figures beneath them, are left in a state of pleasing hesitation between "The Cream of the Valley," "The Out and Out," "The No Mistake," "The Good for Mixing," "The real Knock-me-down," "The celebrated Butter Gin," "The regular Flare-up," and a dozen others, equally inviting and wholesome *liqueurs*. Although places of this description are to be met with in every second street, they are invariably numerous and splendid in precise proportion to the dirt and poverty of the surrounding neighbourhood. The gin-shops in and near Drury Lane, Holborn, St. Giles's, Covent Garden, and Clare Market, are the handsomest in London. There is more of filth and squalid misery near those great thoroughfares than in any part of this mighty city.

We will endeavour to sketch the bar of a large gin-shop, and its ordinary customers, for the edification of such of our readers as may not have had opportunities of observing such scenes; and on the chance of finding one well suited to our purpose, we will make for Drury Lane, through the narrow streets and dirty courts which divide it from Oxford Street, and that classical spot adjoining the brewery at the bottom of Tottenham Court Road, best known to the initiated as the "Rookery."

The filthy and miserable appearance of this part of London can hardly be imagined by those (and there are many such) who have not witnessed it. Wretched houses with broken windows patched with rags and paper, every room let out to a different family and in many instances to two or even three; fruit and "sweet-stuff" manufacturers in the cellars, barbers and red-herring vendors in the front parlours, and cobblers in the back; a bird-fancier on the first floor, three families on the second, starvation in the attics, Irishmen in the passage, a "musician" in the front kitchen, and a charwoman and five hungry children in the back one—filth everywhere—a gutter before the houses and a drain behind them—clothes drying and slops emptying from the windows: girls of fourteen or fifteen, with matted hair, walking about barefooted, and in white greatcoats, almost their only covering; boys of all ages, in

THE GIN SHOP.

coats of all sizes and no coats at all; men and women, in every variety of scanty and dirty apparel, lounging, scolding, drinking, smoking, squabbling, fighting, and swearing.

You turn the corner. What a change! All is light and brilliancy. The hum of many voices issues from that splendid gin-shop which forms the commencement of the two streets opposite, and the gay building with the fantastically ornamented parapet, the illuminated clock, the plate-glass windows surrounded by stucco-rosettes, and its profusion of gas-lights in richly-gilt burners, is perfectly dazzling when contrasted with the darkness and dirt we have just left. The interior is even gayer than the exterior. A bar of French-polished mahogany, elegantly carved, extends the whole width of the place; and there are two side-aisles of great casks, painted green and gold, enclosed within a light brass rail, and bearing such inscriptions as "Old Tom, 549;" "Young Tom, 360;" "Samson, 1421." Beyond the bar is a lofty and spacious saloon, full of the same enticing vessels, with a gallery running round it, equally well furnished. On the counter, in addition to the usual spirit apparatus, are two or three little baskets of cakes and biscuits, which are carefully secured at the top with wickerwork, to prevent their contents being unlawfully abstracted. Behind it, are two showily-dressed damsels with large necklaces, dispensing the spirits and "compounds." They are assisted by the ostensible proprietor of the concern, a stout coarse fellow in a fur cap, put on very much on one side to give him a knowing air, and display his sandy whiskers to the best advantage.

The two old washerwomen, who are seated on the little bench to the left of the bar, are rather overcome by the head-dresses and haughty demeanour of the young ladies who officiate; and receive their half-quartern of gin and peppermint with considerable deference, prefacing a request for "one of them soft biscuits," with a "Jist be good enough, ma'am," &c. They are quite astonished at the impudent air of the young fellow in a brown coat and bright buttons, who, ushering in his two companions, and walking up to the bar in as careless a manner as if he had been used to green and gold ornaments all his life, winks at one of the young ladies with singular coolness, and calls for a "kervorten and a three-out-glass," just as if the place were his own. "Gin for you, sir?" says the young lady when she had drawn it: carefully looking every way but the right one, to show that the wink had no effect upon her. "For me, Mary my dear," replies the gentleman in brown. "My name ain't Mary as it happens," says the young girl, in a most insinuating manner as she delivers the change. "Well, if it ain't, it ought to be," responds the irresistible one; "all the Marys as ever I see, was handsome gals." Here the young lady, not precisely remembering how blushes are managed in

such cases, abruptly ends the flirtation by addressing the
female in the faded feathers who has just entered, and who,
after stating explicitly, to prevent any subsequent misunder-
standing, that "this gentleman pays," calls for "a glass of port
wine and a bit of sugar," the drinking which, and sipping
another, accompanied by sundry whisperings to her companion, and no small quantity of giggling, occupies a
considerable time.

Those two old men who came in "just to have a drain,"
finished their third quartern a few seconds ago; they have
made themselves crying drunk; and the fat comfortable-
looking elderly women, who had "a glass of rum-srub" each,
having chimed in with their complaints on the hardness of the
times, one of the women has agreed to stand a glass round,
jocularly observing that "grief never mended no broken
bones, and as good people's wery scarce, what I says is, make
the most on 'em, and that's all about it;" a sentiment which
appears to afford unlimited satisfaction to those who have
nothing to pay.

It is growing late, and the throng of men, women, and
children, who have been constantly going in and out, dwindles
down to two or three occasional stragglers—cold, wretched-
looking creatures, in the last stage of emaciation and disease.
The knot of Irish labourers at the lower end of the place, who
have been alternately shaking hands with, and threatening the
life of, each other for the last hour, become furious in their
disputes, and finding it impossible to silence one man, who is
particularly anxious to adjust the difference, they resort to
the infallible expedient of knocking him down and jumping on
him afterwards. The man in the fur cap, and the potboy rush
out: a scene of riot and confusion ensues; half the Irishmen
get shut out, and the other half get shut in; the potboy is
knocked among the tubs in no time; the landlord hits everybody, and everybody hits the landlord; the barmaids scream;
the police come in; and the rest is a confused mixture of arms,
legs, staves, torn coats, shouting and struggling. Some of the
party are borne off to the station-house, and the remainder
slink home to beat their wives for complaining, and kick the
children for daring to be hungry.

We have sketched this subject very slightly, not only
because our limits compel us to do so, but because, if it were
pursued further, it would be painful and repulsive. Well-
disposed gentlemen, and charitable ladies, would alike turn
with coldness and disgust from a description of the drunken
besotted men, and wretched broken-down miserable women,
who form no inconsiderable portion of the frequenters of these
haunts; forgetting, in the pleasant consciousness of their own
high rectitude, the poverty of the one, and the temptation of
the other. Gin-drinking is a great vice in England, but

poverty is a greater; and until you can cure it, or persuade a half-famished wretch not to seek relief in the temporary oblivion of his own misery, with the pittance which, divided among his family, would just furnish a morsel of bread for each, gin-shops will increase in number and splendour. If Temperance Societies could suggest an antidote against hunger, distress, or establish dispensaries for the gratuitous distribution of bottles of Lethe-water, gin-palaces would be numbered among the things that were. Until then, their decrease may be despaired of.

CHAPTER XXIII: *The Pawnbroker's Shop*

OF all the numerous receptacles for misery and distress with which the streets of London unhappily abound, there are, perhaps, none which present such striking scenes of vice and poverty as the pawnbrokers' shops. The very nature and description of these places occasions their being but little known, except to the unfortunate beings whose profligacy or misfortune drives them to seek the temporary relief they offer. The subject may appear, at first sight, to be anything but an inviting one, but we venture on it nevertheless, in the hope that, as far as the limits of our present paper are concerned, it will present, at all events, nothing to disgust even the most fastidious reader.

There are some pawnbrokers' shops of a very superior description. There are grades in pawning as in everything else, and distinctions must be observed even in poverty. The aristocratic Spanish cloak and the plebeian calico shirt, the silver fork and the flat iron, the muslin cravat and the Belcher neckerchief, would but ill assort together; so the better sort of pawnbroker calls himself a silversmith and decorates his shop with handsome trinkets and expensive jewellery, while the more humble money-lender boldly advertises his calling, and invites observation. It is with pawnbrokers' shops of the latter class that we have to do. We have selected one for our purpose, and will endeavour to describe it.

The pawnbroker's shop is situated near Drury Lane, at the corner of a court, which affords a side entrance for the accommodation of such customers as may be desirous of avoiding the observation of the passers-by, or the chance of recognition in the public street. It is a low, dirty-looking, dusty shop, the door of which stands always doubtfully, a little way open: half inviting, half repelling the hesitating visitor, who, if he be as yet uninitiated, examines one of the old garnet brooches in the window for a minute or two with affected eagerness, as if he contemplated making a purchase; and then looking cautiously round to ascertain that no one watches him, hastily slinks in: the door closing of itself after him, to just its former width. The shop front and the window-frames bear evident marks of having been once painted; but what the colour was originally, or at what date it was probably laid on, are at this remote period questions which may be asked, but cannot be answered. Tradition states that the transparency in the front door, which displays at night three red balls on a blue ground, once bore also, inscribed in graceful waves, the words "Money advanced on plate, jewels, wearing apparel, and every description of property," but a few illegible hieroglyphics are all that now remain to attest the fact. The plate and jewels would seem to have disappeared together with the announcement, for the articles of stock, which are displayed in some profusion in the window, do not include any very valuable luxuries of either kind. A few old china cups; some modern vases, adorned with paltry paintings of three Spanish cavaliers playing three Spanish guitars; or a party of boors carousing; each boor with one leg painfully elevated in the air, by way of expressing his perfect freedom and gaiety; several sets of chessmen, two or three flutes, a few fiddles, a round-eyed portrait staring in astonishment from a very dark ground; some gaudily-bound prayer-books and testaments, two rows of silver watches quite as clumsy and almost as large as Ferguson's first, numerous old-fashioned table and tea spoons displayed, fan-like, in half-dozens; strings of coral with great broad gilt snaps; cards of rings and brooches, fastened and labelled separately, like the insects in the British Museum; cheap silver pen-holders and snuff-boxes, with a masonic star, complete the jewellery department; while five or six beds in smeary clouded ticks, strings of blankets and sheets, silk and cotton handkerchiefs, and wearing apparel of every description, form the more useful, though even less ornamental, part of the articles exposed for sale. An extensive collection of planes, chisels, saws, and other carpenters' tools, which have been pledged, and never redeemed, form the foreground of the picture; while the large frames full of ticketed bundles which are dimly seen through the dirty casement up-stairs—the squalid neighbourhood—the adjoining houses, straggling, shrunken, and rotten, with one or two filthy, unwholesome-looking heads, thrust out of every window, and old red pans and stunted plants exposed on the tottering parapets, to the manifest hazard of the heads of the passers-by—the noisy men loitering under the archway at the corner of the court, or about the gin-shop next door, and their wives patiently standing on the curb-stone, with large baskets of cheap vegetables slung round them for sale, are its immediate auxiliaries.

If the outside of the pawnbroker's shop be calculated to attract the attention, or excite the interest, of the speculative pedestrian, its interior cannot fail to produce the same effect in a very increased degree. The front door, which we have before noticed, opens into the common shop, which is the resort of all those customers whose habitual acquaintance with such scenes renders them indifferent to the observation of their companions in poverty. The side door opens into a small passage from which some half-dozen doors (which may be secured on the inside by bolts) open into a corresponding number of little dens, or closets, which face the counter. Here the more timid or respectable portion of the crowd shroud themselves from the notice of the remainder, and patiently wait until the gentleman behind the counter, with the curly black hair, diamond ring, and double silver watch-guard, shall feel disposed to favour them with his notice—a consummation which depends considerably on the temper of the aforesaid gentleman for the time being.

At the present moment, this elegantly attired individual is in the act of entering the duplicate he has just made out, in a thick book: a process from which he is diverted occasionally, by a conversation he is carrying on with another young man similarly employed at a little distance from him, whose allusions to "that last bottle of soda-water last night," and "how regularly round my hat he felt himself when the young 'ooman gave 'em in charge," would appear to refer to the consequences of some stolen joviality of the preceding evening. The customers generally, however, seem rather unable to participate in the amusement derivable from this source, for an old sallow-looking woman, who has been leaning with both arms on the counter with a small bundle before her, for half an hour previously, suddenly interrupts the conversation by addressing the jewelled shopman—"Now, Mr. Henry, do make haste, there's a good soul, for my two grandchildren's locked up at home, and I'm afeer'd of the fire." The shopman slightly raises his head, with an air of deep abstraction, and resumes his entry with as much deliberation as if he were engraving. "You're in a hurry, Mrs. Tatham, this ev'nin', ain't you?" is the only notice he deigns to take, after the lapse of five minutes or so. "Yes, I am indeed, Mr. Henry; now, do serve me next, there's a good creetur. I wouldn't worry you, only it's all along o' them botherin' children."—"What have you got here?" inquires the shopman, unpinning the bundle: "old concern, I suppose—pair o' stays and a petticut. You must look up somethin' else, old 'ooman; I can't lend you anything more upon them; they're completely worn out by this time, if it's only by putting in, and taking out again, three times a week."—"Oh! you're a rum 'un, you are," replies the old woman, laughing extremely, as in duty bound; "I wish I'd got the gift of the gab like you; see if I'd be up the spout so often then. No, no; it ain't the petticut; it's a child's frock and a beautiful silk-ankecher, as belongs to my husband,

He gave four shillin' for it, the werry same blessed day as he broke his arm."—"What do you want upon these?" inquires Mr. Henry, slightly glancing at the articles, which in all probability are old acquaintances. "What do you want upon these?"—"Eighteenpence."—"Lend you ninepence."—"Oh, make it a shillin'; there's a dear—do now."—"Not another farden."—"Well, I suppose I must take it." The duplicate is made out, one ticket pinned on the parcel, the other given to the old woman: the parcel is flung carelessly down into a corner, and some other customer prefers his claim to be served without further delay.

The choice falls on an unshaven, dirty, sottish-looking fellow, whose tarnished paper-cap, stuck negligently over one eye, communicates an additionally repulsive expression to his very uninviting countenance. He was enjoying a little relaxation from his sedentary pursuits a quarter of an hour ago, in kicking his wife up the court. He has come to redeem some tools:—probably to complete a job with, on account of which he has already received some money, if his inflamed countenance and drunken stagger, may be taken as evidence of the fact. Having waited some little time, he makes his presence known by venting his ill-humour on a ragged urchin, who, being unable to bring his face on a level with the counter by any other process, has employed himself in climbing up, and then hooking himself on with his elbows—an uneasy perch, from which he has fallen at intervals, generally alighting on the toes of the person in his immediate vicinity. In the present case, the unfortunate little wretch has received a cuff which sends him reeling to the door; and the donor of the blow is immediately the object of general indignation.

"What do you strike the boy for, you brute?" exclaims a slipshod woman, with two flat irons in a little basket. "Do you think he's your wife, you willin?"—"Go and hang yourself!" replies the gentleman addressed, with a drunken look of savage stupidity, aiming at the same time a blow at the woman which fortunately misses its object. "Go and hang yourself; and wait till I come and cut you down."—"Cut you down," rejoins the woman, "I wish I had the cutting of you up, you wagabond! (loud). Oh! you precious wagabond! (rather louder). Where's your wife, you willin? (louder still; women of this class are always sympathetic, and work themselves into a tremendous passion on the shortest notice). Your poor dear wife as you uses worser nor a dog—strike a woman—you a man! (very shrill). I wish I had you—I'd murder you, I would, if I died for it."—"Now be civil," retorts the man fiercely. "Be civil, you wiper!" ejaculates the woman contemptuously. "Ain't it shocking?" she continues, turning round, and appealing to an old woman who is peeping out of one of the little closets we have before described, and who has not the slightest objection to join in the attack, possessing, as she does, the comfortable conviction that she is bolted in. "An't it shocking, ma'am? (Dreadful! says the old woman in a parenthesis, not exactly knowing what the question refers to.) He's got a wife, ma'am, as takes in mangling, and is as 'dustrious and hard-working a young 'ooman as can be, (very fast) as lives in the back parlour of our 'ous, which my husband and me lives in the front one (with great rapidity)—and we hears him a beatin' on her sometimes when he comes home drunk, the whole night through, and not only a beaten' her, but beaten' his own child too, to make her more miserable—ugh, you beast!—and she, poor creater, won't swear the peace agin him, nor do nothin', because she likes the wretch arter all—worse luck!" Here, as the woman has completely run herself out of breath, the pawnbroker himself, who has just appeared behind the counter in a grey dressing-gown, embraces the favourable opportunity of putting in a word: "Now I won't have none of this sort of thing on my premises," he interposes with an air of authority; "Mrs. Mackin, keep yourself to yourself, or you don't get fourpence for a flat-iron here; and Jinkins, you leave your ticket here till you're sober, and send your wife for them two planes, for I won't have you in my shop at no price; so make yourself scarce, before I make you scarcer."

This eloquent address produces anything but the effect desired; the women rail in concert; the man hits about him in all directions, and is in the act of establishing an indisputable claim to gratuitous lodgings for the night, when the entrance of his wife, a wretched worn-out woman, apparently in the last stage of consumption, whose face bears evident marks of recent ill-usage, and whose strength seems hardly equal to the burden—light enough, God knows!—of the thin, sickly child she carries in her arms, turns his cowardly rage in a safer direction. "Come home, dear," cries the miserable creature, in an imploring tone; "do come home, there's a good fellow, and go to bed."— "Go home yourself," rejoins the furious ruffian, accompanying an epithet we will not repeat, with a kick we will not describe. "Do come home quietly," repeats the wife, bursting into tears. "Go home yourself," retorts the husband again, enforcing his argument by the application we have before hinted at. The poor creature flies out of the shop, with the impetus thus administered, and her "natural protector" follows her up the court, alternately venting his rage in accelerating her progress, and in knocking the little scanty blue bonnet of the unfortunate child over its still more scanty and faded-looking face.

In the last box, which is situated in the darkest and most obscure corner of the shop, considerably removed from either of the gas-lights, are a young delicate girl of about twenty, and an elderly female, evidently her mother from the resemblance between them, who stand at some distance back, as if to avoid the observation even of the shopman. It is not their first visit to a pawnbroker's shop, for they answer without a moment's hesitation the usual questions, put in a rather respectful manner, and in a much lower tone than usual, of "What name shall I say?—Your own property of course?—Where do you live, ma'am?—Housekeeper or lodger?" They bargain, too, for a higher loan than the shopman is at first inclined to offer, which a perfect stranger would be little disposed to do; and the elder female urges her daughter on, in scarcely audible whispers, to exert her utmost powers of persuasion to obtain an advance of the sum, and expatiate on the value of the articles they have brought to raise a present supply upon. They are a small gold chain and a "Forget-me-not" ring: the girl's property, for they are both too small for the mother; given her in better times; prized perhaps once for the giver's sake, but parted with now without a struggle, for want has hardened the mother, and her example has hardened the girl, and the prospect of receiving money, coupled with a recollection of the misery they have both endured from the want of it—the coldness of old friends—the stern refusal of some, and the still more galling compassion of others—appears to have obliterated the consciousness of self-humiliation, which the bare idea of their present situation would once have aroused.

In the next box is a young female, whose attire, miserably poor, but extremely gaudy, wretchedly cold but extravagantly fine, too plain bespeaks her station in life. The rich satin gown with its faded trimmings, the worn-out thin shoes, and pink silk stockings, the summer bonnet in winter, and the sunken face, where a daub of rouge only serves as an index to the ravages of squandered health never to be regained, and lost happiness never to be restored, and where the practised smile is a wretched mockery of the misery of the heart, cannot be mistaken. There is something in the glimpse she has just caught of her young neighbour, and in the sight of the little trinkets she has offered in pawn, that seems to have awakened in the woman's mind some long slumbering recollection, and to have changed, for an instant, her whole demeanour. Her first hasty impulse was to bend forward as if to scan more minutely the appearance of her half-concealed companions; her next, on seeing them involuntarily shrink from her, to retreat to the back of the box, cover her face with her hands, and burst into an agony of tears.

There are strange chords in the human heart, which will lie dormant through years of depravity and wickedness, but which will vibrate at last to some slight circumstance apparently trivial in itself, but connected by some undefined and indistinct association, with past days that can never be recalled, and with bitter recollections from which the most degraded creature in existence cannot escape.

There has been another spectator, in the person of a woman in the common shop; the lowest of the low, dirty, unbonneted, flaunting, and slovenly. Her curiosity was at first attracted by the little she could see of the group; then her attention. The half-intoxicated leer changed to an expression of something like interest, and a feeling similar to that we have described, appeared for a moment, and only a moment, to extend itself even to her bosom.

Who shall say how soon these women may change places? The last has but two more stages—the hospital and the grave. How many females situated as her two companions are, and as she may have been once, have terminated the same wretched course, in the same wretched manner. One is already tracing her footsteps with frightful rapidity. How soon may the other follow her example! How many have done the same!

CHAPTER XXIV: *Criminal Courts*

WE shall never forget the mingled feelings of awe and respect with which we used to gaze on the exterior of Newgate in our schoolboy days. How dreadful its rough heavy walls, and low massive doors, appeared to us—the latter looking as if they were made for the express purpose of letting people in, and never letting them out again. Then the fetters over the debtors' door, which we used to think were a *bonâ fide* set of irons, just hung up there, for convenience' sake, ready to be taken down at a moment's notice, and riveted on the limbs of some refractory felon! We were never tired of wondering how the hackney-coachmen on the opposite stand could cut jokes in the presence of such horrors, and drink pots of half-and-half so near the last drop.

Often have we strayed here in sessions time, just to catch a glimpse of the whipping-place, and that dark building on one side of the yard, in which is kept the gibbet with all its dreadful apparatus, and on the door of which we half expected to see a brass plate, with the inscription "Mr. Ketch"; for we never imagined that the distinguished functionary could by possibility live anywhere else. The days of these childish dreams have passed away, and with them many other boyish ideas of a gayer nature. But we still retain so much of our original feeling, that to this hour we never pass the building without something like a shudder.

What London pedestrian is there who has not, at some time or other, cast a hurried glance through the wicket at which prisoners are admitted into this gloomy mansion, and surveyed the few objects he could discern, with an indescribable feeling of curiosity? The thick door, plated with iron and mounted with spikes, just low enough to enable you to see, leaning over them, an ill-looking fellow in a broad-brimmed hat, Belcher handkerchief and top-boots, with a brown coat, something between a great-coat and a "sporting" jacket, on his back, and an immense key in his left hand. Perhaps you are lucky enough to pass, just as the gate is being opened; then you see on the other side of the lodge another gate, the very image of its predecessor, and two or three more turnkeys, who look like multiplications of the first one, seated round a fire which just lights up the white-washed apartment sufficiently to enable you to catch a hasty glimpse of these different objects. We have a great respect for Mrs. Fry, but she certainly ought to have written more romances than Mrs. Radcliffe.

We were walking leisurely down the Old Bailey, some time ago, when, just as we passed this identical gate, it was opened by the officiating turnkey. We turned quickly round, as a matter of course, and saw two persons descending the steps. We could not help stopping and observing them.

They were an elderly woman, of decent appearance, though evidently poor, and a boy of about fourteen or fifteen. The woman was crying bitterly; she carried a small bundle in her hand, and the boy followed at a short distance behind her. Their little history was obvious. The boy was her son, to whose early comfort she had perhaps sacrificed her own—for whose sake she had borne misery without repining, and poverty without a murmur: looking steadily forward to the time, when he who had so long witnessed her struggles for himself, might be enabled to make some exertions for their joint support. He had formed dissolute connections; idleness had led to crime, and he had been committed to take his trial for some petty theft. He had been long in prison, and, after receiving some trifling additional punishment, had been ordered to be discharged that morning. It was his first offence, and his poor old mother, still hoping to reclaim him, had been waiting at the gate to implore him to return home.

We cannot forget the boy; he descended the steps with a dogged look, shaking his head with an air of bravado and obstinate determination. They walked a few paces, and paused. The woman put her hand upon his shoulder in an agony of entreaty, and the boy sullenly raised his head as if in refusal. It was a brilliant morning, and every object looked fresh and happy in the broad, gay sunlight; he gazed round him for a few moments, bewildered with the brightness of the scene, for it was long since he had beheld anything save the gloomy walls of a prison. Perhaps the wretchedness of his mother made some impression on the boy's heart; perhaps some undefined recollection of the time when he was a happy child, and she his only friend, and best companion, crowded on him—he burst into tears; and covering his face with one hand, and hurriedly placing the other in his mother's, they walked away together.

Curiosity has occasionally led us into both Courts at the Old Bailey. Nothing is so likely to strike the person who enters them for the first time, as the calm indifference with which the proceedings are conducted; every trial seems a mere matter of business. There is a great deal of form, but no compassion; considerable interest, but no sympathy. Take the Old Court for example. There sit the Judges, with whose great dignity everybody is acquainted, and of whom therefore we need say no more. Then there is the Lord Mayor in the centre, looking as cool as a Lord Mayor *can* look, with an immense *bouquet* before him, and habited in all the splendour of his office. Then there are the Sheriffs, who are almost as dignified as the Lord Mayor himself; and the Barristers, who are quite dignified enough in their own opinion; and the spectators, who having paid for their admission, look upon the whole scene as if it were got up especially for their amusement. Look upon the whole group in the body of the Court —some wholly engrossed in the morning papers, others carelessly conversing in low whispers, and others, again, quietly dozing away an hour—and you can scarcely believe that the result of the trial is a matter of life or death to one wretched being present. Turn your eyes to the dock; watch the prisoner attentively for a few moments, and the fact is before you, in all its painful reality. Mark how restlessly he has been engaged for the last ten minutes, in forming all sorts of fantastic figures with the herbs which are strewed upon the ledge before him; observe the ashy paleness of his face when a particular witness appears, and how he changes his position and wipes his clammy forehead, and feverish hands, when the case for the prosecution is closed, as if it were a relief to him to feel that the jury knew the worst.

The defence is concluded; the judge proceeds to sum up the evidence; and the prisoner watches the countenance of the jury, as a dying man, clinging to life to the very last, vainly looks in the face of his physician for one slight ray of hope. They turn round to consult; you can almost hear the man's heart beat, as he bites the stalk of rosemary, with a desperate effort to appear composed. They resume their places—a dead silence prevails as the foreman delivers in the verdict—"Guilty!" A shriek bursts from a female in the gallery; the prisoner casts one look at the quarter from whence the noise proceeded, and is immediately hurried from the dock by the gaoler. The clerk directs one of the officers of the court to "take the woman out," and fresh business is proceeded with, as if nothing had occurred.

No imaginary contrast to a case like this, could be as complete as that which is constantly presented in the New Court, the gravity of which is frequently disturbed in no small degree, by the cunning and pertinacity of juvenile offenders. A boy of thirteen is tried, say for picking the pocket of some subject of her Majesty, and the offence is about as clearly proved as an offence can be. He is called upon for his defence, and contents himself with a little declamation about the jurymen and his country—asserts that all the witnesses have committed perjury, and hints that the police force generally have entered into a conspiracy "again" him. However probable this statement may be, it fails to convince the Court, and some such scene as the following then takes place:—

Court : Have you any witnesses to speak to your character, boy?

Boy : Yes, my Lord; fifteen gen'lm'n is a vaten outside, and vos a vaten all day yesterday, vich they told me the night afore my trial vos a comin' on.

Court : Inquire for these witnesses.

Here a very stout beadle runs out, and vociferates for the witnesses at the very top of his voice; for you hear his cry grow fainter and fainter as he descends the steps into the court-yard below. After an absence of five minutes, he returns very warm and hoarse, and informs the Court of what it was perfectly well aware before—namely, that there are no such witnesses in attendance. Hereupon the boy sets up the most awful howling ever heard within or without the walls of a court; screws the lower part of the palms of his hands into the corners of his eyes; and endeavours to look the very picture of injured innocence. The jury at once find him "guilty," and his endeavours to squeeze out a tear or two are redoubled. The governor of the gaol then states, in reply to an inquiry from the bench, that the prisoner has been under his care twice before. This the urchin resolutely denies in some such terms as—"S'elp me God, gen'lm'n, I never vos in trouble afore—indeed, my Lord, I never vos. It's all a howen to my having a twin brother, vich has wrongfully taking to prigging, and vich is so exactly like me, that no vun ever knows the difference atween us."

This representation, like the defence, fails in producing the desired effect, and the boy is sentenced, perhaps, to seven years' transportation. Finding it impossible to excite compassion, he gives vent to his feelings in an imprecation bearing reference to the eyes of "old big vig!" and as he declines to take the trouble of walking from the dock, is forthwith carried out by two men, congratulating himself on having succeeded in giving everybody as much trouble as possible.

CHAPTER XXV: *A visit to Newgate*

"THE force of habit" is a trite phrase in everybody's mouth; and it is not a little remarkable that those who use it most as applied to others, unconsciously afford in their own persons singular examples of the power which habit and custom exercise over the minds of men, and of the little reflection they are apt to bestow on subjects with which every day's experience has rendered them familiar. If Bedlam could be suddenly removed like another Aladdin's palace, and set down on the space now occupied by Newgate, scarcely one man out of a hundred, whose road to business every morning lies through Newgate Street or the Old Bailey, would pass the building without bestowing a hasty glance on its small, grated windows, and a transient thought at least upon the condition of the unhappy beings immured in its dismal cells; and yet these same men, day by day, and hour by hour, pass and repass this gloomy depository of the guilt and misery of London, in one perpetual stream of life and bustle, utterly unmindful of the throng of wretched creatures pent up within it—nay, not even knowing, or if they do, not heeding the fact, that as they pass one particular angle of the massive wall with a light laugh or a merry whistle, they stand within one yard of a fellow-creature, bound and helpless, whose hours are numbered, from whom the last feeble ray of hope has fled for ever, and whose miserable career will shortly terminate in a violent and shameful death. Contact with death even in its least terrible shape is solemn and appalling. How much more awful is it to reflect on this near vicinity to the dying—to men in full health and vigour, in the flower of youth or the prime of life, with all their faculties and perceptions as acute and perfect as your own; but dying, nevertheless—dying as surely—with the hand of death imprinted upon them as indelibly—as if mortal disease had wasted their frames to shadows, and loathsome corruption had already begun!

It was with some such thoughts as these that we determined not many weeks since to visit the interior of Newgate —in an amateur capacity, of course; and, having carried our intention into effect, we proceed to lay its results before our readers, in the hope—founded more upon the nature of the subject, than on any presumptuous confidence in our descriptive powers—that this paper may not be found wholly devoid of interest. We have only to premise, that we do not intend to fatigue the reader with any statistical accounts of the prison: they will be found at length in numerous reports of numerous committees, and a variety of authorities of equal weight. We took no notes, made no memoranda, measured none of the yards, ascertained the exact number of inches in no particular room; are unable even to report of how many apartments the gaol is composed.

We saw the prison, and saw the prisoners; and what we did see, and what we thought, we will tell at once in our own way.

Having delivered our credentials to the servant who answered our knock at the door of the governor's house, we were ushered into the "office;" a little room, on the right-hand side as you enter, with two windows looking into the Old Bailey, fitted up like an ordinary attorney's office, or merchant's counting-house, with the usual fixtures—a wainscoted partition, a shelf or two, a desk, a couple of stools, a pair of clerks, an almanac, a clock, and a few maps. After a little delay, occasioned by sending into the interior of the prison for the officer whose duty it was to conduct us, that functionary arrived; a respectable-looking man of about two or three and fifty, in a broad-brimmed hat, and full suit of black, who, but for his keys, would have looked quite as much like a clergyman as a turnkey: we were quite disappointed; he had not even top-boots on. Following our conductor by a door opposite to that at which we had entered, we arrived at a small room, without any other furniture than a little desk, with a book for visitors' autographs, and a shelf, on which were a few boxes for papers, and casts of the heads and faces of the two notorious murderers, Bishop and Williams; the former, in particular, exhibiting a style of head and set of features, which would have afforded sufficient moral grounds for his instant execution at any time, even had there been no other evidence against him. Leaving this room also by an opposite door, we found ourself in the lodge which opens on the Old Bailey, one side of which is plentifully garnished with a choice collection of heavy sets of irons, including those worn by the redoubtable Jack Sheppard—genuine; and those *said* to have been graced by the sturdy limbs of the no less celebrated Dick Turpin—doubtful. From this lodge a heavy oaken gate, bound with iron, studded with nails of the same material, and guarded by another turnkey, opens on a few steps, if we remember right, which terminate in a narrow and dismal stone passage, running parallel with the Old Bailey, and leading to the different yards, through a number of tortuous and intricate windows, guarded in their turn by huge gates and gratings, whose appearance is sufficient to dispel at once the slightest hope of escape that any new-comer may have entertained; and the very recollection of which, on eventually traversing the place again, involves one in a maze of confusion.

It is necessary to explain here, that the buildings in the prison, or in other words the different wards—form a square of which the four sides abut respectively on the Old Bailey, the old College of Physicians (now forming a part of Newgate Market), the Sessions House and Newgate Street. The intermediate space is divided into several paved yards, in which the prisoners take such air and exercise as can be had in such a place. These yards, with the exception of that in which prisoners under sentence of death are confined (of which we shall presently give a more detailed description), run parallel with Newgate Street and consequently from the Old Bailey, as it were, to Newgate Market. The women's side is in the right wing of the prison nearest the Sessions House; and as we were introduced into this part of the building first, we will adopt the same order, and introduce our readers to it also.

Turning to the right, then, down the passage to which we just now adverted, omitting any mention of intervening gates —for if we noticed every gate that was unlocked for us to pass through, and locked again as soon as we had passed, we should require a gate at every comma—we came to a door composed of thick bars of wood, through which were discernible, passing to and fro in a narrow yard, some twenty women, the majority of whom, however, as soon as they were aware of the presence of strangers, retreated to their wards One side of this yard is railed off at a considerable distance, and formed into a kind of iron cage, about five feet ten inches in height, roofed at the top, and defended in front by iron bars, from which the friends of the female prisoners communicate with them. In one corner of this singular-looking den was a yellow, haggard, decrepit old woman, in a tattered gown that had once been black, and the remains of an old straw bonnet, with faded ribbon of the same hue, in earnest conversation with a young girl—a prisoner of course—of about two-and-twenty. It is impossible to imagine a more poverty-stricken object, or a creature so borne down in soul and body, by excess of misery and destitution. The girl was a good-looking robust female, with a profusion of hair streaming about in the wind—for she had no bonnet on—and a man's silk pocket-handkerchief was loosely thrown over a most ample pair of shoulders. The old woman was talking in that low, stifled tone of voice which tells so forcibly of mental anguish; and every now and then burst into an irrepressible sharp, abrupt cry of grief, the most distressing sound that human ears can hear. The girl was perfectly unmoved. Hardened beyond all hope of redemption, she listened doggedly to her mother's entreaties, whatever they were: and, beyond inquiring after "Jem," and eagerly catching at the few halfpence her miserable parent had brought her, took no more apparent interest in the conversation than the most unconcerned spectators. God knows there were enough of them in the persons of the other prisoners in the yard, who were no more concerned by what was passing before their eyes, and within their hearing, than if they were blind and deaf. Why should they be? Inside the prison, and out, such scenes were too familiar to them, to excite even a passing thought, unless of ridicule or contempt for the display of feelings which they had long since forgotten, and lost all sympathy for.

A little farther on, a squalid-looking woman in a slovenly, thick-bordered cap, with her arms muffled up in a large red shawl, the fringed ends of which straggled nearly to the bottom of a dirty white apron, was communicating some instructions to *her* visitor—her daughter evidently. The girl was thinly clad, and shaking with the cold. Some ordinary word of recognition passed between her and her mother when she appeared at the grating, but neither hope, condolence, regret, nor affection was expressed on either side. The mother whispered her instructions, and the girl received them with her pinched-up half-starved features twisted into an expression of careful cunning. It was some scheme for the woman's defence that she was disclosing; and a sullen smile came over the girl's face for an instant, as if she were pleased, not so much at the probability of her mother's liberation, as at the chance of her "getting off" in spite of her prosecutors. The dialogue was soon concluded; and with the same careless indifference with which they had approached each other, the mother turned towards the inner end of the yard, and the girl to the gate at which she had entered.

The girl belonged to a class—unhappily but too extensive—the very existence of which should make men's hearts bleed. Barely past her childhood, it required but a glance to discover that she was one of those children born and bred in poverty and vice, who have never known what childhood is; who have never been taught to love and court a parent's smile, or to dread a parent's frown. The thousand nameless endearments of childhood, its gaiety and its innocence, are alike unknown to them. They have entered at once upon the stern realities and miseries of life, and to their better nature it is almost hopeless to appeal in aftertimes, by any of the references which will awaken, if it be only for a moment, some good feeling in ordinary bosoms, however corrupt they may have become. Talk to them of parental solicitude, the happy days of childhood, and the merry games of infancy! Tell them of hunger and the streets, beggary and stripes, the ginshop, the station-house, and the pawnbroker's, and they will understand you.

Two or three women were standing at different parts of the grating conversing with their friends, but a very large proportion of the prisoners appeared to have no friends at all, beyond such of their old companions as might happen to be within the walls. So, passing hastily down the yard, and pausing only for an instant to notice the little incidents we have just recorded, we were conducted up a clean and well-lighted flight of stone stairs to one of the wards. There are several in this part of the building, but a description of one is a description of the whole.

It was a spacious, bare, whitewashed apartment, lighted, of course, by windows looking into the interior of the prison, but far more light and airy than one could reasonably expect to find in such a situation. There was a large fire with a deal table before it, round which ten or a dozen women were seated on wooden forms at dinner. Along both sides of the room ran a shelf; and below it, at regular intervals, a row of large hooks were fixed in the wall, on each of which was hung the sleeping mat of a prisoner; her rug and blanket being folded up, and placed on the shelf above. At night these mats are placed on the floor, each beneath the hook on which it hangs during the day; and the ward is thus made to answer the purposes both of a day-room and sleeping apartment. Over the fireplace was a large sheet of pasteboard, on which were displayed a variety of texts from Scripture, which were also scattered about the room in scraps about the size and shape of the copy-slips which are used in schools. On the table was a sufficient provision of a kind of stewed beef, and brown bread, in pewter dishes, which are kept perfectly bright, and displayed on shelves in great order and regularity when they are not in use.

The women rose hastily on our entrance, and retired in a hurried manner to either side of the fireplace. They were all cleanly—many of them decently—attired, and there was nothing peculiar either in their appearance or demeanour. One or two resumed the needlework which they had probably laid aside at the commencement of their meal, others gazed at the visitors with listless curiosity, and a few retired behind their companions to the very end of the room, as if desirous to avoid even the casual observation of the strangers. Some old Irish women, both in this and other wards, to whom the thing was no novelty, appeared perfectly indifferent to our presence, and remained standing close to the seats from which they had just risen; but the general feeling among the females seemed to be one of uneasiness during the period of our stay among them, which was very brief. Not a word was uttered during the time of our remaining, unless indeed by the wardswoman in reply to some question which we put to the turnkey who accompanied us. In every ward on the female side a wardswoman is appointed to preserve order, and a similar regulation is adopted among the males. The wardsmen and wardswomen are all prisoners, selected for good conduct. They alone are allowed the privilege of sleeping on bedsteads; a small stump bedstead being placed in every ward for that purpose. On both sides of the gaol is a small receiving-room to which prisoners are conducted on their first reception, and whence they cannot be removed until they have been examined by the surgeon of the prison.*

Retracing our steps to the dismal passage in which we found ourselves at first (and which, by-the-by, contains three or four dark cells for the accommodation of refractory prisoners), we were led through a narrow yard to the "school"—a portion of the prison set apart for boys under fourteen years of age. In a tolerable-sized room, in which were writing-materials and some copy-books, was the schoolmaster, with a couple of his pupils; the remainder having been fetched from an adjoining apartment, the whole were drawn up in line for our inspection. There were fourteen of them in all, some with shoes, some without; some in pinafores without jackets, others in jackets without pinafores, and one in scarce anything at all. The whole number, without an exception we believe, had been committed for trial on charges of pocket-picking; and fourteen such villainous little faces we never beheld.—There was not one redeeming feature among them—not a glance of honesty—not a wink expressive of anything but the gallows and the hulks, in the whole collection. As to anything like shame or contrition, that was entirely out of the question. They were evidently quite gratified at being thought worth the trouble of looking at; their idea appeared to be that we had come to see Newgate as a grand affair, and that they were an indispensable part of the show: and every boy as he "fell in" to the line, actually seemed as pleased and important as if he had done something excessively meritorious in getting there at all. We never looked upon a more disagreeable sight, because we never saw fourteen such hopeless and irreclaimable wretches before.

On either side of the school-yard is a yard for men, in one of which—that towards Newgate Street—prisoners of the more respectable class are confined. Of the other we have little description to offer, as the different wards necessarily partake of the same character. They are provided, like the

* The regulations of the prison relative to the confinement of prisoners during the day, their sleeping at night, their taking their meals, and other matters of gaol economy, have been all altered—greatly for the better—since this sketch was written three years ago

wards on the women's side, with mats and rugs, which are disposed of in the same manner during the day; and the only very striking difference between their appearance and that of the wards inhabited by the females, is the utter absence of any employment whatever. Huddled together upon two opposite forms, by the fireside, sit twenty men perhaps; here a boy in livery, there a man in a rough great-coat and top-boots; further on, a desperate-looking fellow in his shirt sleeves, with an old Scotch cap upon his shaggy head; near him again, a tall ruffian, in a smock-frock, and next to him a miserable being of distressed appearance, with his head resting on his hand;—but all alike in one respect, all idle and listless: when they do leave the fire, sauntering moodily about, lounging in the window, or leaning against the wall, vacantly swinging their bodies to and fro. With the exception of a man reading an old newspaper in two or three instances, this was the case in every ward we entered.

The only communication these men have with their friends is through two close iron gratings, with an intermediate space of about a yard in width between the two, so that nothing can be handed across, nor can the prisoner have any communication by touch with the person who visits him. The married men have a separate grating, at which to see their wives, but its construction is the same.

The prison chapel is situated at the back of the governor's house, the latter having no windows looking into the interior of the prison. Whether the associations connected with the place—that knowledge that here a portion of the burial service is, on some dreadful occasions, performed over the quick and not upon the dead—cast over it a still more gloomy and sombre air than art has imparted to it, we know not, but its appearance is very striking. There is something in a silent and deserted place of worship highly solemn and impressive at any time; and the very dissimilarity of this one from any we have been accustomed to, only enhances the impression. The meanness of its appointments—the bare and scanty pulpit, with the paltry painted pillars on either side—the women's gallery with its great heavy curtain, the men's with its unpainted benches and dingy front—the tottering little table at the altar, with the commandments on the wall above it, scarcely legible through lack of paint, and dust and damp—so unlike the rich velvet and gilding, the stately marble and polished wood, of a modern church—are the more striking from their powerful contrast. There is one object, too, which rivets the attention and fascinates the gaze, and from which we may turn disgusted and horror-stricken in vain, for the recollection of it will haunt us, waking and sleeping, for months afterwards. Immediately below the reading-desk, on the floor of the chapel and forming the most conspicuous object in its little area, is *the condemned pew*; a huge black pen, in which the wretched men, who are singled out for death, are placed, on the Sunday preceding their execution, in sight of all their fellow-prisoners, from many of whom they may have been separated but a week before, to hear prayers for their own souls, to join in the responses of their own burial service, and to listen to an address, warning their recent companions to take example by their fate, and urging themselves, while there is yet time—nearly four-and-twenty hours—to "turn and flee from the wrath to come!" Imagine what have been the feelings of the men whom that fearful pew has enclosed, and of whom, between the gallows and the knife, no mortal remnant may now remain; think of the hopeless clinging to life to the last, and the wild despair, far exceeding in anguish the felon's death itself, by which they have heard the certainty of their speedy transmission to another world, with all their crimes upon their heads, rung into their ears by the officiating clergyman!

At one time—and at no distant period either—the coffins of the men about to be executed, were placed in that pew, upon the seat by their side, during the whole service. It may seem incredible, but it is strictly true. Let us hope that the increased spirit of civilisation and humanity which abolished this frightful and degrading custom, may extend itself to other usages equally barbarous; usages which have not even the plea of utility in their defence, as every year's experience has shown them to be more and more inefficacious.

Leaving the chapel, descending to the passage so frequently alluded to, and crossing the yard before noticed as being allotted to prisoners of a more respectable description than the generality of men confined here, the visitor arrives at a thick iron gate of great size and strength. Having been admitted through it by the turnkey on duty, he turns sharp round to the left, and pauses before another gate; and, having passed this last barrier, he stands in the most terrible part of this gloomy building—the condemned ward.

The press-yard, well known by name to newspaper readers, from its frequent mention (formerly, thank God!) in accounts of executions, is at the corner of the building, and next to the ordinary's house, in Newgate Street; running from Newgate Street, towards the centre of the prison, parallel with Newgate Market. It is a long, narrow court of which a portion of the wall in Newgate Street forms one end, and the gate the other. At the upper end, on the left-hand—that is, adjoining the wall in Newgate Street—is a cistern of water, and at the bottom a double grating (of which the gate itself forms a part) similar to that before described. Through these grates the prisoners are allowed to see their friends, a turnkey always remaining in the vacant space between, during the whole interview. Immediately on the right as you enter, is a building containing the press-room, day-room, and cells; the yard is on every side surrounded by lofty walls guarded by *chevaux de frise*; and the whole is under the constant inspection of vigilant and experienced turnkeys.

In the first apartment into which we were conducted—which was at the top of a staircase, and immediately over the press-room—were five-and-twenty or thirty prisoners, all under sentence of death, awaiting the result of the Recorder's report—men of all ages and appearances, from a hardened old offender with swarthy face and grizzly beard of three days' growth, to a handsome boy, not fourteen years old, of singularly youthful appearance even for that age, who had been condemned for burglary. There was nothing remarkable in the appearance of these prisoners. One or two decently-dressed men were brooding with a dejected air over the fire; several little groups of two or three had been engaged in conversation at the upper end of the room, or in the windows; and the remainder were crowded round a young man seated at a table, who appeared to be engaged in teaching the younger ones to write. The room was large, airy, and clean. There was very little anxiety or mental suffering depicted in the countenance of any of the men; —they had all been sentenced to death, it is true, and the Recorder's report had not yet been made; but we question whether there was a man among them, notwithstanding, who did not *know* that although he had undergone the ceremony, it never was intended that his life should be sacrificed. On the table lay a Testament, but there were no signs of its having been in recent use.

In the press-room below, were three men, the nature of whose offence rendered it necessary to separate them, even from their companions in guilt. It is a long, sombre room, with two windows sunk into the stone wall, and here the wretched men are pinioned on the morning of their execution, before moving towards the scaffold. The fate of one of these men was uncertain; some mitigatory circumstances having come to light since his trial, which had been humanely represented in the proper quarter. The other two had nothing to expect from the mercy of the Crown; their doom was sealed; no plea could be urged in extenuation of their crime, and they well knew that for them there was no hope in this world. "The two short ones," the turnkey whispered, "were dead men."

The man to whom we have alluded as entertaining some hopes of escape, was lounging at the greatest distance he could place between himself and his companions, in the window nearest the door. He was probably aware of our approach, and had assumed an air of courageous indifference; his face was purposely averted towards the window, and he stirred not an inch while we were present. The other two men were at the upper end of the room. One of them, who was imperfectly seen in the dim light, had his back towards us, and was stooping over the fire with his right arm on the mantelpiece, and his head sunk upon it. The other was leaning on the sill of the farthest window. The light fell full upon him, and communicated to his pale, haggard face, and disordered hair, an appearance which, at that distance, was perfectly ghastly. His cheek rested upon his hand; and, with his face a little raised, and his eyes widely staring before him, he seemed to be unconsciously intent on counting the chinks in the opposite wall. We passed this room again afterwards. The first man was pacing up and down the court with a firm military step—he had been a soldier in the footguards—and a cloth cap jauntily thrown on one side of the head. He bowed respectfully to our conductor, and the salute was returned. The other two still remained in the positions we have described, and were motionless as statues.*

A few paces up the yard, and forming a continuation of the building, in which are the two rooms we have just quitted, lie the condemned cells. The entrance is by a narrow and obscure staircase leading to a dark passage, in which a charcoal stove casts a lurid tint over the objects in its immediate vicinity, and diffuses something like warmth around. From the left-hand side of this passage, the massive door of every cell on the storey opens, and from it alone can they be approached. There are three of these passages, and three of these ranges of cells one above the other, but in size, furniture and appearance, they are all precisely alike. Prior to the Recorder's report being made, all the prisoners under sentence of death are removed from the day-room at five o'clock in the afternoon, and locked up in these cells where they are allowed a candle until ten o'clock, and here they remain until seven next morning. When the warrant for a prisoner's execution arrives, he is immediately removed to the cells and confined in one of them until he leaves it for the scaffold. He is at liberty to walk in the yard, but both in his walks and in his cell, he is constantly attended by a turnkey who never leaves him on any pretence whatever.

We entered the first cell. It was a stone dungeon, eight feet long by six wide, with a bench at the further end, under which were a common horse-rug, a Bible, and prayer-book. An iron candlestick was fixed into the wall at the side; and a small high window in the back admitted as much air and light as could struggle in between a double row of heavy,

* These two men were executed shortly afterwards. The other was respited during his Majesty's pleasure.

crossed iron bars. It contained no other furniture of any description.

Conceive the situation of a man, spending his last night on earth in this cell. Buoyed up with some vague and undefined hope of reprieve, he knew not why—indulging in some wild and visionary idea of escaping, he knew not how—hour after hour of the three preceding days allowed him for preparation, has fled with a speed which no man living would deem possible, for none but this dying man can know. He has wearied his friends with entreaties, exhausted the attendants with importunities, neglected in his feverish restlessness the timely warnings of his spiritual consoler; and now that the illusion is at last dispelled, now that eternity is before him and guilt behind, now that his fears of death amount almost to madness, and an overwhelming sense of his helpless, hopeless state rushes upon him he is lost and stupefied, and has neither thoughts to turn to, nor power to call upon, the Almighty Being, from whom alone he can seek mercy and forgiveness, and before whom his repentance can alone avail.

Hours have glided by, and still he sits upon the same stone bench with folded arms, heedless alike of the fast decreasing time before him, and the urgent entreaties of the good man at his side. The feeble light is wasting gradually, and the deathlike stillness of the street without, broken only by the rumbling of some passing vehicle which echoes mournfully through the empty yards, warns him that the night is waning fast away. The deep bell of St. Paul's strikes—one! He heard it; it has roused him. Seven hours left! He paces the narrow limits of his cell with rapid strides, cold drops of terror starting on his forehead, and every muscle of his frame quivering with agony. Seven hours! He suffers himself to be led to his seat, mechanically takes the Bible which is placed in his hand, and tries to read and listen. No: his thoughts will wander. The book is torn and soiled by use—and how like the book he read his lessons in at school just forty years ago! He has never bestowed a thought upon it since he left it as a child: and yet the place, the time, the room—nay, the very boys he played with, crowd as vividly before him as if they were scenes of yesterday; and some forgotten phrase, some childish word of kindness, rings in his ears like the echo of one uttered but a minute since. The deep voice of the clergyman recalls him to himself. He is reading from the sacred book its solemn promises of pardon for repentance, and its awful denunciation of obdurate men. He falls upon his knees and clasps his hands to pray. Hush! what sound was that? He starts upon his feet. It cannot be two yet. Hark! Two quarters have struck;—the third—the fourth. It is! Six hours left. Tell him not of repentance. Six hours' repentance for eight times six years of guilt and sin! He buries his face in his hands, and throws himself on the bench.

Worn with watching and excitement, he sleeps, and the same unsettled state of mind pursues him in his dreams. An insupportable load is taken from his breast; he is walking with his wife in a pleasant field, with the blue sky above them, and a fresh and boundless prospect on every side—how different from the stone walls of Newgate! She is looking—not as she did when he saw her for the last time in that dreadful place, but as she used when he loved her—long, long ago, before misery and ill-treatment had altered her looks, and vice had changed his nature, and she is leaning upon his arm, and looking up into his face with tenderness and affection —and he does *not* strike her now, nor rudely shake her from him. And oh! how glad he is to tell her all he had forgotten in that last hurried interview, and to fall on his knees before her and fervently beseech her pardon for all the unkindness and cruelty that wasted her form and broke her heart! The scene suddenly changes. He is on his trial again: there are the judge and jury, and prosecutors, and witnesses, just as they were before. How full the court is—what a sea of heads—with a gallows, too, and a scaffold—and how all those people stare at *him!* Verdict, "Guilty." No matter; he will escape.

The night is dark and cold, the gates have been left open, and in an instant he is in the street, flying from the scene of his imprisonment like the wind. The streets are cleared, the open fields are gained and the broad wide country lies before him. Onward he dashes in the midst of darkness, over hedge and ditch, through mud and pool, bounding from spot to spot with a speed and lightness, astonishing even to himself. At length he pauses: he must be safe from pursuit now; he will stretch himself on that bank and sleep till sunrise.

A period of unconsciousness succeeds. He wakes cold and wretched; the dull grey light of morning is stealing into the cell, and falls upon the form of the attendant turnkey. Confused by his dreams, he starts from his uneasy bed in momentary uncertainty. It is but momentary. Every object in that narrow cell is too frightfully real to admit of doubt or mistake. He is the condemned felon again, guilty and despairing; and in two hours more he is a corpse.

CHARACTERS

CHAPTER I: *Thoughts about People*

'TIS strange with how little notice, good, bad, or indifferent, a man may live and die in London. He awakens no sympathy in the breast of any single person; his existence is a matter of interest to no one save himself, and he cannot be said to be forgotten when he dies, for no one remembered him when he was alive. There is a very numerous class of people in this great metropolis who seem not to possess a single friend, and whom nobody appears to care for. Urged by imperative necessity in the first instance, they have resorted to London in search of employment, and the means of subsistence. It is hard, we know, to break the ties which bind us to our homes and friends, and harder still to efface the thousand recollections of happy days and old times, which have been slumbering in our bosoms for years, and only rush upon the mind to bring before it, with startling reality, associations connected with the friends we have left, the scenes we have beheld too probably for the last time, and the hopes we once cherished, but may entertain no more. These men, however, happily, for themselves, have long since forgotten such thoughts. Old country friends have died or emigrated; former correspondents have become lost, like themselves, in the crowd and turmoil of some busy city, and they have gradually settled down into mere passive creatures of habit and endurance.

We were seated in the enclosure of St. James's Park the other day, when our attention was attracted by a man whom we immediately put down in our own mind as one of this class. He was a tall, thin, pale person, in a black coat, scanty gray trousers, little pinched-up gaiters, and brown beaver gloves. He had an umbrella in his hand—not for use, for the day was fine—but evidently because he always carried one to the office in the morning; and he walked up and down before the little patch of grass on which the chairs are placed for hire, not as if he were doing it for pleasure or recreation, but as if it were a matter of compulsion, just as he would walk to the office every morning from the back settlements of Islington. It was Monday, he had escaped for four-and-twenty hours from the thraldom of the desk, and was walking here for exercise and amusement—perhaps for the first time in his life. We were inclined to think he had never had a holiday before, and that even now he did not know what to do with himself. Children were playing on the grass; groups of people were loitering about, chatting and laughing, but the man walked steadily up and down, unheeding and unheeded, his spare pale face looking as if it were incapable of bearing the expression of curiosity or interest.

There was something in the man's manner and appearance which told us, we fancied, his whole life, or rather his whole day, for a man of this sort has no variety. We almost saw the dingy little back office into which he walks every morning, hanging his hat on the same peg, and placing his legs beneath the same desk: first taking off that black coat which lasts the year through, and putting on the one which did duty last year, and which he keeps in his desk to save the other. There he sits till five o'clock, working on all day as regularly as the dial over the mantelpiece, whose loud ticking is as monotonous as his whole existence, only raising his head when some one enters the counting-house, or when, as in the midst of some difficult calculation, he looks up to the ceiling as if there were inspiration in the dusty skylight with a green knot in the centre of every pane of glass. About five, or half-past, he slowly dismounts from his accustomed stool, and again changing his coat, proceeds to his usual dining-place, somewhere near Bucklersbury. The waiter recites the bill of fare in a rather confidential manner—for he is a regular customer—and after inquiring "What's in the best cut?" and "What was up last?" he orders a small plate of roast beef, with green peas, and half-a-pint of porter. He has a small plate to-day, because greens are a penny more than potatoes, and he had "two breads" yesterday, with the additional enormity of "a cheese" the day before. This important point being settled, he hangs up his hat—he took it off the moment he sat down—and bespeaks the paper after the next gentleman. If he can get it while he is at dinner, he appears to eat it with much greater zest; balancing it against the water-bottle, and eating a bit of beef, and reading a line or two, alternately. Exactly at five minutes before the hour is up, he produces a shilling, pays the reckoning, carefully deposits the change in his waistcoat-pocket (first deducting a penny for the waiter), and returns to the office, from which, if it is not foreign post night, he again sallies forth in about half an hour. He then walks home, at his usual pace, to his little back room at Islington, where he has his tea; perhaps solacing himself during the meal with the conversation of his landlady's little boy, whom he occasionally rewards with a penny, for solving problems in simple addition. Sometimes there is a letter or two to take up to his employer's, in Russell Square; and then the wealthy man of business hearing his voice, calls out from the dining-parlour,—"Come in, Mr. Smith:" and Mr. Smith, putting his hat at the feet of one of the hall chairs, walks timidly in, and being condescendingly desired to sit down, carefully tucks his legs under his chair, and sits at a considerable distance from the table while he drinks the glass of sherry which is poured out for him by the eldest boy, and after drinking which, he backs and slides out of the room, in a state of nervous agitation from which he does not perfectly recover, until he finds himself once more in the Islington Road. Poor homeless creatures, these men are; contented but not happy; broken-spirited and humbled, they may feel no pain, but they never know pleasure.

Compare these men with another class of beings who, like them, have neither friend nor companion, but whose position in society is the result of their own choice. These are generally old fellows with white heads and red faces, addicted to port wine and Hessian boots, who from some cause, real or imaginary—generally the former, the excellent reason being that they are rich, and their relations poor—grow suspicious of everybody, and do the misanthropical in chambers, taking great delight in thinking themselves unhappy, and making everybody they come near, miserable. You may see such men as these anywhere; you will know them at coffee-houses by their discontented exclamations and the luxury of their dinners; at theatres, by their always sitting in the same place and looking with a jaundiced eye on all the young people near them; at church, by the pomposity with which they enter, and the loud tone in which they repeat the responses; at parties, by their getting cross at whist and hating music. An old fellow of this kind will have his chambers splendidly furnished, and collect books, plate, and pictures about him in profusion; not so much for his own gratification as to annoy those who have the desire, but not the means, to compete with him. He belongs to two or three clubs, and is envied, and flattered, and hated by the members of them all. Sometimes he will be appealed to by a poor relation—a married nephew perhaps—for some little assistance and relief: and then he will declaim with honest indignation on the improvidence of young married people, the worthlessness of a wife, the insolence of having a family, the atrocity of getting into debt with a hundred and twenty-five pounds a-year, and other unpardonable crimes; winding up his exhortations with a complacent review of his own conduct, and a delicate allusion to parochial relief. He dies some day after dinner of apoplexy, having bequeathed his property to a Bible Society, and the Institution erects a tablet to his memory expressive of their admiration of his Christian conduct in this world, and their comfortable conviction of his happiness in the next.

But next to our very particular friends, hackney-coachmen,

cabmen, and cads, whom we admire in proportion to the extent of their cool impudence and perfect self-possession, there is no class of people who amuse us more than London apprentices. They are no longer an organised body, bound down by solemn compact to terrify his Majesty's subjects whenever it pleases them to take offence in their heads and staves in their hands. They are only bound now by indentures; and as to their valour, it is easily restrained by the wholesome dread of the New Police, and a perspective view of a damp station-house, terminating in a police-office and a reprimand. They are still, however, a peculiar class, and not the less pleasant for being inoffensive. Can any one fail to have noticed them in the streets on Sunday? And were there ever such beautiful attempts at the grand and magnificent as they display in their own proper persons! We walked down the Strand a Sunday or two ago, behind a little group; and they furnished food for our amusement the whole way. They had come out of some part of the City; it was between three and four o'clock in the afternoon, and they were on their way to the Park. There were four of them, all arm-in-arm, with white kid gloves like so many bridegrooms, light trousers of unprecedented patterns, and coats for which the English language has yet no name—a kind of cross between a great-coat and a surtout, with the collar of the one, the skirts of the other, and pockets peculiar to themselves.

Each of the gentlemen carried a thick stick with a large tassel at the top which he occasionally twirled gracefully round, and the whole four, by way of looking easy and unconcerned, were walking with a sort of paralytic swagger irresistibly ludicrous. One of the party had got a watch about the size and shape of a Ribstone pippin, jammed into his waistcoat-pocket, which he carefully compared with the clocks at St. Clement's and the New Church, the illuminated clock at Exeter 'Change, St. Martin's Church, and the Horse Guards, and when they at last arrived in Saint James's Park, the member of the party who had the best-made boots on, hired a second chair expressly for his feet, and flung himself on this two-pennyworth of sylvan luxury with an air which levelled all distinctions between Brookes's and Snooks's, Crockford's and Bagnigge Wells.

We may smile at such people as these, but they can never excite our anger. They are usually on the best of terms with themselves, and it follows almost as a matter of course, in good humour with every one about them. And if they do display a little occasional foolery in their own proper persons, it is surely more tolerable than the precocious puppyism of the Quadrant, the whiskered dandyism of Regent Street and Pall Mall, or gallantry in its dotage anywhere.

CHAPTER II: *A Christmas Dinner*

CHRISTMAS time! The man must be a misanthrope indeed, in whose breast something like a jovial feeling is not roused—in whose mind some pleasant associations are not awakened by the recurrence of Christmas. There are people who will tell you that Christmas is not to them what it used to be: that each succeeding Christmas has found some cherished hope, or happy prospect, of the year before, dimmed or passed away, and that the present only serves to remind them of reduced circumstances and straitened incomes—of the feasts they once bestowed on hollow friends, and of the cold looks that meet them now, in adversity and misfortune. Never heed such dismal reminiscences. There are few men who have lived long enough in the world, who cannot call up such thoughts any day in the year. Then do not select the merriest of the three hundred and sixty-five, for your doleful recollections, but draw your chair nearer the blazing fire—fill the glass and send round the song—and if your room be smaller than it was a dozen years ago, or if your glass be filled with reeking punch, instead of sparkling wine, put a good face on the matter, and empty it off-hand, and fill another, and troll off the old ditty you used to sing, and thank God it's no worse. Look on the merry faces of your children as they sit round the fire. One little seat may be empty; one slight form that gladdened the father's heart, and roused the mother's pride to look upon, may not be there. Dwell not upon the past; think not that one short year ago, the fair child now resolving into dust, sat before you, with the bloom of health upon its cheek, and the gay unconsciousness of infancy in its joyous eye. Reflect upon your present blessings—of which every man has many—not on your past misfortunes, of which all men have some. Fill your glass again, with a merry face and contented heart. Our life on it, but your Christmas shall be merry, and your New Year a happy one.

Who can be insensible to the outpourings of good feeling, and the honest interchange of affectionate attachment, which abound at this season of the year? A Christmas family-party! We know nothing in nature more delightful! There seems a magic in the very name of Christmas. Petty jealousies and discords are forgotten: social feelings are awakened in bosoms to which they have long been strangers: father and son, or brother and sister, who have met and passed with averted gaze, or a look of cold recognition, for months before, proffer and return the cordial embrace, and bury their past animosities in their present happiness. Kindly hearts that have yearned towards each other, but have been withheld by false notions of pride and self-dignity, are again reunited, and all is kindness and benevolence! Would that Christmas lasted the whole year through, and that the prejudices and passions which deform our better nature, were never called into action among those to whom they should ever be strangers!

The Christmas family-party that we mean, is not a mere assemblage of relations, got up at a week or two's notice, originating this year, having no family precedent in the last, and not likely to be repeated in the next. It is an annual gathering of all the accessible members of the family, young or old, rich or poor; and all the children look forward to it, for two months beforehand, in a fever of anticipation. Formerly it was held at grandpapa's; but grandpapa getting old, and grandmamma getting old too, and rather infirm, they have given up housekeeping, and domesticated themselves with uncle George, so the party always takes place at uncle George's house, but grandmamma sends in most of the good things, and grandpapa always *will* toddle down, all the way to Newgate Market, to buy the turkey, which he engages a porter to bring home behind him in triumph, always insisting on the man's being rewarded with a glass of spirits, over and above his hire, to drink "a merry Christmas and a happy New Year" to aunt George. As to grandmamma, she is very secret and mysterious for two or three days beforehand, but not sufficiently so to prevent rumours getting afloat that she has purchased a beautiful new cap with pink ribbons for each of the servants, together with sundry books, and penknives, and pencil-cases, for the younger branches; to say nothing of divers secret additions to the order originally given by aunt George at the pastrycook's, such as another dozen of mince-pies for the dinner, and a large plum-cake for the children.

On Christmas-eve, grandmamma is always in excellent spirits, and after employing all the children, during the day, in stoning the plums and all that, insists regularly every year on uncle George coming down into the kitchen, taking off his coat, and stirring the pudding for half an hour or so, which uncle George good-humouredly does, to the vociferous delight of the children and servants, and the evening concludes with a glorious game of blind-man's-buff, in an early stage of which grandpapa takes great care to be caught, in order that he may have an opportunity of displaying his dexterity.

On the following morning, the old couple, with as many of the children as the pew will hold, go to church in great state, leaving aunt George at home dusting decanters and filling castors, and uncle George carrying bottles into the dining-parlour, and calling for corkscrews, and getting into everybody's way.

When the church-party return to lunch, grandpapa produces a small sprig of mistletoe from his pocket, and tempts the boys to kiss their little cousins under it—a proceeding which affords both the boys and the old gentleman unlimited satisfaction, but which rather outrages grandmamma's ideas of decorum, until grandpapa says, that when he was just thirteen years and three months old, *he* kissed grandmamma under a mistletoe too, on which the children clap their hands, and laugh very heartily, as do aunt George and uncle George; and grandmamma looks pleased, and says, with a benevolent smile, that grandpapa always was an impudent dog, on which the children laugh very heartily again, and grandpapa more heartily than any of them.

But all these diversions are nothing to the subsequent excitement when grandmamma in a high cap, and slate-coloured silk gown, and grandpapa with a beautifully plaited shirt-frill, and white neckerchief, seat themselves on one side of the drawing-room fire, with uncle George's children and little cousins innumerable, seated in the front, waiting the arrival of the anxiously expected visitors. Suddenly a hackney-coach is heard to stop, and uncle George, who has been looking out of the window, exclaims "Here's Jane!" on which the children rush to the door, and helter-skelter down-stairs; and uncle Robert and aunt Jane, and the dear little baby, and the nurse, and the whole party, are ushered up-stairs amidst tumultuous shouts of "Oh, my!" from the children, and frequently repeated warnings not to hurt baby from the nurse: and grandpapa takes the child, and grandmamma kisses her daughter, and the confusion of this first entry has scarcely subsided, when some other aunts and uncles with more cousins arrive, and the grown-up cousins flirt with each other, and so do the little cousins too, for that matter, and nothing is to be heard but a confused din of talking, laughing, and merriment.

A hesitating double-knock at the street-door, heard during a momentary pause in the conversation, excites a general inquiry of "Who's that?" and two or three children, who have been standing at the window, announce in a low voice, that it's "poor aunt Margaret." Upon which aunt George leaves the room to welcome the new-comer, and grandmamma draws herself up rather stiff and stately, for Margaret married a poor man without her consent, and poverty not being a sufficiently weighty punishment for her offence, has been discarded by her friends, and debarred the society of her dearest relatives. But Christmas has come round, and the unkind feelings that have struggled against better dispositions during the year, have melted away before its genial influence, like half-formed ice beneath the morning sun. It is not difficult in a moment of angry feeling for a parent to denounce a disobedient child; but to banish her at a period of general goodwill and hilarity, from the hearth round which she has s..t on so many anniversaries of the same day, expanding by slow degrees from infancy to girlhood, and then bursting, almost imperceptibly, into the high-spirited and beautiful woman, is widely different. The air of conscious rectitude, and cold forgiveness, which the old lady has assumed, sits ill upon her; and when the poor girl is led in by her sister, pale in looks and broken in spirit—not from poverty, for that she could bear, but from the consciousness of undeserved neglect and unmerited unkindness—it is easy to see how much of it is assumed. A momentary pause succeeds; the girl breaks suddenly from her sister and throws herself, sobbing, on her mother's neck. The father steps hastily forward, and grasps her husband's hand. Friends crowd round to offer their hearty congratulations, and happiness and harmony again prevail.

As to the dinner, it's perfectly delightful—nothing goes wrong, and everybody is in the very best of spirits, and disposed to please and be pleased. Grandpapa relates a circumstantial account of the purchase of the turkey, with a slight digression relative to the purchase of previous turkeys, on former Christmas-days, which grandmamma corroborates in the minutest particular. Uncle George tells stories, and carves poultry, and takes wine, and jokes with the children at the side-table, and winks at the cousins that are making love, or being made love to, and exhilarates everybody with his good humour and hospitality; and when at last a stout servant staggers in with a gigantic pudding, with a sprig of holly in the top, there is such a laughing, and shouting, and clapping of little chubby hands, and kicking up of fat dumpy legs, as can only be equalled by the applause with which the astonishing feat of pouring lighted brandy into mince-pies, is received by the younger visitors. Then the desert!—and the wine!—and the fun! Such beautiful speeches, and *such* songs, from aunt Margaret's husband, who turns out to be such a nice man, and *so* attentive to grandmamma! Even grandpapa not only sings his annual song with unprecedented vigour, but on being honoured with an unanimous *encore*, according to annual custom, actually comes out with a new one which nobody but grandmamma ever heard before: and a young scape-grace of a cousin, who has been in some disgrace with the old people, for certain heinous sins of omission and commission—neglecting to call, and persisting in drinking Burton Ale—astonishes everybody into convulsions of laughter by volunteering the most extraordinary comic songs that were ever heard. And thus the evening passes, in a strain of rational good-will and cheerfulness, doing more to awaken the sympathies of every member of the party in behalf of his neighbour, and to perpetuate their good feeling during the ensuing year, than all the homilies that have ever been written, by all the divines that have ever lived.

CHAPTER III: *The New Year*

NEXT to Christmas-day, the most pleasant annual epoch in existence is the advent of the New Year. There are a lachrymose set of people who usher in the New Year with watching and fasting, as if they were bound to attend as chief mourners at the obsequies of the old one. Now, we cannot but think it a great deal more complimentary, both to the old year that has rolled away, and to the New Year that is just beginning to dawn upon us, to see the old fellow out, and the new one in, with gaiety and glee.

There must have been some few occurrences in the past year to which we can look back with a smile of cheerful recollection, if not with a feeling of heartfelt thankfulness. And we are bound by every rule of justice and equity to give the New Year credit for being a good one, until he proves himself unworthy the confidence we repose in him.

This is our view of the matter; and entertaining it, notwithstanding our respect for the old year, one of the few remaining moments of whose existence passes away with every word we write, here we are, seated by our fireside on this last night of the old year, one thousand eight hundred and thirty-six, penning this article with as jolly a face as if nothing extraordinary had happened, or was about to happen, to disturb our equanimity.

Hackney-coaches and carriages keep rattling up the street and down the street in rapid succession, conveying, doubtless, smartly-dressed coachfuls to crowded parties; loud and repeated double-knocks at the house with green blinds, opposite, announce to the whole neighbourhood that there's one large party in the street at all events; and we saw through the window, and through the fog too, till it grew so thick that we rang for candles, and drew our curtains, pastry-cooks' men with green boxes on their heads, and rout-furniture-warehouse-carts, with cane seats and French lamps, hurrying to the numerous houses where an annual festival is held in honour of the occasion.

We can fancy one of these parties, we think, as well as if we were duly dress-coated and pumped, and had just been announced at the drawing-room door.

Take the house with green blinds for instance. We know it is a quadrille party, because we saw a man taking up the front drawing-room carpet while we sat at breakfast this morning, and if further evidence be required, and we must tell the truth, we just now saw one of the young ladies "doing" another of the young ladies' hair, near one of the bedroom windows, in an unusual style of splendour, which nothing else but a quadrille party could possibly justify.

The master of the house with the green blinds is in a public office; we know the fact by the cut of his coat, the tie of his neckcloth, and the self-satisfaction of his gait—the very green blinds themselves have a Somerset House air about them.

Hark!—a cab! That's a junior clerk in the same office; a tidy sort of young man, with a tendency to cold and corns, who comes in a pair of boots with black cloth fronts, and brings his shoes in his coat-pocket, which shoes he is at this very moment putting on in the hall. Now he is announced by the man in the passage to another man in a blue coat, who is a disguised messenger from the office.

The man on the first landing precedes him to the drawing-room door. "Mr. Tupple!" shouts the messenger. "How are you, Tupple?" says the master of the house, advancing from the fire, before which he has been talking politics and airing himself. "My dear, this is Mr. Tupple (a courteous salute from the lady of the house); Tupple, my eldest daughter; Julia, my dear, Mr. Tupple; Tupple, my other daughters; my son, sir;" Tupple rubs his hands very hard, and smiles as if it were all capital fun, and keeps constantly bowing and turning himself round, till the whole family have been intro-duced, when he glides into a chair, at the corner of the sofa, and opens a miscellaneous conversation with the young ladies upon the weather, and the theatres, and the old year, and the last new murder, and the balloon, and the ladies' sleeves, and the festivities of the season, and a great many other topics of small talk beside.

More double-knocks! what an extensive party; what an incessant hum of conversation and general sipping of coffee! We see Tupple now, in our mind's eye, in the very height of his glory. He has just handed that stout old lady's cup to the servant, and now he dives among the crowd of young men by the door, to intercept the other servant, and secure the muffin-plate for the old lady's daughter, before he leaves the room; and as he passes the sofa on his way back, he bestows a glance of recognition and patronage upon the young ladies, as condescending and familiar as if he had known them from their infancy.

Charming person that Mr. Tupple—perfect ladies' man— such a delightful companion, too. Laugh!—nobody ever understood papa's jokes half so well as Mr. Tupple, who laughs himself into convulsions at every fresh burst of facetiousness. Most delightful partner! talks through the whole set; and although he does seem at first rather gay and

frivolous, so romantic and with so *much* feeling! Quite a
love. No great favourite with the young men, certainly, who
sneer at, and affect to despise him; but everybody knows
that's only envy, and they needn't give themselves the trouble
to depreciate his merits at any rate, for Ma says he shall be
asked to every future dinner-party, if it's only to talk to
people between the courses, and to distract their attention
when there's any unexpected delay in the kitchen.

At supper, Mr. Tupple shows to still greater advantage than
he has done throughout the evening, and when Pa requests
every one to fill their glasses for the purpose of drinking
happiness throughout the year, Mr. Tupple is *so* droll, insisting
on all the young ladies having their glasses filled, notwithstanding their repeated assurances that they never can, by
any possibility, think of emptying them: and subsequently
begging permission to say a few words on the sentiment which
has just been uttered by Pa, when he makes one of the most
brilliant and poetical speeches that can possibly be imagined,
about the old year and new one. After the toast has been
drunk, and when the ladies have retired, Mr. Tupple requests
that every gentleman will do him the favour of filling his
glass, for he has a toast to propose: on which all the gentlemen cry "Hear! hear!" and pass the decanters accordingly:
and Mr. Tupple being informed by the master of the house
that they are all charged, and waiting for his toast, rises,
and begs to remind the gentlemen present, how much they
have been delighted by the dazzling array of elegance and
beauty which the drawing-room has exhibited that night,
and how their senses have been charmed, and their hearts
captivated, by the bewitching concentration of female loveli-
ness which that very room has so recently displayed. Loud
cries of "Hear!") Much as he (Tupple) would be disposed to
deplore the absence of the ladies, on other grounds, he cannot
but derive some consolation from the reflection that the very
circumstance of their not being present, enables him to propose a toast, which he would have otherwise been prevented
from giving—that toast he begs to say is—"The Ladies!"
(Great applause.) The Ladies; among whom the fascinating
daughters of their excellent host, are alike conspicuous for
their beauty, their accomplishments, and their elegance. He
begs them to drain a bumper to "The Ladies, and a happy
New Year to them!" (Prolonged approbation; above which
the noise of the ladies dancing the Spanish dance among
themselves, overhead, is distinctly audible.)

The applause consequent on this toast has scarcely subsided,
when a young gentleman in a pink under-waistcoat, sitting
towards the bottom of the table, is observed to grow very
restless and fidgety, and to evince strong indications of some
latent desire to give vent to his feelings in a speech, which

the wary Tupple at once perceiving, determines to forestall by speaking himself. He, therefore, rises again with an air of solemn importance, and trusts he may be permitted to propose another toast (unqualified approbation, and Mr. Tupple proceeds): he is sure they must all be deeply impressed with the hospitality—he may say the splendour—with which they have been that night received by their worthy host and hostess. (Unbounded applause.) Although this is the first occasion on which he has had the pleasure and delight of sitting at that board, he has known his friend Dobble long and intimately; he has been connected with him in business —he wishes everybody present knew Dobble as well as he does. (A cough from the host.) He (Tupple) can lay his hand upon his (Tupple's) heart, and declare his confident belief that a better man, a better husband, a better father, a better brother, a better son, a better relation in any relation of life, than Dobble, never existed. (Loud cries of "Hear!") They have seen him to-night in the peaceful bosom of his family: they should see him in the morning, in the trying duties of his office. Calm in the perusal of the morning papers, uncompromising in the signature of his name, dignified in his replies to the inquiries of stranger applicants, deferential in his behaviour to his superiors, majestic in his deportment to the messengers. (Cheers.) When he bears this merited testimony to the excellent qualities of his friend Dobble, what can he say in approaching such a subject as Mrs. Dobble? Is it requisite for him to expatiate on the qualities of that amiable woman? No; he will spare his friend Dobble's feelings; he will spare the feelings of his friend if he will allow him to have the honour of calling him so—Mr. Dobble, junior. (Here Mr. Dobble, junior, who has been previously distending his mouth to a considerable width, by thrusting a particularly fine orange into that feature, suspends operations, and assumes a proper appearance of intense melancholy.) He will simply say—and he is quite certain it is a sentiment in which all who hear him will readily concur—that his friend Dobble is as superior to any man he ever knew, as Mrs. Dobble is far beyond any woman he ever saw (except her daughters), and he will conclude by proposing their worthy "Host and Hostess, and may they live to enjoy many more New Years."

The toast is drunk with acclamation; Dobble returns thanks, and the whole party rejoin the ladies in the drawing-room. Young men who were too bashful to dance before supper, find tongues and partners; the musicians exhibit unequivocal symptoms of having drunk the New Year in, while the company were out; and dancing is kept up, until far in the first morning of the New Year.

We have scarcely written the last word of the previous sentence, when the first stroke of twelve, peals from the neighbouring churches. There is something awful in the sound. Strictly speaking, it may not be more impressive now, than at any other time; for the hours steal as swiftly on at other periods, and their flight is little heeded. But we measure man's life by years, and it is a solemn knell that warns us we have passed another of the landmarks which stand between us and the grave; disguise it as we may, the reflection will force itself on our minds, that when the next bell announces the arrival of a new year, we may be insensible alike of the timely warning we have so often neglected, and of all the warm feelings that glow within us now.

CHAPTER IV: *Miss Evans and the Eagle*

MR. SAMUEL WILKINS was a carpenter, a journeyman carpenter of small dimensions; decidedly below the middle size—bordering, perhaps, upon the dwarfish. His face was round and shining, and his hair carefully twisted into the outer corner of each eye, till it formed a variety of that description of semi-curls, usually known as "haggerawators." His earnings were all-sufficient for his wants, varying from eighteen shillings to one pound five, weekly; his manner undeniable—his Sabbath waistcoats dazzling. No wonder that, with these qualifications, Samuel Wilkins found favour in the eyes of the other sex; many women have been captivated by far less substantial qualifications. But Samuel was proof against their blandishments, until at length his eyes rested on those of a being for whom, from that time forth, he felt fate had destined him. He came, and conquered—proposed, and was accepted—loved, and was beloved. Mr. Wilkins "kept company" with Jemima Evans.

Miss Evans (or Ivins, to adopt the pronunciation most in vogue with her circle of acquaintance) had adopted in early life the harmless pursuit of shoe-binding, to which she had afterwards superadded the occupation of a straw-bonnet maker. Herself, her maternal parent, and two sisters, formed an harmonious quartet in the most secluded portion of Camden Town; and here it was that Mr. Wilkins presented himself one Monday afternoon in his best attire, with his face more shining and his waistcoat more bright than either had ever appeared before. The family were just going to tea, and were *so* glad to see him. It was quite a little feast; two ounces of seven-and-sixpenny green, and a quarter of a pound of the best fresh; and Mr. Wilkins had brought a pint of shrimps, neatly folded up in a clean Belcher, to give a zest to the meal, and propitiate Mrs. Ivins. Jemima was "cleaning herself" up-stairs; so Mr. Samuel Wilkins sat down and talked domestic economy with Mrs. Ivins, whilst the two youngest Miss Ivinses

poked bits of lighted brown paper between the bars under
the kettle, to make the water boil for tea.

"I vos a thinking," said Mr. Samuel Wilkins, during a pause
in the conversation—"I vos a thinking of taking J'mima to
the Eagle to-night."—"O my!" exclaimed Mrs. Ivins. "Lor!
how nice!" said the youngest Miss Ivins. "Well, I declare!"
added the youngest Miss Ivins but one. "Tell J'mima to
put on her white muslin, Tilly," screamed Mrs. Ivins, with
motherly anxiety; and down came J'mima herself soon
afterwards in a white muslin gown carefully hooked and eyed,
and little red shawl, plentifully pinned, and white straw bonnet
trimmed with red ribbons, and a small necklace, and large
pair of bracelets, and Denmark satin shoes, and open-worked
stockings, white cotton gloves on her fingers, and a cambric
pocket-handkerchief, carefully folded up, in her hand—all
quite genteel and ladylike. And away went Miss J'mima
Ivins and Mr. Samuel Wilkins, and a dress cane, with a gilt
knob at the top, to the admiration and envy of the street in
general, and to the high gratification of Mrs. Ivins, and the
two youngest Miss Ivinses in particular. They had no sooner
turned into the Pancras Road, than who should Miss J'mima
Ivins stumble upon by the most fortunate accident in the
world but a young lady as she knew, with *her* young man;
and it is so strange how things do turn out sometimes—they
were actually going to the Eagle too. So Mr. Samuel Wilkins
was introduced to Miss J'mima Ivins's friend's young man,
and they all walked on together, talking, and laughing, and
joking away like anything; and when they got as far as Pentonville, Miss Ivins's friend's young man, would have the
ladies go into the Crown, to taste some shrub, which, after a
great blushing and giggling, and hiding of faces in elaborate
pocket-handkerchiefs, they consented to do. Having tasted
it once, they were easily prevailed upon to taste it again;
and they sat out in the garden tasting shrub and looking at
the busses alternately, till it was just the proper time to go
to the Eagle; and then they resumed their journey, and
walked very fast, for fear they should lose the beginning of
the concert in the Rotunda.

"How ev'nly!" said Miss J'mima Ivins, and Miss J'mima
Ivins's friend, both at once, when they had passed the gate
and were fairly inside the gardens. There were the walks
beautifully gravelled and planted, and the refreshment-
boxes painted and ornamented like so many snuff-boxes,
and the variegated lamps shedding their rich light upon the
company's heads, and the place for dancing ready chalked
for the company's feet, and a Moorish band playing at one
end of the gardens and an opposition military band playing
away at the other. Then the waiters were rushing to and
fro with glasses of negus, and glasses of brandy-and-water,

and bottles of ale, and bottles of stout; and ginger-beer was going off in one place, and practical jokes going on in another; and people were crowding to the door of the Rotunda; and in short the whole scene was, as Miss J'mima Ivins, inspired by the novelty, or the shrub, or both, observed—"one of dazzling excitement." As to the concert-room, never was anything half so splendid. There was an orchestra for the singers, all paint, gilding, and plate-glass; and such an organ! Miss J'mima Ivins's friend's young man whispered it had cost "four hundred pound," which Mr. Samuel Wilkins said was "not dear neither;" an opinion in which the ladies perfectly coincided. The audience were seated on elevated benches round the room, and crowded into every part of it, and everybody was eating and drinking as comfortably as possible. Just before the concert commenced, Mr. Samuel Wilkins ordered two glasses of rum-and-water "warm with—" and two slices of lemon, for himself and the other young man, together with "a pint o' sherry wine for the ladies, and some sweet carraway-seed biscuits;" and they would have been quite comfortable and happy, only one gentleman with large whiskers *would* stare at Miss J'mima Ivins, and another gentleman in a plaid waistcoat *would* wink at Miss J'mima Ivins's friend, on which Miss J'mima Ivins's friend's young man exhibited symptoms of boiling over, and began to mutter about "people's imperence," and "swells out o' luck;" and to intimate, in oblique terms, a vague intention of knocking somebody's head off; which he was only prevented from announcing more emphatically, by both Miss J'mima Ivins and her friend threatening to faint away on the spot if he said another word.

The concert commenced—overture on the organ. "How solemn!" exclaimed Miss J'mima Ivins, glancing, perhaps unconsciously, at the gentleman with the whiskers. Mr. Samuel Wilkins, who had been muttering apart for some time past, as if he were holding a confidential conversation with the gilt knob of the dress cane, breathed very hard—breathing vengeance, perhaps,—but said nothing. "The soldier tired," Miss Somebody in white satin. "Ancore!" cried Miss J'mima Ivins's friend. "Ancore!" shouted the gentleman in the plaid waistcoat immediately, hammering the table with a stout-bottle. Miss J'mima Ivins's friend's young man eyed the man behind the waistcoat from head to foot, and cast a look of interrogative contempt towards Mr. Samuel Wilkins. Comic song, accompanied on the organ. Miss J'mima Ivins was convulsed with laughter—so was the man with the whiskers. Everything the ladies did, the plaid waistcoat and whiskers did, by way of expressing unity of sentiment and congeniality of soul; and Miss J'mima Ivins, and Miss J'mima Ivins's friend, grew lively and talkative, as Mr. Samuel Wilkins and Miss J'mima Ivins's friend's young man, grew morose and surly in inverse proportion.

Now, if the matter had ended here, the little party might soon have recovered their former equanimity, but Mr. Samuel Wilkins and his friend began to throw looks of defiance upon the waistcoat and whiskers. And the waistcoat and whiskers, by way of intimating the slight degree in which they were affected by the looks aforesaid, bestowed glances of increased admiration upon Miss J'mima Ivins and friend. The concert and vaudeville concluded, they promenaded the gardens. The waistcoat and whiskers did the same; and made divers remarks complimentary to the ankles of Miss J'mima Ivins and friend, in an audible tone. At length, not satisfied with these numerous atrocities, they actually came up and asked Miss J'mima Ivins, and Miss J'mima Ivins's friend to dance, without taking no more notice of Mr. Samuel Wilkins, and Miss J'mima Ivins's friend's young man, than if they was nobody!

"What do you mean by that, scoundrel?" exclaimed Mr. Samuel Wilkins, grasping the gilt-knobbed dress-cane firmly in his right hand. "What's the matter with *you*, you little humbug?" replied the whiskers. "How dare you insult me and my friend?" inquired the friend's young man. "You and your friend be hanged," responded the waistcoat. "Take that," exclaimed Mr. Samuel Wilkins. The ferrule of the gilt-knobbed dress-cane was visible for an instant, and then the light of the variegated lamps shone brightly upon it as it whirled into the air, cane and all. "Give it him," said the waistcoat. "Horficer!" screamed the ladies. Miss J'mima Ivins's beau, and the friend's young man, lay gasping on the gravel, and the waistcoat and whiskers were seen no more.

Miss J'mima Ivins and friend being conscious that the affray was in no slight degree attributable to themselves, of course went into hysterics forthwith; declared themselves the most injured of women, exclaimed in incoherent ravings, that they had been suspected—wrongfully suspected—oh! that they should ever have lived to see the day, and so forth; suffered a relapse every time they opened their eyes and saw their unfortunate little admirers, and were carried to their respective abodes in a hackney-coach, and a state of insensibility, compounded of shrub, sherry, and excitement.

CHAPTER V: *The Parlour Orator*

WE had been lounging one evening, down Oxford Street, Holborn, Cheapside, Coleman Street, Finsbury Square, and so on, with the intention of returning by Pentonville and the New Road, when we began to feel rather thirsty, and disposed to rest for five or ten minutes. So, we turned back towards an old, quiet, decent public-house, which we remembered to have passed but a moment before (it was not far from the City Road), for the purpose of solacing ourself with a glass of ale. The house was none of your stuccoed, French-polished, illuminated palaces, but a modest public-house of the old school, with a little old bar, and a little old landlord, who, with a wife and daughter of the same pattern, was comfortably seated in the bar aforesaid—a snug little room with a cheerful fire, protected by a large screen, from behind which the young lady emerged on our representing our inclination for a glass of ale.

"Won't you walk into the parlour, sir?" said the young lady, in seductive tones.

"You had better walk into the parlour, sir," said the little old landlord, throwing his chair back, and looking round one side of the screen, to survey our appearance. "You had much better step into the parlour, sir," said the little old lady, popping out her head, on the other side of the screen.

We cast a slight glance around, as if to express our ignorance of the locality so much recommended. The little old landlord observed it; bustled out of the small door of the small bar; and forthwith ushered us into the parlour itself.

It was an ancient, dark-looking room, with oaken wainscoting, a sanded floor, and a high mantelpiece. The walls were ornamented with three or four old coloured prints in black frames, each print representing a naval engagement, with a couple of men-of-war banging away at each other most vigorously, while another vessel or two were blowing up in the distance, and the foreground represented a miscellaneous collection of broken masts and blue legs sticking up out of the water. Depending from the ceiling in the centre of the room, were a gas-light and bell-pull; and on each side were three or four long narrow tables, behind which was a thickly-planted row of those slippy, shiny-looking wooden chairs, peculiar to places of this description. The monotonous appearance of the sanded boards was relieved by an occasional spittoon; and a triangular pile of those useful articles adorned the two upper corners of the apartment.

At the furthest table, nearest the fire, with his face towards the door at the bottom of the room, sat a stoutish man of about forty, whose short, stiff, black hair curled closely round a broad high forehead, and a face to which something besides water and exercise had communicated a rather inflamed appearance. He was smoking a cigar, with his eyes fixed on the ceiling, and had that confident oracular air which marked him as the leading politician, general authority, and universal anecdote-relater of the place. He had evidently just delivered himself of something very weighty; for the remainder of the company were puffing at their respective pipes and cigars in a kind of solemn abstraction, as if quite overwhelmed with the magnitude of the subject recently under discussion.

On his right hand sat an elderly gentleman with a white head, and broad-brimmed brown hat; on his left, a sharp-nosed, light-haired man in a brown surtout reaching nearly to his heels, who took a whiff at his pipe, and an admiring glance at the red-faced man, alternately.

"Very extraordinary!" said the light-haired man after a pause of five minutes. A murmur of assent ran through the company.

"Not at all extraordinary—not at all," said the red-faced man, awakening suddenly from his reverie, and turning upon the light-haired man, the moment he had spoken.

"Why should it be extraordinary?—why is it extraordinary? Prove it to be extraordinary!"

"Oh, if you come to that—" said the light-haired man.

"Come to that!" ejaculated the man with the red face; "but we must come to that. We stand, in these times, upon a calm elevation of intellectual attainment, and not in the dark recess of mental deprivation. Proof is what I require —proof, and not assertions, in these stirring times. Every gen'lem'n that knows me, knows what was the nature and effect of my observations, when it was in the contemplation of the Old Street Suburban Representative Discovery Society, to recommend a candidate for that place in Cornwall there— I forget the name of it. 'Mr. Snobee,' said Mr. Wilson, 'is a fit and proper person to represent the borough in Parliament.' 'Prove it,' says I. 'He is a friend to Reform,' says Mr. Wilson. 'Prove it,' says I. 'The abolitionist of the national debt, the unflinching opponent of pensions, the uncompromising advocate of the negro, the reducer of sinecures and the duration of Parliaments; the extender of nothing but the suffrages of the people,' says Mr. Wilson. 'Prove it,' says I. 'His acts prove it,' says he. 'Prove *them*,' says I."

"And he could not prove them," said the red-faced man, looking round triumphantly; "and the borough didn't have him; and if you carried this principle to the full extent, you'd have no debt, no pensions, no sinecures, no negroes, no nothing. And then, standing upon an elevation of intellectual attainment, and having reached the summit of popular prosperity, you might bid defiance to the nations of the earth, and erect yourselves in the proud confidence of wisdom and superiority. This is my argument—this always has been my argument— and if I was a Member of the House of Commons to-morrow, I'd make 'em shake in their shoes with it." And the red-faced man, having struck the table very hard with his clenched fist, by way of adding weight to the declaration, smoked away like a brewery.

"Well!" said the sharp-nosed man, in a very slow and soft voice, addressing the company in general, "I always do say, that of all the gentlemen I have the pleasure of meeting in this room, there is not one whose conversation I like to hear so much as Mr. Rogers's, or who is such improving company."

"Improving company!" said Mr. Rogers, for that was the name of the red-faced man, "You may say I am improving company, for I've improved you all to some purpose, though as to my conversation being as my friend Mr. Ellis here describes it, that is not for me to say anything about. You, gentlemen, are the best judges on that point; but this I will say, when I came into this parish, and first used this room, ten years ago, I don't believe there was one man in it, who knew he was a slave, and now you all know it, and writhe under it. Inscribe that upon my tomb, and I am satisfied."

"Why as to inscribing it on your tomb," said a little green-grocer with a rather chubby face, "of course you can have anything chalked up, as you likes to pay for, so far as it relates to yourself and your affairs, but when you come to talk about slaves, and that there abuse, you'd better keep it in the family, 'cos I for one don't like to be called them names night after night."

"You *are* a slave," said the red-faced man, "and the most pitiable of all slaves."

"Werry hard if I am," interrupted the greengrocer, "for I got no good out of the twenty million that was paid for 'mancipation anyhow."

"A willing slave," ejaculated the red-faced man, getting more red with eloquence, and contradiction—"resigning the dearest birthright of your children—neglecting the sacred call of Liberty—who, standing imploringly before you, appeals to the warmest feelings of your heart, and points to your helpless infants, but in vain."

"Prove it," said the greengrocer.

"Prove it!" sneered the man with the red face. "What! bending beneath the yoke of an insolent and factious oligarchy; bowed down by the domination of cruel laws; groaning beneath tyranny and oppression on every hand, at every side, and in every corner. Prove it!" The red-faced man abruptly broke off, sneered melodramatically, and buried his countenance and his indignation together, in a pint pot.

"Ah, to be sure, Mr. Rogers," said a stout broker in a large waistcoat, who had kept his eyes fixed on this luminary all the time he was speaking. "Ah, to be sure," said the broker with a sigh, "that's the point."

"Of course, of course," said divers members of the company, who understood almost as much about the matter as the broker himself.

"You had better let him alone, Tommy," said the broker,

by way of advice to the little greengrocer, "he can tell what's o'clock by an eight-day, without looking at the minute hand, he can. Try it on, on some other suit; it won't do with him, Tommy."

"What is a man?" continued the red-faced specimen of the species, jerking his hat indignantly from its peg on the wall. "What is an Englishman? Is he to be trampled upon by every oppressor? Is he to be knocked down at everybody's bidding? What's freedom? Not a standing army. What's a standing army? Not freedom. What's general happiness? Not universal misery. Liberty ain't the window-tax, is it? The Lords ain't the Commons, are they?" And the red-faced man, gradually bursting into a radiating sentence, in which such adjectives as "dastardly," "oppressive," "violent," and "sanguinary," formed the most conspicuous words, knocked his hat indignantly over his eyes, left the room, and slammed the door after him.

"Wonderful man!" said he of the sharp nose.

"Splendid speaker!" added the broker.

"Great power!" said everybody but the greengrocer. And as they said it, the whole party shook their heads mysteriously, and one by one retired, leaving us alone in the old parlour.

If we had followed the established precedent in all such instances, we should have fallen into a fit of musing, without delay. The ancient appearance of the room—the old panelling of the wall—the chimney blackened with smoke and age —would have carried us back a hundred years at least, and we should have gone dreaming on, until the pewter-pot on the table, or the little beer-chiller on the fire, had started into life, and addressed to us a long story of days gone by. But, by some means or other, we were not in a romantic humour; and although we tried very hard to invest the furniture with vitality, it remained perfectly unmoved, obstinate, and sullen. Being thus reduced to the unpleasant necessity of musing about ordinary matters, our thoughts reverted to the red-faced man, and his oratorical display.

A numerous race are these red-faced men; there is not a parlour, or club-room, or benefit society, or humble party of any kind, without its red-faced man. Weak-pated dolts they are, and a great deal of mischief they do to their cause, however good. So, just to hold a pattern one up, to know the others by, we took his likeness at once, and put him in here. And that is the reason why we have written this paper.

CHAPTER VI: *The Hospital Patient*

IN our rambles through the streets of London after evening has set in, we often pause beneath the windows of some public hospital, and picture to ourself the gloomy and mournful scenes that are passing within. The sudden moving of a taper as its feeble ray shoots from window after window, until its light gradually disappears, as if it were carried further back into the room to the bedside of some suffering patient, is enough to awaken a whole crowd of reflections; the mere glimmering of the low-burning lamps, which, when all other habitations are wrapped in darkness and slumber, denote the chamber where so many forms are writhing with pain, or wasting with disease, is sufficient to check the most boisterous merriment.

Who can tell the anguish of those weary hours, when the only sound the sick man hears, is the disjointed wanderings of some feverish slumberer near him, the low moan of pain, or perhaps the muttered, long-forgotten prayer of a dying man? Who, but those who have felt it, can imagine the sense of loneliness and desolation which must be the portion of those who in the hour of dangerous illness are left to be tended by strangers; for what hands, be they ever so gentle, can wipe the clammy brow, or smooth the restless bed, like those of mother, wife, or child?

Impressed with these thoughts, we have turned away, through the nearly-deserted streets; and the sight of the few miserable creatures still hovering about them, has not tended to lessen the pain which such meditations awaken. The hospital is a refuge and resting-place for hundreds, who but for such institutions must die in the streets and doorways; but what can be the feelings of outcasts like these when they are stretched on the bed of sickness with scarcely a hope of recovery? The wretched woman who lingers about the pavement, hours after midnight, and the miserable shadow of a man—the ghastly remnant that want and drunkenness have left—which crouches beneath a window-ledge, to sleep where there is some shelter from the rain, have little to bind them to life, but what have they to look back upon, in death? What are the unwonted comforts of a roof and a bed to them, when the recollections of a whole life of debasement stalk before them; when repentance seems a mockery, and sorrow comes too late?

About a twelvemonth ago, as we were strolling through Covent Garden (we had been thinking about these things overnight) we were attracted by the very prepossessing appearance of a pickpocket, who having declined to take the trouble of walking to the Police-office, on the ground that he hadn't the slightest wish to go there at all, was being conveyed thither in a wheelbarrow, to the huge delight of a crowd, but apparently not very much to his own gratification.

Somehow we never can resist joining a crowd, so we turned back with the mob, and entered the office, in company with our friend the pickpocket, a couple of policemen, and as many dirty-faced spectators as could squeeze their way in.

There was a powerful, ill-looking young fellow at the bar, who was undergoing an examination, on the very common charge of having, on the previous night, ill-treated a woman, with whom he lived in some court hard by. Several witnesses bore testimony to acts of the grossest brutality; and a certificate was read from the house-surgeon of a neighbouring hospital, describing the nature of the injuries the woman had received, and intimating that her recovery was extremely doubtful.

Some question appeared to have been raised about the identity of the prisoner; for when it was agreed that the two magistrates should visit the hospital at eight o'clock that evening, to take her deposition, it was settled that the man should be taken there also. He had turned deadly pale at this, and we saw him clench the bar very hard when the order was given. He was removed directly afterwards, and he spoke not a word.

We felt an irrepressible curiosity to witness this interview, although it is hard to tell why, at this instant, for we knew it must be a painful one. It was no very difficult matter for us to gain permission, and we obtained it.

The prisoner, and the officer who had him in custody, were already at the hospital when we reached it, and waiting the arrival of the magistrates in a small room below stairs. The man was handcuffed, and his hat was pulled forward over his eyes. It was easy to see, though, by the livid whiteness of his countenance, and the constant twitching of the muscles of his face, that he dreaded what was to come. After a short interval, the magistrates and clerk were bowed in by the house-surgeon and a couple of young men who smelt very strong of tobacco-smoke—they were introduced as "dressers" —and after one magistrate had complained bitterly of the cold, and the other of the absence of any news in the evening paper, it was announced that the patient was prepared: and we were conducted to the "casualty ward" in which she was lying.

The dim light which burnt in the spacious room, increased rather than diminished the ghastly appearance of the hapless creatures in the beds, which were ranged in two long rows on either side. In one bed lay a child enveloped in bandages, with its body half-consumed by fire; in another, a female, rendered hideous by some dreadful accident, was wildly beating her clenched fists on the coverlet, in an agony of pain; on a third, there lay stretched a young girl, apparently in that heavy stupor so often the immediate precursor of death: her face was stained with blood, and her breast and arms were bound up in folds of linen. Two or three of the beds were

A Pickpocket in Custody.

empty, and their recent occupants were sitting beside them, but with faces so wan, and eyes so bright and glassy, that it was fearful to meet their gaze. On every face was stamped the expression of anguish and suffering.

The object of the visit was lying at the upper end of the room. She was a fine young woman of about two or three and twenty. Her long black hair had been hastily cut from near the wounds on her head, and streamed over the pillow in jagged and matted locks. Her face bore frightful marks of the ill-usage she had received: her hand was pressed upon her side, as if her chief pain were there; her breathing was short and heavy; and it was plain to see that she was dying fast. She murmured a few words in reply to the magistrate's inquiry whether she was in great pain; and having been raised on the pillow by the nurse, looked vacantly upon the strange countenances that surrounded her bed. The magistrate nodded to the officer, to bring the man forward. He did so, and stationed him at the bedside. The girl looked on, with a wild and troubled expression of face; but her sight was dim, and she did not know him.

"Take off his hat," said the magistrate. The officer did as he was desired, and the man's features were fully disclosed. The girl started up, with an energy quite preternatural; the fire gleamed in her heavy eyes, and the blood rushed to her pale and sunken cheeks. It was a convulsive effort. She fell back upon her pillow, and covering her scarred and bruised face with her hands, burst into tears. The man cast an anxious look towards her, but otherwise appeared wholly unmoved. After a brief pause the nature of their errand was explained, and the oath tendered.

"Oh, no, gentlemen," said the girl, raising herself once more, and folding her hands together; "no, gentlemen, for God's sake! I did it myself—it was nobody's fault—it was an accident. He didn't hurt me; he wouldn't for all the world. Jack, dear Jack, you know you wouldn't.'"

Her sight was fast failing her, and her hand groped over the bedclothes in search of his. Brute as the man was, he was not prepared for this. He turned his face from the bed, and sobbed aloud. The girl's colour changed, and her breathing grew more difficult. She was evidently dying.

"We respect these feelings which prompt you to this," said the gentleman who had spoken first, "but let me warn you, not to persist in what you know to be untrue, until it is too late. It cannot save him."

"Jack," murmured the girl, laying her hand upon his arm, 'they shall not persuade me to swear your life away. He didn't do it, gentlemen. He never hurt me." She grasped his arm tightly, and added, in a broken whisper, "I hope God Almighty will forgive me all the wrong I have done, and the

life I have led.   God bless you, Jack.   Some kind gentleman
take my love to my poor old father.   Five years ago, he said
he wished I had died a child.   Oh I wish I had!   I wish I
had!''

The nurse bent over the girl for a few seconds, and then
drew the sheet over her face.   It covered a corpse.

CHAPTER VII: *The misplaced attachment of Mr. John
            Dounce*

IF we had to make a classification of society, there are a
particular kind of men whom we should immediately set down
under the head of "Old Boys''; and a column of most extensive dimensions the old boys would require.   To what precise
causes the rapid advance of old boy population is to be traced,
we are unable to determine; it would be an interesting and
curious speculation, but as we have not sufficient space to
devote to it here, we simply state the fact that the numbers
of the old boys have been gradually augmenting within the
last few years, and that they are at this moment alarmingly
on the increase.

Upon a general review of the subject, and without considering it minutely in detail, we should be disposed to subdivide
the old boys into two distinct classes—the gay old boys, and
the steady old boys.   The gay old boys, are paunchy old
men in the disguise of young ones, who frequent the Quadrant
and Regent Street in the day-time; the theatre (especially
theatres under lady management) at night, and who assume
all the foppishness and levity of boys, without the excuse of
youth or inexperience.   The steady old boys are certain stout
old gentlemen of clean appearance, who are always to be
seen in the same taverns, at the same hours every evening,
smoking and drinking in the same company.

There was once a fine collection of old boys to be seen
round the circular table at Offley's every night, between the
hours of half-past eight and half-past eleven.   We have lost
sight of them for some time.   There were, and may be
still, for aught we know, two splendid specimens in full blossom
at the Rainbow Tavern in Fleet Street, who always used to
sit in the box nearest the fireplace, and smoked long cherry-
stick pipes which went under the table, with the bowls resting
upon the floor.   Grand old boys they were—fat, red-faced,
white-headed old fellows; always there—one on one side the
table, and the other opposite—puffing and drinking away in
great state; everybody knew them, and it was supposed by
some people that they were both immortal.

Mr. John Dounce was an old boy of the latter class (we don't
mean immortal, but steady)—a retired glove and braces

maker, a widower, resident with three daughters—all grown up, and all unmarried—in Cursitor Street, Chancery Lane. He was a short, round, large-faced, tubbish sort of man, with a broad-brimmed hat, and a square coat; and had that grave, but confident, kind of roll, peculiar to old boys in general.   Regular as clockwork—breakfast at nine—dress and tittivate a little—down to the Sir Somebody's Head—a glass of ale and the paper—come back again, and take the daughters out for a walk—dinner at three—glass of grog and a pipe—nap—tea—little walk—Sir Somebody's Head again—capital house—delightful evenings!   There were Mr. Harris, the law-stationer, and Mr. Jennings, the robe-maker (two jolly young fellows like himself), and Jones, the barrister's clerk—rum fellow that Jones—capital company—full of anecdote!—and there they sat every night till just ten minutes before twelve, drinking their brandy-and-water, and smoking their pipes, and telling stories and enjoying themselves with a kind of solemn joviality particularly edifying.

Sometimes Jones would propose a half-price visit to Drury Lane or Covent Garden, to see two acts of a five-act play, and a new farce, perhaps, or a ballet, on which occasions the whole four of them went together; none of your hurrying and nonsense, but having their brandy-and-water first, comfortably, and ordering a steak and some oysters for their supper against they came back, and then walking coolly into the pit, when the "rush" had gone in, as all sensible people do, and did when Mr. Dounce was a young man, except when the celebrated Master Betty was at the height of his popularity, and then, sir—then Mr. Dounce perfectly well remembered getting a holiday from business, and going to the pit doors at eleven o'clock in the forenoon, and waiting there till six in the afternoon, with some sandwiches in a pocket-handkerchief and some wine in a phial, and fainting after all, with the heat and fatigue before the play began; in which situation he was lifted out of the pit into one of the dress boxes, sir, by five of the finest women of that day, sir, who compassionated his situation and administered restoratives, and sent a black servant, six foot high, in blue and silver livery, next morning with their compliments, and to know how he found himself, sir—by G—!   Between the acts Mr. Dounce and Mr. Harris, and Mr. Jennings, used to stand up, and look round the house, and Jones—knowing fellow that Jones—knew every-body—pointed out the fashionable and celebrated Lady So-and-So in the boxes, at the mention of whose name Mr. Dounce, after brushing up his hair, and adjusting his neck-handkerchief, would inspect the aforesaid Lady So-and-So through an immense glass, and remark either that she was a "fine woman—very fine woman, indeed," or that "there might be a little more of her,—eh, Jones?" just as the case might happen to be. When the dancing began, John Dounce, and the other old boys, were particularly anxious to see what was going forward on the stage, and Jones—wicked dog, that Jones—whispered little critical remarks into the ears of John Dounce, which John Dounce retailed to Mr. Harris and Mr. Harris to Mr. Jennings, and then they all four laughed until the tears ran down, out of their eyes.

When the curtain fell, they walked back together, two and two, to the steaks and oysters, and when they came to the second glass of brandy-and-water, Jones—hoaxing scamp, that Jones—used to recount how he had observed a lady in white feathers in one of the pit boxes, gazing intently on Mr. Dounce all the evening, and how he had caught Mr. Dounce, whenever he thought no one was looking at him, bestowing ardent looks of intense devotion on the lady in return; on which Mr. Harris and Mr. Jennings used to laugh very heartily, and John Dounce more heartily than either of them, acknowledging, however, that the time *had* been when he *might* have done such things; upon which Mr. Jones used to poke him in the ribs, and tell him he had been a sad dog in his time, which John Dounce, with chuckles, confessed. And after Mr. Harris and Mr. Jennings had preferred their claims to the character of having been sad dogs too, they separated harmoniously, and trotted home.

The decrees of Fate, and the means by which they are brought about, are mysterious and inscrutable. John Dounce had led this life for twenty years and upwards, without wish for change, or care for variety, when his whole social system was suddenly upset, and turned completely topsy-turvy—not by an earthquake, or some other dreadful convulsion of nature, as the reader would be inclined to suppose, but by the simple agency of an oyster: and thus it happened.

Mr. John Dounce was returning one night from the Sir Somebody's Head, to his residence in Cursitor Street—not tipsy, but rather excited, for it was Mr. Jennings's birthday, and they had had a brace of partridges for supper, and a brace of extra glasses afterwards, and Jones had been more than ordinarily amusing—when his eyes rested on a newly-opened oyster-shop, on a magnificent scale, with natives laid one deep in circular marble basins in the windows, together with little round barrels of oysters directed to Lords and Baronets, and Colonels and Captains, in every part of the habitable globe.

Behind the natives were the barrels, and behind the barrels was a young lady of about five-and-twenty, all in blue, and all alone—splendid creature, charming face, and lovely figure! It is difficult to say whether Mr. John Dounce's red countenance, illuminated as it was by the flickering gas-light in the window before which he paused, excited the lady's risibility, or whether a natural exuberance of animal spirits proved too much for that staidness of demeanour which the forms of society rather dictatorially prescribe. But certain it is, that the lady smiled, then put her finger upon her lip, with a striking recollection of what was due to herself; and finally retired, in oyster-like bashfulness, to the very back of the counter. The sad-dog sort of feeling came strongly upon John Dounce: he lingered—the lady in blue made no sign. He coughed—still she came not. He entered the shop.

"Can you open me an oyster, my dear?" said Mr. John Dounce.

"Dare say I can, sir," replied the lady in blue, with enchanting playfulness. And Mr. Dounce ate one oyster, and then looked at the young lady, and then ate another, and then squeezed the young lady's hand as she was opening the third, and so forth, until he had devoured a dozen of those at eightpence in less than no time.

"Can you open me half-a-dozen more, my dear?" inquired Mr. John Dounce.

"I'll see what I can do for you, sir," replied the young lady in blue, even more bewitchingly than before; and Mr. John Dounce ate half-a-dozen more of those at eightpence, and his gallantry increased.

"You couldn't manage to get me a glass of brandy-and-water, my dear, I suppose?" said Mr. John Dounce, when he had finished the oysters, in a tone which clearly implies his supposition that she could.

"I'll see, sir," said the young lady: and away she ran out of the shop, and down the street, her long auburn ringlets shaking in the wind in the most enchanting manner; and back she came again, tripping over the coal-cellar lids like a whipping-top, with a tumbler of brandy-and-water, which Mr. John Dounce insisted on her taking a share of, as it was regular ladies' grog—hot, strong, sweet, and plenty of it.

So the young lady sat down with Mr. John Dounce in a little red box with a green curtain, and took a small sip of the brandy-and-water, and a small look at Mr. John Dounce, and then turned her head away, and went through various other serio-pantomimic fascinations, which forcibly reminded Mr. John Dounce of the first time he courted his first wife, and which made him feel more affectionate than ever; in pursuance of which affection, and actuated by which feeling, Mr. John Dounce sounded the young lady on her matrimonial engagements, when the young lady denied having formed any such engagements at all—she couldn't abear the men, they were such deceivers; thereupon Mr. John Dounce inquired whether this sweeping condemnation was meant to include other than very young men; on which the young

lady blushed deeply—at least she turned away her head, and
said Mr. John Dounce had made her blush, so of course she
did blush—and Mr. John Dounce was a long time drinking
the brandy-and-water; and the young lady said "Ha' done,
sir," very often; and at last John Dounce went home to bed,
and dreamt of his first wife, and his second wife, and the
young lady, and partridges, and oysters, and brandy-and-
water, and disinterested attachments.

The next morning, John Dounce was rather feverish with
the extra brandy-and-water of the previous night; and partly
in the hope of cooling himself with an oyster, and partly
with the view of ascertaining whether he owed the young
lady anything, or not, went back to the oyster-shop. If the
young lady had appeared beautiful by night, she was perfectly
irresistible by day; and from this time forward a change came
over the spirit of John Dounce's dream. He bought shirt
pins; wore a ring on his third finger; read poetry; bribed a
cheap miniature-painter to perpetrate a faint resemblance
to a youthful face, with a curtain over his head, six large books
in the background, and an open country in the distance (this
he called his portrait): "went on" altogether in such an
uproarious manner, that the three Miss Dounces went off
on small pensions, he having made the tenement in Cursitor
Street too warm to contain them; and in short, comported
and demeaned himself in every respect like an unmitigated old
Saracen, as he was.

As to his ancient friends, the other old boys, at the Sir
Somebody's Head, he dropped off from them by gradual
degrees; for even when he did go there, Jones—vulgar fellow,
that Jones—persisted in asking "when it was to be?" and
"whether he was to have any gloves?" together with other
inquiries of an equally offensive nature, at which not only
Harris laughed, but Jennings also; so he cut the two altogether, and attached himself solely to the blue young lady
at the smart oyster-shop.

Now comes the moral of the story—for it has a moral after
all. The last-mentioned young lady, having derived sufficient
profit and emolument from John Dounce's attachment, not
only refused when matters came to a crisis to take him for
better for worse, but expressly declared, to use her own
forcible words, that she "wouldn't have him at no price;"
and John Dounce, having lost his old friends, alienated his
relations, and rendered himself ridiculous to everybody,
made offers successively to a schoolmistress, a landlady, a
feminine tobacconist, and a housekeeper; and being directly
rejected by each and every of them, was accepted by his cook,
with whom he now lives, a henpecked husband, a melancholy
monument of antiquated misery, and a living warning to all
uxorious old boys.

CHAPTER VIII: *The Mistaken Milliner. A tale of ambition*
MISS AMELIA MARTIN was pale, tallish, thin, and two-and-thirty—what ill-natured people would call plain, and police reports interesting. She was a milliner and dressmaker, living on her business and not above it. If you had been a young lady in service, and wanted Miss Martin, as a great many young ladies in service did, you would just have stepped up, in the evening, to number forty-seven, Drummond Street, George Street, Euston Square, and after casting your eye on a brass door-plate one foot ten by one and a half, ornamented with a great brass nob at each of the four corners, and bearing the inscription—"Miss Martin; millinery and dressmaking, in all its branches;" you'd just have knocked two loud knocks at the street-door; and down would have come Miss Martin herself, in a merino gown of the newest fashion, black velvet bracelets on the genteelest principle, and other little elegancies of the most approved description.

If Miss Martin knew the young lady who called, or if the young lady who called had been recommended by any other young lady whom Miss Martin knew, Miss Martin would forthwith show her up-stairs into the two-pair front, and chat she would—*so* kind, and *so* comfortable—it really wasn't like a matter of business, she was so friendly; and then Miss Martin, after contemplating the figure and general appearance of the young lady in service with great apparent admiration, would say how well she would look, to be sure, in a low dress with short sleeves, made very full in the skirts, with four tucks in the bottom, to which the young lady in service would reply in terms expressive of her entire concurrence in the notion, and the virtuous indignation with which she reflected on the tyranny of "Missis," who wouldn't allow a young girl to wear a short sleeve of an afternoon—no, nor nothing smart, not even a pair of ear-rings; let alone hiding people's heads of hair under them frightful caps: at the termination of which complaint, Miss Amelia Martin would distantly suggest certain dark suspicions that some people were jealous on account of their own daughters, and were obliged to keep their servants' charms under, for fear they should get married first, which was no uncommon circumstance—leastways she had known two or three young ladies in service, who had married a great deal better than their missises, and *they* were not very good-looking either; and then the young lady would inform Miss Martin, in confidence, that how one of their young ladies was engaged to a young man and was a-going to be married, and Missis was so proud about it there was no bearing her; but she needn't hold her head quite so high neither, for, after all, he was only a clerk. And, after expressing a due contempt for clerks in general, and the engaged clerk in particular, and the highest opinion possible of themselves and each other, Miss Martin and the young lady in service would bid each other good-night in a friendly but perfectly genteel manner: and the one went back to her "place," and the other, to her room on the second-floor front.

There is no saying how long Miss Amelia Martin might have continued this course of life; how extensive a connection she might have established among young ladies in service; or what amount her demands upon their quarterly receipts might have ultimately attained, had not an unforeseen train of circumstances directed her thoughts to a sphere of action very different from dress-making or millinery.

A friend of Miss Martin's who had long been keeping company with an ornamental painter and decorator's journeyman, at last consented (on being at last asked to do so) to name the day which would make the aforesaid journeyman a happy husband. It was a Monday that was appointed for the celebration of the nuptials, and Miss Amelia Martin was invited, among others, to honour the wedding-dinner with her presence. It was a charming party; Somers Town the locality, and a front parlour the apartment. The ornamental painter and decorator's journeyman had taken a house—no lodgings nor vulgarity of that kind, but a house—four beautiful rooms, and a delightful little washhouse at the end of the passage, which was the most convenient thing in the world, for the bridesmaids could sit in the front parlour and receive the company, and then run into the little washhouse and see how the pudding and boiled pork were getting on in the copper, and then pop back into the parlour again, as snug and comfortable as possible. And such a parlour as it was too! Beautiful Kidderminster carpet—six bran-new cane-bottomed stained chairs—three wine-glasses and a tumbler on each sideboard—a farmer's girl and a farmer's boy on the mantelpiece: one tumbling over a stile, and the other spitting himself, on the handle of a pitchfork—long white dimity curtains in the window—and, in short, everything on the most genteel scale imaginable.

Then the dinner. There was baked leg of mutton at the top, boiled leg of mutton at the bottom, pair of fowls and leg of pork in the middle; porter-pots at the corners; pepper, mustard, and vinegar in the centre; vegetables on the floor; and plum-pudding and apple-pie and tartlets without number, to say nothing of cheese, and celery, and water-cresses, and all that sort of thing. As to the company! Miss Amelia Martin herself declared, on a subsequent occasion, that much as she had heard of the ornamental painter's journeyman's connection, she never could have supposed it was half so genteel. There was his father, such a funny old gentleman

—and his mother, such a dear old lady—and his sister, such a charming girl—and his brother, such a manly-looking young man—with such a eye! But even all these were as nothing when compared with his musical friends, Mr. and Mrs. Jennings Rodolph, from White Conduit, with whom the ornamental painter's journeyman had been fortunate enough to contract an intimacy while engaged in decorating the concert-room of that noble institution. To hear them sing separately, was perfectly divine, but when they went through the tragic duet of "Red Ruffian, retire!" it was, as Miss Martin afterwards remarked, "thrilling." And why (as Mr. Jennings Rodolph observed)—why were they not engaged at one of the patent theatres? If he was to be told that their voices were not powerful enough to fill the House, his only reply was, that he would back himself for any amount to fill Russell Square—a statement in which the company, after hearing the duet, expressed their full belief; so they all said it was shameful treatment; and both Mr. and Mrs. Jennings Rodolph said it was shameful too, and Mr. Jennings Rodolph looked very serious, and said he knew who his malignant opponents were, but they had better take care how far they went, for if they irritated him too much he had not quite made up his mind whether he wouldn't bring the subject before Parliament; and they all agreed that it "'ud serve 'em quite right, and it was very proper that such people should be made an example of." So Mr. Jennings Rodolph said he'd think of it.

When the conversation resumed its former tone, Mr. Jennings Rodolph claimed his right to call upon a lady, and the right being conceded, trusted Miss Martin would favour the company—a proposal which met with unanimous approbation, whereupon Miss Martin, after sundry hesitatings and coughings, with a preparatory choke or two, and an introductory declaration that she was frightened to death to attempt it before such great judges of the art, commenced a species of treble chirruping containing frequent allusions to some young gentleman of the name of Hen-e-ry, with an occasional reference to madness and damaged hearts. Mr. Jennings Rodolph frequently interrupted the progress of the song by ejaculating "Beautiful!"—"Charming!"— "Brilliant!"—"Oh! splendid," &c.; and at its close the admiration of himself, and his lady, knew no bounds.

"Did you ever hear so sweet a voice, my dear?" inquired Mr. Jennings Rodolph of Mrs. Jennings Rodolph.

"Never; indeed I never did, love," replied Mrs. Jennings Rodolph.

"Don't you think Miss Martin, with a little cultivation, would be very like Signora Marra Boni, my dear?" asked Mr. Jennings Rodolph.

"Just exactly the very thing that struck me, my love," answered Mrs. Jennings Rodolph.

And thus the time passed away; Mr. Jennings Rodolph played tunes on a walking-stick, and then went behind the parlour-door and gave his celebrated imitations of actors, edge-tools, and animals; Miss Martin sang several other songs with increased admiration every time, and even the funny old gentleman began singing; his song had properly seven verses, but as he couldn't recollect more than the first one he sang that over seven times, apparently very much to his own personal gratification. And then all the company sang the national anthem with national independence—each for himself, without reference to the other—and finally separated, all declaring that they never had spent so pleasant an evening, and Miss Martin inwardly resolving to adopt the advice of Mr. Jennings Rodolph, and to "come out" without delay.

Now, "coming out," either in acting, or singing, or society, or facetiousness, or anything else, is all very well, and remarkably pleasant to the individual principally concerned, if he or she can but manage to come out with a burst, and being out, to keep out, and not go in again; but it does unfortunately happen that both consummations are extremely difficult to accomplish, and that the difficulties of getting out at all in the first instance, and if you surmount them, of keeping out in the second, are pretty much on a par, and no slight ones either—and so Miss Amelia Martin shortly discovered. It is a singular fact (there being ladies in the case) that Miss Amelia Martin's principal foible was vanity, and the leading characteristic of Mrs. Jennings Rodolph an attachment to dress. Dismal wailings were heard to issue from the second-floor front, of number forty-seven, Drummond Street, George Street, Euston Square; it was Miss Martin practising. Half-suppressed murmurs disturbed the calm dignity of the White Conduit orchestra at the commencement of the season. It was the appearance of Mrs. Jennings Rodolph in full dress, that occasioned them. Miss Martin studied incessantly—the practising was the consequence. Mrs. Jennings Rodolph taught gratuitously now and then—the dresses were the result.

Weeks passed away; the White Conduit season had begun, and had progressed, and was more than half over. The dress-making business had fallen off from neglect; and its profits had dwindled away almost imperceptibly. A benefit-night approached; Mr. Jennings Rodolph yielded to the earnest solicitations of Miss Amelia Martin, and introduced her personally to the "comic gentleman" whose benefit it was. The comic gentleman was all smiles and blandness—he had composed a duet expressly for the occasion, and Miss Martin should sing it with him. The night arrived; there was an immense room—ninety-seven six-penn'orths of gin-and-water, thirty-two small glasses of brandy-and-water, five-and-twenty bottled ales, and forty-one neguses; and the ornamental painter's journeyman with his wife and a select circle of acquaintance were seated at one of the side-tables near the orchestra. The concert began. Song—sentimental—by a light-haired young gentleman in a blue coat, and bright basket buttons [applause]. Another song, doubtful, by another gentleman in another blue coat and more bright basket buttons—[increased applause]. Duet, Mr. Jennings Rodolph, and Mrs. Jennings Rodolph, "Red Ruffian, retire!"—[great applause]. Solo, Miss Julia Montague (positively on this occasion only)—"I am a Friar"—[enthusiasm]. Original duet, comic—Mr. H. Taplin (the comic gentleman) and Miss Martin—"The Time of Day."—"Brayvo!—Brayvo!" cried the ornamental painter's journeyman's party as Miss Martin was gracefully led in by the comic gentleman. "Go to work, Harry," cried the comic gentleman's personal friends. "Tap—tap—tap," went the leader's bow on the music-desk. The symphony began, and was soon afterwards followed by a faint kind of ventriloquial chirping, proceeding apparently from the deepest recesses of the interior of Miss Amelia Martin.— "Sing out"—shouted one gentleman in a white greatcoat. "Don't be afraid to put the steam on, old gal," exclaimed another. "S—s—s—s—s—s—s"—went the five-and-twenty bottled ales. "Shame, shame!" remonstrated the ornamental painter's journeyman's party. "S—s—s—s" went the bottled ales again, accompanied by all the gins and a majority of the brandies.

"Turn them geese out," cried the ornamental painter's journeyman's party, with great indignation.

"Sing out," whispered Mr. Jennings Rodolph.

"So I do," responded Miss Amelia Martin.

"Sing louder," said Mrs. Jennings Rodolph.

"I can't," replied Miss Amelia Martin.

"Off, off, off," cried the rest of the audience.

"Bray-vo!" shouted the painter's party. It wouldn't do —Miss Amelia Martin left the orchestra with much less ceremony than she had entered it; and, as she couldn't sing out, never came out. The general good humour was not restored until Mr. Jennings Rodolph had become purple in the face, by imitating divers quadrupeds for half an hour without being able to render himself audible; and, to this day, neither has Miss Amelia Martin's good humour been restored, nor the dresses made for and presented to Mrs. Jennings Rodolph, nor the vocal abilities which Mr. Jennings Rodolph once staked his professional reputation that Miss Martin possessed.

CHAPTER IX: *The Dancing Academy*

OF all the dancing academies that ever were established, there never was one more popular in its immediate vicinity than Signor Billsmethi's, of the "King's Theatre." It was not in Spring Gardens, or Newman Street, or Berners Street, or Gower Street, or Charlotte Street, or Percy Street, or any other of the numerous streets which have been devoted time out of mind to professional people, dispensaries, and boarding-houses; it was not in the West-end at all—it rather approximated to the eastern portion of London, being situated in the populous and improving neighbourhood of Gray's Inn Lane. It was not a dear dancing academy—four-and-six-pence a quarter is decidedly cheap upon the whole. It was *very* select, the number of pupils being strictly limited to seventy-five, and a quarter's payment in advance being rigidly exacted. There was public tuition and private tuition—an assembly-room and a parlour. Signor Billsmethi's family were always thrown in with the parlour, and included in parlour price; that is to say, a private pupil had Signor Billsmethi's parlour to dance *in*, and Signor Billsmethi's family to dance *with*; and when he had been sufficiently broken in in the parlour he began to run in couples in the Assembly-room.

Such was the dancing academy of Signor Billsmethi when Mr. Augustus Cooper, of Fetter Lane, first saw an unstamped advertisement walking leisurely down Holborn Hill, announcing to the world that Signor Billsmethi, of the King's Theatre, intended opening for the season with a Grand Ball.

Now, Mr. Augustus Cooper was in the oil and colour line —just of age, with a little money, a little business, and a little mother, who, having managed her husband and *his* business in his lifetime, took to managing her son and *his* business, after his decease; and so, somehow or other, he had been cooped up in the little back parlour behind the shop on week-days, and in a little deal box without a lid (called by courtesy a pew) at Bethel Chapel, on Sundays, and had seen no more of the world than if he had been an infant all his days; whereas young White, at the gas-fitter's over the way, three years younger than him, had been flaring away like winkin'—going to the theatre—supping at harmonic meetings —eating oysters by the barrel—drinking stout by the gallon —even stopping out all night, and coming home as cool in the morning as if nothing had happened. So Mr. Augustus Cooper made up his mind that he would not stand it any longer, and had that very morning expressed to his mother a firm determination to be "blowed," in the event of his not being instantly provided with a street-door key. And he was walking down Holborn Hill thinking about all these things, and wondering how he could manage to get introduced into genteel society for the first time, when his eyes rested on Signor Billsmethi's announcement, which it immediately struck him was just the very thing he wanted; for he should not only be able to select a genteel circle of acquaintance at once out of the five-and-seventy pupils at four-and-sixpence a quarter, but should qualify himself at the same time to go through a hornpipe in private society, with perfect ease to himself and great delight to his friends. So he stopped the unstamped advertisement—an animated sandwich, composed of a boy between two boards—and having procured a very small card with the Signor's address indented thereon, walked straight at once to the Signor's house—and very fast he walked too, for fear the list should be filled up, and the five-and-seventy completed before he got there. The Signor was at home, and, what was still more gratifying, he was an Englishman! Such a nice man—and so polite! The list was not full, but it was a most extraordinary circumstance that there was only just one vacancy, and even that one would have been filled up that very morning, only Signor Billsmethi was dissatisfied with the reference, and being very much afraid that the lady wasn't select, wouldn't take her.

"And very much delighted I am, Mr. Cooper," said Signor Billsmethi, "that I did *not* take her. I assure you, Mr. Cooper—I don't say it to flatter you, for I know you're above it—that I consider myself extremely fortunate in having a gentleman of your manners and appearance, sir."

"I am very glad of it too, sir," said Augustus Cooper.

"And I hope we shall be better acquainted, sir," said Signor Billsmethi.

"And I'm sure I hope we shall too, sir," responded Augustus Cooper. Just then the door opened, and in came a young lady with her hair curled in a crop all over her head, and her shoes tied in sandals all over her legs.

"Don't run away, my dear," said Signor Billsmethi; for the young lady didn't know Mr. Cooper was there when she ran in, and was going to run out again in her modesty, all in confusion-like. "Don't run away, my dear," said Signor Billsmethi, "this is Mr. Cooper—Mr. Cooper, of Fetter Lane. Mr. Cooper, my daughter, sir—Miss Billsmethi, sir, who I hope will have the pleasure of dancing many a quadrille, minuet, gavotte, country-dance, fandango, double-hornpipe, and farinagholkajingo with you, sir. She dances them all, sir; and so shall you, sir, before you're a quarter older, sir."

And Signor Billsmethi slapped Mr. Augustus Cooper on the back as if he had known him a dozen years,—so friendly; and Mr. Cooper bowed to the young lady, and the young lady curtseyed to him, and Signor Billsmethi said they were as handsome a pair as ever he'd wish to see; upon which the young lady exclaimed, "Lor, pa!" and blushed as red as Mr. Cooper himself—you might have thought they were both standing under a red lamp at a chemist's shop; and before Mr. Cooper went away it was settled that he should join the family circle that very night—taking them just as they were—no ceremony nor nonsense of that kind—and learn his positions, in order that he might lose no time and be able to come out at the forthcoming ball.

Well; Mr. Augustus Cooper went away to one of the cheap shoemaker's shops in Holborn, where gentlemen's dress-pumps are seven and sixpence, and men's strong walking just nothing at all, and bought a pair of the regular seven-and-sixpenny, long-quartered, town-mades, in which he astonished himself quite as much as his mother, and sallied forth to Signor Billsmethi's. There were four other private pupils in the parlour: two ladies and two gentlemen. Such nice people! Not a bit of pride about them. One of the ladies in particular, who was in training for a Columbine, was remarkably affable, and she and Miss Billsmethi took such an interest in Mr. Augustus Cooper, and joked and smiled, and looked so bewitching, that he got quite at home and learnt his steps in no time. After the practising was over, Signor Billsmethi, and Miss Billsmethi, and Master Billsmethi, and a young lady, and the two ladies, and the two gentlemen, danced a quadrille—none of your slipping and sliding about, but regular warm work, flying into corners, and diving among chairs, and shooting out at the door,—something like dancing! Signor Billsmethi in particular, notwithstanding his having a little fiddle to play all the time, was out on the landing every figure, and Master Billsmethi, when everybody else was breathless, danced a hornpipe with a cane in his hand, and a cheese-plate on his head, to the unqualified admiration of the whole company. Then Signor Billsmethi insisted as they were so happy, that they should all stay to supper, and proposed sending Master Billsmethi for the beer and spirits, whereupon the two gentlemen swore, "strike 'em wulgar if they'd stand that;" and were just going to quarrel who should pay for it, when Mr. Augustus Cooper said he would, if they'd have the kindness to allow him; and they *had* the kindness to allow him; and Master Billsmethi brought the beer in a can, and the rum in a quart-pot. They had a regular night of it; and Miss Billsmethi squeezed Mr. Augustus Cooper's hand under the table; and Mr. Augustus Cooper returned the squeeze and returned home too, at something to six o'clock in the morning, when he was put to bed by main force by the apprentice, after repeatedly expressing an uncontrollable desire to pitch his reverend parent out of the second-floor window, and to throttle the apprentice with his own neck-handkerchief.

Weeks had worn on, and the seven-and-sixpenny town-mades had nearly worn out, when the night arrived for the grand dress-ball at which the whole of the five-and-seventy pupils were to meet together for the first time that season, and to take out some portion of their respective four-and-sixpences in lamp-oil and fiddlers. Mr. Augustus Cooper had ordered a new coat for the occasion—a two-pound-tenner from Turnstile. It was his first appearance in public; and after a grand Sicilian shawl-dance by fourteen young ladies in character, he was to open the quadrille department with Miss Billsmethi herself, with whom he had become quite intimate since his first introduction. It *was* a night! Everything was admirably arranged. The sandwich-boy took the hats and bonnets at the street-door; there was a turn-up bedstead in the back parlour, on which Miss Billsmethi made tea and coffee for such of the gentlemen as chose to pay for it, and such of the ladies as the gentlemen treated; red port-wine negus and lemonade were handed round at eighteen-pence a head, and, in pursuance of a previous engagement with the public-house at the corner of the street, an extra potboy was laid on for the occasion. In short, nothing could exceed the arrangements, except the company. Such ladies! Such pink silk stockings! Such artificial flowers! Such a number of cabs! No sooner had one cab set down a couple of ladies, than another cab drove up and set down another couple of ladies, and they all knew, not only one another, but the majority of the gentlemen into the bargain, which made it all as pleasant and lively as could be. Signor Billsmethi in black tights, with a large blue bow in his button-hole, introduced the ladies to such of the gentlemen as were strangers: and the ladies talked away—and laughed they did—it was delightful to see them.

As to the shawl-dance, it was the most exciting thing that ever was beheld; there was such a whisking, and rustling, and fanning, and getting ladies into a tangle with artificial flowers, and then disentangling them again; and as to Mr. Augustus Cooper's share in the quadrille, he got through it admirably. He was missing from his partner now and then certainly, and discovered on such occasions to be either dancing with laudable perseverance in another set, or sliding about in perspective, apparently without any definite object; but, generally speaking, they managed to shove him through the figure, until he turned up in the right place. Be this as it may, when he had finished a great many ladies and gentlemen came up and complimented him very much, and said they had never seen a beginner do anything like it before; and Mr. Augustus Cooper was perfectly satisfied with himself, and everybody else into the bargain, and "stood" considerable quantities of spirits-and-water, negus, and compounds, for the use and behoof of two or three dozen very particular friends, selected from the select circle of five-and-seventy pupils.

Now, whether it was the strength of the compounds, or the beauty of the ladies, or what not, it did so happen that Mr. Augustus Cooper encouraged, rather than repelled, the very flattering attentions of a young lady in brown gauze over white calico who had appeared particularly struck with him from the first; and when the encouragements had been prolonged for some time, Miss Billsmethi betrayed her spite and jealousy thereat by calling the young lady in brown gauze a "creetur," which induced the young lady in brown gauze to retort in certain sentences containing a taunt founded on the payment of four-and-sixpence a quarter, and some indistinct reference to a "fancy man"; which reference Mr. Augustus Cooper, being then and there in a state of considerable bewilderment, expressed his entire concurrence in. Miss Billsmethi, thus renounced, forthwith began screaming in the loudest key of her voice at the rate of fourteen screams a minute; and being unsuccessful in an onslaught on the eyes and face, first of the lady in gauze and then of Mr. Augustus Cooper, called distractedly on the other three-and-seventy pupils to furnish her with oxalic acid for her own private drinking, and the call not being honoured, made another rush at Mr. Cooper, and then had her stay-lace cut and was carried off to bed. Mr. Augustus Cooper, not being remarkable for quickness of apprehension, was at a loss to understand what all this meant, till Signor Billsmethi explained it in a most satisfactory manner by stating to the pupils that Mr. Augustus Cooper had made and confirmed divers promises of marriage to his daughter on divers occasions, and had now basely deserted her; on which the indignation of the pupils became universal; and as several chivalrous gentlemen inquired rather pressingly of Mr. Augustus Cooper, whether he required anything for his own use, or, in other words, whether he "wanted anything for himself," he deemed it prudent to make a precipitate retreat. And the upshot of the matter was, that a lawyer's letter came the next day, and an action was commenced next week; and that Mr. Augustus Cooper, after walking twice to the Serpentine for the purpose of drowning himself, and coming twice back without doing it, made a confidante of his mother, who compromised the matter with twenty pounds from the till, which made twenty pounds four shillings and sixpence paid to Signor Billsmethi, exclusive of treats and pumps; and Mr. Augustus Cooper went back and lived with his mother, and there he lives to this day; and as he has lost his ambition for society, and never goes into the world, he will never see this account of himself and will never be any the wiser.

CHAPTER X: *Shabby-Genteel People*

THERE are certain descriptions of people who, oddly enough, appear to appertain exclusively to this metropolis. You meet them every day in the streets of London, but no one ever encounters them elsewhere; they seem to be indigenous to the soil, and to belong as exclusively to London as its own smoke, or the dingy bricks and mortar. We could illustrate the remark by a variety of examples, but in our present sketch we will only advert to one class as a specimen—that class which is so aptly and expressively designated as "shabby genteel."

Now shabby people, God knows, may be found anywhere, and genteel people are not articles of greater scarcity out of London than in it, but this compound of the two—this shabby gentility—is as purely local as the statue at Charing Cross, or the pump at Aldgate. It is worthy of remark too, that only men are shabby-genteel; a woman is always either dirty and slovenly in the extreme, or neat and respectable, however poverty-stricken in appearance. A very poor man, "who has seen better days," as the phrase goes, is a strange compound of dirty-slovenliness and wretched attempts at faded smartness.

We will endeavour to explain our conception of the term which forms the title of this paper. If you meet a man lounging up Drury Lane, or leaning with his back against a post in Long Acre, with his hands in the pockets of a pair of drab trousers plentifully besprinkled with grease-spots: the trousers made very full over the boots, and ornamented with two cords down the outside of each leg—wearing, also what has been a brown coat with bright buttons, and a hat very much pinched up at the sides, cocked over his right eye— don't pity him. He is not shabby-genteel. The "harmonic meetings" at some fourth-rate public-house, or the purlieus of a private theatre, are his chosen haunts; he entertains a rooted antipathy to any kind of work, and is on familiar terms with several pantomime men at the large houses. But if you see hurrying along a bystreet, keeping as close as he can to the area-railings, a man of about forty or fifty, clad in an old rusty suit of threadbare black cloth which shines with constant wear as if it had been bees-waxed, the trousers tightly strapped down, partly for the look of the thing and partly to keep his old shoes from slipping off at the heels,— if you observe too that his yellowish-white neckerchief is carefully pinned up, to conceal the tattered garment underneath, and that his hands are encased in the remains of an old pair of beaver gloves, you may set him down as a shabby-genteel man. A glance at that depressed face, and timorous air of conscious poverty, will make your heart ache—always supposing that you are neither a philosopher, nor a political economist.

We were once haunted by a shabby-genteel man; he was bodily present to our senses all day, and he was in our mind's eye all night. The man of whom Sir Walter Scott speaks in his Demonology, did not suffer half the persecution from his imaginary gentleman-usher in black velvet, that we sustained from our friend in quondam black cloth. He first attracted our notice by sitting opposite to us in the reading-room at the British Museum, and what made the man more remarkable was, that he had always got before him a couple of shabby-genteel books—two old dogs-eared folios, in mouldy worm-eaten covers, which had once been smart. He was in his chair every morning just as the clock struck ten; he was always the last to leave the room in the afternoon, and when he did, he quitted it with the air of a man who knew not where else to go for warmth and quiet. There he used to sit all day, as close to the table as possible in order to conceal the lack of buttons on his coat, with his old hat carefully deposited at his feet where he evidently flattered himself it escaped observation.

About two o'clock you would see him munching a French roll or a penny loaf; not taking it boldly out of his pocket at once, like a man who knew he was only making a lunch, but breaking off little bits in his pocket, and eating them by stealth. He knew too well it was his dinner.

When we first saw this poor object, we thought it quite impossible that his attire could ever become worse. We even went so far as to speculate on the possibility of his shortly appearing in a decent second-hand suit. We knew nothing about the matter; he grew more and more shabby-genteel every day. The buttons dropped off his waistcoat one by one; then he buttoned his coat, and when one side of the coat was reduced to the same condition as the waistcoat, he buttoned it over on the other side. He looked somewhat better at the beginning of the week than at the conclusion, because the neckerchief, though yellow, was not quite so dingy, and in the midst of all this wretchedness he never appeared without gloves and straps. He remained in this state for a week or two. At length one of the buttons on the back of the coat fell off, and then the man himself disappeared, and we thought he was dead.

We were sitting at the same table about a week after his disappearance, and as our eyes rested on his vacant chair, we insensibly fell into a train of meditation on the subject of his retirement from public life. We were wondering whether he had hung himself or thrown himself off a bridge, whether he really was dead or had only been arrested—when our conjectures were suddenly set at rest by the entry of the very man himself. He had undergone some strange meta-morphosis and walked up the centre of the room with an air which showed he was fully conscious of the improvement in his appearance. It was very odd; his clothes were a fine, glossy black, and yet they looked like the same suit; nay, there were the very darns with which old acquaintance had made us familiar. The hat, too—nobody could mistake the shape of that hat, with its high crown gradually increasing in cir-cumference towards the top. Long service had imparted to it a reddish-brown tint, but now it was as black as the coat. The truth flashed suddenly upon us—they had been "revived." It is a deceitful liquid that black and blue reviver; we have watched its effects on many a shabby-genteel man. It betrays its victims into a temporary assumption of importance, possibly into the purchase of a new pair of gloves, or a cheap stock, or some other trifling article of dress. It elevates their spirits for a week, only to depress them, if possible, below their original level. It was so in this case; the transient dignity of the unhappy man decreased, in exact proportion as the "reviver" wore off. The knees of the unmentionables, and the elbows of the coat, and the seams generally, soon began to get alarmingly white. The hat was once more deposited under the table, and its owner crept into his seat as quietly as ever.

There was a week of incessant small rain and mist. At its expiration the "reviver" had entirely vanished, and the shabby-genteel man never afterwards attempted to effect any improvement in his outward appearance.

It would be difficult to name any particular part of town as the principal resort of shabby-genteel men. We have met a great many persons of this description in the neighbour-hood of the Inns of Court. They may be met with in Holborn between eight and ten any morning, and whoever has the curiosity to enter the Insolvent Debtors' Court will observe, both among spectators and practitioners, a great variety of them. We never went on 'Change by any chance without seeing some shabby-genteel men, and we have often wondered what earthly business they can have there. They will sit there for hours, leaning on great, dropsical, mildewed umbrellas, or eating Abernethy biscuits; nobody speaks to them, nor they to any one. On consideration, we remember to have occasionally seen two shabby-genteel men conversing together on 'Change, but our experience assures us that this is an uncommon circumstance, occasioned by the offer of a pinch of snuff, or some such ordinary civility.

It would be a task of equal difficulty either to assign any

particular spot for the residence of these beings, or to endeavour to enumerate their general occupations. We were never engaged in business with more than one shabbygenteel man; he was a drunken engraver and lived in a damp back-parlour in a new row of houses at Camden Town, half street, half brick-field, somewhere near the canal. A shabbygenteel man may have no occupation at all, or he may be a corn agent, or a coal agent, or a wine agent, or a collector of debts, or a broker's assistant, or a broken-down attorney. He may be a clerk of the lowest description, or a contributor to the press of the same grade. Whether our readers have noticed these men in their walks as often as we have, we know not; this we know—that the miserably poor man (no matter whether he owes his distresses to his own conduct, or that of others) who feels his poverty and vainly strives to conceal it, is one of the most pitiable objects in human nature. Such objects, with few exceptions, are shabby-genteel people.

CHAPTER XI: *Making a night of it*

DAMON and Pythias were undoubtedly very good fellows in their way: the former for his extreme readiness to put in special bail for a friend, and the latter for a certain trumplike punctuality in turning up just in the very nick of time, scarcely less remarkable. Many points in their character have however grown obsolete. Damons are rather hard to find in these days of imprisonment for debt (except the sham ones, and they cost half-a-crown); and, as to the Pythiases, the few that have existed in these degenerate times have had an unfortunate knack of making themselves scarce at the very moment when their appearance would have been strictly classical. If the actions of these heroes, however, can find no parallel in modern times, their friendship can. We have Damon and Pythias on the one hand—Potter and Smithers on the other; and lest the two last-mentioned names should never have reached the ears of our enlightened readers, we can do no better than make them acquainted with the owners thereof.

Mr. Thomas Potter, then, was a clerk in the City, and Mr. Robert Smithers was a ditto in the same; their incomes were limited, but their friendship was unbounded. They lived in the same street, walked into town every morning at the same hour, dined at the same slap-bang every day, and revelled in each other's company every night. They were knit together by the closest ties of intimacy and friendship, or, as Mr. Thomas Potter touchingly observed, they were "thick-and-thin pals, and nothing but it." There was a spice of romance in Mr. Smithers' disposition, a ray of poetry, a gleam of misery, a sort of consciousness of he didn't exactly know what, coming across him he didn't precisely know why—which stood out in fine relief against the off-hand, dashing, amateur-pickpocket-sort-of-manner, which distinguished Mr. Potter in an eminent degree.

The peculiarity of their respective dispositions, extended itself to their individual costume. Mr. Smithers generally appeared in public in a surtout and shoes, with a narrow black neckerchief and a brown hat, very much turned up at the sides—peculiarities which Mr. Potter wholly eschewed, for it was his ambition to do something in the celebrated "kiddy" or stage-coach way, and he had even gone so far as to invest capital in the purchase of a rough blue coat with wooden buttons, made upon the fireman's principle, in which, with the addition of a low-crowned, flower-pot-saucer-shaped hat, he had created no inconsiderable sensation at the Albion in Little Russell Street, and divers other places of public and fashionable resort.

Mr. Potter and Mr. Smithers had mutually agreed that, on the receipt of their quarter's salary, they would jointly and in company "spend the evening"—an evident misnomer—the spending applying, as everybody knows, not to the evening itself but to all the money the individual may chance to be possessed of, on the occasion to which reference is made; and they had further agreed that, on the evening aforesaid, they would "make a night of it"—an expressive term, implying the borrowing of several hours from to-morrow morning, adding them to the night before, and manufacturing a compound night of the whole.

The quarter-day arrived at last—we say at last, because quarter-days are as eccentric as comets, moving wonderfully quick when you have a good deal to pay, and marvellously slow when you have a little to receive. Mr. Thomas Potter and Mr. Robert Smithers met by appointment to begin the evening with a dinner; and a nice, snug, comfortable dinner they had, consisting of a little procession of four chops and four kidneys following each other, supported on either side by a pot of the real draught stout, and attended by divers cushions of bread and wedges of cheese.

When the cloth was removed, Mr. Thomas Potter ordered the waiter to bring in, two goes of his best Scotch whiskey, with warm water and sugar, and a couple of his "very mildest" Havannahs, which the waiter did. Mr. Thomas Potter mixed his grog, and lit his cigar; Mr. Robert Smithers did the same; and then Mr. Thomas Potter jocularly proposed as the first toast, "the abolition of all offices whatever" (not sinecures, but counting-houses), which was immediately drunk by Mr. Robert Smithers, with enthusiastic applause. So they went on talking politics, puffing cigars and sipping whiskey-and-

water, till the "goes"—most appropriately so called—were
both gone, which Mr. Robert Smithers perceiving, immediately
ordered in two more goes of the best Scotch whiskey and two
more of the very mildest Havannahs; and the goes kept
coming in, and the mild Havannahs kept going out, until
what with the drinking and lighting, and puffing, and the
stale ashes on the table, and the tallow-grease on the cigars,
Mr. Robert Smithers began to doubt the mildness of the
Havannahs, and to feel very much as if he had been sitting
in a hackney-coach with his back to the horses.

As to Mr. Thomas Potter, he would keep laughing out loud,
and volunteering inarticulate declarations that he was "all
right," in proof of which, he feebly bespoke the evening paper
after the next gentleman, but finding it a matter of some
difficulty to discover any news in its columns or to ascertain
distinctly whether it had any columns at all, he walked slowly
out to look for the moon, and, after coming back quite pale
with looking up at the sky so long, and attempting to express
mirth at Mr. Robert Smithers having fallen asleep, by various
galvanic chuckles, he laid his head on his arm, and went to
sleep also. When he woke again, Mr. Robert Smithers woke
too, and they both very gravely agreed that it was extremely
unwise to eat so many pickled walnuts with the chops, as it
was a notorious fact that they always made people queer and
sleepy; indeed, if it had not been for the whiskey and cigars,
there was no knowing what harm they mightn't have done 'em.
So they took some coffee, and after paying the bill, twelve
and twopence the dinner, and the odd tenpence for the waiter
—thirteen shillings in all—started out on their expedition to
manufacture a night.

It was just half-past eight, so they thought they couldn't
do better than go half-price to the slips at the City Theatre,
which they did accordingly. Mr. Robert Smithers, who had
become extremely poetical after the settlement of the bill,
enlivening the walk by informing Mr. Thomas Potter in
confidence that he felt an inward presentiment of approaching
dissolution and subsequently embellishing the theatre, by
falling asleep, with his head and both arms gracefully drooping
over the front of the boxes.

Such was the quiet demeanour of the unassuming Smithers,
and such were the happy effects of Scotch whiskey and
Havannahs on that interesting person; but Mr. Thomas
Potter, whose great aim it was to be considered as a "knowing
card," a "fast goer" and so forth, conducted himself in a
very different manner, and commenced going very fast
indeed—rather too fast at last, for the patience of the audience
to keep pace with him. On his first entry, he contented
himself by earnestly calling upon the gentlemen in the
gallery to "flare up," accompanying the demand with another

request, expressive of his wish that they would instantaneously "form a union," both which requisitions were responded to, in the manner most in vogue on such occasions.

"Give that dog a bone!" cried one gentleman in his shirt-sleeves.

"Where have you been a having half a pint of intermediate beer?" cried a second. "Tailor!" screamed a third. "Barber's clerk!" shouted a fourth. "Throw him o—ver!" roared a fifth; while numerous voices concurred in desiring Mr. Thomas Potter to return to the arms of his maternal parent, or in common parlance to "go home to his mother!" All these taunts Mr. Thomas Potter received with supreme contempt, cocking the low-crowned hat a little more on one side whenever any reference was made to his personal appearance, and, standing up with his arms a-kimbo, expressing defiance most melodramatically.

The overture—to which these various sounds had been an *ad libitum* accompaniment—concluded, the second piece began, and Mr. Thomas Potter emboldened by impunity, proceeded to behave in a most unprecedented and outrageous manner. First of all, he imitated the shake of the principal female singer; then groaned at the blue fire, then affected to be frightened into convulsions of terror at the appearance of the ghost; and lastly not only made a running commentary in an audible voice, upon the dialogue on the stage, but actually awoke Mr. Robert Smithers who, hearing his companion making a noise, and having a very indistinct notion of where he was, or what was required of him, immediately by way of imitating a good example, set up the most unearthly, unremitting, and appalling howling that ever audience heard. It was too much. "Turn them out!" was the general cry. A noise as of shuffling of feet, and men being knocked up with violence against wainscoting was heard: a hurried dialogue of "Come out!"—"I won't!"—"You shall!"—"I shan't!" —"Give me your card, sir!"—"You're a scoundrel, sir!" and so forth succeeded. A round of applause betokened the approbation of the audience, and Mr. Robert Smithers and Mr. Thomas Potter found themselves shot with astonishing swiftness into the road, without having had the trouble of once putting foot to ground during the whole progress of their rapid descent.

Mr. Robert Smithers being constitutionally one of the slow-goers, and having had quite enough of fast-going, in the course of his recent expulsion to last till the quarter-day then next ensuing at the very least, had no sooner emerged with his companion from the precincts of Milton Street, than he proceeded to indulge in circuitous references to the beauties of sleep, mingled with distant allusions to the propriety of returning to Islington, and testing the influence of their patent Bramahs over the street-door locks to which they respectively belonged. Mr. Thomas Potter, however, was valorous and peremptory. They had come out to make a night of it: and a night must be made. So Mr. Robert Smithers, who was three parts dull, and the other dismal, despairingly assented; and they went into a wine-vaults to get materials for assisting them in making a night, where they found a good many young ladies, and various old gentlemen, and a plentiful sprinkling of hackney-coachmen and cab-drivers, all drinking and talking together; and Mr. Thomas Potter and Mr. Robert Smithers drank small glasses of brandy, and large glasses of soda, till they began to have a very confused idea, either of things in general, or anything in particular; and when they had done treating themselves they began to treat everybody else; and the rest of the entertainment was a confused mixture of heads and heels, black eyes and blue uniforms, mud and gas-lights, thick doors, and a stone paving.

Then, as standard novelists expressively inform us—"all was a blank!" and in the morning the blank was filled up with the words "STATION HOUSE," and the station-house was filled up with Mr. Thomas Potter, Mr. Robert Smithers, and the major part of their wine-vault companions of the preceding night, with a comparatively small portion of clothing of any kind. And it was disclosed at the police office, to the indignation of the Bench, and the astonishment of the spectators, how one Robert Smithers, aided and abetted by one Thomas Potter, had knocked down and beaten, in divers streets, at different times, five men, four boys, and three women; how the said Thomas Potter had feloniously obtained possession of five door-knockers, two bell-handles, and a bonnet: how Robert Smithers, his friend, had sworn at least forty pounds' worth of oaths, at the rate of five shillings a-piece; terrified whole streets full of Her Majesty's subjects with awful shrieks and alarms of fire; destroyed the uniforms of five policemen, and committed various other atrocities, too numerous to recapitulate. And the magistrate, after an appropriate reprimand, fined Mr. Thomas Potter and Mr. Robert Smithers five shillings each, for being, what the law vulgarly terms, drunk, with the trifling addition of thirty-four pounds for seventeen assaults at forty shillings a-head, with liberty to speak to the prosecutors.

The prosecutors *were* spoken to and Messrs. Potter and Smithers lived on credit for a quarter as best they might; and, although the prosecutors expressed their readiness to be assaulted twice a week on the same terms, they have never since been detected in "making a night of it."

CHAPTER XII: *The Prisoners' Van*

WE were passing the corner of Bow Street, on our return from a lounging excursion the other afternoon, when a crowd, assembled round the door of the police office, attracted our attention and we turned up the street accordingly. There were thirty or forty people standing on the pavement and half across the road, and a few stragglers were patiently stationed on the opposite side of the way—all evidently waiting in expectation of some arrival. We waited too, a few minutes, but nothing occurred; so we turned round to an unshaved sallow-looking cobbler, who was standing next us with his hands under the bib of his apron, and put the usual question of "What's the matter?" The cobbler eyed us from head to foot with superlative contempt, and laconically replied "Nuffin."

Now, we were perfectly aware that if two men stop in the street to look at any given object, or even to gaze in the air, two hundred men will be assembled in no time: but as we knew very well that no crowd of people could by possibility remain in a street for five minutes without getting up a little amusement among themselves, unless they had some absorbing object in view, the natural inquiry next in order was, "What are all these people waiting here for?"—"Her Majesty's carriage," replied the cobbler. This was still more extraordinary. We could not imagine what earthly business Her Majesty's carriage could have at the public office, Bow Street, and we were beginning to ruminate upon the possible causes of such an uncommon appearance, when a general exclamation from all the boys in the crowd of "Here's the wan!" caused us to raise our heads and look up the street.

The covered vehicle, in which prisoners are conveyed from the police offices to the different prisons, was coming along at full speed and it then occurred to us for the first time that Her Majesty's carriage was merely another name for the prisoners' van, conferred upon it, not only by reason of the superior gentility of the term, but because the aforesaid van is maintained at Her Majesty's expense, having been originally started for the exclusive accommodation of ladies and gentlemen under the necessity of visiting the various houses of call known by the general denomination of "Her Majesty's Gaols."

The van drew up at the office-door, and the people thronged round the steps, just leaving a little alley for the prisoners to pass through. Our friend the cobbler and the other stragglers crossed over, and we followed their example. The driver, and another man who had been seated by his side in front of the vehicle, dismounted, and were admitted into the office. The office-door was closed after them, and the crowd were on the tiptoe of expectation.

After a few minutes' delay the door again opened, and the two first prisoners appeared. They were a couple of girls, of whom the elder could not be more than sixteen, and the younger of whom had certainly not attained her fourteenth year. That they were sisters was evident from the resemblance which still subsisted between them, though two additional years of depravity had fixed their brand upon the elder girl's features as legibly as if a red-hot iron had seared them. They were both gaudily dressed, the younger one especially, and although there was a strong similarity between them in both respects, which was rendered the more obvious by their being handcuffed together, it is impossible to conceive a greater contrast than the demeanour of the two presented. The younger girl was weeping bitterly—not for display or in the hope of producing effect, but for very shame; her face was buried in her handkerchief, and her whole manner was but too expressive of bitter and unavailing sorrow.

"How long are you for, Emily?" screamed a red-faced woman in the crowd. "Six weeks and labour," replied the elder girl with a flaunting laugh; "and that's better than the stone jug anyhow; the mill's a deal better than the Sessions, and here's Bella a-going too for the first time. Hold up your head, you chicken," she continued boisterously tearing the other girl's handkerchief away; "hold up your head, and show 'em your face, I ain't jealous, but I'm blessed if I ain't game." —"That's right, old gal," exclaimed a man in a paper cap, who, in common with the greater part of the crowd, had been inexpressibly delighted with this little incident.—"Right!" replied the girl; "ah, to be sure; what's the odds, eh?"— "Come, in with you," interrupted the driver.—"Don't you be in a hurry, coachman," replied the girl, "and recollect I want to be set down in Cold-bath Fields—large house with a high garden-wall in front; you can't mistake it. Hallo, Bella, where are you going to—you'll pull my precious arm off?" This was addressed to the young girl, who, in her anxiety to hide herself in the caravan, had ascended the step first, and forgotten the strain upon the handcuff. "Come down, and let's show you the way." And after jerking the miserable girl down with a force which made her stagger on the pavement, she got into the vehicle, and was followed by her wretched companion.

These two girls had been thrown upon London streets, their vices and debauchery, by a sordid and rapacious mother. What the younger girl was then, the elder had been once; and what the elder then was, she must soon become. A melancholy prospect, but how surely to be realised: a tragic drama, but how often acted! Turn to the prisons and police offices of

London—nay, look into the very streets themselves. These things pass before our eyes day after day, and hour after hour —they have become such matters of course that they are utterly disregarded. The progress of these girls in crime will be as rapid as the flight of a pestilence, resembling it too in its baneful influence and wide-spreading infection. Step by step how many wretched females, within the sphere of every man's observation have become involved in a career of vice frightful to contemplate; hopeless at its commencement, loathsome and repulsive in its course, friendless, forlorn, and unpitied at its miserable conclusion!

There were other prisoners—boys of ten, as hardened in vice as men of fifty—a houseless vagrant going joyfully to prison as a place of food and shelter, handcuffed to a man whose prospects were ruined, character lost, and family rendered destitute by his first offence.—Our curiosity, however, was satisfied. The first group had left an impression on our mind we would gladly have avoided, and would willingly have effaced.

The crowd dispersed; the vehicle rolled away with its load of guilt and misfortune, and we saw no more of the Prisoners' Van.

TALES

CHAPTER I: *The Boarding-House.*   *Chapter the First*

Mrs. TIBBS was, beyond all dispute, the most tidy, fidgety, thrifty little personage that ever inhaled the smoke of London; and the house of Mrs. Tibbs was decidedly the neatest in all Great Coram Street. The area and the area-steps, and the street-door, and the street-door steps, and the brass handle, and the door-plate, and the knocker, and the fan-light, were all as clean and bright as indefatigable white-washing, and hearth-stoning, and scrubbing and rubbing could make them. The wonder was, that the brass door-plate, with the interesting inscription "MRS. TIBBS," had never caught fire from constant friction, so perseveringly was it polished. There were meat-safe-looking blinds in the parlour windows, blue and gold curtains in the drawing-room, and spring-roller blinds, as Mrs. Tibbs was wont in the pride of her heart to boast, "all the way up." The bell-lamp in the passage looked as clear as a soap-bubble; you could see yourself in all the tables, and French-polish yourself on any one of the chairs. The banisters were bees-waxed; and the very stair-wires made your eyes wink, they were so glittering.

Mrs. Tibbs was somewhat short of stature, and Mr. Tibbs was by no means a large man. He had, moreover, very short legs, but, by way of indemnification, his face was peculiarly long. He was to his wife what the 0 is in 90—he was of some importance *with* her—he was nothing without her. Mrs. Tibbs was always talking. Mr. Tibbs rarely spoke; but if it were at any time possible to put in a word, just when he should have said nothing at all, he did it. Mrs. Tibbs detested long stories, and Mr. Tibbs had one, the conclusion of which had never been heard by his most intimate friends. It always began, "I recollect when I was in the volunteer corps, in eighteen hundred and six,"—but as he spoke very slowly and softly and his better half very quickly and loudly, he rarely got beyond the introductory sentence. He was a melancholy specimen of the story-teller. He was the wandering Jew of Joe Millerism.

Mr. Tibbs enjoyed a small independence from the pension-list—about 43*l.* 15*s.* 10*d.* a year. His father, mother, and five interesting scions from the same stock drew a like sum from the revenue of a grateful country, though for what particular service was never distinctly known. But, as this said independence was not quite sufficient to furnish two people with *all* the luxuries of this life, it had occurred to the busy little spouse of Tibbs, that the best thing she could do with a legacy of 700*l.*, would be to take and furnish a tolerable house, somewhere in that partially-explored tract of country which lies between the British Museum, and a remote village called Somers Town, for the reception of boarders. Great Coram Street was the spot pitched upon. The house had been furnished accordingly; two female servants and a boy engaged; and an advertisement inserted in the morning papers, informing the public that "Six individuals would meet with all the comforts of a cheerful musical home in a select private family residing within ten minutes' walk of everywhere." Answers out of number were received, with all sorts of initials; all the letters of the alphabet seemed to be seized with a sudden wish to go out boarding and lodging, voluminous was the correspondence between Mrs. Tibbs and the applicants, and most profound was the secrecy which was to be observed. "E." didn't like this, and "I." couldn't think of putting up with that; "I.O.U." didn't think the terms would suit him; and "G. R." had never slept in a French bed. The result, however, was, that three gentlemen became inmates of Mrs. Tibbs's house, on terms which were "agreeable to all parties." In went the advertisement again, and a lady with her two daughters proposed to increase—not their families, but Mrs. Tibbs's.

"Charming woman, that Mrs. Maplesone!" said Mrs. Tibbs, as she and her spouse were sitting by the fire after breakfast; the gentlemen having gone out on their several avocations. "Charming woman, indeed!" repeated little Mrs. Tibbs, more by way of soliloquy than anything else, for she never thought of consulting her husband. "And the two daughters are delightful. We must have some fish to-day; they'll join us at dinner for the first time."

Mr. Tibbs placed the poker at right angles with the fire shovel, and essayed to speak, but recollected he had nothing to say.

"The young ladies," continued Mrs. T., "have kindly volunteered to bring their own piano."

Tibbs thought of the volunteer story, but did not venture it. A bright thought struck him:

"It's very likely," said he.

"Pray don't lean your head against the paper," interrupted Mrs. Tibbs—"and don't put your feet on the steel fender; that's worse."

Tibbs took his head from the paper, and his feet from the fender, and proceeded. "It's very likely one of the young

ladies may set her cap at young Mr. Simpson, and you know a
marriage——"

"A what!" shrieked Mrs. Tibbs. Tibbs modestly repeated
his former suggestion.

"I beg you won't mention such a thing," said Mrs. T. "A
marriage, indeed!—to rob me of my boarders—no, not for
the world."

Tibbs thought in his own mind that the event was by no
means unlikely, but as he never argued with his wife, he put
a stop to the dialogue, by observing it was "time to go to
business." He always went out at ten o'clock in the morning,
and returned at five in the afternoon, with an exceedingly
dirty face, and smelling very mouldy. Nobody knew what he
was, or where he went; but Mrs. Tibbs used to say with an air
of great importance, that he was engaged in the City.

The Miss Maplesones and their accomplished parent arrived
in the course of the afternoon in a hackney-coach, and
accompanied by a most astonishing number of packages.
Trunks, bonnet-boxes, muff-boxes and parasols, guitar-cases,
and parcels of all imaginable shapes, done up in brown paper,
and fastened with pins, filled the passage. Then, there was
such a running up and down with the luggage, such scampering
for warm water for the ladies to wash in, and such a bustle, and
confusion, and heating of servants and curling-irons, as had
never been known in Great Coram Street before. Little Mrs.
Tibbs was quite in her element, bustling about, talking
incessantly, and distributing towels and soap, and all the
etceteras, like a head nurse in a hospital. The house was not
restored to its usual state of quiet repose until the ladies were
safely shut up in their respective bedrooms, engaged in the
important occupation of dressing for dinner.

"Are these gals 'andsome?" inquired Mr. Simpson of Mr.
Septimus Hicks, another of the boarders, as they were
amusing themselves in the drawing-room before dinner, by
lolling on sofas, and contemplating their pumps.

"Don't know," replied Mr. Septimus Hicks, who was a
tallish, white-faced young man, with spectacles, and a black
ribbon round his neck instead of a neckerchief—a most
interesting person; a poetical walker of the hospitals, and a
"very talented young man." He was fond of "lugging" into
conversation all sorts of quotations from Don Juan, without
fettering himself by the propriety of their application, in which
particular he was remarkably independent. The other, Mr.
Simpson, was one of those young men who are in society what
walking gentlemen are upon the stage, only infinitely worse
skilled in his vocation than the most indifferent artist. He
was as empty-headed as the great bell of St. Paul's; always
dressed according to the caricatures published in the monthly
fashions, and spelt Character with a K.

"I saw a devilish number of parcels in the passage when I came home," simpered Simpson.

"Materials for the toilet, no doubt," rejoined the Don Juan reader.

> ——"*Much linen, lace, and several pair*
> *Of stockings, slippers, brushes, combs, complete* ;
> *With other articles of ladies' fair,*
> *To keep them beautiful, or leave them neat.*"

"Is that from Milton?" inquired Mr. Simpson.

"No—from Byron," returned Mr. Hicks, with a look of profound contempt. He was quite sure of his author, because he had never read any other.—"Hush!" said the sapient hospital-walker, "here come the gals," and they both commenced talking in a very loud key.

"Mrs. Maplesone and the Miss Maplesones, Mr. Hicks. Mr. Hicks—Mrs. Maplesone and the Miss Maplesones," said Mrs. Tibbs with a very red face, for she had been superintending the cooking operations below stairs, and looked like a wax doll on a sunny day. "Mr. Simpson, I beg your pardon—Mr. Simpson —Mrs. Maplesone and the Miss Maplesones"—and vice versa. The gentlemen immediately began to slide about with much politeness, and to look as if they wished their arms had been legs, so little did they know what to do with them. The ladies smiled, curtsyed, and glided into chairs, and dived for dropped pocket-handkerchiefs: the gentlemen leant against two of the curtain-pegs; Mrs. Tibbs went through an admirable bit of serious pantomime with a servant who had come up to ask some question about the fish-sauce, and then the two young ladies looked at each other; and everybody else appeared to discover something very attractive in the pattern of the fender.

"Julia, my love," said Mrs. Maplesone to her youngest daughter, in a tone just loud enough for the remainder of the company to hear,—"Julia."

"Yes, Ma."

"Don't stoop."—This was said for the purpose of directing general attention to Miss Julia's figure, which was undeniable. Everybody looked at her accordingly, and there was another pause.

"We had the most uncivil hackney-coachman to-day you can imagine," said Mrs. Maplesone to Mrs. Tibbs, in a confidential tone.

"Dear me!" replied the hostess, with an air of great commiseration. She couldn't say more, for the servant again appeared at the door, and commenced telegraphing most earnestly to her "Missis."

"I think hackney-coachmen generally are uncivil," said Mr. Hicks in his most insinuating tone.

"Positively I think they are," replied Mrs. Maplesone, as if the idea had never struck her before.

"And cabmen, too," said Mr. Simpson. This remark was a failure, for no one intimated by word or sign the slightest knowledge of the manners and customs of cabmen.

"Robinson, what *do* you want?" said Mrs. Tibbs to the servant who, by way of making her presence known to her mistress, had been giving sundry hems and sniffs outside the door during the preceding five minutes.

"Please, ma'am, master wants his clean things," replied the servant, completely taken off her guard. There was no resisting this: the two young men turned their faces to the window, and "went off" like a couple of bottles of ginger-beer; the ladies put their handkerchiefs to their mouths, and little Mrs. Tibbs bustled out of the room to give Tibbs his clean linen,—and the servant warning.

Mr. Calton, the remaining boarder, shortly afterwards made his appearance, and proved a surprising promoter of the conversation. Mr. Calton was a superannuated beau—an old boy. He used to say of himself that although his features were not regularly handsome, they were striking. They certainly were; it was impossible to look at his face without being forcibly reminded of a chubby street-door knocker, half-lion half-monkey; and the comparison might be extended to his whole character and conversation. He had stood still while everything else had been moving. He never originated a conversation, or started a new idea; but if any commonplace topic were broached, or, to pursue the comparison, if anybody *lifted him up*, he would hammer away with surprising rapidity. He had the tic-douloureux occasionally, and then he might be said to be muffled, because he did not make quite as much noise as at other times when he would go on prosing, rat-rat-tat the same thing over and over again. He had never been married; but he was still on the look-out for a wife with money. He had a life interest worth about 300*l.* a year—he was exceedingly vain, and inordinately selfish. He had acquired the reputation of being the very pink of politeness, and he walked round the park, and up Regent Street, every day.

This respectable personage had made up his mind to render himself exceedingly agreeable to Mrs. Maplesone—indeed, the desire of being as amiable as possible extended itself to the whole party; Mrs. Tibbs having considered it an admirable little bit of management to represent to the gentlemen that she had *some* reason to believe the ladies were fortunes, and to hint to the ladies, that all the gentlemen were "eligible." A little flirtation, she thought, might keep her house full, without leading to any other result.

Mrs. Maplesone was an enterprising widow of about fifty: shrewd, scheming, and good-looking. She was amiably anxious on behalf of her daughters; in proof whereof she used to remark, that she would have no objection to marry again, if it would benefit her dear girls—she could have no other motive. The "dear girls" themselves were not at all insensible to the merits of "a good establishment." One of them was twenty-five, the other three years younger. They had been at different watering-places for four seasons; they had gambled at libraries, read books in balconies, sold at fancy fairs, danced at assemblies, talked sentiment—in short, they had done all that industrious girls could do—and all to no purpose.

"What a magnificent dresser Mr. Simpson is!" whispered Matilda Maplesone to her sister Julia.

"Splendid!" returned the youngest. The magnificent individual alluded to wore a sort of maroon-coloured dress-coat, with a velvet collar and cuffs of the same tint—very like that which usually invests the form of the distinguished unknown who condescends to play the "swell" in the pantomime at "Richardson's Show."

"What whiskers!" said Miss Julia.

"Charming!" responded her sister; "and what hair!" His hair was like a wig, and distinguished by that insinuating wave which graces the shining locks of those *chefs-d'œuvre* of perruquerian art surmounting the waxen images in Bartellot's window in Regent Street; his whiskers meeting beneath his chin seemed strings wherewith to tie it on, ere science had rendered them unnecessary by her patent invisible springs.

"Dinner's on the table, ma'am, if you please," said the boy, who now appeared for the first time, in a revived black coat of his master's.

"Oh! Mr. Calton, will you lead Mrs. Maplesone?—Thank you." Mr. Simpson offered his arm to Miss Julia; Mr. Septimus Hicks escorted the lovely Matilda; and then Mrs. Tibbs directed James to take off the covers. Salmon, lobster-sauce, giblet-soup, and the usual accompaniments were *disc*overed: potatoes like petrifactions, and bits of toasted bread, the shape and size of blank dice.

"Soup for Mrs. Maplesone, my dear," said the bustling Mrs. Tibbs. She always called her husband "my dear" before company. Tibbs who had been eating his bread, and calculating how long it would be before he should get any fish, helped the soup in a hurry, made a small island on the tablecloth, and put his glass upon it, to hide it from his wife.

"Miss Julia, shall I assist you to some fish?"

"If you please—very little—oh! plenty, thank you" (a bit about the size of a walnut put upon the plate).

"Julia is a *very* little eater," said Mrs. Maplesone to Mr. Calton.

The knocker gave a single rap. He was busy eating the fish with his eyes: so he only ejaculated, "Ah!"

"My dear," said Mrs. Tibbs to her spouse after every one else had been helped, "What do *you* take?" The inquiry was accompanied with a look intimating that he mustn't say fish, because there was not much left. Tibbs thought the frown referred to the island on the tablecloth; he therefore coolly replied, "Why—I'll take a little—fish, I think."

"Did you say fish, my dear?" (another frown).

"Yes, dear," replied the villain, with an expression of acute hunger depicted in his countenance. The tears almost started to Mrs. Tibbs's eyes, as she helped her "wretch of a husband," as she inwardly called him, to the last eatable bit of salmon on the dish.

"James, take this to your master, and take away your master's knife." This was deliberate revenge, as Tibbs never could eat fish without one. He was, however, constrained to chase small particles of salmon round and round his plate with a piece of bread and a fork, occasionally securing a bit; the number of successful attempts being about one in seventeen.

"Take away, James," said Mrs. Tibbs, just as Tibbs swallowed the fourth mouthful—and away went the plates like lightning.

"I'll take a bit of bread, James," said the poor "*master* of the house," more hungry than ever.

"Never mind your master now, James," said Mrs. Tibbs, "see about the meat."—This was conveyed in the tone in which ladies usually give admonitions to servants in company, that is to say, a low one; but which, like a stage whisper, from its peculiar emphasis, is most distinctly heard by everybody present.

A pause ensued before the table was replenished—a sort of parenthesis in which Mr. Simpson, Mr. Calton, and Mr. Hicks produced respectively a bottle of sauterne, bucellas, and sherry, and took wine with everybody—except Tibbs; no one ever thought of him.

Between the fish and an intimated sirloin there was a prolonged interval.

Here was an opportunity for Mr. Hicks. He could not resist the singularly appropriate quotation:

"But beef is rare within these oxless isles ;
Goats' flesh there is, no doubt, and kid, and mutton,
And, when a holiday upon them smiles,
A joint upon their barbarous spits they put on."

"Very ungentlemanly behaviour," thought little Mrs. Tibbs, "to talk in that way."

"Ah," said Mr. Calton, filling his glass. "Tom Moore is my poet."

"And mine," said Mrs. Maplesone.

"And mine," said Miss Julia.

"And mine," added Mr. Simpson.

"Look at his compositions," resumed the knocker.

"To be sure," said Simpson, with confidence.

"Look at Don Juan," replied Mr. Septimus Hicks.

"Julia's letter," suggested Miss Matilda.

"Can anything be grander than the Fire Worshippers?" inquired Miss Julia.

"To be sure," said Simpson.

"Or Paradise and the Peri," said the old beau.

"Yes; or Paradise and the Peer," repeated Simpson, who thought he was getting through it capitally.

"It's all very well," replied Mr. Septimus Hicks, who, as we have before hinted, never read anything but Don Juan. "Where will you find anything finer than the description of the siege, at the commencement of the seventh canto?"

"Talking of a siege," said Tibbs, with a mouthful of bread— "when I was in the volunteer corps, in eighteen hundred and six, our commanding officer was Sir Charles Rampart; and one day, when we were exercising on the ground on which the London University now stands, he says, says he, Tibbs (calling me from the ranks), Tibbs——"

"Tell your master, James," interrupted Mrs. Tibbs, in an awfully distinct tone, "tell your master if he *won't* carve those fowls, to send them to me." The discomfited volunteer instantly set to work, and carved the fowls almost as expeditiously as his wife operated on the haunch of mutton. Whether he ever finished the story is not exactly known, but if he did nobody heard it.

As the ice was now broken, and the new inmates more at home, every member of the company felt more at ease. Tibbs himself most certainly did, because he went to sleep immediately after dinner. Mr. Hicks and the ladies discoursed most eloquently about poetry, and the theatres, and Lord Chesterfield's Letters; and Mr. Calton followed up what everybody said, with continuous double-knocks. Mrs. Tibbs highly approved of every observation that fell from Mrs. Maplesone; and as Mr. Simpson sat with a smile upon his face and said "Yes," or "Certainly," at intervals of about four minutes each, he received full credit for understanding what was going forward. The gentlemen rejoined the ladies in the drawing-room very shortly after they had left the dining-parlour. Mrs. Maplesone and Mr. Calton played cribbage, and the "young people" amused themselves with music and conversation. The Miss Maplesones sang the most fascinating duets, and accompanied themselves on guitars, ornamented with bits of ethereal blue ribbon. Mr. Simpson put on a pink waistcoat, and said he was in raptures; and Mr. Hicks felt in the seventh heaven of poetry, or the seventh canto of Don Juan—it was the same thing to him. Mrs. Tibbs was quite charmed with the new-comers, and Mr. Tibbs spent the evening in his usual way—he went to sleep, and woke up, and went to sleep again, and woke at supper-time.

We are not about to adopt the license of novel-writers, and to let "years roll on"; but we will take the liberty of requesting the reader to suppose that six months have elapsed since the dinner we have just described, and that Mrs. Tibbs's boarders have, during that period, sung, and danced, and gone to theatres and exhibitions together, as ladies and gentlemen, wherever they board, often do; and we will beg them, the period we have mentioned having elapsed, to imagine further, that Mr. Septimus Hicks received, in his own bedroom (a front attic), at an early hour one morning, a note from Mr. Calton, requesting the favour of seeing him, as soon as convenient to himself, in his (Calton's) dressing-room on the second-floor back.

"Tell Mr. Calton I'll come down directly," said Mr. Septimus to the boy. "Stop—is Mr. Calton unwell?" inquired the excited walker of hospitals, as he put on a bed-furniture-looking dressing-gown.

"Not as I know on, sir," replied the boy. "Please, sir, he looked rather rum, as it might be."

"Ah, that's no proof of his being ill," returned Hicks, unconsciously. "Very well: I'll be down directly." Downstairs ran the boy with the message, and down went the excited Hicks himself, almost as soon as the message was delivered. "Tap, tap." "Come in."—Door opens, and discovers Mr. Calton sitting in an easy chair, and looking more like a knocker than ever. Mutual shakes of the hand exchanged, and Mr. Septimus Hicks motioned to a seat. A short pause. Mr. Hicks coughed, and Mr. Calton took a pinch of snuff. It was just one of those interviews where neither party knows what to say. Mr. Septimus Hicks broke silence.

"I received a note—" he said, very tremulously, in a voice like a Punch with a cold.

"Yes," returned the other, "you did."

"Exactly."

"Yes."

Now, although this dialogue must have been satisfactory, both gentlemen felt there was something more important to be said; so they did as many in such a situation would have done —they looked at the table with a most determined aspect. The conversation had been opened, however, and Mr. Calton had made up his mind to continue it with a regular double-knock. He always spoke very pompously.

"Hicks," said he, "I have sent for you in consequence of certain arrangements which are pending in this house, connected with a marriage."

"With a marriage!" gasped Hicks, compared with whose expression of countenance, Hamlet's, when he sees his father's ghost, is pleasing and composed.

"With a marriage," returned the knocker. "I have sent for you to prove the great confidence I can repose in you."

"And will you betray me?" eagerly inquired Hicks, who in his alarm had even forgotten to quote.

"*I* betray *you!* Won't *you* betray *me?*"

"Never: no one shall know to my dying day, that you had a hand in the business," responded the agitated Hicks, with an inflamed countenance, and his hair standing on end as if he were on the stool of an electrifying machine in full operation.

"People must know that, some time or other—within a year, I imagine," said Mr. Calton, with an air of great self-complacency. "We *may* have a family, you know."

"*We!*—That won't affect you, surely?"

"The devil it won't!"

"No! how can it?" said the bewildered Hicks. Calton was too much inwrapped in the contemplation of happiness to see the equivoque between Hicks and himself, and threw himself back in his chair. "Oh, Matilda!" sighed the antique beau, in a lack-a-daisical voice, and applying his right hand a little to the left of the fourth button of his waistcoat, counting from the bottom. This was meant to be pathetic.—"Oh, Matilda!"

"What Matilda?" inquired Hicks, starting up.

"Matilda Maplesone," responded the other, doing the same.

"I marry her to-morrow morning," said Hicks, furiously.

"It's false," rejoined his companion: "I marry her!"

"You marry her!"

"I marry her!"

"You marry Matilda Maplesone?"

"Matilda Maplesone."

"*Miss* Maplesone marry *you?*"

"Miss Maplesone! No: Mrs. Maplesone."

"Good God!" said Hicks, falling into his chair: "You marry the mother, and I the daughter!"

"Most extraordinary circumstance!" replied Mr. Calton, "and rather inconvenient too; for the fact is, that owing to

Matilda's wishing to keep her intention secret from her daughters until the ceremony has taken place, she doesn't like applying to any of her friends to give her away. I entertain an objection to making the affair known to my acquaintance just now; and the consequence is, that I sent to you to know whether you'd oblige me by acting as father."

"I should have been most happy, I assure you," said Hicks, in a tone of condolence; "but you see I shall be acting as bridegroom. One character is frequently a consequence of the other; but it is not usual to act in both at the same time. There's Simpson—I have no doubt he'll do it for you."

"I don't like to ask him," replied Calton; "he's such a donkey."

Mr. Septimus Hicks looked up at the ceiling, and down at the floor; at last an idea struck him.—"Let the man of the house, Tibbs, be the father," he suggested; and then he quoted, as peculiarly applicable to Tibbs and the pair:

> "*Oh Powers of Heaven! what dark eyes meets she there?*
> *'Tis—'tis her father's—fixed upon the pair.*"

"The idea has struck me already," said Mr. Calton: "but, you see, Matilda, for what reason I know not, is very anxious that Mrs. Tibbs should know nothing about it till it's all over. It's a natural delicacy, after all, you know."

"He's the best-natured little man in existence, if you manage him properly," said Mr. Septimus Hicks. "Tell him not to mention it to his wife, and assure him she won't mind it, and he'll do it directly. My marriage is to be a secret one, on account of the mother and *my* father: therefore he must be enjoined to secrecy."

A small double-knock, like a presumptuous single one, was that instant heard at the street-door. It was Tibbs; it could be no one else, for no one else occupied five minutes in rubbing their shoes. He had been out to pay the baker's bill.

"Mr. Tibbs," called Mr. Calton in a very bland tone, looking over the banisters.

"Sir!" replied he of the dirty face.

"Will you have the kindness to step upstairs for a moment?"

"Certainly, sir," said Tibbs, delighted to be taken notice of. The bedroom door was carefully closed, and Tibbs, having put his hat on the floor (as all timid men do), and been accommodated with a seat, looked as astounded as if he were suddenly summoned before the familiars of the Inquisition.

"A rather unpleasant occurrence, Mr. Tibbs," said Calton, in a very portentous manner, "obliges me to consult you, and to beg you will not communicate what I am about to say to your wife."

Tibbs acquiesced, wondering in his own mind what the deuce

the other could have done, and imagining that at least he must have broken the best decanters.

Mr. Calton resumed: "I am placed, Mr. Tibbs, in rather an unpleasant situation."

Tibbs looked at Mr. Septimus Hicks, as if he thought his being in the immediate vicinity of his fellow-boarder might constitute the unpleasantness of his situation; but as he did not exactly know what to say, he merely ejaculated the monosyllable "Lor!"

"Now," continued the knocker, "let me beg you will exhibit no manifestations of surprise, which may be overheard by the domestics, when I tell you—command your feelings of astonishment—that two inmates of this house intend to be married to-morrow morning,"—and he drew back his chair several feet to perceive the effect of the unlooked-for announcement.

If Tibbs had rushed from the room, staggered down-stairs, and fainted in the passage—if he had instantaneously jumped out of the window into the mews behind the house, in an agony of surprise—his behaviour would have been much less inexplicable to Mr. Calton than it was, when he put his hands into his inexpressible pockets, and said with a half-chuckle, "Just so."

"You are not surprised, Mr. Tibbs?" inquired Mr. Calton.

"Bless you, no, sir," returned Tibbs; "after all it's very natural. When two young people get together, you know——"

"Certainly, certainly," said Calton, with an indescribable air of self-satisfaction.

"You don't think it's at all an out-of-the-way affair then?" asked Mr. Septimus Hicks, who had watched the countenance of Tibbs in mute astonishment.

"No, sir," replied Tibbs; "I was just the same at his age." He actually smiled when he said this.

"How devilish well I must carry my years!" thought the delighted old beau, knowing he was at least ten years older than Tibbs at that moment.

"Well, then, to come to the point at once," he continued, "I have to ask you whether you will object to act as father on the occasion?"

"Certainly not," replied Tibbs; still without evincing an atom of surprise.

"You will not?"

"Decidedly not," reiterated Tibbs, who appeared as calm as a pot of porter with the head off.

Mr. Calton seized the hand of the petticoat-governed little man, and vowed eternal friendship from that hour. Hicks, who was all admiration and surprise, did the same.

"Now confess," asked Mr. Calton of Tibbs, as he picked up his hat, "were you not a little surprised?"

"I b'lieve you!" replied that illustrious person, holding up one hand; "I b'lieve you! When I first heard of it."

"So sudden," said Septimus Hicks.

"So strange to ask *me*, you know," said Tibbs.

"So odd altogether," said the superannuated love-maker; and then all three laughed.

"I say," said Tibbs, shutting the door which he had previously opened, and giving full vent to a hitherto corked-up giggle, "what bothers me is, what *will* his father say?"

Mr. Septimus Hicks looked at Mr. Calton.

"Yes; but the best of it is," said the latter, giggling in his turn, "I haven't got a father—he! he! he!"

"*You* haven't got a father. No; but *he* has," said Tibbs.

"*Who* has?" inquired Septimus Hicks, almost rabid.

"Why *him*."

"Him, who? Do you know my secret? Do you mean me?"

"You! No; you know who I mean," returned Tibbs, with a knowing wink.

"For Heaven's sake whom *do* you mean?" inquired Mr. Calton, who, like Septimus Hicks, was all but out of his senses at the strange confusion.

"Why, Mr. Simpson, of course," replied Tibbs; "who else could I mean?"

"I see it all," said the Byron-quoter; "Simpson marries Julia Maplesone to-morrow morning!"

"Undoubtedly," replied Tibbs, thoroughly satisfied; "of course he does."

It would require the pencil of Hogarth to illustrate—our feeble pen is inadequate to describe—the expression which the countenances of Mr. Calton and Mr. Septimus Hicks respectively assumed at this unexpected announcement. Equally impossible is it to describe, although it is much easier for our lady readers to imagine, what arts the three ladies could have used so completely to entangle their separate partners. Whatever they were, however, they were successful. The mother was perfectly aware of the intended marriage of both daughters; and the young ladies were equally acquainted with the intention of their estimable parent. They agreed, however, that it would have a much better appearance if each feigned ignorance of the other's engagement; and it was equally desirable that all the marriages should take place on the same day, to prevent the discovery of one clandestine alliance operating prejudicially on the others. Hence the mystification of Mr. Calton and Mr. Septimus Hicks, and the pre-engagement of the unwary Tibbs.

On the following morning Mr. Septimus Hicks was united to Miss Matilda Maplesone. Mr. Simpson also entered into a "holy alliance" with Miss Julia: Tibbs acting as father, "his first appearance in that character." Mr. Calton, not being quite so eager as the two young men, was rather struck by the double discovery; and as he had found some difficulty in getting any one to give the lady away, it occurred to him that the best mode of obviating the inconvenience would be not to take her at all. The lady, however, "appealed," as her counsel said on the trial of the cause, *Maplesone* v. *Calton*, for a breach of promise, "with a broken heart, to the outraged laws of her country." She recovered damages to the amount of 1000*l*., which the unfortunate knocker was compelled to pay. Mr. Septimus Hicks having walked the hospitals, took it into his head to walk off altogether. His injured wife is at present residing with her mother at Boulogne. Mr. Simpson, having the misfortune to lose his wife six weeks after marriage (by her eloping with an officer during his temporary sojourn in the Fleet Prison, in consequence of his inability to discharge her little mantuamaker's bill), and being disinherited by his father, who died soon afterwards, was fortunate enough to obtain a permanent engagement at a fashionable hair-cutter's; hairdressing being a science to which he had frequently directed his attention. In this situation he had necessarily many opportunities of making himself acquainted with the habits and style of thinking of the exclusive portion of the nobility of this kingdom. To this fortunate circumstance are we indebted for the production of those brilliant efforts of genius, his fashionable novels, which so long as good taste, unsullied by exaggeration, cant, and maudlin quackery, continues to exist, cannot fail to instruct and amuse the thinking portion of the community.

It only remains to add, that this complication of disorders completely deprived poor Mrs. Tibbs of all her inmates, except the one whom it would have afforded her the greatest pleasure to lose—her husband. That wretched little man returned home on the day of the wedding in a state of partial intoxication; and under the influence of wine, excitement, and despair, actually dared to brave the anger of his wife. Since that ill-fated hour he has constantly taken his meals in the kitchen, to which apartment it is understood his witticisms will be in future confined: a turn-up bedstead having been conveyed there by Mrs. Tibbs's order for his exclusive accommodation. It is very likely that he will be enabled to finish there his story of the volunteers.

The advertisement has again appeared in the morning papers. Results must be reserved for another chapter.

Chapter the Second

"WELL," said little Mrs. Tibbs to herself, as she sat in the front parlour of the Coram Street mansion one morning, mending a piece of stair-carpet off the first landing;—"Well!

things have not turned out so badly either, and if I only get a favourable answer to the advertisement, we shall be full again."

Mrs. Tibbs resumed her occupation of making worsted lattice-work in the carpet, anxiously listening to the twopenny postman, who was hammering his way down the street at the rate of a penny a knock. The house was as quiet as possible. There was only one low sound to be heard—it was the unhappy Tibbs cleaning the gentlemen's boots in the back kitchen, and accompanying himself with a buzzing noise, in wretched mockery of humming a tune.

The postman drew near the house. He paused—so did Mrs. Tibbs. A knock—a bustle—a letter—post paid.

T. I. presents compt. to I. T. and T. I. begs To say that i see the advertisement And she will Do Herself the pleasure of calling On you at 12 o'clock to-morrow morning.

T. I. as To apologise to I. T. for the shortness Of the notice But i hope it will not unconvenience you.

I remain yours Truly
Wednesday evening.

Little Mrs. Tibbs perused the document over and over again; and the more she read it, the more was she confused by the mixture of the first and third person; the substitution of the "I" for the "T. I."; and the transition from the "I. T." to the "you." The writing looked like a skein of thread in a tangle, and the note was ingeniously folded into a perfect square, with the direction squeezed up into the right-hand corner, as if it were ashamed of itself. The back of the epistle was pleasingly ornamented with a large red wafer, which, with the addition of divers ink-stains, bore a marvellous resemblance to a black beetle trodden upon. One thing, however, was perfectly clear to the perplexed Mrs. Tibbs. Somebody was to call at twelve.

The drawing-room was forthwith dusted for the third time that morning; three or four chairs were pulled out of their places, and a corresponding number of books carefully upset, in order that there might be a due absence of formality. Down went the piece of stair-carpet before noticed, and up ran Mrs. Tibbs "to make herself tidy."

The clock of New Saint Pancras Church struck twelve, and the Foundling, with laudable politeness, did the same ten minutes afterwards. Saint something else struck the quarter, and then there arrived a single lady with a double-knock, in a pelisse the colour of the interior of a damson pie; a bonnet of the same, with a regular conservatory of artificial flowers; a white veil, and a green parasol, with a cobweb border.

The visitor (who was very fat and red-faced) was shown into the drawing-room; Mrs. Tibbs presented herself, and the negotiation commenced.

"I called in consequence of an advertisement," said the stranger, in a voice as if she had been playing a set of Pan's pipes for a fortnight without leaving off.

"Yes!" said Mrs. Tibbs, rubbing her hands very slowly, and looking the applicant full in the face—two things she always did on such occasions.

"Money isn't no object whatever to me," said the *lady*, "so much as living in a state of retirement and obtrusion."

Mrs. Tibbs, as a matter of course, acquiesced in such an exceedingly natural desire.

"I am constantly attended by a medical man," resumed the pelisse wearer; "I have been a shocking unitarian for some time—I, indeed, have had very little peace since the death of Mr. Bloss."

Mrs. Tibbs looked at the relict of the departed Bloss, and thought he must have had very little peace in his time. Of course she could not say so; so she looked very sympathising.

"I shall be a good deal of trouble to you," said Mrs. Bloss; "but for that trouble I am willing to pay. I am going through a course of treatment which renders attention necessary. I have one mutton chop in bed at half-past eight, and another at ten, every morning."

Mrs. Tibbs, as in duty bound, expressed the pity she felt for anybody placed in such a distressing situation; and the carnivorous Mrs. Bloss proceeded to arrange the various preliminaries with wonderful despatch. "Now mind," said that lady, after terms were arranged; "I am to have the second-floor front for my bedroom?"

"Yes, ma'am."

"And you'll find room for my little servant Agnes?"

"Oh! certainly."

"And I can have one of the cellars in the area for my bottled porter."

"With the greatest pleasure;—James shall get it ready for you by Saturday."

"And I'll join the company at the breakfast-table on Sunday morning," said Mrs. Bloss. "I shall get up on purpose."

"Very well," returned Mrs. Tibbs, in her most amiable tone; for satisfactory references had "been given and required," and it was quite certain that the new-comer had plenty of money. "It's rather singular," continued Mrs. Tibbs, with what was meant for a most bewitching smile, "that we have a gentleman now with us, who is in a very delicate state of health—a Mr. Gobler. His apartment is the back drawing-room."

"The next room?" inquired Mrs. Bloss.

"The next room," repeated the hostess.

"How very promiscuous!" ejaculated the widow.

"He hardly ever gets up," said Mrs. Tibbs in a whisper.

"Lor!" cried Mrs. Bloss, in an equally low tone.

"And when he is up," said Mrs. Tibbs, "we never can persuade him to go to bed again."

"Dear me!" said the astonished Mrs. Bloss, drawing her chair nearer Mrs. Tibbs. "What is his complaint?"

"Why, the fact is," replied Mrs. Tibbs, with a most communicative air, "he has no stomach whatever."

"No what?" inquired Mrs. Bloss, with a look of the most indescribable alarm.

"No stomach," repeated Mrs. Tibbs, with a shake of the head.

"Lord bless us! what an extraordinary case!" gasped Mrs. Bloss, as if she understood the communication in its literal sense, and was astonished at a gentleman without a stomach finding it necessary to board anywhere.

"When I say he has no stomach," explained the chatty little Mrs. Tibbs, "I mean that his digestion is so much impaired, and his interior so deranged, that his stomach is not of the least use to him;—in fact, it's rather an inconvenience than otherwise."

"Never heard such a case in my life!" exclaimed Mrs. Bloss. "Why, he's worse than I am."

"Oh, yes!" replied Mrs. Tibbs;—"certainly." She said this with great confidence, for the damson pelisse satisfactorily proved that Mrs. Bloss, at all events, was not suffering under Mr. Gobler's complaint.

"You have quite incited my curiosity," said Mrs. Bloss, as she rose to depart. "How I long to see him!"

"He generally comes down once a week," replied Mrs. Tibbs; "I dare say you'll see him on Sunday." With this consolatory promise Mrs. Bloss was obliged to be contented. She accordingly walked slowly down the stairs, detailing her complaints all the way; and Mrs. Tibbs followed her, uttering an exclamation of compassion at every step. James (who looked very gritty, for he was cleaning the knives) fell up the kitchen stairs, and opened the street-door; and, after mutual farewells, Mrs. Bloss slowly departed down the shady side of the street.

It is almost superfluous to say, that the lady whom we have just shown out at the street-door (and whom the two female servants are now inspecting from the second-floor windows) was exceedingly vulgar, ignorant, and selfish. Her deceased better-half had been an eminent cork-cutter, in which capacity he had amassed a decent fortune. He had no relative but his nephew, and no friend but his cook. The former had the insolence one morning to ask for the loan of fifteen pounds, and by way of retaliation he married the latter next day; he made a will immediately afterwards, containing a burst of honest indignation against his nephew (who supported himself and two sisters on 100*l.* a-year), and a bequest of his whole property to his wife. He felt ill after breakfast, and died after dinner. There is a mantelpiece-looking tablet in a civic parish church, setting forth his virtues, and deploring his loss. He never dishonoured a bill, or gave away a halfpenny!

The relict and sole executrix of this noble-minded man was an odd mixture of shrewdness and simplicity, liberality and meanness. Bred up as she had been, she knew no mode of living so agreeable as a boarding-house; and having nothing to do, and nothing to wish for, she naturally imagined she must be very ill—an impression which was most assiduously promoted by her medical attendant, Dr. Wosky, and her hand-maid, Agnes, both of whom, doubtless for excellent reasons, encouraged all her extravagant notions.

Since the catastrophe recorded in the last chapter, Mrs. Tibbs had been very shy of young-lady boarders. Her present inmates were all lords of the creation, and she availed herself of the opportunity of their assemblage at the dinner-table, to announce the expected arrival of Mrs. Bloss. The gentlemen received the communication with stoical indifference, and Mrs. Tibbs devoted all her energies to prepare for the reception of the valetudinarian. The second-floor front was scrubbed, and washed, and flannelled, till the wet went through to the drawing-room ceiling. Clean white counterpanes, and curtains, and napkins; water-bottles as clear as crystal, blue jugs, and mahogany furniture, added to the splendour and increased the comfort of the apartment. The warming-pan was in constant requisition, and a fire lighted in the room every day. The chattels of Mrs. Bloss were forwarded by instalments. First there came a large hamper of Guinness's stout and an umbrella; then a train of trunks; then a pair of clogs and a bandbox; then an easy-chair with an air-cushion, then a variety of suspicious looking packages; and—"though last not least"—Mrs. Bloss and Agnes, the latter in a cherry-coloured merino dress, open-work stockings, and shoes with sandals; looking like a disguised Columbine.

The installation of the Duke of Wellington, as Chancellor of the University of Oxford, was nothing in point of bustle and turmoil to the installation of Mrs. Bloss in her new quarters. True, there was no bright doctor of civil law to deliver a classical address on the occasion; but there were several other old women present, who spoke quite as much to the purpose, and understood themselves equally well. The chop-eater was so fatigued with the process of removal that she declined leaving her room until the following morning; so a mutton-chop, pickle, a two-grain calomel pill, a pint bottle of stout, and other medicines, were carried up-stairs for her consumption.

"Why, what *do* you think, ma'am?" inquired the inquisitive Agnes of her mistress, after they had been in the house some three hours; "what *do* you think, ma'am? the lady of the house is married."

"Married!" said Mrs. Bloss, taking the pill and a draught of Guinness—"married! Unpossible!"

"She is indeed, ma'am," returned the Columbine; "and her husband, ma'am, lives—he—he—he—lives in the kitchen, ma'am."

"In the kitchen!"

"Yes, ma'am; and he—he—he—the housemaid says, he never goes into the parlour except on Sundays; and that Mrs. Tibbs makes him clean the gentlemen's boots; and that he cleans the windows, too, sometimes; and that one morning early, when he was in the front balcony cleaning the drawing-room windows, he called out to a gentleman on the opposite side of the way, who used to live here—'Ah! Mr. Calton, sir, how are you?'" Here the attendant laughed till Mrs. Bloss was in serious apprehension of her chuckling herself into a fit.

"Well, I never!" said Mrs. Bloss.

"Yes, and please, ma'am, the servants gives him gin-and-water sometimes; and then he cries and says he hates his wife and the boarders, and wants to tickle them."

"Tickle the boarders!" exclaimed Mrs. Bloss, seriously alarmed.

"No, ma'am, not the boarders, the servants."

"Oh, is that all!" said Mrs. Bloss, quite satisfied.

"He wanted to kiss me as I came up the kitchen-stairs, just now," said Agnes, indignantly; "but I gave it him—a little wretch!"

This intelligence was but too true. A long course of snubbing and neglect; his days spent in the kitchen, and his nights in the turn-up bedstead, had completely broken the little spirit that the unfortunate volunteer had ever possessed. He had no one to whom he could detail his injuries but the servants, and they were almost of necessity his chosen confidants. It is no less strange than true, however, that the little weaknesses which he had incurred, most probably during his military career, seemed to increase as his comforts diminished. He was actually a sort of journeyman Giovanni in the basement story.

The next morning, being Sunday, breakfast was laid in the front parlour at ten o'clock. Nine was the usual time, but the family always breakfasted an hour later on Sabbath. Tibbs enrobed himself in his Sunday costume—a black coat, and exceedingly short, thin trousers, with a very large white

waistcoat, white stockings and cravat, and Blucher boots—
and mounted to the parlour aforesaid. Nobody had come
down, and he amused himself by drinking the contents of the
milkpot with a teaspoon.

A pair of slippers were heard descending the stairs; Tibbs
flew to a chair, and a stern-looking man, of about fifty, with
very little hair on his head, and a Sunday paper in his hand,
entered the room.

"Good morning, Mr. Evenson," said Tibbs, very humbly,
with something between a nod and a bow.

"How do you do, Mr. Tibbs?" replied he of the slippers, as
he sat himself down, and began to read his paper without
saying another word.

"Is Mr. Wisbottle in town to-day, do you know, sir?"
inquired Tibbs, just for the sake of saying something.

"I should think he was," replied the stern gentleman. "He
was whistling 'The Light Guitar,' in the next room to mine,
at five o'clock this morning."

"He's very fond of whistling," said Tibbs with a slight
smirk.

"Yes—I ain't," was the laconic reply.

Mr. John Evenson was in the receipt of an independent
income, arising chiefly from various houses he owned in the
different suburbs. He was very morose and discontented.
He was a thorough Radical, and used to attend a great variety
of public meetings, for the express purpose of finding fault
with everything that was proposed. Mr. Wisbottle, on the
other hand, was a high Tory. He was a clerk in the Woods
and Forests Office, which he considered rather an aristocratic
employment; he knew the peerage by heart, and could tell you
off-hand where any illustrious personage lived. He had a
good set of teeth, and a capital tailor. Mr. Evenson looked
on all these qualifications with profound contempt; and the
consequence was that the two were always disputing, much to
the edification of the rest of the house. It should be added,
that, in addition to his partiality for whistling, Mr. Wisbottle
had a great idea of his singing powers. There were two other
boarders besides the gentleman in the back drawing-room—
Mr. Alfred Tomkins and Mr. Frederick O'Bleary. Mr.
Tomkins was a clerk in a wine-house; he was a connoisseur
in paintings, and had a wonderful eye for the picturesque.
Mr. O'Bleary was an Irishman, recently imported; he was in a
perfectly wild state, and had come over to England to be an
apothecary, a clerk in a government office, an actor, a reporter,
or anything else that turned up—he was not particular. He
was on familiar terms with two small Irish members, and got
franks for everybody in the house. He felt convinced that his
intrinsic merits must procure him a high destiny. He wore
shepherd's-plaid inexpressibles, and used to look under all the

ladies' bonnets as he walked along the streets. His manners
and appearance always forcibly reminded one of Orson.

"Here comes Mr. Wisbottle," said Tibbs; and Mr. Wisbottle
forthwith appeared in blue slippers, and a shawl dressing-
gown, whistling "*Di piacer.*"

"Good morning, sir," said Tibbs again. It was about the
only thing he ever said to anybody.

"How are you, Tibbs?" condescendingly replied the
amateur; and he walked to the window, and whistled louder
than ever.

"Pretty air, that!" said Evenson with a snarl, and without
taking his eyes off the paper.

"Glad you like it," replied Wisbottle, highly gratified.

"Don't you think it would sound better, if you whistled
it a little louder?" inquired the mastiff.

"No; I don't think it would," rejoined the unconscious
Wisbottle.

"I'll tell you what, Wisbottle," said Evenson, who had been
bottling up his anger for some hours—"the next time you
feel disposed to whistle 'The Light Guitar' at five o'clock in
the morning, I'll trouble you to whistle it with your head out
o' window. If you don't, I'll learn the triangle—I will
by——"

The entrance of Mrs. Tibbs (with the keys in a little basket)
interrupted the threat, and prevented its conclusion.

Mrs. Tibbs apologised for being down rather late; the bell
was rung; James brought up the urn, and received an unlimited order for dry toast and bacon. Tibbs sat down at
the bottom of the table, and began eating water-cresses like
a second Nebuchadnezzar. Mr. O'Bleary appeared, and Mr.
Alfred Tomkins. The compliments of the morning were
exchanged, and the tea was made.

"God bless me!" exclaimed Tomkins, who had been looking out at the window. "Here—Wisbottle—pray come here:
make haste."

Mr. Wisbottle started from the table, and every one looked
up.

"Do you see," said the connoisseur, placing Wisbottle in
the right position—"a little more this way: there—do you
see how splendidly the light falls upon the left side of that
broken chimney-pot at No. 48?"

"Dear me! I see," replied Wisbottle, in a tone of
admiration.

"I never saw an object stand out so beautifully against the
clear sky in my life," ejaculated Alfred. Everybody (except
John Evenson) echoed the sentiment, for Mr. Tomkins had a
great character for finding out beauties which no one else
could discover—he certainly deserved it.

"I have frequently observed a chimney-pot in College

Green, Dublin, which has a much better effect," said the patriotic O'Bleary, who never allowed Ireland to be outdone on any point.

The assertion was received with obvious incredulity, for Mr. Tomkins declared that no other chimney-pot in the United Kingdom, broken or unbroken, could be so beautiful as the one at No. 48.

The room-door was suddenly thrown open, and Agnes appeared leading in Mrs. Bloss, who was dressed in a geranium-coloured muslin gown, and displayed a gold watch of huge dimensions; a chain to match, and a splendid assortment of rings, with enormous stones. A general rush was made for a chair, and a regular introduction took place. Mr. John Evenson made a slight inclination of the head; Mr. Frederick O'Bleary, Mr. Alfred Tomkins, and Mr. Wisbottle, bowed like the mandarins in a grocer's shop; Tibbs rubbed hands, and went round in circles. He was observed to close one eye, and to assume a clock-work sort of expression with the other; this has been considered as a wink, and it has been reported that Agnes was its object. We repel the calumny, and challenge contradiction.

Mrs. Tibbs inquired after Mrs. Bloss's health in a low tone. Mrs. Bloss, with a supreme contempt for the memory of Lindley Murray, answered the various questions in a most satisfactory manner; and a pause ensued, during which the eatables disappeared with awful rapidity.

"You must have been very much pleased with the appearance of the ladies going to the Drawing-room the other day, Mr. O'Bleary?" said Mrs. Tibbs, hoping to start a topic.

"Yes," replied Orson, with a mouthful of toast.

"Never saw anything like it before, I suppose?" suggested Wisbottle.

"No—except the Lord Lieutenant's levees," replied O'Bleary.

"Are they at all equal to our drawing-rooms?"

"Oh, infinitely superior."

"Gad! I don't know," said the aristocratic Wisbottle, "the Dowager Marchioness of Publiccash was most magnificently dressed, and so was the Baron Slappenbachenhausen."

"What was he presented on?" inquired Evenson.

"On his arrival in England."

"I thought so," growled the Radical; "you never hear of these fellows being presented on their going away again. They know better than that."

"Unless somebody pervades them with an apintment," said Mrs. Bloss, joining in the conversation in a faint voice.

"Well," said Wisbottle, evading the point, "it's a splendid sight."

"And did it never occur to you," inquired the Radical,

who never would be quiet—"did it never occur to you,
that you pay for these precious ornaments of society?"

"It certainly *has* occurred to me," said Wisbottle, who
thought this answer was a poser; "it *has* occurred to me,
and I am willing to pay for them."

"Well, and it has occurred to me too," replied John Evenson, "and I ain't willing to pay for 'em. Then why should
I?—I say, why should I?" continued the politician, laying
down the paper, and knocking his knuckles on the table.
"There are two great principles—demand——"

"A cup of tea if you please, dear," interrupted Tibbs.

"And supply——"

"May I trouble you to hand this tea to Mr. Tibbs?" said
Mrs. Tibbs, interrupting the argument, and unconsciously
illustrating it.

The thread of the orator's discourse was broken. He drank
his tea and resumed the paper.

"If it's very fine," said Mr. Alfred Tomkins, addressing
the company in general, "I shall ride down to Richmond
to-day, and come back by the steamer. There are some
splendid effects of light and shade on the Thames; the contrast between the blueness of the sky and the yellow water
is frequently exceedingly beautiful." Mr. Wisbottle hummed,
"Flow on, thou shining river."

"We have some splendid steam-vessels in Ireland," said
O'Bleary.

"Certainly," said Mrs. Bloss, delighted to find a subject
broached in which she could take part.

"The accommodations are extraordinary," said O'Bleary.

"Extraordinary indeed," returned Mrs. Bloss. "When Mr.
Bloss was alive he was promiscuously obligated to go to Ireland on business. I went with him, and raly the manner in
which the ladies and gentlemen were accommodated with
berths is not creditable."

Tibbs, who had been listening to the dialogue, looked very
aghast, and evinced a strong inclination to ask a question,
but was checked by a look from his wife. Mr. Wisbottle
laughed, and said Tomkins had made a pun; and Tomkins
laughed too, and said he had not.

The remainder of the meal passed off as breakfasts usually
do. Conversation flagged, and people played with their
teaspoons. The gentlemen looked out at the window, walked
about the room, and when they got near the door, dropped off
one by one. Tibbs retired to the back parlour by his wife's
orders, to check the greengrocer's weekly account; and
ultimately Mrs. Tibbs and Mrs. Bloss were left alone
together.

"Oh dear!" said the latter, "I feel alarmingly faint; it's
very singular." (It certainly was, for she had eaten four

pounds of solids that morning.) "By-the-by," said Mrs.
Bloss, "I have not seen Mr. What's-his-name yet."

"Mr. Gobler?" suggested Mrs. Tibbs.

"Yes."

"Oh!" said Mrs. Tibbs, "he is a most mysterious person.
He has his meals regularly sent up-stairs, and sometimes
don't leave his room for weeks together."

"I haven't seen or heard nothing of him," repeated Mrs.
Bloss.

"I dare say you'll hear him to-night," replied Mrs. Tibbs;
"he generally groans a good deal on Sunday evenings."

"I never felt such an interest in any one in my life," ejacu-
ated Mrs. Bloss. A finicking double-knock interrupted the
conversation; Dr. Wosky was announced, and duly shown
in. He was a little man with a red face,—dressed of course
in black, with a stiff white neckerchief. He had a very good
practice, and plenty of money, which he had amassed by
invariably humouring the worst fancies of all the females of
all the families he had ever been introduced into. Mrs.
Tibbs offered to retire, but was entreated to stay.

"Well, my dear ma'am, and how are we?" inquired Wosky
in a soothing tone.

"Very ill, doctor—very ill," said Mrs. Bloss in a whisper.

"Ah! we must take care of ourselves;—we must, indeed,"
said the obsequious Wosky, as he felt the pulse of his interesting patient.

"How is our appetite?"

Mrs. Bloss shook her head.

"Our friend requires great care," said Wosky, appealing to
Mrs. Tibbs, who of course assented. "I hope, however, with
the blessing of Providence," continued the doctor, "that we
shall be enabled to make her quite stout again."

Mrs. Tibbs wondered in her own mind what the patient
would be when she had got quite stout.

"We must take stimulants," said the cunning Wosky—
"plenty of nourishment, and, above all, we must keep our
nerves quiet; we positively must not give way to our sensibilities. We must take all we can get," concluded the
doctor as he pocketed his fee, "and we must keep quiet."

"Dear man!" exclaimed Mrs. Bloss as the doctor stepped
into his carriage.

"Charming creature indeed—quite a lady's man," said
Mrs. Tibbs, and Doctor Wosky rattled away to make fresh
culls of delicate females, and pocket fresh fees.

As we had occasion in a former paper to describe a dinner
at Mrs. Tibbs's, and as one meal went off very like another on
all ordinary occasions, we will not fatigue our readers by
entering into any other detailed account of the domestic
economy of the establishment. We will therefore proceed to

events, merely premising that the mysterious tenant of the back drawing-room was a lazy, selfish hypochondriac; always complaining and never ill.   As his character in many respects closely assimilated to that of Mrs. Bloss, a very warm friendship soon sprang up between them.   He was tall, thin, and pale; he always fancied he had a severe pain somewhere or other, and his face invariably wore a pinched, screwed-up expression; he looked, indeed, like a man who had got his feet in a tub of exceedingly hot water against his will.

For two or three months after Mrs. Bloss's first appearance in Coram Street, John Evenson was observed to become every day more sarcastic and more ill-natured, and there was a degree of additional importance in his manner, which clearly showed that he fancied he had discovered something, which he only wanted a proper opportunity of divulging.   He found it at last.

One evening, the different inmates of the house were assembled in the drawing-room engaged in their ordinary occupations.   Mr. Gobler and Mrs. Bloss were sitting at a small card-table near the centre window playing cribbage; Mr. Wisbottle was describing semicircles on the music-stool, turning over the leaves of a book on the piano, and humming most melodiously; Alfred Tomkins was sitting at the round table with his elbows duly squared, making a pencil sketch of a head considerably larger than his own; O'Bleary was reading Horace, and trying to look as if he understood it; and John Evenson had drawn his chair close to Mrs. Tibbs's work-table, and was talking to her very earnestly in a low tone.

"I can assure you, Mrs. Tibbs," said the Radical, laying his forefinger on the muslin she was at work on; "I can assure you, Mrs. Tibbs, that nothing but the interest I take in your welfare would induce me to make this communication.   I repeat I fear Wisbottle is endeavouring to gain the affections of that young woman, Agnes, and that he is in the habit of meeting her in the store-room on the first floor, over the leads. From my bedroom I distinctly heard voices there last night. I opened my door immediately, and crept very softly on to the landing; there I saw Mr. Tibbs, who, it seems, had been disturbed also.—Bless me, Mrs. Tibbs, you change colour!"

"No, no—it's nothing," returned Mrs. T. in a hurried manner; "it's only the heat of the room."

"A flush!" ejaculated Mrs. Bloss from the card-table; "that's good for four."

"If I thought it was Mr. Wisbottle," said Mrs. Tibbs, after a pause, "he should leave this house instantly."

"Go!" said Mrs. Bloss again.

"And if I thought," continued the hostess with a most threatening air, "if I thought he was assisted by Mr. Tibbs——"

"One for his nob!" said Gobler.

"Oh," said Evenson, in a most soothing tone—he liked to make mischief—"I should hope Mr. Tibbs was not in any way implicated. He always appeared to me very harmless."

"I have generally found him so," sobbed poor little Mrs. Tibbs; crying like a watering-pot in full play.

"Hush! hush! pray—Mrs. Tibbs—consider—we shall be observed—pray, don't!" said John Evenson, fearing his whole plan would be interrupted. "We will set the matter at rest with the utmost care, and I shall be most happy to assist you in doing so."

Mrs. Tibbs murmured her thanks.

"When you think every one has retired to rest to-night," said Evenson very pompously, "if you'll meet me without a light, just outside my bedroom-door, by the staircase-window, I think we can ascertain who the parties really are, and you will afterwards be enabled to proceed as you think proper."

Mrs. Tibbs was easily persuaded; her curiosity was excited, her jealousy was roused, and the arrangement was forthwith made. She resumed her work, and John Evenson walked up and down the room with his hands in his pockets, looking as if nothing had happened. The game of cribbage was over, and conversation began again.

"Well, Mr. O'Bleary," said the humming top, turning round on his pivot, and facing the company, "what did you think of Vauxhall the other night?"

"Oh, it's very fair," replied Orson, who had been enthusiastically delighted with the whole exhibition.

"Never saw anything like that Captain Ross's set-out—eh?"

"No," returned the patriot with his usual reservation—"except in Dublin."

"I saw the Count de Canky and Captain Fitzthompson in the Gardens," said Wisbottle; "they appeared much delighted."

"Then it must be beautiful!" snarled Evenson.

"I think the white bears is partickerlerly well done," suggested Mrs. Bloss. "In their shaggy white coats, they look just like Polar bears—don't you think they do, Mr. Evenson?"

"I think they look a great deal more like omnibus cads on all fours," replied the discontented one.

"Upon the whole, I should have liked our evening very well," gasped Gobler; "only I caught a desperate cold which increased my pain dreadfully. I was obliged to have several shower-baths, before I could leave my room."

"Capital things those shower-baths!" ejaculated Wisbottle.

"Excellent!" said Tomkins.

"Delightful!" chimed in O'Bleary. (He had once seen one outside a tinman's.)

"Disgusting machines!" rejoined Evenson, who extended

his dislike to almost every created object, masculine, feminine, or neuter.

"Disgusting, Mr. Evenson!" said Gobler, in a tone of strong indignation.—"Disgusting! Look at their utility—consider how many lives they have saved by promoting perspiration."

"Promoting perspiration, indeed," growled John Evenson, stopping short in his walk across the large squares in the pattern of the carpet—"I was ass enough to be persuaded some time ago to have one in my bedroom. 'Gad, I was in it once, and it effectually cured *me* certainly, for the mere sight of it threw me into a profuse perspiration for six months afterwards."

A general titter followed this announcement, and before it had subsided James brought up "the tray," containing the remains of a leg of lamb which had made its *début* at dinner; bread, cheese; an atom of butter in a forest of parsley; one pickled walnut and the third of another, and so forth. The boy disappeared, and returned again with another tray, containing glasses and jugs of hot and cold water. The gentlemen brought in their spirit-bottles; the housemaid placed divers plated bedroom candlesticks under the card-table, and the servants retired for the night.

Chairs were drawn round the table, and the conversation proceeded in the customary manner. John Evenson, who never ate supper, lolled on the sofa, and amused himself by contradicting everybody. O'Bleary ate as much as he could conveniently carry, and Mrs. Tibbs felt a due degree of indignation thereat; Mr. Gobler and Mrs. Bloss conversed most affectionately on the subject of pill-taking and other innocent amusements; and Tomkins and Wisbottle "got into an argument"; that is to say, they both talked very loudly and vehemently, each flattering himself that he had got some advantage about something, and neither of them having more than a very indistinct idea of what they were talking about. An hour or two passed away; and the boarders and the brass candlesticks retired in pairs to their respective bedrooms. John Evenson pulled off his boots, locked his door, and determined to sit up until Mr. Gobler had retired. He always sat in the drawing-room about an hour after everybody else had left it, taking medicine, and groaning.

Great Coram Street was hushed into a state of the most profound repose: it was nearly two o'clock. A hackney-coach now and then rumbled slowly by; and occasionally some stray lawyer's clerk on his way home to Somers Town struck his iron heel on the top of the coal-cellar with a noise resembling the click of a smoke-jack. A low, monotonous, gushing sound was heard, which added considerably to the romantic dreariness of the scene. It was the water "coming in" at number eleven.

"He must be asleep by this time," said John Evenson to himself after waiting with exemplary patience for nearly an hour after Mr. Gobler had left the drawing-room. He listened for a few moments; the house was perfectly quiet; he extinguished his rushlight, and opened his bedroom-door. The staircase was so dark that it was impossible to see anything.

"S—s—s!" whispered the mischief-maker, making a noise like the first indication a catherine-wheel gives of the probability of its going off.

"Hush!" whispered somebody else.

"Is that you, Mrs. Tibbs?"

"Yes, sir."

"Where?"

"Here"; and the misty outline of Mrs. Tibbs appeared at the staircase window, like the ghost of Queen Anne in the tent scene in Richard.

"This way, Mrs. Tibbs," whispered the delighted busybody: "give me your hand—there. Whoever these people are, they are in the store-room now, for I have been looking down from my window, and I could see that they accidentally upset their candlestick, and are now in darkness. You have no shoes on, have you?"

"No," said little Mrs. Tibbs, who could hardly speak for trembling.

"Well; I have taken my boots off, so we can go down close to the store-room-door and listen over the banisters," continued Evenson; and down-stairs they both crept accordingly, every board creaking like a patent mangle on a Saturday afternoon.

"It's Wisbottle and somebody I'll swear," exclaimed the Radical in an energetic whisper, when they had listened for a few moments.

"Hush—pray let's hear what they say!" exclaimed Mrs. Tibbs, the gratification of whose curiosity was now paramount to every other consideration.

"Ah! if I could but believe you," said a female voice coquettishly, "I'd be bound to settle my missis for life."

"What does she say?" inquired Mr. Evenson, who was not quite so well situated as his companion.

"She says she'll settle her missis's life," replied Mrs. Tibbs. "The wretch! they're plotting murder."

"I know you want money," continued the voice, which belonged to Agnes; "and if you'd secure me the five hundred pounds, I warrant she should take fire soon enough."

"What's that?" inquired Evenson again. He could just hear enough to want to hear more.

"I think she says she'll set the house on fire," replied the affrighted Mrs. Tibbs. "But thank God I'm insured in the Phœnix!"

"The moment I have secured your mistress, my dear," said a man's voice in a strong Irish brogue, "you may depend on having the money."

"Bless my soul, it's Mr. O'Bleary!" exclaimed Mrs. Tibbs in a parenthesis.

"The villain!" said the indignant Mr. Evenson.

"The first thing to be done," continued the Hibernian, "is to poison Mr. Gobler's mind."

"Oh, certainly!" returned Agnes, with the utmost coolness.

"What's that?" inquired Evenson again, in an agony of curiosity and a whisper.

"He says she's to mind and poison Mr. Gobler," replied Mrs. Tibbs, perfectly aghast at this awful sacrifice of human life.

"And in regard to Mrs. Tibbs," continued O'Bleary.—Mrs. Tibbs shuddered.

"Hush!" exclaimed Agnes, in a tone of the greatest alarm, just as Mrs. Tibbs was on the extreme verge of a fainting fit. "Hush!"

"Hush!" exclaimed Evenson, at the same moment to Mrs. Tibbs.

"There's somebody coming *up*-stairs," said Agnes to O'Bleary.

"There's somebody coming *down*-stairs," whispered Evenson to Mrs. Tibbs.

"Go into the parlour, sir," said Agnes to her companion. "You will get there, before whoever it is gets to the top of the kitchen stairs."

"The drawing-room, Mrs. Tibbs!" whispered the astonished Evenson to his equally astonished companion; and for the drawing-room they both made, plainly hearing the rustling of two persons, one coming down-stairs, and one coming up.

"What can it be?" exclaimed Mrs. Tibbs. "It's like a dream. I wouldn't be found in this situation for the world!"

"Nor I," returned Evenson, who could never bear a joke at his own expense. "Hush! here they are at the door."

"What fun!" whispered one of the newcomers.—It was Wisbottle.

"Glorious!" replied his companion, in an equally low tone.—This was Alfred Tomkins. "Who would have thought it?"

"I told you so," said Wisbottle, in a most knowing whisper. "Lord bless you, he has paid her most extraordinary attention for the last two months. I saw 'em when I was sitting at the piano to-night."

"Well, do you know I didn't notice it?" interrupted Tomkins.

"Not notice it!" continued Wisbottle. "Bless you; I saw him whispering to her, and she crying; and then I'll swear I heard him say something about to-night when we were all in bed."

"They're talking of *us!*" exclaimed the agonised Mrs. Tibbs, as the painful suspicion, and a sense of their situation, flashed upon her mind.

"I know it—I know it," replied Evenson, with a melancholy consciousness that there was no mode of escape.

"What's to be done? we cannot both stop here!" ejaculated Mrs. Tibbs, in a state of partial derangement.

"I'll get up the chimney," replied Evenson, who really meant what he said.

"You can't," said Mrs. Tibbs, in despair. "You can't—it's a register stove."

"Hush!" repeated John Evenson.

"Hush—hush!" cried somebody down-stairs.

"What a d—d hushing!" said Alfred Tomkins, who began to get rather bewildered.

"There they are!" exclaimed the sapient Wisbottle, as a rustling noise was heard in the store-room.

"Hark!" whispered both the young men.

"Hark!" repeated Mrs. Tibbs and Evenson.

"Let me alone, sir," said a female voice in the store-room.

"Oh, Hagnes!" cried another voice, which clearly belonged to Tibbs, for nobody else ever owned one like it. "Oh, Hagnes—lovely creature!"

"Be quiet, sir!" (A bounce.)

"Hag——"

"Be quiet, sir—I am ashamed of you. Think of your wife, Mr. Tibbs. Be quiet, sir!"

"My wife!" exclaimed the valorous Tibbs, who was clearly under the influence of gin-and-water, and a misplaced attachment; "I 'ate her! Oh, Hagnes! when I was in the volunteer corps, in eighteen hundred and——"

"I declare I'll scream. Be quiet, sir, will you?" (Another bounce and a scuffle.)

"What's that?" exclaimed Tibbs, with a start.

"What's what?" said Agnes, stopping short.

"Why, that!"

"Ah! you have done it nicely now, sir," sobbed the frightened Agnes, as a tapping was heard at Mrs. Tibbs's bedroom door, which would have beaten any twelve woodpeckers hollow.

"Mrs. Tibbs! Mrs. Tibbs!" called out Mrs. Bloss. "Mrs. Tibbs, pray get up." (Here the imitation of a woodpecker was resumed with tenfold violence.)

"Oh, dear—dear!" exclaimed the wretched partner of the depraved Tibbs. "She's knocking at my door. We must be discovered! What will they think?"

"Mrs. Tibbs! Mrs. Tibbs!" screamed the woodpecker again.

"What's the matter!" shouted Gobler, bursting out of the back drawing-room like the dragon at Astley's—only without the portable gas in his countenance.

"Oh, Mr. Gobler!" cried Mrs. Bloss, with a proper approximation to hysterics; "I think the house is on fire, or else there's thieves in it. I have heard the most dreadful noises!"

"The devil you have!" shouted Gobler again, bouncing back into his den, in happy imitation of the aforesaid dragon, and returning immediately with a lighted candle. "Why, what's this? Wisbottle! Tomkins! O'Bleary! Agnes! What the deuce! all up and dressed?"

"Astonishing!" said Mrs. Bloss, who had run down-stairs, and taken Mr. Gobler's arm.

"Call Mrs. Tibbs directly, somebody," said Gobler, turning into the front drawing-room.—"What! Mrs. Tibbs and Mr. Evenson!!"

"Mrs. Tibbs and Mr. Evenson!" repeated everybody, as that unhappy pair were discovered, Mrs. Tibbs seated in an arm-chair by the fireplace, and Mr. Evenson standing by her side.

We must leave the scene that ensued to the reader's imagination. We could tell how Mrs. Tibbs forthwith fainted away, and how it required the united strength of Mr. Wisbottle and Mr. Alfred Tomkins to hold her in her chair; how Mr. Evenson explained, and how his explanation was evidently disbelieved; how Agnes repelled the accusations of Mrs. Tibbs, by proving that she was negotiating with Mr. O'Bleary to influence her mistress's affections in his behalf; and how Mr. Gobler threw a damp counterpane on the hopes of Mr. O'Bleary by avowing that he (Gobler) had already proposed to, and been accepted by, Mrs. Bloss; how Agnes was discharged from that lady's service; how Mr. O'Bleary discharged himself from Mrs. Tibb's house, without going through the form of previously discharging his bill; and how that disappointed young gentleman rails against England and the English, and vows there is no virtue or fine feeling extant, "except in Ireland." We repeat that we *could* tell all this, but we love to exercise our self-denial, and we therefore prefer leaving it to be imagined.

The lady whom we have hitherto described as Mrs. Bloss is no more. Mrs. Gobler exists: Mrs. Bloss has left us for ever. In a secluded retreat in Newington Butts, far—far removed from the noisy strife of that great boarding-house, the world, the enviable Gobler and his pleasing wife revel in retirement; happy in their complaints, their table, and their medicine; wafted through life by the grateful prayers of all the purveyors of animal food within three miles round.

We would willingly stop here, but we have a painful duty imposed upon us, which we must discharge. Mr. and Mrs. Tibbs have separated by mutual consent, Mrs. Tibbs receiving one moiety of 43*l*. 15*s*. 10*d*., which we before stated to be the amount of her husband's annual income, and Mr. Tibbs the other. He is spending the evening of his days in retirement, and he is spending also annually that small but honourable independence. He resides among the original settlers at Walworth, and it has been stated, on unquestionable authority, that the conclusion of the volunteer story has been heard in a small tavern in that respectable neighbourhood.

The unfortunate Mrs. Tibbs has determined to dispose of the whole of her furniture by public auction, and to retire from a residence in which she has suffered so much. Mr. Robins has been applied to, to conduct the sale, and the transcendent abilities of the literary gentlemen connected with his establishment are now devoted to the task of drawing up the preliminary advertisement. It is to contain, among a variety of brilliant matter, seventy-eight words in large capitals, and six *original* quotations in inverted commas.

CHAPTER II: *Mr. Minns and his Cousin*

MR. AUGUSTUS MINNS was a bachelor, of about forty as he said—of about eight-and-forty as his friends said. He was always exceedingly clean, precise, and tidy; perhaps somewhat priggish and the most retiring man in the world. He usually wore a brown frock-coat without a wrinkle, light inexplicables without a spot, a neat neckerchief with a remarkably neat tie, and boots without a fault: moreover, he always carried a brown silk umbrella with an ivory handle. He was a clerk in Somerset House, or, as he said himself, he held "a responsible situation under Government." He had a good and increasing salary, in addition to some 10,000*l*. of his own (invested in the funds), and he occupied a first floor in Tavistock Street, Covent Garden, where he had resided for twenty years, having been in the habit of quarrelling with his landlord the whole time, regularly giving notice of his intention to quit on the first day of every quarter, and as regularly countermanding it on the second. There were two classes of created objects which he held in the deepest and most unmingled horror: they were dogs and children. He was not unamiable, but he could at any time have viewed the execution of a dog, or the assassination of an infant, with the liveliest satisfaction. Their habits were at variance with his love of order; and his love of order was as powerful as his love of life. Mr. Augustus Minns had no relations, in or near London, with the exception of his cousin Mr. Octavius Budden, to whose son, whom he had never seen (for he disliked the father) he had consented to become godfather by proxy. Mr. Budden having realised a moderate fortune by exercising the trade or calling of a corn-chandler, and having a great predilection for the country, had purchased a cottage in the vicinity of Stamford Hill, whither he retired with the wife of his bosom, and his only son, Master Alexander Augustus Budden. One evening, as Mr. and Mrs. B. were admiring their son, discussing his various merits, talking over his education, and disputing whether the classics should be made an essential part thereof, the lady pressed so strongly upon her husband the propriety of cultivating the friendship of Mr. Minns in behalf of their son, that Mr. Budden at last made up his mind, that it should not be his fault if he and his cousin were not in future more intimate.

"I'll break the ice, my love," said Mr. Budden, stirring up the sugar at the bottom of his glass of brandy-and-water, and casting a sidelong look at his spouse to see the effect of the announcement of his determination, "by asking Minns down to dine with us, on Sunday."

"Then pray, Mr. Budden, write to your cousin at once," replied Mrs. Budden. "Who knows, if we could only get him down here, but that he might take a fancy to our Alexander, and leave him his property?—Alick, my dear, take your legs off the rail of the chair!"

"Very true," said Mr. Budden, musing, "very true, indeed, my love!"

On the following morning, as Mr. Minns was sitting at his breakfast-table, alternately biting his dry toast and casting a look upon the columns of his morning paper, which he always read from the title to the printer's name, he heard a loud knock at the street-door which was shortly afterwards followed by the entrance of his servant, who put into his hand a particularly small card, on which was engraved in immense letters, "Mr. Octavius Budden, Amelia Cottage (Mrs. B.'s name was Amelia), Poplar Walk, Stamford Hill."

"Budden," ejaculated Minns, "what the deuce can bring that vulgar fellow here!—say I'm asleep—say I'm out, and shall never be home again—anything to keep him downstairs."

"But please, sir, the gentleman's coming up," replied the servant; and the fact was made perfectly evident, by an appalling creaking of boots on the stair-case accompanied by a pattering noise, the cause of which Minns could not for the life of him divine.

"Hem!—show the gentleman in," said the unfortunate bachelor. Exit servant, and enter Octavius preceded by a large white dog, dressed in a suit of fleecy hosiery, with pink eyes, large ears, and no perceptible tail.

The cause of the pattering on the stairs was but too plain. Mr. Augustus Minns staggered beneath the shock of the dog's appearance.

"My dear fellow, how are you?" said Budden as he entered. He always spoke at the top of his voice, and always said the same thing half a dozen times.

"How are you, my hearty?"

"How do you do, Mr. Budden?—pray take a chair!" politely stammered the discomfited Minns.

"Thank you—thank you—well—how are you, eh?"

"Uncommonly well, thank ye," said Minns casting a diabolical look at the dog, who with his hind-legs on the floor, and his forepaws resting on the table, was dragging a bit of bread and butter out of a plate, preparatory to devouring it, with the buttered side next the carpet.

"Ah, you rogue!" said Budden to his dog; "you see, Minns, he's like me, always at home, eh, my boy?—Egad, I'm precious hot and hungry! I've walked all the way from Stamford Hill this morning."

"Have you breakfasted?" inquired Minns.

"Oh, no!—came to breakfast with you; so ring the bell, my dear fellow, will you? and let's have another cup and saucer, and the cold ham.—Make myself at home you see!" continued Budden, dusting his boots with a table-napkin. "Ha!—ha!—ha!—'pon my life, I'm hungry."

Minns rang the bell, and tried to smile.

"I decidedly never was so hot in my life," continued Octavius, wiping his forehead: "well, but how are you, Minns? 'Pon my soul you wear capitally!"

"D'ye think so?" said Minns; and he tried another smile.

"'Pon my life, I do!"

"Mrs. B. and—what's his name—quite well?"

"Alick—my son, you mean, never better—never better. But at such a place as we've got at Poplar Walk, you know, he couldn't be ill if he tried. When I first saw it, by Jove! it looked so knowing, with the front garden, and the green railings, and the brass knocker, and all that—I really thought it was a cut above me."

"Don't you think you'd like the ham better," interrupted Minns, "if you cut it the other way?" He saw, with feelings which it is impossible to describe, that his visitor was cutting or rather maiming the ham, in utter violation of all established rules.

"No, thank ye," returned Budden, with the most barbarous indifference to crime, "I prefer it this way—it eats short. But I say, Minns, when will you come down and see us? You will be delighted with the place; I know you will. Amelia and I were talking about you the other night, and Amelia said—another lump of sugar, please; thank ye—she said,

don't you think you could contrive, my dear, to say to Mr.
Minns, in a friendly way—come down, sir—damn the dog!
he's spoiling your curtains, Minns—ha!—ha!—ha!" Minns
leaped from his seat as though he had received the discharge
from a galvanic battery.

"Come out, sir!—go out, hoo!" cried poor Augustus, keeping nevertheless, at a very respectful distance from the dog,
having read of a case of hydrophobia in the paper of that
morning. By dint of great exertion, much shouting, and a
marvellous deal of poking under the tables with a stick and
umbrella, the dog was at last dislodged, and placed on the
landing outside the door, where he immediately commenced
a most appalling howling; at the same time vehemently
scratching the paint off the two nicely-varnished bottom panels
of the door, until they resembled the interior of a back-
gammon-board.

"A good dog for the country that!" coolly observed Budden
to the distracted Minns—"he's not much used to confinement,
though. But now, Minns, when will you come down? I'll
take no denial, positively. Let's see, to-day's Thursday.—
Will you come on Sunday? We dine at five, don't say no—
do."

After a great deal of pressing, Mr. Augustus Minns, driven
to despair, accepted the invitation and promised to be at
Poplar Walk on the ensuing Sunday, at a quarter before five
to the minute.

"Now mind the direction," said Budden; "the coach goes
from the Flower-pot, in Bishopsgate Street, every half-hour.
When the coach stops at the Swan, you'll see, immediately
opposite you a white house."

"Which is your house—I understand," said Minns, wishing
to cut short the visit and the story at the same time.

"No, no, that's not mine; that's Grogus's, the great iron-
monger's. I was going to say—you turn down by the side of the
white house till you can't go another step further—mind that
—and then you turn to your right, by some stables—well;
close to you, you'll see a wall with 'Beware of the Dog'
written upon it in large letters—(Minns shuddered)—go along
by the side of that wall for about a quarter of a mile, and
anybody will show you which is my place."

"Very well—thank ye—good-bye."

"Be punctual."

"Certainly: good-morning."

"I say, Minns, you've got a card?"

"Yes, I have: thank ye." And Mr. Octavius Budden
departed leaving his cousin looking forward to his visit of
the following Sunday, with the feelings of a penniless poet to
the weekly visit of his Scotch landlady.

Sunday arrived; the sky was bright and clear; crowds of

people were hurrying along the streets, intent on their different schemes of pleasure for the day; and everything and everybody looked cheerful and happy but Augustus Minns.

The day was fine, but the heat was considerable; and by the time Mr. Minns had fagged up the shady side of Fleet Street, Cheapside, and Threadneedle Street, he had become pretty warm, tolerably dusty, and it was getting late into the bargain. By the most extraordinary good fortune, however, a coach was waiting at the Flowerpot, into which Mr. Augustus Minns got, on the solemn assurance of the cad that the vehicle would start in three minutes—that being the very utmost extremity of time it was allowed to wait by Act of Parliament. A quarter of an hour elapsed, and there were no signs of moving. Minns looked at his watch for the sixth time.

"Coachman, are you going or not?" bawled Mr. Minns, with his head and half his body out of the coach-window.

"Di—rectly, sir," said the coachman, with his hands in his pockets, looking as much unlike a man in a hurry as possible.

"Bill, take them cloths off." Five minutes more elapsed: at the end of which time the coachman mounted the box, from whence he looked down the street and up the street, and hailed all the pedestrians for another five minutes.

"Coachman! if you don't go this moment, I shall get out," said Mr. Minns, rendered desperate by the lateness of the hour, and the impossibility of being in Poplar Walk at the appointed time.

"Going this minute, sir," was the reply;—and, accordingly the machine trundled on for a couple of hundred yards, and then stopped again. Minns doubled himself up into a corner of the coach, and abandoned himself to fate, as a child, a mother, a bandbox, and a parasol became his fellow passengers.

The child was an affectionate and an amiable infant; the little dear mistook Minns for its other parent, and screamed to embrace him.

"Be quiet, dear," said the mamma, restraining the impetuosity of the darling, whose little fat legs were kicking, and stamping, and twining themselves into the most complicated forms, in an ecstasy of impatience. "Be quiet, dear, that's not your papa."

"Thank Heaven I am not!" thought Minns, as the first gleam of pleasure he had experienced that morning shone like a meteor through his wretchedness.

Playfulness was agreeably mingled with affection in the disposition of the boy. When satisfied that Mr. Minns was not his parent he endeavoured to attract his notice by scraping his drab trousers with his dirty shoes, poking his chest with his mamma's parasol, and other nameless endearments peculiar to infancy, with which he beguiled the tediousness of the ride, apparently very much to his own satisfaction.

When the unfortunate gentleman arrived at the Swan, he found to his great dismay, that it was a quarter-past five. The white house, the stables, the "Beware of the Dog,"— every landmark was passed, with a rapidity not unusual to a gentleman of a certain age when too late for dinner. After the lapse of a few minutes, Mr. Minns found himself opposite a yellow brick house with a green door, brass knocker and door-plate, green window-frames and ditto railings, with "a garden" in front, that is to say, a small loose bit of gravelled ground, with one round and two scalene triangular beds, containing a fir-tree, twenty or thirty bulbs, and an unlimited number of marigolds. The taste of Mr. and Mrs. Budden was further displayed by the appearance of a Cupid on each side of the door, perched upon a heap of large chalk flints, variegated with pink conch-shells. His knock at the door was answered by a stumpy boy, in drab livery, cotton stockings and highlows, who, after hanging his hat on one of the dozen brass pegs which ornamented the passage, denominated by courtesy "The Hall," ushered him into a front drawing-room commanding a very extensive view of the backs of the neighbouring houses. The usual ceremony of introduction, and so forth, over, Mr. Minns took his seat, not a little agitated at finding that he was the last comer, and, somehow or other, the Lion of about a dozen people, sitting together in a small drawing-room, getting rid of that most tedious of all time, the time preceding dinner.

"Well, Brogson," said Budden, addressing an elderly gentleman in a black coat, drab knee-breeches, and long gaiters, who, under pretence of inspecting the prints in an Annual, had been engaged in satisfying himself upon the subject of Mr. Minns's general appearance, by looking at him over the tops of the leaves—"Well, Brogson, what do Ministers mean to do? Will they go out, or what?"

"Oh—why—really, you know, I'm the last person in the world to ask for news. Your cousin, from his situation, is the most likely person to answer the question."

Mr. Minns assured the last speaker, that although he was in Somerset House, he possessed no official communication relative to the projects of his Majesty's Ministers. But his remark was evidently received incredulously; and no further conjectures being hazarded on the subject, a long pause ensued, during which the company occupied themselves in coughing and blowing their noses, until the entrance of Mrs. Budden caused a general rise.

The ceremony of introduction being over, dinner was announced, and down-stairs the party proceeded accordingly

—Mr. Minns escorting Mrs. Budden as far as the drawing-room door, but being prevented, by the narrowness of the staircase, from extending his gallantry any farther. The dinner passed off as such dinners usually do. Ever and anon amidst the clatter of knives and forks, and the hum of conversation, Mr. B.'s voice might be heard, asking a friend to take wine, and assuring him he was glad to see him; and a great deal of by-play took place between Mrs. B. and the servants, respecting the removal of the dishes, during which her countenance assumed all the variations of a weather-glass, from "stormy" to "set fair."

Upon the dessert and wine being placed on the table, the servant, in compliance with a significant look from Mrs. B., brought down "Master Alexander," habited in a sky-blue suit with silver buttons, and with hair of nearly the same colour as the metal. After sundry praises from his mother, and various admonitions as to his behaviour from his pa, he was introduced to his godfather.

"Well, my little fellow—you are a fine boy, ain't you?" said Mr. Minns, as happy as a tomtit on birdlime.

"Yes."

"How old are you?"

"Eight, next We'nsday. How old are *you*?"

"Alexander," interrupted his mother, "how dare you ask Mr. Minns how old he is!"

"He asked me how old *I* was," said the precocious child to whom Minns had from that moment internally resolved he never would bequeath one shilling. As soon as the titter occasioned by the observation had subsided, a little smirking man with red whiskers, sitting at the bottom of the table, who during the whole of dinner had been endeavouring to obtain a listener to some stories about Sheridan, called out, with a very patronising air—"Alick, what part of speech is *be*?"

"A verb."

"That's a good boy," said Mrs. Budden, with all a mother's pride. "Now, you know what a verb is?"

"A verb is a word which signifies to be, to do, or to suffer; as, I am—I rule—I am ruled. Give me an apple, ma."

"I'll give you an apple," replied the man with the red whiskers, who was an established friend of the family, or in other words was always invited by Mrs. Budden, whether Mr. Budden liked it or not, "if you'll tell me what is the meaning of *be*."

"Be?" said the prodigy, after a little hesitation—"an insect that gathers honey."

"No, dear," frowned Mrs. Budden.—"B double E is the substantive."

"I don't think he knows much yet about *common* substantives," said the smirking gentleman, who thought this an admirable opportunity for letting off a joke. "It's clear he's not very well acquainted with *proper names*. He! he! he!"

"Gentlemen," called out Mr. Budden, from the end of the table, in a stentorian voice, and with a very important air, "will you have the goodness to charge your glasses? I have a toast to propose."

"Hear! hear!" cried the gentlemen, passing the decanters. After they had made the round of the table, Mr. Budden proceeded—"Gentlemen; there is an individual present——"

"Hear! hear!" said the little man with red whiskers.

"*Pray* be quiet, Jones," remonstrated Budden.

"I say, gentlemen, there is an individual present," resumed the host, "in whose society, I am sure we must take great delight—and—and—the conversation of that individual must have afforded to every one present the utmost pleasure." ["Thank Heaven, he does not mean me!" thought Minns, conscious that his diffidence and exclusiveness had prevented his saying above a dozen words since he entered the house.] "Gentlemen, I am but a humble individual myself, and I perhaps ought to apologise for allowing any individual feelings of friendship and affection for the person I allude to, to induce me to venture to rise, to propose the health of that person—a person that, I am sure—that is to say, a person whose virtues must endear him to those who know him—and those who have not the pleasure of knowing him, cannot dislike him."

"Hear! hear!" said the company, in a tone of encouragement and approval.

"Gentlemen," continued Budden, "my cousin is a man who—who is a relation of my own." (Hear! hear!) Minns groaned audibly. "Who I am most happy to see here, and who, if he were not here, would certainly have deprived us of the great pleasure we all feel in seeing him. (Loud cries of hear!) Gentlemen, I feel that I have already trespassed on your attention for too long a time. With every feeling—of—with every sentiment—of—of——"

"Gratification"—suggested the friend of the family.

"—Of gratification, I beg to propose the health of Mr. Minns."

"Standing, gentlemen!" shouted the indefatigable little man with the whiskers—"and with the honours. Take your time from me, if you please. Hip! hip! hip!—Za!—Hip! hip! hip!—Za!—Hip! hip!—Za—a—a!"

All eyes were now fixed on the subject of the toast, who by gulping down port wine at the imminent hazard of suffocation, endeavoured to conceal his confusion. After as long a pause as decency would admit, he rose, but, as the newspapers sometimes say in their reports, "we regret that we are quite unable to give even the substance of the honourable gentleman's observations." The words "present company—honour—present occasion," and "great happiness"—heard occasionally, and repeated at intervals, with a countenance expressive of the utmost confusion and misery, convinced the company that he was making an excellent speech; and accordingly, on his resuming his seat, they cried "Bravo!" and manifested tumultuous applause. Jones, who had been long watching his opportunity, then darted up.

"Budden," said he, "will you allow *me* to propose a toast?"

"Certainly," replied Budden, adding in an undertone to Minns right across the table—"Devilish sharp fellow that: you'll be very much pleased with his speech. He talks equally well on any subject." Minns bowed, and Mr. Jones proceeded:

"It has on several occasions, in various instances, under many circumstances, and in different companies, fallen to my lot to propose a toast to those by whom, at the time, I have had the honour to be surrounded. I have sometimes, I will cheerfully own—for why should I deny it?—felt the overwhelming nature of the task I have undertaken, and my own utter incapability to do justice to the subject. If such have been my feelings, however, on former occasions, what must they be now—now—under the extraordinary circumstances in which I am placed. (Hear! hear!)—To describe my feelings accurately would be impossible; but I cannot give you a better idea of them, gentlemen, than by referring to a circumstance which happens, oddly enough, to occur to my mind at the moment. On one occasion, when that truly great and illustrious man, Sheridan, was——"

Now, there is no knowing what new villainy in the form of a joke would have been heaped upon the memory of that very ill-used man, Mr. Sheridan, if the boy in drab had not at that moment entered the room in a breathless state, to report that, as it was a very wet night, the nine o'clock stage had come round to know whether there was anybody going to town, as, in that case, he (the nine o'clock) had room for one inside.

Mr. Minns started up; and, despite countless exclamations of surprise, and entreaties to stay, persisted in his determination to accept the vacant place. But the brown silk umbrella was nowhere to be found; and as the coachman couldn't wait, he drove back to the Swan, leaving word for Mr. Minns to "run round" and catch him. But as it did not occur to Mr. Minns for some ten minutes or so, that he had left the brown silk umbrella with the ivory handle in the other coach, coming down; and, moreover, as he was by no means remarkable for speed, it is no matter of surprise that when he accomplished the feat of "running round" to the Swan, the coach—the last coach—had gone without him.

It was somewhere about three o'clock in the morning, when Mr. Augustus Minns knocked feebly at the street-door of his lodgings in Tavistock Street, cold, wet, cross, and miserable. He made his will next morning, and his professional man informs us, in that strict confidence in which we inform the public, that neither the name of Mr. Octavius Budden, nor of Mrs. Amelia Budden, nor of Master Alexander Augustus Budden, appears therein.

CHAPTER III: *Sentiment*

THE Miss Crumptons, or to quote the authority of the inscription on the garden-gate of Minerva House, Hammersmith—"The Misses Crumpton," were two unusually tall, particularly thin, and exceedingly skinny personages: very upright, and very yellow. Miss Amelia Crumpton owned to thirty-eight, and Miss Maria Crumpton admitted she was forty; an admission which was rendered perfectly unnecessary by the self-evident fact of her being fifty at least. They dressed in the most interesting manner—like twins, and looked about as happy and comfortable as a couple of marigolds run to seed. They were very precise, had the strictest possible ideas of propriety, wore false hair, and always smelt very strongly of lavender.

Minerva House, conducted under the auspices of the two sisters, was a "finishing establishment for young ladies," where some twenty girls of the ages of from thirteen to nineteen inclusive, acquired a smattering of everything, and a knowledge of nothing; instruction in French and Italian, dancing lessons twice a-week, and other necessaries of life. The house was a white one, a little removed from the road-side, with close palings in front. The bedroom windows were always left partly open to afford a bird's-eye view of numerous little bedsteads with very white dimity furniture, and thereby impress the passer-by with a due sense of the luxuries of the establishment; and there was a front parlour hung round with highly varnished maps which nobody ever looked at, and filled with books which no one ever read, appropriated exclusively to the reception of parents, who, whenever they called, could not fail to be struck with the very knowledge-imparting appearance of the place.

"Amelia, my dear," said Miss Maria Crumpton, entering the school-room one morning, with her false hair in papers, as she occasionally did, in order to impress the young ladies with a conviction of its reality—"Amelia, my dear, here's a most gratifying note I have just received. You needn't mind reading it aloud."

Miss Amelia thus advised, proceeded to read the following note with an air of great triumph:

"*Cornelius Brook Dingwall, Esq., M.P., presents his compliments to Miss Crumpton, and will feel much obliged by Miss Crumpton's calling on him, if she conveniently can, to-morrow morning at one o'clock, as Cornelius Brook Dingwall, Esq., M.P., is anxious to see Miss Crumpton on the subject of placing Miss Brook Dingwall under her charge.*

Adelphi.

Monday morning."

"A Member of Parliament's daughter!" ejaculated Amelia, in an ecstatic tone.

"A Member of Parliament's daughter!" repeated Miss Maria, with a smile of delight, which of course elicited a concurrent titter of pleasure from all the young ladies.

"It's exceedingly delightful!" said Miss Amelia; whereupon all the young ladies murmured their admiration again. Courtiers are but school-boys, and court-ladies school-girls.

So important an announcement at once superseded the business of the day. A holiday was declared in commemoration of the great event: the Miss Crumptons retired to their private apartment to talk it over; the smaller girls discussed the probable manners and customs of the daughter of a Member of Parliament; and the young ladies verging on eighteen wondered whether she was engaged, whether she was pretty, whether she wore much bustle, and many other *whethers* of equal importance.

The two Miss Crumptons proceeded to the Adelphi at the appointed time next day, dressed, of course, in their best style, and looking as amiable as they possibly could—which, by-the-by, is not saying much for them. Having sent in their cards, through the medium of a red-hot looking footman in bright livery, they were ushered into the august presence of the profound Dingwall.

Cornelius Brook Dingwall, Esq., M.P., was very haughty, solemn, and portentous. He had naturally a somewhat spasmodic expression of countenance, which was not rendered the less remarkable by his wearing an extremely stiff cravat. He was wonderfully proud of the M.P. attached to his name, and never lost an opportunity of reminding people of his dignity. He had a great idea of his own abilities, which must have been a great comfort to him, as no one else had; and in diplomacy, on a small scale in his own family arrangements, he considered himself unrivalled. He was a country magistrate, and discharged the duties of his station with all due justice and impartiality, frequently committing poachers, and occasionally committing himself. Miss Brook Dingwall was one of that numerous class of young ladies, who, like adverbs, may be known by their answering to a common-place question, and doing nothing else.

On the present occasion this talented individual was seated in a small library at a table covered with papers, doing nothing, but trying to look busy—playing at shop. Acts of Parliament, and letters directed to "Cornelius Brook Dingwall, Esq., M.P.," were ostentatiously scattered over the table, at a little distance from which Mrs. Brook Dingwall was seated at work. One of those public nuisances, a spoiled child, was playing about the room, dressed after the most approved fashion, in a blue tunic with a black belt a quarter of a yard wide, fastened with an immense buckle, and looking like a robber in a melodrama, seen through a diminishing glass.

After a little pleasantry from the sweet child, who amused himself by running away with Miss Maria Crumpton's chair as fast as it was placed for her, the visitors were seated, and Cornelius Brook Dingwall, Esq., opened the conversation.

He had sent for Miss Crumpton, he said, in consequence of the high character he had received of her establishment from his friend Sir Alfred Muggs.

Miss Crumpton murmured her acknowledgments to him (Muggs), and Cornelius proceeded.

"One of my principal reasons, Miss Crumpton, for parting with my daughter is, that she has lately acquired some sentimental ideas, which it is most desirable to eradicate from her young mind." (Here the little innocent before noticed fell out of an arm-chair with an awful crash.)

"Naughty boy!" said his mamma, who appeared more surprised at his taking the liberty of falling down, than at anything else; "I'll ring the bell for James to take him away."

"Pray don't check him, my love," said the diplomatist, as soon as he could make himself heard amidst the unearthly howling consequent upon the threat and the tumble. "It all arises from his great flow of spirits." This last explanation was addressed to Miss Crumpton.

"Certainly, sir," replied the antique Maria, not exactly seeing, however, the connection between a flow of animal spirits and a fall from an arm-chair.

Silence was restored, and the M.P. resumed: "Now, I know nothing so likely to effect this object, Miss Crumpton, as her mixing constantly in the society of girls of her own age; and as I know that in your establishment she will meet such as are not likely to contaminate her young mind, I propose to send her to you."

The youngest Miss Crumpton expressed the acknowledgments of the establishment generally. Maria was rendered perfectly speechless by bodily pain—the dear little fellow, having recovered his spirits, was standing upon her most tender foot, by way of getting his face (which looked like a capital O in a red-lettered play-bill) on a level with the writing-table.

"Of course, Lavinia will be a parlour boarder," continued the enviable father; "and on one point I wish my directions to be strictly observed. The fact is, that some ridiculous love affair with a person much her inferior in life has been the cause of her present state of mind. Knowing that of course, under your care, she can have no opportunity of meeting this person, I do not object to—indeed, I should rather prefer—her mixing with such society as you see yourself."

The important statement was again interrupted by the high-spirited little creature, in the excess of his joyousness, breaking a pane of glass, and nearly precipitating himself into an adjacent area. James was rung for; considerable confusion and screaming succeeded, two little blue legs about the size of hoop-sticks were seen to kick violently in the air as the man left the room, and the child was gone.

"Mr. Brook Dingwall would like Miss Brook Dingwall to learn everything," said Mrs. Brook Dingwall, who hardly ever said anything at all.

"Certainly," said both the Miss Crumptons together.

"And as I trust the plan I have devised will be effectual in weaning my daughter from this absurd idea, Miss Crumpton," continued the legislator, "I hope you will have the goodness to comply in all respects with any request I may forward to you."

The promise was of course made; and after a lengthened discussion, conducted on behalf of the Dingwalls with the most becoming diplomatic gravity, and on that of the Crumptons with profound respect, it was finally arranged that Miss Lavinia should be forwarded to Hammersmith on the next day but one, on which occasion the half-yearly ball given at the establishment was to take place. It might divert the dear girl's mind. This, by the way, was another bit of diplomacy.

Miss Lavinia was introduced to her future governess, and both the Miss Crumptons pronounced her "a most charming girl;" an opinion which, by a singular coincidence, they always entertained of any new pupil.

Courtesies were made, acknowledgments expressed, condescension exhibited, and the interview terminated.

Preparations, to make use of theatrical phraseology, "on a scale of magnitude never before attempted," were incessantly made at Minerva House to give every effect to the forthcoming ball. The largest room in the house was pleasingly ornamented with blue calico roses, plaid tulips, and other equally natural-looking artificial flowers, the work of the young ladies themselves. The carpet was taken up, the folding-doors were taken down, the furniture was taken out, and rout-seats were taken in. The linen-drapers of Hammersmith were astounded at the sudden demand for blue sarsenet ribbon, and long white gloves. Dozens of geraniums were purchased for bouquets, and a harp and two violins were bespoke from town, in addition to the grand piano already on the premises. The young ladies who were selected to show off on the occasion, and do credit to the establishment, practised incessantly, much to their own satisfaction, and greatly to the annoyance of the lame old gentleman over the way; and a constant correspondence was kept up, between the Misses Crumpton and the Hammersmith pastrycook.

The evening came; and then there was such a lacing of stays, and tying of sandals, and dressing of hair, as never can take place with a proper degree of bustle out of a boarding-school. The smaller girls managed to be in everybody's way, and were pushed about accordingly; and the elder ones dressed, and tied, and flattered and envied one another, as earnestly and sincerely as if they had actually *come out*.

"How do I look, dear?" inquired Miss Emily Smithers, the belle of the house, of Miss Caroline Wilson, who was her bosom friend, because she was the ugliest girl in Hammersmith, or out of it.

"Oh! charming, dear. How do I?"

"Delightful! you never looked so handsome," returned the belle, adjusting her own dress, and not bestowing a glance on her poor companion.

"I hope young Hilton will come early," said another young lady to Miss somebody else, in a fever of expectation.

"I'm sure he'd be highly flattered if he knew it," returned the other, who was practising *l'été* for effect.

"Oh! he's so handsome," said the first.

"Such a charming person!" added a second.

"Such a *distingué* air!" said a third.

"Oh, what *do* you think?" said another girl, running into the room; "Miss Crumpton says her cousin's coming."

"What! Theodosius Butler?" said everybody in raptures.

"Is *he* handsome?" inquired a novice.

"No, not particularly handsome," was the general reply; "but, oh, so clever!"

Mr. Theodosius Butler was one of those immortal geniuses who are to be met with in almost every circle. They have usually very deep monotonous voices. They always persuade themselves that they are wonderful persons, and that they ought to be very miserable, though they don't precisely know why. They are very conceited, and usually possess exactly half an idea; but with enthusiastic young ladies, and silly young gentlemen, they are very wonderful persons. The individual in question, Mr. Theodosius, had written a pamphlet containing some very weighty considerations on the expediency of doing something or other; and as every sentence contained at least fifty words of four syllables, his admirers took it for granted that he meant a good deal.

"Perhaps that's he," exclaimed several young ladies, as the first pull of the evening threatened destruction to the bell of the gate.

An awful pause ensued. Some boxes arrived, and a young lady—it was Miss Brook Dingwall, in full ball costume, with an immense gold chain round her neck, and her dress looped up with a single rose. An ivory fan in her hand, and a most interesting expression of despair in her face.

The Miss Crumptons inquired after the family with the most excruciating anxiety, and Miss Brook Dingwall was formally introduced to her future companions. The Miss Crumptons conversed with the young ladies in the most mellifluous tones, in order that Miss Brook Dingwall might be properly impressed with their amiable treatment.

Another pull at the bell. Mr. Dadson, the writing master, and his wife. The wife in green silk, with shoes and cap-trimmings to correspond, and the writing-master in a white waistcoat, black knee-shorts, and ditto silk stockings, displaying a leg large enough for two writing-masters, at least. The young ladies whispered one another, and the writing-master and his wife flattered the Miss Crumptons, who were dressed in amber, with long sashes, like dolls.

Repeated pulls at the bell, and arrivals too numerous to particularise: papas and mammas, and aunts and uncles, the owners and guardians of the different pupils; the singing-master, Signor Lobskini, in a black wig; the pianoforte player and the violins; the harp, in a state of intoxication; and some twenty young men, who stood near the door, and talked to one another, occasionally bursting into a giggle. A general hum of conversation. Coffee handed round and plentifully partaken of by fat mammas, looking like the stout people who come on in pantomimes for the sole purpose of being knocked down.

The popular Mr. Hilton was the next arrival; and having, at the request of the Miss Crumptons, undertaken the office of Master of the Ceremonies, the quadrilles commenced with considerable spirit. The young men by the door gradually advanced into the middle of the room, and in time became sufficiently at ease to consent to be introduced to partners. The writing-master danced every set, springing about with the most fearful agility, and his wife played a rubber in the back-parlour—a little room with five book-shelves, dignified by the name of the study. Setting her down to whist was a half-yearly piece of generalship on the part of the Miss Crumptons, as it was necessary to hide her somewhere on account of her being a fright.

The interesting Lavinia Brook Dingwall was the only girl present who appeared to take no interest in the proceedings of the evening. In vain was she solicited to dance; in vain was the universal homage paid to her as the daughter of a Member of Parliament. She was equally unmoved by the splendid tenor of the inimitable Lobskini, and the brilliant execution of Miss Lætitia Parsons, whose performance of "The Recollections of Ireland" was universally declared to be almost equal to that of Moscheles himself. Not even the announcement of the arrival of Mr. Theodosius Butler could induce her to leave the corner of the back drawing-room in which she was seated.

"Now, Theodosius," said Miss Maria Crumpton, after that enlightened pamphleteer had nearly run the gauntlet of the whole company, "I must introduce you to our new pupil."

Theodosius looked as if he cared for nothing earthly.

"She's the daughter of a Member of Parliament," said Maria.—Theodosius started.

"And her name is——?" he inquired.

"Miss Brook Dingwall."

"Great Heaven!" poetically exclaimed Theodosius in a low tone.

Miss Crumpton commenced the introduction in due form. Miss Brook Dingwall languidly raised her head.

"Edward!" she exclaimed, with a half-shriek, on seeing the well-known nankeen legs.

Fortunately, as Miss Maria Crumpton possessed no remarkable share of penetration, and as it was one of the diplomatic arrangements that no attention was to be paid to Miss Lavinia's incoherent exclamations, she was perfectly unconscious of the mutual agitation of the parties; and therefore, seeing that the offer of his hand for the next quadrille was accepted, she left him by the side of Miss Brook Dingwall.

"Oh, Edward!" exclaimed that most romantic of all romantic young ladies, as the light of science seated himself beside her, "Oh, Edward! is it you?"

Mr. Theodosius assured the dear creature, in the most impassioned manner, that he was not conscious of being anybody but himself.

"Then why—why—this disguise? Oh! Edward M'Neville Walter, what have I not suffered on your account!"

"Lavinia, hear me," replied the hero, in his most poetic strain. "Do not condemn me unheard. If anything that emanates from the soul of such a wretch as I can occupy a place in your recollection—if any being so vile deserve your notice—you may remember that I once published a pamphlet (and paid for its publication) entitled 'Considerations on the Policy of Removing the Duty on Bees'-wax.'"

"I do—I do!" sobbed Lavinia.

"That," continued the lover, "was a subject to which your father was devoted heart and soul."

"He was—he was!" reiterated the sentimentalist.

"I knew it," continued Theodosius, tragically; "I knew it—I forwarded him a copy. He wished to know me. Could I disclose my real name? Never! No, I assumed that name which you have so often pronounced in tones of endearment. As M'Neville Walter, I devoted myself to the stirring cause; as M'Neville Walter I gained your heart; in the same character I was ejected from your house by your father's domestics, and in no character at all have I since been enabled to see you. We now meet again, and I proudly own that I am—Theodosius Butler."

The young lady appeared perfectly satisfied with this very argumentative address, and bestowed a look of the most ardent affection on the immortal advocate of bees'-wax.

"May I hope," said he, "that the promise your father's violent behaviour interrupted may be renewed?"

"Let us join this set," replied Lavinia, coquettishly—for girls of nineteen can coquette.

"No," ejaculated he of the nankeens; "I stir not from this spot writhing under this torture of suspense. May I—may I—hope?"

"You may."

"The promise is renewed?"

"It is."

"I have your permission?"

"You have."

"To the fullest extent?"

"You know it," returned the blushing Lavinia. The contortions of the interesting Butler's visage expressed his raptures.

We could dilate upon the occurrences that ensued. How Mr. Theodosius and Miss Lavinia danced, and talked, and sighed for the remainder of the evening—how the Miss Crumptons were delighted thereat. How the writing-master continued to frisk about with one-horse power, and how his wife, from some unaccountable freak, left the whist-table in the little back-parlour, and persisted in displaying her green head-dress in the most conspicuous part of the drawing-room. How the supper consisted of small triangular sandwiches in trays, and a tart here and there by way of variety; and how the visitors consumed warm water disguised with lemon, and dotted with nutmeg, under the denomination of negus. These, and other matters of as much interest, however, we pass over, for the purpose of describing a scene of even more importance.

A fortnight after the date of the ball, Cornelius Brook Dingwall, Esq., M.P., was seated at the same library-table, and in the same room as we have before described. He was alone, and his face bore an expression of deep thought and solemn gravity—he was drawing up "A Bill for the better observance of Easter Monday."

The footman tapped at the door—the legislator started from his reverie, and "Miss Crumpton" was announced. Permission was given for Miss Crumpton to enter the *sanctum ;* Maria came sliding in, and having taken her seat with a due portion of affectation, the footman retired, and the governess was left alone with the M.P. Oh! how she longed for the presence of a third party! Even the facetious young gentleman would have been a relief.

Miss Crumpton began the duet. She hoped Mrs. Brook Dingwall and the handsome little boy were in good health.

They were. Mrs. Brook Dingwall and little Frederick were at Brighton.

"Much obliged to you, Miss Crumpton," said Cornelius, in his most dignified manner, "for your attention in calling this morning. I should have driven down to Hammersmith to see Lavinia, but your account was so very satisfactory, and my duties in the House occupy me so much, that I determined to postpone it for a week. How has she gone on?"

"Very well indeed, sir," returned Maria, dreading to inform the father that she had gone off.

"Ah, I thought the plan on which I proceeded would be a match for her."

Here was a favourable opportunity to say that somebody else had been a match for her. The unfortunate governess was unequal to the task.

"You have persevered strictly in the line of conduct I prescribed, Miss Crumpton?"

"Strictly, sir."

"You tell me in your note that her spirits gradually improved."

"Very much indeed, sir."

"To be sure. I was convinced they would."

"But I fear, sir," said Miss Crumpton, with visible emotion, "I fear the plan has not succeeded quite so well as we could have wished.

"No!" exclaimed the prophet. "Bless me! Miss Crumpton, you look alarmed. What has happened?"

"Miss Brook Dingwall, sir——"

"Yes, ma'am?"

"Has gone, sir"—said Maria. exhibiting a strong inclination to faint.

"Gone!"

"Eloped, sir."

"Eloped! — Who with — when — where — how?" almost shrieked the agitated diplomatist.

The natural yellow of the unfortunate Maria's face changed to all the hues of the rainbow, as she laid a small packet upon the Member's table.

He hurriedly opened it. A letter from his daughter, and another from Theodosius. He glanced over their contents—"Ere this reaches you, far distant—appeal to feelings—love to distraction—bees'-wax—slavery," &c., &c. He dashed his hand to his forehead, and paced the room with fearfully long strides, to the great alarm of the precise Maria.

"Now mind; from this time forward," said Mr. Brook Dingwall, suddenly stopping at the table, and beating time upon it with his hand—"from this time forward, I never will, under any circumstances whatever, permit a man who writes pamphlets to enter any room of this house but the kitchen. —I'll allow my daughter and her husband one hundred and fifty pounds a-year, and never see their faces again; —and, damme! ma'am, I'll bring in a bill for the abolition of finishing schools!"

Some time has elapsed since this passionate declaration. Mr. and Mrs. Butler are at present rusticating in a small cottage at Ball's Pond, pleasantly situated in the immediate vicinity of a brickfield. They have no family. Mr. Theodosius looks very important, and writes incessantly; but, in consequence of some gross combination on the part of publishers, none of his productions appear in print. His young wife begins to think that ideal misery is preferable to real unhappiness; and that a marriage contracted in haste, and repented at leisure, is the cause of more substantial wretchedness than she ever anticipated.

On cool reflection, Cornelius Brook Dingwall, Esq., M.P., was reluctantly compelled to admit that the untoward result of his admirable arrangements was attributable, not to the Miss Crumptons, but his own diplomacy. He however consoles himself, like some other small diplomatists, by satisfactorily proving that if his plans did not succeed, they ought to have done so. Minerva House is in *statu quo*, and "The Misses Crumpton" remain in the peaceable and undisturbed enjoyment of all the advantages resulting from their Finishing School.

CHAPTER IV: *The Tuggs's at Ramsgate*

ONCE upon a time there dwelt, in a narrow street on the Surrey side of the water within three minutes' walk of the old London Bridge, Mr. Joseph Tuggs—a little dark-faced man, with shiny hair, twinkling eyes, short legs, and a body of very considerable thickness, measuring from the centre button of his waistcoat in front, to the ornamental buttons of his coat behind. The figure of the amiable Mrs. Tuggs, if not perfectly symmetrical, was decidedly comfortable; and the form of her only daughter, the accomplished Miss Charlotte Tuggs, was fast ripening into that state of luxuriant plumpness which had enchanted the eyes, and captivated the heart, of Mr. Joseph Tuggs in his earlier days. Mr. Simon Tuggs, his only son, and Miss Charlotte Tuggs's only brother, was as differently formed in body, as he was differently constituted in mind, from the remainder of his family. There was that elongation in his thoughtful face, and that tendency to weakness in his interesting legs, which tell so forcibly of a great mind and romantic disposition. The slightest traits of character in such a being, possess no mean interest to speculative minds. He usually appeared in public in capacious shoes with black cotton stockings; and was observed to be particularly attached to a black glazed stock, without tie or ornament of any description.

There is perhaps no profession, however useful, no pursuit, however meritorious, which can escape the petty attacks of vulgar minds. Mr. Joseph Tuggs was a grocer. It might be supposed that a grocer was beyond the breath of calumny: but no—the neighbours stigmatised him as a chandler; and the poisonous voice of envy distinctly asserted that he dispensed tea and coffee by the quartern, retailed sugar by the ounce, cheese by the slice, tobacco by the screw, and butter by the pat. These taunts, however, were lost upon the Tuggs's. Mr. Tuggs attended to the grocery department, Mrs. Tuggs to the cheesemongery, and Miss Tuggs to her education. Mr. Simon Tuggs kept his father's books, and his own counsel.

One fine spring afternoon, the latter gentleman was seated on a tub of weekly Dorset behind the little red desk with a wooden rail, which ornamented a corner of the counter, when a stranger dismounted from a cab, and hastily entered the shop. He was habited in black cloth, and bore with him a green umbrella and a blue bag.

"Mr. Tuggs?" said the stranger, inquiringly.

"*My* name is Tuggs," replied Mr. Simon.

"It's the other Mr. Tuggs," said the stranger, looking towards the glass door which led into the parlour behind the shop, and on the inside of which, the round face of Mr. Tuggs, senior, was distinctly visible, peeping over the curtain.

Mr. Simon gracefully waved his pen, as if in intimation of his wish that his father would advance, and Mr. Joseph Tuggs, with considerable celerity, removed his face from the curtain, and placed it before the stranger.

"I come from the Temple," said the man with the bag.

"From the Temple!" said Mrs. Tuggs, flinging open the door of the little parlour, and disclosing Miss Tuggs in perspective.

"From the Temple!" said Miss Tuggs and Mr. Simon Tuggs at the same moment.

"From the Temple!" said Mr. Joseph Tuggs, turning as pale as a Dutch cheese.

"From the Temple," repeated the man with the bag; "from Mr. Cower's, the solicitor's. Mr. Tuggs, I congratulate you, sir. Ladies, I wish you joy of your prosperity! We have been successful!" And the man with the bag leisurely divested himself of his umbrella and glove, as a preliminary to shaking hands with Mr. Joseph Tuggs.

Now the words "we have been successful" had no sooner issued from the mouth of the man with the bag, than Mr. Simon Tuggs rose from the tub of weekly Dorset, opened his eyes very wide, gasped for breath, made figures of eight in the air with his pen, and finally fell into the arms of his anxious mother, and fainted away, without the slightest ostensible cause or pretence.

"Water!" screamed Mrs. Tuggs.

"Look up, my son," exclaimed Mr. Tuggs.

"Simon! dear Simon!" shrieked Miss Tuggs.

"I'm better now," said Mr. Simon Tuggs.—"What! successful!" And then, as corroborative evidence of his being better, he fainted away again, and was borne into the little parlour by the united efforts of the remainder of the family and the man with the bag.

To a casual spectator, or to any one unacquainted with the position of the family, this fainting would have been unaccountable. To those who understood the mission of the man with the bag, and were moreover acquainted with the excitability of the nerves of Mr. Simon Tuggs, it was quite comprehensible. A long-pending law-suit respecting the validity of a will, had been unexpectedly decided; and Mr. Joseph Tuggs was the possessor of twenty thousand pounds.

A prolonged consultation took place that night in the little parlour—a consultation that was to settle the future destinies of the Tuggs's. The shop was shut up at an unusually early hour; and many were the unavailing kicks bestowed upon the closed door by applicants for quarterns of sugar, or half-quarterns of bread, or penn'orths of pepper, which were to have been "left till Saturday," but which fortune had decreed were to be left alone altogether.

"We must certainly give up business," said Miss Tuggs.

"Oh, decidedly," said Mrs. Tuggs.

"Simon shall go to the bar," said Mr. Joseph Tuggs.

"And I shall always sign myself 'Cymon' in future," said his son.

"And I shall call myself Charlotta," said Miss Tuggs.

"And you must always call *me* 'Ma,' and father 'Pa,'" said Mrs. Tuggs.

"Yes, and pa must leave off all his vulgar habits," interposed Miss Tuggs.

"I'll take care of all that," responded Mr. Joseph Tuggs, complacently.—He was at that very moment eating pickled salmon with a pocket-knife.

"We must leave town immediately," said Mr. Cymon Tuggs.

Everybody concurred that this was an indispensable preliminary to being genteel. The question then rose—Where should they go?

"Gravesend," mildly suggested Mr. Joseph Tuggs. The idea was unanimously scouted. Gravesend was *low*.

"Margate," insinuated Mrs. Tuggs. Worse and worse—nobody there but tradespeople.

"Brighton!" Mr. Cymon Tuggs opposed an insurmountable objection. All the coaches had been upset in their turn within the last three weeks; each coach had averaged two passengers killed and six wounded; and in every case the newspapers had distinctly understood that "no blame whatever was attributable to the coachman."

"Ramsgate!" ejaculated Mr. Cymon, thoughtfully.—To be sure; how stupid they must have been not to have thought of that before! Ramsgate was just the place of all others that they ought to go to.

Two months after this conversation the City of London Ramsgate steamer was running gaily down the river. Her flag was flying, her band was playing, her passengers were conversing; everything about her seemed gay and lively.—No wonder—the Tuggs's were on board.

"Charming, ain't it?" said Mr. Joseph Tuggs, in a bottle-green greatcoat, with a velvet collar of the same, and a blue travelling-cap with a gold band.

"Soul-inspiring," replied Mr. Cymon Tuggs—he was entered at the bar.—"Soul-inspiring!"

"Delightful morning, sir," said a stoutish, military-looking gentleman in a blue surtout buttoned up to his chin, and white trousers chained down to the soles of his boots.

Mr. Cymon Tuggs took upon himself the responsibility of answering the observation. "Heavenly!" he replied.

"You are an enthusiastic admirer of the beauties of nature, sir?" said the military gentleman, deferentially.

"I am, sir," replied Mr. Cymon Tuggs.

"Travelled much, sir?" inquired the military gentleman.

"Not much," replied Mr. Cymon Tuggs.

"You've been on the continent, of course?" inquired the military gentleman.

"Not exactly," replied Mr. Cymon Tuggs, in a qualified tone, as if he wished it to be implied that he had gone half-way and come back again.

"You of course intend your son to make the grand tour, sir?" said the military gentleman, addressing Mr. Joseph Tuggs.

As Mr. Joseph Tuggs did not precisely understand what the grand tour was, or how such an article was manufactured, he replied, "Of course." Just as he said the word, there came tripping up from her seat at the stern of the vessel, a young lady in a puce-coloured silk cloak and boots of the same, with long black ringlets, large black eyes, brief petti-coats, and unexceptionable ankles.

"Walter, my dear," said the young lady to the military gentleman.

"Yes, Belinda, my love," responded the military gentleman to the black-eyed young lady.

"What have you left me alone so long for?" said the young lady. "I have been stared out of countenance by those rude young men."

"What! stared at?" exclaimed the military gentleman, with an emphasis which made Mr. Cymon Tuggs withdraw his eyes from the young lady's face with inconceivable rapidity. "Which young men—where?" and the military gentleman clenched his fist, and glared fearfully on the cigar-smokers around.

"Be calm, Walter, I entreat," said the young lady.

"I won't," said the military gentleman.

"Do, sir," interposed Mr. Cymon Tuggs. "They ain't worth your notice."

"No—no—they are not, indeed," urged the young lady.

"I *will* be calm," said the military gentleman. "You speak truly, sir. I thank you for a timely remonstrance, which may have spared me the guilt of manslaughter." Calming his wrath, the military gentleman wrung Mr. Cymon Tuggs by the hand.

"My sister, sir," said Mr. Cymon Tuggs; seeing that the military gentleman was casting an admiring look towards Miss Charlotta.

"My wife, ma'am—Mrs. Captain Waters," said the military gentleman, presenting the black-eyed young lady.

"My mother, ma'am—Mrs. Tuggs," said Mr. Cymon. The military gentleman and his wife murmured enchanting courtesies; and the Tuggs's looked as unembarrassed as they could.

"Walter, my dear," said the black-eyed young lady, after they had sat chatting with the Tuggs's some half-hour.

"Yes, my love," said the military gentleman.

"Don't you think this gentleman (with an inclination of the head towards Mr. Cymon Tuggs) is very much like the Marquis Carriwini?"

"God bless me, very!" said the military gentleman.

"It struck me, the moment I saw him," said the young lady: gazing intently, and with a melancholy air, on the scarlet countenance of Mr. Cymon Tuggs. Mr. Cymon Tuggs looked at everybody; and finding that everybody was looking at him, appeared to feel some temporary difficulty in disposing of his eye-sight.

"So exactly the air of the marquis," said the military gentleman.

"Quite extraordinary!" sighed the military gentleman's lady.

"You don't know the marquis, sir?" inquired the military gentleman.

Mr. Cymon Tuggs stammered a negative.

"If you did," continued Captain Walter Waters, "you would feel how much reason you have to be proud of the resemblance—a most elegant man, with a most prepossessing appearance.

"He is—he is indeed!" exclaimed Belinda Waters energetically: and as her eye caught that of Mr. Cymon Tuggs, she withdrew it from his features in bashful confusion.

All this was highly gratifying to the feelings of the Tuggs's: and when, in the course of further conversation, it was discovered that Miss Charlotta Tuggs was the *facsimile* of a titled relative of Mrs. Belinda Waters, and that Mrs. Tuggs herself was the very picture of the Dowager Duchess of Dobbleton, their delight, in the acquisition of so genteel and friendly an acquaintance, knew no bounds. Even the dignity of Captain Walter Waters relaxed to that degree, that he suffered himself to be prevailed upon by Mrs. Joseph Tuggs to partake of cold pigeon-pie and sherry on deck; and a most delightful conversation, aided by these agreeable stimulants, was prolonged until they ran alongside Ramsgate Pier.

"Good-bye, dear!" said Mrs. Captain Waters to Miss Charlotta Tuggs, just before the bustle of landing commenced; "we shall see you on the sands in the morning: and as we are sure to have found lodgings before then, I hope we shall be inseparables for many weeks to come."

"Oh! I hope so," said Miss Charlotta Tuggs, emphatically.

"Tickets, ladies and gen'l'm'n," said the man on the paddle-box.

"Want a porter, sir?" inquired a dozen men in smock-frocks.

"Now, my dear!" said Captain Waters.

"Good-bye!" said Mrs. Captain Waters—"good-bye,

Mr. Cymon! and with a pressure of the hand that threw the amiable young man's nerves into a state of considerable derangement, Mrs. Captain Waters disappeared among the crowd. A pair of puce-coloured boots were seen ascending the steps, a white handkerchief fluttered, a black eye gleamed. The Waterses were gone, and Mr. Cymon Tuggs was alone in a heartless world.

Silently and abstractedly did that too sensitive youth follow his revered parents and a train of smock-frocks and wheelbarrows, along the pier, until the bustle of the scene around, recalled him to himself. The sun was shining brightly; the sea, dancing to its own music, rolled merrily in; crowds of people promenaded to and fro, young ladies tittered, old ladies talked, nurse-maids displayed their charms to the greatest possible advantage, and their sweet little charges ran up and down, and to and fro, and in and out, under the feet, and between the legs of the assembled concourse, in the most playful and exhilarating manner possible. There were old gentlemen trying to make out objects through long telescopes, and young ones making objects of themselves in open shirt-collars; ladies carrying about portable chairs, and portable chairs carrying about invalids; parties waiting on the pier for parties who had come by the steamboat; and nothing was to be heard but talking, laughing, welcoming, and merriment.

"Fly, sir?" exclaimed a chorus of fourteen men and six boys the moment that Mr. Joseph Tuggs, at the head of his little party, had set foot in the street.

"Here's the gen'l'm'n at last!" said one, touching his hat with mock politeness. "Werry glad to see you, sir,—been waitin' for you these six weeks. Jump in, if you please, sir."

"Nice light fly and a fast trotter, sir," said another: "fourteen mile a hour, and surroundin' objects invisible by hextreme welocity!"

"Large fly for your luggage, sir," cried a third. "Werry large fly here, sir—reg'lar bluebottle!"

"Here's your fly, sir!" shouted another aspiring charioteer, mounting the box, and inducing an old grey horse to indulge in some imperfect reminiscences of a canter. "Look at him, sir!—temper of a lamb and haction of a steamingein."

Resisting even the temptation of securing the services of so valuable a quadruped as the last named, Mr. Joseph Tuggs beckoned to the proprietor of a dingy conveyance of a greenish hue, lined with faded striped calico; and, the luggage and the family having been deposited therein, the animal in the shafts, after describing circles in the road for a quarter of an hour, at last consented to depart in quest of lodgings.

"How many beds have you got?" screamed Mrs. Tuggs

out of the fly, to the woman who opened the door of the first
house which displayed a bill intimating that apartments
were to be let within.

"How many did you want, ma'am?" was of course the
reply.

"Three."

"Will you step in, ma'am?" Down got Mrs. Tuggs. The
family were delighted. Splendid view of the sea from the
front windows—charming! A short pause. Back came
Mrs. Tuggs again.—One parlour, and a mattress.

"Why the devil didn't they say so at first?" inquired
Mr. Joseph Tuggs, rather pettishly.

"Don't know," said Mrs. Tuggs.

"Wretches!" exclaimed the nervous Cymon. Another bill
—another stoppage. Same question—same answer—similar
result.

"What do they mean by this?" inquired Mr. Joseph Tuggs,
thoroughly out of temper.

"Don't know," said the placid Mrs. Tuggs.

"Orvis the vay here, sir," said the driver, by way of
accounting for the circumstance in a satisfactory manner;
and off they went again, to make fresh inquiries, and encounter fresh disappointments.

It had grown dusk when the "fly"—the rate of whose
progress greatly belied its name—after climbing up four or
five perpendicular hills, stopped before the door of a dusty
house, with a bay window, from which you could obtain a
beautiful glimpse of the sea—if you thrust half your body
out of it, at the imminent peril of falling in the area. Mrs.
Tuggs alighted. One ground-floor sitting-room, and three
cells with beds in them up-stairs—a double house—family on
the opposite side—five children milk-and-watering in the
parlour, and one little boy, expelled for bad behaviour,
screaming on his back in the passage.

"What's the terms?" said Mrs. Tuggs. The mistress of
the house was deliberating on the expediency of putting on
an extra guinea; so she coughed slightly, and affected not to
hear the question.

"What's the terms?" said Mrs. Tuggs, in a louder key.

"Five guineas a week, ma'am, *with* attendance," replied
the lodging-house keeper. (Attendance means the privilege
of ringing the bell as often as you like, for your own amusement).

"Rather dear," said Mrs. Tuggs.

"Oh dear, no, ma'am," replied the mistress of the house,
with a benign smile of pity at the ignorance of manners and
customs, which the observation betrayed. "Very cheap."

Such an authority was indisputable. Mrs. Tuggs paid a
week's rent in advance, and took the lodgings for a month.

In an hour's time the family were seated at tea in their new abode.

"Capital srimps!" said Mr. Joseph Tuggs.

Mr. Cymon eyed his father with a rebellious scowl, as he emphatically said "*Shrimps*."

"Well then, shrimps," said Mr. Joseph Tuggs. "Srimps or shrimps, don't much matter."

There was pity, blended with malignity, in Mr. Cymon's eye, as he replied, "Don't matter, father! What would Captain Waters say, if he heard such vulgarity?"

"Or what would dear Mrs. Captain Waters say," added Charlotta, "if she saw mother—ma, I mean—eating them whole, heads and all?"

"It won't bear thinking of!" ejaculated Mr. Cymon, with a shudder. "How different," he thought, "from the Dowager Duchess of Dobbleton!"

"Very pretty woman, Mrs. Captain Waters, is she not, Cymon?" inquired Miss Charlotta.

A glow of nervous excitement passed over the countenance of Mr. Cymon Tuggs, as he replied, "An angel of beauty!"

"Hallo!" said Mr. Joseph Tuggs, "hallo, Cymon, my boy, take care.—Married lady, you know;" and he winked one of his twinkling eyes knowingly.

"Why," exclaimed Cymon, starting up with an ebullition of fury, as unexpected as alarming, "why am I to be reminded of that blight of my happiness, and ruin of my hopes? Why am I to be taunted with the miseries which are heaped upon my head? Is it not enough to—to—to—" and the orator paused; but whether for want of words, or lack of breath, was never distinctly ascertained.

There was an impressive solemnity in the tone of this address, and in the air with which the romantic Cymon at its conclusion, rang the bell, and demanded a flat candlestick, which effectually forbade a reply. He stalked dramatically to bed, and the Tuggses went to bed too, half an hour afterwards, in a state of considerable mystification and perplexity.

If the pier had presented a scene of life and bustle to the Tuggs's on their first landing at Ramsgate, it was far surpassed by the appearance of the sands on the morning after their arrival. It was a fine, bright, clear day, with a light breeze from the sea. There were the same ladies and gentlemen, the same children, the same nursemaids, the same telescopes, the same portable chairs; the ladies were employed in needlework, or watch-guard making, or knitting, or reading novels; the gentlemen were reading newspapers and magazines, the children were digging holes in the sand with wooden spades, and collecting water therein: the nursemaids with their youngest charges in their arms, were running in after the waves, and then running back with the waves after them;

and now and then a little sailing-boat either departed with a gay and talkative cargo of passengers, or returned with a very silent, and particularly uncomfortable-looking one.

"Well, I never!" exclaimed Mrs. Tuggs, as she and Mr. Joseph Tuggs, and Miss Charlotta Tuggs, and Mr. Cymon Tuggs, with their eight feet in a corresponding number of yellow shoes, seated themselves on four rush-bottomed chairs, which, being placed in a soft part of the sand, forthwith sank down some two feet and a half.—"Well, I never!"

Mr. Cymon, by an exertion of great personal strength, uprooted the chairs, and removed them further back.

"Why, I'm blessed if there ain't some ladies a-going in!" exclaimed Mr. Joseph Tuggs, with intense astonishment.

"Lor, pa!" exclaimed Miss Charlotta.

"There is, my dear," said Mr. Joseph Tuggs. And sure enough, four young ladies, each furnished with a towel, tripped up the steps of a bathing-machine; in went the horse, floundering about in the water; round turned the machine, down sat the driver, and presently out burst the young ladies aforesaid, with four distinct splashes.

"Well, that's sing'ler, too!" ejaculated Mr. Joseph Tuggs, after an awkward pause. Mr. Cymon coughed slightly.

"Why, here's some gentlemen a-going in on this side," exclaimed Mrs. Tuggs in a tone of horror.

Three machines—three horses—three flounderings—three turnings round—three splashes—three gentlemen, disporting themselves in the water like so many dolphins.

"Well that's sing'ler!" said Mr. Joseph Tuggs again.

Miss Charlotta coughed this time, and another pause ensued. It was agreeably broken.

"How d'ye do, dear? We have been looking for you all the morning," said a voice to Miss Charlotta Tuggs. Mrs. Captain Waters was the owner of it.

"How d'ye do?" said Captain Walter Waters, all suavity; and a most cordial interchange of greetings ensued.

"Belinda, my love," said Captain Walter Waters, applying his glass to his eye, and looking in the direction of the sea.

"Yes, my dear," replied Mrs. Captain Waters.

"There's Harry Thompson."

"Where?" said Belinda, applying her glass to her eye.

"Bathing."

"Lor, so it is! He don't see us, does he?"

"No, I don't think he does," replied the captain. "Bless my soul, how very singular!"

"What?" inquired Belinda.

"There's Mary Goring, too."

"Lor!—where?" (Up went the glass again.)

"There!" said the captain, pointing to one of the young ladies before noticed, who, in her bathing costume, looked as if she was enveloped in a patent mackintosh of scanty dimensions.

"So it is, I declare!" exclaimed Mrs. Captain Waters. "How very curious we should see them both!"

"Very," said the captain, with perfect coolness.

"It's the reg'lar thing here, you see," whispered Mr. Cymon Tuggs to his father.

"I see it is," whispered Mr. Joseph Tuggs in reply. "Queer, though—ain't it?" Mr. Cymon Tuggs nodded assent.

"What do you think of doing with yourself this morning?" inquired the captain. "Shall we lunch at Pegwell?"

"I should like that very much indeed," interposed Mrs. Tuggs. She had never heard of Pegwell before; but the word "lunch" had reached her ears, and it sounded agreeably.

"How shall we go?" inquired the captain; "it's too warm to walk."

"A shay?" suggested Mr. Joseph Tuggs.

"Chaise," whispered Mr. Cymon.

"I should think one would be enough," said Mr. Joseph Tuggs aloud, quite unconscious of the meaning of the correction. "However, two shays if you like."

"I should like a donkey so much," said Belinda.

"Oh, so should I!" echoed Charlotta Tuggs.

"Well, we can have a fly," suggested the captain, "and you can have a couple of donkeys."

A fresh difficulty arose. Mrs. Captain Waters declared it would be decidedly improper for two ladies to ride alone. The remedy was obvious. Perhaps young Mr. Tuggs would be gallant enough to accompany them.

Mr. Cymon Tuggs blushed, smiled, looked vacant, and faintly protested he was no horseman. The objection was at once overruled. A fly was speedily found; and three donkeys—which the proprietor declared on his solemn asseveration to be "three parts blood, and the other corn" —were engaged in the service.

"Kim up!" shouted one of the two boys who followed behind to propel the donkeys, when Belinda Waters and Charlotta Tuggs had been hoisted and pushed and pulled into their respective saddles.

"Hi—hi—hi!" groaned the other boy behind Mr. Cymon Tuggs. Away went the donkey, with the stirrups jingling against the heels of Cymon's boots, and Cymon's boots nearly scraping the ground.

"Way—way! Wo—o—o—o— !" cried Mr. Cymon Tuggs as well as he could, in the midst of the jolting.

"Don't make it gallop!" screamed Mrs. Captain Waters, behind.

"My donkey will go into the public-house!" shrieked Miss Tuggs, in the rear.

"Hi—hi—hi!" groaned both the boys together; and on went the donkeys as if nothing would ever stop them.

Everything has an end, however; and even the galloping of donkeys will cease in time. The animal which Mr. Cymon Tuggs bestrode, feeling sundry uncomfortable tugs at the bit, the intent of which he could by no means divine, abruptly sidled against a brick wall, and expressed his uneasiness by grinding Mr. Cymon Tuggs's leg on the rough surface. Mrs. Captain Waters's donkey, apparently under the influence of some playfulness of spirit, rushed suddenly, head first, into a hedge, and declined to come out again: and the quadruped on which Miss Tuggs was mounted expressed his delight at this humorous proceeding by firmly planting his fore-feet against the ground, and kicking up his hind-legs in a very agile, but somewhat alarming manner.

This abrupt termination to the rapidity of the ride naturally occasioned some confusion. Both the ladies indulged in vehement screaming for several minutes; and Mr. Cymon Tuggs, besides sustaining intense bodily pain, had the additional mental anguish of witnessing their distressing situation, without the power to rescue them, by reason of his leg being firmly screwed in between the animal and the wall. The efforts of the boys, however, assisted by the ingenious expedient of twisting the tail of the most rebellious donkey, restored order in a much shorter time than could have reasonably been expected, and the little party jogged slowly on together.

"Now let 'em walk," said Mr. Cymon Tuggs. "It's cruel to overdrive 'em."

"Werry well, sir," replied the boy, with a grin at his companion, as if he understood Mr. Cymon to mean that the cruelty applied less to the animals than to their riders.

"What a lovely day, dear!" said Charlotta.

"Charming; enchanting, dear!" responded Mrs. Captain Waters. "What a beautiful prospect, Mr. Tuggs!"

Cymon looked full in Belinda's face, as he responded—"Beautiful, indeed!" The lady cast down her eyes, and suffered the animal she was riding to fall a little back. Cymon Tuggs instinctively did the same.

There was a brief silence, broken only by a sigh from Mr. Cymon Tuggs.

"Mr. Cymon," said the lady suddenly, in a low tone, "Mr. Cymon—I am another's."

Mr. Cymon expressed his perfect concurrence in a statement which it was quite impossible to controvert.

"If I had not been," resumed Belinda; and there she stopped.

"What—what?" said Mr. Cymon earnestly. "Do not torture me. What would you say?"

"If I had not been"—continued Mrs. Captain Waters—

"if in earlier life, it had been my fate to have known, and been beloved by a noble youth—a kindred soul—a congenial spirit—one capable of feeling and appreciating the sentiments which——"

"Heavens! what do I hear?" exclaimed Mr. Cymon Tuggs. "Is it possible! can I believe my—Come up!" (This last unsentimental parenthesis was addressed to the donkey, who with his head between his forelegs, appeared to be examining the state of his shoes with great anxiety.)

"Hi—hi—hi," said the boys behind. "Come up," expostulated Cymon Tuggs again. "Hi—hi—hi," repeated the boys: and whether it was that the animal felt indignant at the tone of Mr. Tuggs's command, or alarmed by the noise of the deputy proprietor's boots running behind him, or whether he burned with a noble emulation to outstrip the other donkeys, certain it is that he no sooner heard the second series of "hi—hi's" than he started away with a celerity of pace which jerked Mr. Cymon's hat off instantaneously, and carried him to the Pegwell Bay hotel in no time, where he deposited his rider without giving him the trouble of dismounting, by sagaciously pitching him over his head, into the very door of the tavern.

Great was the confusion of Mr. Cymon Tuggs, when he was put right end uppermost by two waiters; considerable was the alarm of Mrs. Tuggs in behalf of her son; and agonising were the apprehensions of Mrs. Captain Waters on his account. It was speedily discovered, however, that he had not sustained much more injury than the donkey—he was grazed, and the animal was grazing—and then it *was* a delightful party to be sure! Mr. and Mrs. Tuggs, and the captain, had ordered lunch in the little garden behind:—small saucers of large shrimps, dabs of butter, crusty loaves, and bottled ale. The sky was without a cloud; there were flower-pots and turf before them; the sea at the foot of the cliff stretching away as far as the eye could discern anything at all; and vessels in the distance with sails as white, and as small, as nicely-got-up cambric handkerchiefs. The shrimps were delightful the ale better, and the captain even more pleasant than either Mrs. Captain Waters was in *such* spirits after lunch—chasing, first the captain across the turf, and among the flower-pots, and then Mr. Cymon Tuggs, and then Miss Tuggs, and laughing too, quite boisterously. But as the captain said, it didn't matter; who knew what they were, there? For all the people of the house knew, they might be common people. To which Mr. Joseph Tuggs responded, "To be sure"; and then they went down the steep wooden steps a little further on, which led to the bottom of the cliff, and looked at the crabs, and the seaweed, and the eels, till it was more than fully time to go back to Ramsgate again; and finally Mr. Cymon

Tuggs ascended the steps last, and Mrs. Captain Waters last but one; and Mr. Cymon Tuggs discovered that the foot and ankle of Mrs. Captain Waters were even more unexceptionable than he had at first supposed.

Taking a donkey towards his ordinary place of residence, is a very different thing, and a feat much more easily to be accomplished, than taking him from it. It requires a great deal of foresight and presence of mind in the one case, to anticipate the numerous flights of his discursive imagination; whereas in the other, all you have to do is to hold on, and place a blind confidence in the animal. Mr. Cymon Tuggs adopted the latter expedient on his return; and his nerves were so little discomposed by the journey, that he distinctly understood they were all to meet again at the library in the evening.

The library was crowded. There were the same ladies and the same gentlemen who had been on the sands in the morning, and on the pier the day before. There were young ladies in maroon-coloured gowns and black velvet bracelets, dispensing fancy articles in the shop, and presiding over games of chance in the concert-room. There were marriageable daughters, and marriage-making mammas, gaming, and promenading, and turning over music, and flirting. There were some male beaux doing the sentimental in whispers, and others doing the ferocious in moustache. There were Mrs. Tuggs in amber, Miss Tuggs in sky-blue, and Mrs. Captain Waters in pink. There was Captain Waters in a braided surtout; there was Mr. Cymon Tuggs in pumps and a gilt waistcoat; and, moreover, there was Mr. Joseph Tuggs in a blue coat and a shirt-frill.

"Number three, eight, and eleven," cried one of the young ladies in the maroon-coloured gowns.

"Number three, eight, and eleven," echoed another young lady in the same uniform.

"Number three's gone," said the first young lady. "Number eight and eleven."

"Number eight and eleven," echoed the second young lady.

"Number eight's gone, Mary Ann," said the first young lady.

"Number eleven," screamed the second.

"The numbers are all taken now, ladies, if you please," said the first. The representatives of numbers three, eight, and eleven, and the rest of the numbers, crowded round the table.

"Will you throw, ma'am?" said the presiding goddess, handing the dice-box to the eldest daughter of a stout lady, with four girls.

There was a profound silence among the lookers-on.

"Throw, Jane, my dear," said the stout lady. An interesting display of bashfulness—a little blushing in a cambric handkerchief—a whispering to a younger sister.

"Amelia, my dear, throw for your sister," said the stout lady; and then she turned to a walking advertisement of Rowlands' Macassar Oil, who stood next her, and said, "Jane is so *very* modest and retiring; but I can't be angry with her for it. An artless and unsophisticated girl is *so* truly amiable, that I often wish Amelia was more like her sister."

The gentleman with the whiskers whispered his admiring approval; and the artless young lady glanced across to observe the effect of her most unqualified simplicity.

"Now, my dear!" said the stout lady. Miss Amelia threw —eight for her sister, ten for herself.

"Nice figure, Amelia," whispered the stout lady to a thin youth beside her.

"Beautiful!"

"And *such* a spirit. I am like you in that respect. I can *not* help admiring that life and vivacity. Ah! (a sigh) I wish I could make poor Jane a little more like my dear Amelia!"

The young gentleman cordially acquiesced in the sentiment; both he, and the individual first addressed, were perfectly contented.

"Who's this?" inquired Mr. Cymon Tuggs of Mrs. Captain Waters, as a short female, in a blue velvet hat and feathers, was led into the orchestra, by a fat man in black tights, and cloudy Berlins.

"Mrs. Tippin, of the London theatres," replied Belinda, referring to the programme of the concert.

The talented Tippin having condescendingly acknowledged the clapping of hands, and shouts of "bravo!" which greeted her appearance, proceeded to sing the popular cavatina of "Bid me discourse," accompanied on the piano by Mr. Tippin; after which Mr. Tippin sang a comic song, accompanied on the piano by Mrs. Tippin, the applause consequent upon which was only to be exceeded by the enthusiastic approbation bestowed upon an air with variations on the guitar, by Miss Tippin, accompanied on the chin by Master Tippin.

Thus passed the evening; and thus passed the days and evenings of the Tuggs's, and the Waters's, for six weeks afterwards. Sands in the morning—donkeys at noon—pier in the afternoon—library at night; and the same people everywhere.

On that very night six weeks, the moon was shining brightly over the calm sea, which dashed against the feet of the tall gaunt cliffs with just enough noise to lull the old fish to sleep, without disturbing the young ones, when two figures were discernible—or would have been, if anybody had looked for

them—seated on one of the wooden benches which are
stationed near the verge of the western cliff. The moon had
climbed higher into the heavens, by two hours' journeying,
since those figures first sat down, and yet they had moved not.
The crowd of loungers had thinned and dispersed, the noise of
itinerant musicians had died away; light after light had
appeared in the windows of the different houses in the
distance, blockade-man after blockade-man had passed the
spot, wending his way towards his solitary post, and yet those
figures had remained stationary. Some portions of the two
forms were in deep shadow, but the light of the moon fell
strongly on a puce-coloured boot and a glazed stock. Mr.
Cymon Tuggs and Mrs. Captain Waters were seated on that
bench. They spoke not, but were silently gazing on the sea.

"Walter will return to-morrow," said Mrs. Captain Waters,
mournfully breaking silence.

Mr. Cymon Tuggs sighed like a gust of wind through a forest
of gooseberry bushes, as he replied—"Alas! he will."

"Oh, Cymon!" resumed Belinda, "the chaste delight, the
calm happiness, of this one week of Platonic love is too much
for me."

Cymon was about to suggest that it was too little for him,
but he stopped himself, and murmured unintelligibly.

"And to think that even this glimpse of happiness, innocent
as it is," exclaimed Belinda, "is now to be lost for ever!"

"Oh, do not say for ever, Belinda," exclaimed the excitable
Cymon, as two strongly-defined tears chased each other down
his pale face—it was so long that there was plenty of room for
a chase. "Do not say for ever!"

"I must," replied Belinda.

"Why?" urged Cymon, "oh why? Such Platonic acquaintance as ours is so harmless, that even your husband can
never object to it."

"My husband!" exclaimed Belinda. "You little know him.
Jealous and revengeful; ferocious in his revenge—a maniac in
his jealousy! Would you be assassinated before my eyes?"
Mr. Cymon Tuggs, in a voice broken by emotion, expressed his
disinclination to undergo the process of assassination before
the eyes of anybody.

"Then leave me," said Mrs. Captain Waters. "Leave me,
this night, for ever. It is late; let us return."

Mr. Cymon Tuggs sadly offered the lady his arm, and
escorted her to her lodgings. He paused at the door—he felt
a Platonic pressure of his hand. "Good-night," he said,
hesitating.

"Good-night," sobbed the lady. Mr. Cymon Tuggs paused
again.

"Won't you walk in, sir?" said the servant. Mr. Tuggs
hesitated. Oh, that hesitation! He *did* walk in

"Good-night," said Mr. Cymon Tuggs again, when he reached the drawing-room.

"Good-night!" replied Belinda; "and, if at any period of my life, I—Hush!" The lady paused, and stared, with a steady gaze of horror, on the ashy countenance of Mr. Cymon Tuggs. There was a double-knock at the street-door.

"It is my husband!" said Belinda, as the captain's voice was heard below.

"And my family!" added Cymon Tuggs, as the voices of his relatives floated up the staircase.

"The curtain! The curtain!" gasped Mrs. Captain Waters, pointing to the window, before which some chintz hangings were closely drawn.

"But I have done nothing wrong," said the hesitating Cymon.

"The curtain!" reiterated the frantic lady; "you will be murdered." This last appeal to his feelings was irresistible. The dismayed Cymon concealed himself behind the curtain, with pantomimic suddenness.

Enter the captain, Joseph Tuggs, Mrs. Tuggs, and Charlotta.

"My dear," said the captain, "Lieutenant Slaughter." Two iron-shod boots, and one gruff voice were heard by Mr. Cymon to advance, and acknowledge the honour of the introduction. The sabre of the lieutenant rattled heavily upon the floor, as he seated himself at the table. Mr. Cymon's fears almost overcame his reason.

"The brandy, my dear," said the captain. Here was a situation! They were going to make a night of it: and Mr. Cymon Tuggs was pent up behind the curtain, and afraid to breathe.

"Slaughter," said the captain, "a cigar?"

Now, Mr. Cymon Tuggs never could smoke without feeling it indispensably necessary to retire immediately, and never could smell smoke without a strong disposition to cough. The cigars were introduced; the captain was a professed smoker, so was the lieutenant, so was Joseph Tuggs. The apartment was small, the door was closed, the smoke powerful: it hung in heavy wreaths over the room, and at length found its way behind the curtain. Cymon Tuggs held his nose, then his mouth, then his breath. It was all of no use—out came the cough.

"Bless my soul!" said the captain, "I beg your pardon, Miss Tuggs. You dislike smoking?"

"Oh, no; I don't indeed," said Charlotta.

"It makes you cough."

"Oh dear no."

"You coughed just now."

"Me, Captain Waters! Lor! how can you say so?"

"Somebody coughed," said the captain

"I certainly thought so," said Slaughter. No; everybody denied it.

"Fancy," said the captain.

"Must be," echoed Slaughter.

Cigars resumed—more smoke, another cough—smothered, but violent.

"Damned odd!" said the captain, staring about him.

"Sing'ler!" ejaculated the unconscious Mr. Joseph Tuggs.

Lieutenant Slaughter looked first at one person mysteriously, then at another, then laid down his cigar; then approached the window on tiptoe, and pointed with his right thumb over his shoulder, in the direction of the curtain.

"Slaughter!" ejaculated the captain, rising from table, "what do you mean?"

The lieutenant, in reply, drew back the curtain, and discovered Mr. Cymon Tuggs behind it: pallid with apprehension, and blue with wanting to cough.

"Ah!" exclaimed the captain, furiously, "what do I see? Slaughter, your sabre!"

"Cymon!" screamed the Tuggs's.

"Mercy!" said Belinda.

"Platonic!" gasped Cymon.

"Your sabre!" roared the captain: "Slaughter—unhand me—the villain's life!"

"Murder!" screamed the Tuggs's.

"Hold him fast, sir!" faintly articulated Cymon.

"Water!" exclaimed Joseph Tuggs—and Mr. Cymon Tuggs and all the ladies forthwith fainted away, and formed a tableau.

Most willingly would we conceal the disastrous termination of the six weeks' acquaintance. A troublesome form, and an arbitrary custom, however, prescribe that a story should have a conclusion in addition to a commencement; and we have therefore no alternative. Lieutenant Slaughter brought a message—the captain brought an action. Mr. Joseph Tuggs interposed—the lieutenant negotiated. When Mr. Cymon Tuggs recovered from the nervous disorder into which misplaced affection, and exciting circumstances had plunged him, he found that his family had lost their pleasant acquaintance; that his father was minus fifteen hundred pounds; and the captain plus the precise sum. The money was paid to hush the matter up, but it got abroad notwithstanding; and there are not wanting those who affirm that three designing impostors never found more easy dupes, than did Captain Waters, Mrs. Waters, and Lieutenant Slaughter, in the Tuggs's at Ramsgate.

CHAPTER V: *Horatio Sparkins*

"INDEED, my love, he paid Teresa very great attention on the last assembly night," said Mrs. Malderton, addressing her spouse, who, after the fatigues of the day in the City, was sitting with a silk handkerchief over his head, and his feet on the fender, drinking his port;—"very great attention; and I say again, every possible encouragement ought to be given him. He positively must be asked down here to dine."

"Who must?" inquired Mr. Malderton.

"Why, you know whom I mean, my dear—the young man with the black whiskers and the white cravat, who has just come out at our assembly, and whom all the girls are talking about. Young—dear me! what's his name?—Marianne, what *is* his name?" continued Mrs. Malderton, addressing her youngest daughter, who was engaged in netting a purse, and endeavouring to look sentimental.

"Mr. Horatio Sparkins, ma," replied Miss Marianne, with a Juliet-like sigh.

"Oh! yes, to be sure—Horatio Sparkins," said Mrs. Malderton. "Decidedly the most gentleman-like young man I ever saw. I am sure, in the beautifully made coat he wore the other night, he looked like—like——"

"Like Prince Leopold, ma—so noble, so full of sentiment!" suggested Miss Marianne, in a tone of enthusiastic admiration.

"You should recollect, my dear," resumed Mrs. Malderton, "that Teresa is now eight-and-twenty; and that it really is very important that something should be done."

Miss Teresa Malderton was a very little girl, rather fat, with vermilion cheeks, but good-humoured, and still disengaged, although, to do her justice, the misfortune arose from no lack of perseverance on her part. In vain had she flirted for ten years; in vain had Mr. and Mrs. Malderton assiduously kept up an extensive acquaintance among the eligible young bachelors of Camberwell, and even of Wandsworth and Brixton; to say nothing of those who "dropped in" from town. Miss Malderton was as well known as the lion on the top of Northumberland House, and had an equal chance of "going off."

"I am quite sure you'd like him," continued Mrs. Malderton; "he is so gentlemanly!"

"So clever!" said Miss Marianne.

"And has such a flow of language!" added Miss Teresa.

"He has a great respect for you, my dear," said Mrs. Malderton to her husband, in a confident tone. Mr. Malderton coughed, and looked at the fire.

"Yes, I'm sure he's very much attached to pa's society," said Miss Marianne.

"No doubt of it," echoed Miss Teresa.

"Indeed, he said as much to me in confidence," observed Mrs. Malderton.

"Well, well," returned Mr. Malderton, somewhat flattered; "if I see him at the assembly to-morrow, perhaps I'll ask him down here. I hope he knows we live at Oak Lodge, Camberwell, my dear?"

"Of course—and that you keep a one-horse carriage."

"I'll see about it," said Mr. Malderton, composing himself for a nap; "I'll see about it."

Mr. Malderton was a man whose whole scope of ideas was limited to Lloyd's, the Exchange, the India House, and the Bank. A few successful speculations had raised him from a situation of obscurity and comparative poverty to a state of affluence. As it frequently happens in such cases, the ideas of himself and his family became elevated to an extraordinary pitch as their means increased; they affected fashion, taste, and many other fooleries, in imitation of their betters, and had a very decided and becoming horror of anything which could by possibility be considered *low*. He was hospitable from ostentation, illiberal from ignorance, and prejudiced from conceit. Egotism and the love of display induced him to keep an excellent table: convenience, and a love of the good things of this life, ensured him plenty of guests. He liked to have clever men, or what he considered such, at his table, because it was a great thing to talk about; but he never could endure what he called "sharp fellows." Probably he cherished this feeling out of compliment to his two sons, who gave their respected parent no uneasiness in that particular. The family were ambitious of forming acquaintances and connections in some sphere of society superior to that in which they themselves moved; and one of the necessary consequences of this desire, added to their utter ignorance of the world beyond their own small circle, was, that any one who could plausibly lay claim to an acquaintance with people of rank and title had a sure passport to the table at Oak Lodge, Camberwell.

The appearance of Mr. Horatio Sparkins at the assembly had excited no small degree of surprise and curiosity among its regular frequenters. Who could he be? He was evidently reserved, and apparently melancholy. Was he a clergyman? —He danced too well. A barrister?—He was not called. He used very fine words, and said a great deal. Could he be a distinguished foreigner come to England for the purpose of describing the country, its manners and customs; and frequenting public balls and public dinners, with the view of becoming acquainted with high life, polished etiquette, and English refinement?—No, he had not a foreign accent. Was he a surgeon, a contributor to the magazines, a writer of fashionable novels, or an artist?—No; to each and all of these surmises there existed some valid objection.—"Then," said everybody, "he must be *somebody*."—"I should think he must be," reasoned Mr. Malderton, with himself, "because he perceives our superiority, and pays us so much attention."

The night succeeding the conversation we have just recorded

HORATIO SPARKINS.

was "assembly night." The double-fly was ordered to be at the door of Oak Lodge at nine o'clock precisely. The Miss Maldertons were dressed in sky-blue satin trimmed with artificial flowers; and Mrs. M. (who was a little fat woman), in ditto ditto, looked like her eldest daughter multiplied by two. Mr. Frederick Malderton the eldest son, in full-dress costume, was the very *beau ideal* of a smart waiter; and Mr. Thomas Malderton, the youngest, with his white dress-stock, blue coat, bright buttons, and red watch-ribbon, strongly resembled the portrait of that interesting, though somewhat rash young gentleman, George Barnwell. Every member of the party had made up his or her mind to cultivate the acquaintance of Mr. Horatio Sparkins. Miss Teresa, of course, was to be as amiable and interesting as ladies of eight-and-twenty on the look-out for a husband usually are; Mrs. Malderton would be all smiles and graces; Miss Marianne would request the favour of some verses for her album; Mr. Malderton would patronise the great unknown by asking him to dinner; and Tom intended to ascertain the extent of his information on the interesting topics of snuff and cigars. Even Mr. Frederick Malderton himself, the family authority on all points of taste, dress, and fashionable arrangement—who had lodgings of his own in town, who had a free admission to Covent Garden theatre, who always dressed according to the fashions of the months, who went up the water twice a week in the season, and who actually had an intimate friend who once knew a gentleman who formerly lived in the Albany,—even he had determined that Mr. Horatio Sparkins must be a devilish good fellow, and that he would do him the honour of challenging him to a game of billiards.

The first object that met the anxious eyes of the expectant family, on their entrance into the ball-room, was the interesting Horatio, with his hair brushed off his forehead, and his eyes fixed on the ceiling, reclining in a contemplative attitude on one of the seats.

"There he is, my dear," anxiously whispered Mrs. Malderton to Mr. Malderton.

"How like Lord Byron!" murmured Miss Teresa.

"Or Montgomery!" whispered Miss Marianne.

"Or the portraits of Captain Ross!" suggested Tom.

"Tom—don't be an ass!" said his father, who checked him upon all occasions, probably with a view to prevent his becoming "sharp"—which was very unnecessary.

The elegant Sparkins attitudinised with admirable effect until the family had crossed the room. He then started up with the most natural appearance of surprise and delight; accosted Mrs. Malderton with the utmost cordiality, saluted the young ladies in the most enchanting manner; bowed to, and shook hands with Mr. Malderton, with a degree of respect amounting almost to veneration, and returned the greetings of the two young men in a half-gratified, half-patronizing manner, which fully convinced them that he must be an important, and, at the same time, condescending personage.

"Miss Malderton," said Horatio, after the ordinary salutations, and bowing very low, "may I be permitted to presume to hope that you will allow me to have the pleasure——"

"I don't think I am engaged," said Miss Teresa, with a dreadful affectation of indifference; "but, really—so many——"

Horatio looked as handsomely miserable as a Hamlet sliding upon a bit of orange-peel.

"I shall be most happy," simpered the interesting Teresa, at last; and Horatio's countenance brightened up like an old hat in a shower of rain.

"A very genteel young man, certainly!" said the gratified Mr. Malderton, as the obsequious Sparkins and his partner joined the quadrille which was just forming.

"He has a remarkably good address," said Mr. Frederick.

"Yes, he is a prime fellow," interposed Tom, who always managed to put his foot in it—"he talks just like an auctioneer."

"Tom!" said his father solemnly, "I think I desired you before not to be a fool."—Tom looked as happy as a cock on a drizzly morning.

"How delightful!" said the interesting Horatio to his partner, as they promenaded the room at the conclusion of the set—"how delightful, how refreshing it is, to retire from the cloudy storms, the vicissitudes, and the troubles of life, even if it be but for a few short, fleeting moments; and to spend those moments, fading and evanescent though they be, in the delightful, the blessed society of one individual—of her whose frowns would be death, whose coldness would be madness, whose falsehood would be ruin, whose constancy would be bliss; the possession of whose affection would be the brightest and best reward that Heaven could bestow on man."

"What feeling! what sentiment!" thought Miss Teresa, as she leaned more heavily upon her companion's arm.

"But enough—enough!" resumed the elegant Sparkins, with a theatrical air. "What have I said? what have I—I—to do with sentiments like these! Miss Malderton—" here he stopped short—"may I hope to be permitted to offer the humble tribute of——"

"Really, Mr. Sparkins," returned the enraptured Teresa, blushing in the sweetest confusion, "I must refer you to papa. I never can, without his consent, venture to—to——"

"Surely he cannot object——"

"Oh, yes. Indeed, indeed, you know him not," interrupted Miss Teresa, well knowing there was nothing to fear, but wishing to make the interview resemble a scene in some romantic novel.

"He cannot object to my offering you a glass of negus," returned the adorable Sparkins, with some surprise.

"Is that all?" thought the disappointed Teresa to herself. "What a fuss about nothing!"

"It will give me the greatest pleasure, sir, to see you to dinner at Oak Lodge, Camberwell, on Sunday next at five o'clock, if you have no better engagement," said Mr. Malderton, at the conclusion of the evening, as he and his sons were standing in conversation with Mr. Horatio Sparkins.

Horatio bowed his acknowledgments, and accepted the flattering invitation.

"I must confess," continued the manœuvring father, offering his snuff-box to his new acquaintance, "that I don't enjoy these assemblies half so much as the comfort—I had almost said the luxury—of Oak Lodge: they have no great charms for an elderly man."

"And after all, sir, what is man?" said the metaphysical Sparkins—"I say, what is man?"

"Ah! very true," said Mr. Malderton—"very true."

"We know that we live and breathe," continued Horatio; "that we have wants and wishes, desires and appetites——"

"Certainly," said Mr. Frederick Malderton, looking very profound.

"I say, we know that we exist," repeated Horatio, raising his voice, "but there we stop; there is an end to our knowledge; there is the summit of our attainments; there is the termination of our ends. What more do we know?"

"Nothing," replied Mr. Frederick—than whom no one was more capable of answering for himself in that particular. Tom was about to hazard something, but, fortunately for his reputation, he caught his father's angry eye, and slunk off like a puppy convicted of petty larceny.

"Upon my word," said Mr. Malderton the elder, as they were returning home in the fly, "that Mr. Sparkins is a wonderful young man. Such surprising knowledge! such extraordinary information! and such a splendid mode of expressing himself!"

"I think he must be somebody in disguise," said Miss Marianne. "How charmingly romantic!"

"He talks very loud and nicely," timidly observed Tom, "but I don't exactly understand what he means."

"I almost begin to despair of *your* understanding anything, sir," said his father, who, of course, had been much enlightened by Mr. Horatio Sparkins's conversations.

"It strikes me, Tom," said Miss Teresa, "that you have made yourself very ridiculous this evening."

"No doubt of it," cried everybody—and the unfortunate

Tom reduced himself into the least possible space. That night Mr. and Mrs. Malderton had a long conversation respecting their daughter's prospects and future arrangements. Miss Teresa went to bed, considering whether, in the event of her marrying a title, she could conscientiously encourage the visits of her present associates; and dreamt all night, of disguised noblemen, large routs, ostrich plumes, bridal favours, and Horatio Sparkins.

Various surmises were hazarded on the Sunday morning as to the mode of conveyance which the anxiously-expected Horatio would adopt. Did he keep a gig?—was it possible he could come on horseback?—or would he patronise the stage? These, and various other conjectures of equal importance, engrossed the attention of Mrs. Malderton during the whole morning.

"Upon my word, my dear, it's a most annoying thing that that vulgar brother of yours should have invited himself to dine here to-day," said Mr. Malderton to his wife. "On account of Mr. Sparkins's coming down, I purposely abstained from asking any one but Flamwell. And then to think of your brother—a tradesman—it's insufferable. I declare I wouldn't have him mention his shop before our new guests—no, not for a thousand pounds! I wouldn't care if he had the good sense to conceal the disgrace he is to the family; but he's so cursedly fond of his horrid business, that he *will* let people know what he is."

Mr. Jacob Barton, the individual alluded to, was a large grocer; so vulgar, and so lost to all sense of feeling, that he actually never scrupled to avow that he wasn't above his business: "he'd made his money by it, and he didn't care who know'd it."

"Ah! Flamwell, my dear fellow, how d'ye do?" said Mr. Malderton, as a little spoffish man, with green spectacles, entered the room. "You got my note?"

"Yes, I did; and here I am in consequence."

"You don't happen to know this Mr. Sparkins by name? You know everybody."

Mr. Flamwell was one of those gentlemen of remarkably extensive information whom one occasionally meets in society, who pretend to know everybody, but in reality know nobody. At Malderton's, where any stories about great people were received with a greedy ear, he was an especial favourite; and knowing the kind of people he had to deal with, he carried his passion of claiming acquaintance with everybody to the most immoderate length. He had rather a singular way of telling his greatest lies in a parenthesis, and with an air of self-denial, as if he feared being thought egotistical.

"Why, no, I don't know him by that name," returned Flamwell, in a low tone, and with an air of immense impor-

tance. "I have no doubt I know him though. Is he
tall?"

"Middle sized," said Miss Teresa.

"With black hair?" inquired Flamwell, hazarding a bold
guess.

"Yes," returned Miss Teresa, eagerly.

"Rather a snub nose?"

"No," said the disappointed Teresa, "he has a Roman nose."

"I said a Roman nose, didn't I?" inquired Flamwell.
"He's an elegant young man?"

"Oh, certainly."

"With remarkably prepossessing manners?"

"Oh, yes!" said all the family together. "You must know
him."

"Yes, I thought you knew him, if he was anybody,"
triumphantly exclaimed Mr. Malderton. "Who d'ye think
he is?"

"Why, from your description," said Flamwell, ruminating,
and sinking his voice almost to a whisper, "he bears a strong
resemblance to the Honourable Augustus Fitz-Edward Fitz-
John Fitz-Osborne. He's a very talented young man, and
rather eccentric. It's extremely probable he may have
changed his name for some temporary purpose."

Teresa's heart beat high. Could he be the Honourable
Augustus Fitz-Edward Fitz-John Fitz-Osborne! What a
name to be elegantly engraved upon two glazed cards, tied
together with a piece of white satin ribbon! "The Honourable Mrs. Augustus Fitz-Edward Fitz-John Fitz-Osborne!"
The thought was transport.

"It's five minutes to five," said Mr. Malderton, looking at
his watch: "I hope he's not going to disappoint us."

"There he is!" exclaimed Miss Teresa, as a loud double-
knock was heard at the door. Everybody endeavoured to
look—as people when they particularly expect a visitor always
do—as if they were perfectly unsuspicious of the approach of
anybody.

The room-door opened. "Mr. Barton!" said the servant.

"Confound the man!" murmured Malderton. "Ah! my
dear sir, how d'ye do! Any news?"

"Why, no," returned the grocer, in his usual honest, bluff
manner. "No, none partickler. None that I am much
aware of.—How d'ye do, gals and boys?—Mr. Flamwell, sir—
glad to see you."

"Here's Mr. Sparkins!" said Tom, who had been looking
out at the window, "on *such* a black horse!"—There was
Horatio, sure enough, on a large black horse, curveting and
prancing along like an Astley's supernumerary. After a great
deal of reining in and pulling up, with the usual accompaniments of snorting, rearing, and kicking, the animal consented

to stop at about a hundred yards from the gate, where Mr. Sparkins dismounted, and confided him to the care of Mr. Malderton's groom. The ceremony of introduction was gone through in all due form. Mr. Flamwell looked from behind his green spectacles at Horatio with an air of mysterious importance; and the gallant Horatio looked unutterable things at Teresa, who tried in her turn to appear uncommonly lackadaisical.

"Is he the Honourable Mr. Augustus—what's his name?" whispered Mrs. Malderton to Flamwell, as he was escorting her to the dining-room.

"Why, no—at least not exactly," returned that great authority—"not exactly."

"Who *is* he then?"

"Hush!" said Flamwell, nodding his head with a grave air, importing that he knew very well; but was prevented by some grave reasons of state from disclosing the important secret. It might be one of the ministers making himself acquainted with the views of the people.

"Mr. Sparkins," said the delighted Mrs. Malderton, "pray divide the ladies. John, put a chair for the gentleman between Miss Teresa and Miss Marianne." This was addressed to a man who on ordinary occasions acted as half-groom, half-gardener; but who, as it was most important to make an impression on Mr. Sparkins, had been forced into a white neckerchief and shoes, and touched up and brushed to look like a second footman.

The dinner was excellent; Horatio was most attentive to Miss Teresa, and every one felt in high spirits, except Mr. Malderton, who, knowing the propensity of his brother-in-law, Mr. Barton, endured that sort of agony which the newspapers inform us is experienced by the surrounding neighbourhood when a pot-boy hangs himself in a hay-loft, and which is "much easier to be imagined than described."

"Have you seen your friend, Sir Thomas Noland, lately, Flamwell?" inquired Mr. Malderton, casting a sidelong look at Horatio, to see what effect the mention of so great a man had upon him.

"Why, no—not very lately; I saw Lord Gubbleton the day before yesterday."

"Ah! I hope his lordship is very well," said Malderton, in a tone of the greatest interest. It is scarcely necessary to say that until that moment he had been quite innocent of the existence of such a person.

"Why, yes; he was very well—very well indeed. He's a devilish good fellow; I met him in the City, and had a long chat with him. Indeed, I'm rather intimate with him. I couldn't stop to talk to him as long as I could wish though, because I was on my way to a banker's, a very rich man, and a member of Parliament, with whom I am also rather, indeed I may say very, intimate."

"I know whom you mean," returned the host, consequentially, in reality knowing as much about the matter as Flamwell himself. "He has a capital business."

This was touching on a dangerous topic.

"Talking of business," interposed Mr. Barton, from the centre of the table. "A gentleman that you knew very well, Malderton, before you made that first lucky spec of yours, called at our shop the other day, and——"

"Barton, may I trouble you for a potato," interrupted the wretched master of the house, hoping to nip the story in the bud.

"Certainly," returned the grocer, quite insensible of his brother-in-law's object—"and he said in a very plain manner——"

"*Floury*, if you please," interrupted Malderton again; dreading the termination of the anecdote, and fearing a repetition of the word "shop."

"He said, says he," continued the culprit, after despatching the potato—"says he, how goes on your business? So I said jokingly—you know my way—says I, I'm never above my business, and I hope my business will never be above me. Ha, ha!"

"Mr. Sparkins," said the host, vainly endeavouring to conceal his dismay, "a glass of wine?"

"With the utmost pleasure, sir."

"Happy to see you."

"Thank you."

"We were talking the other evening," resumed the host, addressing Horatio, partly with the view of displaying the conversational powers of his new acquaintance, and partly in the hope of drowning the grocer's stories—"we were talking the other day about the nature of man. Your argument struck me very forcibly."

"And me," said Mr. Frederick. Horatio made a graceful inclination of the head.

"Pray, what is your opinion of woman, Mr. Sparkins?" inquired Mrs. Malderton. The young ladies simpered.

"Man," replied Horatio, "man, whether he ranged the bright, gay, flowery plains of a second Eden, or the more sterile, barren, and, I may say, commonplace regions, to which we are compelled to accustom ourselves in times such as these; man, I say, under any circumstances, or in any place—whether he were bending beneath the withering blasts of the frigid zone, or scorching under the rays of a vertical sun—man, without woman, would be—alone."

"I am very happy to find you entertain such honourable opinions, Mr. Sparkins," said Mrs. Malderton.

"And I," added Miss Teresa. Horatio looked his delight, and the young lady blushed like a full-blown peony.

"Now it's my opinion," said Mr. Barton——

"I know what you're going to say," interposed Malderton, determined not to give his relation another opportunity, "and I don't agree with you."

"What!" inquired the astonished grocer.

"I am sorry to differ from you, Barton," said the host, in as positive a manner as if he really were contradicting a position which the other had laid down, "but I cannot give my assent to what I consider a very monstrous proposition."

"But I meant to say——"

"You never can convince me," said Malderton, with an air of obstinate determination. "Never."

"And I," said Mr. Frederick, following up his father's attack, "cannot entirely agree in Mr. Sparkins's argument."

"What!" said Horatio, who became more metaphysical, and more argumentative, as he saw the female part of the family listening in wondering delight—"what? Is effect the consequence of cause? Is cause the precursor of effect?"

"That's the point," said Flamwell.

"To be sure," said Mr. Malderton.

"Because, if effect is the consequence of cause, and if cause does precede effect, I apprehend you are decidedly wrong," added Horatio.

"Decidedly," said the toad-eating Flamwell.

"At least, I apprehend that to be the just and logical deduction?" said Sparkins, in a tone of interrogation.

"No doubt of it," chimed in Flamwell again. "It settles the point."

"Well, perhaps it does," said Mr. Frederick; "I didn't see it before."

"I don't exactly see it now," thought the grocer; "but I suppose it's all right."

"How wonderfully clever he is! ' whispered Mrs. Malderton to her daughters, as they retired to the drawing-room.

"Oh, he's quite a love!" said both the young ladies together; "he talks like an oracle. He must have seen a great deal of life."

The gentlemen being left to themselves, a pause ensued, during which everybody looked very grave, as if they were quite overcome by the profound nature of the previous discussion. Flamwell, who had made up his mind to find out who and what Mr. Horatio Sparkins really was, first broke silence.

"Excuse me, sir, ' said that distinguished personage—"I presume you have studied for the bar? I thought of entering once myself—indeed, I'm rather intimate with some of the highest ornaments of that distinguished profession."

"No—no!" said Horatio, with a little hesitation; "not exactly."

"But you have been much among the silk gowns, or I mistake?" inquired Flamwell, deferentially.

"Nearly all my life," returned Sparkins.

The question was thus pretty well settled in the mind of Mr. Flamwell.—He was a young gentleman "about to be called."

"I shouldn't like to be a barrister," said Tom, speaking for the first time, and looking round the table to find somebody who would notice the remark.

No one made any reply.

"I shouldn't like to wear a wig," added Tom, hazarding another observation.

"Tom, I beg you will not make yourself ridiculous," said his father. "Pray listen and improve yourself by the conversation you hear, and don't be constantly making these absurd remarks."

"Very well, father," replied the unfortunate Tom, who had not spoken a word since he had asked for another slice of beef at a quarter-past five o'clock, P.M., and it was then eight.

"Well, Tom," observed his good-natured uncle, "never mind; I think with you. *I* shouldn't like to wear a wig. I'd rather wear an apron."

Mr. Malderton coughed violently. Mr. Barton resumed—"For if a man's above his business——"

The cough returned with tenfold violence, and did not cease until the unfortunate cause of it, in his alarm, had quite forgotten what he intended to say.

"Mr. Sparkins," said Flamwell, returning to the charge, "do you happen to know Mr. Delafontaine, of Bedford Square?"

"I have exchanged cards with him; since which, indeed, I have had an opportunity of serving him considerably," replied Horatio, slightly colouring, no doubt, at having been betrayed into making the acknowledgment.

"You are very lucky, if you have had an opportunity of obliging that great man," observed Flamwell, with an air of profound respect.

"I don't know who he is," he whispered to Mr. Malderton confidentially, as they followed Horatio up to the drawing-room. "It's quite clear, however, that he belongs to the law, and that he is somebody of great importance, and very highly connected."

"No doubt, no doubt," returned his companion.

The remainder of the evening passed away most delightfully. Mr. Malderton, relieved from his apprehensions by the circumstance of Mr. Barton's falling into a profound sleep, was as affable and gracious as possible. Miss Teresa played the "Fall of Paris," as Mr. Sparkins declared, in a most masterly manner, and both of them, assisted by Mr. Frederick, tried over glees and trios without number; they having made the pleasing discovery that their voices harmonised beautifully. To be sure, they all sang the first part: and Horatio, in addition to the slight drawback of having no ear, was perfectly innocent of knowing a note of music; still they passed the time very agreeably, and it was past twelve o'clock before Mr. Sparkins ordered the mourning-coach-looking steed to be brought out —an order which was only complied with, upon the distinct understanding that he was to repeat his visit on the following Sunday.

"But, perhaps, Mr. Sparkins will form one of our party to-morrow evening?" suggested Mrs. M. "Mr. Malderton intends taking the girls to see the pantomime."—Mr. Sparkins bowed, and promised to join the party in box 48, in the course of the evening.

"We will not tax you for the morning," said Miss Teresa, bewitchingly; "for ma is going to take us to all sorts of places, shopping. But I know that gentlemen have a great horror of that employment." Mr. Sparkins bowed again, and declared that he should be delighted, but business of importance occupied him in the morning. Flamwell looked at Malderton significantly.—"It's term time!" he whispered.

At twelve o'clock on the following morning, the "fly" was at the door of Oak Lodge, to convey Mrs. Malderton and her daughters on their expedition for the day. They were to dine and dress for the play at a friend's house; first driving thither with their band-boxes, they departed on their first errand to make some purchases at Messrs. Jones, Spruggins, and Smith's, of Tottenham Court Road; after which they were to go to Redmayne's, in Bond Street; and thence to innumerable places that no one ever heard of. The young ladies beguiled the tediousness of the ride by eulogising Mr. Horatio Sparkins, scolding their mamma for taking them so far to save a shilling, and wondering whether they should ever reach their destination. At length the vehicle stopped before a dirty-looking ticketed linendraper's shop, with goods of all kinds, and labels of all sorts and sizes in the window. There were dropsical figures of a seven with a little three farthings in the corner, something like the aquatic animalculæ disclosed by the gas microscope, "perfectly invisible to the naked eye;" three hundred and fifty thousand ladies' boas, *from* one shilling and a penny half-penny; real French kid shoes, at two and ninepence per pair; green parasols with handles like carving-forks, at an equally cheap rate; and "every description of goods," as the proprietors said—and they must know best—"fifty per cent. under cost price."

"La! ma, what a place you have brought us to!" said Miss Teresa; "what *would* Mr. Sparkins say if he could see us!"

"Ah! what, indeed!" said Miss Marianne, horrified at the idea.

"Pray be seated, ladies. What is the first article?" inquired the obsequious master of the ceremonies of the establishment, who, in his large white neckcloth and formal tie, looked like a bad "portrait of a gentleman" in the Somerset House exhibition.

"I want to see some silks," answered Mrs. Malderton.

"Directly, ma'am.—Mr. Smith! Where *is* Mr. Smith?"

"Here, sir," cried a voice at the back of the shop.

"Pray make haste, Mr. Smith," said the M.C. "You never are to be found when you're wanted, sir."

Mr. Smith, thus enjoined to use all possible despatch, leaped over the counter with great agility, and placed himself before the newly-arrived customers. Mrs. Malderton uttered a faint scream; Miss Teresa, who had been stooping down to talk to her sister, raised her head, and beheld—Horatio Sparkins!

"We will draw a veil," as novel writers say, over the scene that ensued. The mysterious, philosophical, romantic, metaphysical Sparkins—he who, to the interesting Teresa, seemed like the embodied idea of the young dukes and poetical exquisites in blue silk dressing-gowns, and ditto ditto slippers, of whom she had read and dreamt, but had never expected to behold—was suddenly converted into Mr. Samuel Smith, the assistant at a "cheap shop"; the junior partner in a slippery firm of some three weeks' existence. The dignified evanishment of the hero of Oak Lodge on this unexpected recognition could only be equalled by that of a furtive dog with a considerable kettle at his tail. All the hopes of the Maldertons were destined at once to melt away, like the lemon ices at a Company's dinner; Almacks was still to them as distant as the North Pole; and Miss Teresa had about as much chance of a husband as Captain Ross had of the north-west passage.

Years have elapsed since the occurrence of this dreadful morning. The daisies have thrice bloomed on Camberwell Green—the sparrows have thrice repeated their vernal chirps in Camberwell Grove; but the Miss Maldertons are still unmated. Miss Teresa's case is more desperate than ever; but Flamwell is yet in the zenith of his reputation; and the family have the same predilection for aristocratic personages, with an increased aversion to anything *low*.

CHAPTER VI: *The Black Veil*

ONE winter's evening towards the close of the year 1800, or within a year or two of that time, a young medical practitioner, recently established in business, was seated by a cheer-

ful fire in his little parlour, listening to the wind which was
beating the rain in pattering drops against the window, and
rumbling dismally in the chimney. The night was wet and
cold; he had been walking through mud and water the whole
day, and was now comfortably reposing in his dressing-gown
and slippers, more than half asleep and less than half awake,
revolving a thousand matters in his wandering imagination.
First he thought how hard the wind was blowing, and how
the cold sharp rain would be at that moment beating in his
face if he were not comfortably housed at home. Then his
mind reverted to his annual Christmas visit to his native place
and dearest friends; he thought how glad they would all be
to see him, and how happy it would make Rose if he could
only tell her that he had got a patient at last, and hoped to
have more, and to come down again in a few months' time
and marry her, and take her home to gladden his lonely
fireside, and stimulate him to fresh exertions. Then he began
to wonder when his first patient would appear, or whether
he was destined by special dispensation of Providence never
to have any patients at all; and then he thought about Rose
again, and dropped to sleep and dreamed about her, till the
very tones of her sweet merry voice sounded in his ears,
and her soft tiny hand rested on his shoulder.

There *was* a hand upon his shoulder, but it was neither soft
nor tiny; its owner being a corpulent round-headed boy, who,
in consideration of the sum of one shilling per week and his
food, was let out by the parish to carry medicine and messages.
As there was no demand for the one, however, and no necessity
for the other, he usually occupied his unemployed hours—
averaging fourteen a day—in abstracting peppermint drops,
taking animal nourishment, and going to sleep.

"A lady, sir—a lady!" whispered the boy, rousing his
master with a shake.

"What lady?" cried our friend, starting up, not quite
certain that his dream was an illusion, and half expecting
that it might be Rose herself. "What lady? Where?"

"*There*, sir," replied the boy, pointing to the glass door
leading into the surgery, with an expression of alarm which
the very unusual apparition of a customer might have tended
to excite.

The surgeon looked towards the door, and started himself
for an instant on beholding the appearance of his unlooked-
for visitor.

It was a singularly tall female, dressed in deep mourning,
and standing so close to the door that her face almost touched
the glass. The upper part of her person was carefully muffled
in a black shawl, as if for the purpose of concealment, and
her face was shrouded by a thick black veil. She stood
perfectly erect; her figure was drawn up to its full height,

and though the surgeon *felt* that the eyes beneath the veil
were fixed on him, she stood perfectly motionless, and
evinced, by no gesture whatever, the slightest consciousness
of his having turned towards her.

"Do you wish to consult me?" he inquired, with some
hesitation, holding open the door. It opened inwards, and
therefore the action did not alter the position of the figure,
which still remained motionless on the same spot.

The female slightly inclined her head, in token of
acquiescence.

"Pray walk in," said the surgeon.

The figure moved a step forward; and then turning its
head in the direction of the boy—to his infinite horror—
appeared to hesitate.

"Leave the room, Tom," said the young man, addressing
the boy, whose large round eyes had been extended to their
utmost width during this brief interview. "Draw the curtain,
and shut the door."

The boy drew a green curtain across the glass part of the
door, retired into the surgery, closed the door after him, and
immediately applied one of his large eyes to the keyhole on
the other side.

The surgeon drew a chair to the fire, and motioned the
visitor to a seat. The mysterious figure slowly moved
towards it, and as the blaze shone upon the black dress, the
surgeon observed that the bottom of it was saturated with
mud and rain.

"You are very wet," he said.

"I am," said the stranger, in a low deep voice.

"And you are ill?" added the surgeon, compassionately, for
the tone was that of a person in severe pain.

"I am," was the reply—"very ill: not bodily, but mentally.
It is not for myself, or on my own behalf," continued the
stranger, "that I come to you. If I laboured under bodily
disease, I should not be out alone at such an hour, or on such
a night as this; and if I were afflicted with it twenty-four
hours hence, God knows how gladly I would lie down and
pray to die. It is for another that I beseech your aid, sir.
I may be mad to ask it for him—I think I am; but, night after
night through the long dreary hours of watching and weeping,
the thought has been ever present to my mind; and though
even *I* see the hopelessness of human assistance availing him,
the bare thought of laying him in his grave without it makes
my blood run cold!" And a shudder, such as the surgeon
well knew art could not produce, trembled through the
speaker's frame.

There was a desperate earnestness in this woman's manner
that went to the young man's heart. He was young in his
profession, and had not yet witnessed enough of the miseries

which are daily presented before the eyes of its members, to have grown comparatively callous to human suffering.

"If," he said, rising hastily, "the person of whom you speak be in so hopeless a condition as you describe, not a moment is to be lost. I will go with you instantly. Why did you not obtain medical advice before?"

"Because it would have been useless before—because it is useless even now," replied the woman, clasping her hands passionately.

The surgeon gazed for a moment on the black veil, as if to ascertain the expression of the features beneath it; its thickness, however, rendered such a result impossible.

"You *are* ill," he said, gently, "although you do not know it. The fever which has enabled you to bear without feeling it the fatigue you have evidently undergone, is burning within you now. Put that to your lips," he continued, pouring out a glass of water—"compose yourself for a few moments, and then tell me, as calmly as you can, what the disease of the patient is, and how long he has been ill. The moment I know what it is necessary I should know, to render my visit serviceable to him, I am ready to accompany you."

The stranger lifted the glass of water to her mouth without raising the veil, put it down again untasted, and burst into tears.

"I know," she said, sobbing aloud, "that what I say to you now, seems like the ravings of fever. I have been told so before, less kindly than by you. I am not a young woman, sir; and they do say, that as life steals on towards its final close, the last short remnant, worthless as it may seem to all beside, is dearer to its possessor than all the years that have gone before, connected though they be with the recollection of old friends long since dead, and young ones—children perhaps—who have fallen off from, and forgotten one as completely as if they had died too. My natural term of life cannot be many years longer, and should be dear on that account; but I would lay it down without a sigh—with cheerfulness—with joy—if what I tell you now were only false, or imaginary. To-morrow morning he of whom I speak will be, I *know*, though I would fain think otherwise, beyond the reach of human aid; and yet, to-night, though he is in deadly peril, you must not see, and could not serve him."

"I am unwilling to increase your distress," said the surgeon, after a short pause, "by making any comment on what you have just said, or appearing desirous to investigate a subject you seem so anxious to conceal; but there is an inconsistency in your statement which I cannot reconcile with probability. This person is dying to-night, and I cannot see him when my assistance might possibly avail; you apprehend it will be useless to-morrow, and yet you would have me see him then.

If he be indeed as dear to you, as your words and manner would imply, why not try to save his life before delay and the progress of his disease render it impracticable?"

"God help me!" exclaimed the woman, weeping bitterly, "how can I hope strangers will believe what appears incredible, even to myself? You will *not* see him then, sir?" she added, rising suddenly.

"I did not say that I declined to see him," replied the surgeon: "but I warn you, that if you persist in this extraordinary procrastination, and the individual dies, a fearful responsibility rests with you."

"The responsibility will rest heavily somewhere," replied the stranger bitterly. "Whatever responsibility rests with me, I am content to bear and ready to answer."

"As I incur none," continued the surgeon, "by acceding to your request, I will see him in the morning, if you leave me the address. At what hour can he be seen?"

"*Nine*," replied the stranger.

"You must excuse my pressing these inquiries," said the surgeon. "But is he in your charge now?"

"He is not," was the rejoinder.

"Then if I gave you instructions for his treatment through the night, you could not assist him?"

The woman wept bitterly, as she replied, "I could not."

Finding that there was but little prospect of obtaining further information by prolonging the interview; and anxious to spare the woman's feelings, which, subdued at first by a violent effort, were now irrepressible and most painful to witness, the surgeon repeated his promise of calling in the morning at the appointed hour; and his visitor, after giving him a direction to an obscure part of Walworth, left the house in the same mysterious manner as she had entered it.

It will be readily believed that so extraordinary a visit produced a considerable impression on the mind of the young surgeon, and that he speculated a great deal and to very little purpose on the possible circumstances of the case. In common with the generality of people, he had often heard and read of singular instances, in which a presentiment of death at a particular day or even minute had been entertained and realised. At one moment he was inclined to think that the present might be such a case, but then it occurred to him that all the anecdotes of the kind he had ever heard, were of persons who had been troubled with a foreboding of their own death. This woman, however, spoke of another person —a man; and it was impossible to suppose that a mere dream or delusion of fancy would induce her to speak of his approaching dissolution with such terrible certainty as she had done. It could not be that the man was to be murdered in the morning, and that the woman, originally a consenting party

an l bound to secrecy by an oath, had relented, and, thoug
unable to prevent the commission of some outrage on th
victim, had determined to prevent his death if possible b
the timely interposition of medical aid. The idea of suc
things happening within two miles of the metropolis appeare
too wild and preposterous to be entertained beyond the instan
Then his original impression that the woman's intellects wer
disordered, recurred; and as it was the only mode of solvin
the difficulty with any degree of satisfaction, he obstinatel
made up his mind to believe she was mad. Certain misgiving
upon this point, however, stole upon his thoughts at the time
and presented themselves again and again through the lon
dull course of a sleepless night, during which, in spite of al
his efforts to the contrary, he was unable to banish the blac
veil from his disturbed imagination.

The back part of Walworth, at its greatest distance from
town, is a straggling, miserable place enough, even in thes
days; but five-and-thirty years ago the greater portion of i
was little better than a dreary waste, inhabited by a few
scattered people of most questionable character, whos
poverty prevented their living in any better neighbourhood
or whose pursuits and mode of life rendered its solitud
desirable. Very many of the houses which have since sprun
up on all sides, were not built until some years afterwards
and the great majority even of those which were sprinkle
about at irregular intervals, were of the rudest and mos
miserable description.

The appearance of the place through which he walked wa
not calculated to raise the spirits of the young surgeon, o
to dispel any feeling of anxiety or depression which th
singular kind of visit he was about to make, had awakened
Striking off from the high road, his way lay across a marshy
common, through irregular lanes, with here and there a
ruinous and dismantled cottage fast falling to pieces wit
decay and neglect. A stunted tree, or pool of stagnant water
roused into a creeping sluggish action by the heavy rain o
the preceding night, skirted the path occasionally; and now
and then a miserable patch of garden-ground, with a few
old boards knocked together for a summer-house, and old
palings imperfectly mended with stakes pilfered from the
neighbouring hedges, bore testimony at once to the poverty
of the inhabitants, and the little scruple they entertained in
appropriating the property of other people to their own
use. Occasionally, a filthy-looking woman would make her
appearance from the door of a dirty house, to empty the contents of some cooking utensil into the gutter in front, or to
scream after a little slipshod girl, who had contrived to stagger
a few yards from the door under the weight of a sallow
infant almost as big as herself; but scarcely anything

was stirring around, and so much of the prospect as could be faintly traced through the cold damp mist which hung heavily over it presented a lonely and dreary appearance perfectly in keeping with the objects we have described.

After plodding wearily through the mud and mire; making many inquiries for the place to which he had been directed; and receiving as many contradictory and unsatisfactory replies in return, the young man at length arrived before the house which had been pointed out to him as the object of his destination. It was a small low building, one storey above the ground, with a more desolate and unpromising exterior than any he had yet passed. An old yellow curtain was closely drawn across the window up-stairs, and the parlour shutters were closed, but not fastened. The house was detached from any other, and, as it stood at an angle of a narrow lane, there was no other habitation in sight.

When we say that the surgeon hesitated, and walked a few paces beyond the house before he could prevail upon himself to lift the knocker, we say nothing that need raise a smile upon the face of the boldest reader. The police of London were a very different body in that day to what they are now: the isolated position of the suburbs, when the rage for building and the progress of improvement had not yet begun to connect them with the main body of the city and its environs, rendered many of them (and this in particular) a place of resort for the worst and most depraved characters. Even the streets in the gayest parts of London were imperfectly lighted at that time, and such places as these were left entirely to the mercy of the moon and stars. The chances of detecting desperate characters, or of tracing them to their haunts, were thus rendered very few, and their offences naturally increased in boldness, as the consciousness of comparative security became the more impressed upon them by daily experience. Added to these considerations, it must be remembered that the young man had spent some time in the public hospitals of the metropolis; and although neither Burke nor Bishop had then gained a horrible notoriety, still his own observation might have suggested to him how easily the atrocities to which the former has since given his name, might be committed. Be this as it may, whatever reflection made him hesitate, he *did* hesitate; but, being a young man of strong mind and great personal daring, it was only for an instant;—he stepped briskly back, and knocked gently at the door.

A low whispering was audible immediately afterwards, as if some person at the end of the passage were conversing stealthily with another on the landing above. It was succeeded by the noise of a pair of heavy boots upon the bare floor. The door-chain was softly unfastened; the door opened, and a tall, ill-favoured man, with black hair, and a face, as the surgeon often declared afterwards, as pale and haggard as the countenance of any dead man he ever saw, presented himself.

"Walk in, sir," he said in a low tone.

The surgeon did so, and the man having secured the door again by the chain, led the way to a small back parlour at the extremity of the passage.

"Am I in time?"

"Too soon," replied the man. The surgeon turned hastily round, with a gesture of astonishment not unmixed with alarm, which he found it impossible to repress, though he would gladly have recalled it.

"If you'll step in here, sir," said the man, who had evidently noticed the action—"if you'll step in here, sir, you won't be detained five minutes, I assure you."

The surgeon at once walked into the room. The man closed the door, and left him alone.

It was a little cold room, with no other furniture than two deal chairs and a table of the same material. A handful of fire unguarded by any fender, was burning in the grate, which brought out the damp if it served no more comfortable purpose; for the unwholesome moisture was stealing down the walls in long slug-like tracks. The window, which was broken and patched in many places, looked into a small enclosed piece of ground almost covered with water. Not a sound was to be heard, either within the house or without. The young surgeon sat down by the fire-place, to await the result of his first professional visit.

He had not remained in this position many minutes when the noise of some approaching vehicle struck his ear. It stopped; the street-door was opened; a low talking succeeded, accompanied with a shuffling noise of footsteps along the passage and on the stairs, as if two or three men were engaged in carrying some heavy body to the room above. The creaking of the stairs a few seconds afterwards, announced that the new-comers having completed their task, whatever it was, were leaving the house. The door was again closed, and the former silence was restored.

Another five minutes elapsed, and the surgeon had just resolved to explore the house in search of some one to whom he might make his errand known, when the room-door opened, and his last night's visitor, dressed in exactly the same manner, with the veil lowered as before, motioned him to advance. The singular height of her form, coupled with the circumstance of her not speaking, caused the idea to pass across his brain for an instant that it might be a man disguised in woman's attire. The hysteric sobs which issued from beneath the veil, and the convulsive attitude of grief of the whole figure, however, at once exposed the absurdity of the suspicion, and he hastily followed.

The woman led the way up-stairs to the front room, and paused at the door to let him enter first. It was scantily furnished with an old deal box, a few chairs, and a tent bedstead without hangings or cross-rails, which was covered with a patchwork counterpane. The dim light admitted through the curtain which he had noticed from the outside, rendered the objects in the room so indistinct, and communicated to all of them so uniform a hue, that he did not at first perceive the object on which his eye at once rested when the woman rushed frantically past him, and flung herself on her knees by the bedside.

Stretched upon the bed, closely enveloped in a linen wrapper, and covered with blankets, lay a human form stiff and motionless. The head and face, which were those of a man, were uncovered, save by a bandage which passed over the head and under the chin. The eyes were closed. The left arm lay heavily across the bed, and the woman held the passive hand.

The surgeon gently pushed the woman aside, and took the hand in his.

"My God!" he exclaimed, letting it fall involuntarily— "the man is dead!"

The woman started to her feet and beat her hands together. "Oh! don't say so, sir," she exclaimed, with a burst of passion, amounting almost to frenzy—"Oh! don't say so, sir! I can't bear it, indeed I can't! Men have been brought to life before when unskilful people have given them up for lost; and men have died who might have been restored, if proper means had been resorted to. Don't let him lie here, sir, without one effort to save him. This very moment life may be passing away. Do try, sir—do, for God's sake!" And while speaking, she hurriedly chafed, first the forehead and then the breast of the senseless form before her, and then wildly beat the cold hands, which, when she ceased to hold them, fell listlessly and heavily back on the coverlet.

"It is of no use, my good woman," said the surgeon, sooth-ingly, as he withdrew his hand from the man's breast. "Stay —undo that curtain."

"Why?" said the woman, starting up.

"Undo that curtain," repeated the surgeon, in an agitated tone.

"*I* darkened the room on purpose," said the woman, throwing herself before him as he rose to undraw it. "Oh! sir, have pity on me! If it can be of no use, and he is really dead, do not—do not expose that corpse to other eyes than mine!"

"This man died no natural or easy death," said the surgeon.

"I *must* see the body!" And with a motion so sudden, that the woman hardly knew that he had slipped from beside her, he tore open the curtain, admitted the full light of day, and returned to the bedside.

"There has been violence here," he said, pointing towards the body, and gazing intently on the face, from which the black veil was now for the first time removed. In the excitement of a minute before, the female had dashed off the bonnet and veil, and now stood with her eyes fixed upon him. Her features were those of a woman of about fifty, who had once been handsome. Sorrow and weeping had left traces upon them which not time itself would ever have produced without their aid: her face was deadly pale, and there was a nervous contortion of the lip, and an unnatural fire in her eye, which showed too plainly that her bodily and mental powers had nearly sunk beneath an accumulation of misery.

"There has been violence here," said the surgeon, preserving his searching glance.

"There has!" replied the woman.

"This man has been murdered."

"That I call God to witness he has," said the woman, passionately; "pitilessly, inhumanly murdered!"

"By whom?" said the surgeon, seizing the woman by the arm.

"Look at the butchers' marks, and then ask me," she replied.

The surgeon turned his face towards the bed, and bent over the body which lay full in the light of the window. The throat was swollen, and a blue livid mark encircled it. The truth flashed suddenly upon him.

"This is one of the men who were hanged this morning!" he exclaimed, turning away with a shudder.

"It is," replied the woman, with a cold, unmeaning stare.

"Who was he?" inquired the surgeon.

"*My son,*" rejoined the woman; and fell senseless at his feet.

It was true. A companion, equally guilty with himself, had been acquitted for want of evidence; and this man had been left for death, and executed. To recount the circumstances of the case at this distant period must be unnecessary, and might give pain to some persons still alive. The history was an every-day one. The mother was a widow without friends or money, and had denied herself necessaries to bestow them on her orphan boy. That boy, unmindful of her prayers, and forgetful of the sufferings she had endured for him—incessant anxiety of mind, and voluntary starvation of body—had plunged into a career of dissipation and crime. And this was the result: his own death by the hangman's hands, and his mother's shame, and incurable insanity.

For many years after this occurrence, and when profitable

and arduous avocations would have led many men to forget that such a miserable being existed, the young surgeon was a daily visitor at the side of the harmless mad woman; not only soothing her by his presence and kindness, but alleviating the rigour of her condition by pecuniary donations for her comfort and support, bestowed with no sparing hand. In the transient gleam of recollection and consciousness which preceded her death, a prayer for his welfare and protection, as fervent as mortal ever breathed, rose from the lips of this poor friendless creature. That prayer flew to Heaven, and was heard. The blessings he was instrumental in conferring have been repaid to him a thousand-fold; but, amid all the honours of rank and station which have since been heaped upon him, and which he has so well earned, he can have no one reminiscence more gratifying to his feelings than that connected with—The Black Veil.

CHAPTER VII: *The Steam Excursion*

Mr. PERCY NOAKES was a law student, inhabiting a set of chambers on the fourth floor, in one of those houses in Gray's Inn Square which command an extensive view of the gardens, and their usual adjuncts—flaunting nursery-maids, and town-made children, with parenthetical legs. Mr. Percy Noakes was what is generally termed—"a devilish good fellow." He had a large circle of acquaintance, and seldom dined at his own expense. He used to talk politics to papas, flatter the vanity of mammas, do the amiable to their daughters, make pleasure engagements with their sons, and romp with the younger branches. Like those paragons of perfection, advertising footmen out of place, he was always "willing to make himself generally useful." If any old lady, whose son was in India, gave a ball, Mr. Percy Noakes was master of the ceremonies; if any young lady made a stolen match, Mr. Percy Noakes gave her away; if a juvenile wife presented her husband with a blooming cherub, Mr. Percy Noakes was either godfather, or deputy-godfather; and if any member of a friend's family died, Mr. Percy Noakes was invariably to be seen in the second mourning coach, with a white hand-kerchief to his eyes, sobbing—to use his own appropriate and expressive description—"like winkin'!"

It may readily be imagined that these numerous avocations were rather calculated to interfere with Mr. Percy Noakes's professional studies. Mr. Percy Noakes was perfectly aware of the fact, and he had, therefore, after mature reflection, made up his mind not to study at all—a laudable determina-tion, to which he adhered in the most praiseworthy manner. His sitting-room presented a strange chaos of dress-gloves, boxing-gloves, caricatures, albums, invitation-cards, foils, cricket-bats, card-board drawings, paste, gum, and fifty other extraordinary articles, heaped together in the strangest confusion. He was always making something for somebody, or planning some party of pleasure, which was his great *forte*. He invariably spoke with astonishing rapidity; was smart, spoffish, and eight-and-twenty.

"Splendid idea, 'pon my life!" soliloquised Mr. Percy Noakes, over his morning's coffee, as his mind reverted to a suggestion which had been thrown out the previous night, by a lady at whose house he had spent the evening. "Glorious idea!—Mrs. Stubbs," cried the student, raising his voice.

"Yes, sir," replied a dirty old woman with an inflamed countenance, emerging from the bedroom, with a barrel of dirt and cinders.—This was the laundress. "Did you call, sir?"

"Oh! Mrs. Stubbs, I'm going out: if that tailor should call again, you'd better say—you'd better say I'm out of town, and shan't be back for a fortnight; and if that boot-maker should come, tell him I've lost his address, or I'd have sent him that little amount. Mind he writes it down; and if Mr. Hardy should call—you know Mr. Hardy?"

"The funny gentleman, sir?"

"Ah! the funny gentleman. If Mr. Hardy should call, say I've gone to Mrs. Taunton's about that water-party."

"Yes, sir."

"And if any fellow calls, and says he's come about a steamer, tell him to be here at five o'clock this afternoon, Mrs. Stubbs."

"Very well, sir."

Mr. Percy Noakes brushed his hat, whisked the crumbs off his inexplicables with a silk handkerchief, gave the ends of his hair a persuasive roll round his forefinger, and sallied forth for Mrs. Taunton's domicile in Great Marlborough Street, where she and her daughters occupied the upper part of a house. She was a good-looking widow of fifty, with the form of a giantess and the mind of a child. The pursuit of pleasure, and some means of killing time, appeared the sole end of her existence. She doted on her daughters, who were as frivolous as herself.

A general exclamation of satisfaction hailed the arrival of Mr. Percy Noakes, who went through the ordinary salutations and threw himself into an easy-chair near the ladies' work-table, with all the ease of a regularly established friend of the family. Mrs. Taunton was busily engaged in planting immense bright bows on every part of a smart cap on which it was possible to stick one; Miss Emily Taunton was making a watch-guard; and Miss Sophia was at the piano, practising a new song—poetry by the young officer, or the police-officer, or the custom-house officer, or some equally interesting amateur.

"You good creature!" said Mrs. Taunton, addressing the gallant Percy. "You really are a good soul! You've come about the water-party, I know."

"I should rather suspect I had," replied Mr. Noakes, triumphantly. "Now, come here, girls, and I'll tell you all about it." Miss Emily and Miss Sophia advanced to the table, with that ballet-sort of step which some young ladies seem to think so fascinating—something between a skip and a canter.

"Now," continued Mr. Percy Noakes, "it seems to me that the best way will be to have a committee of ten, to make all the arrangements, and manage the whole set-out. Then I propose that the expenses shall be paid by these ten fellows jointly."

"Excellent, indeed!" said Mrs. Taunton, who highly approved of this part of the arrangements.

"Then my plan is, that each of these ten fellows shall have the power of asking five people. There must be a meeting of the committee at my chambers, to make all the arrangements, and these people shall be then named; every member of the committee shall have the power of black-balling any one who is proposed, and one black ball shall exclude that person. This will ensure our having a pleasant party, you know."

"What a manager you are!" interrupted Mrs. Taunton again.

"Charming!" said the lovely Emily.

"I never did!" ejaculated Sophia.

"Yes, I think it'll do," replied Mr. Percy Noakes, who was now quite in his element. "I think it'll do. Then you know we shall go down to the Nore and back, and have a regular capital cold dinner laid out in the cabin before we start, so that everything may be ready without any confusion; and we shall have the lunch laid out on deck in those little tea-garden-looking concerns by the paddle-boxes—I don't know what you call 'em. Then we shall hire a steamer expressly for our party, and a band, and have the deck chalked, and we shall be able to dance quadrilles all day: and then whoever we know that's musical, you know, why they'll make themselves useful and agreeable; and—and—upon the whole, I really hope we shall have a glorious day, you know."

The announcement of these arrangements was received with the utmost enthusiasm. Mrs. Taunton, Emily, and Sophia, were loud in their praises.

"Well, but tell me, Percy," said Mrs. Taunton, "who are the ten gentlemen to be?"

"O! I know plenty of fellows who'll be delighted with the scheme," replied Mr. Percy Noakes; "of course, we shall have——"

"Mr. Hardy," interrupted the servant, announcing a visitor. Miss Sophia and Miss Emily hastily assumed the most interesting attitudes that could be adopted on so short a notice.

"How are you?" said a stout gentleman of about forty, pausing at the door in the attitude of an awkward harlequin. This was Mr. Hardy, whom we have before described, on the authority of Mrs. Stubbs, as "the funny gentleman." He was an Astley-Cooperish Joe Miller—a practical joker, immensely popular with married ladies, and a general favourite with young men. He was always engaged in some pleasure excursion or other, and delighted in getting somebody into a scrape on such occasions. He could sing comic songs, imitate hackney-coachmen and fowls, play airs on his chin, and execute concertos on the Jews'-harp. He always ate and drank most immoderately, and was the bosom friend of Mr. Percy Noakes. He had a red face, a somewhat husky voice, and a tremendously loud laugh.

"How are you?" said this worthy, laughing, as if it were the finest joke in the world to make a morning call, and shaking hands with the ladies with as much vehemence as if their arms were so many pump-handles.

"You're just the very man I wanted," said Mr. Percy Noakes, who proceeded to explain the cause of his being in requisition.

"Ha! ha! ha!" shouted Hardy, after hearing the statement, and receiving a detailed account of the proposed excursion. "Oh, capital! glorious! What a day it will be! what fun!— But, I say, when are you going to begin making the arrangements?

"No time like the present—at once, if you please."

"Oh, charming!" cried the ladies. "Pray, do."

Writing materials were laid before Mr. Percy Noakes, and the names of the different members of the committee were agreed on, after as much discussion between him and Mr. Hardy as if at least the fate of nations had depended on their appointment. It was then agreed that a meeting should take place at Mr. Percy Noakes's chambers on the ensuing Wednesday evening at eight o'clock, and the visitors departed.

Wednesday evening arrived; eight o'clock came, and eight members of the committee were punctual in their attendance. Mr. Loggins, the solicitor, of Boswell Court, sent an excuse, and Mr. Samuel Briggs, the ditto of Furnival's Inn, sent his brother, much to his (the brother's) satisfaction, and greatly to the discomfiture of Mr. Percy Noakes. Between the Briggses and the Tauntons there existed a degree of implacable hatred, quite unprecedented. The animosity between the Montagues and Capulets was nothing to that which prevailed between these two illustrious houses. Mrs. Briggs was a widow, with three daughters and two sons; Mr. Samuel, the eldest, was an attorney, and Mr. Alexander, the youngest, was under articles to his brother. They resided in Portland Street, Oxford Street, and moved in the same orbit as the Tauntons—hence their mutual dislike. If the Miss Briggses appeared in smart bonnets, the Miss Tauntons eclipsed them with smarter. If Mrs. Taunton appeared in a cap of all the hues of the rainbow, Mrs. Briggs forthwith mounted a toque, with all the patterns of a kaleidoscope. If Miss Sophia Taunton learnt a new song, two of the Miss Briggses came out with a new duet. The Tauntons had once gained a temporary triumph with the assistance of a harp, but the Briggses brought three guitars into the field, and effectually routed the enemy. There was no end to the rivalry between them.

Now, as Mr. Samuel Briggs was a mere machine, a sort of self-acting legal walking-stick; and as the party was known to have originated, however remotely, with Mrs. Taunton, the female branches of the Briggs family had arranged that Mr. Alexander should attend instead of his brother; and as the said Mr. Alexander was deservedly celebrated for possessing all the pertinacity of a bankruptcy-court attorney, combined with the obstinacy of that pleasing animal which browses upon the thistle, he required but little tuition. He was especially enjoined to make himself as disagreeable as possible; and, above all, to blackball the Tauntons at every hazard.

The proceedings of the evening were opened by Mr. Percy Noakes. After successfully urging upon the gentlemen present the propriety of their mixing some brandy-and-water, he briefly stated the object of the meeting, and concluded by observing that the first step must be the selection of a chairman, necessarily possessing some arbitrary—he trusted not unconstitutional—powers, to whom the personal direction of the whole of the arrangements (subject to the approval of the committee) should be confided. A pale young gentleman in a green stock and spectacles of the same, a member of the honourable society of the Inner Temple, immediately rose for the purpose of proposing Mr. Percy Noakes. He had known him long, and this he would say, that a more honourable, a more excellent, or a better-hearted fellow, never existed—(Hear, hear!) The young gentleman, who was a member of a debating society, took this opportunity of entering into an examination of the state of the English law, from the days of William the Conqueror down to the present period: he briefly adverted to the code established by the ancient Druids; slightly glanced at the principles laid down by the Athenian law-givers; and concluded with a most glowing eulogium on picnics and constitutional rights.

Mr. Alexander Briggs opposed the motion. He had the

highest esteem for Mr. Percy Noakes as an individual, but he did consider that he ought not to be intrusted with these immense powers—(Oh, oh!)—He believed that in the proposed capacity Mr. Percy Noakes would not act fairly, impartially, or honourably; but he begged it to be distinctly understood, that he said this without the slightest personal disrespect.   Mr. Hardy defended his honourable friend, in a voice rendered partially unintelligible by emotion and brandy-and-water.   The proposition was put to the vote, and there appearing to be only one dissentient voice, Mr. Percy Noakes was declared duly elected, and took the chair accordingly.

The business of the meeting now proceeded with great rapidity.   The chairman delivered in his estimate of the probable expense of the excursion, and every one present subscribed his proportion thereof.   The question was put that "The Endeavour" be hired for the occasion; Mr. Alexander Briggs moved as an amendment, that the word "Fly" be substituted for the word "Endeavour"; but after some debate consented to withdraw his opposition.   The important ceremony of balloting then commenced.   A tea-caddy was placed on a table in a dark corner of the apartment, and every one was provided with two backgammon men, one black and one white.

The chairman with great solemnity then read the following list of the guests whom he proposed to introduce: Mrs. Taunton and two daughters, Mr. Wizzle, Mr. Simson.   The names were respectively balloted for, and Mrs. Taunton and her daughters were declared to be black-balled.   Mr. Percy Noakes and Mr. Hardy exchanged glances.

"Is your list prepared, Mr. Briggs?" inquired the chairman.

"It is," replied Alexander, delivering in the following: "Mrs. Briggs and three daughters, Mr. Samuel Briggs." The previous ceremony was repeated, and Mrs. Briggs and three daughters were declared to be black-balled.   Mr. Alexander Briggs looked rather foolish, and the remainder of the company appeared somewhat overawed by the mysterious nature of the proceedings.

The balloting proceeded; but one little circumstance which Mr. Percy Noakes had not originally foreseen, prevented the system from working quite as well as he had anticipated—everybody was black-balled.   Mr. Alexander Briggs, by way of retaliation, exercised his power of exclusion in every instance, and the result was, that after three hours had been consumed in incessant balloting, the names of only three gentlemen were found to have been agreed to.   In this dilemma what was to be done? either the whole plan must fall to the ground, or a compromise must be effected.   The latter alternative was preferable; and Mr. Percy Noakes therefore proposed that the form of balloting should be dispensed with, and that every gentleman should merely be required to state whom he intended to bring. The proposal was readily acceded to; the Tauntons and the Briggses were reinstated, and the party was formed.

The next Wednesday was fixed for the eventful day, and it was unanimously resolved that every member of the committee should wear a piece of blue sarcenet ribbon round his left arm. It appeared from the statement of Mr. Percy Noakes, that the boat belonged to the General Steam Navigation Company, and was then lying off the Custom House; and as he proposed that the dinner and wines should be provided by an eminent City purveyor, it was arranged that Mr. Percy Noakes should be on board by seven o'clock to superintend the arrangements, and that the remaining members of the committee, together with the company generally, should be expected to join her by nine o'clock. More brandy-and-water was despatched; several speeches were made by the different law students present; thanks were voted to the chairman, and the meeting separated.

The weather had been beautiful up to this period, and beautiful it continued to be. Sunday passed over, and Mr. Percy Noakes became unusually fidgety—rushing constantly to and from the Steam Packet Wharf, to the astonishment of the clerks, and the great emolument of the Holborn cabmen. Tuesday arrived, and the anxiety of Mr. Percy Noakes knew no bounds; he was every instant running to the window to look out for clouds; and Mr. Hardy astonished the whole square by practising a new comic song for the occasion, in the chairman's chambers.

Uneasy were the slumbers of Mr. Percy Noakes that night: he tossed and tumbled about, and had confused dreams of steamers starting off, and gigantic clocks with the hands pointing to a quarter-past nine, and the ugly face of Mr. Alexander Briggs looking over the boat's side, and grinning as if in derision of his fruitless attempts to move. He made a violent effort to get on board, and awoke. The bright sun was shining cheerfully into the bedroom, and Mr. Percy Noakes started up for his watch, in the dreadful expectation of finding his worst dreams realised.

It was just five o'clock. He calculated the time—he should be a good half-hour dressing himself; and as it was a lovely morning, and the tide would be then running down, he would walk leisurely to Strand Lane, and have a boat to the Custom House.

He dressed himself, took a hasty apology for a breakfast, and sallied forth. The streets looked as lonely and deserted as if they had been crowded overnight for the last time. Here and there an early apprentice, with quenched-looking sleepy eyes, was taking down the shutters of a shop; and a police-man or milk-woman might occasionally be seen pacing slowly along; the servants had not yet begun to clean the doors, or light the fires, and London looked the picture of desolation. At the corner of a by-street, near Temple Bar, was stationed a "street-breakfast." The coffee was boiling over a charcoal fire, and large slices of bread and butter were piled one upon the other, like deals in a timber-yard. The company were seated on a form, which, with a view both to security and comfort, was placed against a neighbouring wall. Two young men, whose uproarious mirth and dis-ordered dress bespoke the conviviality of the preceding evening, were treating three "ladies" and an Irish labourer. A little sweep was standing at a short distance, casting a longing eye at the tempting delicacies; and a policeman was watching the group from the opposite side of the street. The wan looks, and gaudy finery of the wretched thinly-clad females contrasted as strangely with the gay sunlight, as did their forced merriment with the boisterous hilarity of the two young men, who now and then varied their amusements by "bonneting" the proprietor of this itinerant coffee-house.

Mr. Percy Noakes walked briskly by, and when he turned down Strand Lane, and caught a glimpse of the glistening water, he thought he had never felt so important or so happy in his life.

"Boat, sir!" cried one of the three watermen who were mopping out their boats, and all whistling different tunes. "Boat, sir!"

"No," replied Mr. Percy Noakes, rather sharply; for the inquiry was not made in a manner at all suitable to his dignity.

"Would you prefer a wessel, sir?" inquired another, to the infinite delight of the "Jack-in-the-water."

Mr. Percy Noakes replied with a look of the most supreme contempt.

"Did you want to be put on board a steamer, sir?" inquired an old fireman-waterman, very confidentially. He was dressed in a faded red suit, just the colour of the cover of a very old Court-guide.

"Yes, make haste—the Endeavour—off the Custom House."

"Endeavour!" cried the man who had convulsed the "Jack" before. "Vy, I see the Endeavour go up half an hour ago."

"So did I," said another; "and I should think she'd gone down by this time, for she's a precious sight too full of ladies and gen'lemen."

Mr. Percy Noakes affected to disregard these represen-tations, and stepped into the boat, which the old man, by dint of scrambling, and shoving, and grating, had brought up to the causeway. "Shove her off," cried Mr. Percy Noakes, and away the boat glided down the river; Mr. Percy Noakes seated on the recently mopped seat, and the watermen at the stairs offering to bet him any reasonable sum that he'd never reach the "Custum-us."

"Here she is, by Jove!" said the delighted Percy, as they ran alongside the Endeavour.

"Hold hard!" cried the steward over the side, and Mr. Percy Noakes jumped on board.

"Hope you'll find everything as you wished, sir. She looks uncommon well this morning."

"She does, indeed," replied the manager, in a state of ecstasy which it is impossible to describe. The deck was scrubbed, and the seats were scrubbed, and there was a bench for the band, and a place for dancing, and a pile of camp-stools, and an awning; and then Mr. Percy Noakes bustled down below, and there were the pastrycook's men, and the steward's wife laying out the dinner on two tables the whole length of the cabin; and then Mr. Percy Noakes took off his coat, and rushed backwards and forwards, doing nothing, but quite convinced he was assisting everybody; and the steward's wife laughed till she cried, and Mr. Percy Noakes panted with the violence of his exertions. And then the bell at London Bridge wharf rang, and a Margate boat was just starting, and a Gravesend boat just starting, and people shouted, and porters ran down the steps with luggage that would crush any men but porters; and sloping boards, with bits of wood nailed on them, were placed between the outside boat and the inside boat; and the passengers ran along them, and looked like so many fowls coming out of an area; and then the bell ceased, and the boards were taken away, and the boats started; and the whole scene was one of the most delightful bustle and confusion that can be imagined.

The time wore on; half-past eight o'clock arrived; the pastrycook's men went ashore; the dinner was completely laid out, and Mr. Percy Noakes locked the principal cabin, and put the key into his pocket, in order that it might be suddenly disclosed in all its magnificence to the eyes of the astonished company. The band came on board and so did the wine.

Ten minutes to nine, and the committee embarked in a body. There was Mr. Hardy in a blue jacket and waistcoat, white trousers, silk stockings, and pumps; habited in full aquatic costume, with a straw hat on his head, and an immense telescope under his arm; and there was the young gentleman with the green spectacles, in nankeen inexplicables, with a ditto waistcoat and bright buttons, like the pictures of Paul —not the saint, but he of Virginia notoriety. The remainder of the committee, dressed in white hats, light jackets, waist-coats, and trousers, looked something between waiters and West India planters.

Nine o'clock struck, and the company arrived in shoals. Mr. Samuel Briggs, Mrs. Briggs, and the Misses Briggs made their appearance in a smart private wherry. The three guitars, in their respective dark green cases, were carefully stowed away in the bottom of the boat, accompanied by two immense portfolios of music, which it would take at least a week's incessant playing to get through. The Tauntons arrived at the same moment with more music, and a lion—a gentleman with a bass voice and an incipient red moustache. The colours of the Taunton party were pink; those of the Briggses a light blue. The Tauntons had artificial flowers in their bonnets; here the Briggses gained a decided advantage—they wore feathers.

"How d'ye do, dear?" said the Misses Briggs to the Misses Taunton. (The word "dear" among girls is frequently synonymous with "wretch.")

"Quite well, thank you, dear," replied the Misses Taunton to the Misses Briggs; and then there was such a kissing, and congratulating, and shaking of hands, as would induce one to suppose that the two families were the best friends in the world, instead of each wishing the other overboard, as they most sincerely did.

Mr. Percy Noakes received the visitors, and bowed to the strange gentleman, as if he should like to know who he was. This was just what Mrs. Taunton wanted. Here was an opportunity to astonish the Briggses.

"Oh! I beg your pardon," said the general of the Taunton party, with a careless air. "Captain Helves—Mr. Percy Noakes—Mrs. Briggs—Captain Helves."

Mr. Percy Noakes bowed very low; the gallant captain did the same with all due ferocity, and the Briggses were clearly overcome.

"Our friend, Mr. Wizzle, being unfortunately prevented from coming," resumed Mrs. Taunton, "I did myself the pleasure of bringing the captain, whose musical talents I knew would be a great acquisition."

"In the name of the committee I have to thank you for doing so, and to offer you a most sincere welcome, sir," replied Percy. (Here the scraping was renewed.) "But pray be seated—won't you walk aft? Captain, will you conduct Miss Taunton?—Miss Briggs, will you allow me?"

"Where could they have picked up that military man?" inquired Mrs. Briggs of Miss Kate Briggs, as they followed the little party.

"I can't imagine," replied Miss Kate, bursting with vexa-tion; for the very fierce air with which the gallant captain regarded the company, had impressed her with a high sense of his importance.

Boat after boat came alongside, and guest after guest arrived. The invites had been excellently arranged, Mr. Percy Noakes having considered it as important that the number of young men should exactly tally with that of the young ladies, as that the quantity of knives on board should be in precise proportion to the forks.

"Now, is every one on board?" inquired Mr. Percy Noakes. The committee (who, with their bits of blue ribbon, looked as if they were all going to be bled) bustled about to ascertain the fact, and reported that they might safely start.

"Go on," cried the master of the boat from the top of one of the paddle-boxes.

"Go on," echoed the boy, who was stationed over the hatchway to pass the directions down to the engineer; and away went the vessel with that agreeable noise which is peculiar to steamers, and which is composed of a pleasant mixture of creaking, gushing, clanging, and snorting.

"Hoi—oi—oi—oi—oi—oi—o—i—i—i!" shouted half a dozen voices from a boat about a quarter of a mile astern.

"Ease her!" cried the captain: "do these people belong to us, sir?"

"Noakes," exclaimed Hardy, who had been looking at every object, far and near, through the large telescope, "it's the Fleetwoods and the Wakefields—and two children with them, by Jove!"

"What a shame to bring children!" said everybody; "how very inconsiderate!"

"I say, it would be a good joke to pretend not to see 'em, wouldn't it?" suggested Hardy, to the immense delight of the company generally. A council of war was hastily held, and it was resolved that the new-comers should be taken on board, on Mr. Hardy's solemnly pledging himself to tease the children during the whole of the day.

"Stop her!" cried the captain.

"Stop her," repeated the boy; whizz went the steam, and all the young ladies, as in duty bound, screamed in concert. They were only appeased by the assurance of the martial Helves, that the escape of steam consequent on stopping a vessel was seldom attended with any great loss of human life.

Two men ran to the side, and after a good deal of shouting, and swearing, and angling for the wherry with a boat-hook, Mr. Fleetwood, and Mrs. Fleetwood, and Master Fleetwood, and Mr. Wakefield, and Mrs. Wakefield, and Miss Wakefield, were safely deposited on the deck. The girl was about six years old, the boy about four; the former was dressed in a white frock with a pink sash and a dog's-eared-looking little spencer, a straw bonnet and green veil, six inches by three and a half:

the latter was attired for the occasion in a nankeen frock, between the bottom of which and the top of his plaid socks a considerable portion of two small mottled legs was discernible. He had a light blue cap with a gold band and tassel on his head, and a damp piece of gingerbread in his hand, with which he had slightly embossed his countenance.

The boat once more started off; the band played "Off she goes"; the major part of the company conversed cheerfully in groups, and the old gentlemen walked up and down the deck in pairs, as perseveringly and gravely as if they were doing a match against time for an immense stake. They ran briskly down the Pool; the gentlemen pointed out the Docks, the Thames Police Office, and other elegant public edifices; and the young ladies exhibited a proper display of horror at the appearance of the coal-whippers and ballast-heavers. Mr. Hardy told stories to the married ladies, at which they laughed very much, in their pocket-handkerchiefs, and hit him on the knuckles with their fans, declaring him to be "a naughty man—a shocking creature"—and so forth; and Captain Helves gave slight descriptions of battles and duels, with a most blood-thirsty air, which made him the admiration of the women, and the envy of the men. Quadrilling commenced; Captain Helves danced one set with Miss Emily Taunton, and another set with Miss Sophia Taunton. Mrs. Taunton was in ecstasies. The victory appeared to be complete; but, alas! the inconstancy of man! Having performed this necessary duty, he attached himself solely to Miss Julia Briggs, with whom he danced no less than three sets consecutively, and from whose side he evinced no intention of stirring for the remainder of the day.

Mr. Hardy having played one or two very brilliant fantasias on the Jews'-harp, and having frequently repeated the exquisitely amusing joke of slily chalking a large cross on the back of some member of the committee, Mr. Percy Noakes expressed his hope that some of their musical friends would oblige the company by a display of their abilities.

"Perhaps," he said in a very insinuating manner, "Captain Helves will oblige us." Mrs. Taunton's countenance lighted up, for the captain only sang duets, and couldn't sing them with anybody but one of her daughters.

"Really," said that warlike individual, "I should be very happy, but——"

"Oh! pray do," cried all the young ladies.

"Miss Sophia, have you any objection to join in a duet?"

"Oh! not the slightest," returned the young lady, in a tone which clearly showed she had the greatest possible objection.

"Shall I accompany you, dear?" inquired one of the Miss Briggses, with the bland intention of spoiling the effect.

"Very much obliged to you, Miss Briggs," sharply retorted

Mrs. Taunton, who saw through the manœuvre; "my daughters always sing without accompaniments."

"And without voices," tittered Mrs. Briggs, in a low tone.

"Perhaps," said Mrs. Taunton, reddening, for she guessed the tenor of the observation, though she had not heard it clearly—"perhaps it would be as well for some people, if their voices were not quite so audible as they are to other people."

"And perhaps, if gentlemen who are kidnapped to pay attention to some persons' daughters, had not sufficient discernment to pay attention to other persons' daughters," returned Mrs. Briggs, "some persons would not be so ready to display that ill-temper which, thank God, distinguishes them from other persons."

"Persons!" ejaculated Mrs. Taunton.

"Yes; persons, ma'am," replied Mrs. Briggs.

"Insolence!"

"Creature!"

"Hush! hush!" interrupted Mr. Percy Noakes, who was one of the very few by whom this dialogue had been overheard. "Hush!—pray, silence for the duet."

After a great deal of preparatory crowing and humming, the captain began the following duet from the opera of "Paul and Virginia," in that grunting tone in which a man gets down, Heaven knows where, without the remotest chance of ever getting up again. This, in private circles, is frequently designated "a bass voice."

> "See (sung the captain) from o—ce—an ri—sing
> Bright flames the or—b of d—ay.
> From yon gro—ve, the varied so—ngs—"

Here the singer was interrupted by varied cries of the most dreadful description, proceeding from some grove in the immediate vicinity of the starboard paddle-box.

"My child!" screamed Mrs. Fleetwood. "My child! it is his voice—I know it."

Mr. Fleetwood, accompanied by several gentlemen, here rushed to the quarter from whence the noise proceeded, and an exclamation of horror burst from the company; the general impression being, that the little innocent had either got his head in the water, or his legs in the machinery.

"What is the matter?" shouted the agonised father, as he returned with the child in his arms.

"Oh! oh! oh!" screamed the small sufferer again.

"What is the matter, dear?" inquired the father once more—hastily stripping off the nankeen frock, for the purpose of ascertaining whether the child had one bone which was not smashed to pieces.

"Oh! oh!—I'm so frightened."

"What at, dear?—what at?" said the mother, soothing the sweet infant.

"Oh! he's been making such dreadful faces at me," cried the boy, relapsing into convulsions at the bare recollection.

"He!—who?" cried everybody, crowding round him.

"Oh!—him," replied the child, pointing at Hardy, who affected to be the most concerned of the whole group.

The real state of the case at once flashed upon the minds of all present, with the exception of the Fleetwoods and the Wakefields. The facetious Hardy, in fulfilment of his promise, had watched the child to a remote part of the vessel, and, suddenly appearing before him with the most awful contortions of visage, had produced his paroxysm of terror. Of course, he now observed that it was hardly necessary for him to deny the accusation; and the unfortunate little victim was accordingly led below, after receiving sundry thumps on the head from both his parents, for having the wickedness to tell a story.

This little interruption having been adjusted, the captain resumed and Miss Emily chimed in, in due course. The duet was loudly applauded, and, certainly, the perfect independence of the parties deserved great commendation. Miss Emily sang her part without the slightest reference to the captain, and the captain sang so loud that he had not the slightest idea of what was being done by his partner. After having gone through the last few eighteen or nineteen bars by himself, therefore, he acknowledged the plaudits of the circle with that air of self-denial which men always assume when they think they have done something to astonish the company, though they don't exactly know what.

"Now," said Mr. Percy Noakes, who had just ascended from the fore-cabin, where he had been busily engaged in decanting the wine, "if the Misses Briggs will oblige us with something before dinner, I am sure we shall be very much delighted."

One of those hums of admiration followed the suggestion which one frequently hears in society, when nobody has the most distant notion what he is expressing his approval of. The three Misses Briggs looked modestly at their mamma, and the mamma looked approvingly at her daughters, and Mrs. Taunton looked scornfully at all of them. The Misses Briggs asked for their guitars, and several gentlemen seriously damaged the cases in their anxiety to present them. Then there was a very interesting production of three little keys for the aforesaid cases, and a melodramatic expression of horror at finding a string broken; and a vast deal of screwing and tightening, and winding and tuning, during which Mrs. Briggs expatiated to those near her on the immense difficulty of playing a guitar, and hinted at the wondrous proficiency of her daughters in that mystic art. Mrs. Taunton whispered to a neighbour that it was "quite sickening!" and the Misses Taunton tried to look as if they knew how to play, but disdained to do so.

At length the Misses Briggs began in real earnest. It was a new Spanish composition, for three voices and three guitars. The effect was electrical. All eyes were turned upon the captain, who was reported to have once passed through Spain with his regiment, and who, of course, must be well acquainted with the national music. He was in raptures. This was sufficient; the trio was encored—the applause was universal, and never had the Tauntons suffered such a complete defeat.

"Bravo! bravo!" ejaculated the captain. "Bravo!"

"Pretty! isn't it, sir?" inquired Mr. Samuel Briggs, with the air of a self-satisfied showman. By-the-by, these were the first words he had been heard to utter since he left Boswell Court the evening before.

"De—lightful!" returned the captain, with a flourish, and a military cough;—"de—lightful!"

"Sweet instrument!" said an old gentleman with a bald head, who had been trying all the morning to look through a telescope, inside the glass of which Mr. Hardy had fixed a large black wafer.

"Did you ever hear a Portuguese tambourine?" inquired that jocular individual.

"Did *you* ever hear a tom-tom, sir?" sternly inquired the captain, who lost no opportunity of showing off his travels, real or pretended.

"A what?" asked Hardy, rather taken aback.

"A tom-tom."

"Never."

"Nor a gum-gum?"

"Never!"

"What *is* a gum-gum?" eagerly inquired several young ladies.

"When I was in the East Indies," replied the captain (here was a discovery—he had been in the East Indies!)—"when I was in the East Indies, I was once stopping a few thousand miles up the country, on a visit at the house of a very particular friend of mine, Ram Chowdar Doss Azuph Al Bowlar—a devilish pleasant fellow. As we were enjoying our hookahs one evening in the cool veranda in front of his villa, we were rather surprised by the sudden appearance of thirty-four of his Kit-ma-gars (for he had rather a large establishment there), accompanied by an equal number of Con-su-mars, approaching the house with a threatening aspect, and beating a tom-tom. The Ram started up——"

"The who?" inquired the bald gentleman, intensely interested.

"The Ram—Ram Chowdar——"

"Oh!" said the old gentleman, "I beg your pardon, it really didn't occur to me; pray go on."

"—Started up and drew a pistol. 'Helves,' said he, 'my boy,'—he always called me, my boy—'Helves,' said he, 'do you hear that tom-tom?'—'I do,' said I. His countenance, which before was pale, assumed a most frightful appearance; his whole visage was distorted, and his frame shaken by violent emotions. 'Do you see that gum-gum?' said he. 'No,' said I, staring about me. 'You don't?' said he. 'No, I'll be damned if I do,' said I; 'and what's more, I don't know what a gum-gum is,' said I. I really thought the man would have dropped. He drew me aside, and with an expression of agony I shall never forget, said in a low whisper——"

"Dinner's on the table, ladies," interrupted the steward's wife.

"Will you allow me?" said the captain, immediately suiting the action to the word, and escorting Miss Julia Briggs to the cabin, with as much ease as if he had finished the story.

"What an extraordinary circumstance!" ejaculated the same old gentleman, preserving his listening attitude.

"What a traveller!" said the young ladies.

"What a singular name!" exclaimed the gentlemen, rather confused by the coolness of the whole affair.

"I wish he had finished the story," said an old lady. "I wonder what a gum-gum really is?"

"By Jove!" exclaimed Hardy, who until now had been lost in utter amazement, "I don't know what it may be in India, but in England I think a gum-gum has very much the same meaning as a hum-bug."

"How illiberal! how envious!" said everybody, as they made for the cabin, fully impressed with a belief in the captain's amazing adventures. Helves was the sole lion for the remainder of the day—impudence and the marvellous are sure passports to any society.

The party had by this time reached their destination, and put about on their return home. The wind, which had been with them the whole day, was now directly in their teeth; the weather had become gradually more and more overcast; and the sky, water, and shore, were all of that dull, heavy, uniform lead-colour, which house-painters daub in the first instance over a street-door which is gradually approaching a state of convalescence. It had been "spitting" with rain for the last half-hour, and now began to pour in good earnest. The wind was freshening very fast, and the waterman at the wheel had unequivocally expressed his opinion that there would shortly be a squall. A slight emotion on the part of the vessel now and then, seemed to suggest the possibility of its pitching to a very uncomfortable extent in the event of its blowing harder; and every timber began to creak as if the boat were an overladen clothes-basket. Sea-sickness, however, is like a belief in ghosts—every one entertains some misgivings on the subject, but few will acknowledge them. The majority of the company, therefore, endeavoured to look peculiarly happy, feeling all the while especially miserable.

"Don't it rain?" inquired the old gentleman before noticed, when, by dint of squeezing and jamming, they were all seated at table.

"I think it does—a little," replied Mr. Percy Noakes, who could hardly hear himself speak, in consequence of the pattering on the deck.

"Don't it blow?" inquired some one else.

"No—I don't think it does," responded Hardy, sincerely wishing that he could persuade himself it did not, for he sat near the door, and was almost blown off his seat.

"It'll soon clear up," said Mr. Percy Noakes, in a cheerful tone.

"Oh, certainly!" ejaculated the committee generally.

"No doubt of it," said the remainder of the company, whose attention was now pretty well engrossed by the serious business of eating, carving, taking wine, and so forth.

The throbbing motion of the engine was but too perceptible. There was a large, substantial cold boiled leg of mutton at the bottom of the table, shaking like blancmange; a hearty sirloin of beef looked as if it had been suddenly seized with the palsy; and some tongues, which were placed on dishes rather too large for them, were going through the most surprising evolutions, darting from side to side, and from end to end, like a fly in an inverted wine-glass. Then, the sweets shook and trembled till it was quite impossible to help them, and people gave up the attempt in despair; and the pigeon-pies looked as if the birds, whose legs were stuck outside, were trying to get them in. The table vibrated and started like a feverish pulse, and the very legs were slightly convulsed—everything was shaking and jarring. The beams in the roof of the cabin seemed as if they were put there for the sole purpose of giving people headaches, and several elderly gentlemen became ill-tempered in consequence. As fast as the steward put the fire-irons up, they would fall down again; and the more the ladies and gentlemen tried to sit comfortably on their seats, the more the seats seemed to slide away from the ladies and gentlemen. Several ominous demands were made for small glasses of brandy; the countenances of the company gradually underwent the most extraordinary changes; and one gentleman was observed suddenly to rush from table without the slightest ostensible reason, and dart up the steps with incredible swiftness, thereby greatly damaging both himself and the steward, who happened to be coming down at the same moment.

The cloth was removed; the dessert was laid on the table; and the glasses were filled. The motion of the boat increased, several members of the party began to feel rather vague and misty, and looked as if they had only just got up. The young gentleman with the spectacles, who had been in a fluctuating state for some time—one moment bright, and another dismal, like a revolving light on the sea-coast—rashly announced his wish to propose a toast. After several ineffectual attempts to preserve his perpendicular, the young gentleman, having managed to hook himself to the centre leg of the table with his left hand, proceeded as follows:

"Ladies and gentlemen. A gentleman is among us—I may say a stranger (here some painful thought seemed to strike the orator; he paused, and looked extremely odd) whose talents, whose travels, whose cheerfulness——"

"I beg your pardon, Edkins," hastily interrupted Mr. Percy Noakes.—"Hardy, what's the matter?"

"Nothing," replied the "funny gentleman," who had just life enough left to utter two consecutive syllables.

"Will you have some brandy?"

"No," replied Hardy, in a tone of great indignation, and looking about as comfortable as Temple Bar in a Scotch mist; "what should I want brandy for?"

"Will you go on deck?"

"No, I will not." This was said with a most determined air, and in a voice which might have been taken for an imitation of anything; it was quite as much like a guinea-pig as a bassoon.

"I beg your pardon, Edkins," said the courteous Percy; "I thought our friend was ill. Pray go on."

A pause.

"Pray go on."

"Mr. Edkins *is* gone," cried somebody.

"I beg your pardon, Edkins," said the steward, running up to Mr. Percy Noakes, "I beg your pardon, sir, but the gentleman as just went on deck—him with the green spectacles—is uncommon bad, to be sure; and the young man as played the wiolin says, that unless he has some brandy he can't answer for the consequences. He says he has a wife and two children, whose werry subsistence depends on his breaking a wessel, and that he expects to do so every moment. The flageolet's been very ill, but he's better, only he's in such a dreadful prusperation."

All disguise was now useless; the company staggered on deck, the gentlemen tried to see nothing but the clouds, and the ladies, muffled up in such shawls and cloaks as they had brought with them, lay about on the seats and under the seats, in the most wretched condition. Never was such a blowing, and raining, and pitching, and tossing, endured by any pleasure party before. Several remonstrances were sent down below on the subject of Master Fleetwood, but they were totally unheeded in consequence of the indisposition of his natural protectors. That interesting child screamed at the

STEAM EXCURSION.

very top of his voice, until he had no voice left to scream with and then Miss Wakefield began, and screamed for the remainder of the passage.

Mr. Hardy was observed some hours afterwards in an attitude which induced his friends to suppose that he was busily engaged in contemplating the beauties of the deep; they only regretted that his taste for the picturesque should lead him to remain so long in a position, very injurious at all times, but especially so to an individual labouring under a tendency of blood to the head.

The party arrived off the Custom House at about two o'clock on the Thursday morning—dispirited and worn out. The Tauntons were too ill to quarrel with the Briggses and the Briggses were too wretched to annoy the Tauntons. One of the guitar-cases was lost on its passage to a hackney-coach, and Mrs. Briggs has not scrupled to state that the Tauntons bribed a porter to throw it down an area. Mr. Alexander Briggs opposes vote by ballot—he says from personal experience of its inefficacy; and Mr. Samuel Briggs whenever he is asked to express his sentiments on the point says that he has no opinion on that or any other subject.

Mr. Edkins—the young gentleman in the green spectacles—makes a speech on every occasion on which a speech can possibly be made, the eloquence of which can only be equalled by its length. In the event of his not being previously appointed to a judgeship it is most probable that he will practise as a barrister in the New Central Criminal Court.

Captain Helves continued his attention to Miss Julia Briggs whom he might possibly have espoused if it had not unfortunately happened that Mr. Samuel arrested him in the way of business pursuant to instructions received from Messrs. Scroggins and Payne, whose town debts the gallant captain had condescended to collect, but whose accounts, with the indiscretion so peculiar to military minds, he had omitted to keep with that dull accuracy which custom has rendered necessary. Mrs. Taunton complains that she has been much deceived in him. He introduced himself to the family on board a Gravesend steam-packet, and certainly, therefore, ought to have proved respectable.

Mr. Percy Noakes is as light-hearted and careless as ever. We have described him as a general favourite in his private circle, and trust he may find a kindly-disposed friend or two in public.

CHAPTER VIII: *The Great Winglebury Duel*

THE little town of Great Winglebury is exactly forty-two miles and three-quarters from Hyde Park Corner. It has a long, straggling, quiet High Street, with a great black and white

clock at a small red Town Hall, half-way up—a market-place
—a cage—an assembly-room—a church—a bridge—a chapel
—a theatre—a library—an inn—a pump—and a post office.
Tradition tells of a "Little Winglebury" down some cross-road
about two miles off; and as a square mass of dirty paper,
supposed to have been originally intended for a letter, with
certain tremulous characters inscribed thereon, in which a
lively imagination might trace a remote resemblance to the
word "Little," was once stuck up to be owned in the sunny
window of the Great Winglebury Post Office, from which it
only disappeared when it fell to pieces with dust and extreme
old age, there would appear to be some foundation for the
legend.   Common belief is inclined to bestow the name upon
a little hole at the end of a muddy lane about a couple of miles
long, colonised by one wheelwright, four paupers, and a beer-
shop; but even this authority, slight as it is, must be regarded
with extreme suspicion, inasmuch as the inhabitants of the
hole aforesaid concur in opining that it never had any name at
all, from the earliest ages down to the present day.

The Winglebury Arms in the centre of the High Street,
opposite the small building with the big clock, is the principal
inn of Great Winglebury—the commercial-inn, posting-house
and excise office; the "Blue" house at every election, and the
Judges' house at every assizes.   It is the head-quarters of the
Gentlemen's Whist Club of Winglebury Blues (so called in
opposition to the Gentlemen's Whist Club of Winglebury
Buffs, held at the other house, a little further down); and
whenever a juggler, or waxwork man, or concert-giver, takes
Great Winglebury in his circuit, it is immediately placarded
all over the town that Mr. So-and-so, "trusting to that liberal
support which the inhabitants of Great Winglebury have long
been so liberal in bestowing, has at a great expense engaged
the elegant and commodious assembly-rooms, attached to the
Winglebury Arms."   The house is a large one, with a red
brick and stone front; a pretty spacious hall ornamented with
evergreen plants, terminates in a perspective view of the bar,
and a glass case, in which are displayed a choice variety of
delicacies ready for dressing, to catch the eye of a new-comer
the moment he enters, and excite his appetite to the highest
possible pitch.   Opposite doors lead to the "coffee" and
"commercial" rooms; and a great wide, rambling staircase,—
three stairs and a landing—four stairs and another landing—
one step and another landing—half a dozen stairs and another
landing—and so on—conducts to galleries of bedrooms, and
labyrinths of sitting-rooms, denominated "private," where you
may enjoy yourself as privately as you can in any place where
some bewildered being or other walks into your room every
five minutes by mistake, and then walks out again, to open all
the doors along the gallery till he finds his own.

Such is the Winglebury Arms at this day, and such was the Winglebury Arms some time since—no matter when—two or three minutes before the arrival of the London stage. Four horses with cloths on—change for a coach—were standing quietly at the corner of the yard, surrounded by a listless group of post-boys in shiny hats and smock-frocks, engaged in discussing the merits of the cattle; half a dozen ragged boys were standing a little apart, listening with evident interest to the conversation of these worthies; and a few loungers were collected round the horse-trough, awaiting the arrival of the coach.

The day was hot and sunny, the town in the zenith of its dulness, and with the exception of these few idlers, not a living creature was to be seen. Suddenly the loud notes of a key-bugle broke the monotonous stillness of the street; in came the coach, rattling over the uneven paving with a noise startling enough to stop even the large-faced clock itself. Down got the outsides, up went the windows in all directions; out came the waiters, up started the ostlers, and the loungers, and the post-boys, and the ragged boys, as if they were electrified—unstrapping, and unchaining, and unbuckling, and dragging willing horses out, and forcing reluctant horses in, and making a most exhilarating bustle. "Lady inside, here," said the guard. "Please to alight, ma'am," said the waiter. "Private sitting-room?" interrogated the lady. "Certainly, ma'am," responded the chambermaid. "Nothing but these 'ere trunks, ma'am?" inquired the guard. "Nothing more," replied the lady. Up got the outsides again, and the guard, and the coachman; off came the cloths, with a jerk; "All right!" was the cry; and away they went. The loungers lingered a minute or two in the road, watching the coach till it turned the corner, and then loitered away one by one. The street was clear again, and the town, by contrast, quieter than ever.

"Lady in number twenty-five," screamed the landlady. "Thomas!"

"Yes, ma'am."

"Letter just been left for the gentleman in number nineteen. Boots at the Lion left it. No answer."

"Letter for you, sir," said Thomas, depositing the letter on number nineteen's table.

"For me?" said number nineteen, turning from the window, out of which he had been surveying the scene we have just described.

"Yes, sir"—(waiters always speak in hints, and never utter complete sentences)—"yes, sir—Boots at the Lion, sir—Bar, sir—Missis said number nineteen, sir—Alexander Trott, Esq., sir?—Your card at the bar, sir, I think, sir?"

"My name *is* Trott," replied number nineteen, breaking the seal. "You may go, waiter." The waiter pulled down the

window-blind, and then pulled it up again—for a regular
waiter must do something before he leaves the room—
adjusted the glasses on the sideboard, brushed a place which
was *not* dusty, rubbed his hands very hard, walked stealthily
to the door, and evaporated.

There was evidently something in the contents of the letter
of a nature, if not wholly unexpected, certainly extremely
disagreeable. Mr. Alexander Trott laid it down and took it
up again, and walked about the room on particular squares of
the carpet, and even attempted, though very unsuccessfully,
to whistle an air. It wouldn't do. He threw himself into a
chair and read the following epistle aloud:—

> BLUE LION AND STOMACH-WARMER,
> GREAT WINGLEBURY.
> *Wednesday Morning.*
>
> SIR,
> *Immediately on discovering your intentions, I left our counting-
> house and followed you. I know the purport of your journey—
> that journey shall never be completed.*
> *I have no friend here just now, on whose secrecy I can rely.
> This shall be no obstacle to my revenge. Neither shall Emily
> Brown be exposed to the mercenary solicitations of a scoundrel,
> odious in her eyes, and contemptible in everybody else's : nor will
> I tamely submit to the clandestine attacks of a base umbrella-maker.*
> *Sir, from Great Winglebury church, a footpath leads through
> four meadows to a retired spot known to the townspeople as
> Stiffun's Acre.* [Mr. Trott shuddered.] *I shall be waiting there
> alone, at twenty minutes before six o'clock to-morrow morning.
> Should I be disappointed of seeing you there, I will do myself the
> pleasure of calling with a horsewhip.*
>
> HORACE HUNTER.
>
> *P.S. There is a gunsmith's in the High Street ; and they
> won't sell gunpowder after dark—you understand me.*
> *PP.S. You had better not order your breakfast in the morning
> till you have seen me. It may be an unnecessary expense.*

"Desperate-minded villain! I knew how it would be!"
ejaculated the terrified Trott. "I always told father, that
once start me on this expedition, and Hunter would pursue
me like the Wandering Jew. It's bad enough as it is, to
marry with the old people's commands, and without the girl's
consent; but what will Emily think of me, if I go down there,
breathless with running away from this infernal salamander?
What *shall* I do? What *can* I do? If I go back to the City,
I'm disgraced for ever—lose the girl, and what's more lose the
money too. Even if I did go on to the Browns' by the coach,
Hunter would be after me in a post-chaise; and if I go to this
place, this Stiffun's Acre (another shudder), I'm as good as

dead. I've seen him hit the man, at the Pall Mall shooting-gallery, in the second button-hole of the waistcoat five times out of every six, and when he didn't hit him there, he hit him in the head." And with this consolatory reminiscence Mr. Alexander Trott again ejaculated, "What shall I do?"

Long and weary were his reflections as, burying his face in his hands, he sat ruminating on the best course to be pursued. His mental direction-post pointed to London. He thought of the "governor's" anger, and the loss of the fortune which the paternal Brown had promised the paternal Trott his daughter should contribute to the coffers of his son. Then the words "To Brown's" were legibly inscribed on the said direction-post, but Horace Hunter's denunciation rung in his ears;—last of all it bore, in red letters, the words, "To Stiffun's Acre"; and then Mr. Alexander Trott decided on adopting a plan which he presently matured.

First and foremost he despatched the under-boots to the Blue Lion and Stomach-warmer, with a gentlemanly note to Mr. Horace Hunter, intimating that he thirsted for his destruction and would do himself the pleasure of slaughtering him next morning without fail. He then wrote another letter, and requested the attendance of the other boots—for they kept a pair. A modest knock at the room-door was heard. "Come in," said Mr. Trott. A man thrust in a red head with one eye in it, and being again desired to "come in," brought in the body and legs to which the head belonged, and a fur cap which belonged to the head.

"You are the upper-boots, I think," inquired Mr. Trott.

"Yes, I am the upper-boots," replied a voice from inside a velveteen case with mother-of-pearl buttons—"that is, I'm the boots as b'longs to the house; the other man's my man, as goes errands and does odd jobs—top boots and half-boots, I calls us."

"You're from London?" inquired Mr. Trott.

"Driv a cab once," was the laconic reply.

"Why don't you drive it now?" asked Mr. Trott.

"Cos I over-driv the cab, and driv over a 'ooman," replied the top-boots, with brevity.

"Do you know the mayor's house?" inquired Trott.

"Rather," replied the boots, significantly, as if he had some good reason to remember it.

"Do you think you could manage to leave a letter there?" interrogated Trott.

"Shouldn't wonder," responded boots.

"But this letter," said Trott, holding a deformed note with a paralytic direction in one hand, and five shillings in the other —"this letter is anonymous."

"A—what?" interrupted the boots.

"Anonymous—he's not to know who it comes from."

"Oh! I see," responded the reg'lar, with a knowing wink, but without evincing the slightest disinclination to undertake the charge—"I see—bit o' Sving, eh?" and his one eye wandered round the room as if in quest of a dark lantern and phosphorus-box. "But I say," he continued, recalling the eye from his search, and bringing it to bear on Mr. Trott. "I say, he's a lawyer, our mayor, and insured in the County. If you've a spite agen him, you'd better not burn his house down —blessed if I don't think it would be the greatest favour you could do him." And he chuckled inwardly.

If Mr. Alexander Trott had been in any other situation, his first act would have been to kick the man down-stairs by deputy; or, in other words, to ring the bell, and desire the landlord to take his boots off. He contented himself, however, with doubling the fee and explaining that the letter merely related to a breach of the peace. The top-boots retired, solemnly pledged to secrecy; and Mr. Alexander Trott sat down to a fried sole, maintenon cutlet, Madeira, and sundries, with much greater composure than he had experienced since the receipt of Horace Hunter's letter of defiance.

The lady who alighted from the London coach had no sooner been installed in number twenty-five, and made some alteration in her travelling-dress, than she indited a note to Joseph Overton, Esquire, solicitor, and mayor of Great Winglebury, requesting his immediate attendance on private business of paramount importance—a summons which that worthy functionary lost no time in obeying; for after sundry openings of his eyes, divers ejaculations of "Bless me!" and other manifestations of surprise, he took his broad-brimmed hat from its accustomed peg in his little front office, and walked briskly down the High Street to the Winglebury Arms; through the hall and up the staircase of which establishment he was ushered by the landlady, and a crowd of officious waiters, to the door of number twenty-five.

"Show the gentleman in," said the stranger lady, in reply to the foremost waiter's announcement. The gentleman was shown in accordingly.

The lady rose from the sofa; the mayor advanced a step from the door, and there they both paused for a minute or two, looking at one another as if by mutual consent. The mayor saw before him a buxom richly-dressed female of about forty; and the lady looked upon a sleek man about ten years older, in drab shorts and continuations, black coat, neckcloth, and gloves.

"Miss Julia Manners!" exclaimed the mayor at length, "you astonish me."

"That's very unfair of you, Overton," replied Miss Julia, "for I have known you long enough not to be surprised at anything you do, and you might extend equal courtesy to me."

"But to run away—actually run away—with a young man!" remonstrated the mayor.

"You wouldn't have me actually run away with an old one, I presume?" was the cool rejoinder.

"And then to ask me—me—of all people in the world—a man of my age and appearance—mayor of the town—to promote such a scheme!" pettishly ejaculated Joseph Overton; throwing himself into an arm-chair, and producing Miss Julia's letter from his pocket, as if to corroborate the assertion that he had been asked.

"Now, Overton," replied the lady, impatiently, "I want your assistance in this matter, and I must have it. In the lifetime of that poor old dear, Mr. Cornberry, who—who——"

"Who was to have married you, and didn't, because he died first; and who left you his property unencumbered with the addition of himself," suggested the mayor, in a sarcastic tone.

"Well," replied Miss Julia, reddening slightly, "in the lifetime of the poor old dear, the property had the encumbrance of your management; and all I will say of that is, that I only wonder it didn't die of consumption instead of its master. You helped yourself then: help me now."

Mr. Joseph Overton was a man of the world, and an attorney; and as certain indistinct recollections of an odd thousand pounds or two, appropriated by mistake, passed across his mind, he hemmed deprecatingly, smiled blandly, remained silent for a few seconds; and finally inquired, "What do you wish me to do?"

"I'll tell you," replied Miss Julia—"I'll tell you in three words. Dear Lord Peter——"

"That's the young man, I suppose—" interrupted the mayor.

"That's the young nobleman," replied the lady, with a great stress on the last word. "Dear Lord Peter is considerably afraid of the resentment of his family; and we have therefore thought it better to make the match a stolen one. He left town to avoid suspicion, on a visit to his friend, the Honourable Augustus Flair, whose seat, as you know, is about thirty miles from this, accompanied only by his favourite tiger. We arranged that I should come here alone in the London coach; and that he, leaving his tiger and cab behind him, should come on, and arrive here as soon as possible this afternoon."

"Very well," observed Joseph Overton, "and then he can order the chaise, and you can go on to Gretna Green together, without requiring the presence or interference of a third party, can't you?"

"No," replied Miss Julia. "We have every reason to believe—dear Lord Peter not being considered very prudent or sagacious by his friends, and they having discovered his attachment to me—that immediately on his absence being observed, pursuit will be made in this direction: to elude which, and to prevent our being traced, I wish it to be understood in this house that dear Lord Peter is slightly deranged, though perfectly harmless; and that I am, unknown to him, waiting his arrival to convey him in a post-chaise to a private asylum—at Berwick, say. If I don't show myself much, I dare say I can manage to pass for his mother."

The thought occurred to the mayor's mind that the lady might show herself a good deal without fear of detection; seeing that she was about double the age of her intended husband. He said nothing, however, and the lady proceeded.

"With the whole of this arrangement, dear Lord Peter is acquainted: and all I want you to do is, to make the delusion more complete by giving it the sanction of your influence in this place, and assigning this as a reason to the people of the house for my taking the young gentleman away. As it would not be consistent with the story that I should see him until after he has entered the chaise, I also wish you to communicate with him, and inform him that it is all going on well."

"Has he arrived?" inquired Overton.

"I don't know," replied the lady.

"Then how am I to know?" inquired the mayor. "Of course he will not give his own name at the bar."

"I begged him, immediately on his arrival, to write you a note," replied Miss Manners; "and to prevent the possibility of our project being discovered through its means, I desired him to write anonymously, and in mysterious terms to acquaint you with the number of his room."

"God bless me!" exclaimed the mayor, rising from his seat, and searching his pockets—"most extraordinary circumstance —he *has* arrived—mysterious note left at my house in a most mysterious manner, just before yours—didn't know what to make of it before, and certainly shouldn't have attended to it.—Oh! here it is." And Joseph Overton pulled out of an inner coat-pocket the identical letter penned by Alexander Trott. "Is this his lordship's hand?"

"Oh yes," replied Julia; "good, punctual creature! I have not seen it more than once or twice, but I know he writes very badly and very large. These dear, wild young noblemen, you know, Overton——"

"Ay, ay, I see," replied the mayor. "Horses and dogs, play and wine—grooms, actresses, and cigars—the stable, the green-room, the saloon, the brothel, and the tavern; and the legislative assembly at last."

"Here's what he says," pursued the mayor: "'Sir,—A young gentleman in number nineteen at the Winglebury

Arms, is bent on committing a rash act to-morrow morning at an early hour.' (That's good—he means marrying.) 'If you have any regard for the peace of this town, or the preservation of one—it may be two—human lives'—What the deuce does he mean by that?"

"'That he's so anxious for the ceremony, he will expire if it's put off, and that I may possibly do the same," replied the lady with great complacency.

"Oh! I see—not much fear of that;—well—'two human lives, you will cause him to be removed to-night.'—(He wants to start at once.) 'Fear not to do this on your responsibility: for to-morrow, the absolute necessity of the proceeding will be but too apparent. Remember: number nineteen. The name is Trott. No delay; for life and death depend upon your promptitude.'—Passionate language, certainly. Shall I see him?"

"Do," replied Miss Julia; "and entreat him to act his part well. I am half afraid of him. Tell him to be cautious."

"I will," said the mayor.

"Settle all the arrangements."

"I will," said the mayor again.

"And say I think the chaise had better be ordered for one o'clock."

"Very well," cried the mayor once more; and ruminating on the absurdity of the situation in which fate and old acquaintance had placed him, he desired a waiter to herald his approach to the temporary representative of number nineteen.

The announcement, "Gentleman to speak with you, sir," induced Mr. Trott to pause half-way in the glass of port, the contents of which he was in the act of imbibing at the moment; to rise from his chair, and retreat a few paces towards the window, as if to secure a retreat in the event of the visitor assuming the form and appearance of Horace Hunter. One glance at Joseph Overton, however, quieted his apprehensions. He courteously motioned the stranger to a seat. The waiter after a little jingling with the decanter and glasses, consented to leave the room; and Joseph Overton placing the broad-brimmed hat on the chair next him, and bending his body gently forward, opened the business by saying in a very low and cautious tone:

"My lord——"

"Eh?" said Mr. Alexander Trott in a very loud key, with the vacant and mystified stare of a chilly somnambulist.

"Hush—hush!" said the cautious attorney: "to be sure—quite right—no titles here—my name is Overton, sir."

"Overton?"

"Yes: the mayor of this place—you sent me a letter with anonymous information, this afternoon."

"I, sir?" exclaimed Trott with ill-dissembled surprise; for, coward as he was, he would willingly have repudiated the authorship of the letter in question. "I, sir?"

"Yes, you, sir; did you not?" responded Overton, annoyed with what he supposed to be an extreme degree of unnecessary suspicion. "Either this letter is yours, or it is not. If it be, we can converse securely upon the subject at once. If it be not, of course I have no more to say."

"Stay, stay," said Trott, "it *is* mine; I *did* write it. What could I do, sir? I had no friend here."

"To be sure, to be sure," said the mayor, encouragingly, "you could not have managed it better. Well, sir; it will be necessary for you to leave here to-night in a post-chaise and four. And the harder the boys drive the better. You are not safe from pursuit here."

"Bless me!" exclaimed Trott, in an agony of apprehension, "can such things happen in a country like this? Such unrelenting and cold-blooded hostility!" He wiped off the concentrated essence of cowardice that was oozing fast down his forehead, and looked aghast at Joseph Overton.

"It certainly is a very hard case," replied the mayor with a smile, "that, in a free country, people can't marry whom they like without being hunted down as if they were criminals. However, in the present instance the lady is willing, you know, and that's the main point, after all."

"Lady willing!" repeated Trott, mechanically. "How do you know the lady's willing?"

"Come, that's a good one," said the mayor, benevolently tapping Mr. Trott on the arm with his broad-brimmed hat. "I have known her well for a long time, and if anybody could entertain the remotest doubt on the subject, I assure you I have none, nor need you."

"Dear me!" said Mr. Trott, ruminating. "Dear me! This is *very* extraordinary!"

"Well, Lord Peter," said the mayor, rising.

"Lord Peter!" repeated Mr. Trott.

"Oh—ah, I forgot; well, Mr. Trott, then—Trott—very good, ha! ha! Well, sir, the chaise shall be ready at half-past twelve."

"And what is to become of me till then?" inquired Mr. Trott, anxiously. "Wouldn't it save appearances if I were placed under some restraint?"

"Ah!" replied Overton, "very good thought—capital idea indeed. I'll send somebody up directly. And if you make a little resistance when we put you in the chaise it wouldn't be amiss—look as if you didn't want to be taken away, you know."

"To be sure," said Trott—"to be sure."

"Well, my lord," said Overton, in a low tone, "till then, I wish your lordship a good evening."

"Lord—lordship!" ejaculated Trott again, falling back a

step or two, and gazing in unutterable wonder on the countenance of the mayor.

"Ha-ha! I see, my lord—practising the madman?—very good indeed—very vacant look—capital, my lord, capital—good evening, Mr.—Trott—ha! ha! ha!"

"That mayor's decidedly drunk," soliloquised Mr. Trott, throwing himself back in his chair, in an attitude of reflection.

"He is a much cleverer fellow than I thought him, that young nobleman—he carries it off uncommonly well," thought Overton, as he wended his way to the bar, there to complete his arrangements. This was soon done: every word of the story was implicitly believed, and the one-eyed boots was immediately instructed to repair to number nineteen, to act as custodian of the person of the supposed lunatic until half-past twelve o'clock. In pursuance of this direction, that somewhat eccentric gentleman armed himself with a walking-stick of gigantic dimensions, and repaired with his usual equanimity of manner to Mr. Trott's apartment, which he entered without any ceremony and mounted guard in by quietly depositing himself upon a chair near the door, where he proceeded to beguile the time by whistling a popular air with great apparent satisfaction.

"What do you want here, you scoundrel?" exclaimed Mr. Alexander Trott, with a proper appearance of indignation at his detention.

The boots beat time with his head as he looked gently round at Mr. Trott with a smile of pity, and whistled an *adagio* movement.

"Do you attend in this room by Mr. Overton's desire?" inquired Trott, rather astonished at the man's demeanour.

"Keep yourself to yourself, young feller," calmly responded the boots, "and don't say nothin' to nobody." And he whistled again.

"Now, mind," ejaculated Mr. Trott, anxious to keep up the face of wishing with great earnestness to fight a duel if they'd let him. "I protest against being kept here. I deny that I have any intention of fighting with anybody. But as it's useless contending with superior numbers, I shall sit quietly down."

"You'd better," observed the placid boots, shaking the large stick expressively.

"Under protest, however," added Alexander Trott, seating himself, with indignation in his face but great content in his heart. "Under protest."

"Oh, certainly!" responded the boots; "anything you please. If you're happy, I'm transported; only don't talk too much—it'll make you worse."

"Make me worse!" exclaimed Trott, in unfeigned astonishment: "the man's drunk!"

"You'd better be quiet, young feller," remarked the boots, going through a most threatening piece of pantomime with the stick.

"Or mad!" said Mr. Trott, rather alarmed. "Leave the room, sir, and tell them to send somebody else."

"Wor't do!" replied the boots.

"Leave the room!" shouted Trott, ringing the bell violently; for he began to be alarmed on a new score.

"Leave that 'ere bell alone, you wretched loo-nattic!" said the boots, suddenly forcing the unfortunate Trott back into his chair, and brandishing the stick aloft. "Be quiet, you miserable object, and don't let everybody know there's a madman in the house."

"He *is* a madman! He *is* a madman!" exclaimed the terrified Mr. Trott, gazing on the one eye of the red-headed boots with a look of abject horror.

"Madman!" replied the boots—"damme, I think he *is* a madman with a vengeance! Listen to me, you unfort'nate. Ah! would you?"—[a slight tap on the head with the large stick, as Mr. Trott made another move towards the bell-handle] "I caught you there! did I?"

"Spare my life!" exclaimed Trott, raising his hands imploringly.

"I don't want your life," replied the boots, disdainfully, "though I think it 'ud be a charity if somebody took it."

"No, no, it wouldn't," interrupted poor Mr. Trott, hurriedly; "no, no, it wouldn't! I—I—'d rather keep it!"

"O werry well," said the boots; "that's a mere matter of taste—ev'ry one to his liking. Hows'ever, all I've got to say is this here: You sit quietly down in that chair, and I'll sit hoppersite you here, and if you keep quiet and don't stir, I won't damage you; but, if you move hand or foot till half-past twelve o'clock, I shall alter the expression of your countenance so completely, that the next time you look in the glass you'll ask vether you're gone out of town, and ven you're likely to come back again. So sit down."

"I will—I will," responded the victim of mistakes; and down sat Mr. Trott and down sat the boots too, exactly opposite him, with the stick ready for immediate action in case of emergency.

Long and dreary were the hours that followed. The bell of Great Winglebury church had just struck ten, and two hours and a half would probably elapse before succour arrived.

For half an hour the noise occasioned by shutting up the shops in the street beneath betokened something like life in the town, and rendered Mr. Trott's situation a little less insupportable; but when even these ceased, and nothing was heard beyond the occasional rattling of a post-chaise as it drove up the yard to change horses, and then drove away again, or the clattering of horses' hoofs in the stables behind, it became almost unbearable. The boots occasionally moved an inch or two, to knock superfluous bits of wax off the candles, which were burning low, but instantaneously resumed his former position; and as he remembered to have heard somewhere or other that the human eye had an unfailing effect in controlling mad people, he kept his solitary organ of vision constantly fixed on Mr. Alexander Trott. That unfortunate individual stared at his companion in his turn, until his features grew more and more indistinct—his hair gradually less red—and the room more misty and obscure. Mr. Alexander Trott fell into a sound sleep, from which he was awakened by a rumbling in the street, and a cry of—"Chaise-and-four for number twenty-five!" A bustle on the stairs succeeded; the room door was hastily thrown open; and Mr. Joseph Overton entered, followed by four stout waiters, and Mrs. Williamson, the stout landlady of the Winglebury Arms.

"Mr. Overton!" exclaimed Mr. Alexander Trott, jumping up in a frenzy of passionate excitement, "look at this man, sir; consider the situation in which I have been placed for three hours past—the person you sent to guard me, sir, was a madman—a madman—a raging, ravaging, furious madman."

"Bravo!" whispered Overton.

"Poor dear!" said the compassionate Mrs. Williamson, "mad people always think other people's mad."

"Poor dear!" ejaculated Mr. Alexander Trott. "What the devil do you mean by poor dear! Are you the landlady of this house?"

"Yes, yes," replied the stout old lady, "don't exert yourself, there's a dear! Consider your health, now; do."

"Exert myself!" shouted Mr. Alexander Trott, "it's a mercy, ma'am, that I have any breath to exert myself with! I might have been assassinated three hours ago by that one-eyed monster with the oakum head. How dare you have a madman, ma'am—how dare you have a madman, to assault and terrify the visitors to your house?"

"I'll never have another," said Mrs. Williamson, casting a look of reproach at the mayor.

"Capital, capital," whispered Overton again, as he enveloped Mr. Alexander Trott in a thick travelling-cloak.

"Capital, sir!" exclaimed Trott, aloud, "it's horrible. The very recollection makes me shudder. I'd rather fight four duels in three hours, if I survived the first three, than I'd sit for that time face to face with a madman."

"Keep it up, as you go down-stairs," whispered Overton; "your bill is paid, and your portmanteau in the chaise." And then he added aloud, "Now, waiters, the gentleman's ready."

At this signal the waiters crowded round Mr. Alexander

Trott. One took one arm, another the other, a third walked
before with a candle, the fourth behind with another candle;
the boots and Mrs. Williamson brought up the rear, and down-
stairs they went, Mr. Alexander Trott expressing alternately
at the very top of his voice either his feigned reluctance to go,
or his unfeigned indignation at being shut up with a madman.

Mr. Overton was waiting at the chaise-door, the boys were
ready mounted and a few ostlers and stable nondescripts
were standing round to witness the departure of "the mad
gentleman." Mr. Alexander Trott's foot was on the step;
when he observed (which the dim light had prevented his
doing before) a human figure seated in the chaise, closely
muffled up in a cloak like his own.

"Who's that?" he inquired of Overton, in a whisper.

"Hush, hush," replied the mayor; "the other party, of
course."

"The other party!" exclaimed Trott, with an effort to
retreat.

"Yes, yes; you'll soon find that out, before you go far, I
should think—but make a noise, you'll excite suspicion if
you whisper to me so much."

"I won't go in this chaise!" shouted Mr. Alexander Trott,
all his original fears recurring with tenfold violence. "I
shall be assassinated—I shall be——"

"Bravo, bravo," whispered Overton. "I'll push you in."

"But I won't go," exclaimed Mr. Trott. "Help here,
help! They're carrying me away against my will. This is
a plot to murder me."

"Poor dear!" said Mrs. Williamson again.

"Now, boys, put 'em along," cried the mayor, pushing Trott
in and slamming the door. "Off with you as quick as you
can, and stop for nothing till you come to the next stage—
all right."

"Horses are paid, Tom," screamed Mrs. Williamson; and
away went the chaise at the rate of fourteen miles an hour,
with Mr. Alexander Trott and Miss Julia Manners carefully
shut up in the inside.

Mr. Alexander Trott remained coiled up in one corner of
the chaise, and his mysterious companion in the other, for
the first two or three miles; Mr. Trott edging more and more
into his corner as he felt his companion gradually edging more
and more from hers; and vainly endeavouring in the darkness
to catch a glimpse of the furious face of the supposed Horace
Hunter.

"We may speak now," said his fellow traveller, at length;
"the post-boys can neither see nor hear us."

"That's not Hunter's voice!" thought Alexander,
astonished.

"Dear Lord Peter!" said Miss Julia, most winningly:

putting her arm on Mr. Trott's shoulder. "Dear Lord Peter. Not a word?"

"Why, it's a woman!" exclaimed Mr. Trott, in a low tone of excessive wonder.

"Ah! Whose voice is that?" said Julia; "'tis not Lord Peter's."

"No,—it's mine," replied Mr. Trott.

"Yours!" ejaculated Miss Julia Manners; "a strange man! Gracious heaven! How came you here?"

"Whoever you are, you might have known that I came against my will, ma'am," replied Alexander, "for I made noise enough when I got in."

"Do you come from Lord Peter?" inquired Miss Manners.

"Damn Lord Peter," replied Trott pettishly. "I don't know any Lord Peter. I never heard of him before to-night, when I've been Lord Peter'd by one and Lord Peter'd by another, till I verily believe I'm mad, or dreaming——"

"Whither are we going?" inquired the lady tragically.

"How should *I* know, ma'am?" replied Trott with singular coolness; for the events of the evening had completely hardened him.

"Stop! stop!" cried the lady, letting down the front glasses of the chaise.

"Stay, my dear ma'am!" said Mr. Trott, pulling the glasses up again with one hand, and gently squeezing Miss Julia's waist with the other. "There is some mistake here; give me till the end of this stage to explain my share of it. We must go so far; you cannot be set down here alone, at this hour of the night."

The lady consented; the mistake was mutually explained. Mr. Trott was a young man, had highly promising whiskers, an undeniable tailor, and an insinuating address—he wanted nothing but valour, and who wants that with three thousand a-year? The lady had this, and more; she wanted a young husband, and the only course open to Mr. Trott to retrieve his disgrace was a rich wife. So, they came to the conclusion that it would be a pity to have all this trouble and expense for nothing, and that as they were so far on the road already, they had better go to Gretna Green, and marry each other, and they did so. And the very next preceding entry in the Blacksmith's book was an entry of the marriage of Emily Brown with Horace Hunter. Mr. Hunter took his wife home, and begged pardon, and *was* pardoned; and Mr. Trott took *his* wife home, begged pardon too, and was pardoned also. And Lord Peter, who had been detained beyond his time by drinking champagne and riding a steeple-chase, went back to the Honourable Augustus Flair's, and drank more champagne, and rode another steeple-chase, and was thrown and killed. And Horace Hunter took great credit to himself for practising on the cowardice of Alexander Trott; and all these circumstances were discovered in time, and carefully noted down; and if ever you stop a week at the Winglebury Arms, they will give you just this account of The Great Winglebury Duel.

CHAPTER IX: *Mrs. Joseph Porter*

MOST extensive were the preparations at Rose Villa, Clapham Rise, in the occupation of Mr. Gattleton (a stockbroker in especially comfortable circumstances), and great was the anxiety of Mr. Gattleton's interesting family, as the day fixed for the representation of the Private Play which had been "many months in preparation," approached. The whole family was infected with the mania for Private Theatricals; the house, usually so clean and tidy, was, to use Mr. Gattleton's expressive description, "regularly turned out o' windows;" the large dining-room, dismantled of its furniture and ornaments, presented a strange jumble of flats, flies, wings, lamps, bridges, clouds, thunder and lightning, festoons and flowers, daggers and foil, and all the other messes which in theatrical slang are included under the comprehensive name of "properties."

The bedrooms were crowded with scenery, the kitchen was occupied by carpenters. Rehearsals took place every other night in the drawing-room, and every sofa in the house was more or less damaged by the perseverance and spirit with which Mr. Sempronius Gattleton, and Miss Lucina, rehearsed the smothering scene in "Othello"—it having been determined that that tragedy should form the first portion of the evening's entertainments.

"When we're a *leetle* more perfect, I think it will go off admirably," said Mr. Sempronius, addressing his *corps dramatique*, at the conclusion of the hundred and fiftieth rehearsal. In consideration of his sustaining the trifling inconvenience of bearing all the expenses of the play, Mr. Sempronius had been in the most handsome manner unanimously elected stage-manager. "Evans," continued Mr. Gattleton, jun., addressing a tall, thin, pale young gentleman, with extensive whiskers, "Evans, 'pon my word you play *Roderigo* beautifully."

"Beautifully!" echoed the three Miss Gattletons; for Mr. Evans was pronounced by all his lady friends to be "quite a dear." He looked so interesting, and had such lovely whiskers, to say nothing of his talent for writing verses in albums and playing the flute! The interesting *Roderigo* simpered and bowed.

"But I think," added the manager, "you are hardly perfect in the—fall—in the fencing-scene, where you are—you understand?"

"It's very difficult," said Mr. Evans, thoughtfully; "I've fallen about a good deal in our counting-house lately for practice, only I find it hurts one so. Being obliged to fall backwards, you see, it bruises one's head a good deal."

"But you must take care you don't knock a wing down," said Mr. Gattleton, sen., who had been appointed prompter, and who took as much interest in the play as the youngest of the company. "The stage is very narrow, you know."

"Oh! don't be afraid," said Mr. Evans, with a very self-satisfied air: "I shall fall with my head 'off,' and then I can't do any harm."

"But, egad!" said the manager, rubbing his hands, "we shall make a decided hit in 'Masaniello.' Harleigh sings that music admirably."

Everybody echoed the sentiment. Mr. Harleigh smiled, and looked foolish—not an unusual thing with him, hummed, "Behold how brightly breaks the morning," and blushed as red as the fisherman's nightcap he was trying on.

"Let's see," resumed the manager, telling the number on his fingers, "we shall have three dancing female peasants, besides *Fenella*, and four fishermen. Then there's our man Tom, he can have a pair of ducks of mine, and a check shirt of Bob's, and a red nightcap, and he'll do for another—that's five. In the choruses, of course, we can sing at the sides, and in the market-scene we can walk about in cloaks and things. When the revolt takes place, Tom must keep rushing in on one side and out on the other, with a pickaxe, as fast as he can. The effect will be electrical; 'twill look exactly as if there were a great number of 'em; and in the eruption scene we must burn the red fire, and upset the tea-trays, and hallo and make all sorts of noises—and it's sure to do."

"Sure! sure!" cried all the performers *unâ voce*—and away hurried Mr. Sempronius Gattleton to wash the burnt cork off his face, and superintend the "setting up" of some of the amateur-painted but never-sufficiently-to-be-admired scenery.

Mrs. Gattleton was a kind, good-tempered, vulgar soul, exceedingly fond of her husband and children, and entertaining only three dislikes. In the first place, she had a natural antipathy to anybody else's unmarried daughters; and in the second, she was in bodily fear of anything in the shape of ridicule; and, lastly—almost a necessary consequence of this feeling—she regarded with feelings of the utmost horror one Mrs. Joseph Porter over the way. However, the good folks of Clapham and its vicinity stood very much in awe of scandal and sarcasm; and thus Mrs. Joseph Porter was courted, and flattered, and caressed, and invited, for very much the same reason that a poor author, without a farthing in his pocket, behaves with the most extraordinary civility to a two-penny postman.

"Never mind, ma," said Miss Emma Porter, in colloquy with her respected relative, and trying to look unconcerned; "if they had invited me, you know that neither you nor pa would have allowed me to take part in such an exhibition."

"Just what I should have thought from your high sense of propriety," returned the mother. "I am glad to see, Emma, you know how to designate the proceeding." Miss P., by-the-by, had only the week before made "an exhibition" of herself for four days, behind a counter at a fancy fair, to all and every of her Majesty's liege subjects who were disposed to pay a shilling each for the privilege of seeing some four dozen girls flirting with strangers, and playing at shop.

"There!" said Mrs. Porter, looking out of window; "there are two rounds of beef and a ham going in, clearly for sandwiches; and Thomas, the pastry-cook, says there have been twelve dozen tarts ordered, besides blanc-mange and jellies. Upon my word! think of the Miss Gattletons in fancy dresses too!"

"Oh, it's too ridiculous!" said Miss Porter, with a sort of hysterical chuckle.

"I'll manage to put them a little out of conceit with the business, however," said Mrs. Porter; and out she went on her charitable errand.

"Well, my dear Mrs. Gattleton," said Mrs. Joseph Porter —after they had been closeted for some time, and when by dint of indefatigable pumping, she had managed to extract all the news about the play—"well, my dear, people may say what they please; indeed we know they will, for some folks are so ill-natured. Ah, my dear Miss Lucina, how d'ye do?— I was just telling your mamma that I have heard it said, that——"

"What?"

"Mrs. Porter is alluding to the play, my dear," said Mrs. Gattleton; "she was, I am sorry to say, just informing me that——"

"Oh, now pray don't mention it," interrupted Mrs. Porter; "it's most absurd—quite as absurd as young What's-his-name saying he wondered how Miss Caroline with such a foot and ankle, could have the vanity to play *Fenella*."

"Highly impertinent, whoever said it," said Mrs. Gattleton, bridling up.

"Certainly, my dear," chimed in the delighted Mrs. Porter; "most undoubtedly. Because, as I said, if Miss Caroline *does* play *Fenella*, it doesn't follow, as a matter of course, that she should think she has a pretty foot; and then—such puppies as these young men are—he had the impudence to say, that——"

How far the amiable Mrs. Porter might have succeeded in her pleasant purpose it is impossible to say, had not the entrance of Mr. Thomas Balderstone, Mrs. Gattleton's brother, familiarly called in the family "Uncle Tom," changed the course of conversation, and suggested to her mind an excellent plan of operation on the evening of the play.

Uncle Tom was very rich, and exceedingly fond of his nephews and nieces: as a matter of course, therefore, he was an object of great importance in his own family. He was one of the best-hearted men in existence; always in a good temper, and always talking. It was his boast that he wore top-boots on all occasions, and had never worn a black silk neckerchief; and it was his pride that he remembered all the principal plays of Shakspeare from beginning to end—and so he did. The result of this parrot-like accomplishment was, that he was not only perpetually quoting himself, but that he could never sit by and hear a misquotation from the "Swan of Avon" without setting the unfortunate delinquent right. He was also something of a wag; never missed an opportunity of saying what he considered a good thing, and invariably laughed till he cried at anything that appeared to him mirth-moving or ridiculous.

"Well, girls!" said Uncle Tom, after the preparatory ceremony of kissing and how-d'ye-do-ing had been gone through—"how d'ye get on? Know your parts, eh?—Lucina, my dear, act ii., scene 1—place, left—cue—'Unknown fate,' —What's next, ha?—Go on—'The Heavens——'"

"Oh, yes," said Miss Lucina, "I recollect—

> *"The heavens forbid*
> *But that our loves and comforts should increase*
> *Even as our days do grow!"*

"Make a pause here and there," said the old gentleman, who was a great critic in his own estimation.—"'But that our loves and comforts should increase'—emphasis on the last syllable, 'crease,'—loud 'even,'—one, two, three, four; then loud again, 'as our days do grow;' emphasis on *days*. That's the way, my dear; trust to your uncle for emphasis. —Ah! Sem, my boy, how are you?"

"Very well, thankee, uncle," returned Mr. Sempronius, who had just appeared, looking something like a ring-dove, with a small circle round each eye, the result of his constant corking. "Of course we see you on Thursday."

"Of course, of course, my dear boy."

"What a pity it is your nephew didn't think of making you prompter, Mr. Balderstone," whispered Mrs. Joseph Porter; "you would have been invaluable."

"Well, I flatter myself, I *should* have been tolerably up to the thing," responded Uncle Tom.

"I must bespeak sitting next you on the night," resumed Mrs. Porter; "and then, if our dear young friends here, should be at all wrong, you will be able to enlighten me. I shall be *so* interested."

"I am sure I shall be most happy to give you any assistance in my power."

"Mind, it's a bargain."

"Certainly."

"I don't know how it is," said Mrs. Gattleton to her daughters, as they were sitting round the fire in the evening, looking over their parts, "but I really very much wish Mrs. Joseph Porter wasn't coming on Thursday. I am sure she's scheming something."

"She can't make *us* ridiculous, however," observed Mr. Sempronius Gattleton, haughtily.

The long-looked-for Thursday arrived in due course, and brought with it, as Mr. Gattleton, senior, philosophically observed, "no disappointments, to speak of." True, it was yet a matter of doubt whether *Cassio* would be enabled to get into the dress which had been sent for him from the masquerade warehouse. It was equally uncertain whether the principal female singer would be sufficiently recovered from the influenza to make her appearance; Mr. Harleigh, the *Masaniello* of the night, was hoarse, and rather unwell, in consequence of the great quantity of lemon and sugar-candy he had eaten to improve his voice; and two flutes and a violoncello had pleaded severe colds. What of that? the audience were all coming. Everybody knew his part; the dresses were covered with tinsel and spangles; the white plumes looked beautiful; Mr. Evans had practised falling until he was bruised from head to foot and quite perfect; and *Iago* was perfectly sure that, in the stabbing-scene, he should make "a decided hit." A self-taught deaf gentleman, who had kindly offered to bring his flute, would be a most valuable addition to the orchestra; Miss Jenkins's talent for the piano was too well know to be doubted for an instant; Mr. Cape had practised the violin accompaniment with her frequently, and Mr. Brown, who had kindly undertaken at a few hours' notice, to bring his violoncello, would, no doubt, manage extremely well.

Seven o'clock came, and so did the audience; all the rank and fashion of Clapham and its vicinity was fast filling the theatre. There were the Smiths, the Gubbinses, the Nixons, the Dixons, the Hicksons, people with all sorts of names, two aldermen, a sheriff in perspective, Sir Thomas Glumper (who had been knighted in the last reign for carrying up an address on somebody's escaping from something); and last not least, there were Mrs. Joseph Porter and Uncle Tom, seated in the centre of the third row from the stage; Mrs. P. amusing Uncle Tom with all sorts of stories, and Uncle Tom amusing every one else by laughing most immoderately.

Ting, ting, ting! went the prompter's bell at eight o'clock precisely, and dash went the orchestra into the overture to "The Men of Prometheus." The pianoforte player hammered away with the most laudable perseverance; and the violoncello, which struck in at intervals, "sounded very well, considering." The unfortunate individual, however, who had undertaken to play the flute accompaniment "at sight," found, from fatal experience, the perfect truth of the old adage, "out of sight, out of mind;" for being very near-sighted, and being placed at a considerable distance from his music-book, all he had an opportunity of doing was to play a bar now and then in the wrong place, and put the other performers out. It is, however, but justice to Mr. Brown to say that he did this to admiration. The overture, in fact, was not unlike a race between the different instruments; the piano came in first by several bars, and the violoncello next, quite distancing the poor flute; for the deaf gentleman *too-too'd* away, quite unconscious that he was at all wrong, until apprised, by the applause of the audience, that the overture was concluded. A considerable bustle and shuffling of feet was then heard upon the stage, accompanied by whispers of "Here's a pretty go!—what's to be done?" &c. The audience applauded again, by way of raising the spirits of the performers; and then Mr. Sempronius desired the prompter, in a very audible voice, to "clear the stage, and ring up."

Ting, ting, ting! went the bell again. Everybody sat down; the curtain shook, rose sufficiently high to display several pair of yellow boots paddling about, and there it remained.

Ting, ting, ting! went the bell again. The curtain was violently convulsed, but rose no higher; the audience tittered; Mrs. Porter looked at Uncle Tom, and Uncle Tom looked at everybody, rubbing his hands, and laughing with perfect rapture. After as much ringing with the little bell as a muffin-boy would make in going down a tolerably long street, and a vast deal of whispering, hammering, and calling for nails and cord, the curtain at length rose, and discovered Mr. Sempronius Gattleton *solus*, and decked for *Othello*. After three distinct rounds of applause, during which Mr. Sempronius applied his right hand to his left breast, and bowed in the most approved manner, the manager advanced, and said:

"Ladies and Gentlemen—I assure you it is with sincere regret, that I regret to be compelled to inform you, that *Iago* who was to have played Mr. Wilson—I beg your pardon, Ladies and Gentlemen, but I am naturally somewhat agitated (applause)—I mean, Mr. Wilson, who was to have played *Iago*, is—that is, has been—or, in other words, Ladies and Gentlemen, the fact is, that I have just received a note, in which I am informed that *Iago* is unavoidably detained at the Post Office this evening. Under these circumstances, I trust—a—a—

amateur performance—a—another gentleman undertaken to
read the part—request indulgence for a short time—courtesy
and kindness of a British audience."—(Overwhelming
applause.) Exit Mr. Sempronius Gattleton, and curtain falls.

The audience were, of course, exceedingly good-humoured;
the whole business was a joke; and accordingly they waited for
an hour with the utmost patience, being enlivened by an
interlude of rout-cakes and lemonade. It appeared by Mr.
Sempronius's subsequent explanation, that the delay would
not have been so great, had it not so happened that when the
substitute *Iago* had finished dressing, and just as the play was
on the point of commencing, the original *Iago* unexpectedly
arrived. The former was therefore compelled to undress, and
the latter to dress for his part; which, as he found some difficulty in getting into his clothes, occupied no inconsiderable
time. At last the tragedy began in real earnest. It went off
well enough, until the third scene of the first act, in which
Othello addresses the Senate, the only remarkable circumstance
being, that as *Iago* could not get on any of the stage boots, in
consequence of his feet being violently swelled with the heat
and excitement, he was under the necessity of playing the part
in a pair of common Hessians, which contrasted rather oddly
with his richly embroidered pantaloons. When *Othello* started
with his address to the Senate (whose dignity was represented
by the *Duke*, a carpenter, two men engaged on the recommen-
dation of the gardener, and a boy) Mrs. Porter found the
opportunity she so anxiously sought.

Mr. Sempronius proceeded:

> "*Most potent, grave, and reverend signiors,*
> *My very noble and approv'd good masters,*
> *That I have ta'en away this old man's daughter,*
> *It is most true ;—rude am I in my speech——*"

"Is that right?" whispered Mrs. Porter to Uncle Tom.

"No."

"Tell him so, then."

"I will.—Sem!" called out Uncle Tom, "that's wrong, my
boy."

"What's wrong, Uncle?" demanded *Othello*, quite forgetting
the dignity of his situation.

"You've left out something. 'True I have married—'"

"Oh, ah!" said Mr. Sempronius, endeavouring to hide his
confusion as much and as ineffectually as the audience
attempted to conceal their half-suppressed tittering, by
coughing with the most extraordinary violence—

> ——"*true I have married her ;—*
> *The very head and front of my offending*
> *Hath this extent ; no more.*

(*Aside*) Why don't you prompt, father?"

"Because I've mislaid my spectacles," said poor Mr. Gattle-ton, almost dead with the heat and bustle.

"There, now it's 'rude am I,'" said Uncle Tom.

"Yes, I know it is," returned the unfortunate manager, proceeding with his part.

It would be useless and tiresome to quote the number of instances in which Uncle Tom, now completely in his element, and instigated by the mischievous Mrs. Porter, corrected the mistakes of the performers; suffice it to say, that having mounted his hobby, nothing could induce him to dismount; so, during the whole remainder of the play, he performed a kind of running accompaniment, by muttering everybody's part as it was being delivered, in an undertone. The audience were highly amused, Mrs. Porter delighted, the performers embarrassed; Uncle Tom never was better pleased in all his life; and Uncle Tom's nephews and nieces had never, although the declared heirs to his large property, so heartily wished him gathered to his fathers as on that memorable occasion.

Several other minor causes, too, united to damp the ardour of the *dramatis personæ*. None of the performers could walk in their tights, or move their arms in their jackets; the panta-loons were too small, the boots too large, and the swords of all shapes and sizes. Mr. Evans, naturally too tall for the scenery, wore a black velvet hat with immense white plumes, the glory of which was lost in "the flies"; and the only other inconvenience of which was, that when it was off his head he could not put it on, and when it was on he could not take it off. Notwithstanding all his practice, too, he fell with his head and shoulders as neatly through one of the side-scenes as a harlequin would jump through a panel in a Christmas pantomime. The pianoforte player, overpowered by the extreme heat of the room, fainted away at the commencement of the entertainments, leaving the music of "Masaniello" to the flute and violoncello. The orchestra complained that Mr. Harleigh put them out, and Mr. Harleigh declared that the orchestra prevented his singing at all. The fishermen, who were hired for the occasion, revolted to the very life, positively refusing to play without an increased allowance of spirits; and their demand being complied with, they got drunk in the eruption scene as naturally as possible. The red fire, which was burnt at the conclusion of the second act, not only nearly suffocated the audience, but nearly set the house on fire into the bargain; and, as it was, the remainder of the piece was acted in a thick fog.

In short, the whole affair was, as Mrs. Joseph Porter triumphantly told everybody, "a complete failure." The audience went home at four o'clock in the morning, exhausted with laughter, suffering from severe headaches, and smelling terribly of brimstone and gunpowder. The Messrs. Gattleton, senior and junior, retired to rest with the vague idea of emigrating to Swan River early in the ensuing week.

Rose Villa has once again resumed its wonted appearance: the dining-room furniture has been replaced; the tables are as nicely polished as formerly; the horsehair chairs are ranged against the wall as regularly as ever; Venetian blinds have been fitted to every window in the house to intercept the prying gaze of Mrs. Joseph Porter. The subject of theatricals is now never mentioned in the Gattleton family, unless, indeed, by Uncle Tom, who cannot refrain from sometimes expressing his surprise and regret at finding that his nephews and nieces appear to have lost the relish they once possessed for the beauties of Shakspeare, and quotations from the works of the immortal bard.

CHAPTER X: *A passage in the life of Mr. Watkins Tottle.* *Chapter the First*

MATRIMONY is proverbially a serious undertaking. Like an overweening predilection for brandy-and-water, it is a misfortune into which a man easily falls, and from which he finds it remarkably difficult to extricate himself. It is no use telling a man who is timorous on these points that it is but one plunge, and all is over. They say the same thing at the Old Bailey, and the unfortunate victims derive about as much comfort from the assurance in the one case as in the other.

Mr. Watkins Tottle was a rather uncommon compound of strong uxorious inclinations, and an unparalleled degree of anti-connubial timidity. He was about fifty years of age; stood four feet six inches and three-quarters in his socks—for he never stood in stockings at all—plump, clean, and rosy. He looked something like a vignette to one of Richardson's novels, and had a clean, cravatish formality of manner, and kitchen-pokerness of carriage, which Sir Charles Grandison himself might have envied. He lived on an annuity, which was well adapted to the individual who received it, in one respect—it was rather small. He received it in periodical payments on every alternate Monday; but he ran himself out about a day after the expiration of the first week as regularly as an eight-day clock, and then, to make the comparison complete, his landlady wound him up, and he went on with a regular tick.

Mr. Watkins Tottle had long lived in a state of single blessedness, as bachelors say, or single cursedness, as spinsters think; but the idea of matrimony had never ceased to haunt him. Wrapt in profound reveries on this never-failing theme, fancy transformed his small parlour in Cecil Street into a neat house in the suburbs—the half-hundredweight of coal under the kitchen-stairs suddenly sprang up into three tons of the best

Wallsend—his small French bedstead was converted into a regular matrimonial four-poster—and on the empty chair on the opposite side of the fireplace, imagination seated a beautiful young lady with a very little independence or will of her own, and a very large independence under a will of her father's.

"Who's there?" inquired Mr. Watkins Tottle, as a gentle tap at his room-door disturbed these meditations one evening.

"Tottle, my dear fellow, how *do* you do?" said a short elderly gentleman with a gruffish voice, bursting into the room, and replying to the question by asking another; and then they shook hands with a great deal of solemnity.

"Told you I should drop in some evening," said the short gentleman, as he delivered his hat into Tottle's hand, after a little struggling and dodging.

"Delighted to see you, I'm sure," said Mr. Watkins Tottle, wishing internally that his visitor had "dropped in" to the Thames at the bottom of the street, instead of dropping into his parlour. The fortnight was nearly up, and Watkins was hard up.

"How is Mrs. Gabriel Parsons?" inquired Tottle.

"Quite well, thank you," replied Mr. Gabriel Parsons, for that was the name the short gentleman revelled in. Here there was a pause; the short gentleman looked at the left hob of the fireplace, and Mr. Watkins Tottle stared vacancy out of countenance.

"Quite well," repeated the short gentleman, when five minutes had expired. "I may say remarkably well." And he rubbed the palms of his hands together as hard as if he were going to strike a light by friction.

"What will you take?" inquired Tottle, with the desperate suddenness of a man who knew that unless the visitor took his leave he stood very little chance of taking anything else.

"Oh, I don't know. Have you any whiskey?"

"Why," replied Tottle, very slowly, for all this was gaining time, "I *had* some capital and remarkably strong whiskey last week; but it's all gone—and therefore its strength——"

"Is much beyond proof; or, in other words, impossible to be proved," said the short gentleman; and he laughed very heartily, and seemed quite glad the whiskey had been drunk. Mr. Tottle smiled—but it was the smile of despair. When Mr. Gabriel Parsons had done laughing, he delicately insinuated that, in the absence of whiskey he would not be averse to brandy. And Mr. Watkins Tottle, lighting a flat candle very ostentatiously, and displaying an immense key, which belonged to the street-door, but which for the sake of appearances occasionally did duty in an imaginary wine-cellar, left the room to entreat his landlady to charge their glasses, and charge them in the bill. The application was successful—the spirits were speedily called;—not from "the vasty deep" but the adjacent wine-vaults. The two short gentlemen mixed their grog; and then sat cosily down before the fire—a pair of shorts, airing themselves.

"Tottle," said Mr. Gabrielle Parsons, "you know my way—off-hand, open, say what I mean, mean what I say, damn reserve, and can't bear affectation. One is a bad domino which only hides what good people have about 'em, without making the bad look better; and the other is much about the same thing as pinking a white cotton stocking to make it look like a silk one.—Now listen to what I'm going to say."

Here the little gentleman paused, and took a long pull at his brandy-and-water. Mr. Watkins Tottle took a sip of his, stirred the fire, and assumed an air of profound attention.

"It's no use humming and ha'ing about the matter," resumed the short gentleman. "You want to get married—don't you?"

"Why—" replied Mr. Watkins Tottle, evasively; for he trembled violently, and felt a sudden tingling throughout his whole frame—"why—I should certainly—at least, I *think* I should like it."

"Won't do," said the short gentleman. "Plain and free—or there's an end of the matter. Do you want money?"

"You know I do."

"You admire the sex?"

"I do."

"And you'd like to be married?"

"Certainly."

"Then you shall be. There's an end of that." And thus saying, Mr. Gabriel Parsons took a pinch of snuff, and mixed another glass.

"Let me entreat you to be more explanatory," said Tottle. "Really, as the party principally interested, I cannot consent to be disposed of in this way."

"I'll tell you," replied Mr. Gabriel Parsons, warming with the subject, and the brandy-and-water. "I know a lady—she's stopping with my wife now—who is just the thing for you. Well educated; talks French; plays the piano; knows a good deal about flowers and shells, and all that sort of thing; and has five hundred a year, with an uncontrolled power of disposing of it, by her last will and testament."

"I'll pay my addresses to her," said Mr. Watkins Tottle. "She isn't *very* young—is she?"

"Not very; just the thing for you.—I've said that already."

"What coloured hair has the lady?" inquired Mr. Watkins Tottle.

"Egad! I hardly recollect," replied Gabriel, with great coolness. "Perhaps I ought to have observed, at first, she wears a front."

"A what!" ejaculated Tottle.

"One of those things with curls along here," said Parsons drawing a straight line across his forehead, just over his eyes, in illustration of his meaning. "I know the front's black; I can't speak quite positively about her own hair; because, unless one walks behind her, and catches a glimpse of it under her bonnet one seldom sees it; but I should say, that it was lighter than the front—just a shade of greyish tinge, perhaps."

Mr. Watkins Tottle looked as if he had certain misgivings of mind. Mr. Gabriel Parsons perceived it, and thought it would be safe to begin the next attack without delay.

"Now, were you ever in love, Tottle?" he inquired.

Mr. Watkins Tottle blushed up to the eyes, and down to the chin, and exhibited a most extensive combination of colours as he confessed the soft impeachment.

"I suppose you popped the question more than once, when you were a young—I beg your pardon—a younger—man," said Parsons.

"Never in my life," replied his friend, apparently indignant at being suspected of such an act. "Never! The fact is, that I entertain, as you know, peculiar opinions on these subjects. I am not afraid of ladies, young or old—far from it; but I think, that in compliance with the custom of the present day, they allow too much freedom of speech and manner to marriageable men. Now the fact is, that anything like this easy freedom I never could acquire; and as I am always afraid of going too far, I am generally, I dare say, considered formal and cold."

"I shouldn't wonder if you were," replied Parsons gravely; "I shouldn't wonder. However, you'll be all right in this case; for the strictness and delicacy of this lady's ideas greatly exceed your own. Lord bless you, why when she came to our house, there was an old portrait of some man or other with two large black staring eyes hanging up in her bedroom; she positively refused to go to bed there till it was taken down, considering it decidedly improper."

"I think so, too," said Mr. Watkins Tottle; "certainly."

"And then the other night—I never laughed so much in my life," resumed Mr. Gabriel Parsons; "I had driven home in an easterly wind, and caught a devil of a face-ache. Well; as Fanny—that's Mrs. Parsons, you know—and this friend of hers, and I, and Frank Ross, were playing a rubber, I said, jokingly, that when I went to bed I should wrap my head in Fanny's flannel petticoat. She instantly threw up her cards, and left the room."

"Quite right," said Mr. Watkins Tottle, "she could not possibly have behaved in a more dignified manner. What did you do?"

"Do? Frank took dummy; and I won sixpence."

"But didn't you apologise for hurting her feelings?"

"Devil a bit. Next morning, at breakfast, we talked it over. She contended that any reference to a flannel petticoat was highly improper;—men ought not to be supposed to know that such things were. I pleaded my coverture; being a married man."

"And what did the lady say to that?" inquired Tottle, deeply interested.

"Changed her ground, and said that Frank being a single man its impropriety was obvious."

"Noble-minded creature!" exclaimed the enraptured Tottle.

"Oh! both Fanny and I said at once that she was regularly cut out for you."

A gleam of placid satisfaction shone on the circular face of Mr. Watkins Tottle, as he heard the prophecy.

"There's one thing I can't understand," said Mr. Gabriel Parsons, as he rose to depart: "I cannot for the life and soul of me imagine how the deuce you'll ever manage to come together. The lady would certainly go into convulsions if the subject were mentioned." And Mr. Gabriel Parsons sat down again, and laughed till he was weak. Tottle owed him money, so he had a perfect right to laugh at his expense.

Mr. Watkins Tottle feared in his own mind that this was another characteristic which he had in common with this modern Lucretia. He, however, accepted the invitation to dine with the Parsonses on the next day but one, with great firmness; and looked forward to the introduction, when again left alone, with tolerable composure.

The sun that rose on the next day but one had never beheld a sprucer personage on the outside of the Norwood stage than Mr. Watkins Tottle, and when the coach drew up before a cardboard-looking house with disguised chimneys, and a lawn like a large sheet of green letter-paper, he certainly had never lighted to his place of destination a gentleman who felt more awkward or uncomfortable.

The coach stopped, and Mr. Watkins Tottle jumped—we beg his pardon—alighted with great dignity. "All right!" said he, and away went the coach up the hill with that beautiful equanimity of pace for which "short" stages are generally remarkable.

Mr. Watkins Tottle gave a faltering jerk to the handle of the garden-gate bell. He essayed a more energetic tug, and his previous nervousness was not at all diminished by hearing the bell ringing like a fire alarm.

"Is Mr. Parsons at home?" inquired Tottle of the man who opened the gate. He could hardly hear himself speak, for the bell had not yet done tolling.

"Here I am," shouted a voice on the lawn,—and there was Mr. Gabriel Parsons in a flannel jacket, running backwards and forwards from a wicket to two hats piled on each other, and then from the two hats to the wicket, in the most violent manner, while another gentleman with his coat off was getting down the area of the house, after a ball. When the gentleman without the coat had found it—which he did in less than ten minutes—he ran back to the hats, and Gabriel Parsons pulled up. Then the gentleman without the coat called out "play," very loudly, and bowled: Mr. Gabriel Parsons knocked the ball several yards, and took another run. Then the other gentleman aimed at the wicket, and didn't hit it; and Mr. Gabriel Parsons, having finished running on his own account, laid down the bat and ran after the ball, which went into a neighbouring field.

They called this cricket.

"Tottle, will you 'go in?'" inquired Mr. Gabriel Parsons, as he approached him, wiping the perspiration off his face.

Mr. Watkins Tottle declined the offer, the bare idea of accepting which made him even warmer than his friend.

"Then we'll go into the house as it's past four, and I shall have to wash my hands before dinner," said Mr. Gabriel Parsons. "Here, I hate ceremony, you know—Timson, that is Tottle—Tottle, that's Timson, bred for the church, which I fear will never be bread for him;" and he chuckled at the old joke. Mr. Timson bowed carelessly. Mr. Watkins Tottle bowed stiffly, and Mr. Gabriel Parsons led the way to the house. He was a rich sugar-baker, and mistook rudeness for honesty, and abrupt bluntness for an open and candid manner; many besides Gabriel mistake bluntness for sincerity.

Mrs. Gabriel Parsons received the visitors most graciously on the steps, and preceded them to the drawing-room. On the sofa was seated a lady of very prim appearance, and remarkably inanimate. She was just one of those persons at whose age it is impossible to make any reasonable guess; her features might have been remarkably pretty when she was younger, and they might always have presented the same appearance. Her complexion—with a slight trace of powder here and there—was as clear as that of a well-made wax-doll, and her face as expressive.

She was handsomely dressed, and was winding up a gold watch for effect.

"Miss Lillerton, my dear, this is our friend Mr. Watkins Tottle; a very old acquaintance, I assure you," said Mrs. Parsons, presenting the Strephon of Cecil Street, Strand. The lady rose, and made a deep curtsy; Mr. Watkins Tottle made a serio-comic bow.

"Splendid, majestic creature!" thought Watkins Tottle. She was his *beau idéal* of a desirable female.

Mr. Timson advanced, and Mr. Watkins Tottle began to hate him. Men generally discover a rival instinctively, and Mr. Watkins Tottle felt that his hate was deserved.

"May I beg," said the reverend gentleman,—"may I beg to call upon you, Miss Lillerton, for some trifling donation to my soup, coals, and blanket distribution society?"

"Put my name down for two sovereigns, if you please," responded Miss Lillerton.

"You are truly charitable, madam," said the Reverend Mr. Timson, "and we know that charity will cover a multitude of sins. Let me beg you to understand that I do not say this from the supposition that you have many sins which require palliation: believe me when I say that I never yet met any one who had fewer to atone for than Miss Lillerton."

Something like a bad imitation of animation lighted up the lady's face, as she acknowledged the compliment. Watkins Tottle incurred the sin of wishing that the ashes of the Reverend Charles Timson were quietly deposited in the churchyard of his curacy, wherever it might be.

"I'll tell you what," interrupted Parsons, who had just appeared with clean hands, and a black coat; "it's my private opinion, Timson, that your 'distribution society' is rather a humbug."

"You are so severe," replied Timson, with a Christian smile; he disliked Parsons, but liked his dinners.

"So positively unjust," said Miss Lillerton.

"Certainly," observed Tottle. The lady looked up; her eyes met those of Mr. Watkins Tottle. She withdrew them in a sweet confusion, and Watkins Tottle did the same— the confusion was mutual.

"Why," urged Mr. Parsons, pursuing his objections, "what on earth is the use of giving a man coals who has nothing to cook, or giving him blankets when he hasn't a bed, or giving him soup when he requires substantial food?—'like sending them ruffles when wanting a shirt.' Why not give 'em a trifle of money, as I do, when I think they deserve it, and let them purchase what they think best. Why?—because your subscribers wouldn't see their names flourishing in print on the church-door—that's the reason."

"Really, Mr. Parsons, I hope you don't mean to insinuate that I wish to see my name in print, on the church-door," interrupted Miss Lillerton.

"I hope not," said Mr. Watkins Tottle, putting in another word, and getting another glance.

"Certainly not," replied Parsons. "I dare say you wouldn't mind seeing it in writing, though, in the church register—eh?"

"Register! What register?" inquired the lady, gravely.

"Why, the register of marriages, to be sure," replied Parsons, chuckling at the sally, and glancing at Tottle. Mr. Watkins Tottle thought he should have fainted for shame, and it is quite impossible to imagine what effect the joke would have had upon the lady, if dinner had not been that moment announced. Mr. Watkins Tottle, with an unprecedented effort of gallantry, offered the tip of his little finger; Miss Lillerton accepted it gracefully, with maiden modesty; and they proceeded in due state to the dinner-table, where they were soon deposited side by side. The room was very snug, the dinner very good, and the little party in tolerable spirits. The conversation became pretty general, and when Mr. Watkins Tottle had extracted one or two cold observations from his neighbour, and taken wine with her, he began to acquire confidence rapidly. The cloth was removed; Mrs. Gabriel Parsons drank four glasses of port on the plea of her being a nurse just then, and Miss Lillerton took about the same number of sips, on the plea of her not wanting any at all. At length the ladies retired, to the great gratification of Mr. Gabriel Parsons, who had been coughing and frowning at his wife, for half an hour previously—signals which Mrs. Parsons never happened to observe, until she had been pressed to take her ordinary quantum, which, to avoid giving trouble, she generally did at once.

"What do you think of her?" inquired Mr. Gabriel Parsons of Mr. Watkins Tottle, in an undertone.

"I dote on her with enthusiasm already," replied Mr. Watkins Tottle.

"Gentlemen, pray let us drink 'the ladies,'" said the Reverend Mr. Timson.

"The ladies!" said Mr. Watkins Tottle, emptying his glass. In the fulness of his confidence he felt as if he could make love to a dozen ladies, off-hand.

"Ah!" said Mr. Gabriel Parsons, "I remember when I was a younger man—fill your glass, Timson."

"I have this moment emptied it."

"Then fill it again."

"I will," said Timson, readily suiting the action to the word.

"I remember," resumed Mr. Gabriel Parsons, "when I was a younger man, with what a strange compound of feelings I used to drink that toast, and how I used to think that every woman was an angel—quite a superior being."

"Was that before you were married?" mildly inquired Mr. Watkins Tottle.

"Oh! certainly," replied Mr. Gabriel Parsons. "I have never thought so since; and a precious milksop I must have been, ever to have thought so at all. But, you know, I married Fanny under the oddest and most ridiculous circumstances possible."

"What were they, if one may inquire?" asked Timson, who had heard the story, on an average twice a week for the last six months. Mr. Watkins Tottle listened attentively, in the hope of picking up some suggestion that might be useful to him in his new undertaking.

"I spent my wedding-night in a back-kitchen chimney," said Parsons, by way of a beginning.

"In a back-kitchen chimney!" ejaculated Watkins Tottle. "How dreadful."

"Yes, it wasn't very pleasant," replied the small host. "The fact is that Fanny's father and mother liked me well enough as an individual, but had a decided objection to my becoming a husband. You see, I hadn't any money in those days and they had; and so they wanted Fanny to pick up somebody else. However, we managed to discover the state of each other's affections somehow. I used to meet her at some mutual friends' parties; at first we danced together, and talked, and flirted, and all that sort of thing; then I used to like nothing so well as sitting by her side—we didn't talk so much then, but I remember I used to have a great notion of looking at her out of the extreme corner of my left eye, and then I got very miserable and sentimental, and began to write verses, and use Macassar. At last I couldn't bear it any longer, and after I had walked up and down the sunny side of Oxford Street in tight boots for a week—and a devilish hot summer it was too—in the hope of meeting her, I sat down and wrote a letter, and begged her to manage to see me clandestinely, for I wanted to hear her decision from her own mouth. I said I had discovered, to my perfect satisfaction, that I couldn't live without her, and that if she didn't have me, I had made up my mind to take prussic acid, or take to drinking, or emigrate, so as to take myself off in some way or other. Well, I borrowed a pound, and bribed the housemaid to give her the note, which she did."

"And what was the reply?" inquired Timson, who had found before, that encouraging the repetition of old stories is sure to end in a general invitation.

"Oh, the usual one, you know. Fanny expressed herself very miserable; hinted at the possibility of an early grave; said that nothing should induce her to swerve from the duty she owed her parents; and implored me to forget her, and find out somebody more deserving, and all that sort of thing. She said she could on no account think of meeting me unknown to her pa and ma; and entreated me, as she should be in a particular part of Kensington Gardens at eleven o'clock next morning, not to attempt to meet her there."

"You didn't go, of course?" said Watkins Tottle.

"Didn't I? Of course I did. There she was, with the identical housemaid in perspective, in order that there might be no interruption. We walked about for a couple of hours; made ourselves delightfully miserable; and were regularly engaged. Then we began to 'correspond'—that is to say, we used to exchange about four letters a day; what we used to say in 'em I can't imagine. And I used to have an interview in the kitchen, or in the cellar, or some such place, every evening. Well, things went on in this way for some time; and we got fonder of each other every day. At last, as our love was raised to such a pitch, and as my salary had been raised too, shortly before, we determined on a secret marriage. Fanny arranged to sleep at a friend's the previous night; we were to be married early in the morning, and then we were to return to her home and be pathetic. She was to fall at the old gentleman's feet, and bathe his boots with her tears; and I was to hug the old lady and call her 'mother,' and use my pocket-handkerchief as much as possible. Married we were the next morning; two girls—friends of Fanny's—acting as bridesmaids, and a man, who was hired for five shillings and a pint of porter, officiating as father. Now, the old lady unfortunately put off her return from Ramsgate where she had been paying a visit, until the next morning; and as we placed great reliance upon her, we agreed to postpone our confession for four-and-twenty hours. My newly-made wife returned home, and I spent my wedding-day in strolling about Hampstead Heath and damning my father-in-law. Of course I went to comfort my dear little wife at night as much as I could, with the assurance that our troubles would soon be over. I opened the garden-gate of which I had a key, and was shown by the servant to our old place of meeting —a back kitchen, with a stone-floor and a dresser, upon which, in the absence of chairs, we used to sit and make love."

"Make love upon a kitchen dresser!" interrupted Mr. Watkins Tottle, whose ideas of decorum were greatly outraged.

"Ah! On a kitchen-dresser!" replied Parsons. "And let me tell you, old fellow, that, if you were really over head-and-ears in love, and had no other place to make love in, you'd be devilish glad to avail yourself of such an opportunity. However, let me see;—where was I?"

"On the dresser," suggested Timson.

"Oh—ah! Well, here I found poor Fanny, quite disconsolate and uncomfortable. The old boy had been very cross all day, which made her feel still more lonely; and she was quite out of spirits. So I put a good face on the matter, and laughed it off, and said we should enjoy the pleasures of a matrimonial life more by contrast; and, at length, poor Fanny brightened up a little. I stopped there till about eleven o'clock, and, just as I was taking my leave for the fourteenth time, the girl came running down-stairs, without her shoes, in a great fright, to tell us that the old villain— God forgive me for calling him so, for he is dead and gone now—prompted I suppose by the Prince of Darkness, was coming down to draw his own beer for supper—a thing he had not done before for six months to my certain knowledge;

for the cask stood in that very back kitchen. If he discovered me there, explanation would have been out of the question; for he was so outrageously violent, when at all excited, that he never would have listened to me. There was only one thing to be done.—The chimney was a very wide one: it had been originally built for an oven; went up perpendicularly for a few feet, and then shot backward and formed a sort of small cavern. My hopes and fortune—the means of our joint existence almost—were at stake. I scrambled in like a squirrel; coiled myself up in this recess; and, as Fanny and the girl replaced the deal chimney-board, I could see the light of the candle which my unconscious father-in-law carried in his hand. I heard him draw the beer; and I never heard beer run so slowly. He was just leaving the kitchen, and I was preparing to descend, when down came the infernal chimney-board with a tremendous crash. He stopped, and put down the candle and the jug of beer on the dresser; he was a nervous old fellow, and any unexpected noise annoyed him. He coolly observed that the fireplace was never used, and sending the frightened servant into the next kitchen for a hammer and nails, actually nailed up the board, and locked the door on the outside. So there was I on my wedding-night, in the light kerseymere trousers, fancy waistcoat, and blue coat, that I had been married in in the morning, in a back-kitchen chimney, the bottom of which was nailed up, and the top of which had been formerly raised some fifteen feet, to prevent the smoke from annoying the neighbours. And there," added Mr. Gabriel Parsons, as he passed the bottle, "there I remained till half-past seven the next morning, when the housemaid's sweetheart, who was a carpenter, unshelled me. The old dog had nailed me up so securely, that, to this very hour, I firmly believe that no one but a carpenter could ever have got me out."

"And what did Mrs. Parsons's father say, when he found you were married?" inquired Watkins Tottle, who, although he never saw a joke, was not satisfied until he heard a story to the very end.

"Why, the affair of the chimney so tickled his fancy that he pardoned us off-hand, and allowed us something to live on till he went the way of all flesh. I spent the next night in his second-floor front much more comfortably than I had spent the preceding one; for, as you will probably guess——"

"Please, sir, missis has made tea," said a middle-aged female servant, bobbing into the room.

"That's the very housemaid that figures in my story," said Mr. Gabriel Parsons. "She went into Fanny's service when we were first married, and has been with us ever since; but I don't think she has felt one atom of respect for me since the morning she saw me released, when she went into violent hysterics, to which she has been subject ever since. Now, shall we join the ladies?"

"If you please," said Mr. Watkins Tottle.

"By all means," added the obsequious Mr. Timson; and the trio made for the drawing-room accordingly.

Tea being concluded, and the toast and cups having been duly handed, and occasionally upset, by Mr. Watkins Tottle, a rubber was proposed. They cut for partners—Mr. and Mrs. Parsons; and Mr. Watkins Tottle and Miss Lillerton. Mr. Timson being a clergyman, having conscientious scruples on the subject of card-playing, drank brandy-and-water, and kept up a running spar with Mr. Watkins Tottle. The evening went off well; Mr. Watkins Tottle was in high spirits, having some reason to be gratified with his reception by Miss Lillerton; and before he left, a small party was made up to visit the Beulah Spa on the following Saturday.

"It's all right, I think," said Mr. Gabriel Parsons to Mr. Watkins Tottle, as he opened the garden gate for him.

"I hope so," he replied, squeezing his friend's hand.

"You'll be down by the first coach on Saturday," said Mr. Gabriel Parsons.

"Certainly," replied Mr. Watkins Tottle. "Undoubtedly."

But fortune had decreed that Mr. Watkins Tottle should not be down by the first coach on Saturday. His adventures on that day, however, and the success of his wooing, are subjects for another chapter.

Chapter the Second

"The first coach has not come in yet, has it, Tom?" inquired Mr. Gabriel Parsons, as he very complacently paced up and down the fourteen feet of gravel which bordered the "lawn," on the Saturday morning which had been fixed upon for the Beulah Spa jaunt.

"No, sir; I haven't seen it," replied a gardener in a blue apron, who let himself out to do the ornamental for half-a-crown a day and his "keep."

"Time Tottle was down," said Mr. Gabriel Parsons, ruminating—"Oh, here he is, no doubt," added Gabriel, as a cab drove rapidly up the hill; and he buttoned his dressing-gown, and opened the gate to receive the expected visitor. The cab stopped, and out jumped a man in a coarse Petersham great-coat, whity-brown neckerchief, faded black suit, gamboge-coloured top-boots, and one of those large-crowned hats, formerly seldom met with, but now very generally patronised by gentlemen and costermongers.

"Mr. Parsons?" said the man, looking at the superscription of a note he held in his hand, and addressing Gabriel with an inquiring air.

"*My* name is Parsons," responded the sugar-baker.

"I've brought this here note," replied the individual in the painted tops, in a hoarse whisper; "I've brought this here note from a gen'l'm'n as come to our house this mornin'."

"I expected the gentleman at my house," said Parsons, as he broke the seal, which bore the impression of her Majesty's profile as it is seen on a sixpence.

"I've no doubt the gen'l'm'n would ha' been here," replied the stranger, "if he hadn't happened to call at our house first; but we never trusts no gen'l'm'n no furder nor we can see him —no mistake about that there"—added the unknown, with a facetious grin; "beg yer pardon, sir, no offence meant, only— once in, and I wish you may—catch the idea, sir?"

Mr. Gabriel Parsons was not remarkable for catching anything suddenly, but a cold. He therefore only bestowed a glance of profound astonishment on his mysterious companion, and proceeded to unfold the note of which he had been the bearer. Once opened and the idea was caught with very little difficulty. Mr. Watkins Tottle had been suddenly arrested for 33*l.* 10*s.* 4*d.*, and dated his communication from a lock-up house in the vicinity of Chancery Lane.

"Unfortunate affair this!" said Parsons, refolding the note.

"Oh! nothin' ven you're used to it," coolly observed the man in the Petersham.

"Tom!" exclaimed Parsons, after a few minutes' consideration, "just put the horse in, will you?—Tell the gentleman that I shall be there almost as soon as you are," he continued, addressing the sheriff-officer's Mercury.

"Werry well," replied that important functionary; adding, in a confidential manner, "I'd adwise the gen'l'm'n's friends to settle. You see it's a mere trifle, and, unless the gen'l'm'n means to go up afore the court, it's hardly worth while waiting for detainers you know. Our governor's wide awake, he is. I'll never say nothin' agin him, nor no man; but he knows what's o'clock, he does, uncommon." Having delivered this eloquent, and, to Parsons, particularly intelligible harangue, the meaning of which was eked out by divers nods and winks, the gentleman in the boots reseated himself in the cab, which went rapidly off, and was soon out of sight. Mr. Gabriel Parsons continued to pace up and down the pathway for some minutes, apparently absorbed in deep meditation. The result of his cogitations seemed to be perfectly satisfactory to himself, for he ran briskly into the house; said that business had suddenly summoned him to town; that he had desired the messenger to inform Mr. Watkins Tottle of the fact; and that they would return together to dinner. He then hastily equipped himself for a drive, and mounting his gig, was soon on his way to the establishment of Mr. Solomon Jacobs.

situate (as Mr. Watkins Tottle had informed him) in Cursitor Street, Chancery Lane.

When a man is in a violent hurry to get on, and has a specific object in view, the attainment of which depends on the completion of his journey, the difficulties which interpose themselves in his way appear not only to be innumerable, but to have been called into existence especially for the occasion. The remark is by no means a new one, and Mr. Gabriel Parsons had practical and painful experience of its justice in the course of his drive. There are three classes of animated objects which prevent your driving with any degree of comfort or celerity through streets which are but little frequented—they are pigs, children, and old women. On the occasion we are describing, the pigs were luxuriating on cabbage-stalks, and the shuttlecocks fluttered from the little deal battledores, and the children played in the road; and women, with a basket in one hand and the street-door key in the other, *would* cross just before the horse's head, until Mr. Gabriel Parsons was perfectly savage with vexation, and quite hoarse with hoi-ing and imprecating. Then, when he got into Fleet Street, there was "a stoppage," in which people in vehicles have the satisfaction of remaining stationary for half an hour, and envying the slowest pedestrians; and where policemen rush about, and seize hold of horses' bridles, and back them into shop-windows, by way of clearing the road and preventing confusion. At length Mr. Gabriel Parsons turned into Chancery Lane, and having inquired for and been directed to Cursitor Street (for it was a locality of which he was quite ignorant), he soon found himself opposite the house of Mr. Solomon Jacobs. Confiding his horse and gig to the care of one of the fourteen boys who had followed him from the other side of Blackfriars Bridge on the chance of his requiring their services, Mr. Gabriel Parsons crossed the road and knocked at an inner door, the upper part of which was of glass, grated like the windows of this inviting mansion with iron bars—painted white to look comfortable.

The knock was answered by a sallow-faced red-haired sulky boy, who, after surveying Mr. Gabriel Parsons through the glass, applied a large key to an immense wooden excrescence, which was in reality a lock, but which, taken in conjunction with the iron nails with which the panels were studded, gave the door the appearance of being subject to warts.

"I want to see Mr. Watkins Tottle," said Parsons.

"It's the gentleman that come in this morning, Jem," screamed a voice from the top of the kitchen-stairs, which belonged to a dirty woman who had just brought her chin to a level with the passage-floor. "The gentleman's in the coffee-room."

"Up-stairs, sir," said the boy, just opening the door wide enough to let Parsons in without squeezing him, and double-

locking it the moment he had made his way through the
aperture. "First floor—door on the left."

Mr. Gabriel Parsons, thus instructed, ascended the un-
carpeted and ill-lighted staircase, and after giving several
subdued taps at the before-mentioned "door on the left,"
which were rendered inaudible by the hum of voices within the
room, and the hissing noise attendant on some frying operations which were carrying on below-stairs, turned the handle,
and entered the apartment. Being informed that the unfortunate object of his visit had just gone up-stairs to write
a letter, he had leisure to sit down and observe the scene
before him.

The room—which was a small, confined den—was partitioned off into boxes, like the common-room of some inferior
eating-house. The dirty floor had evidently been as long a
stranger to the scrubbing-brush as to carpet or floor-cloth; and
the ceiling was completely blackened by the flare of the oil-
lamp by which the room was lighted at night. The grey ashes
on the edges of the tables, and the cigar-ends which were
plentifully scattered about the dusty grate, fully accounted
for the intolerable smell of tobacco which pervaded the place;
and the empty glasses and half-saturated slices of lemon on the
tables, together with the porter pots beneath them, bore
testimony to the frequent libations in which the individuals
who honoured Mr. Solomon Jacobs by a temporary residence
in his house indulged. Over the mantelshelf was a paltry
looking-glass, extending about half the width of the chimney-
piece; but, by way of counterpoise, the ashes were confined by
a rusty fender about twice as long as the hearth.

From this cheerful room itself, the attention of Mr. Gabriel
Parsons was naturally directed to its inmates. In one of the
boxes two men were playing at cribbage with a very dirty
pack of cards, some with blue, some with green, and some with
red backs—selections from decayed packs. The cribbage
board had been long ago formed on the table by some ingenious
visitor with the assistance of a pocket-knife and a two-pronged
fork, with which the necessary number of holes had been made
in the table at proper distances for the reception of the
wooden pegs. In another box a stout, hearty-looking man, of
about forty, was eating some dinner, which his wife—an
equally comfortable-looking personage—had brought him in
a basket; and in a third, a genteel-looking young man was
talking earnestly, and in a low tone to a young female, whose
face was concealed by a thick veil, but whom Mr. Gabriel
Parsons immediately set down in his own mind as the debtor's
wife. A young fellow of vulgar manners, dressed in the very
extreme of the prevailing fashion, was pacing up and down the
room, with a lighted cigar in his mouth and his hands in his
pockets, ever and anon puffing forth volumes of smoke, and

occasionally applying, with much apparent relish, to a pint pot, the contents of which were "chilling" on the hob.

"Fourpence more, by gum!" exclaimed one of the cribbage-players, lighting a pipe, and addressing his adversary at the close of the game; "one 'ud think you'd got luck in a pepper-cruet, and shook it out when you wanted it."

"Well, that ain't a bad un," replied the other, who was a horse-dealer from Islington.

"No; I'm blessed if it is," interposed the jolly-looking fellow, who, having finished his dinner, was drinking out of the same glass as his wife, in truly conjugal harmony, some hot gin-and-water. The faithful partner of his cares had brought a plentiful supply of the anti-temperance fluid in a large flat stone bottle, which looked like a half-gallon jar that had been successfully tapped for the dropsy. "You're a rum chap, you are, Mr. Walker—will you dip your beak into this, sir?"

"Thankee, sir," replied Mr. Walker, leaving his box, and advancing to the other to accept the proffered glass. "Here's your health, sir, and your good 'ooman's here. Gentlemen all —yours, and better luck still. Well, Mr. Willis," continued the facetious prisoner, addressing the young man with the cigar, "you seem rather down to-day—floored, as one may say. What's the matter, sir? Never say die, you know."

"Oh! I'm all right," replied the smoker. "I shall be bailed out to-morrow."

"Shall you, though?" inquired the other. "Damme, I wish I could say the same. I am as regularly over head and ears as the Royal George, and stand about as much chance of being *bailed out.* Ha! ha! ha!"

"Why," said the young man, stopping short, and speaking in a very loud key, "look at me. What d'ye think I've stopped here two days for?"

"'Cause you couldn't get out, I suppose," interrupted Mr. Walker, winking to the company. "Not that you're exactly obliged to stop here, only you can't help it. No compulsion, you know, only you must—eh?"

"Ain't he a rum un?" inquired the delighted individual, who had offered the gin-and-water, of his wife.

"Oh, he just is!" replied the lady, who was quite overcome by these flashes of imagination.

"Why, my case," frowned the victim, throwing the end of his cigar into the fire, and illustrating his argument by knocking the bottom of the pot on the table, at intervals,— "my case is a very singular one. My father's a man of large property, and I am his son."

"That's a very strange circumstance!" interrupted the jocose Mr. Walker, *en passant.*

"—I am his son, and have received a liberal education. I don't owe no man nothing—not the value of a farthing, but I was induced, you see, to put my name to some bills for a friend —bills to a large amount, I may say a very large amount, for which I didn't receive no consideration. What's the consequence?"

"Why, I suppose the bills went out, and you came in. The acceptances weren't taken up, and you were, eh?" inquired Walker.

"To be sure," replied the liberally-educated young gentleman. "To be sure; and so here I am, locked up for a matter of twelve hundred pound."

"Why don't you ask your old governor to stump up?" inquired Walker, with a somewhat sceptical air.

"Oh! bless you, he'd never do it," replied the other, in a tone of expostulation—"Never!"

"Well, it is very odd to—be—sure," interposed the owner of the flat bottle, mixing another glass, "but I've been in difficulties, as one may say, now for thirty year. I went to pieces when I was in a milk-walk, thirty year ago; arterwards, when I was a fruiterer, and kept a spring wan; and arter that again in the coal and 'tatur line—but all that time I never see a youngish chap come into a place of this kind, who wasn't going out again directly, and who hadn't been arrested on bills which he'd given a friend and for which he'd received nothing whatsomever—not a fraction."

"Oh! it's always the cry," said Walker. "I can't see the use on it; that's what makes me so wild. Why, I should have a much better opinion of an individual, if he'd say at once in an honourable and gentlemanly manner as he'd done everybody he possible could."

"Ay, to be sure," interposed the horse-dealer, with whose notions of bargain and sale the axiom perfectly coincided, "so should I."

The young gentleman, who had given rise to these observations, was on the point of offering a rather angry reply to these sneers, but the rising of the young man before noticed, and of the female who had been sitting by him, to leave the room, interrupted the conversation. She had been weeping bitterly, and the noxious atmosphere of the room acting upon her excited feelings and delicate frame, rendered the support of her companion necessary as they quitted it together.

There was an air of superiority about them both, and something in their appearance so unusual in such a place, that a respectful silence was observed until the *whirr—r—bang* of the spring door announced that they were out of hearing. It was broken by the wife of the ex-fruiterer.

"Poor creetur!" said she, quenching a sigh in a rivulet of gin-and-water. "She's very young."

"She's a nice-looking 'ooman too," added the horse-dealer.

"What's he in for, Ikey?" inquired Walker, of an individual

who was spreading a cloth with numerous blotches of mustard upon it, on one of the tables, and whom Mr. Gabriel Parsons had no difficulty in recognising as the man who had called upon him in the morning.

"Vy," responded the factotum, "it's one of the rummest rigs you ever heard on. He come in here last Vensday, which by-the-by he's a-going over the water to-night—hows'ever that's neither here nor there. You see I've been a-going back-ards and for-ards about his business, and ha' managed to pick up some of his story from the servants and them; and so far as I can make it out, it seems to be summat to this here effect——"

"Cut it short, old fellow," interrupted Walker, who knew from former experience that he of the top-boots was neither very concise nor intelligible in his narratives.

"Let me alone," replied Ikey, "and I'll ha' vound up, and made my lucky in five seconds. This here young gen'l'm'n's father—so I'm told, mind ye—and the father o' the young voman, have always been on very bad, out-and-out, rig'lar knock-me-down sort o' terms; but somehow or another, when he was a wisitin' at some gentlefolk's house, as he knowed at college, he come into contract with the young lady. He seed her several times, and then he up and said he'd keep company with her, if so be as she vos agreeable. Vell, she vos as sweet upon him as he vos upon her, and so I s'pose they made it all right; for they got married 'bout six months arterwards, unbeknown, mind ye, to the two fathers—leastways, so I'm told. When they heard on it—my eyes, there was such a combustion! Starvation vos the very least that vos to be done to 'em. The young gen'l'm'n's father cut him off vith a bob, 'cos he'd cut himself off vith a wife; and the young lady's father he behaved even worser and more unnat'ral, for he not only blow'd her up dreadful, and swore he'd never see her again, but he employed a chap as I knows—and as you knows, Mr. Valker, a precious sight too well—to go about and buy up the bills and them things on which the young husband, thinking his governor 'ud come round agin, had raised the vind just to blow himself on vith for a time; besides vich, he made all the interest he could to set other people agin him. Consequence vos, that he paid as long as he could; but things he never expected to have to meet till he'd had time to turn himself round, come fast upon him, and he vos nabbed. He vos brought here, as I said afore, last Vensday, and I think there's about—ah, half a dozen detainers agin him down-stairs now. I have been," added Ikey, "in the purfession these fifteen year, and I never met vith such windictiveness afore!"

"Poor creeturs!" exclaimed the coal-dealer's wife once more: again resorting to the same excellent prescription for nipping a sigh in the bud. "Ah! when they've seen as much trouble as I and my old man here have, they'll be as comfortable under it as we are."

"The young lady's a pretty creature," said Walker, "only she's a little too delicate for my taste—there ain't enough of her. As to the young cove, he may be very respectable and what not, but he's too down in the mouth for me—he ain't game."

"Game!" exclaimed Ikey, who had been altering the position of a green-handled knife and fork at least a dozen times, in order that he might remain in the room under the pretext of having something to do. "He's game enough ven there's anything to be fierce about; but who could be game as you call it, Mr. Walker, with a pale young creetur like that, hanging about him? It's enough to drive any man's heart into his boots to see 'em together—and no mistake at all about it. I never shall forget her first comin' here; he wrote to her on the Thursday to come—I know he did, 'cos I took the letter. Uncommon fidgety he was all day, to be sure, and in the evening he goes down into the office, and he says to Jacobs, says he, 'Sir, can I have the loan of a private room for a few minutes this evening, without incurring any additional expense—just to see my wife in?' says he. Jacobs looked as much as to say, 'Strike me bountiful if you ain't one of the modest sort!' but as the gen'l'm'n who had been in the back parlour had just gone out, and had paid for it for that day, he says—werry grave—'Sir,' says he, 'it's agin our rules to let private rooms to our lodgers on gratis terms, but,' says he, 'for a gentleman, I don't mind breaking through them for once.' So then he turns round to me, and says, 'Ikey, put two mould candles in the back parlour, and charge 'em to this gen'l'm'n's account,' vich I did. Vell, by-and-by a hackney-coach comes up to the door, and there, sure enough, was the young lady, wrapped up in a hopera-cloak, as it might be, and all alone. I opened the gate that night, so I went up when the coach come, and he vos a waitin' at the parlour-door—and wasn't he a trembling, neither? The poor creetur see him, and could hardly walk to meet him. 'Oh, Harry!' she says, 'that it should have come to this! and all for my sake,' says she, putting her hand upon his shoulder. So he puts his arm round her pretty little waist, and leading her gently a little way into the room, so that he might be able to shut the door, he says, so kind and soft-like, 'Why, Kate,' says he——"

"Here's the gentleman you want," said Ikey, abruptly breaking off in his story, and introducing Mr. Gabriel Parsons to the crestfallen Watkins Tottle, who at that moment entered the room. Watkins advanced with a wooden expression of passive endurance, and accepted the hand which Mr. Gabriel Parsons held out.

"I want to speak to you," said Gabriel, with a look strongly expressive of his dislike of the company.

"This way," replied the imprisoned one, leading the way to the front drawing-room, where rich debtors did the luxurious at the rate of a couple of guineas a day.

"Well, here I am," said Watkins, as he sat down on the sofa; and placing the palms of his hands on his knees, anxiously glanced at his friend's countenance.

"Yes; and here you're likely to be," said Gabriel, coolly, as he rattled the money in his unmentionable pockets, and looked out of the window.

"What's the amount with the costs?" inquired Parsons, after an awkward pause.

"37l. 3s. 10d."

"Have you any money?"

"Nine and sixpence halfpenny."

Mr. Gabriel Parsons walked up and down the room for a few seconds, before he could make up his mind to disclose the plan he had formed; he was accustomed to drive hard bargains, but was always most anxious to conceal his avarice. At length he stopped short, and said, "Tottle, you owe me fifty pounds."

"I do."

"And from all I see, I infer that you are likely to owe it me."

"I fear I am."

"Though you have every disposition to pay me if you could?"

"Certainly."

"Then," said Mr. Gabriel Parsons, "listen; here's my proposition. You know my way of old. Accept it—yes or no—I will or I won't. I'll pay the debt and costs, and I'll lend you ten pound more (which, added to your annuity, will enable you to carry on the war well), if you'll give me your note of hand to pay me one hundred and fifty pounds within six months after you are married to Miss Lillerton."

"My dear——"

"Stop a minute—on one condition; and that is, that you propose to Miss Lillerton at once."

"At once! My dear Parsons, consider."

"It's for you to consider, not me. She knows you well from reputation, though she did not know you personally until lately. Notwithstanding all her maiden modesty, I think she'd be devilish glad to get married out of hand, with as little delay as possible. My wife has sounded her on the subject, and she has confessed."

"What—what?" eagerly interrupted the enamoured Watkins.

"Why," replied Parsons, "to say exactly what she has confessed, would be rather difficult, because they only spoke in hints, and so forth; but my wife, who is no bad judge in these cases, declared to me that what she had confessed was as good as to say that she was not insensible of your merits—in fact, that no other man should have her."

Mr. Watkins Tottle rose hastily from his seat, and rang the bell.

"What's that for?" inquired Parsons.

"I want to send the man for the bill stamp," replied Mr. Watkins Tottle.

"Then you've made up your mind?"

"I have,"—and they shook hands most cordially. The note of hand was given—the debt and costs were paid—Ikey was satisfied for his trouble, and the two friends soon found themselves on that side of Mr. Solomon Jacobs's establishment, on which most of his visitors were very happy when they found themselves once again—to wit, the *outside*.

"Now," said Mr. Gabriel Parsons, as they drove to Norwood together—"you shall have an opportunity to make the disclosure to-night, and mind you speak out, Tottle."

"I will—I will!" replied Watkins, valorously.

"How I should like to see you together!" ejaculated Mr. Gabriel Parsons. "What fun!" And he laughed so long and so loudly, that he disconcerted Mr. Watkins Tottle, and frightened the horse.

"There's Fanny and your intended, walking about on the lawn," said Gabriel, as they approached the house. "Mind your eye, Tottle."

"Never fear," replied Watkins, resolutely, as he made his way to the spot where the ladies were walking.

"Here's Mr. Tottle, my dear," said Mrs. Parsons, addressing Miss Lillerton. The lady turned quickly round, and acknowledged his courteous salute with the same sort of confusion that Watkins had noticed on their first interview, but with something like a slight expression of disappointment or carelessness.

"Did you see how glad she was to see you?" whispered Parsons to his friend.

"Why, I really thought she looked as if she would rather have seen somebody else," replied Tottle.

"Pooh, nonsense!" whispered Parsons again; "it's always the way with the women, young or old. They never show how delighted they are to see those whose presence makes their hearts beat. It's the way with the whole sex, and no man should have lived to your time of life without knowing it. Fanny confessed it to me, when we were first married, over and over again—see what it is to have a wife."

"Certainly," whispered Tottle, whose courage was vanishing fast.

'Well now, you'd better begin to pave the way," said

Parsons, who, having invested some money in the speculation, assumed the office of director.

"Yes, yes, I will—presently," replied Tottle, greatly flurried.

"Say something to her, man," urged Parsons again. "Confound it! pay her a compliment, can't you?"

"No! not till after dinner," replied the bashful Tottle, anxious to postpone the evil moment.

"Well, gentlemen," said Mrs. Parsons, "you are really very polite; you stay away the whole morning, after promising to take us out, and when you do come home, you stand whispering together and take no notice of us."

"We were talking of the *business*, my dear, which detained us this morning," replied Parsons, looking significantly at Tottle.

"Dear me! how very quickly the morning has gone," said Miss Lillerton, referring to the gold watch, which was wound up on state occasions, whether it required it or not.

"*I* think it has passed very slowly," mildly suggested Tottle.

("That's right—bravo!" whispered Parsons.)

"Indeed!" said Miss Lillerton, with an air of majestic surprise.

"I can only impute it to my unavoidable absence from your society, madam," said Watkins, "and that of Mrs. Parsons."

During this short dialogue, the ladies had been leading the way to the house.

"What the deuce did you stick Fanny into that last compliment for?" inquired Parsons, as they followed together; "it quite spoilt the effect."

"Oh! it really would have been too broad without," replied Watkins Tottle, "much too broad!"

"He's mad!" Parsons whispered his wife, as they entered the drawing-room, "mad from modesty."

"Dear me!" ejaculated the lady, "I never heard of such a thing."

"You'll find we have quite a family dinner, Mr. Tottle," said Mrs. Parsons, when they sat down to table: "Miss Lillerton is one of us, and, of course, we make no stranger of you."

Mr. Watkins Tottle expressed a hope that the Parsons family never would make a stranger of him; and wished internally that his bashfulness would allow him to feel a little less like a stranger himself.

"Take off the covers, Martha," said Mrs. Parsons, directing the shifting of the scenery with great anxiety. The order was obeyed, and a pair of boiled fowls, with tongue and et ceteras, were displayed at the top, and a fillet of veal at the bottom. On one side of the table two green sauce-tureens, with ladles of the same, were setting to each other in a green dish; and on the other was a curried rabbit, in a brown suit, turned up with lemon.

"Miss Lillerton, my dear," said Mrs. Parsons, "shall I assist you?"

"Thank you, no; I think I'll trouble Mr. Tottle."

Watkins started—trembled—helped the rabbit—and broke a tumbler. The countenance of the lady of the house, which had been all smiles previously, underwent an awful change.

"Extremely sorry," stammered Watkins, assisting himself to curry and parsley and butter, in the extremity of his confusion.

"Not the least consequence," replied Mrs. Parsons, in a tone which implied that it was of the greatest consequence possible,—directing aside the researches of the boy, who was groping under the table for the bits of broken glass.

"I presume," said Miss Lillerton, "that Mr. Tottle is aware of the interest which bachelors usually pay in such cases; a dozen glasses for one is the lowest penalty."

Mr. Gabriel Parsons gave his friend an admonitory tread on the toe. Here was a clear hint that the sooner he ceased to be a bachelor, and emancipated himself from such penalties, the better. Mr. Watkins Tottle viewed the observation in the same light, and challenged Mrs. Parsons to take wine, with a degree of presence of mind, which, under all the circumstances, was really extraordinary.

"Miss Lillerton," said Gabriel, "may I have the pleasure?"

"I shall be most happy."

"Tottle, will you assist Miss Lillerton, and pass the decanter. Thank you." (The usual pantomimic ceremony of nodding and sipping gone through)—

"Tottle, were you ever in Suffolk?" inquired the master of the house, who was burning to tell one of his seven stock stories.

"No," responded Watkins, adding, by way of a saving clause, "but I've been in Devonshire."

"Ah!" replied Gabriel, "it was in Suffolk that a rather singular circumstance happened to me many years ago. Did you ever happen to hear me mention it?"

Mr. Watkins Tottle *had* happened to hear his friend mention it some four hundred times. Of course he expressed great curiosity, and evinced the utmost impatience to hear the story again. Mr. Gabriel Parsons forthwith attempted to proceed, in spite of the interruptions to which, as our readers must frequently have observed, the master of the house is often exposed in such cases. We will attempt to give them an idea of our meaning.

"When I was in Suffolk," said Mr. Gabriel Parsons——

"Take off the fowls first, Martha," said Mrs. Parsons. "I beg your pardon, my dear."

"When I was in Suffolk," resumed Mr. Parsons, with an impatient glance at his wife, who pretended not to observe it, "which is now some years ago, business led me to the town of Bury St. Edmund's. I had to stop at the principal places in my way, and therefore, for the sake of convenience, I travelled in a gig. I left Sudbury one dark night—it was winter time—about nine o'clock; the rain poured in torrents, the wind howled among the trees that skirted the road-side, and I was obliged to proceed at a foot-pace, for I could hardly see my hand before me, it was so dark——"

"John," interrupted Mrs. Parsons, in a low, hollow voice, "don't spill that gravy."

"Fanny," said Parsons impatiently, "I wish you'd defer these domestic reproofs to some more suitable time. Really, my dear, these constant interruptions are very annoying."

"My dear, I didn't interrupt you," said Mrs. Parsons.

"But, my dear, you *did* interrupt me," remonstrated Mr. Parsons.

"How very absurd you are, my love! I must give directions to the servants; I am quite sure that if I sat here and allowed John to spill the gravy over the new carpet, you'd be the first to find fault when you saw the stain to-morrow morning."

"Well," continued Gabriel, with a resigned air, as if he knew there was no getting over the point about the carpet, "I was just saying, it was so dark that I could hardly see my hand before me. The road was very lonely, and I assure you, Tottle (this was a device to arrest the wandering attention of that individual, which was distracted by a confidential communication between Mrs. Parsons and Martha, accompanied by the delivery of a large bunch of keys), I assure you, Tottle, I became somehow impressed with a sense of the loneliness of my situation——"

"Pie to your master," interrupted Mrs. Parsons, again directing the servant.

"Now, pray, my dear," remonstrated Parsons once more, very pettishly. Mrs. P. turned up her hands and eyebrows, and appealed in dumb show to Miss Lillerton. "As I turned a corner of the road," resumed Gabriel, "the horse stopped short, and reared tremendously. I pulled up, jumped out, ran to his head, and found a man lying on his back in the middle of the road, with his eyes fixed on the sky. I thought he was dead; but no, he was alive, and there appeared to be nothing the matter with him. He jumped up, and putting his hand to his chest, and fixing upon me the most earnest gaze you can imagine, exclaimed——"

"Pudding here," said Mrs. Parsons.

"Oh! it's no use," exclaimed the host, now rendered desperate. "Here, Tottle; a glass of wine. It's useless to attempt relating anything when Mrs. Parsons is present."

This attack was received in the usual way. Mrs. Parsons talked *to* Miss Lillerton and *at* her better half; expatiated on the impatience of men generally; hinted that her husband was peculiarly vicious in this respect, and wound up by insinuating that she must be one of the best tempers that ever existed, or she never could put up with it. Really what she had to endure sometimes, was more than any one who saw her in every-day life could by possibility suppose.—The story was now a painful subject, and therefore Mr. Parsons declined to enter into any details, and contented himself by stating that the man was a maniac, who had escaped from a neighbouring mad-house.

The cloth was removed; the ladies soon afterwards retired, and Miss Lillerton played the piano in the drawing-room overhead, very loudly, for the edification of the visitor. Mr. Watkins Tottle and Mr. Gabriel Parsons sat chatting comfortably enough, until the conclusion of the second bottle, when the latter, in proposing an adjournment to the drawing-room, informed Watkins that he had concerted a plan with his wife, for leaving him and Miss Lillerton alone, soon after tea.

"I say," said Tottle, as they went up-stairs, "don't you think it would be better if we put it off till—till—to-morrow?"

"Don't *you* think it would have been much better if I had left you in that wretched hole I found you in this morning?" retorted Parsons bluntly.

"Well—well—I only made a suggestion," said poor Watkins Tottle, with a deep sigh.

Tea was soon concluded, and Miss Lillerton, drawing a small work-table on one side of the fire, and placing a little wooden frame upon it, something like a miniature clay-mill without the horse, was soon busily engaged in making a watch-guard with brown silk.

"God bless me!" exclaimed Parsons, starting up with well-feigned surprise, "I've forgotten those confounded letters. Tottle, I know you'll excuse me."

If Tottle had been a free agent, he would have allowed no one to leave the room on any pretence, except himself. As it was, however, he was obliged to look cheerful when Parsons quitted the apartment.

He had scarcely left, when Martha put her head into the room, with—"Please, ma'am, you're wanted."

Mrs. Parsons left the room, shut the door carefully after her, and Mr. Watkins Tottle was left alone with Miss Lillerton.

For the first five minutes there was a dead silence. Mr. Watkins Tottle was thinking how he should begin, and Miss Lillerton appeared to be thinking of nothing. The fire was burning low; Mr. Watkins Tottle stirred it, and put some coals on.

"Hem!" coughed Miss Lillerton; Mr. Watkins Tottle thought the fair creature had spoken. "I beg your pardon," said he.

"Eh?"

"I thought you spoke.'

"No."

"Oh!"

"There are some books on the sofa, Mr. Tottle, if you would like to look at them," said Miss Lillerton, after the lapse of another five minutes.

"No, thank you," returned Watkins: and then he added, with a courage which was perfectly astonishing, even to himself, "Madam, that is Miss Lillerton, I wish to speak to you."

"To me!" said Miss Lillerton, letting the silk drop from her hand, and sliding her chair back a few paces. "Speak— to me!"

"To you, madam—and on the subject of the state of your affections." The lady hastily rose, and would have left the room; but Mr. Watkins Tottle gently detained her by the hand, and holding it as far from him as the joint length of their arms would permit, he thus proceeded: "Pray do not misunderstand me, or suppose that I am led to address you, after so short an acquaintance, by any feeling of my own merits—for merits I have none which could give me a claim to your hand. I hope you will acquit me of any presumption when I explain that I have been acquainted through Mrs. Parsons, with the state—that is, that Mrs. Parsons has told me—at least, not Mrs. Parsons, but—" here Watkins began to wander, but Miss Lillerton relieved him.

"Am I to understand, Mr. Tottle, that Mrs. Parsons has acquainted you with my feeling—my affection—I mean my respect, for an individual of the opposite sex?"

"She has."

"Then, what," inquired Miss Lillerton, averting her face, with a girlish air, "what could induce *you* to seek such an interview as this? What can your object be? How can I promote your happiness, Mr. Tottle?"

Here was the time for a flourish. "By allowing me," replied Watkins, falling bump on his knees, and breaking two brace-buttons and a waistcoat-string, in the act—"by allowing me to be your slave, your servant—in short, by unreservedly making me the confidant of your heart's feelings —may I say, for the promotion of your own happiness—may I say, in order that you may become the wife of a kind and affectionate husband?"

"Disinterested creature!" exclaimed Miss Lillerton, hiding her face in a white pocket-handkerchief with an eyelet-hole border.

Mr. Watkins Tottle thought that if the lady knew all,

she might possibly alter her opinion on this last point. He raised the tip of her middle finger ceremoniously to his lips, and got off his knees as gracefully as he could. "My information was correct?" he tremulously inquired, when he was once more on his feet.

"It was." Watkins elevated his hands, and looked up to the ornament in the centre of the ceiling, which had been made for a lamp, by way of expressing his rapture.

"Our situation, Mr. Tottle," resumed the lady, glancing at him through one of the eyelet-holes, "is a most peculiar and delicate one."

"It is," said Mr. Tottle.

"Our acquaintance has been of *so* short duration," said Miss Lillerton.

"Only a week," assented Watkins Tottle.

"Oh! more than that," exclaimed the lady, in a tone of surprise.

"Indeed!" said Tottle.

"More than a month—more than two months!" said Miss Lillerton.

"Rather odd, this," thought Watkins.

"Oh!" he said, recollecting Parsons's assurance that she had known him from report, "I understand. But, my dear madam, pray consider. The longer this acquaintance has existed, the less reason is there for delay now. Why not at once fix a period for gratifying the hopes of your devoted admirer?"

"It has been represented to me again and again that this is the course I ought to pursue," replied Miss Lillerton; "but pardon my feelings of delicacy, Mr. Tottle—pray excuse this embarrassment—I have peculiar ideas on such subjects, and I am quite sure that I never could summon up fortitude enough to name the day to my future husband."

"Then allow *me* to name it," said Tottle eagerly.

"I should like to fix it myself," replied Miss Lillerton, bashfully, "but I cannot do so without at once resorting to a third party."

"A third party!" thought Watkins Tottle; "who the deuce is that to be, I wonder!"

"Mr. Tottle," continued Miss Lillerton, "you have made me a most disinterested and kind offer—that offer I accept. Will you at once be the bearer of a note from me to—to Mr. Timson?"

"Mr. Timson!" said Watkins.

"After what has passed between us," responded Miss Lillerton, still averting her head, "you must understand whom I mean; Mr. Timson, the—the—clergyman."

"Mr. Timson, the clergyman!" ejaculated Watkins Tottle, in a state of inexpressible beatitude, and positive wonder at his own success. "Angel! Certainly—this moment!"

"I'll prepare it immediately," said Miss Lillerton, making for the door; "the events of this day have flurried me so much, Mr. Tottle, that I shall not leave my room again this evening; I will send you the note by the servant."

"Stay—stay," cried Watkins Tottle, still keeping a most respectful distance from the lady; "when shall we meet again?"

"Oh! Mr. Tottle," replied Miss Lillerton, coquettishly, "when *we* are married, I can never see you too often, nor thank you too much;" and she left the room.

Mr. Watkins Tottle flung himself into an arm-chair, and indulged in the most delicious reveries of future bliss, in which the idea of "Five hundred pounds per annum, with an uncontrolled power of disposing of it by her last will and testament," was somehow or other the foremost. He had gone through the interview so well, and it had terminated so admirably, that he almost began to wish he had expressly stipulated for the settlement of the annual five hundred on himself.

"May I come in?" said Mr. Gabriel Parsons, peeping in at the door.

"You may," replied Watkins.

"Well, have you done it?" anxiously inquired Gabriel.

"Have I done it!" said Watkins Tottle. "Hush—I'm going to the clergyman."

"No!" said Parsons. "How well you have managed it!"

"Where does Timson live?" inquired Watkins.

"At his uncle's," replied Gabriel, "just round the lane. He's waiting for a living, and has been assisting his uncle here for the last two or three months. But how well you have done it—I didn't think you could have carried it off so!"

Mr. Watkins Tottle was proceeding to demonstrate that the Richardsonian principle was the best on which love could possibly be made, when he was interrupted by the entrance of Martha, with a little pink note folded like a fancy cocked-hat.

"Miss Lillerton's compliments," said Martha, as she delivered it into Tottle's hands, and vanished.

"Do you observe the delicacy?" said Tottle, appealing to Mr. Gabriel Parsons. "*Compliments* not *love*, by the servant, eh?"

Mr. Gabriel Parsons didn't exactly know what reply to make, so he poked the forefinger of his right hand between the third and fourth ribs of Mr. Watkins Tottle.

"Come," said Watkins, when the explosion of mirth, consequent on this practical jest, had subsided, "we'll be off at once—let's lose no time."

"Capital!" echoed Gabriel Parsons; and in five minutes they were at the garden-gate of the villa tenanted by the uncle of Mr. Timson.

"Is Mr. Charles Timson at home?" inquired Mr. Watkins Tottle of Mr. Charles Timson's uncle's man.

"Mr. Charles *is* at home," replied the man, stammering; "but he desired me to say he couldn't be interrupted, sir, by any of the parishioners."

"*I* am not a parishioner," replied Watkins.

"Is Mr. Charles writing a sermon, Tom?" inquired Parsons, thrusting himself forward.

"No, Mr. Parsons, sir; he's not exactly writing a sermon, but he is practising the violoncello in his own bedroom, and gave strict orders not to be disturbed."

"Say I'm here," replied Gabriel, leading the way across the garden; "Mr. Parsons and Mr. Tottle, on private and particular business."

They were shown into the parlour, and the servant departed to deliver his message. The distant groaning of the violoncello ceased; footsteps were heard on the stairs; and Mr. Timson presented himself, and shook hands with Parsons with the utmost cordiality.

"How do you do, sir?" said Watkins Tottle, with great solemnity.

"How do *you* do, sir?" replied Timson, with as much coldness as if it were a matter of perfect indifference to him how he did, as it very likely was.

"I beg to deliver this note to you," said Watkins Tottle, producing the cocked-hat.

"From Miss Lillerton!" said Timson, suddenly changing colour. "Pray sit down."

Mr. Watkins Tottle sat down; and while Timson perused the note, fixed his eyes on an oyster-sauce-coloured portrait of the Archbishop of Canterbury, which hung over the fireplace.

Mr. Timson rose from his seat when he had concluded the note, and looked dubiously at Parsons. "May I ask," he inquired, appealing to Watkins Tottle, "whether our friend here is acquainted with the object of your visit?"

"Our friend is in *my* confidence," replied Watkins, with considerable importance.

"Then, sir," said Timson, seizing both Tottle's hands, "allow me in his presence to thank you, most unfeignedly and cordially, for the noble part you have acted in this affair."

"He thinks I recommended him," thought Tottle. "Confound these fellows! they never think of anything but their fees."

"I deeply regret having misunderstood your intentions, my dear sir," continued Timson. "Disinterested and manly indeed! There are very few men who would have acted as you have done."

Mr. Watkins Tottle could not help thinking that this last remark was anything but complimentary. He therefore inquired, rather hastily, "When is it to be?"

"On Thursday," replied Timson—"on Thursday morning at half-past eight."

"Uncommonly early," observed Watkins Tottle, with an air of triumphant self-denial. "I shall hardly be able to get down here by that hour." (This was intended for a joke.)

"Never mind, my dear fellow," replied Timson, all suavity, shaking hands with Tottle again most heartily, "so long as we see you to breakfast, you know——"

"Eh!" said Parsons, with one of the most extraordinary expressions of countenance that ever appeared in a human face.

"What!" ejaculated Watkins Tottle, at the same moment.

"I say that so long as we see you to breakfast," repeated Timson, "we will excuse your being absent from the ceremony, though of course your presence at it would give us the utmost pleasure."

Mr. Watkins Tottle staggered against the wall, and fixed his eyes on Timson with appalling perseverance.

"Timson," said Parsons, hurriedly brushing his hat with his left arm, "when you say 'us,' whom do you mean?"

Mr. Timson looked foolish in his turn, when he replied, "Why—Mrs. Timson that will be this day week: Miss Lillerton that is——"

"Now don't stare at that idiot in the corner," angrily exclaimed Parsons, as the extraordinary convulsions of Watkins Tottle's countenance excited the wondering gaze of Timson,—"but have the goodness to tell me in three words the contents of that note."

"This note," replied Timson, "is from Miss Lillerton, to whom I have been for the last five weeks regularly engaged. Her singular scruples and strange feeling on some points have hitherto prevented my bringing the engagement to that termination which I so anxiously desire. She informs me here, that she sounded Mrs. Parsons with the view of making her her confidante and go-between, that Mrs. Parsons informed this elderly gentleman, Mr. Tottle, of the circumstance, and that he, in the most kind and delicate terms, offered to assist us in any way, and even undertook to convey this note, which contains the promise I have long sought in vain—an act of kindness for which I can never be sufficiently grateful."

"Good-night, Timson," said Parsons, hurrying off, and carrying the bewildered Tottle with him.

"Won't you stay—and have something?" said Timson.

"No, thank ye," replied Parsons, "I've had quite enough."

And away he went, followed by Watkins Tottle in a state of stupefaction.

Mr. Gabriel Parsons whistled until they had walked some quarter of a mile past his own gate, when he suddenly stopped, and said:

"You are a clever fellow, Tottle, ain't you?"

"I don't know," said the unfortunate Watkins.

"I suppose you'll say this is Fanny's fault, won't you?" inquired Gabriel.

"I don't know anything about it," replied the bewildered Tottle.

"Well," said Parsons, turning on his heel to go home, "the next time you make an offer, you had better speak plainly, and don't throw a chance away. And the next time you're locked up in a sponging-house, just wait there till I come and take you out, there's a good fellow."

How, or at what hour, Mr. Watkins Tottle returned to Cecil Street is unknown. His boots were seen outside his bedroom-door next morning, but we have the authority of his landlady for stating that he neither emerged therefrom, nor accepted sustenance for four-and-twenty hours. At the expiration of that period, and when a council of war was being held in the kitchen on the propriety of summoning the parochial beadle to break his door open, he rang his bell, and demanded a cup of milk-and-water. The next morning he went through the formalities of eating and drinking as usual, but a week afterwards he was seized with a relapse, while perusing the list of marriages in a morning paper, from which he never perfectly recovered.

A few weeks after the last-named occurrence, the body of a gentleman unknown, was found in the Regent's Canal. In the trousers-pockets were four shillings and threepence halfpenny; a matrimonial advertisement from a lady, which appeared to have been cut out of a Sunday paper; a toothpick, and a card-case, which it is confidently believed would have led to the identification of the unfortunate gentleman, but for the circumstance of there being none but blank cards in it. Mr. Watkins Tottle absented himself from his lodgings shortly before. A bill which has not been taken up was presented next morning; and a bill which has not been taken down was soon afterwards affixed in his parlour-window.

CHAPTER XI: *The Bloomsbury Christening*

[The author may be permitted to observe that this sketch was published some time before the Farce entitled "The Christening" was first represented.]

MR. NICODEMUS DUMPS, or, as his acquaintance called him, "long Dumps," was a bachelor, six feet high, and fifty years old; cross, cadaverous, odd, and ill-natured. He was never happy but when he was miserable; and always miserable when he had the best reason to be happy. The only real comfort of his existence was to make everybody about him wretched—then he might be truly said to enjoy life. He was afflicted with a situation in the Bank worth five hundred a year, and he rented a "first-floor furnished," at Pentonville, which he originally took because it commanded a dismal prospect of an adjacent churchyard. He was familiar with the face of every tombstone, and the burial service seemed to excite his strongest sympathy. His friends said he was surly —he insisted he was nervous; they thought him a lucky dog, but he protested that he was "the most unfortunate man in the world." Cold as he was, and wretched as he declared himself to be, he was not wholly unsusceptible of attachments. He revered the memory of Hoyle, as he was himself an admirable and imperturbable whist-player, and he chuckled with delight at a fretful and impatient adversary. He adored King Herod for his massacre of the innocents; and if he hated one thing more than another, it was a child. However, he could hardly be said to hate anything in particular, because he disliked everything in general; but perhaps his greatest antipathies were cabs, old women, doors that would not shut, musical amateurs, and omnibus cads. He subscribed to the Society for the Suppression of Vice for the pleasure of putting a stop to any harmless amusements; and he contributed largely towards the support of two itinerant Methodist parsons, in the amiable hope that if circumstances rendered any people happy in this world, they might perchance be rendered miserable by fears for the next.

Mr. Dumps had a nephew who had been married about a year, and who was somewhat of a favourite with his uncle, because he was an admirable subject to exercise his misery-creating powers upon. Mr. Charles Kitterbell was a small, sharp, spare man, with a very large head, and a broad, good-humoured countenance. He looked like a faded giant, with the head and face partially restored; and he had a cast in his eye which rendered it quite impossible for any one with whom he conversed to know where he was looking. His eyes appeared fixed on the wall, and he was staring you out of countenance; in short, there was no catching his eye, and perhaps it is a merciful dispensation of Providence that such eyes are not catching. In addition to these characteristics, it may be added that Mr. Charles Kitterbell was one of the most credulous and matter-of-fact little personages that ever took *to* himself a wife, and *for* himself a house in Great Russell Street, Bedford Square. (Uncle Dumps always dropped the "Bedford Square," and inserted in lieu thereof the dreadful words "Tottenham Court Road.")

"No, but uncle, 'pon my life you must—you must promise to be godfather," said Mr. Kitterbell, as he sat in conversation with his respected relative one morning.

"I cannot, indeed I cannot," returned Dumps.

"Well, but why not? Jemima will think it very unkind. It's very little trouble."

"As to the trouble," rejoined the most unhappy man in existence, "I don't mind that; but my nerves are in that state—I cannot go through the ceremony. You know I don't like going out.—For God's sake, Charles, don't fidget with that stool so, you'll drive me mad." Mr. Kitterbell, quite regardless of his uncle's nerves, had occupied himself for some ten minutes in describing a circle on the floor with one leg of the office-stool on which he was seated, keeping the other three up in the air, and holding fast on by the desk.

"I beg your pardon, uncle," said Kitterbell, quite abashed, suddenly releasing his hold of the desk, and bringing the three wandering legs back to the floor, with a force sufficient to drive them through it.

"But come, don't refuse. If it's a boy, you know, we must have two godfathers."

"*If* it's a boy!" said Dumps, "why can't you say at once whether it *is* a boy or not?"

"I should be very happy to tell you, but it's impossible I can undertake to say whether it's a girl or a boy, if the child isn't born yet."

"Not born yet!" echoed Dumps, with a gleam of hope lighting up his lugubrious visage. "Oh, well, it *may* be a girl, and then you won't want me, or if it is a boy, it *may* die before it is christened."

"I hope not," said the father that expected to be, looking very grave.

"I hope not," acquiesced Dumps, evidently pleased with the subject. He was beginning to get happy. "*I* hope not, but distressing cases frequently occur during the first two or three days of a child's life; fits, I am told, are exceedingly common, and alarming convulsions are almost matters of course."

"Lord, uncle!" ejaculated little Kitterbell, gasping for breath.

"Yes; my landlady was confined—let me see—last Tuesday: an uncommonly fine boy. On the Thursday night the nurse was sitting with him upon her knee before the fire, and he was as well as possible. Suddenly he became black in the face, and alarmingly spasmodic. The medical man was instantly sent for, and every remedy was tried, but——"

"How frightful!" interrupted the horror-stricken Kitterbell.

"The child died of course. However your child *may* not die, and if it should be a boy, and should *live* to be christened, why I suppose I must be one of the sponsors." Dumps was evidently good-natured on the faith of his anticipations.

"Thank you, uncle," said his agitated nephew, grasping his hand as warmly as if he had done him some essential service. "Perhaps I had better not tell Mrs. K. what you have mentioned."

"Why, if she's low spirited, perhaps you had better not mention the melancholy case to her," returned Dumps, who of course had invented the whole story, "though perhaps it would be but doing your duty as a husband to prepare her for the *worst.*"

A day or two afterwards, as Dumps was perusing a morning paper at the chop-house which he regularly frequented, the following paragraph met his eyes:

Births.—On Saturday, the 18th inst., in Great Russell Street, the lady of Charles Kitterbell, Esq., of a son."

"It *is* a boy!" he exclaimed, dashing down the paper to the astonishment of the waiters. "It *is* a boy!" But he speedily regained his composure as his eye rested on a paragraph quoting the number of infant deaths from the bills of mortality.

Six weeks passed away, and as no communication had been received from the Kitterbells, Dumps was beginning to flatter himself that the child was dead, when the following note painfully resolved his doubts:

GREAT RUSSELL STREET,
Monday morning.

DEAR UNCLE,

You will be delighted to hear that my dear Jemima has left her room, and that your future godson is getting on capitally. He was very thin at first, but he is getting much larger, and nurse says he is filling out every day. He cries a good deal, and is a very singular colour, which made Jemima and me rather uncomfortable ; but as nurse says it's natural, and as of course we know nothing about these things yet, we are quite satisfied with what nurse says. We think he will be a sharp child ; and nurse says she's sure he will, because he never goes to sleep. You will readily believe that we are all very happy, only we're a little worn out for want of rest, as he keeps us awake all night ; but this we must expect, nurse says, for the first six or eight months. He has been vaccinated, but in consequence of the operation being rather awkwardly performed, some small particles of glass were introduced into the arm with the matter. Perhaps this may in some degree account for his being rather fractious ; at least, so nurse says. We propose to have him christened at twelve o'clock on Friday, at Saint George's Church, in Hart Street, by the name of Frederick Charles William. Pray don't be later than a quarter before twelve. We shall have a very few friends in the evening, when of course we shall see you. I am sorry to say that the dear boy appears rather restless and uneasy to-day ; the cause, I fear, is fever.

> *Believe me, dear Uncle,*
> *Yours affectionately,*
> CHARLES KITTERBELL.

P.S.—I open this note to say that we have just discovered the cause of little Frederick's restlessness. It is not fever, as I apprehended, but a small pin, which nurse accidentally stuck in his leg yesterday evening. We have taken it out, and he appears more composed, though he still sobs a good deal.

It is almost unnecessary to say that the perusal of the above interesting statement was no great relief to the mind of the hypochondriacal Dumps. It was impossible to recede, however, and so he put the best face—that is to say, an uncommonly miserable one—upon the matter; and purchased a handsome silver mug for the infant Kitterbell, upon which he ordered the initials "F. C. W. K.," with the customary untrained grape-vine-looking flourishes, and a large full stop, to be engraved forthwith.

Monday was a fine day, Tuesday was delightful, Wednesday was equal to either, and Thursday was finer than ever; four successive fine days in London! Hackney-coachmen became revolutionary, and crossing-sweepers began to doubt the existence of a First Cause. The *Morning Herald* informed its readers that an old woman in Camden Town had been heard to say that the fineness of the season was "unprecedented in the memory of the oldest inhabitant;" and Islington clerks, with large families and small salaries, left off their black gaiters, disdained to carry their once green cotton umbrellas, and walked to town in the conscious pride of white stockings and cleanly brushed Bluchers. Dumps beheld all this with an eye of supreme contempt—his triumph was at hand. He knew that if it had been fine for four weeks instead of four days, it would rain when he went out; he was lugubriously happy in the conviction that Friday would be a wretched day —and so it was. "I knew how it would be," said Dumps, as he turned round opposite the Mansion House at half-past eleven o'clock on the Friday morning. "I knew how it would be; *I* am concerned, and that's enough." And certainly the appearance of the day was sufficient to depress the spirits of a much more buoyant-hearted individual than himself. It had rained, without a moment's cessation, since eight o'clock; everybody that passed up Cheapside, and down Cheapside, looked wet, cold, and dirty. All sorts of forgotten and long-concealed umbrellas had been put into requisition. Cabs whisked about, with the "fare" as carefully boxed up behind two glazed calico curtains as any mysterious picture in any one of Mrs. Radcliffe's castles; omnibus horses smoked like steam-engines; nobody thought of "standing up" under door-ways or arches; they were painfully convinced it was a hopeless case; and so everybody went hastily along, jumping and jostling, and swearing and perspiring, and slipping about, like amateur skaters behind wooden chairs on the Serpentine on a frosty Sunday.

Dumps paused; he could not think of walking, being rather smart for the christening. If he took a cab he was sure to be spilt, and a hackney-coach was too expensive for his economical ideas. An omnibus was waiting at the opposite corner—it was a desperate case—he had never heard of an omnibus upsetting or running away, and if the cad did knock him down, he could "pull him up" in return.

"Now, sir!" cried the young gentleman who officiated as "cad" to the "Lads of the Village," which was the name of the machine just noticed. Dumps crossed.

"This vay, sir!" shouted the driver of the "Hark-away," pulling up his vehicle immediately across the door of the opposition—"this vay, sir—he's full." Dumps hesitated, whereupon the "Lads of the Village" commenced pouring out a torrent of abuse against the "Hark-away"; but the con-ductor of the "Admiral Napier" settled the contest in a most satisfactory manner for all parties, by seizing Dumps round the waist, and thrusting him into the middle of his vehicle which had just come up and only wanted the sixteenth inside.

"All right," said the "Admiral," and off the thing thundered, like a fire-engine at full gallop, with the kidnapped customer inside, standing in the position of a half doubled-up bootjack, and falling about with every jerk of the machine, first on one side and then on the other, like a "Jack-in-the-Green," on May-day, setting to the lady with a brass ladle.

"For Heaven's sake, where am I to sit?" inquired the miserable man of an old gentleman, into whose stomach he had just fallen for the fourth time.

"Anywhere but on my *chest*, sir," replied the old gentleman, in a surly tone.

"Perhaps the *box* would suit the gentleman better," sug-gested a very damp lawyer's clerk, in a pink shirt, and a smirking countenance.

After a great deal of struggling and falling about, Dumps at last managed to squeeze himself into a seat, which, in addition to the slight disadvantage of being between a window that would not shut, and a door that must be open, placed him in close contact with a passenger, who had been walking about all the morning without an umbrella, and who looked as if he had spent the day in a full water-butt—only wetter.

"Don't bang the door so," said Dumps to the conductor, as he shut it, after letting out four of the passengers; "I am very nervous—it destroys me."

"Did any gen'l'm'n say anythink?" replied the cad, thrusting in his head, and trying to look as if he didn't understand the request.

"I told you not to bang the door so!" repeated Dumps, with an expression of countenance like the knave of clubs in convulsions.

"Oh! vy, it's rather a sing'ler circumstance about this here door, sir, that it von't shut without banging," replied the conductor; and he opened the door very wide, and shut it with a terrific bang, in proof of the assertion.

"I beg your pardon, sir," said a little prim, wheezing old gentleman, sitting opposite Dumps, "I beg your pardon; but have you ever observed, when you have been in an omnibus on a wet day, that four people out of five always come in with large cotton umbrellas, without a handle at the top, or the brass spike at the bottom?"

"Why, sir," returned Dumps, as he heard the clock strike twelve, "it never struck me before; but now you mention it, I—Hollo! hollo!" shouted the persecuted individual, as the omnibus dashed past Drury Lane, where he had directed to be set down. "Where is the cad?"

"I think he's on the box, sir," said the young gentleman before noticed in the pink shirt, which looked like a white one ruled with red ink.

"I want to be set down!" said Dumps, in a faint voice, overcome by his previous efforts.

"I think these cads want to be *set down*," returned the attorney's clerk, chuckling at his sally.

"Hollo!" cried Dumps again.

"Hollo!" echoed the passengers. The omnibus passed St. Giles's Church.

"Hold hard!" said the conductor; "I'm blowed if we hain't forgot the gen'l'm'n as vas to be set down at Doory Lane.— Now, sir, make haste, if you please," he added, opening the door, and assisting Dumps out with as much coolness as if it was "all right." Dumps's indignation was for once getting the better of his cynical equanimity. "Drury Lane!" he gasped, with the voice of a boy in a cold bath for the first time.

"Doory Lane, sir?—yes, sir,—third turning on the right-hand side, sir."

Dumps's passion was paramount; he clutched his umbrella, and was striding off with the firm determination of not paying the fare. The cad, by a remarkable coincidence, happened to entertain a directly contrary opinion, and Heaven knows how far the altercation would have proceeded, if it had not been most ably and satisfactorily brought to a close by the driver.

"Hollo!" said that respectable person, standing up on the box, and leaning with one hand on the roof of the omnibus. "Hollo, Tom! tell the gentleman if so be as he feels aggrieved, we will take him up to the Edge-er (Edgware) Road for nothing, and set him down at Doory Lane when we comes back. He can't reject that, anyhow."

The argument was irresistible: Dumps paid the disputed sixpence, and in a quarter of an hour was on the staircase of No. 14, Great Russell Street.

Everything indicated that preparations were making for the reception of "a few friends" in the evening. Two dozen extra tumblers, and four ditto wine-glasses—looking anything but transparent, with little bits of straw in them—were on the slab in the passage, just arrived. There was a great smell of nutmeg, port wine, and almonds, on the staircase; the covers were taken off the stair-carpet, and the figure of Venus on the first landing looked as if she were ashamed of the composition-candle in her right hand, which contrasted beautifully with the lamp-blacked drapery of the goddess of love. The female servant (who looked very warm and bustling) ushered Dumps into a front drawing-room, very prettily furnished, with a plentiful sprinkling of little baskets, paper table-mats, china watchmen, pink and gold albums, and rainbow-bound little books on the different tables.

"Ah, uncle!" said Mr. Kitterbell, "how d'ye do? Allow me —Jemima, my dear—my uncle. I think you've seen Jemima before, sir?"

"Have had the *pleasure*," returned big Dumps, his tone and look making it doubtful whether in his life he had ever experienced the sensation.

"I'm sure," said Mrs. Kitterbell, with a languid smile, and a slight cough, "I'm sure—hem—any friend—of Charles's—hem—much less a relation, is——"

"I knew you'd say so, my love," said little Kitterbell, who, while he appeared to be gazing on the opposite houses, was looking at his wife with a most affectionate air. "Bless you!" The last two words were accompanied with a simper, and a squeeze of the hand, which stirred up all Uncle Dumps's bile.

"Jane, tell nurse to bring down baby," said Mrs. Kitterbell, addressing the servant. Mrs. Kitterbell was a tall, thin young lady, with very light hair, and a particularly white face—one of those young women who almost invariably, though one hardly knows why, recall to one's mind the idea of a cold fillet of veal.	Out went the servant, and in came the nurse, with a remarkably small parcel in her arms, packed up in a blue mantle trimmed with white fur.	This was the baby.

"Now, uncle," said Mr. Kitterbell, lifting up that part of the mantle which covered the infant's face, with an air of great triumph, "*who* do you think he's like?"

"He! he! Yes, who?" said Mrs. K., putting her arm through her husband's, and looking up into Dumps's face with an expression of as much interest as she was capable of displaying.

"Good God, how small he is!" cried the amiable uncle, starting back with well-feigned surprise; "*remarkably* small indeed."

"Do you think so?" inquired poor little Kitterbell, rather alarmed.	"He's a monster to what he was—ain't he, nurse?"

"He's a dear," said the nurse, squeezing the child, and evading the question—not because she scrupled to disguise the fact, but because she couldn't afford to throw away the chance of Dumps's half-crown.

"Well, but who is he like?" inquired little Kitterbell.

Dumps looked at the little pink heap before him, and only thought at the moment of the best mode of mortifying the youthful parents.

"I really don't know *who* he's like," he answered, very well knowing the reply expected of him.

"Don't you think he's like *me*?" inquired his nephew, with a knowing air.

"Oh, *decidedly* not!" returned Dumps, with an emphasis not to be misunderstood.	"Decidedly not like you.	Oh, certainly not."

"Like Jemima?" asked Kitterbell, faintly.

"Oh dear, no; not in the least.	I'm no judge, of course, in such cases; but I really think he's more like one of those little carved representations that one sometimes sees blowing a trumpet on a tombstone!"	The nurse stooped down over the child, and with great difficulty prevented an explosion of mirth. Pa and ma looked almost as miserable as their amiable uncle.

"Well!" said the disappointed little father, "you'll be better able to tell what he's like by-and-by.	You shall see him this evening with his mantle off."

"Thank you," said Dumps, feeling particularly grateful.

"Now, my love," said Kitterbell to his wife, "it's time we were off.	We're to meet the other godfather and the godmother at the church, uncle,—Mr. and Mrs. Wilson from over the way—uncommonly nice people.	My love, are you well wrapped up?"

"Yes, dear."

"Are you sure you won't have another shawl?" inquired the anxious husband.

"No, sweet," returned the charming mother, accepting Dumps's proffered arm; and the little party entered the hackney-coach that was to take them to the church; Dumps amusing Mrs. Kitterbell by expatiating largely on the danger of measles, thrush, teeth-cutting, and other interesting diseases to which children are subject.

The ceremony (which occupied about five minutes) passed off without anything particular occurring. The clergyman had to dine some distance from town, and had two churchings, three christenings, and a funeral to perform in something less than an hour. The godfathers and godmother, therefore, promised to renounce the devil and all his works—"and all that sort of thing," as little Kitterbell said—"in less than no time;" and, with the exception of Dumps nearly letting the child fall into the font when he handed it to the clergyman, the whole affair went off in the usual business-like and matter-of-course manner, and Dumps re-entered the Bank gates at two o'clock with a heavy heart, and the painful conviction that he was regularly booked for an evening party.

Evening came—and so did Dumps's pumps, black silk stockings, and white cravat which he had ordered to be forwarded, per boy, from Pentonville. The depressed godfather dressed himself at a friend's counting-house, from whence, with his spirits fifty degrees below proof, he sallied forth—as the weather had cleared up, and the evening was tolerably fine—to walk to Great Russell Street. Slowly he paced up Cheapside, Newgate Street, down Snow Hill, and up Holborn ditto, looking as grim as the figure-head of a man-of-war, and finding out fresh causes of misery at every step. As he was crossing the corner of Hatton Garden, a man apparently intoxicated, rushed against him, and would have knocked him down had he not been providentially caught by a very genteel young man who happened to be close to him at the time. The shock so disarranged Dumps's nerves, as well as his dress, that he could hardly stand. The gentleman took his arm, and in the kindest manner walked with him as far as Furnival's Inn. Dumps, for about the first time in his life, felt grateful and polite; and he and the gentlemanly-looking young man parted with mutual expressions of goodwill.

"There are at least some well-disposed men in the world," ruminated the misanthropical Dumps, as he proceeded towards his destination.

Rat—tat—ta-ra-ra-ra-ra-ra-rat—knocked a hackney-coachman at Kitterbell's door, in imitation of a gentleman's servant, just as Dumps reached it; and out came an old lady in a large toque, and an old gentleman in a blue coat, and three female copies of the old lady in pink dresses, and shoes to match.

"It's a large party," sighed the unhappy godfather, wiping the perspiration from his forehead, and leaning against the area-railings. It was some time before the miserable man could muster up courage to knock at the door, and when he did, the smart appearance of a neighbouring greengrocer (who had been hired to wait for seven and sixpence, and whose calves alone were worth double the money), the lamp in the passage, and the Venus on the landing, added to the hum of many voices, and the sound of a harp and two violins, painfully convinced him that his surmises were but too well founded.

"How are you?" said little Kitterbell, in a greater bustle than ever, bolting out of the little back parlour with a cork-screw in his hand, and various particles of sawdust, looking like so many inverted commas, on his inexpressibles.

"Good God!" said Dumps, turning into the aforesaid parlour to put his shoes on which he had brought in his coat-pocket, and still more appalled by the sight of seven fresh-drawn corks, and a corresponding number of decanters. "How many people are there up-stairs?"

"Oh, not above thirty-five. We've had the carpet taken up in the back drawing-room, and the piano and the card-tables are in the front. Jemima thought we'd better have a regular sit-down supper, in the front parlour, because of the speechifying, and all that. But, Lord! uncle, what's the matter?" continued the little man, as Dumps stood with one shoe on, rummaging his pockets with the most frightful distortion of visage. "What have you lost? Your pocket-book?"

"No," returned Dumps, diving first into one pocket and then into the other, and speaking in a voice like Desdemona with the pillow over her mouth.

"Your card-case? snuff-box? the key of your lodgings?" continued Kitterbell, pouring question on question with the rapidity of lightning.

"No! no!" ejaculated Dumps, still diving eagerly into his empty pocket.

"Not—not—the *mug* you spoke of this morning?"

"Yes, the *mug*!" replied Dumps, sinking into a chair.

"How *could* you have done it?" inquired Kitterbell. "Are you sure you brought it out?"

"Yes! yes! I see it all," said Dumps, starting up as the idea flashed across his mind; "miserable dog that I am—I was born to suffer. I see it all; it was the gentlemanly-looking young man!"

"Mr. Dumps!" shouted the greengrocer in a stentorian voice, as he ushered the somewhat recovered godfather into the drawing-room half an hour after the above declaration.

"Mr. Dumps!"—everybody looked at the door, and in came Dumps, feeling about as much out of place as a salmon might be supposed to be on a gravel-walk.

"Happy to see you again," said Mrs. Kitterbell, quite unconscious of the unfortunate man's confusion and misery; "you must allow me to introduce you to a few of our friends: my mamma, Mr. Dumps—my papa and sisters." Dumps seized the hand of the mother as warmly as if she was his own parent, bowed *to* the young ladies, and *against* a gentleman behind him, and took no notice whatever of the father, who had been bowing incessantly for three minutes and a quarter.

"Uncle," said little Kitterbell, after Dumps had been introduced to a select dozen or two, "you must let me lead you to the other end of the room, to introduce you to my friend Danton. Such a splendid fellow! I'm sure you'll like him —this way." Dumps followed as tractably as a tame bear.

Mr. Danton was a young man of about five-and-twenty, with a considerable stock of impudence, and a very small share of ideas: he was a great favourite, especially with young ladies of from sixteen to twenty-six years of age, both inclusive. He could imitate the French-horn to admiration, sang comic songs most inimitably, and had the most insinuating way of saying impertinent nothings to his doting female admirers. He had acquired, somehow or other, the reputation of being a great wit, and, accordingly whenever he opened his mouth, everybody who knew him laughed very heartily.

The introduction took place in due form. Mr. Danton bowed and twirled a lady's handkerchief, which he held in his hand, in a most comic way. Everybody smiled.

"Very warm," said Dumps, feeling it necessary to say something.

"Yes. It was warmer yesterday," returned the brilliant Mr. Danton.—A general laugh.

"I have great pleasure in congratulating you on your first appearance in the character of a father, sir," he continued, addressing Dumps—"godfather, I mean."—The young ladies were convulsed, and the gentlemen in ecstasies.

A general hum of admiration interrupted the conversation, and announced the entrance of nurse with the baby. An universal rush of the young ladies immediately took place. (Girls are always *so* fond of babies in company.)

"Oh, you dear!" said one.

"How sweet!" cried another, in a low tone of the most enthusiastic admiration.

"Heavenly!" added a third.

"Oh! what dear little arms!" said a fourth, holding up an arm and fist about the size and shape of the leg of a fowl cleanly picked.

"Did you ever!" said a little coquette with a large bustle, who looked like a French lithograph, appealing to a gentleman in three waistcoats—"did you ever!"

"Never, in my life," returned her admirer, pulling up his collar.

"Oh! *do* let me take it, nurse," cried another young lady. "The love!"

"Can it open its eyes, nurse?" inquired another, affecting the utmost innocence.—Suffice it to say, that the single ladies unanimously voted him an angel, and that the married ones, *nem. con.*, agreed that he was decidedly the finest baby they had ever beheld—except their own.

The quadrilles were resumed with great spirit. Mr. Danton was universally admitted to be beyond himself, several young ladies enchanted the company and gained admirers by singing "We met"—"I saw her at the Fancy Fair"—and other equally sentimental and interesting ballads. "The young men," as Mrs. Kitterbell said, "made themselves very agreeable;" the girls did not lose their opportunity; and the evening promised to go off excellently. Dumps didn't mind it: he had devised a plan for himself—a little bit of fun in his own way—and he was almost happy! He played a rubber and lost every point. Mr. Danton said he could not have lost every point, because he made a point of losing: everybody laughed tremendously. Dumps retorted with a better joke, and nobody smiled, with the exception of the host, who seemed to consider it his duty to laugh till he was black in the face, at everything. There was only one drawback— the musicians did not play with quite as much spirit as could have been wished. The cause, however, was satisfactorily explained; for it appeared on the testimony of a gentleman who had come up from Gravesend in the afternoon, that they had been engaged on board a steamer all day, and had played almost without cessation all the way to Gravesend, and all the way back again.

The "sit-down supper" was excellent; there were four barley-sugar temples on the table, which would have looked beautiful if they had not melted away when the supper began; and a water-mill, whose only fault was that instead of going round, it ran over the table-cloth. Then there were fowls, and tongue, and trifle, and sweets, and lobster salad, and potted beef—and everything. And little Kitterbell kept calling out for clean plates, and the clean plates did not come: and then the gentlemen who wanted the plates said they didn't mind, they'd take a lady's; and then Mrs. Kitterbell applauded their gallantry, and the greengrocer ran about till he thought his seven and sixpence was very hardly earned; and the young ladies didn't eat much for fear it shouldn't look romantic, and the married ladies ate as much as possible, for fear they shouldn't have enough; and a great deal of wine was drunk, and everybody talked and laughed considerably.

"Hush! hush!" said Mr. Kitterbell, rising and looking very important. "My love (this was addressed to his wife at the other end of the table), take care of Mrs. Maxwell, and your mamma, and the rest of the married ladies; the gentlemen will persuade the young ladies to fill their glasses, I am sure."

"Ladies and gentlemen," said long Dumps, in a very sepulchral voice and rueful accent, rising from his chair like the ghost in Don Juan, "will you have the kindness to charge your glasses? I am desirous of proposing a toast."

A dead silence ensued, and the glasses were filled—everybody looked serious.

"Ladies and gentlemen," slowly continued the ominous Dumps, "I"—(here Mr. Danton imitated two notes from the French-horn, in a very loud key, which electrified the nervous toast-proposer, and convulsed his audience).

"Order! order!" said little Kitterbell, endeavouring to suppress his laughter.

"Order!" said the gentlemen.

"Danton, be quiet," said a particular friend on the opposite side of the table.

"Ladies and gentlemen," resumed Dumps, somewhat recovered, and not much disconcerted, for he was always a pretty good hand at a speech: "In accordance with what is, I believe, the established usage on these occasions, I, as one of the godfathers of Master Frederick Charles William Kitterbell —(here the speaker's voice faltered, for he remembered the mug)—venture to rise to propose a toast. I need hardly say that it is the health and prosperity of that young gentleman, the particular event of whose early life we are here met to celebrate—(applause). Ladies and gentlemen, it is impossible to suppose that our friends here, whose sincere well-wishers we all are, can pass through life without some trials, considerable suffering, severe affliction, and heavy losses!"— Here the arch-traitor paused, and slowly drew forth a long white pocket-handkerchief—his example was followed by several ladies. "That these trials may be long spared them is my most earnest prayer, my most fervent wish (a distinct sob from the grandmother). I hope and trust, ladies and gentlemen, that the infant whose christening we have this evening met to celebrate, may not be removed from the arms of his parents by premature decay (several cambrics were in requisition): that his young and now *apparently* healthy form, may not be wasted by lingering disease. (Here Dumps cast a sardonic glance around, for a great sensation was manifest among the married ladies.) You, I

am sure, will concur with me in wishing that he may live to
be a comfort and a blessing to his parents. (Hear, hear!
and an audible sob from Mr. Kitterbell). But should he not
be what we could wish—should he forget in after-times the
duty which he owes to them—should they unhappily experience that distracting truth, 'how sharper than a serpent's
tooth it is to have a thankless child'"—Here Mrs. Kitterbell,
with her handkerchief to her eyes, and accompanied by
several ladies, rushed from the room, and went into violent
hysterics in the passage, leaving her better half in almost
as bad a condition, and a general impression in Dumps's
favour; for people like sentiment, after all.

It need hardly be added, that this occurrence quite put a
stop to the harmony of the evening. Vinegar, hartshorn, and
cold water, were now as much in request as negus, rout-cakes,
and *bon-bons* had been a short time before. Mrs. Kitterbell
was immediately conveyed to her apartment, the musicians
were silenced, flirting ceased, and the company slowly departed. Dumps left the house at the commencement of
the bustle, and walked home with a light step, and (for him)
a cheerful heart. His landlady, who slept in the next room,
has offered to make oath that she heard him laugh in his
peculiar manner, after he had locked his door. The assertion,
however, is so improbable, and bears on the face of it such
strong evidence of untruth, that it has never obtained
credence to this hour.

The family of Mr. Kitterbell has considerably increased
since the period to which we have referred; he has now two
sons and a daughter: and as he expects, at no distant period,
to have another addition to his blooming progeny, he is anxious
to secure an eligible godfather for the occasion. He is determined, however, to impose upon him two conditions. He
must bind himself, by a solemn obligation, not to make any
speech after supper; and it is indispensable that he should
be in no way connected with "the most miserable man in
the world."

CHAPTER XII: *The Drunkard's Death*

WE will be bold to say that there is scarcely a man in the
constant habit of walking, day after day, through any of
the crowded thoroughfares of London, who cannot recollect
among the people whom he "knows by sight," to use a
familiar phrase, some being of abject and wretched appearance
whom he remembers to have seen in a very different condition,
whom he has observed sinking lower and lower by almost
imperceptible degrees, and the shabbiness and utter destitution of whose appearance, at last, strike forcibly and painfully

upon him, as he passes by. Is there any man who has mixed much with society, or whose avocations have caused him to mingle, at one time or other, with a great number of people, who cannot call to mind the time when some shabby, miserable wretch, in rags and filth, who shuffles past him now in all the squalor of disease and poverty, was a respectable tradesman, or clerk, or a man following some thriving pursuit, with good prospects, and decent means;—or cannot any of our readers call to mind from among the list of their *quondam* acquaintance, some fallen and degraded man, who lingers about the pavement in hungry misery—from whom every one turns coldly away, and who preserves himself from sheer starvation, nobody knows how? Alas! such cases are of too frequent occurrence to be rare items in any man's experience; and but too often arise from one cause—drunkenness, that fierce rage for the slow, sure poison, that oversteps every other consideration: that casts aside wife, children, friends, happiness, and station; and hurries its victims madly on to degradation and death.

Some of these men have been impelled by misfortune and misery to the vice that has degraded them. The ruin of worldly expectations, the death of those they loved, the sorrow that slowly consumes, but will not break the heart, has driven them wild; and they present the hideous spectacle of madmen, slowly dying by their own hands. But, by far the greater part have wilfully, and with open eyes, plunged into the gulf from which the man who once enters it never rises more, but into which he sinks deeper and deeper down, until recovery is hopeless.

Such a man as this once stood by the bedside of his dying wife, while his children knelt around, and mingled low bursts of grief with their innocent prayers. The room was scantily and meanly furnished; and it needed but a glance at the pale form from which the light of life was fast passing away, to know that grief, and want, and anxious care, had been busy at the heart for many a weary year. An elderly female, with her face bathed in tears, was supporting the head of the dying woman—her daughter—on her arm. But it was not towards her that the wan face turned; it was not her hand that the cold and trembling fingers clasped; they pressed the husband's arm; the eyes so soon to be closed in death rested on his face, and the man shook beneath their gaze. His dress was slovenly and disordered, his face inflamed, his eyes bloodshot and heavy. He had been summoned from some wild debauch to the bed of sorrow and death.

A shaded lamp by the bed-side cast a dim light on the figures around, and left the remainder of the room in thick, deep shadow. The silence of night prevailed without the house, and the stillness of death was in the chamber. A watch hung over the mantelshelf; its low ticking was the only sound that broke the profound quiet, but it was a solemn one, for well they knew, who heard it, that before it had recorded the passing of another hour, it would beat the knell of a departed spirit.

It is a dreadful thing to wait and watch for the approach of death; to know that hope is gone, and recovery impossible; and to sit and count the dreary hours through long, long nights—such nights as only watchers by the bed of sickness know. It chills the blood to hear the dearest secrets of the heart, the pent-up, hidden secrets of many years, poured forth by the unconscious helpless being before you; and to think how little the reserve and cunning of a whole life will avail, when fever and delirium tear off the mask at last. Strange tales have been told in the wanderings of dying men; tales so full of guilt and crime, that those who stood by the sick person's couch have fled in horror and affright, lest they should be scared to madness by what they heard and saw; and many a wretch has died alone, raving of deeds the very name of which has driven the boldest man away.

But no such ravings were to be heard at the bed-side by which the children knelt. Their half-stifled sobs and moanings alone broke the silence of the lonely chamber. And when at last the mother's grasp relaxed, and, turning one look from the children to their father, she vainly strove to speak, and fell backward on the pillow, all was so calm and tranquil that she seemed to sink to sleep. They leant over her; they called upon her name, softly at first, and then in the loud and piercing tones of desperation. But there was no reply. They listened for her breath, but no sound came. They felt for the palpitation of the heart, but no faint throb responded to the touch. That heart was broken, and she was dead!

The husband sank into a chair by the bed-side, and clasped his hands upon his burning forehead. He gazed from child to child, but when a weeping eye met his, he quailed beneath its look. No word of comfort was whispered in his ear, no look of kindness lighted on his face. All shrank from and avoided him; and when at last he staggered from the room, no one sought to follow or console the widower.

The time had been when many a friend would have crowded round him in his affliction, and many a heartfelt condolence would have met him in his grief. Where were they now? One by one, friends, relations, the commonest acquaintance even, had fallen off from and deserted the drunkard. His wife alone had clung to him in good and evil, in sickness and poverty; and how had he rewarded her? He had reeled from the tavern to her bed-side in time to see her die.

He rushed from the house, and walked swiftly through the

streets. Remorse, fear, shame, all crowded on his mind. Stupefied with drink, and bewildered with the scene he had just witnessed, he re-entered the tavern he had quitted shortly before. Glass succeeded glass. His blood mounted, and his brain whirled round. Death! Every one must die, and why not *she*. She was too good for him; her relations had often told him so. Curses on them! Had they not deserted her, and left her to whine away the time at home? Well; she was dead, and happy perhaps. It was better as it was. Another glass—one more! Hurrah! It was a merry life while it lasted; and he would make the most of it.

Time went on; the three children who were left to him, grew up, and were children no longer. The father remained the same—poorer, shabbier, and more dissolute-looking, but the same confirmed and irreclaimable drunkard. The boys had, long ago, run wild in the streets, and left him; the girl alone remained, but she worked hard, and words or blows could always procure him something for the tavern. So he went on in the old course, and a merry life he led.

One night, as early as ten o'clock—for the girl had been sick for many days, and there was, consequently, little to spend at the public-house—he bent his steps homewards, bethinking himself that if he would have her able to earn money, it would be as well to apply to the parish surgeon, or, at all events, to take the trouble of inquiring what ailed her, which he had not yet thought it worth while to do. It was a wet December night; the wind blew piercing cold, and the rain poured heavily down. He begged a few halfpence from a passer-by, and having bought a small loaf (for it was his interest to keep the girl alive, if he could), he shuffled onwards as fast as the wind and rain would let him.

At the back of Fleet Street, and lying between it and the water-side, are several mean and narrow courts, which form a portion of Whitefriars; it was to one of these that he directed his steps.

The alley into which he turned, might, for filth and misery, have competed with the darkest corner of this ancient sanctuary in its dirtiest and most lawless time. The houses, varying from two stories in height to four, were stained with every indescribable hue that long exposure to the weather, damp, and rottenness can impart to tenements composed originally of the roughest and coarsest materials. The windows were patched with paper, and stuffed with the foulest rags; the doors were falling from their hinges; poles with lines on which to dry clothes, projected from every casement, and sounds of quarrelling or drunkenness issued from every room.

The solitary oil lamp in the centre of the court had been blown out, either by the violence of the wind or the act of some inhabitant who had excellent reasons for objecting to his residence being rendered too conspicuous: and the only light which fell upon the broken and uneven pavement, was derived from the miserable candles that here and there twinkled in the rooms of such of the more fortunate residents as could afford to indulge in so expensive a luxury. A gutter ran down the centre of the alley—all the sluggish odours of which had been called forth by the rain; and as the wind whistled through the old houses, the doors and shutters creaked upon their hinges, and the windows shook in their frames, with a violence which every moment seemed to threaten the destruction of the whole place.

The man whom we have followed into his den, walked on in the darkness, sometimes stumbling into the main gutter, and at others into some branch repositories of garbage which had been formed by the rain, until he reached the last house in the court. The door, or rather what was left of it, stood ajar, for the convenience of the numerous lodgers; and he proceeded to grope his way up the old and broken stair, to the attic story.

He was within a step or two of his room door, when it opened, and a girl, whose miserable and emaciated appearance was only to be equalled by that of the candle which she shaded with her hand, peeped anxiously out.

"Is that you, father?" said the girl.

"Who else should it be?" replied the man gruffly. "What are you trembling at? It's little enough that I've had to drink to-day, for there's no drink without money, and no money without work. What the devil's the matter with the girl?"

"I am not well, father—not at all well," said the girl, bursting into tears.

"Ah!" replied the man, in the tone of a person who is compelled to admit a very unpleasant fact, to which he would rather remain blind, if he could. "You must get better somehow, for we must have money. You must go to the parish doctor, and make him give you some medicine. They're paid for it, damn 'em. What are you standing before the door for? Let me come in, can't you?"

"Father," whispered the girl, shutting the door behind her, and placing herself before it, "William has come back."

"Who!" said the man, with a start.

"Hush," replied the girl. "William; brother William."

"And what does he want?" said the man, with an effort at composure—"money? meat? drink? He's come to the wrong shop for that, if he does. Give me the candle—give me the candle, fool—I ain't going to hurt him." He snatched the candle from her hand, and walked into the room.

Sitting on an old box, with his head resting on his hand, and his eyes fixed on a wretched cinder fire that was smouldering on the hearth, was a young man of about two-and-twenty, miserably clad in an old coarse jacket and trousers. He started up when his father entered.

"Fasten the door, Mary," said the young man hastily— "fasten the door. You look as if you didn't know me, father. It's long enough since you drove me from home; you may well forget me."

"And what do you want here, now?" said the father, seating himself on a stool, on the other side of the fireplace. "What do you want here, now?"

"Shelter," replied the son. "I'm in trouble; that's enough. If I'm caught I shall swing; that's certain. Caught I shall be, unless I stop here; that's *as* certain. And there's an end of it."

"You mean to say, you've been robbing, or murdering, then?" said the father.

"Yes, I do," replied the son. "Does it surprise you, father?" He looked steadily in the man's face, but he withdrew his eyes and bent them on the ground.

"Where's your brothers?" he said, after a long pause.

"Where they'll never trouble you," replied his son: "John's gone to America, and Henry's dead."

"Dead!" said the father, with a shudder, which even he could not repress.

"Dead," replied the young man. "He died in my arms— shot like a dog, by a gamekeeper. He staggered back, I caught him, and his blood trickled down my hands. It poured out from his side like water. He was weak, and it blinded him, but he threw himself down on his knees, on the grass, and prayed to God, that if his mother was in heaven, He would hear her prayers for pardon for her youngest son. 'I was her favourite boy, Will,' he said, 'and I am glad to think, now, that when she was dying, though I was a very young child then, and my little heart was almost bursting, I knelt down at the foot of the bed, and thanked God for having made me so fond of her as to have never once done anything to bring the tears into her eyes. O Will, why was she taken away, and father left!' There's his dying words, father," said the young man; "make the best you can of 'em. You struck him across the face, in a drunken fit, the morning we ran away; and here's the end of it."

The girl wept aloud; and the father sinking, his head upon his knees, rocked himself to and fro.

"If I am taken," said the young man, "I shall be carried back into the country, and hung for that man's murder. They cannot trace me here, without your assistance, father. For aught I know, you may give me up to justice; but unless you do, here I stop, until I can venture to escape abroad."

For two whole days, all three remained in the wretched room, without stirring out. On the third evening, however, the girl was worse than she had been yet, and the few scraps of food they had were gone. It was indispensably necessary that somebody should go out; and as the girl was too weak and ill, the father went, just at nightfall.

He got some medicine for the girl, and a trifle in the way of pecuniary assistance. On his way back, he earned sixpence by holding a horse; and he turned homewards with enough money to supply their most pressing wants for two or three days to come. He had to pass the public-house. He lingered for an instant, walked past it, turned back again, lingered once more, and finally slunk in. Two men whom he had not observed were on the watch. They were on the point of giving up their search in despair, when his loitering attracted their attention; and when he entered the public-house, they followed him.

"You'll drink with me. master," said one of them, proffering him a glass of liquor.

"And me too," said the other, replenishing the glass as soon as it was drained of its contents.

The man thought of his hungry children, and his son's danger. But they were nothing to the drunkard. He *did* drink; and his reason left him.

"A wet night, Warden," whispered one of the men in his ear, as he at length turned to go away, after spending in liquor one-half of the money on which, perhaps, his daughter's life depended.

"The right sort of night for our friends in hiding, Master Warden," whispered the other.

"Sit down here," said the one who had spoken first, drawing him into a corner. "We have been looking arter the young un. We came to tell him it's all right now, but we couldn't find him 'cause we hadn't got the precise direction. But that ain't strange, for I don't think he know'd it himself, when he came to London, did he?"

"No, he didn't," replied the fath

The two men exchanged glances.

"There's a vessel down at the docks, to sail at midnight, when it's high water," resumed the first speaker, "and we'll put him on board. His passage is taken in another name, and what's better than that, it's paid for. It's lucky we met you."

"Very," said the second.

"Capital luck," said the first, with a wink to his companion.

"Great," replied the second, with a slight nod of intelligence.

"Another glass here; quick," said the first speaker. And in five minutes more, the father had unconsciously yielded up his own son into the hangman's hands.

Slowly and heavily the time dragged along, as the brother and sister, in their miserable hiding-place, listened in anxious suspense to the slightest sound. At length, a heavy footstep was heard upon the stair; it approached nearer; it reached the landing; and the father staggered into the room.

The girl saw that he was intoxicated, and advanced with the candle in her hand to meet him; she stopped short, gave a loud scream, and fell senseless on the ground. She had caught sight of the shadow of a man, reflected on the floor. They both rushed in, and in another instant the young man was a prisoner, and handcuffed.

"Very quietly done," said one of the men to his companion, "thanks to the old man. Lift up the girl, Tom—come, come, it's no use crying, young woman. It's all over now, and can't be helped."

The young man stooped for an instant over the girl, and then turned fiercely round upon his father, who had reeled against the wall, and was gazing on the group with drunken stupidity.

"Listen to me, father," he said, in a tone that made the drunkard's flesh creep. "My brother's blood, and mine, is on your head: I never had kind look, or word, or care, from you, and alive or dead, I never will forgive you. Die when you will, or how, I will be with you. I speak as a dead man now, and I warn you, father, that as surely as you must one day stand before your Maker so surely shall your children be there, hand in hand, to cry for judgment against you." He raised his manacled hands in a threatening attitude, fixed his eyes on his shrinking parent, and slowly left the room; and neither father nor sister ever beheld him more, on this side of the grave.

When the dim and misty light of a winter's morning penetrated into the narrow court, and struggled through the begrimed window of the wretched room, Warden awoke from his heavy sleep, and found himself alone. He rose, and looked round him; the old flock mattress on the floor was undisturbed; everything was just as he remembered to have seen it last: and there were no signs of any one, save himself, having occupied the room during the night. He inquired of the other lodgers, and of the neighbours; but his daughter had not been seen or heard of. He rambled through the streets, and scrutinised each wretched face among the crowds that thronged them, with anxious eyes. But his search was fruitless, and he returned to his garret when night came on, desolate and weary.

For many days he occupied himself in the same manner, but no trace of his daughter did he meet with, and no word of her reached his ears. At length he gave up the pursuit as hopeless. He had long thought of the probability of her leaving him, and endeavouring to gain her bread in quiet, elsewhere. She had left him at last to starve alone. He ground his teeth, and cursed her!

He begged his bread from door to door. Every halfpenny he could wring from the pity or credulity of those to whom he addressed himself was spent in the old way. A year passed over his head; the roof of a jail was the only one that had sheltered him for many months. He slept under archways, and in brickfields—anywhere, where there was some warmth or shelter from the cold and rain. But in the last stage of poverty, disease, and houseless want, he was a drunkard still.

At last, one bitter night, he sank down on a door-step faint and ill. The premature decay of vice and profligacy had worn him to the bone. His cheeks were hollow and livid; his eyes were sunken, and their sight was dim. His legs trembled beneath his weight, and a cold shiver ran through every limb.

And now the long-forgotten scenes of a misspent life crowded thick and fast upon him. He thought of the time when he had a home—a happy, cheerful home—and of those who peopled it, and flocked about him then, until the forms of his elder children seemed to rise from the grave, and stand about him—so plain, so clear, and so distinct they were that he could touch and feel them. Looks that he had long forgotten were fixed upon him once more; voices long since hushed in death sounded in his ears like the music of village bells. But it was only for an instant. The rain beat heavily upon him; and cold and hunger were gnawing at his heart again.

He rose, and dragged his feeble limbs a few paces further. The street was silent and empty; the few passengers who passed by, at that late hour, hurried quickly on, and his tremulous voice was lost in the violence of the storm. Again that heavy chill struck through his frame, and his blood seemed to stagnate beneath it. He coiled himself up in a projecting doorway, and tried to sleep.

But sleep had fled from his dull and glazed eyes. His mind wandered strangely, but he was awake, and conscious. The well-known shout of drunken mirth sounded in his ear, the glass was at his lips, the board was covered with choice rich food—they were before him: he could see them all, he had but to reach out his hand, and take them—and, though the illusion was reality itself, he knew that he was sitting alone in the deserted street, watching the rain-drops as they pattered on the stones; that death was coming upon him by inches—and that there were none to care for or help him.

Suddenly, he started up, in the extremity of terror. He

had heard his own voice shouting in the night air, he knew not what, or why. Hark! A groan! another! His senses were leaving him: half-formed and incoherent words burst from his lips; and his hands sought to tear and lacerate his flesh. He was going mad, and he shrieked for help till his voice failed him,

He raised his head, and looked up the long dismal street. He recollected that outcasts like himself, condemned to wander day and night in those dreadful streets, had sometimes gone distracted with their own loneliness. He remembered to have heard many years before that a homeless wretch had once been found in a solitary corner, sharpening a rusty knife to plunge into his own heart, preferring death to that endless, weary, wandering to and fro. In an instant his resolve was taken, his limbs received new life; he ran quickly from the spot, and paused not for breath until he reached the river-side.

He crept softly down the steep stone stairs that lead from the commencement of Waterloo Bridge, down to the water's level. He crouched into a corner, and held his breath, as he patrol passed. Never did prisoner's heart throb with the hope of liberty and life half so eagerly as did that of the wretched man at the prospect of death. The watch passed close to him, but he remained unobserved; and after waiting till the sound of footsteps had died away in the distance, he cautiously descended, and stood beneath the gloomy arch that forms the landing-place from the river.

The tide was in, and the water flowed at his feet. The rain had ceased, the wind was lulled, and all was, for the moment, still and quiet—so quiet that the slightest sound on the opposite bank, even the rippling of the water against the barges that were moored there, was distinctly audible to his ear. The stream stole languidly and sluggishly on. Strange and fantastic forms rose to the surface, and beckoned him to approach; dark gleaming eyes peered from the water, and seemed to mock his hesitation, while hollow murmurs from behind urged him onwards. He retreated a few paces, took a short run, desperate leap, and plunged into the river.

Not five seconds had passed when he rose to the water's surface—but what a change had taken place in that short time, in all his thoughts and feelings! Life—life—in any form, poverty, misery, starvation—anything but death. He fought and struggled with the water that closed over his head, and screamed in agonies of terror. The curse of his own son rang in his ears. The shore—but one foot of dry ground—he could almost touch the step. One hand's breadth nearer, and he was saved—but the tide bore him onward, under the dark arches of the bridge, and he sank to the bottom.

Again he rose, and struggled for life. For one instant—for one brief instant—the buildings on the river's banks, the lights on the bridge through which the current had borne him, the black water, and the fast-flying clouds, were distinctly visible—once more he sank, and once again he rose. Bright flames of fire shot up from earth to heaven, and reeled before his eyes, while the water thundered in his ears, and stunned him with its furious roar.

A week afterwards the body was washed ashore, some miles down the river, a swollen and disfigured mass. Unrecognised and unpitied, it was borne to the grave; and there it has long since mouldered away!

HARD TIMES

STEPHEN AND RACHAEL IN THE SICK ROOM.

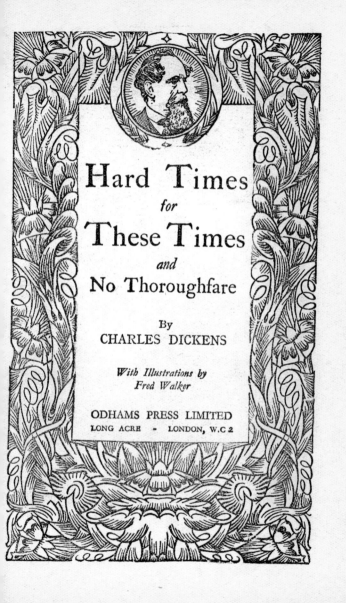

Hard Times
for
These Times
and
No Thoroughfare

By
CHARLES DICKENS

With Illustrations by
Fred Walker

ODHAMS PRESS LIMITED
LONG ACRE - LONDON, W.C 2

CONTENTS

BOOK THE FIRST : SOWING

CHAPTER   PAGE

   I. The One Thing Needful 9

  II. Murdering the Innocents . . . 10

 III. A Loophole 14

 IV. Mr. Bounderby 18

  V. The Key-note 24

 VI. Sleary's Horsemanship . . . 28

VII. Mrs. Sparsit 39

VIII. Never Wonder 44

 IX. Sissy's Progress 48

  X. Stephen Blackpool 54

 XI. No Way Out 59

XII. The Old Woman 64

XIII. Rachael 68

XIV. The Great Manufacturer . . . 74

 XV. Father and Daughter . . . 78

XVI. Husband and Wife 84

BOOK THE SECOND: REAPING

   I. Effects in the Bank 89

  II. Mr. James Harthouse 99

 III. The Whelp 107

 IV. Men and Brothers 111

  V. Men and Masters 117

 VI. Fading Away 122

VII. Gunpowder 132

VIII. Explosion 142

 IX. Hearing the Last of It . . . 154

  X. Mrs. Sparsit's Staircase . . . 160

 XI. Lower and Lower 163

XII. Down 170

CONTENTS

BOOK THE THIRD: GARNERING

CHAPTER		PAGE
I. Another Thing Needful	. . . .	174
II. Very Ridiculous	. . . .	178
III. Very Decided	. . . .	186
IV. Lost	. . . .	192
V. Found	. . . .	200
VI. The Starlight	. . . .	206
VII. Whelp-hunting	. . . .	216
VIII. Philosophical	. . . .	225
IX. Final	. . . .	230

NO THOROUGHFARE

THE OVERTURE	. . . .	237
ACT I: The Curtain Rises	. . .	241
Enter the Housekeeper	. .	248
The Housekeeper Speaks	. .	250
New Characters on the Scene	.	257
Exit Wilding	. . . .	270
ACT II: Vendale Makes Love	. .	281
Vendale makes Mischief	. .	294
ACT III: In the Valley	. .	304
On the Mountain	. . .	314
ACT IV: The Clock-lock	. . .	323
Obenreizer's Victory	. .	330
The Curtain Falls	. .	338

HARD TIMES

BOOK THE FIRST: SOWING

CHAPTER I: *The One Thing Needful*

"Now, what I want is, Facts. Teach these boys and girls nothing but Facts. Facts alone are wanted in life. Plant nothing else, and root out everything else. You can only form the minds of reasoning animals upon Facts: nothing else will ever be of any service to them. This is the principle on which I bring up my own children, and this is the principle on which I bring up these children. Stick to Facts, sir!"

The scene was a plain, bare, monotonous vault of a schoolroom, and the speaker's square forefinger emphasised his observations, by underscoring every sentence with a line on the schoolmaster's sleeve. The emphasis was helped by the speaker's square wall of a forehead, which had his eyebrows for its base, while his eyes found commodious cellarage in two dark caves, overshadowed by the wall. The emphasis was helped by the speaker's mouth, which was wide, thin, and hard set. The emphasis was helped by the speaker's voice, which was inflexible, dry and dictatorial. The emphasis was helped by the speaker's hair, which bristled on the skirts of his bald head, a plantation of firs to keep the wind from its shining surface, all covered with knobs, like the crust of a plum-pie, as if the head had scarcely warehouse-room for the hard facts stored inside. The speaker's obstinate carriage, square coat, square legs, square shoulders,—nay, his very neckcloth, trained to take him by the throat with an unaccommodating grasp, like a stubborn fact, as it was,—all helped the emphasis.

"In this life, we want nothing but Facts, sir; nothing but Facts!"

The speaker, and the schoolmaster, and the third grown person present, all backed a little, and swept with their eyes the inclined plane of little vessels then and there arranged in order, ready to have imperial gallons of facts poured into them until they were full to the brim.

CHAPTER II: *Murdering the Innocents*

THOMAS GRADGRIND, sir. A man of realities. A man of facts
and calculations. A man who proceeds upon the principle
that two and two are four, and nothing over, and who is not
to be talked into allowing for anything over. Thomas Gradgrind, sir—peremptorily Thomas—Thomas Gradgrind. With
a rule and a pair of scales, and the multiplication table always
in his pocket, sir, ready to weigh and measure any parcel of
human nature, and tell you exactly what it comes to. It is a
mere question of figures, a case of simple arithmetic. You
might hope to get some other nonsensical belief into the head
of George Gradgrind, or Augustus Gradgrind, or John Gradgrind, or Joseph Gradgrind (all supposititious, non-existent
persons), but into the head of Thomas Gradgrind—no, sir!

In such terms Mr. Gradgrind always mentally introduced
himself, whether to his private circle of acquaintance, or to the
public in general. In such terms, no doubt, substituting the
words "boys and girls" for "sir," Thomas Gradgrind now
presented Thomas Gradgrind to the little pitchers before him,
who were to be filled so full of facts.

Indeed, as he eagerly sparkled at them from the cellarage
before mentioned, he seemed a kind of cannon loaded to the
muzzle with facts, and prepared to blow them clean out of
the regions of childhood at one discharge. He seemed a gal-
vanising apparatus, too, charged with a grim mechanical
substitute for the tender young imaginations that were to be
stormed away.

"Girl number twenty," said Mr. Gradgrind, squarely pointing with his square forefinger, "I don't know that girl. Who
is that girl?"

"Sissy Jupe, sir," explained number twenty, blushing,
standing up, and curtseying.

"Sissy is not a name," said Mr. Gradgrind. "Don't call
yourself Sissy. Call yourself Cecilia."

"It's father as calls me Sissy, sir," returned the young girl
in a trembling voice, and with another curtsey.

"Then he has no business to do it," said Mr. Gradgrind.
"Tell him he mustn't. Cecilia Jupe. Let me see. What is
your father?"

"He belongs to the horse-riding, if you please, sir."

Mr. Gradgrind frowned, and waved off the objectionable
calling with his hand.

"We don't want to know anything about that, here. You
mustn't tell us about that, here. Your father breaks horses,
don't he?"

"If you please, sir, when they can get any to break, they do
break horses in the ring, sir."

"You mustn't tell us about the ring, here. Very well, then. Describe your father as a horsebreaker. He doctors sick horses, I dare say?"

"Oh yes, sir."

"Very well, then. He is a veterinary surgeon, a farrier, and horsebreaker. Give me your definition of a horse."

(Sissy Jupe thrown into the greatest alarm by this demand.)

"Girl number twenty unable to define a horse!" said Mr. Gradgrind, for the general behoof of all the little pitchers. "Girl number twenty possessed of no facts, in reference to one of the commonest of animals! Some boy's definition of a horse. Bitzer, yours."

The square finger, moving here and there, lighted suddenly on Bitzer, perhaps because he chanced to sit in the same ray of sunlight which, darting in at one of the bare windows of the intensely white-washed room, irradiated Sissy. For, the boys and girls sat on the face of the inclined plane in two compact bodies, divided up the centre by a narrow interval; and Sissy, being at the corner of a row on the sunny side, came in for the beginning of a sunbeam, of which Bitzer, being at the corner of a row on the other side, a few rows in advance, caught the end. But, whereas the girl was so dark-eyed and dark-haired, that she seemed to receive a deeper and more lustrous colour from the sun, when it shone upon her, the boy was so light-eyed and light-haired, that the self-same rays appeared to draw out of him what little colour he ever possessed. His cold eyes would hardly have been eyes, but for the short ends of lashes which, by bringing them into immediate contrast with something paler than themselves, expressed their form. His short-cropped hair might have been a mere continuation of the sandy freckles on his forehead and face. His skin was so unwholesomely deficient in the natural tinge, that he looked as though, if it were cut, he would bleed white.

"Bitzer," said Thomas Gradgrind, "your definition of a horse."

"Quadruped. Graminivorous. Forty teeth, namely twenty-four grinders, four eye-teeth, and twelve incisive. Sheds coat in the spring; in marshy countries, sheds hoofs, too. Hoofs hard, but requiring to be shod with iron. Age known by marks in mouth." Thus (and much more) Bitzer.

"Now girl number twenty," said Mr. Gradgrind. "You know what a horse is."

She curtseyed again, and would have blushed deeper, if she could have blushed deeper than she had blushed all this time. Bitzer, after rapidly blinking at Thomas Gradgrind with both eyes at once, and so catching the light upon his quivering ends of lashes that they looked like the antennæ of busy insects, put his knuckles to his freckled forehead, and sat down again.

The third gentleman now stepped forth. A mighty man at

cutting and drying, he was; a government officer; in his way
(and in most other people's too), a professed pugilist; always
training, always with a system to force down the general
throat like a bolus, always to be heard of at the bar of his little
Public-office, ready to fight all England. To continue in
fistic phraseology, he had a genius for coming up to the
scratch, wherever and whatever it was, and proving himself
an ugly customer. He would go in and damage any subject
whatever with his right, follow up with his left, stop, exchange,
counter, bore his opponent (he always fought all England) to
the ropes, and fall upon him neatly. He was certain to knock
the wind out of common sense, and render that unlucky
adversary deaf to the call of time. And he had it in charge
from high authority to bring about the great public-office
Millennium, when Commissioners should reign upon earth.

"Very well," said this gentleman, briskly smiling, and folding his arms. "That's a horse. Now, let me ask you girls
and boys, Would you paper a room with representations of
horses?"

After a pause, one half of the children cried in chorus, "Yes,
sir!" Upon which the other half, seeing in the gentleman's
face that Yes was wrong, cried out in chorus, "No, sir!"—as
the custom is in these examinations.

"Of course, No. Why wouldn't you?"

A pause. One corpulent slow boy, with a wheezy manner of
breathing, ventured the answer, Because he wouldn't paper
a room at all, but would paint it.

"You *must* paper it," said the gentleman, rather warmly.

"You must paper it," said Thomas Gradgrind, "whether
you like it or not. Don't tell *us* you wouldn't paper it. What
do you mean, boy?"

"I'll explain to you then," said the gentleman, after another
and a dismal pause, "why you wouldn't paper a room with
representations of horses. Do you ever see horses walking up
and down the sides of rooms in reality—in fact? Do you?"

"Yes, sir!" from one half. "No, sir!" from the other.

"Of course no," said the gentleman, with an indignant look
at the wrong half. "Why, then, you are not to see anywhere,
what you don't see in fact; you are not to have anywhere,
what you don't have in fact. What is called Taste, is only
another name for Fact."

Thomas Gradgrind nodded his approbation.

"This is a new principle, a discovery, a great discovery,"
said the gentleman.

"Now, I'll try you again. Suppose you were going to carpet
a room. Would you use a carpet having a representation of
flowers upon it?"

There being a general conviction by this time that "No,
sir!" was always the right answer to this gentleman, the

chorus of No was very strong. Only a few feeble stragglers said Yes; among them Sissy Jupe.

"Girl number twenty," said the gentleman, smiling in the calm strength of knowledge.

Sissy blushed, and stood up.

"So you would carpet your room—or your husband's room, if you were a grown woman, and had a husband—with representations of flowers, would you?" said the gentleman. "Why would you?"

"If you please, sir, I am very fond of flowers," returned the girl.

"And is that why you would put tables and chairs upon them, and have people walking over them with heavy boots?"

"It wouldn't hurt them, sir. They wouldn't crush and wither, if you please, sir. They would be the pictures of what was very pretty, and pleasant, and I would fancy——"

"Ay, ay, ay! But you mustn't fancy," cried the gentleman, quite elated by coming so happily to his point. "That's it! You are never to fancy."

"You are not Cecilia Jupe," Thomas Gradgrind solemnly repeated, "to do anything of that kind."

"Fact, fact, fact!" said the gentleman. And "Fact, fact, fact!" repeated Thomas Gradgrind.

"You are to be in all things regulated and governed," said the gentleman, "by fact. We hope to have, before long, a board of fact, composed of commissioners of fact, who will force the people to be a people of fact, and of nothing but fact. You must discard the word Fancy altogether. You have nothing to do with it. You are not to have, in any object of use or ornament, what would be a contradiction in fact. You don't walk upon flowers in fact; you cannot be allowed to walk upon flowers in carpets. You don't find that foreign birds and butterflies come and perch upon your crockery; you cannot be permitted to paint foreign birds and butterflies upon your crockery. You never meet with quadrupeds going up and down walls; you must not have quadrupeds represented upon walls. You must use," said the gentleman, "for all these purposes, combinations and modifications (in primary colours) of mathematical figures which are susceptible of proof and demonstration. This is the new discovery. This is fact. This is taste."

The girl curtseyed, and sat down. She was very young, and she looked as if she were frightened by the matter of fact prospect the world afforded.

"Now, if Mr. M'Choakumchild," said the gentleman, "will proceed to give his first lesson here, Mr. Gradgrind, I shall be happy, at your request, to observe his mode of procedure."

Mr. Gradgrind was much obliged. "Mr. M'Choakumchild, we only wait for you."

So, Mr. M'Choakumchild began in his best manner. He and some one hundred and forty other schoolmasters had been lately turned at the same time, in the same factory, on the same principles, like so many pianoforte legs. He had been put through an immense variety of paces, and had answered volumes of head-breaking questions. Orthography, etymology, syntax, and prosody, biography, astronomy, geography, and general cosmography, the sciences of compound proportion, algebra, land-surveying and levelling, vocal music, and drawing from models, were all at the ends of his ten chilled fingers. He had worked his stony way into Her Majesty's most Honourable Privy Council's Schedule B, and had taken the bloom off the higher branches of mathematics and physical science, French, German, Latin, and Greek. He knew all about all the Water Sheds of all the world (whatever they are), and all the histories of all the peoples, and all the names of all the rivers and mountains, and all the productions, manners, and customs of all the countries, and all their boundaries and bearings on the two-and-thirty points of the compass. Ah, rather overdone, M'Choakumchild. If he had only learnt a little less, how infinitely better he might have taught much more!

He went to work in this preparatory lesson, not unlike Morgiana in the Forty Thieves: looking into all the vessels ranged before him, one after another, to see what they contained. Say, good M'Choakumchild. When from thy boiling store, thou shalt fill each jar brim full by-and-by, dost thou think that thou wilt always kill outright the robber Fancy lurking within—or sometimes only maim him and distort him!

CHAPTER III: *A Loophole*

MR. GRADGRIND walked homeward from the school, in a state of considerable satisfaction. It was his school, and he intended it to be a model. He intended every child in it to be a model—just as the young Gradgrinds were all models.

There were five young Gradgrinds, and they were models every one. They had been lectured at, from their tenderest years; coursed, like little hares. Almost as soon as they could run alone, they had been made to run to the lecture-room. The first object with which they had an association, or of which they had a remembrance, was a large black board with a dry Ogre chalking ghastly white figures on it.

Not that they knew, by name or nature, anything about an Ogre. Fact forbid! I only use the word to express a monster in a lecturing castle, with Heaven knows how many heads manipulated into one, taking childhood captive, and dragging it into gloomy statistical dens by the hair.

No little Gradgrind had ever seen a face in the moon; it was up in the moon before it could speak distinctly. No little Gradgrind had ever learnt the silly jingle, Twinkle, twinkle little star; how I wonder what you are! No little Gradgrind had ever known wonder on the subject, each little Gradgrind having at five years old dissected the Great Bear like a Professor Owen, and driven Charles's Wain like a locomotive engine-driver. No little Gradgrind had ever associated a cow in a field with that famous cow with the crumpled horn who tossed the dog who worried the cat who killed the rat who ate the malt, or with that yet more famous cow who swallowed Tom Thumb: it had never heard of those celebrities, and had only been introduced to a cow as a graminivorous ruminating quadruped with several stomachs.

To his matter of fact home, which was called Stone Lodge, Mr. Gradgrind directed his steps. He had virtually retired from the wholesale hardware trade before he built Stone Lodge, and was now looking about for a suitable opportunity of making an arithmetical figure in Parliament. Stone Lodge was situated on a moor within a mile or two of a great town —called Coketown in the present faithful guide-book.

A very regular feature on the face of the country, Stone Lodge was. Not the least disguise toned down or shaded off that uncompromising fact in the landscape. A great square house, with a heavy portico darkening the principal windows, as its master's heavy brows overshadowed his eyes. A calculated, cast up, balanced, and proved house. Six windows on this side of the door, six on that side; a total of twelve in this wing, a total of twelve in the other wing; four-and-twenty carried over to the back wings. A lawn and garden and an infant avenue, all ruled straight like a botanical account-book. Gas and ventilation, drainage and water-service, all of the primest quality. Iron clamps and girders, fire-proof from top to bottom; mechanical lifts for the housemaids, with all their brushes and brooms; everything that heart could desire.

Everything? Well, I suppose so. The little Gradgrinds had cabinets in various departments of science too. They had a little conchological cabinet, and a little metallurgical cabinet, and a little mineralogical cabinet; and the specimens were all arranged and labelled, and the bits of stone and ore looked as though they might have been broken from the parent substances by those tremendously hard instruments their own names; and, to paraphrase the idle legend of Peter Piper, who had never found his way into their nursery. If the greedy little Gradgrinds grasped at more than this, what was it for good gracious goodness' sake, that the greedy little Gradgrinds grasped at!

Their father walked on in a hopeful and satisfied frame of mind. He was an affectionate father, after his manner; but he would probably have described himself (if he had been put like Sissy Jupe, upon a definition) as "an eminently practical" father. He had a particular pride in the phrase eminently practical, which was considered to have a special application to him. Whatsoever the public meeting held in Coketown, and whatsoever the subject of such meeting, some Coketowner was sure to seize the occasion of alluding to his eminently practical friend Gradgrind. This always pleased the eminently practical friend. He knew it to be his due, but his due was acceptable.

He had reached the neutral ground upon the outskirts of the town, which was neither town nor country, and yet was either spoiled, when his ears were invaded by the sound of music. The clashing and banging band attached to the horse-riding establishment which had there set up its rest in a wooden pavilion was in full bray. A flag, floating from the summit of the temple, proclaimed to mankind that it was "Sleary's Horse-riding" which claimed their suffrages. Sleary himself, a stout modern statue with a money-box at its elbow, in an ecclesiastical niche of early Gothic architecture, took the money. Miss Josephine Sleary, as some very long and very narrow strips of printed bill announced, was then inaugurating the entertainments with her graceful equestrian Tyrolean flower-act. Among the other pleasing but always strictly moral wonders which must be seen to be believed, Signor Jupe was that afternoon to "elucidate the diverting accomplishments of his highly trained performing dog Merrylegs." He was also to exhibit "his astounding feat of throwing seventy-five hundredweight in rapid succession backhanded over his head, thus forming a fountain of solid iron in mid-air, a feat never before attempted in this or any other country, and which having elicited such rapturous plaudits from enthusiastic throngs, it cannot be withdrawn." The same Signor Jupe was to "enliven the varied performances at frequent intervals with his chaste Shaksperean quips and retorts." Lastly, he was to wind them up by appearing in his favourite character of Mr. William Button, of Tooley street, in "the highly novel and laughable hippo-comedietta of The Tailor's Journey to Brentford."

Thomas Gradgrind took no heed of these trivialities of course, but passed on as a practical man ought to pass on, either brushing the noisy insects from his thoughts, or consigning them to the House of Correction. But, the turning of the road took him by the back of the booth, and at the back of the booth a number of children were congregated in a number of stealthy attitudes, striving to peep in at the hidden glories of the place.

This brought him to a stop. "Now, to think of these vagabonds," said he, "attracting the young rabble from a model school."

A space of stunted grass and dry rubbish being between him and the young rabble, he took his eyeglass out of his waistcoat to look for any child he knew by name, and might order off. Phenomenon almost incredible though distinctly seen, what did he then behold but his own metallurgical Louisa, peeping with all her might through a hole in a deal board, and his own mathematical Thomas abasing himself on the ground to catch but a hoof of the graceful equestrian Tyrolean flower-act!

Dumb with amazement, Mr. Gradgrind crossed to the spot where his family was thus disgraced, laid his hand upon each erring child, and said:

"Louisa!! Thomas!!"

Both rose, red and disconcerted. But, Louisa looked at her father with more boldness than Thomas did. Indeed, Thomas did not look at him, but gave himself up to be taken home like a machine.

"In the name of wonder, idleness, and folly!" said Mr. Gradgrind, leading each away by a hand; "what do you do here?"

"Wanted to see what it was like," returned Louisa shortly.

"What it was like?"

"Yes, father."

There was an air of jaded sullenness in them both, and particularly in the girl: yet, struggling through the dissatisfaction of her face, there was a light with nothing to rest upon, a fire with nothing to burn, a starved imagination keeping life in itself somehow, which brightened its expression. Not with the brightness natural to cheerful youth, but with uncertain, eager, doubtful flashes, which had something painful in them, analogous to the changes on a blind face groping its way.

She was a child now, of fifteen or sixteen; but at no distant day would seem to become a woman all at once. Her father thought so as he looked at her. She was pretty. Would have been self-willed (he thought in his eminently practical way) but for her bringing-up.

"Thomas, though I have the fact before me, I find it difficult to believe that you, with your education and resources, should have brought your sister to a scene like this."

"I brought *him*, father," said Louisa, quickly. "I asked him to come."

"I am sorry to hear it. I am very sorry indeed to hear it. It makes Thomas no better, and it makes you worse, Louisa."

She looked at her father again, but no tear fell down her cheek.

"You! Thomas and you, to whom the circle of the sciences is open; Thomas and you, who may be said to be replete with facts; Thomas and you, who have been trained to mathe-

matical exactness; Thomas and you, here!" cried Mr. Gradgrind. "In this degraded position! I am amazed."

"I was tired, father. I have been tired a long time," said
Louisa.

"Tired? Of what?" asked the astonished father.

"I don't know of what—of everything I think."

"Say not another word," returned Mr. Gradgrind. "You are
childish. I will hear no more." He did not speak again until
they had walked some half-a-mile, in silence, when he gravely
broke out with: "What would your best friends say, Louisa?
Do you attach no value to their good opinion? What would
Mr. Bounderby say?"

At the mention of this name, his daughter stole a look at
him, remarkable for its intense and searching character. He
saw nothing of it, for before he looked at her, she had again
cast down her eyes!

"What," he repeated presently, "would Mr. Bounderby
say?" All the way to Stone Lodge, as with grave indignation
he led the two delinquents home, he repeated at intervals,
"What would Mr. Bounderby say!"—as if Mr. Bounderby
had been Mrs. Grundy.

CHAPTER IV: *Mr. Bounderby*

Not being Mrs. Grundy, who *was* Mr. Bounderby?

Why, Mr. Bounderby was as near Mr. Gradgrind's bosom
friend, as a man perfectly devoid of sentiment can approach
that spiritual relationship towards another man perfectly
devoid of sentiment. So near was Mr. Bounderby—or, if the
reader should prefer it, so far off.

He was a rich man: banker, merchant, manufacturer, and
what not. A big, loud man, with a stare, and a metallic
laugh. A man made out of a coarse material, which seemed
to have been stretched to make so much of him. A man with
a great puffed head and forehead, swelled veins in his temples,
and such a strained skin to his face that it seemed to hold his
eyes open, and lift his eyebrows up. A man with a pervading
appearance on him, of being inflated like a balloon, and ready
to start. A man who could never sufficiently vaunt himself a
self-made man. A man who was always proclaiming, through
that brassy speaking-trumpet of a voice of his, his old ignorance
and his old poverty. A man who was the Bully of humility.

A year or two younger than his eminently practical friend,
Mr. Bounderby looked older; his seven or eight and forty
might have had the seven or eight added to it again, without
surprising anybody. He had not much hair. One might
have fancied he had talked it off; and that what was left, all
standing up in disorder, was in that condition from being
constantly blown about by his windy boastfulness.

In the formal drawing-room of Stone Lodge, standing on the hearth-rug, warming himself before the fire, Mr. Bounderby delivered some observations to Mrs. Gradgrind on the circumstance of its being his birthday. He stood before the fire, partly because it was a cool spring afternoon, though the sun shone; partly because the shade of Stone Lodge was always haunted by the ghost of damp mortar; partly because he thus took up a commanding position, from which to subdue Mrs. Gradgrind.

"I hadn't a shoe to my foot. As to a stocking, I didn't know such a thing by name. I passed the day in a ditch, and the night in a pigsty. That's the way I spent my tenth birthday. Not that a ditch was new to me, for I was born in a ditch."

Mrs. Gradgrind, a little, thin, white, pink-eyed bundle of shawls, of surpassing feebleness, mental and bodily; who was always taking physic without any effect, and who, whenever she showed a symptom of coming to life, was invariably stunned by some weighty piece of fact tumbling on her; Mrs. Gradgrind hoped it was a dry ditch?

"No! As wet as a sop. A foot of water in it," said Mr. Bounderby.

"Enough to give a baby cold," Mrs. Gradgrind considered.

"Cold? I was born with inflammation of the lungs, and of everything else, I believe, that was capable of inflammation," returned Mr. Bounderby. "For years, ma'am, I was one of the most miserable little wretches ever seen. I was so sickly, that I was always moaning and groaning. I was so ragged and dirty, that you wouldn't have touched me with a pair of tongs."

Mrs. Gradgrind faintly looked at the tongs, as the most appropriate thing her imbecility could think of doing.

"How I fought through it, *I* don't know," said Bounderby. "I was determined I suppose. I have been a determined character in later life, and I suppose I was then. Here I am, Mrs. Gradgrind, anyhow, and nobody to thank for my being here, but myself."

Mrs. Gradgrind meekly and weakly hoped that his mother—

"*My* mother? Bolted, ma'am!" said Bounderby.

Mrs. Gradgrind, stunned as usual, collapsed and gave it up.

"My mother left me to my grandmother," said Bounderby; "and according to the best of my remembrance, my grandmother was the wickedest and the worst old woman that ever lived. If I got a little pair of shoes by any chance, she would take 'em off and sell 'em for drink. Why, I have known that grandmother of mine lie in her bed and drink her four-teen glasses of liquor before breakfast!"

Mrs. Gradgrind, weakly smiling, and giving no other sign of vitality, looked (as she always did) like an indifferently executed transparency of a small female figure, without enough light behind it.

"She kept a chandler's shop," pursued Bounderby, "and kept me in an egg-box. That was the cot of *my* infancy; an old egg-box. As soon as I was big enough to run away, of course I ran away. Then I became a young vagabond; and instead of one old woman knocking me about and starving me, everybody of all ages knocked me about and starved me. They were right; they had no business to do anything else. I was a nuisance, an incumbrance, and a pest. I know that very well."

His pride in having at any time of his life achieved such a great social distinction as to be a nuisance, an incumbrance, and a pest, was only to be satisfied by three sonorous repetitions of the boast.

"I was to pull through it I suppose, Mrs. Gradgrind. Whether I was to do it or not, ma'am, I did it. I pulled through it, though nobody threw me out a rope. Vagabond, errand-boy, vagabond, labourer, porter, clerk, chief manager, small partner, Josiah Bounderby of Coketown. Those are the antecedents, and the culmination. Josiah Bounderby of Coketown learnt his letters from the outsides of the shops, Mrs. Gradgrind, and was first able to tell the time upon a dial-plate, from studying the steeple clock of St. Giles's Church, London, under the direction of a drunken cripple, who was a convicted thief, and an incorrigible vagrant. Tell Josiah Bounderby of Coketown, of your district schools and your model schools, and your training schools, and your whole kettle-of-fish of schools; and Josiah Bounderby of Coketown tells you plainly, all right, all correct—he hadn't such advantages—but let us have hard-headed, solid-fisted people—the education that made him won't do for everybody, he knows well—such and such his education was, however, and you may force him to swallow boiling fat, but you shall never force him to suppress the facts of his life."

Being heated when he arrived at this climax, Josiah Bounderby of Coketown stopped. He stopped just as his eminently practical friend, still accompanied by the two young culprits, entered the room. His eminently practical friend, on seeing him, stopped also, and gave Louisa a reproachful look that plainly said, "Behold your Bounderby!"

"Well!" blustered Mr. Bounderby, "what's the matter? What is young Thomas in the dumps about?"

He spoke of young Thomas, but he looked at Louisa.

"We were peeping at the circus," muttered Louisa, haughtily, without lifting up her eyes, "and father caught us."

"And Mrs. Gradgrind," said her husband, in a lofty manner, "I should as soon have expected to find my children reading poetry."

"Dear me," whimpered Mrs. Gradgrind. "How can you, Louisa and Thomas! I wonder at you. I declare you're enough to make one regret ever having had a family at all. I have a great mind to say I wish I hadn't. *Then* what would you have done, I should like to know."

Mr. Gradgrind did not seem favourably impressed by these cogent remarks. He frowned impatiently.

"As if, with my head in its present throbbing state, you couldn't go and look at the shells and minerals and things provided for you, instead of circuses!" said Mrs. Gradgrind. "You know, as well as I do, no young people have circus masters, or keep circuses in cabinets, or attend lectures about circuses. What can you possibly want to know of circuses then? I am sure you have enough to do, if that's what you want. With my head in its present state, I couldn't remember the mere names of half the facts you have got to attend to."

"That's the reason!" pouted Louisa.

"Don't tell me that's the reason, because it can be nothing of the sort," said Mrs. Gradgrind. "Go and be something ological directly." Mrs. Gradgrind was not a scientific character, and usually dismissed her children to their studies with this general injunction to choose their pursuit.

In truth, Mrs. Gradgrind's stock of facts in general was woefully defective; but Mr. Gradgrind, in raising her to her high matrimonial position, had been influenced by two reasons. Firstly, she was most satisfactory as a question of figures; and, secondly, she had "no nonsense" about her. By nonsense he meant fancy; and truly it is probable she was as free from any alloy of that nature, as any human being not arrived at the perfection of an absolute idiot, ever was.

The simple circumstance of being left alone with her husband and Mr. Bounderby, was sufficient to stun this admirable lady again without collision between herself and any other fact. So, she once more died away, and nobody minded her.

"Bounderby," said Mr. Gradgrind, drawing a chair to the fireside, "you are always so interested in my young people—particularly in Louisa—that I make no apology for saying to you, I am very much vexed by this discovery. I have systematically devoted myself (as you know) to the education of the reason of my family. The reason is (as you know) the only faculty to which education should be addressed. And yet, Bounderby, it would appear from this unexpected circumstance of to-day, though in itself a trifling one, as if something had crept into Thomas's and Louisa's minds which is—or rather, which is not—I don't know that I can express myself better than by saying—which has never been intended to be developed, and in which their reason has no part."

"There certainly is no reason in looking with interest at a

parcel of vagabonds," returned Bounderby. "When I was a
vagabond myself, nobody looked with any interest at *me;* I
know that."

"Then comes the question," said the eminently practical
father, with his eyes on the fire, "in what has this vulgar
curiosity its rise?"

"I'll tell you in what. In idle imagination."

"I hope not," said the eminently practical; "I confess, however, that the misgiving *has* crossed me on my way home."

"In idle imagination, Gradgrind," repeated Bounderby. "A
very bad thing for anybody, but a cursed bad thing for a girl
like Louisa. I should ask Mrs. Gradgrind's pardon for strong
expressions, but that she knows very well I am not a refined
character. Whoever expects refinement in *me* will be disappointed. I hadn't a refined bringing up."

"Whether," said Mr. Gradgrind, pondering with his hands
in his pockets, and his cavernous eyes on the fire, "whether
any instructor or servant can have suggested anything?
Whether Louisa or Thomas can have been reading anything?
Whether, in spite of all precautions, any idle storybook can
have got into the house? Because, in minds that have been
practically formed by rule and line, from the cradle upwards,
this is so curious, so incomprehensible."

"Stop a bit!" cried Bounderby, who all this time had been
standing, as before, on the hearth, bursting at the very
furniture of the room with explosive humility. "You have
one of those strollers' children in the school."

"Cecilia Jupe, by name," said Mr. Gradgrind, with something of a stricken look at his friend.

"Now, stop a bit!" cried Bounderby again. "How did she
come there?"

"Why the fact is, I saw the girl myself, for the first time,
only just now. She specially applied here at the house to be
admitted, as not regularly belonging to our town, and—yes,
you are right, Bounderby, you are right."

"Now, stop a bit!" cried Bounderby, once more. "Louisa
saw her when she came?"

"Louisa certainly did see her, for she mentioned the application to me. But Louisa saw her, I have no doubt, in Mrs.
Gradgrind's presence."

"Pray, Mrs. Gradgrind," said Bounderby, "what passed?"

"Oh, my poor health!" returned Mrs. Gradgrind. "The
girl wanted to come to the school, and Mr. Gradgrind wanted
girls to come to the school, and Louisa and Thomas both said
that the girl wanted to come, and that Mr. Gradgrind wanted
girls to come, and how was it possible to contradict them when
such was the fact!"

"Now I tell you what, Gradgrind!" said Mr. Bounderby.
"Turn this girl to the right about, and there's an end of it."

"I am much of your opinion."

"Do it at once," said Bounderby, "has always been my motto from a child. When I thought I would run away from my egg-box and my grandmother, I did it at once. Do you the same. Do this at once!"

"Are you walking?" asked his friend. "I have the father's address. Perhaps you would not mind walking to town with me?"

"Not the least in the world," said Mr. Bounderby, "as long as you do it at once!"

So, Mr. Bounderby threw on his hat—he always threw it on, as expressing a man who had been far too busily employed in making himself, to acquire any fashion of wearing his hat—and with his hands in his pockets, sauntered out into the hall. "I never wear gloves," it was his custom to say. "I didn't climb up the ladder in *them*. Shouldn't be so high up, if I had."

Being left to saunter in the hall a minute or two while Mr. Gradgrind went upstairs for the address, he opened the door of the children's study and looked into that serene floor-clothed apartment, which, notwithstanding its bookcases and its cabinets, and its variety of learned and philosophical appliances, had much of the genial aspect of a room devoted to haircutting. Louisa languidly leaned upon the window looking out, without looking at anything, while young Thomas stood sniffing revengefully at the fire. Adam Smith and Malthus, two younger Gradgrinds, were out at lecture in custody; and little Jane, after manufacturing a good deal of moist pipe-clay on her face with slate-pencil and tears, had fallen asleep over vulgar fractions.

"It's all right now, Louisa: it's all right, young Thomas," said Mr. Bounderby; "you won't do so any more. I'll answer for its being all over with father. Well, Louisa, that's worth a kiss, isn't it?"

"You can take one, Mr. Bounderby," returned Louisa, when she had coldly paused, and slowly walked across the room, and ungraciously raised her cheek towards him, with her face turned away.

"Always my pet; ain't you, Louisa?" said Mr. Bounderby. "Good-bye, Louisa!"

He went his way, but she stood on the same spot, rubbing the cheek he had kissed, with her handkerchief, until it was burning red. She was still doing this, five minutes afterwards.

"What are you about, Loo?" her brother sulkily remonstrated. "You'll rub a hole in your face."

"You may cut the piece out with a penknife, if you like, Tom. I wouldn't cry!"

CHAPTER V: *The Key-note*

COKETOWN, to which Messrs. Bounderby and Gradgrind now walked, was a triumph of fact; it had no greater taint of fancy in it than Mrs. Gradgrind herself.   Let us strike the key-note, Coketown, before pursuing our tune.

It was a town of red brick, or of brick that would have been red if the smoke and ashes had allowed it; but as matters stood it was a town of unnatural red and black like the painted face of a savage.

It was a town of machinery and tall chimneys, out of which interminable serpents of smoke trailed themselves for ever and ever, and never got uncoiled.

It had a black canal in it, and a river that ran purple with ill-smelling dye, and vast piles of building full of windows where there was a rattling and a trembling all day long, and where the piston of the steam-engine worked monotonously up and down like the head of an elephant in a state of melancholy madness.   It contained several large streets all very like one another, and many small streets still more like one another, inhabited by people equally like one another, who all went in and out at the same hours, with the same sound upon the same pavements, to do the same work, and to whom every day was the same as yesterday and to-morrow, and every year the counterpart of the last and the next.

These attributes of Coketown were in the main inseparable from the work by which it was sustained; against them were to be set off, comforts of life which found their way all over the world, and elegancies of life which made, we will not ask how much of the fine lady, who could scarcely bear to hear the place mentioned.   The rest of its features were voluntary, and they were these.

You saw nothing in Coketown but what was severely work-ful.   If the members of a religious persuasion built a chapel there—as the members of eighteen religious persuasions had done—they made it a pious warehouse of red brick, with some-times (but this is only in highly ornamented examples) a bell in a birdcage on the top of it.   The solitary exception was the New Church: a stuccoed edifice with a square steeple over the door, terminating in four short pinnacles like florid wooden legs.   All the public inscriptions in the town were painted alike, in severe characters of black and white.   The jail might have been the infirmary, the infirmary might have been the jail, the town-hall might have been either, or both, or anything else, for anything that appeared to the contrary in the graces of their construction.   Fact, fact, fact, everywhere in the material aspect of the town; fact, fact, fact, everywhere in the immaterial.   The M'Choakumchild school was all fact, and the school of design was all fact, and the relations between master and man were all fact, and everything was fact between the lying-in hospital and the cemetery, and what you couldn't state in figures, or show to be purchasable in the cheapest market and saleable in the dearest, was not, and never should be, world without end, Amen.

A town so sacred to fact, and so triumphant in its assertion, of course got on well? Why no, not quite well. No? Dear me!

No. Coketown did not come out of its own furnaces, in all respects like gold that had stood the fire. First, the perplexing mystery of the place was, Who belonged to the eighteen denominations? Because, whoever did, the labouring people did not. It was very strange to walk through the streets on a Sunday morning, and note how few of *them* the barbarous jangling of bells that was driving the sick and nervous mad, called away from their own quarter, from their own close rooms, from the corners of their own streets, where they lounged listlessly, gazing at all the church and chapel going, as at a thing with which they had no manner of concern. Nor was it merely the stranger who noticed this, because there was a native organisation in Coketown itself, whose members were to be heard of in the House of Commons every session, indignantly petitioning for acts of parliament that should make these people religious by main force. Then came the Teetotal Society, who complained that these same people *would* get drunk, and showed in tabular statements that they did get drunk, and proved at tea parties that no inducement, human or Divine (except a medal), would induce them to forego their custom of getting drunk. Then came the chemist and druggist, with other tabular statements, showing that when they didn't get drunk, they took opium. Then came the experienced chaplain of the jail, with more tabular statements, outdoing all the previous tabular statements, and showing that the same people *would* resort to low haunts, hidden from the public eye, where they heard low singing and saw low dancing, and mayhap joined in it; and where A. B., aged twenty-four next birthday, and committed for eighteen months' solitary, had himself said (not that he had ever shown himself particularly worthy of belief) his ruin began, as he was perfectly sure and confident that otherwise he would have been a tip-top moral specimen. Then came Mr. Gradgrind and Mr. Bounderby, the two gentlemen at this present moment walking through Coketown, and both eminently practical, who could, on occasion, furnish more tabular statements derived from their own personal experience, and illustrated by cases they had known and seen, from which it clearly appeared—in short, it was the only clear thing in the case—that these same people were a bad lot altogether, gentlemen; that do

what you would for them they were never thankful for it,
gentlemen; that they were restless, gentlemen; that they never
knew what they wanted; that they lived upon the best, and
bought fresh butter; and insisted on Mocha coffee, and rejected all but prime parts of meat, and yet were eternally
dissatisfied and unmanageable. In short it was the moral
of the old nursery fable:

> *There was an old woman, and what do you think,*
> *She lived upon nothing but victuals and drink ;*
> *Victuals and drink were the whole of her diet,*
> *And yet this old woman would never be quiet.*

Is it possible, I wonder, that there was any analogy between
the case of the Coketown population and the case of the little
Gradgrinds? Surely, none of us in our sober senses and
acquainted with figures, are to be told at this time of day, that
one of the foremost elements in the existence of the Coketown
working-people had been for scores of years deliberately set
at nought? That there was any Fancy in them demanding
to be brought into healthy existence instead of struggling on
in convulsions? That exactly in the ratio as they worked long
and monotonously, the craving grew within them for some
physical relief—some relaxation, encouraging good humour
and good spirits, and giving them a vent—some recognised
holiday though it were but for an honest dance to a stirring
band of music—some occasional light pie in which even
M'Choakumchild had no finger—which craving must and
would be satisfied aright, or must and would inevitably go
wrong, until the laws of the Creation were repealed?

"This man lives at Pod's End, and I don't quite know Pod's
End," said Mr. Gradgrind. "Which is it, Bounderby?"

Mr. Bounderby knew it was somewhere down town, but
knew no more respecting it. So they stopped for a moment,
looking about.

Almost as they did so, there came running round the corner
of the street at a quick pace and with a frightened look, a girl
whom Mr. Gradgrind recognised. "Halloa!" said he. "Stop!
Where are you going? Stop!" Girl number twenty stopped
then, palpitating, and made him a curtsey.

"Why are you tearing about the streets," said Mr. Gradgrind, "in this improper manner?"

"I was—I was run after, sir," the girl panted, "and I
wanted to get away."

"Run after?" repeated Mr. Gradgrind. "Who would run
after *you?*"

The question was unexpectedly and suddenly answered for
her, by the colourless boy, Bitzer, who came round the corner
with such blind speed and so little anticipating a stoppage on

the pavement, that he brought himself up against **Mr. Grad-grind's** waistcoat and rebounded into the road.

"What do you mean, boy?" said Mr. Gradgrind. "What are you doing? How dare you dash against—everybody— in this manner?"

Bitzer picked up his cap, which the concussion had knocked off; and backing, and knuckling his forehead, pleaded that it was an accident.

"Was this boy running after you, Jupe?" asked Mr. Gradgrind.

"Yes, sir," said the girl reluctantly.

"No, I wasn't, sir!" cried Bitzer. "Not till she ran away from me. But the horse-riders never mind what they say, sir; they're famous for it. You know the horse-riders are famous for never minding what they say," addressing Sissy. "It's as well known in the town as—please, sir, as the multi-plication table isn't known to the horse-riders." Bitzer tried Mr. Bounderby with this.

"He frightened me so," said the girl, "with his cruel faces!"

"Oh!" cried Bitzer. "Oh! An't you one of the rest! An't you a horse-rider! I never looked at her, sir. I asked her if she would know how to define a horse to-morrow, and offered to tell her again, and she ran away, and I ran after her, sir, that she might know how to answer when she was asked. You wouldn't have thought of saying such mischief if you hadn't been a horse-rider!"

"Her calling seems to be pretty well known among 'em," observed Mr. Bounderby. "You'd have had the whole school peeping in a row, in a week."

"Truly, I think so," returned his friend. "Bitzer, turn you about and take yourself home. Jupe, stay here a moment. Let me hear of your running in this manner any more, boy, and you will hear of me through the master of the school. You understand what I mean. Go along."

The boy stopped in his rapid blinking, knuckled his fore-head again, glanced at Sissy, turned about, and retreated.

"Now, girl," said Mr. Gradgrind, "take this gentleman and me to your father's; we are going there. What have you got in that bottle you are carrying?"

"Gin," said Mr. Bounderby.

"Dear, no, sir! It's the nine oils."

"The what?" cried Mr. Bounderby.

"The nine oils, sir. To rub father with." Then said Mr. Bounderby, with a loud short laugh, "what the devil do you rub your father with nine oils for?"

"It's what our people always use, sir, when they get any hurts in the ring," replied the girl, looking over her shoulder, to assure herself that her pursuer was gone. "They bruise themselves very bad sometimes."

"Serve 'em right," said Mr. Bounderby, "for being idle." She glanced up at his face, with mingled astonishment and dread.

"By George!" said Mr. Bounderby, "when I was four or five years younger than you, I had worse bruises upon me than ten oils, twenty oils, forty oils, would have rubbed off. I didn't get 'em by posture-making but by being banged about. There was no rope-dancing for me; I danced on the bare ground and was larruped with the rope."

Mr. Gradgrind, though hard enough, was by no means so rough a man as Mr. Bounderby. His character was not unkind, all things considered; it might have been a very kind one indeed, if he had only made some round mistake in the arithmetic that balanced it, years ago. He said, in what he meant for a reassuring tone, as they turned down a narrow road, "And this is Pod's End; is it, Jupe?"

"This is it, sir, and—if you wouldn't mind, sir—this is the house."

She stopped, at twilight, at the door of a mean little public-house, with dim red lights in it. As haggard and as shabby, as if, for want of custom, it had itself taken to drinking, and had gone the way all drunkards go, and was very near the end of it.

"It's only crossing the bar, sir, and up the stairs, if you wouldn't mind, and waiting there for a moment till I get a candle. If you should hear a dog, sir, it's only Merrylegs, and he only barks."

"Merrylegs and nine oils, eh!" said Mr. Bounderby, entering last with his metallic laugh. "Pretty well this, for a self-made man!"

CHAPTER VI : *Sleary's Horsemanship*
THE name of the public-house was the Pegasus's Arms. The Pegasus's legs might have been more to the purpose; but, underneath the winged horse upon the signboard, the Pegasus's Arms was incribed in Roman letters. Beneath this inscription again, in a flowing scroll, the painter had touched off the lines:

> *Good malt makes good beer,*
> *Walk in and they'll draw it here ;*
> *Good wine makes good brandy,*
> *Give us a call, and you'll find it handy.*

Framed and glazed upon the wall behind the dingy little bar, was another Pegasus—a theatrical one—with real gauze let in for his wings, golden stars stuck on all over him, and his ethereal harness made of red silk.

As it had grown too dusky without to see the sign, and as it had not grown light enough within to see the picture, Mr. Gradgrind and Mr. Bounderby received no offence from these idealities. They followed the girl up some steep corner-stairs without meeting any one, and stopped in the dark while she went for a candle. They expected every moment to hear Merrylegs give tongue, but the highly trained performing dog had not barked when the girl and the candle appeared together.

"Father is not in our room, sir," she said, with a face of great surprise. "If you wouldn't mind walking in, I'll find him directly."

They walked in; and Sissy, having set two chairs for them, sped away with a quick light step. It was a mean, shabbily furnished room, with a bed in it. The white night-cap, embellished with two peacock's feathers and a pigtail bolt upright, in which Signor Jupe had that very afternoon enlivened the varied performances with his chaste Shaksperean quips and retorts, hung upon a nail; but no other portion of his wardrobe, or other token of himself or his pursuits, was to be seen anywhere. As to Merrylegs, that respectable ancestor of the highly trained animal who went aboard the ark, might have been accidentally shut out of it, for any sign of a dog that was manifest to eye or ear in the Pegasus's Arms.

They heard the doors of rooms above, opening and shutting as Sissy went from one to another in quest of her father; and presently they heard voices expressing surprise. She came bounding down again in a great hurry, opened a battered and mangy old hair trunk, found it empty, and looked round with her hands clasped and her face full of terror.

"Father must have gone down to the Booth, sir. I don't know why he should go there, but he must be there; I'll bring him in a minute!" She was gone directly, without her bonnet; with her long, dark, childish hair streaming behind her.

"What does she mean!" said Mr. Gradgrind. "Back in a minute? It's more than a mile off."

Before Mr. Bounderby could reply, a young man appeared at the door, and introducing himself with the words, "By your leaves, gentlemen!" walked in with his hands in his pockets. His face, close-shaven, thin, and sallow, was shaded by a great quantity of dark hair, brushed into a roll all round his head, and parted up the centre. His legs were very robust, but shorter than legs of good proportions should have been. His chest and back were as much too broad, as his legs were too short. He was dressed in a Newmarket coat and tight-fitting trousers; wore a shawl round his neck; smelt of lamp-oil, straw, orange-peel, horses' provender, and sawdust; and looked a most remarkable sort of Centaur, compounded of the stable and the play-house. Where the one began, and the other ended, nobody could have told with any precision. This gentleman was mentioned in the bills of the day as Mr. E. W. B. Childers, so justly celebrated for his daring vaulting act as the Wild Huntsman of the North American Prairies; in which popular performance, a diminutive boy with an old face, who now accompanied him, assisted as his infant son: being carried upside down over his father's shoulder, by one foot, and held by the crown of his head, heels upward, in the palm of his father's hand, according to the violent paternal manner in which wild huntsmen may be observed to fondle their offspring. Made up with curls, wreaths, wings, white bismuth, and carmine, this hopeful young person soared into so pleasing a Cupid as to constitute the chief delight of the maternal part of the spectators; but in private, where his characteristics were a precocious cutaway coat and an extremely gruff voice, he became of the Turf, turfy.

"By your leaves, gentlemen," said Mr. E. W. B. Childers, glancing round the room. "It was you, I believe, that were wishing to see Jupe!"

"It was," said Mr. Gradgrind. "His daughter has gone to fetch him, but I can't wait; therefore, if you please, I will leave a message for him with you."

"You see, my friend," Mr. Bounderby put in, "we are the kind of people who know the value of time, and you are the kind of people who don't know the value of time."

"I have not," retorted Mr. Childers, after surveying him from head to foot, "the honour of knowing *you*,—but if you mean that you can make more money of your time than I can of mine, I should judge from your appearance, that you are about right."

"And when you have made it, you can keep it too, I should think," said Cupid.

"Kidderminster, stow that!" said Mr. Childers. (Master Kidderminster was Cupid's mortal name.)

"What does he come here cheeking us for, then?" cried Master Kidderminster, showing a very irascible temperament. "If you want to cheek us, pay your ochre at the doors and take it out."

"Kidderminster," said Mr. Childers, raising his voice, "stow that!—Sir," to Mr. Gradgrind, "I was addressing myself to you. You may or you may not be aware (for perhaps you have not been much in the audience), that Jupe has missed his tip very often lately."

"Has—what has he missed?" asked Mr. Gradgrind, glancing at the potent Bounderby for assistance.

"Missed his tip."

"Offered at the garters four times last night, and never don em once," said Master Kidderminster. "Missed his tip at the banners, too, and was loose in his ponging."

"Didn't do what he ought to. Was short in his leaps and bad in his tumbling," Mr. Childers interpreted.

"Oh!" said Mr. Gradgrind, "that is tip, is it?"

"In a general way that's missing his tip," Mr. E. W. B. Childers answered.

"Nine oils, Merrylegs, missing tips, garters, banners, and ponging, eh!" ejaculated Bounderby, with his laugh of laughs. "Queer sort of company, too, for a man who has raised himself."

"Lower yourself, then," retorted Cupid. "O Lord! if you've raised yourself so high as all that comes to, let yourself down a bit."

"This is a very obtrusive lad!" said Mr. Gradgrind, turning, and knitting his brows on him.

"We'd have had a young gentleman to meet you, if we had known you were coming," retorted Master Kidderminster, nothing abashed. "It's a pity you don't have a bespeak, being so particular. You're on the Tight-Jeff, ain't you?"

"What does this unmannerly boy mean," asked Mr. Gradgrind, eyeing him in a sort of desperation, "by Tight-Jeff?"

"There! Get out, get out!" said Mr. Childers, thrusting his young friend from the room, rather in the prairie manner. "Tight-Jeff or Slack-Jeff, it don't much signify: it's only tight-rope and slack-rope. You were going to give me a message for Jupe?"

"Yes I was."

"Then," continued Mr. Childers, quickly, "my opinion is, he will never receive it. Do you know much of him?"

"I never saw the man in my life."

"I doubt if you ever _will_ see him now. It's pretty plain to me, he's off."

"Do you mean that he has deserted his daughter?"

"Ay! I mean," said Mr. Childers, with a nod, "that he has cut. He was goosed last night, he was goosed the night before last, he was goosed to-day. He has lately got in the way of being always goosed, and he can't stand it."

"Why has he been—so very much—Goosed?" asked Mr. Gradgrind, forcing the words out of himself, with great solemnity and reluctance.

"His joints are turning stiff, and he is getting used up," said Childers. "He has his points as a Cackler still, but he can't get a living out of _them_."

"A Cackler!" Bounderby repeated. "Here we go again!"

"A speaker, if the gentleman likes it better," said Mr. E. W. B. Childers, superciliously throwing the interpretation over his shoulder, and accompanying it with a shake of his long hair—which all shook at once. "Now, it's a remarkable fact,

sir, that it cut that man deeper, to know that his daughter
knew of his being goosed, than to go through with it."

"Good!" interrupted Mr. Bounderby. "This is good,
Gradgrind! A man so fond of his daughter, that he runs away
from her! This is devilish good! Ha! ha! Now, I'll tell you
what, young man. I haven't always occupied my present
station of life. I know what these things are. You may be
astonished to hear it, but my mother ran away from *me*."

E. W. B. Childers replied pointedly, that he was not at all
astonished to hear it.

"Very well," said Bounderby. "I was born in a ditch, and
my mother ran away from me. Do I excuse her for it? No.
Have I ever excused her for it? Not I. What do I call her
for it? I call her probably the very worst woman that ever
lived in the world, except my drunken grandmother. There's
no family pride about me, there's no imaginative sentimental
humbug about me. I call a spade a spade; and I call the
mother of Josiah Bounderby of Coketown, without any fear or
any favour, what I should call her if she had been the mother of
Dick Jones of Wapping. So, with this man. He is a runaway
rogue and a vagabond, that's what he is, in English."

"It's all the same to me what he is or what he is not, whether
in English or whether in French," retorted Mr. E. W. B.
Childers, facing about. "I am telling your friend what's the
fact; if you don't like to hear it, you can avail yourself of the
open air. You give it mouth enough, you do; but give it
mouth in your own building at least," remonstrated E. W. B.
with stern irony. "You have got some building of your own,
I dare say?"

"Perhaps so," replied Mr. Bounderby rattling his money
and laughing.,

"Then give it mouth in your own building, will you, if you
please!" said Childers. "Because this isn't a strong building
and too much of you might bring it down!"

Eyeing Mr Bounderby from head to foot again, he turned
from him, as from a man finally disposed of, to Mr. Gradgrind.

"Jupe sent his daughter out on an errand not an hour ago,
and then was seen to slip out himself, with his hat over his
eyes, and a bundle tied up in a handkerchief under his arm.
She will never believe it of him, but he has cut away and left
her."

"Pray," said Mr. Gradgrind, "why will she never believe
of him?"

"Because those two were one. Because they were never
asunder. Because, up to this time, he seemed to dote upon
her," said Childers, taking a step or two to look into the
empty trunk. Both Mr. Childers and Master Kidderminster
walked in a curious manner; with their legs wider apart than
the general run of men, and with a very knowing assumption

of being stiff in the knees. This walk was common to all the male members of Sleary's company, and was understood to express, that they were always on horseback.

"Poor Sissy! He had better have apprenticed her," said Childers giving his hair another shake, as he looked up from the empty box. "Now, he leaves her without anything to take to."

"It is creditable to you, who have never been apprenticed, to express that opinion," returned Mr. Gradgrind, approvingly.

"*I* never apprenticed? I was apprenticed when I was seven years old."

"Oh! Indeed?" said Mr. Gradgrind, rather resentfully, as having been defrauded of his good opinion. "I was not aware of its being the custom to apprentice young persons to——"

"Idleness," Mr. Bounderby put in with a loud laugh. "No, by the Lord Harry! Nor I!"

"Her father always had it in his head," resumed Childers, feigning unconsciousness of Mr. Bounderby's existence, "that she was to be taught the deuce-and-all of education. How it got into his head, I can't say; I can only say that it never got out. He has been picking up a bit of reading for her, here —and a bit of writing for her, there—and a bit of ciphering for her, somewhere else—these seven years."

Mr. E. W. B. Childers took one of his hands out of his pockets, stroked his face and chin, and looked, with a good deal of doubt and a little hope, at Mr. Gradgrind. From the first he had sought to conciliate that gentleman, for the sake of the deserted girl.

"When Sissy got into the school here," he pursued, "her father was as pleased as Punch. I couldn't altogether make out why, myself, as we were not stationary here, being but comers and goers anywhere. I suppose, however, he had this move in his mind—he was always half-cracked—and then considered her provided for. If you should happen to have looked in to-night for the purpose of telling him that you were going to do her any little service," said Mr. Childers, stroking his face again, and repeating his look, "it would be very fortunate and well-timed; *very* fortunate and well-timed."

"On the contrary," returned Mr. Gradgrind. "I came to tell him that her connections made her not an object for the school, and that she must not attend any more. Still, if her father really has left her without any connivance on her part— Bounderby, let me have a word with you."

Upon this, Mr. Childers politely took himself, with his equestrian walk, to the landing outside the door, and there stood stroking his face, and softly whistling. While thus engaged, he overheard such phrases in Mr. Bounderby's voice as "No. *I* say no. I advise you not. *I* say by no means." While, from Mr. Gradgrind, he heard in his much lower tone the words, "But even as an example to Louisa, of what this pursuit which has been the subject of a vulgar curiosity, leads to and ends in. Think of it, Bounderby, in that point of view."

Meanwhile, the various members of Sleary's company gradually gathered together from the upper regions, where they were quartered, and, from standing about, talking in low voices to one another and to Mr. Childers, gradually insinuated themselves and him into the room. There were two or three handsome young women among them, with their two or three husbands, and their two or three mothers, and their eight or nine little children, who did the fairy business when required. The father of one of the families was in the habit of balancing the father of another of the families on the top of a great pole; the father of a third family often made a pyramid of both those fathers, with Master Kidderminster for the apex, and himself for the base; all the fathers could dance upon rolling casks, stand upon bottles, catch knives and balls, twirl hand-basins, ride upon anything, jump over everything, and stick at nothing. All the mothers could (and did) dance, upon the slack-wire and the tight-rope, and perform rapid acts on bare-backed steeds; none of them were at all particular in respect of showing their legs; and one of them, alone in a Greek chariot, drove six in hand into every town they came to. They all assumed to be mighty rakish and knowing, they were not very tidy in their private dresses, they were not at all orderly in their domestic arrangements, and the combined literature of the whole company would have produced but a poor letter on any subject. Yet there was a remarkable gentleness and childishness about these people, a special inaptitude for any kind of sharp practice, and an untiring readiness to help and pity one another, deserving often of as much respect, and always of as much generous construction, as the every-day virtues of any class of people in the world.

Last of all appeared Mr. Sleary: a stout man as already mentioned, with one fixed eye, and one loose eye, a voice (if it can be called so) like the efforts of a broken old pair of bellows, a flabby surface, and a muddled head which was never sober and never drunk.

"Thquire!" said Mr. Sleary, who was troubled with asthma, and whose breath came far to quick and heavy for the letter s, "Your thervant! Thith ith a bad piethe of bithnith, thith ith. You've heard of my Clown and hith dog being thuppothed to have morrithed?"

He addressed Mr. Gradgrind, who answered "Yes."

"Well, Thquire," he returned, taking off his hat, and rubbing the lining with his pocket-handkerchief, which he kept inside for the purpose. "Ith it your intenthion to do anything for the poor girl, Thquire?"

"I shall have something to propose to her when she comes back," said Mr. Gradgrind.

"Glad to hear it, Thquire. Not that I want to get rid of the child, any more than I want to thtand in her way. I'm willing to take her prentith, though at her age ith late. My voithe ith a little huthky, Thquire, and not eathy heard by them ath don't know me; but if you'd been chilled and heated, heated and chilled, chilled and heated in the ring when you wath young, ath often ath I have been, *your* voithe wouldn't have lathted out, Thquire no more than mine."

"I dare say not," said Mr. Gradgrind.

"What thall it be, Thquire, while you wait? Thall t be Therry? Give it a name, Thquire!" said Mr. Sleary, *r*ith hospitable ease.

"Nothing for me, I thank you," said Mr. Gradgrind.

"Don't thay nothing, Thquire. What doth your friend thay? If you haven't took your feed yet, have a glath of bitterth."

Here his daughter Josephine—a pretty fair-haired girl of eighteen who had been tied on a horse at two years old, and had made a will at twelve, which she always carried about with her, expressive of her dying desire to be drawn to the grave by the two piebald ponies—cried, "Father, hush! she has come back!" Then came Sissy Jupe, running into the room as she had run out of it. And when she saw them all assembled, and saw their looks, and saw no father there, she broke into a most deplorable cry, and took refuge on the bosom of the most accomplished tight-rope lady (herself in the family-way), who knelt down on the floor to nurse her and to weep over her.

"Ith an infernal thame, upon my thoul it ith," said Sleary.

"O my dear father, my good kind father, where are you gone? You are gone to try to do me some good, I know! You are gone away for my sake, I am sure! And how miserable and helpless you will be without me, poor, poor father, until you come back!" It was so pathetic to hear her saying many things of this kind, with her face turned upward, and her arms stretched out as if she were trying to stop his departing shadow and embrace it, that no one spoke a word until Mr. Bounderby (growing impatient) took the case in hand.

"Now, good people all," said he, "this is wanton waste of time. Let the girl understand the fact. Let her take it from me, if you like, who have been run away from myself. Here, what's your name! Your father has absconded—deserted you—and you mustn't expect to see him again as long as you live."

They cared so little for plain Fact, these people, and were in that advanced state of degeneracy on the subject, that instead of being impressed by the speaker's strong common sense, they took it in extraordinary dudgeon. The men muttered "Shame!"

and the women "Brute!" and Sleary, in some haste, communicated the following hint, apart to Mr. Bounderby.

"I tell you what, Thquire. To thpeak plain to you, my opinion ith that you had better cut it thort, and drop it. They're a very good-natur'd people, my people, but they're accuthtomed to be quick in their movementh; and if you don't act upon my advithe, I'm damned if I don't believe they'll pith you out o' winder."

Mr. Bounderby being restrained by this mild suggestion, Mr. Gradgrind found an opening for his eminently practical exposition of the subject.

"It is of no moment," said he, "whether this person is to be expected back at any time, or the contrary. He is gone away, and there is no present expectation of his return. That, I believe, is agreed on all hands."

"Thath agreed, Thquire. Thtick to that!" From Sleary.

"Well then. I, who came here to inform the father of the poor girl, Jupe, that she could not be received at the school any more, in consequence of there being practical objections, into which I need not enter, to the reception there of the children of people so employed, am prepared in these altered circumstances to make a proposal. I am willing to take charge of you, Jupe, and to educate you, and provide for you. The only condition (over and above your good behaviour) I make is, that you decide now, at once, whether to accompany me or remain here. Also, that if you accompany me now, it is understood that you communicate no more with any of your friends who are here present. These observations comprise the whole of the case."

"At the thame time," said Sleary, "I mutht put in my word, Thquire, tho that both thideth of the banner may be equally theen. If you like, Thethilia, to be prentitht, you know the natur of the work and you know your companionth. Emma Gordon, in whothe lap you're a lying at prethent would be a mother to you, and Joth'phine would be a thithter to you. I don't pretend to be of the angel breed mythelf, and I don't thay but what, when you mith'd your tip, you'd find me cut up rough, and thwear an oath or two at you. But what I thay, Thquire, ith, that good tempered or bad tempered, I never did a horthe a injury yet, no more than thwearing at him went, and that I don't expect I thall begin otherwithe at my time of life, with a rider. I never wath much of a Cackler, Thquire, and I have thed my thay."

The latter part of this speech was addressed to Mr. Gradgrind, who received it with a grave inclination of his head, and then remarked:

"The only observation I will make to you, Jupe, in the way of influencing your decision, is, that it is highly desirable to have a sound practical education. and that even your father himself (from what I understand) appears, on your behalf, to have known and felt that much."

The last words had a visible effect upon her. She stopped in her wild crying, a little detached herself from Emma Gordon, and turned her face full upon her patron. The whole company perceived the force of the change, and drew a long breath together, that plainly said, "she will go!"

"Be sure you know your own mind, Jupe," Mr. Gradgrind cautioned her; "I say no more. Be sure you know your own mind!"

"When father comes back," cried the girl, bursting into tears again after a minute's silence, "how will he ever find me if I go away!"

"You may be quite at ease," said Mr. Gradgrind, calmly; he worked out the whole matter like a sum: "you may be quite at ease, Jupe, on that score. In such a case, your father, I apprehend, must find out Mr.——"

"Thleary. Thath my name, Thquire. Not athamed of it. Known all over England, and alwayth payth ith way."

"Must find out Mr. Sleary, who would then let him know where you went. I should have no power of keeping you against his wish, and he would have no difficulty, at any time, in finding Mr. Gradgrind of Coketown. I am well known."

"Well known," assented Mr. Sleary, rolling his loose eye. "You're one of the thort, Thquire, that keepth a prethiouth thight of money out of the houthe. But never mind that at prethent."

There was another silence; and then she exclaimed, sobbing with her hands before her face, "Oh give me my clothes, give me my clothes, and let me go away before I break my heart!"

The women sadly bestirred themselves to get the clothes together—it was soon done, for they were not many—and to pack them in a basket which had often travelled with them. Sissy sat all the time, upon the ground, still sobbing, and covering her eyes. Mr. Gradgrind and his friend Bounderby stood near the door, ready to take her away. Mr. Sleary stood in the middle of the room, with the male members of the company about him, exactly as he would have stood in the centre of the ring during his daughter Josephine's performance. He wanted nothing but his whip.

The basket packed in silence, they brought her bonnet to her, and smoothed her disordered hair, and put it on. Then they pressed about her, and bent over her in very natural attitudes, kissing and embracing her: and brought the children to take leave of her; and were a tender-hearted, simple, foolish set of women altogether.

"Now, Jupe," said Mr. Gradgrind. "If you are quite determined, come!"

But she had to take her farewell of the male part of the

company yet, and every one of them had to unfold his arms (for they all assumed the professional attitude when they found themselves near Sleary), and give her a parting kiss—Master Kidderminster excepted, in whose young nature there was an original flavour of the misanthrope, who was also known to have harboured matrimonial views, and who moodily withdrew. Mr. Sleary was reserved until the last. Opening his arms wide he took her by both her hands, and would have sprung her up and down, after the riding-master manner of congratulating young ladies on their dismounting from a rapid act; but there was no rebound in Sissy, and she only stood before him crying.

"Good-bye, my dear!" said Sleary. "You'll make your fortun, I hope, and none of our poor folkth will ever trouble you, I'll pound it. I with your father hadn't taken hith dog with him; ith a ill-conwenienth to have the dog out of the billth. But on thecond thoughth, he wouldn't have performed without hith mathter, tho ith ath broad ath ith long!"

With that he regarded her attentively with his fixed eye, surveyed his company with his loose one, kissed her, shook his head, and handed her to Mr. Gradgrind as to a horse.

"There the ith, Thquire," he said, sweeping her with a professional glance as if she were being adjusted in her seat, "and the'll do you juthtithe. Good-bye, Thethilia!"

"Good-bye, Cecilia!" "Good-bye, Sissy!" "God bless you, dear!" In a variety of voices from all the room.

But the riding-master eye had observed the bottle of the nine oils in her bosom, and he now interposed with "Leave the bottle, my dear; ith large to carry; it will be of no uthe to you now. Give it to me!"

"No, no!" she said, in another burst of tears. "Oh, no! Pray let me keep it for father till he comes back! He will want it when he comes back. He had never thought of going away, when he sent me for it. I must keep it for him, if you please!"

"Tho be it, my dear. (You see how it ith, Thquire!) Farewell, Thethilia! My latht wordth to you ith thith, Thtick to the termth of your engagement, be obedient to the Thquire, and forget uth. But if, when you're grown up and married and well off, you come upon any horthe-riding ever, don't be hard upon it, don't be croth with it, give it a Bethpeak if you can, and think you might do wurth. People mutht be amuthed, Thquire, thomehow," continued Sleary, rendered more pursy than ever, by so much talking; "they can't be alwayth a working, nor yet they can't be alwayth a learning. Make the betht of uth; not the wurtht. I've got my living out of the horthe-riding all my life, I know; but I conthider that I lay down the philothophy of the thubject when I thay to you, Thquire, make the betht of uth: not the wurtht!"

The Sleary philosophy was propounded as they went downstairs; and the fixed eye of Philosophy—and its rolling eye, too—soon lost the three figures and the basket in the darkness of the street.

CHAPTER VII : *Mrs. Sparsit*

MR. BOUNDERBY being a bachelor, an elderly lady presided over his establishment, in consideration of a certain annual stipend. Mrs. Sparsit was this lady's name; and she was a prominent figure in attendance on Mr. Bounderby's car, as it rolled along in triumph with the Bully of humility inside.

For, Mrs. Sparsit had not only seen different days, but was highly connected. She had a great aunt living in these very times called Lady Scadgers. Mr. Sparsit, deceased, of whom she was the relict, had been by the mother's side what Mrs. Sparsit still called "a Powler." Strangers of limited information and dull apprehension were sometimes observed not to know what a Powler was, and even to appear uncertain whether it might be a business, or a political party, or a profession of faith. The better class of minds, however, did not need to be informed that the Powlers were an ancient stock, who could trace themselves so exceedingly far back that it was not surprising if they sometimes lost themselves—which they had rather frequently done, as respected horse-flesh, blind-hookey, Hebrew monetary transactions, and the Insolvent Debtors Court.

The late Mr. Sparsit, being by the mother's side a Powler, married this lady, being by the father's side a Scadgers. Lady Scadgers (an immensely fat old woman, with an inordinate appetite for butcher's meat, and a mysterious leg which had now refused to get out of bed for fourteen years) contrived the marriage, at a period when Sparsit was just of age, and chiefly noticeable for a slender body, weakly supported on two long slim props, and surmounted by no head worth mentioning. He inherited a fair fortune from his uncle, but owed it all before he came into it, and spent it twice over immediately afterwards. Thus, when he died, at twenty-four (the scene of his decease, Calais, and the cause, brandy), he did not leave his widow, from whom he had been separated soon after the honeymoon, in affluent circumstances. That bereaved lady, fifteen years older than he, fell presently at deadly feud with her only relative, Lady Scadgers; and, partly to spite her ladyship, and partly to maintain herself, went out at a salary. And here she was now, in her elderly days, with the Coriolanian style of nose and the dense black eyebrows which had captivated Sparsit, making Mr. Bounderby's tea as he took his breakfast.

If Bounderby had been a Conqueror, and Mrs. Sparsit a captive Princess whom he took about as a feature in his state-processions, he could not have made a greater flourish with her than he habitually did. Just as it belonged to his boastfulness to depreciate his own extraction, so it belonged to it to exalt Mrs. Sparsit's. In the measure that he would not allow his own youth to have been attended by a single favourable circumstance, he brightened Mrs. Sparsit's juvenile career with every possible advantage, and showered wagon-loads of early roses all over that lady's path. "And yet, sir," he would say, "how does it turn out after all? Why here she is at a hundred a year (I give her a hundred, which she is pleased to term handsome), keeping the house of Josiah Bounderby of Coketown!"

Nay, he made this foil of his so very widely known, that third parties took it up, and handled it on some occasions with considerable briskness. It was one of the most exasperating attributes of Bounderby, that he not only sang his own praises but stimulated other men to sing them. There was a moral infection of clap-trap in him. Strangers, modest enough elsewhere, started up at dinners in Coketown, and boasted, in quite a rampant way, of Bounderby. They made him out to be the Royal arms, the Union-Jack, Magna Charta, John Bull, Habeas Corpus, the Bill of Rights, An Englishman's house is his castle, Church and State, and God save the Queen, all put together. And as often (and it was very often) as an orator of this kind brought into his peroration,

> "*Princes and lords may flourish or may fade,*
> *A breath can make them, as a breath has made*,"

—it was, for certain, more or less understood among the company that he had heard of Mrs. Sparsit.

"Mr. Bounderby," said Mrs. Sparsit, "you are unusually slow, sir, with your breakfast this morning."

"Why, ma'am," he returned, "I am thinking about Tom Gradgrind's whim"; Tom Gradgrind, for a bluff independent manner of speaking—as if somebody were always endeavouring to bribe him with immense sums to say Thomas, and he wouldn't; "Tom Gradgrind's whim, ma'am, of bringing up the tumbling-girl."

"The girl is now waiting to know," said Mrs. Sparsit, "whether she is to go straight to the school, or up to the Lodge."

"She must wait, ma'am," answered Bounderby, "till I know myself. We shall have Tom Gradgrind down here presently, I suppose. If he should wish her to remain here a day or two longer, of course she can, ma'am."

"Of course she can if you wish it, Mr. Bounderby."

"I told him I would give her a shake-down here, last night, in order that he might sleep on it before he decided to let her have any association with Louisa."

"Indeed, Mr. Bounderby? Very thoughtful of you!"

Mrs. Sparsit's Coriolanian nose underwent a slight expansion of the nostrils, and her black eyebrows contracted as she took a sip of tea.

"It's tolerably clear to *me*," said Bounderby, "that the little puss can get small good out of such companionship."

"Are you speaking of young Miss Gradgrind, Mr. Bounderby?"

"Yes, ma'am, I'm speaking of Louisa."

"Your observation being limited to 'little puss,'" said Mrs. Sparsit, "and there being two little girls in question, I did not know which might be indicated by the expression."

"Louisa," repeated Mr. Bounderby. "Louisa, Louisa."

"You are quite another father to Louisa, sir." Mrs. Sparsit took a little more tea; and, as she bent her again contracted eyebrows over her steaming cup, rather looked as if her classical countenance were invoking the infernal gods.

"If you had said I was another father to Tom—young Tom, I mean, not my friend Tom Gradgrind—you might have been nearer the mark. I am going to take young Tom into my office. Going to have him under my wing, ma'am."

"Indeed? Rather young for that, is he not, sir?" Mrs. Sparsit's "sir," in addressing Mr. Bounderby, was a word of ceremony, rather exacting consideration for herself in the use, than honouring him.

"I'm not going to take him at once; he is to finish his educational cramming before then," said Bounderby. "By the Lord Harry, he'll have enough of it, first and last! He'd open his eyes, that boy would, if he knew how empty of learning *my* young maw was, at his time of life." Which, by-the-by, he probably did know, for he had heard of it often enough. "But it's extraordinary the difficulty I have on scores of such subjects, in speaking to any one on equal terms. Here, for example, I have been speaking to you this morning about tumblers. Why, what do *you* know about tumblers? At the time when, to have been a tumbler in the mud of the streets, would have been a godsend to me, a prize in the lottery to me, you were at the Italian Opera. You were coming out of the Italian Opera, ma'am, in white satin and jewels, a blaze of splendour, when I hadn't a penny to buy a link to light you."

"I certainly, sir," returned Mrs. Sparsit, with a dignity serenely mournful, "was familiar with the Italian Opera at a very early age."

"Egad, ma'am, so was I," said Bounderby, "—with the wrong side of it. A hard bed the pavement of its Arcade used to make, I assure you. People like you, ma'am, accustomed from infancy to lie on down feathers, have no idea *now* hard a paving-stone is, without trying it. No, no, it's of no use my talking to *you* about tumblers. I should speak of foreign dancers, and the West End of London, and May Fair, and lords and ladies and honourables."

"I trust, sir," rejoined Mrs. Sparsit, with decent resignation, "it is not necessary that you should do anything of that kind. I hope I have learnt how to accommodate myself to the changes of life. If I have acquired an interest in hearing of your instructive experiences, and can scarcely hear enough of them, I claim no merit for that, since I believe it is a general sentiment."

"Well, ma'am," said her patron, "perhaps some people may be pleased to say that they do like to hear, in his own unpolished way, what Josiah Bounderby, of Coketown, has gone through. But you must confess that you were born in the lap of luxury, yourself. Come, ma'am, you know you were born in the lap of luxury."

"I do not, sir," returned Mrs. Sparsit with a shake of her head, "deny it."

Mr. Bounderby was obliged to get up from table, and stand with his back to the fire, looking at her; she was such an enhancement of his position.

"And you were in crack society. Devilish high society," he said, warming his legs.

"It is true, sir," returned Mrs. Sparsit, with an affectation of humility the very opposite of his, and therefore in no danger of jostling it.

"You were in the tip-top fashion, and all the rest of it," said Mr. Bounderby.

"Yes, sir," returned Mrs. Sparsit, with a kind of social widowhood upon her. "It is unquestionably true."

Mr. Bounderby, bending himself at the knees, literally embraced his legs in his great satisfaction and laughed aloud. Mr. and Miss Gradgrind being then announced, he received the former with a shake of the hand, and the latter with a kiss.

"Can Jupe be sent here, Bounderby?" asked Mr. Gradgrind.

Certainly. So Jupe was sent there. On coming in, she curtseyed to Mr. Bounderby, and to his friend Tom Gradgrind, and also to Louisa; but in her confusion unluckily omitted Mrs. Sparsit. Observing this, the blustrous Bounderby had the following remarks to make:

"Now, I tell you what, my girl. The name of that lady by the tea-pot, is Mrs. Sparsit. That lady acts as mistress of this house, and she is a highly connected lady. Consequently, if ever you come again into any room in this house, you will make a short stay in it if you don't behave towards that lady in your most respectful manner. Now, I don't care a button what you do to *me*, because I don't affect to be anybody. So far from having high connections I have no connections at all, and I come of the scum of the earth. But towards that lady, I do care what you do; and you shall do what is deferential and respectful, or you shall not come here."

"I hope, Bounderby," said Mr. Gradgrind, in a conciliatory voice, "that this was merely an oversight."

"My friend Tom Gradgrind suggests, Mrs. Sparsit," said Bounderby, "that this was merely an oversight. Very likely. However, as you are aware, ma'am, I don't allow of even oversights towards you."

"You are very good indeed, sir," returned Mrs. Sparsit, shaking her head with her state humility. "It is not worth speaking of."

Sissy, who all this time had been faintly excusing herself with tears in her eyes, was now waved over by the master of the house to Mr. Gradgrind. She stood looking intently at him, and Louisa stood coldly by, with her eyes upon the ground, while he proceeded thus:

"Jupe, I have made up my mind to take you into my house; and, when you are not in attendance at the school, to employ you about Mrs. Gradgrind, who is rather an invalid. I have explained to Miss Louisa—this is Miss Louisa—the miserable but natural end of your late career; and you are to expressly understand that the whole of that subject is past, and is not to be referred to any more. From this time you begin your history. You are, at present, ignorant, I know."

"Yes, sir, very," she answered, curtseying.

"I shall have the satisfaction of causing you to be strictly educated; and you will be a living proof to all who come into communication with you, of the advantages of the training you will receive. You will be reclaimed and formed. You have been in the habit now of reading to your father, and those people I found you among, I dare say?" said Mr. Gradgrind, beckoning her nearer to him before he said so, and dropping his voice.

"Only to father and Merrylegs, sir. At least I mean to father, when Merrylegs was always there."

"Never mind Merrylegs, Jupe," said Mr. Gradgrind, with a passing frown. "I don't ask about him. I understand you to have been in the habit of reading to your father?"

"O yes, sir, thousands of times. They were the happiest —O, of all the happy times we had together, sir!"

It was only now when her sorrow broke out, that Louisa looked at her.

"And what," asked Mr. Gradgrind, in a still lower voice, "did you read to your father, Jupe?"

"About the Fairies, sir, and the Dwarf, and the Hunchback and the Genies," she sobbed out; "and about——"

"Hush!" said Mr. Gradgrind, "that is enough. Never

breathe a word of such destructive nonsense any more. Bounderby, this is a case for rigid training, and I shall observe it with interest."

"Well," returned Mr. Bounderby, "I have given you my opinion already, and I shouldn't do as you do. But, very well, very well. Since you are bent upon it, *very* well!"

So, Mr. Gradgrind and his daughter took Cecilia Jupe off with them to Stone Lodge, and on the way Louisa never spoke one word, good or bad. And Mr. Bounderby went about his daily pursuits. And Mrs. Sparsit got behind her eyebrows and meditated in the gloom of that retreat, all the evening.

CHAPTER VIII: *Never Wonder*

LET us strike the key-note again, before pursuing the tune.

When she was half a dozen years younger, Louisa had been overheard to begin a conversation with her brother one day, by saying, "Tom, I wonder"—upon which Mr. Gradgrind, who was the person over-hearing, stepped forth into the light and said, "Louisa, never wonder!"

Herein lay the spring of the mechanical art and mystery of educating the reason without stooping to the cultivation of the sentiments and affections. Never wonder. By means of addition, subtraction, multiplication, and division, settle everything somehow, and never wonder. Bring to me, says M'Choakumchild, yonder baby just able to walk, and I will engage that it shall never wonder.

Now, besides very many babies just able to walk, there happened to be in Coketown a considerable population of babies who had been walking against time towards the infinite world, twenty, thirty, forty, fifty years and more. These portentous infants being alarming creatures to stalk about in any human society, the eighteen denominations incessantly scratched one another's faces and pulled one another's hair by way of agreeing on the steps to be taken for their improvement—which they never did; a surprising circumstance, when the happy adaptation of the means to the end is considered. Still, although they differed in every other particular, conceivable and inconceivable (especially inconceivable), they were pretty well united on the point that these unlucky infants were never to wonder. Body number one, said they must take every thing on trust. Body number two said they must take everything on political economy. Body number three, wrote leaden little books for them, showing how the good grown-up baby invariably got to the Savings-bank, and the bad grown-up baby invariably got transported. Body number four, under dreary pretences of being droll (when it was very melancholy indeed), made the shallowest pretences of concealing pitfalls of knowledge, into which it was the duty of these babies to be smuggled and inveigled. But, all the bodies agreed that they were never to wonder.

There was a library in Coketown, to which general access was easy. Mr. Gradgrind greatly tormented his mind about what the people read in this library: a point whereon little rivers of tabular statements periodically flowed into the howling ocean of tabular statements, which no diver ever got to any depth in and came up sane. It was a disheartening circumstance, but a melancholy fact, that even these readers persisted in wondering. They wondered about human nature, human passions, human hopes and fears, the struggles, triumphs and defeats, the cares and joys and sorrows, the lives and deaths of common men and women! They sometimes, after fifteen hours' work, sat down to read mere fables about men and women, more or less like themselves, and about children, more or less like their own. They took Defoe to their bosoms, instead of Euclid, and seemed to be on the whole more comforted by Goldsmith than by Cocker. Mr. Gradgrind was for ever working, in print and out of print, at this eccentric sum, and he never could make out how it yielded this unaccountable product.

"I am sick of my life, Loo. I hate it altogether, and I hate everybody except you," said the unnatural young Thomas Gradgrind in the hair-cutting chamber at twilight.

"You don't hate Sissy, Tom?"

"I hate to be obliged to call her Jupe. And she hates me," said Tom, moodily.

"No, she does not, Tom, I am sure!"

"She must," said Tom. "She must just hate and detest the whole set-out of us. They'll bother her head off, I think, before they have done with her. Already she is getting as pale as wax, and as heavy as—I am."

Young Thomas expressed these sentiments sitting astride of a chair before the fire, with his arms on the back, and his sulky face on his arms. His sister sat in the darker corner by the fireside, now looking at him, now looking at the bright sparks as they dropped upon the hearth.

"As to me," said Tom, tumbling his hair all manner of ways with his sulky hands, "I am a Donkey, that's what *I* am. I am as obstinate as one, I am more stupid than one, I get as much pleasure as one, and I should like to kick like one."

"Not me, I hope, Tom?"

"No, Loo; I wouldn't hurt *you*. I made an exception of you at first. I don't know what this—jolly old—Jaundiced Jail," Tom had paused to find a sufficiently complimentary and expressive name for the parental roof, and seemed to relieve his mind for a moment by the strong alliteration of this one, "would be without you."

"Indeed, Tom? Do you really and truly say so?"

"Why, of course I do. What's the use of talking about it!" returned Tom, chafing his face on his coat-sleeve, as if to mortify his flesh, and have it in unison with his spirit.

"Because, Tom," said his sister, after silently watching the sparks awhile, "as I get older, and nearer growing up, I often sit wondering here, and think how unfortunate it is for me that I can't reconcile you to home better than I am able to do. I don't know what other girls know. I can't play to you, or sing to you. I can't talk to you so as to lighten your mind, for I never see any amusing sights or read any amusing books that it would be a pleasure or a relief to you to talk about, when you are tired."

"Well, no more do I. I am as bad as you in that respect; and I am a Mule too, which you're not. If father was determined to make me either a Prig or a Mule, and I am not a Prig, why, it stands to reason, I must be a Mule. And so I am," said Tom, desperately.

"It's a great pity," said Louisa, after another pause, and speaking thoughtfully out of her dark corner; "it's a great pity, Tom. It's very unfortunate for both of us."

"Oh! You," said Tom; "you are a girl, Loo, and a girl comes out of it better than a boy does. I don't miss anything in you. You are the only pleasure I have—you can brighten even this place—and you can always lead me as you like."

"You are a dear brother, Tom; and while you think I can do such things, I don't so much mind knowing better. Though I do know better, Tom, and am very sorry for it." She came and kissed him, and went back into her corner again.

"I wish I could collect all the Facts we hear so much about," said Tom, spitefully setting his teeth; "and all the Figures, and all the people who found them out: and I wish I could put a thousand barrels of gunpowder under them, and blow them all up together! However, when I go to live with old Bounderby, I'll have my revenge."

"Your revenge, Tom?"

"I mean, I'll enjoy myself a little, and go about and see something, and hear something. I'll recompense myself for the way in which I have been brought up."

"But don't disappoint yourself beforehand, Tom. Mr. Bounderby thinks as father thinks, and is a great deal rougher, and not half so kind."

"Oh," said Tom, laughing; "I don't mind that. I shall very well know how to manage and smooth old Bounderby!"

Their shadows were defined upon the wall, but those of the high presses in the room were all blended together on the wall and on the ceiling, as if the brother and sister were overhung by a dark cavern. Or, a fanciful imagination—if such treason could have been there—might have made it out to be the shadow of their subject, and of its lowering association with their future.

"What is your great mode of smoothing and managing, Tom? Is it a secret?"

"Oh!" said Tom, "if it is a secret, it's not far off. It's you. You are his little pet, you are his favourite; he'll do anything for you. When he says to me what I don't like, I shall say to him, 'My sister Loo will be hurt and disappointed, Mr. Bounderby. She always used to tell me she was sure you would be easier with me than this.' That'll bring him about, or nothing will."

After waiting for some answering remark, and getting none, Tom wearily relapsed into the present time, and twined himself yawning round and about the rails of his chair, and rumpled his head more and more, until he suddenly looked up, and asked:

"Have you gone to sleep, Loo?"

"No, Tom. I am looking at the fire."

"You seem to find more to look at in it than ever I could find," said Tom. "Another of the advantages, I suppose, of being a girl."

"Tom," inquired his sister, slowly, and in a curious tone, as if she were reading what she asked in the fire, and it were not quite plainly written there, "do you look forward with any satisfaction to this change to Mr. Bounderby's?"

"Why, there's one thing to be said of it," returned Tom, pushing his chair from him, and standing up; "it will be getting away from home."

"There is one thing to be said of it," Louisa repeated in her former curious tone; "it will be getting away from home. Yes."

"Not but what I shall be very unwilling, both to leave you, Loo, and to leave you here. But I must go, you know, whether I like it or not; and I had better go where I can take with me some advantage of your influence, than where I should lose it altogether. Don't you see?"

"Yes, Tom."

The answer was so long in coming, though there was no indecision in it, that Tom went and leaned on the back of her chair, to contemplate the fire which so engrossed her, from her point of view, and see what he could make of it.

"Except that it is a fire," said Tom, "it looks to me as stupid and blank as everything else looks. What do you see in it? Not a circus?"

"I don't see anything in it, Tom, particularly. But since I have been looking at it, I have been wondering about you and me, grown up."

"Wondering again!" said Tom.

"I have such unmanageable thoughts," returned his sister, "that they *will* wonder."

"Then I beg of you, Louisa," said Mrs. Gradgrind, who had opened the door without being heard, "to do nothing of that description, for goodness' sake, you inconsiderate girl, or I shall never hear the last of it from your father. And Thomas, it is really shameful, with my poor head continually wearing me out, that a boy brought up as you have been, and whose education has cost what yours has, should be found encouraging his sister to wonder, when he knows his father has expressly said that she is not to do it."

Louisa denied Tom's participation in the offence; but her mother stopped her with the conclusive answer, "Louisa, don't tell me, in my state of health; for unless you have been encouraged, it is morally and physically impossible that you could have done it."

"I was encouraged by nothing, mother, but by looking at the red sparks dropping out of the fire, and whitening and dying. It made me think, after all, how short my life would be, and how little I could hope to do in it."

"Nonsense!" said Mrs. Gradgrind, rendered almost energetic. "Nonsense! Don't stand there and tell me such stuff, Louisa, to my face, when you know very well that if it was ever to reach your father's ears I should never hear the last of it. After all the trouble that has been taken with you! After the lectures you have attended, and the experiments you have seen! After I have heard you myself, when the whole of my right side has been benumbed, going on with your master about combustion, and calcination, and calorification, and I may say every kind of ation that could drive a poor invalid distracted, to hear you talking in this absurd way about sparks and ashes! I wish," whimpered Mrs. Gradgrind, taking a chair, and discharging her strongest point before succumbing under these mere shadows of facts, "yes, I really *do* wish that I had never had a family, and then you would have known what it was to do without me!"

CHAPTER IX: *Sissy's Progress*

SISSY JUPE had not an easy time of it between Mr. M'Choakumchild and Mrs. Gradgrind, and was not without strong impulses, in the first months of her probation, to run away. It hailed facts all day long so very hard, and life in general was opened to her as such a closely ruled ciphering-book, that assuredly she would have run away, but for only one restraint.

It is lamentable to think of; but this restraint was the result of no arithmetical process, was self-imposed in defiance of all calculation, and went dead against any table of probabilities that any Actuary would have drawn up from the premises. The girl believed that her father had not deserted her; she lived in the hope that he would come back, and in the faith that he would be made the happier by her remaining where she was.

The wretched ignorance with which Jupe clung to this consolation, rejecting the superior comfort of knowing, on a sound arithmetical basis, that her father was an unnatural vagabond, filled Mr. Gradgrind with pity. Yet, what was to be done? M'Choakumchild reported that she had a very dense head for figures; that, once possessed with a general idea of the globe, she took the smallest conceivable interest in its exact measurements; that she was extremely slow in the acquisition of dates, unless some pitiful incident happened to be connected therewith; that she would burst into tears on being required (by the mental process) immediately to name the cost of two hundred and forty-seven muslin caps at fourteen-pence halfpenny; that she was as low down, in the school, as low could be; that after eight weeks of induction into the elements of Political Economy, she had only yesterday been set right by a prattler three feet high, for returning to the question, "What is the first principle of this science?" the absurd answer, "To do unto others as I would that they should do unto me."

Mr. Gradgrind observed, shaking his head, that all this was very bad; that it showed the necessity of infinite grinding at the mill of knowledge, as per system, schedule, blue-book, report, and tabular statements A to Z; and that Jupe "must be kept to it." So Jupe was kept to it, and became low-spirited, but no wiser.

"It would be a fine thing to be you, Miss Louisa!" she said, one night, when Louisa had endeavoured to make her perplexities for next day something clearer to her.

"Do you think so?"

"I should know so much, Miss Louisa. All that is difficult to me now, would be so easy then."

"You might not be the better for it, Sissy."

Sissy submitted, after a little hesitation. "I should not be the worse, Miss Louisa." To which Miss Louisa answered, "I don't know that."

There had been so little communication between these two —both because life at Stone Lodge went monotonously round like a piece of machinery which discouraged human interference, and because of the prohibition relative to Sissy's past career—that they were still almost strangers. Sissy, with her dark eyes wanderingly directed to Louisa's face, was uncertain whether to say more or to remain silent.

"You are more useful to my mother, and more pleasant with her than I can ever be," Louisa resumed. "You are pleasanter to yourself, than *I* am to *my*self."

"But, if you please, Miss Louisa," Sissy pleaded, "I am—
O so stupid!"

Louisa, with a brighter laugh than usual, told her she would
be wiser by-and-by.

"You don't know," said Sissy, half crying, "what a stupid
girl I am. All through school hours I make mistakes. Mr. and
Mrs. M'Choakumchild call me up, over and over again,
regularly to make mistakes. I can't help them. They seem to
come natural to me."

"Mr. and Mrs. M'Choakumchild never make any mistakes
themselves, I suppose, Sissy?"

"O no!" she eagerly returned. "They know everything."

"Tell me some of your mistakes."

"I am almost ashamed," said Sissy, with reluctance. "But
to-day, for instance, Mr. M'Choakumchild was explaining to
us about Natural Prosperity."

"National, I think it must have been," observed Louisa.

"Yes, it was.—But isn't it the same?" she timidly asked.

"You had better say, National, as he said so," returned
Louisa, with her dry reserve.

"National Prosperity. And he said, Now, this schoolroom
is a Nation. And in this nation, there are fifty millions of
money. Isn't this a prosperous nation? Girl number twenty,
isn't this a prosperous nation, and a'n't you in a thriving
state?"

"What did you say?" asked Louisa.

"Miss Louisa, I said I didn't know. I thought I couldn't
know whether it was a prosperous nation or not, and whether
I was in a thriving state or not, unless I knew who had got
the money, and whether any of it was mine. But that had
nothing to do with it. It was not in the figures at all," said
Sissy, wiping her eyes.

"That was a great mistake of yours," observed Louisa.

"Yes, Miss Louisa, I know it was, now. Then Mr. M'Choakumchild said he would try me again. And he said, This school-
room is an immense town, and in it there are a million of
inhabitants, and only five-and-twenty are starved to death in
the streets, in the course of a year. What is your remark on
that proportion? And my remark was—for I couldn't think
of a better one—that I thought it must be just as hard upon
those who were starved, whether the others were a million,
or a million million. And that was wrong, too."

"Of course it was."

"Then Mr. M'Choakumchild said he would try me once
more. And he said, Here are the stutterings——"

"Statistics," said Louisa.

"Yes, Miss Louisa—they always remind me of stutterings,
and that's another of my mistakes—of accidents upon the sea.
And I find (Mr. M'Choakumchild said) that in a given time

a hundred thousand persons went to sea on long voyages, and only five hundred of them were drowned or burnt to death. What is the percentage? And I said, Miss;" here Sissy fairly sobbed as confessing with extreme contrition to her greatest error; "I said it was nothing."

"Nothing, Sissy?"

"Nothing, Miss—to the relations and friends of the people who were killed. I shall never learn," said Sissy. "And the worst of all is, that although my poor father wished me so much to learn, and although I am so anxious to learn, because he wished me to, I am afraid I don't like it."

Louisa stood looking at the pretty modest head, as it drooped abashed before her, until it was raised again to glance at her face. Then she asked:

"Did your father know so much himself, that he wished you to be well taught too, Sissy?"

Sissy hesitated before replying, and so plainly showed her sense that they were entering on forbidden ground, that Louisa added, "No one hears us; and if any one did, I am sure no harm could be found in such an innocent question."

"No, Miss Louisa," answered Sissy, upon this encouragement, shaking her head; "father knows very little indeed. It's as much as he can do to write; and it's more than people in general can do to read his writing. Though it's plain to me."

"Your mother!"

"Father says she was quite a scholar. She died when I was born. She was;" Sissy made the terrible communication nervously; "she was a dancer."

"Did your father love her?" Louisa asked these questions with a strong, wild, wandering interest peculiar to her; an interest gone astray like a banished creature, and hiding in solitary places.

"O yes! As dearly as he loves me. Father loved me, first, for her sake. He carried me about with him when I was quite a baby. We have never been asunder from that time."

"Yet he leaves you now, Sissy?"

"Only for my good. Nobody understands him as I do; nobody knows him as I do. When he left me for my good—he never would have left me for his own—I know he was almost broken-hearted with the trial. He will not be happy for a single minute, till he comes back."

"Tell me more about him," said Louisa, "I will never ask you again. Where did you live?"

"We travelled about the country, and had no fixed place to live in. Father's a;" Sissy whispered the awful word; "a clown."

"To make the people laugh?" said Louisa, with a nod of intelligence.

"Yes. But they wouldn't laugh sometimes, and then father

cried. Lately, they very often wouldn't laugh, and he used to come home despairing. Father's not like most. Those who didn't know him as well as I do, and didn't love him as dearly as I do, might believe he was not quite right. Sometimes they played tricks upon him; but they never knew how he felt them, and shrunk up, when he was alone with me. He was far, far timider than they thought!"

"And you were his comfort through everything?"

She nodded, with the tears rolling down her face. "I hope so, and father said I was. It was because he grew so scared and trembling, and because he felt himself to be a poor, weak, ignorant, helpless man (those used to be his words), that he wanted me so much to know a great deal, and be different from him. I used to read to him to cheer his courage, and he was very fond of that. They were wrong books—I am never to speak of them here—but we didn't know there was any harm in them."

"And he liked them?" said Louisa, with a searching gaze on Sissy all this time.

"O very much! They kept him, many times, from what did him real harm. And often and often of a night, he used to forget all his troubles in wondering whether the Sultan would let the lady go on with the story, or would have her head cut off before it was finished."

"And your father was always kind? To the last?" asked Louisa; contravening the great principle, and wondering very much.

"Always, always!" returned Sissy, clasping her hands. "Kinder and kinder than I can tell. He was angry only one night, and that was not to me, but Merrylegs. Merrylegs;" she whispered the awful fact; "is his performing dog."

"Why was he angry with the dog?" Louisa demanded.

"Father, soon after they came home from performing, told Merrylegs to jump up on the backs of the two chairs and stand across them—which is one of his tricks. He looked at father, and didn't do it at once. Everything of father's had gone wrong that night, and he hadn't pleased the public at all. He cried out that the very dog knew he was failing, and had no compassion on him. Then he beat the dog, and I was frightened, and said, 'Father, father! Pray don't hurt the creature who is so fond of you! O Heaven forgive you, father, stop!' And he stopped, and the dog was bloody, and father lay down crying on the floor with the dog in his arms, and the dog licked his face."

Louisa saw that she was sobbing; and going to her, kissed her, took her hand, and sat down beside her.

"Finish by telling me how your father left you, Sissy. Now that I have asked you so much, tell me the end. The blame, if there is any blame is mine, not yours."

"Dear Miss Louisa," said Sissy, covering her eyes, and sobbing yet; "I came home from the school that afternoon, and found poor father just come home too, from the booth. And he sat rocking himself over the fire, as if he was in pain. And I said, 'Have you hurt yourself, father?' (as he did sometimes, like they all did), and he said, 'A little, my darling.' And when I came to stoop down and look up at his face, I saw that he was crying. The more I spoke to him, the more he hid his face; and at first he shook all over, and said nothing but 'My darling!' and 'My love!'"

Here Tom came lounging in, and stared at the two with a coolness not particularly savouring of interest in anything but himself, and not much of that at present.

"I am asking Sissy a few questions, Tom," observed his sister. "You have no occasion to go away; but don't interrupt us for a moment, Tom dear."

"Oh! very well!" returned Tom. "Only father has brought old Bounderby home, and I want you to come into the drawing room. Because if you come, there's a good chance of old Bounderby's asking me to dinner; and if you don't, there's none."

"I'll come directly."

"I'll wait for you," said Tom, "to make sure."

Sissy resumed in a lower voice. "At last poor father said that he had given no satisfaction again, and never did give any satisfaction now, and that he was a shame and disgrace, and I should have done better without him all along. I said all the affectionate things to him that came into my heart, and presently he was quiet and I sat down by him, and told him all about the school and everything that had been said and done there. When I had no more left to tell, he put his arms round my neck, and kissed me a great many times. Then he asked me to fetch some of the stuff he used, for the little hurt he had had, and to get it at the best place, which was at the other end of the town from there; and then, after kissing me again, he let me go. When I had gone downstairs, I turned back that I might be a little bit more company to him yet, and looked in at the door, and said, 'Father dear, shall I take Merrylegs?' Father shook his head and said, 'No, Sissy, no; take nothing that's known to be mine, my darling;' and I left him sitting by the fire. Then the thought must have come upon him, poor, poor father! of going away to try something for my sake; for when I came back, he was gone."

"I say! Look sharp for old Bounderby, Loo!" Tom remonstrated.

"There's no more to tell, Miss Louisa. I keep the nine oils ready for him, and I know he will come back. Every letter that I see in Mr. Gradgrind's hand takes my breath away and blinds my eyes, for I think it comes from father, or from

Mr. Sleary about father. Mr. Sleary promised to write as soon as ever father should be heard of, and I trust to him to keep his word."

"Do look sharp for old Bounderby, Loo!" said Tom, with an impatient whistle. "He'll be off if you don't look sharp!"

After this, whenever Sissy dropped a curtsey to Mr. Gradgrind in the presence of his family, and said in a faltering way, "I beg your pardon, sir, for being troublesome—but—have you had any letter yet about me?" Louisa would suspend the occupation of the moment, whatever it was, and look for the reply as earnestly as Sissy did. And when Mr. Gradgrind regularly answered, "No, Jupe, nothing of the sort," the trembling of Sissy's lip would be repeated in Louisa's face, and her eyes would follow Sissy with compassion to the door. Mr. Gradgrind usually improved these occasions by remarking, when she was gone, that if Jupe had been properly trained from an early age she would have remonstrated to herself on sound principles the baselessness of these fantastic hopes. Yet it did seem (though not to him, for he saw nothing of it) as if fantastic hope could take as strong a hold as Fact.

This observation must be limited exclusively to his daughter. As to Tom, he was becoming that not unprecedented triumph of calculation which is usually at work on number one. As to Mrs. Gradgrind, if she said anything on the subject, she would come a little way out of her wrappers, like a feminine dormouse, and say:

"Good gracious bless me, how my poor head is vexed and worried by that girl Jupe's so perseveringly asking, over and over again, about her tiresome letters! Upon my word and honour I seem to be fated, and destined, and ordained, to live in the midst of things that I am never to hear the last of. It really is a most extraordinary circumstance that it appears as if I never was to hear the last of anything!"

At about this point, Mr. Gradgrind's eye would fall upon her; and under the influence of that wintry piece of fact, she would become torpid again.

CHAPTER X: *Stephen Blackpool*

I ENTERTAIN a weak idea that the English people are as hard-worked as any people upon whom the sun shines. I acknowledge to this ridiculous idiosyncrasy, as a reason why I would give them a little more play.

In the hardest working part of Coketown; in the innermost fortifications of that ugly citadel, where Nature was as strongly bricked out as killing airs and gases were bricked in; at the heart of the labyrinth of narrow courts upon courts, and close streets upon streets, which had come into existence piecemeal, every piece in a violent hurry for some one man's purpose, and the whole an unnatural family, shouldering, and trampling, and pressing one another to death; in the last close nook of this great exhausted receiver, where the chimneys, for want of air to make a draught, were built in an immense variety of stunted and crooked shapes, as though every house put out a sign of the kind of people who might be expected to be born in it; among the multitude of Coketown, generically called "the Hands,"—a race who would have found more favour with some people, if Providence had seen fit to make them only hands, or, like the lower creatures of the seashore, only hands and stomachs—lived a certain Stephen Blackpool, forty years of age.

Stephen looked older, but he had had a hard life. It is said that every life has its roses and thorns; there seemed, however, to have been a misadventure or mistake in Stephen's case, whereby somebody else had become possessed of his roses, and he had become possessed of the same somebody else's thorns in addition to his own.

He had known, to use his words, a peck of trouble. He was usually called Old Stephen, in a kind of rough homage to the fact. A rather stooping man, with a knitted brow, a pondering expression of face, and a hard-looking head sufficiently capacious, on which his iron-grey hair lay long and thin, Old Stephen might have passed for a particularly intelligent man in his condition. Yet he was not. He took no place among those remarkable "Hands," who, piecing together their broken intervals of leisure through many years, had mastered difficult sciences, and acquired a knowledge of most unlikely things. He held no station among the Hands who could make speeches and carry on debates. Thousands of his compeers could talk much better than he, at any time. He was a good power-loom weaver, and a man of perfect integrity. What more he was, or what else he had in him, if anything, let him show for himself.

The lights in the great factories, which looked, when they were illuminated, like Fairy palaces—or the travellers by express-train said so—were all extinguished; and the bells had rung for knocking off for the night, and had ceased again; and the Hands, men and women, boy and girl, were clattering home. Old Stephen was standing in the street, with the old sensation upon him which the stoppage of the machinery always produced—the sensation of its having worked and stopped in his own head.

"Yet I don't see Rachael, still!" said he.

It was a wet night, and many groups of young women passed him, with their shawls drawn over their bare heads and held close under their chins to keep the rain out. He knew Rachael well, for a glance at any one of these groups was sufficient to show him that she was not there. At last, there were no more to come; and then he turned away, saying in a tone of disappointment, "Why, then, I ha' missed her!"

But, he had not gone the length of three streets, when he saw another of the shawled figures in advance of him, at which he looked so keenly that perhaps its mere shadow indistinctly reflected on the wet pavement—if he could have seen it without the figure itself moving along from lamp to lamp, brightening and fading as it went—would have been enough to tell him who was there. Making his pace at once much quicker and much softer, he darted on until he was very near this figure, then fell into his former walk, and called "Rachael!"

She turned, being then in the brightness of a lamp; and raising her hood a little, showed a quiet oval face, dark and rather delicate, irradiated by a pair of very gentle eyes, and further set off by the perfect order of her shining black hair. It was not a face in its first bloom; she was a woman five-and thirty years of age.

"Ah, lad! 'Tis thou?" When she had said this, with a smile which would have been quite expressed, though nothing of her had been seen but her pleasant eyes, she replaced her hood again, and they went on together.

"I thought thou wast ahind me, Rachael!"

"No."

"Early t'night, lass?"

"'Times I'm a little early, Stephen! 'times a little late. I'm never to be counted on, going home."

"Nor going t'other way, neither, 't seems to me, Rachael?"

"No, Stephen."

He looked at her with some disappointment in his face, but with a respectful and patient conviction that she must be right in whatever she did. The expression was not lost upon her; she laid her hand lightly on his arm a moment as if to thank him for it.

"We are such true friends, lad, and such old friends, and getting to be such old folk now."

"No, Rachael, thou'rt as young as ever thou wast."

"One of us would be puzzled how to get old, Stephen, without t'other getting so too, both being alive," she answered, laughing; "but, anyways, we're such old friends, that t'hide a word of honest truth fro' one another would be a sin and a pity. 'Tis better not to walk too much together. 'Times, yes! 'Twould be hard, indeed, if 'twas not to be at all," she said, with a cheerfulness she sought to communicate to him.

"'Tis hard, anyways, Rachael."

"Try to think not; and 'twill seem better."

"I've tried a long time, and 'ta'nt got better. But thou'rt right; 'tmight mak fok talk, even of thee. Thou hast been that to me, Rachael, through so many year: thou hast done me so much good, and heartened of me in that cheering way, that thy word is a law to me. Ah, lass, and a bright good law! Better than some real ones."

"Never fret about them, Stephen," she answered quickly, and not without an anxious glance at his face. "Let the laws be."

"Yes," he said, with a slow nod or two. "Let 'em be. Let everything be. Let all sorts alone. 'Tis a muddle, and that's aw."

"Always a muddle?" said Rachael, with another gentle touch upon his arm, as if to recall him out of the thoughtfulness, in which he was biting the long ends of his loose neckerchief as he walked along. The touch had its instantaneous effect. He let them fall, turned a smiling face upon her, and said, as he broke into a good-humoured laugh, "Ay, Rachael, lass, awlus a muddle. That's where I stick. I come to the muddle many times and agen, and I never get beyond it."

They had walked some distance, and were near their own homes. The woman's was the first reached. It was in one of the many small streets for which the favourite undertaker (who turned a handsome sum out of the one poor ghastly pomp of the neighbourhood) kept a black ladder, in order that those who had done their daily groping up and down the narrow stairs might slide out of this working world by the windows. She stopped at the street corner, and putting her hand in his, wished him good night."

"Good night, dear lass; good night!"

She went, with her neat figure and her sober womanly step, down the dark street, and he stood looking after her until she turned into one of the small houses. There was not a flutter of her coarse shawl, perhaps, but had its interest in this man's eyes; not a tone of her voice but had its echo in his innermost heart.

When she was lost to his view, he pursued his homeward way, glancing up sometimes at the sky, where the clouds were sailing fast and wildly. But, they were broken now, and the rain had ceased, and the moon shone,—looking down the high chimneys of Coketown on the deep furnaces below, and casting Titanic shadows of the steam-engines at rest, upon the walls where they were lodged. The man seemed to have brightened with the night, as he went on.

His home, in such another street as the first, saving that it was narrower, was over a little shop. How it came to pass that any people found it worth their while to sell or buy the wretched little toys, mixed up in its window with cheap newspapers and pork (there was a leg to be raffled for to-morrow night), matters not here. He took his end of candle from a shelf, lighted it at another end of candle on the counter, without disturbing the mistress of the shop who was asleep in her little room, and went upstairs into his lodging.

It was a room, not unacquainted with the black ladder under various tenants; but as neat, at present, as such a room could be. A few books and writings were on an old bureau in a corner, the furniture was decent and sufficient, and, though the atmosphere was tainted, the room was clean.

Going to the hearth to set the candle down upon a round three-legged table standing there, he stumbled against something. As he recoiled, looking down at it, it raised itself up into the form of a woman in a sitting attitude.

"Heaven's mercy, woman!" he cried, falling farther off from the figure. "Hast thou come back again!"

Such a woman! A disabled, drunken creature, barely able to preserve her sitting posture by steadying herself with one begrimed hand on the floor, while the other was so purposeless in trying to push away her tangled hair from her face, that it only blinded her the more with the dirt upon it. A creature so foul to look at, in her tatters, stains and splashes, but so much fouler than that in her moral infamy, that it was a shameful thing even to see her.

After an impatient oath or two, and some stupid clawing of herself with the hand not necessary to her support, she got her hair away from her eyes sufficiently to obtain a sight of him. Then she sat swaying her body to and fro, and making gestures with her unnerved arm, which seemed intended as the accompaniment to a fit of laughter, though her face was stolid and drowsy.

"Eigh, lad? What, yo'r there?" Some hoarse sounds meant for this, came mockingly out of her at last; and her head dropped forward on her breast.

"Back agen?" she screeched, after some minutes, as if he had that moment said it. "Yes! And back agen. Back agen ever and ever so often. Back? Yes, back. Why not?"

Roused by the unmeaning violence with which she cried it out, she scrambled up, and stood supporting herself with her shoulders against the wall; dangling in one hand by the string, a dunghill-fragment of a bonnet, and trying to look scornfully at him.

"I'll sell thee off again, and I'll sell thee off again, and I'll sell thee off a score of times!" she cried, with something between a furious menace and an effort at a defiant dance. "Come awa' from th' bed!" He was sitting on the side of it, with his face hidden in his hands. "Come awa' from 't. 'Tis mine, and I've a right to 't!"

As she staggered to it, he avoided her with a shudder, and passed—his face still hidden—to the opposite end of the room. She threw herself upon the bed heavily, and soon was snoring hard. He sunk into a chair, and moved but once all that night. It was to throw a covering over her; as if his hands were not enough to hide her, even in the darkness.

CHAPTER XI: *No Way Out*

THE Fairy palaces burst into illumination, before pale morning showed the monstrous serpents of smoke trailing themselves over Coketown. A clattering of clogs upon the pavement; a rapid ringing of bells; and all the melancholy mad elephants, polished and oiled up for the day's monotony, were at their heavy exercise again.

Stephen bent over his loom, quiet, watchful, and steady. A special contrast, as every man was in the forest of looms where Stephen worked, to the crashing, smashing, tearing piece of mechanism at which he laboured. Never fear, good people of an anxious turn of mind, that Art will consign Nature to oblivion. Set anywhere, side by side, the work of GOD and the work of man; and the former, even though it be a troop of Hands of very small account, will gain in dignity from the comparison.

So many hundred Hands in this Mill; so many hundred horse Steam Power. It is known, to the force of a single pound weight, what the engine will do; but, not all the calculators of the National Debt can tell me the capacity for good or evil, for love or hatred, for patriotism or discontent, for the decomposition of virtue into vice, or the reverse, at any single moment in the soul of one of these its quiet servants, with the composed faces and the regulated actions. There is no mystery in it; there is an unfathomable mystery in the meanest of them, for ever.—Supposing we were to reserve our arithmetic for material objects, and to govern these awful quantities by other means!

The day grew strong, and showed itself outside, even against the flaming lights within. The lights were turned out, and the work went on. The rain fell, and the Smoke-serpents, submissive to the curse of all that tribe, trailed themselves upon the earth. In the waste-yard outside, the steam from the escape pipe, the litter of barrels and old iron, the shining heaps of coals, the ashes everywhere, were shrouded in a veil of mist and rain.

The work went on, until the noon-bell rang. More clattering upon the pavements. The looms, and wheels, and Hands all out of gear for an hour.

Stephen came out of the hot mill into the damp wind and cold wet streets, haggard and worn. He turned from his own class and his own quarter, taking nothing but a little bread as he walked along, towards the hill on which his principal employer lived, in a red house with black outside shutters, green inside blinds, a black street door, up two white steps, BOUNDERBY (in letters very like himself) upon a brazen plate.

and a round brazen door-handle underneath it, like a brazen full-stop.

Mr. Bounderby was at his lunch. So Stephen had expected. Would his servant say that one of the Hands begged leave to speak to him? Message in return, requiring name of such Hand. Stephen Blackpool. There was nothing troublesome against Stephen Blackpool; yes, he might come in.

Stephen Blackpool in the parlour. Mr. Bounderby (whom he just knew by sight) at lunch on chop and sherry. Mrs. Sparsit netting at the fireside, in a side-saddle attitude, with one foot in a cotton stirrup. It was a part, at once of Mrs. Sparsit's dignity and service, not to lunch. She supervised the meal officially, but implied that in her own stately person she considered lunch a weakness.

"Now, Stephen," said Mr. Bounderby, "what's the matter with *you?*"

Stephen made a bow. Not a servile one—these Hands will never do that! Lord bless you, sir, you'll never catch them at that, if they had been with you twenty years!—and, as a complimentary toilet for Mrs. Sparsit, tucked his neckerchief ends into his waistcoat.

"Now, you know," said Mr. Bounderby, taking some sherry, "we have never had any difficulty with you, and you have never been one of the unreasonable ones. You don't expect to be set up in a coach and six, and to be fed on turtle soup and venison, with a gold spoon, as a good many of 'em do!" Mr. Bounderby always represented this to be the sole, immediate, and direct object of any Hand who was not entirely satisfied; "and therefore I know already that you have not come here to make a complaint. Now, you know, I am certain of that, beforehand."

"No, sir, sure I ha' not coom for nowt o' th' kind."

Mr. Bounderby seemed agreeably surprised, notwithstanding his previous strong conviction. "Very well," he returned. "You're a steady Hand, and I was not mistaken. Now, let me hear what it's all about. As it's not that, let me hear what it is. What have you got to say? Out with it, lad!"

Stephen happened to glance towards Mrs. Sparsit. "I can go, Mr. Bounderby, if you wish it," said that self-sacrificing lady, making a feint of taking her foot out of the stirrup.

Mr. Bounderby stayed her, by holding a mouthful of chop in suspension before swallowing it, and putting out his left hand. Then, withdrawing his hand and swallowing his mouthful of chop, he said to Stephen:

"Now you know, this good lady is a born lady, a high lady. You are not to suppose because she keeps my house for me, that she hasn't been very high up the tree—ah, up at the top of the tree! Now, if you have got anything to say that can't be said before a born lady, this lady will leave the room. If what you have got to say *can* be said before a born lady, this lady will stay where she is."

"Sir, I hope I never had nowt to say, not fitten for a born lady to year, sin' I were born mysen'," was the reply, accompanied with a slight flush.

"Very well," said Mr. Bounderby, pushing away his plate, and leaning back. "Fire away!"

"I ha' coom," Stephen began, raising his eyes from the floor, after a moment's consideration, "to ask yo yor advice. I need't overmuch. I were married on Eas'r Monday nineteen year sin, long and dree. She were a young lass—pretty enow —wi' good accounts of herseln. Well! She went bad—soon. Not along of me. Gonnows I were not a unkind husband to her."

"I have heard all this before," said Mr. Bounderby. "She took to drinking, left off working, sold the furniture, pawned the clothes, and played old Gooseberry."

"I were patient wi' her."

("The more fool you, I think," said Mr. Bounderby, in confidence to his wine-glass.)

"I were very patient wi' her. I tried to wean her fra't ower and ower agen. I tried this, I tried that, I tried t'other. I ha' gone home, many's the time, and found all vanished as I had in the world, and her without a sense left to bless herseln lying on bare ground. I ha' dun't not once, not twice—twenty time!"

Every line in his face deepened as he said it, and put in its affecting evidence of the suffering he had undergone.

"From bad to worse, from worse to worsen. She left me. She disgraced herseln everyways, bitter and bad. She coom back, she coom back, she coom back. What could I do t' hinder her? I ha' walked the streets nights long, ere ever I'd go home. I ha' gone t' th' brigg, minded to fling myseln ower, and ha' no more on't. I ha' bore that much, that I were owd when I were young."

Mrs. Sparsit, easily ambling along with her netting-needles, raised the Coriolanian eyebrows and shook her head, as much as to say, "The great know trouble as well as the small. Please to turn your humble eye in My direction."

"I ha' paid her to keep awa' fra' me. These five year I ha' paid her. I ha' gotten decent fewtrils about me agen. I ha' lived hard and sad, but not ashamed and fearfo' a' the minnits o' my life. Last night, I went home. There she lay upon my har-stone! There she is!"

In the strength of his misfortune, and the energy of his distress, he fired for the moment like a proud man. In another moment, he stood as he had stood all the time—his usual stoop upon him; his pondering face addressed to Mr. Bounderby, with a curious expression on it, half shrewd, half perplexed, as if his mind were set upon unravelling something very difficult; his hat held tight in his left hand, which rested on his hip; his right arm, with a rugged propriety and force of action, very earnestly emphasising what he said: not least so when it always paused, a little bent, but not withdrawn, as he paused.

"I was acquainted with all this, you know," said Mr. Bounderby, "except the last clause, long ago. It's a bad job; that's what it is. You had better have been satisfied as you were, and not have got married. However, it's too late to say that."

"Was it an unequal marriage, sir, in point of years?" asked Mrs. Sparsit.

"You hear what this lady asks. Was it an unequal marriage in point of years, this unlucky job of yours?" said Mr. Bounderby.

"Not e'en so. I were one-and-twenty myseln; she were twenty nighbut."

"Indeed, sir?" said Mrs. Sparsit to her Chief, with great placidity. "I inferred, from its being so miserable a marriage, that it was probably an unequal one in point of years."

Mr. Bounderby looked very hard at the good lady in a sidelong way that had an odd sheepishness about it. He fortified himself with a little more sherry.

"Well? Why don't you go on?" he then asked, turning rather irritably on Stephen Blackpool.

"I ha' coom to ask yo, sir, how I am to be ridded o' this woman." Stephen infused a yet deeper gravity into the mixed expression of his attentive face. Mrs. Sparsit uttered a gentle ejaculation, as having received a moral shock.

"What do you mean?" said Bounderby, getting up to lean his back against the chimney-piece. "What are you talking about? You took her for better for worse."

"I mun' be ridden o' her. I cannot bear't nommore. I ha' lived under't so long, for that I ha' hadn' the pity and comforting words o' th' best lass living or dead. Haply, but for her, I should ha' gone hottering mad."

"He wishes to be free, to marry the female of whom he speaks, I fear, sir," observed Mrs. Sparsit in an undertone, and much dejected by the immorality of the people.

"I do. The lady says what's right. I do. I were a coming to 't. I ha' read i' th' papers that great fok (fair faw 'em a'! I wishes 'em no hurt!) are not bonded together for better for worse so fast, but that they can be set free fro' their misfortnet marriages, an marry ower agen. When they dunnot agree, for that their tempers is ill-sorted, they has rooms o' one kind an another in their houses, above a bit, and they can live asunders. We fok ha' only one room, and we can't. When that won't do, they ha' gowd an other cash, an 'they can say

'This for yo' an that for me,' an they can go their separate ways. We can't. Spite o' all that, they can be set free for smaller wrongs than mine. So, I mun' be ridden o' this woman, and I want t' know how?"

"No how," returned Mr. Bounderby.

"If I do her any hurt, sir, there's a law to punish me?"

"Of course there is."

"If I flee from her, there's a law to punish me?"

"Of course there is."

"If I marry t'oother dear lass, there's a law to punish me?"

"Of course there is."

"If I was to live wi' her and not marry her—saying such a thing could be, which it never could or would, an' her so good—there's a law to punish me, in every innocent child belonging to me?"

"Of course there is."

"Now, a' God's name," said Stephen Blackpool, "show me the law to help me!"

"Hem! There's a sanctity in this relation of life," said Mr. Bounderby, "and—and—it must be kept up."

"No, no, dunnot say that, sir. 'Tan't kep' up that way. Not that way. 'Tis kep' down that way. I'm a weaver, I were in a fact'ry when a chilt, but I ha' gotten een to see wi' and eern to year wi'. I read in th' papers every 'Sizes, every Sessions—and you read too—I know it!—with dismay—how th' supposed unpossibility o' ever getting unchained from one another, at any price, on any terms, brings blood upon this land, and brings many common married fok to battle, murder, and sudden death. Let us ha' this, right understood. Mine's a grievous case, and I want—if yo will be so good—t' know the law that helps me."

"Now, I tell you what!" said Mr. Bounderby, putting his hands in his pockets. "There *is* such a law."

Stephen, subsiding into his quiet manner, and never wandering in his attention, gave a nod.

"But it's not for you at all. It costs money. It costs a mint of money."

"How much might that be?" Stephen calmly asked.

"Why, you'd have to go to Doctors' Commons with a suit, and you'd have to go to a court of Common Law with a suit, and you'd have to go to the House of Lords with a suit, and you'd have to get an Act of Parliament to enable you to marry again, and it would cost you (if it was a case of very plain sailing), I suppose from a thousand to fifteen hundred pound," said Mr. Bounderby. "Perhaps twice the money."

"There's no other law?"

"Certainly not."

"Why then, sir," said Stephen, turning white, and motioning with that right hand of his, as if he gave everything to the four winds, "'*tis* a muddle. 'Tis just a muddle a'toogether, an the sooner I'm dead, the better."

(Mrs. Sparsit again dejected by the impiety of the people.)

"Pooh, pooh! Don't you talk nonsense, my good fellow," said Mr. Bounderby, "about things you don't understand; and don't you call the Institutions of your country a muddle, or you'll get yourself into a real muddle one of these fine mornings. The Institutions of your country are not your piece-work, and the only thing you have got to do, is, to mind your piece-work. You didn't take your wife for fast and for loose; but for better for worse. If she has turned out worse—why, all we have got to say is, she might have turned out better."

"'Tis a muddle," said Stephen, shaking his head as he moved to the door. "'Tis a' a muddle!"

"Now, I'll tell you what!" Mr. Bounderby resumed, as a valedictory address. "With what I shall call your unhallowed opinions, you have been quite shocking this lady: who, as I have already told you, is a born lady, and who, as I have not already told you, has had her own marriage misfortunes to the tune of tens of thousands of pounds—tens of Thousands of Pounds!" (he repeated it with great relish). "Now, you have always been a steady Hand hitherto; but my opinion is, and so I tell you plainly, that you are turning into the wrong road. You have been listening to some mischievous stranger or other—they're always about—and the best thing you can do is, to come out of that. Now you know;" here his countenance expressed marvellous acuteness; "I can see as far into a grindstone as another man; farther than a good many, perhaps, because I had my nose well kept to it when I was young. I see traces of the turtle soup, and venison, and gold spoon in this. Yes, I do!" cried Mr. Bounderby, shaking his head with obstinate cunning. "By the Lord Harry, I do!"

With a very different shake of the head and deep sigh, Stephen said, "Thank you, sir, I wish you good day." So he left Mr. Bounderby swelling at his own portrait on the wall, as if he were going to explode himself into it; and Mrs. Sparsit still ambling on with her foot in her stirrup, looking quite cast down by the popular vices.

CHAPTER XII: *The Old Woman*

OLD STEPHEN descended the two white steps, shutting the black door with the brazen door-plate, by the aid of the brazen full-stop, to which he gave a parting polish with the sleeve of his coat, observing that his hot hand clouded it. He crossed the street with his eyes bent upon the ground, and thus was walking sorrowfully away, when he felt a touch upon his arm.

It was not the touch he needed most at such a moment—the touch that could calm the wild waters of his soul, as the uplifted hand of the sublimest love and patience could abate the raging of the sea—yet it was a woman's hand too. It was an old woman, tall and shapely still, though withered by time, on whom his eyes fell when he stopped and turned. She was very cleanly and plainly dressed, had country mud upon her shoes, and was newly come from a journey. The flutter of her manner, in the unwonted noise of the streets; the spare shawl, carried unfolded on her arm; the heavy umbrella, and little basket; the loose long-fingered gloves, to which her hands were unused; all bespoke an old woman from the country, in her plain holiday clothes, come into Coketown on an expedition of rare occurrence. Remarking this at a glance, with the quick observation of his class, Stephen Blackpool bent his attentive face—his face, which, like the faces of many of his order, by dint of long working with eyes and hands in the midst of a prodigious noise, had acquired the concentrated look with which we are familiar in the countenances of the deaf—the better to hear what she asked him.

"Pray, sir," said the old woman, "didn't I see you come out of that gentleman's house?" pointing back to Mr. Bounderby's. "I believe it was you, unless I have had the bad luck to mistake the person in following?"

"Yes, missus," returned Stephen, "it were me."

"Have you—you'll excuse an old woman's curiosity—have you seen the gentleman?"

"Yes, missus."

"And how did he look, sir? Was he portly, bold, outspoken, and hearty?" As she straightened her own figure, and held up her head in adapting her action to her words, the idea crossed Stephen that he had seen this old woman before, and had not quite liked her.

"O yes," he returned, observing her more attentively, "he were all that."

"And healthy," said the old woman, "as the fresh wind?"

"Yes," returned Stephen. "He were ett'n and drinking—as large and as loud as a Hummobee."

"Thank you!" said the old woman, with infinite content. "Thank you!"

He certainly never had seen this old woman before. Yet there was a vague remembrance in his mind, as if he had more than once dreamed of some old woman like her.

She walked along at his side, and, gently accommodating himself to her humour, he said Coketown was a busy place, was it not? to which she answered "Eigh sure! Dreadful busy!" Then he said, she came from the country, he saw? To which she answered in the affirmative.

"By Parliamentary, this morning. I came forty mile by Parliamentary this morning, and I'm going back the same forty mile this afternoon. I walked nine mile to the station this morning, and if I find nobody on the road to give me a lift, I shall walk the nine mile back to-night. That's pretty well, sir, at my age!" said the chatty old woman, her eye brightening with exultation.

"'Deed 'tis. Don't do't too often, missus."

"No, no. Once a year," she answered, shaking her head. "I spend my savings so, once every year. I come regular, to tramp about the streets, and see the gentlemen."

"Only to see 'em?" returned Stephen.

"That's enough for me," she replied, with great earnestness and interest of manner. "I ask no more! I have been standing about, on this side of the way, to see that gentleman," turning her head back towards Mr. Bounderby's again, "come out. But, he's late this year, and I have not seen him. You came out instead. Now, if I am obliged to go back without a glimpse of him—I only want a glimpse—well! I have seen you, and you have seen him, and I must make that do." Saying this, she looked at Stephen as if to fix his features in her mind, and her eye was not so bright as it had been.

With a large allowance for difference of tastes, and with all submission to the patricians of Coketown, this seemed so extraordinary a source of interest to take so much trouble about, that it perplexed him. But they were passing the church now, and as his eye caught the clock, he quickened his pace.

He was going to his work? the old woman said, quickening hers, too, quite easily. Yes, time was nearly out. On his telling her where he worked, the old woman became a more singular old woman than before.

"An't you happy?" she asked him.

"Why—there's awmost nobbody but has their troubles, missus." He answered evasively, because the old woman appeared to take it for granted that he would be very happy indeed, and he had not the heart to disappoint her. He knew that there was trouble enough in the world; and if the old woman had lived so long, and could count upon his having so little, why so much the better for her, and none the worse for him.

"Ay, ay! You have your troubles at home, you mean?" she said.

"Times. Just now and then," he answered, slightly.

"But, working under such a gentleman, they don't follow you to the Factory?"

No, no; they didn't follow him there, said Stephen. All correct there. Everything accordant there. (He did not go so far as to say, for her pleasure, that there was a sort of Divine Right there; but, I have heard claims almost as magnificent of late years.)

They were now in the black by-road near the place, and the

Hands were crowding in. The bell was ringing, and the Serpent was a Serpent of many coils, and the Elephant was getting ready. The strange old woman was delighted with the very bell. It was the beautifullest bell she had ever heard, she said, and sounded grand!

She asked him, when he stopped good-naturedly to shake hands with her before going in, how long he had worked there?

"A dozen year," he told her.

"I must kiss the hand," said she, "that has worked in this fine factory for a dozen year!" And she lifted it, though he would have prevented her, and put it to her lips. What harmony, besides her age and her simplicity, surrounded her, he did not know, but even in this fantastic action there was a something neither out of time nor place: a something which it seemed as if nobody else could have made as serious, or done with such a natural and touching air.

He had been at his loom full half an hour, thinking about this old woman, when, having occasion to move round the loom for its adjustment, he glanced through a window which was in his corner, and saw her still looking up at the pile of building, lost in admiration. Heedless of the smoke and mud and wet, and of her two long journeys, she was gazing at it, as if the heavy thrum that issued from its many stories were proud music to her.

She was gone by-and-by, and the day after her, and the lights sprung up again, and the Express whirled in full sight of the Fairy Palace over the arches near: little felt amid the jarring of the machinery, and scarcely heard above its crash and rattle. Long before then his thoughts had gone back to the dreary room above the little shop, and to the shameful figure heavy on the bed, but heavier on his heart.

Machinery slackened; throbbing feebly like a fainting pulse; stopped. The bell again; the glare of light and heat dispelled; the factories, looming heavy in the black wet night—their tall chimneys rising up into the air like competing Towers of Babel.

He had spoken to Rachael only last night, it was true, and had walked with her a little way; but he had his new misfortune on him, in which no one else could give him a moment's relief, and, for the sake of it, and because he knew himself to want that softening of his anger which no voice but hers could effect, he felt he might so far disregard what she had said as to wait for her again. He waited, but she had eluded him. She was gone. On no other night in the year could he so ill have spared her patient face.

Oh! Better to have no home in which to lay his head, than to have a home and dread to go to it, through such a cause. He ate and drank, for he was exhausted—but he little knew or cared what: and he wandered about in the chill rain, thinking and thinking, and brooding and brooding.

No word of a new marriage had ever passed between them; but Rachael had taken great pity on him years ago, and to her alone he had opened his closed heart all this time, on the subject of his miseries; and he knew very well that if he were free to ask her, she would take him. He thought of the home he might at that moment have been seeking with pleasure and pride; of the different man he might have been that night; of the lightness then in his now heavy-laden breast; of the then restored honour, self-respect, and tranquillity all torn to pieces. He thought of the waste of the best part of his life, of the change it made in his character for the worse every day, of the dreadful nature of his existence, bound hand and foot, to a dead woman, and tormented by a demon in her shape. He thought of Rachael, how young when they were first brought together in these circumstances, how mature now, how soon to grow old. He thought of the number of girls and women she had seen marry, how many homes with children in them she had seen grow up around her, how she had contentedly pursued her own lone quiet path—for him—and how he had sometimes seen a shade of melancholy on her blessed face, that smote him with remorse and despair. He set the picture of her up, beside the infamous image of last night; and thought, Could it be, that the whole earthly course of one so gentle, good, and self-denying, was subjugate to such a wretch as that!

Filled with these thoughts—so filled that he had an unwholesome sense of growing larger, of being placed in some new and diseased relation towards the objects among which he passed, of seeing the iris round every misty light turn red—he went home for shelter.

CHAPTER XIII: *Rachael*

A CANDLE faintly burned in the window, to which the black ladder had often been raised for the sliding away of all that was most precious in this world to a striving wife and a brood of hungry babies; and Stephen added to his other thoughts the stern reflection, that of all the casualties of this existence upon earth, not one was dealt out with so unequal a hand as Death. The inequality of Birth was nothing to it. For, say that the child of a King and the child of a Weaver were born to-night in the same moment, what was that disparity, to the death of any human creature who was serviceable to, or beloved by, another, while this abandoned woman lived on!

From the outside of his home he gloomily passed to the inside, with suspended breath and with a slow footstep. He went up to his door, opened it, and so into the room.

Quiet and peace were there. Rachael was there, sitting by the bed.

She turned her head, and the light of her face shone in upon the midnight of his mind. She sat by the bed, watching and tending his wife. That is to say, he saw that some one lay there, and he knew too well it must be she; but Rachael's hands had put a curtain up, so that she was screened from his eyes. Her disgraceful garments were removed, and some of Rachael's were in the room. Everything was in its place and order as he had always kept it, the little fire was newly trimmed, and the hearth was freshly swept. It appeared to him that he saw all this in Rachael's face, and looked at nothing besides. While looking at it, it was shut out from his view by the softened tears that filled his eyes; but not before he had seen how earnestly she looked at him, and how her own eyes were filled too.

She turned again towards the bed, and satisfying herself that all was quiet there, spoke in a low, calm, cheerful voice.

"I am glad you have come at last, Stephen. You are very late."

"I ha' been walking up an' down."

"I thought so. But 'tis too bad a night for that. The rain falls very heavy, and the wind has risen."

The wind? True. It was blowing hard. Hark to the thundering in the chimney, and the surging noise! To have been out in such a wind, and not to have known it was blowing!

"I have been here once before, to-day, Stephen. Landlady came round for me at dinner-time. There was some one here that needed looking to, she said. And 'deed she was right. All wandering and lost, Stephen. Wounded too, and bruised."

He slowly moved to a chair and sat down, drooping his head before her.

"I came to do what little I could, Stephen; first, for that she worked with me when we were girls both, and for that you courted her and married her when I was her friend——"

He laid his furrowed forehead on his hand, with a low groan.

"And next, for that I know your heart, and am right sure and certain that 'tis far too merciful to let her die, or even so much as suffer, for want of aid. Thou knowest who said, 'Let him who is without sin among you cast the first stone at her!' There have been plenty to do that. Thou art not the man to cast the last stone, Stephen, when she is brought so low."

"O Rachael, Rachael!"

"Thou hast been a cruel sufferer, Heaven reward thee!" she said, in compassionate accents. "I am thy poor friend, with all my heart and mind."

The wounds of which she had spoken, seemed to be about the neck of the self-made outcast. She dressed them now, still without showing her. She steeped a piece of linen in a basin, into which she poured some liquid from a bottle, and laid it with a gentle hand upon the sore. The three-legged table had been drawn close to the bedside, and on it there were two bottles. This was one.

It was not so far off, but that Stephen, following her hands with his eyes, could read what was printed on it in large letters. He turned of a deadly hue, and a sudden horror seemed to fall upon him.

"I will stay here, Stephen," said Rachael, quietly resuming her seat, "till the bells go Three. 'Tis to be done again at three, and then she may be left till morning."

"But thy rest agen to-morrow's work, my dear."

"I slept sound last night. I can wake many nights, when I am put to it. 'Tis thou who art in need of rest—so white and tired. Try to sleep in the chair there, while I watch. Thou hadst no sleep last night, I can well believe. To-morrow's work is far harder for thee than for me."

He heard the thundering and surging out of doors, and it seemed to him as if his late angry mood were going about trying to get at him. She had cast it out; she would keep it out; he trusted to her to defend him from himself.

"She don't know me, Stephen; she just drowsily mutters and stares. I have spoken to her times and again, but she didn't notice! 'Tis as well so. When she comes to her right mind once more, I shall have done what I can, and she never the wiser."

"How long, Rachael, is't looked for, that she'll be so?"

"Doctor said she would haply come to her mind to-morrow."

His eyes fell again on the bottle, and a tremble passed over him, causing him to shiver in every limb. She thought he was chilled with the wet. "No," he said, "it was not that. He had had a fright."

"A fright?"

"Ay, ay! coming in. When I were walking. When I were thinking. When I——" It seized him again; and he stood up, holding by the mantel-shelf, as he pressed his dank cold hair down with a hand that shook as if it were palsied.

"Stephen!"

She was coming to him, but he stretched out his arm to stop her.

"No! Don't, please; don't. Let me see thee setten by the bed. Let me see thee, a' so good, and so forgiving. Let me see thee as I see thee when I coom in. I can never see thee better than so. Never, never, never!"

He had a violent fit of trembling, and then sunk into his chair. After a time he controlled himself, and, resting with an elbow on one knee, and his head upon that hand, could look towards Rachael. Seen across the dim candle with his moistened eyes, she looked as if she had a glory shining round her head. He could have believed she had. He did believe it, as the noise without shook the window, rattled at the door below, and went about the house clamouring and lamenting.

"When she gets better, Stephen, 'tis to be hoped she'll leave thee to thyself again, and do thee no more hurt. Anyways we will hope so now. And now I shall keep silence, for I want thee to sleep."

He closed his eyes, more to please her than to rest his weary head; but, by slow degrees as he listened to the great noise of the wind, he ceased to hear it, or it changed into the working of his loom, or even into the voices of the day (his own included) saying what had been really said. Even this imperfect consciousness faded away at last, and he dreamed a long, troubled dream.

He thought that he, and some one on whom his heart had long been set—but she was not Rachael, and that surprised him, even in the midst of his imaginary happiness—stood in the church being married. While the ceremony was performing, and while he recognised among the witnesses some whom he knew to be living, and many whom he knew to be dead, darkness came on, succeeded by the shining of a tremendous light. It broke from one line in the table of commandments at the altar, and illuminated the building with the words. They were sounded through the church, too, as if there were voices in the fiery letters. Upon this, the whole appearance before him and around him changed, and nothing was left as it had been, but himself and the clergyman. They stood in the daylight before a crowd so vast, that if all the people in the world could have been brought together into one space, they could not have looked, he thought, more numerous; and they all abhorred him, and there was not one pitying or friendly eye among the millions that were fastened on his face. He stood on a raised stage, under his own loom; and, looking up at the shape the loom took, and hearing the burial service distinctly read, he knew that he was there to suffer death. In an instant what he stood on fell below him, and he was gone.

Out of what mystery he came back to his usual life, and to places that he knew, he was unable to consider; but he was back in those places by some means, and with this condemnation upon him, that he was never, in this world or the next, through all the unimaginable ages of eternity, to look on Rachael's face or hear her voice. Wandering to and fro, unceasingly, without hope, and in search of he knew not what (he only knew that he was doomed to seek it), he was the subject of a nameless, horrible dread, a mortal fear of one particular shape which everything took. Whatsoever he looked at, grew into that form sooner or later. The object of his miserable existence was to prevent its recognition by any one among the various people he encountered. Hopeless labour! If he led them out of rooms where it was, if he shut up drawers and closets where it stood, if he drew the curious from places where he knew it to be secreted, and got them out into the streets, the very chimneys of the mills assumed that shape, and round them was the printed word.

The wind was blowing again, the rain was beating on the housetops, and the larger spaces through which he had strayed contracted to the four walls of his room. Saving that the fire had died out, it was as his eyes had closed upon it. Rachael seemed to have fallen into a doze, in the chair by the bed. She sat wrapped in her shawl, perfectly still. The table stood in the same place, close by the bedside, and on it, in its real proportions and appearance, was the shape so often repeated.

He thought he saw the curtain move. He looked again, and he was sure it moved. He saw a hand come forth and grope about a little. Then the curtain moved more perceptibly, and the woman in the bed put it back, and sat up.

With her woful eyes, so haggard and wild, so heavy and large, she looked all round the room, and passed the corner where he slept in his chair. Her eyes returned to that corner, and she put her hand over them as a shade, while she looked into it. Again they went all round the room, scarcely heeding Rachael if at all, and returned to that corner. He thought, as she once more shaded them—not so much looking at him, as looking for him with a brutish instinct that he was there—that no single trace was left in those debauched features, or in the mind that went along with them, of the woman he had married eighteen years before. But that he had seen her come to this by inches, he never could have believed her to be the same.

All this time, as if a spell were on him, he was motionless and powerless, except to watch her.

Stupidly dozing, or communing with her incapable self about nothing, she sat for a little while with her hands at her ears, and her head resting on them. Presently, she resumed her staring round the room. And now, for the first time, her eyes stopped at the table with the bottles on it.

Straightway she turned her eyes back to his corner, with the defiance of last night, and moving very cautiously and softly, stretched out her greedy hand. She drew a mug into the bed, and sat for a while considering which of the two bottles she should choose. Finally, she laid her insensate grasp upon the bottle that had swift and certain death in it, and before his eyes, pulled out the cork with her teeth.

Dream or reality, he had no voice, nor had he the power to stir. If this be real, and her allotted time be not yet come, wake, Rachael, wake!

She thought of that, too. She looked at Rachael, and very slowly, very cautiously, poured out the contents. The draught was at her lips. A moment and she would be past all help, let the whole world wake and come about her with its utmost power. But in that moment Rachael started up with a suppressed cry. The creature struggled, struck her, seized her by the hair; but Rachael had the cup.

Stephen broke out of his chair. "Rachael, am I wakin' or dreamin' this dreadfo' night?"

"'Tis all well, Stephen. I have been asleep myself. 'Tis near three. Hush! I hear the bells."

The wind brought the sound of the church clock to the window. They listened, and it struck three. Stephen looked at her, saw how pale she was, noted the disorder of her hair, and the red marks of fingers on her forehead, and felt assured that his senses of sight and hearing had been awake. She held the cup in her hand even now.

"I thought it must be near three," she said, calmly pouring from the cup into the basin, and steeping the linen as before. "I am thankful I stayed! 'Tis done now, when I have put this on. There! And now she's quiet again. The few drops in the basin I'll pour away, for 'tis bad stuff to leave about, though ever so little of it." As she spoke, she drained the basin into the ashes of the fire, and broke the bottle on the hearth.

She had nothing to do, then, but to cover herself with her shawl before going out into the wind and rain.

"Thou'lt let me walk wi' thee at this hour, Rachael?"

"No, Stephen. 'Tis but a minute, and I'm home."

"Thou'rt not fearfo';" he said it in a low voice, as they went out at the door; "to leave me alone wi' her!"

As she looked at him, saying, "Stephen?" he went down on his knee before her, on the poor mean stairs, and put an end of her shawl to his lips.

"Thou art an Angel. Bless thee, bless thee."

"I am, as I have told thee, Stephen, thy poor friend. Angels are not like me. Between them, and a working woman fu' of faults, there is a deep gulf set. My little sister is among them, but she is changed."

She raised her eyes for a moment as she said the words; and then they fell again, in all their gentleness and mildness, on his face.

"Thou changest me from bad to good. Thou mak'st me humbly wishfo' to be more like thee, and fearfo' to lose thee when this life is ower, and a' the muddle cleared awa.' Thou'rt an Angel; it may be, thou hast saved my soul alive!"

She looked at him, on his knee at her feet, with her shawl still in his hand, and the reproof on her lips died away when she saw the working of his face.

"I coom home desp'rate. I coom home wi'out a hope, and
mad wi' thinking that when I said a word o' complaint I was
reckoned a onreasonable Hand. I told thee I had had a fright.
It were the Poison-bottle on table. I never hurt a livin'
creetur; but happenin' so suddenly upon 't, I thowt, 'How
can *I* say what I might ha' done to myseln, or her, or both!'"

She put her two hands on his mouth, with a face of terror,
to stop him from saying more. He caught them in his unoccu-
pied hand, and holding them, and still clasping the border of
her shawl, said hurriedly:

"But I see thee, Rachael, setten by the bed. I ha' seen thee,
aw this night. In my troublous sleep I ha' known thee still to
be there. Evermore I will see thee there. I nevermore will
see her or think o' her, but thou shalt be beside her. I
nevermore will see or think o' anything that angers me, but
thou, so much better than me, shalt be by th' side on't. And
so I will try t' look t' th' time, and so I will try t' trust t' th'
time, when thou and me at last shall walk together far awa',
beyond the deep gulf, in th' country where thy little sister is."

He kissed the border of her shawl again, and let her go.
She bade him good night in a broken voice, and went out into
the street.

The wind blew from the quarter where the day would soon
appear, and still blew strongly. It had cleared the sky before
it, and the rain had spent itself or travelled elsewhere, and the
stars were bright. He stood bareheaded in the road, watching
her quick disappearance. As the shining stars were to the
heavy candle in the window, so was Rachael, in the rugged
fancy of this man, to the common experiences of his life.

CHAPTER XIV: *The Great Manufacturer*

TIME went on in Coketown like its own machinery; so much
material wrought up, so much fuel consumed, so many powers
worn out, so much money made. But, less inexorable than
iron, steel, and brass, it brought its varying seasons even into
that wilderness of smoke and brick, and made the only stand
that ever *was* made in the place against its direful uniformity.

"Louisa is becoming," said Mr. Gradgrind, "almost a young
woman."

Time with his innumerable horse-power, worked away, not
minding what anybody said, and presently turned out young
Thomas a foot taller than when his father had last taken particular notice of him.

"Thomas is becoming," said Mr. Gradgrind, "almost a
young man."

Time passed Thomas on in the mill, while his father was
thinking about it, and there he stood in a long-tailed coat and
a stiff shirt-collar.

"Really," said Mr. Gradgrind, "the period has arrived when Thomas ought to go to Bounderby."

Time, sticking to him, passed him on into Bounderby's bank, made him an inmate of Bounderby's house, necessitated the purchase of his first razor, and exercised him diligently in his calculations relative to number one.

The same great manufacturer, always with an immense variety of work on hand, in every stage of development, passed Sissy onward in his mill, and worked her up into a very pretty article indeed.

"I fear, Jupe," said Mr. Gradgrind, "that your continuance at the school any longer would be useless."

"I am afraid it would, sir," Sissy answered with a curtsey.

"I cannot disguise from you, Jupe," said Mr. Gradgrind, knitting his brow, "that the result of your probation there has disappointed me; has greatly disappointed me. You have not acquired, under Mr. and Mrs. M'Choakumchild, anything like that amount of exact knowledge which I looked for. You are extremely deficient in your facts. Your acquaintance with figures is very limited. You are altogether backward, and below the mark."

"I am sorry, sir," she returned; "but I know it is quite true. Yet I have tried hard, sir."

"Yes," said Mr. Gradgrind, "yes, I believe you have tried hard; I have observed you, and I can find no fault in that respect."

"Thank you, sir. I have thought sometimes;" Sissy very timid here; "that perhaps I tried to learn too much, and that if I had asked to be allowed to try a little less, I might have——"

"No, Jupe, no," said Mr. Gradgrind, shaking his head in his profoundest and most eminently practical way. "No. The course you pursued, you pursued according to the system —the system—and there is no more to be said about it. I can only suppose that the circumstances of your early life were too unfavourable to the development of your reasoning powers, and that we began too late. Still, as I have said already, I am disappointed."

"I wish I could have made a better acknowledgment, sir, of your kindness to a poor forlorn girl who had no claim upon you, and of your protection of her."

"Don't shed tears," said Mr. Gradgrind. "Don't shed tears. I don't complain of you. You are an affectionate, earnest, good young woman—and—and we must make that do."

"Thank you, sir, very much," said Sissy, with a grateful curtsey.

"You are useful to Mrs. Gradgrind, and (in a generally pervading way) you are serviceable in the family also; so I understand from Miss Louisa, and, indeed, so I have observed myself. I therefore hope," said Mr. Gradgrind, "that you can make yourself happy in those relations."

"I should have nothing to wish, sir, if——"

"I understand you," said Mr. Gradgrind; "you still refer to your father. I have heard from Miss Louisa that you still preserve that bottle. Well! If your training in the science of arriving at exact results had been more successful, you would have been wiser on these points. I will say no more."

He really liked Sissy too well to have a contempt for her; otherwise he held her calculating powers in such very slight estimation that he must have fallen upon that conclusion. Somehow or other, he had become possessed by an idea that there was something in this girl which could hardly be set forth in a tabular form. Her capacity of definition might be easily stated at a very low figure, her mathematical knowledge at nothing; yet he was not sure that if he had been required, for example, to tick her off into columns in a parliamentary return, he would have quite known how to divide her.

In some stages of his manufacture of the human fabric, the processes of Time are very rapid. Young Thomas and Sissy being both at such a stage of their working up, these changes were effected in a year or two; while Mr. Gradgrind himself seemed stationary in his course, and underwent no alteration.

Except one, which was apart from his necessary progress through the mill. Time hustled him into a little noisy and rather dirty machinery, in a by-corner, and made him Member of Parliament for Coketown: one of the respected members for ounce weights and measures, one of the representatives of the multiplication table, one of the deaf honourable gentlemen, dumb honourable gentlemen, blind honourable gentlemen, lame honourable gentlemen, dead honourable gentlemen, to every other consideration. Else wherefore live we in a Christian land, eighteen hundred and odd years after our Master?

All this while, Louisa had been passing on, so quiet and reserved, and so much given to watching the bright ashes at twilight as they fell into the grate and became extinct, that from the period when her father had said she was almost a young woman—which seemed but yesterday—she had scarcely attracted his notice again, when he found her quite a young woman.

"Quite a young woman," said Mr. Gradgrind, musing. "Dear me!"

Soon after this discovery, he became more thoughtful than usual for several days, and seemed much engrossed by one subject. On a certain night, when he was going out, and Louisa came to bid him good-bye before his departure—as he was not to be home until late and she would not see him again until the morning—he held her in his arms, looking at her in his kindest manner, and said:

"My dear Louisa, you are a woman!"

She answered with the old, quick, searching look of the night when she was found at the Circus; then cast down her eyes. "Yes, father."

"My dear," said Mr. Gradgrind, "I must speak with you alone and seriously. Come to me in my room after breakfast to-morrow, will you?"

"Yes, father."

"Your hands are rather cold, Louisa. Are you not well?"

"Quite well, father."

"And cheerful?"

She looked at him again, and smiled in her peculiar manner. "I am as cheerful, father, as I usually am, or usually have been."

"That's well," said Mr. Gradgrind. So, he kissed her and went away; and Louisa returned to the serene apartment of the hair-cutting character, and leaning her elbow on her hand, looked again at the short-lived sparks that so soon subsided into ashes.

"Are you there, Loo?" said her brother, looking in at the door. He was quite a young gentleman of pleasure now, and not quite a prepossessing one.

"Dear Tom," she answered, rising and embracing him, "how long it is since you have been to see me!"

"Why, I have been otherwise engaged, Loo, in the evenings; and in the daytime old Bounderby has been keeping me at it rather. But I touch him up with you when he comes it too strong, and so we preserve an understanding. I say! Has father said anything particular to you to-day or yesterday, Loo?"

"No, Tom. But he told me to-night that he wished to do so in the morning."

"Ah! That's what I mean," said Tom. "Do you know where he is to-night?"—with a very deep expression.

"No."

"Then I'll tell you. He's with old Bounderby. They are having a regular confab together up at the Bank. Why at the Bank, do you think? Well, I'll tell you again. To keep Mrs. Sparsit's ears as far off as possible, I expect."

With her hand upon her brother's shoulder, Louisa still stood looking at the fire. Her brother glanced at her face with greater interest than usual, and, encircling her waist with his arm, drew her coaxingly to him.

"You are very fond of me, an't you, Loo?"

"Indeed I am, Tom, though you do let such long intervals go by without coming to see me."

"Well, sister of mine," said Tom, "when you say that, you

are near my thoughts. We might be so much oftener together—mightn't we? Always together, almost—mightn't we? It would do me a great deal of good if you were to make up your mind to I know what, Loo. It would be a splendid thing for me. It would be uncommonly jolly!"

Her thoughtfulness baffled his cunning scrutiny. He could make nothing of her face. He pressed her in his arm, and kissed her cheek. She returned the kiss, but still looked at the fire.

"I say, Loo! I thought I'd come, and just hint to you what was going on; though I supposed you'd most likely guess, even if you didn't know. I can't stay, because I'm engaged to some fellows to-night. You won't forget how fond you are of me?"

"No, dear Tom, I won't forget."

"That's a capital girl," said Tom. "Good-bye, Loo."

She gave him an affectionate good night, and went out with him to the door, whence the fires of Coketown could be seen, making the distance lurid. She stood there, looking stead-fastly towards them, and listening to his departing steps. They retreated quickly, as glad to get away from Stone Lodge; and she stood there yet, when he was gone and all was quiet. It seemed as if, first in her own fire within the house, and then in the fiery haze without, she tried to discover what kind of woof Old Time, that greatest and longest-established Spinner of all, would weave from the threads he had already spun into a woman. But his factory is a secret place, his work is noiseless, and his Hands are mutes.

CHAPTER XV: *Father and Daughter*

ALTHOUGH Mr. Gradgrind did not take after Blue Beard, his room was quite a blue chamber in its abundance of blue books. Whatever they could prove (which is usually anything you like), they proved there, in an army constantly strengthening by the arrival of new recruits. In that charmed apartment, the most complicated social questions were cast up, got into exact totals, and finally settled—if those concerned could only have been brought to know it. As if an astronomical observatory should be made without any windows, and the astronomer within should arrange the starry universe solely by pen, ink, and paper, so Mr. Gradgrind, in *his* Observatory (and there are many like it) had no need to cast an eye upon the teeming myriads of human beings around him, but could settle all their destinies on a slate, and wipe out all their tears with one dirty little bit of sponge.

To this Observatory, then: a stern room, with a deadly statistical clock in it, which measured every second with a beat like a rap upon a coffin-lid; Louisa repaired on the appointed morning. A window looked towards Coketown; and when she sat down near her father's table, she saw the high chimneys and the long tracts of smoke looming in the heavy distance gloomily.

"My dear Louisa," said her father, "I prepared you last night to give me your serious attention in the conversation we are now going to have together. You have been so well trained, and you do, I am happy to say, so much justice to the education you have received, that I have perfect confidence in your good sense. You are not impulsive, you are not romantic, you are accustomed to view everything from the strong dispassionate ground of reason and calculation. From that ground alone, I know you will view and consider what I am going to communicate."

He waited, as if he would have been glad that she said something. But she said never a word.

"Louisa, my dear, you are the subject of a proposal of marriage that has been made to me."

Again he waited, and again she answered not one word. This so far surprised him, as to induce him gently to repeat, "a proposal of marriage, my dear." To which she returned, without any visible emotion whatever:

"I hear you, father. I am attending, I assure you."

"Well!" said Mr. Gradgrind, breaking into a smile, after being for the moment at a loss, "you are even more dispassionate than I expected, Louisa. Or, perhaps, you are not unprepared for the announcement I have it in charge to make?"

"I cannot say that, father, until I hear it. Prepared or unprepared, I wish to hear it all from you. I wish to hear you state it to me, father."

Strange to relate, Mr. Gradgrind was not so collected at this moment as his daughter was. He took a paper-knife in his hand, turned it over, laid it down, took it up again, and even then had to look along the blade of it, considering how to go on.

"What you say, my dear Louisa, is perfectly reasonable. I have undertaken then to let you know that—in short, that Mr. Bounderby has informed me that he has long watched your progress with particular interest and pleasure, and has long hoped that the time might ultimately arrive when he should offer you his hand in marriage. That time, to which he has so long, and certainly with great constancy, looked forward, is now come. Mr. Bounderby has made his proposal of marriage to me, and has entreated me to make it known to you, and to express his hope that you will take it into your favourable consideration."

Silence between them. The deadly statistical clock very hollow. The distant smoke very black and heavy.

"Father," said Louisa, "do you think I love Mr. Bounderby?"

Mr. Gradgrind was extremely discomfited by this unexpected question. "Well, my child," he returned, "I—really—cannot take upon myself to say."

"Father," pursued Louisa in exactly the same voice as before, "do you ask me to love Mr. Bounderby?"

"My dear Louisa, no. No. I ask nothing."

"Father," she still pursued, "does Mr. Bounderby ask me to love him?"

"Really, my dear," said Mr. Gradgrind, "it is difficult to answer your question——"

"Difficult to answer it, Yes or No, father?"

"Certainly, my dear. Because;" here was something to demonstrate, and it set him up again; "because the reply depends so materially, Louisa, on the sense in which we use the expression. Now, Mr. Bounderby does not do you the injustice, and does not do himself the injustice, of pretending to anything, fanciful, fantastic, or (I am using synonymous terms) sentimental. Mr. Bounderby would have seen you grow up under his eyes, to very little purpose, if he could so far forget what is due to your good sense, not to say to his, as to address you from any such ground. Therefore, perhaps the expression itself—I merely suggest this to you, my dear—may be a little misplaced."

"What would you advise me to use in its stead, father?"

"Why, my dear Louisa," said Mr. Gradgrind, completely recovered by this time, "I would advise you (since you ask me) to consider this question, as you have been accustomed to consider every other question, simply as one of tangible Fact. The ignorant and the giddy may embarrass such subjects with irrelevant fancies, and other absurdities that have no existence, properly viewed—really no existence—but it is no compliment to you to say, that you know better. Now, what are the Facts of this case? You are, we will say in round numbers, twenty years of age; Mr. Bounderby is, we will say in round numbers, fifty. There is some disparity in your respective years, but in your means and positions there is none; on the contrary, there is a great suitability. Then the question arises, Is this one disparity sufficient to operate as a bar to such a marriage? In considering this question, it is not unimportant to take into account the statistics of marriage, so far as they have been yet obtained, in England and Wales. I find, on reference to the figures, that a large proportion of these marriages are contracted between parties of very unequal ages, and that the elder of these contracting parties is, in rather more than three-fourths of these instances, the bridegroom. It is remarkable as showing the wide prevalence of this law, that among the natives of the British possessions in India, also in a considerable part of China, and among the Calmucks of Tartary, the best means of computation yet furnished us by travellers, yield similar results. The disparity I have mentioned, therefore, almost ceases to be disparity, and (virtually) all but disappears."

"What do you recommend, father," asked Louisa, her reserved composure not in the least affected by these gratifying results, "that I should substitute for the term I used just now? For the misplaced expression?"

"Louisa," returned her father, "it appears to me that nothing can be plainer. Confining yourself rigidly to Fact, the question of Fact you state to yourself is: Does Mr. Bounderby ask me to marry him? Yes, he does. The sole remaining question then is: Shall I marry him? I think nothing can be plainer than that?"

"Shall I marry him?" repeated Louisa, with great deliberation.

"Precisely. And it is satisfactory to me, as your father, my dear Louisa, to know that you do not come to the consideration of that question with the previous habits of mind, and habits of life, that belong to many young women."

"No, father," she returned, "I do not."

"I now leave you to judge for yourself," said Mr. Gradgrind. "I have stated the case, as such cases are usually stated among practical minds, I have stated it, as the case of your mother and myself was stated in its time. The rest, my dear Louisa, is for you to decide."

From the beginning, she had sat looking at him fixedly. As he now leaned back in his chair, and bent his deep-set eyes upon her in his turn, perhaps he might have seen one wavering moment in her, when she was impelled to throw herself upon his breast, and give him the pent-up confidences of her heart. But, to see it, he must have overleaped at a bound the artificial barriers he had for many years been erecting, between himself and all those subtle essences of humanity which will elude the utmost cunning of algebra until the last trumpet ever to be sounded shall blow even algebra to wreck. The barriers were too many and too high for such a leap. With his unbending, utilitarian, matter-of-fact face, he hardened her again; and the moment shot away into the plumbless depth of the past, to mingle with all the lost opportunities that are drowned there.

Removing her eyes from him, she sat so long looking silently towards the town, that he said, at length: "Are you consulting the chimneys of the Coketown works, Louisa?"

"There seems to be nothing there but languid and monotonous smoke. Yet when the night comes, Fire bursts out, father!" she answered, turning quickly.

"Of course I know that, Louisa. I do not see the application of the remark." To do him justice he did not, at all.

She passed it away with a slight motion of her hand, and

concentrating her attention upon him again, said, "Father, I have often thought that life is very short,"—This was so distinctly one of his subjects that he interposed.

"It is short, no doubt, my dear.   Still, the average duration of human life is proved to have increased of late years.   The calculations of various life assurance and annuity offices, among other figures which cannot go wrong, have established the fact."

"I speak of my own life, father."

"O indeed?   Still," said Mr. Gradgrind, "I need not point out to you, Louisa, that it is governed by the laws which govern lives in the aggregate."

"While it lasts, I would wish to do the little I can, and the little I am fit for.   What does it matter?"

Mr. Gradgrind seemed rather at a loss to understand the last four words; replying, "How, matter? What matter, my dear?"

"Mr. Bounderby," she went on in a steady, straight way, without regarding this, "asks me to marry him.   The question I have to ask myself is, shall I marry him?   That is so, father, is it not?   You have told me so, father.   Have you not?"

"Certainly, my dear."

"Let it be so.   Since Mr. Bounderby likes to take me thus, I am satisfied to accept his proposal.   Tell him, father, as soon as you please, that this was my answer.   Repeat it, word for word, if you can, because I should wish him to know what I said."

"It is quite right, my dear," retorted her father approvingly, "to be exact.   I will observe your very proper request.   Have you any wish in reference to the period of your marriage, my child?"

"None, father.   What does it matter?"

Mr. Gradgrind had drawn his chair a little nearer to her, and taken her hand.   But, her repetition of these words seemed to strike with some little discord on his ear.   He paused to look at her, and, still holding her hand, said:

"Louisa, I have not considered it essential to ask you one question, because the possibility implied in it appeared to me to be too remote.   But perhaps I ought to do so.   You have never entertained in secret any other proposal?"

"Father," she returned, almost scornfully, "what other proposal can have been made to *me?*   Whom have I seen? Where have *I* been?   What are my heart's experiences?"

"My dear Louisa" returned Mr. Gradgrind, reassured and satisfied.   "You correct me justly.   I merely wished to discharge my duty."

"What do *I* know, father," said Louisa in her quiet manner, "of tastes and fancies; of aspirations and affections; of all that part of my nature in which such light things might have been nourished? What escape have I had from problems that could be demonstrated, and realities that could be grasped?" As she said it, she unconsciously closed her hand, as if upon a solid object, and slowly opened it as though she were releasing dust or ash.

"My dear," assented her eminently practical parent, "quite true, quite true."

"Why, father," she pursued, "what a strange question to ask *me!* The baby-preference that even I have heard of as common among children, has never had its innocent resting-place in my breast. You have been so careful of me, that I never had a child's heart. You have trained me so well that I never dreamed a child's dream. You have dealt so wisely with me, father, from my cradle to this hour, that I never had a child's belief or a child's fear."

Mr. Gradgrind was quite moved by his success, and by this testimony to it. "My dear Louisa," said he, "you abundantly repay my care. Kiss me, my dear girl."

So, his daughter kissed him. Detaining her in his embrace, he said, "I may assure you now, my favourite child, that I am made happy by the sound decision at which you have arrived. Mr. Bounderby is a very remarkable man; and what little disparity can be said to exist between you—if any—is more than counterbalanced by the tone your mind has acquired. It has always been my object so to educate you, as that you might, while still in your early youth, be (if I may so express myself) almost any age. Kiss me once more, Louisa. Now, let us go and find your mother."

Accordingly, they went down to the drawing-room, where the esteemed lady with no nonsense about her, was recumbent as usual, while Sissy worked beside her. She gave some feeble signs of returning animation when they entered, and presently the faint transparency was presented in a sitting attitude.

"Mrs. Gradgrind," said her husband, who had waited for the achievement of this feat with some impatience, "allow me to present to you Mrs. Bounderby."

"Oh!" said Mrs. Gradgrind, "so you have settled it! Well, I'm sure I hope your health may be good, Louisa; for if your head begins to split as soon as you are married, which was the case with mine, I cannot consider that you are to be envied, though I have no doubt you think you are, as all girls do. However, I give you joy, my dear—and I hope you may now turn all your ological studies to good account, I am sure I do! I must give you a kiss of congratulation, Louisa; but don't touch my right shoulder, for there's something running down it all day long. And now you see," whimpered Mrs. Gradgrind, adjusting her shawls after the affectionate ceremony, "I shall be worrying myself, morning, noon, and night, to know what I am to call him!"

"Mrs. Gradgrind," said her husband, solemnly, "what do you mean?"

"Whatever I am to call him, Mr. Gradgrind, when he is married to Louisa! I must call him something. It's impossible," said Mrs. Gradgrind, with a mingled sense of politeness and injury, "to be constantly addressing him and never giving him a name. I cannot call him Josiah, for the name is insupportable to me. You yourself wouldn't hear of Joe, you very well know. Am I to call my own son-in-law, Mister. Not, I believe, unless the time has arrived when, as an invalid, I am to be trampled upon by my relations. Then, what am I to call him!"

Nobody present having any suggestion to offer in the remarkable emergency, Mrs. Gradgrind departed this life for the time being, after delivering the following codicil to her remarks already executed:

"As to the wedding, all I ask, Louisa, is,—and I ask it with a fluttering in my chest, which actually extends to the soles of my feet,—that it may take place soon. Otherwise, I know it is one of those subjects I shall never hear the last of."

When Mr. Gradgrind had presented Mrs. Bounderby, Sissy had suddenly turned her head, and looked in wonder, in pity, in sorrow, in doubt, in a multitude of emotions, towards Louisa. Louisa had known it, and seen it, without looking at her. From that moment she was impassive, proud and cold—held Sissy at a distance—changed to her altogether.

CHAPTER XVI: *Husband and Wife*

MR. BOUNDERBY'S first disquietude on hearing of his happiness, was occasioned by the necessity of imparting it to Mrs. Sparsit. He could not make up his mind how to do that, or what the consequences of the step might be. Whether she would instantly depart, bag and baggage, to Lady Scadgers, or would positively refuse to budge from the premises; whether she would be plaintive or abusive, tearful or tearing; whether she would break her heart, or break the looking-glass; Mr. Bounderby could not at all foresee. However, as it must be done, he had no choice but to do it; so, after attempting several letters, and failing in them all, he resolved to do it by word of mouth.

On his way home, on the evening he set aside for this momentous purpose, he took the precaution of stepping into a chemist's shop and buying a bottle of the very strongest smelling-salts. "By George!" said Mr. Bounderby, "if she takes it in the fainting way, I'll have the skin off her nose, at all events!" But, in spite of being thus forearmed, he entered his own house with anything but a courageous air; and appeared before the object of his misgivings, like a dog who was conscious of coming direct from the pantry.

"Good evening, Mr. Bounderby!"

"Good evening, ma'am, good evening," He drew up his chair, and Mrs. Sparsit drew back hers, as who should say, "Your fireside, sir. I freely admit it. It is for you to occupy it all, if you think proper."

"Don't go to the North Pole, ma'am!" said Mr. Bounderby.

"Thank you, sir," said Mrs. Sparsit, and returned, though short of her former position.

Mr. Bounderby sat looking at her, as, with the points of a stiff, sharp pair of scissors, she picked out holes for some inscrutable ornamental purpose, in a piece of cambric. An operation which, taken in connection with the bushy eyebrows and the Roman nose, suggested with some liveliness the idea of a hawk engaged upon the eyes of a tough little bird. She was so steadfastly occupied, that many minutes elapsed before she looked up from her work; when she did so Mr. Bounderby bespoke her attention with a hitch of his head.

"Mrs. Sparsit, ma'am," said Mr. Bounderby, putting his hands in his pockets, and assuring himself with his right hand that the cork of the little bottle was ready for use, "I have no occasion to say to you, that you are not only a lady born and bred, but a devilish sensible woman."

"Sir," returned the lady, "this is indeed not the first time that you have honoured me with similar expressions of your good opinion."

"Mrs. Sparsit, ma'am," said Mr. Bounderby, "I am going to astonish you."

"Yes, sir?" returned Mrs. Sparsit, interrogatively, and in the most tranquil manner possible. She generally wore mittens, and she now laid down her work, and smoothed those mittens.

"I am going, ma'am," said Bounderby, "to marry Tom Gradgrind's daughter."

"Yes, sir," returned Mrs. Sparsit. "I hope you may be happy, Mr. Bounderby. Oh, indeed I hope you may be happy, sir!" And she said it with such great condescension as well as with such great compassion for him, that Bounderby, —far more disconcerted than if she had thrown her work-box at the mirror, or swooned on the hearth-rug,—corked up the smelling-salts tight in his pocket, and thought, "Now confound this woman, who could have ever guessed that she would take it in this way!"

"I wish with all my heart, sir," said Mrs. Sparsit, in a highly superior manner; somehow she seemed in a moment, to have established a right to pity him ever afterwards; "that you may be in all respects very happy."

"Well, ma'am," returned Bounderby, with some resentment in his tone; which was clearly lowered, though in spite of himself, "I am obliged to you. I hope I shall be."

"*Do* you, sir!" said Mrs. Sparsit, with great affability. "But naturally you do; of course you do."

A very awkward pause on Mr. Bounderby's part succeeded. Mrs. Sparsit sedately resumed her work and occasionally gave a small cough, which sounded like the cough of conscious strength and forbearance.

"Well, ma'am," resumed Bounderby, "under these circumstances, I imagine it would not be agreeable to a character like yours to remain here, though you would be very welcome here."

"Oh, dear no, sir, I could on no account think of that!" Mrs. Sparsit shook her head, still in her highly superior manner and a little changed the small cough—coughing now, as if the spirit of prophecy rose within her, but had better be coughed down.

"However, ma'am," said Bounderby, "there are apartments at the Bank, where a born and bred lady, as keeper of the place, would be rather a catch than otherwise; and if the same terms——"

"I beg your pardon, sir. You were so good as to promise that you would always substitute the phrase, annual compliment."

"Well, ma'am, annual compliment. If the same annual compliment would be acceptable there, why, I see nothing to part us, unless you do."

"Sir," returned Mrs. Sparsit. "The proposal is like yourself, and if the position I shall assume at the Bank is one that I could occupy without descending lower in the social scale——"

"Why, of course it is," said Bounderby. "If it was not, ma'am, you don't suppose that I should offer it to a lady who has moved in the society you have moved in. Not that *I* care for such society, you know! But *you* do."

"Mr. Bounderby, you are very considerate."

"You'll have your own private apartments, and you'll have your coals and your candles, and all the rest of it, and you'll have your maid to attend upon you, and you'll have your light porter to protect you, and you'll be what I take the liberty of considering precious comfortable," said Bounderby.

"Sir," rejoined Mrs. Sparsit, "say no more. In yielding up my trust here, I shall not be freed from the necessity of eating the bread of dependence:" she might have said the sweetbread, for that delicate article in a savoury brown sauce was her favourite supper; "and I would rather receive it from your hand, than from any other. Therefore, sir, I accept your offer gratefully, and with many sincere acknowledgments for past favours. And I hope, sir," said Mrs. Sparsit concluding in an impressively compassionate manner, "I fondly hope that Miss Gradgrind may be all you desire, and deserve!"

Nothing moved Mrs. Sparsit from that position any more. It was in vain for Bounderby to bluster or to assert himself in any of his explosive ways; Mrs. Sparsit was resolved to have compassion on him, as a Victim. She was polite, obliging, cheerful, hopeful; but, the more polite, the more obliging, the more cheerful, the more hopeful, the more exemplary altogether, she; the forlorner Sacrifice and Victim, he. She had that tenderness for his melancholy fate, that his great red countenance used to break out into cold perspirations when she looked at him.

Meanwhile the marriage was appointed to be solemnized in eight weeks' time, and Mr. Bounderby went every evening to Stone Lodge as an accepted wooer. Love was made on these occasions in the form of bracelets; and, on all occasions during the period of betrothal, took a manufacturing aspect. Dresses were made, jewellery was made, cakes and gloves were made, settlements were made, and an extensive assortment of Facts did appropriate honour to the contract. The business was all Fact, from first to last. The Hours did not go through any of those rosy performances, which foolish poets have ascribed to them at such times; neither did the clocks go any faster, or any slower, than at other seasons. The deadly statistical recorder in the Gradgrind observatory knocked every second on the head as it was born, and buried it with his accustomed regularity.

So the day came, as all other days come to people who will only stick to reason; and when it came, they were married in the church of the florid wooden legs—that popular order of architecture—Josiah Bounderby Esquire of Coketown, to Louisa eldest daughter of Thomas Gradgrind Esquire of Stone Lodge, M.P. for that borough. And when they were united in holy matrimony, they went home to breakfast at Stone Lodge aforesaid.

There was an improving party assembled on the auspicious occasion, who knew what everything they had to eat and drink was made of, and how it was imported or exported, and in what quantities, and in what bottoms, whether native or foreign, and all about it. The bridesmaids, down to little Jane Gradgrind, were, in an intellectual point of view, fit helpmates for the calculating boy; and there was no nonsense about any of the company.

After breakfast, the bridegroom addressed them in the following terms:

"Ladies and gentlemen, I am Josiah Bounderby of Coketown. Since you have done my wife and myself the honour of drinking our healths and happiness, I suppose I must acknowledge the same; though, as you all know me, and know what my extraction was, you won't expect a speech from a man who, when he sees a Post, says, 'that's a Post,' and when he sees a Pump, says, 'that's a Pump,' and is not to be got to call a Pump a Post, or a Pump a Post, or either of them a Toothpick. If you want a speech this morning, my friend and father-in-law, Tom Gradgrind, is a Member of Parliament, and you know where to get it. I am not your man. However, if I feel a little independent when I look around this table to-day, and reflect how little I thought of marrying Tom Gradgrind's daughter when I was a ragged street-boy, who never washed his face unless it was at a pump, and that not oftener than once a fortnight, I hope I may be excused. So, I hope you like my feeling independent; if you don't, I can't help it. I *do* feel independent. Now I have mentioned, and you have mentioned, that I am this day married to Tom Gradgrind's daughter. I am very glad to be so. It has long been my wish to be so. I have watched her bringing-up, and I believe she is worthy of me. At the same time—not to deceive you—I believe I am worthy of her. So, I thank you, on both our parts, for the goodwill you have shown towards us; and the best wish I can give the unmarried part of the present company, is this: I hope every bachelor may find as good a wife as I have found. And I hope every spinster may find as good a husband as my wife has found."

Shortly after which oration, as they were going on a nuptial trip to Lyons, in order that Mr. Bounderby might take the opportunity of seeing how the Hands got on in those parts, and whether they, too, required to be fed with gold spoons; the happy pair departed for the railroad. The Bride, in passing downstairs, dressed for her journey, found Tom waiting for her—flushed, either with his feelings or the vinous part of the breakfast.

"What a game girl you are, to be such a first-rate sister, Loo!" whispered Tom.

She clung to him as she should have clung to some far better nature that day, and was a little shaken in her reserved composure for the first time.

"Old Bounderby's quite ready, said Tom. "Time's up. Good-bye. I shall be on the look-out for you, when you come back. I say, my dear Loo! An't it uncommonly jolly now!"

[END OF THE FIRST BOOK

BOOK THE SECOND: REAPING

CHAPTER I: *Effects in the Bank*

A SUNNY midsummer day. There was such a thing sometimes, even in Coketown.

Seen from a distance in such weather, Coketown lay shrouded in a haze of its own, which appeared impervious to the sun's rays. You only knew the town was there, because you knew there could have been no such sulky blotch upon the prospect without a town. A blur of soot and smoke, now confusedly tending this way, now that way, now aspiring to the vault of Heaven, now murkily creeping along the earth, as the wind rose and fell, or changed its quarter: a dense formless jumble, with sheets of cross light in it, that showed nothing but masses of darkness:—Coketown in the distance was suggestive of itself, though not a brick of it could be seen.

The wonder was, it was there at all. It had been ruined so often, that it was amazing how it had borne so many shocks. Surely there never was such fragile china-ware as that of which the millers of Coketown were made. Handle them never so lightly, and they fell to pieces with such ease that you might suspect them of having been flawed before. They were ruined, when they were required to send labouring children to school; they were ruined, when inspectors were appointed to look into their works; they were ruined, when such inspectors considered it doubtful whether they were quite justified in chopping people up with their machinery; they were utterly undone, when it was hinted that perhaps they need not always make quite so much smoke. Besides Mr. Bounderby's gold spoon which was generally received in Coketown, another prevalent fiction was very popular there. It took the form of a threat. Whenever a Coketowner felt he was ill-used—that is to say, whenever he was not left entirely alone, and it was proposed to hold him accountable for the consequences of any of his acts—he was sure to come out with the awful menace, that he would "sooner pitch his property into the Atlantic." This had terrified the Home Secretary within an inch of his life, on several occasions.

However, the Coketowners were so patriotic after all, that they never had pitched their property into the Atlantic yet, but, on the contrary, had been kind enough to take mighty

good care of it. So there it was, in the haze yonder; and it
increased and multiplied.

The streets were hot and dusty on the summer day, and the
sun was so bright that it even shone through the heavy vapour
drooping over Coketown, and could not be looked at steadily.
Stokers emerged from low underground doorways into factory
yards, and sat on steps, and posts, and palings, wiping their
swarthy visages, and contemplating coals. The whole town
seemed to be frying in oil. There was a stifling smell of hot
oil everywhere. The steam-engines shone with it, the dresses
of the Hands were soiled with it, the mills throughout their
many stories oozed and trickled it. The atmosphere of those
Fairy palaces was like the breath of the simoom: and their
inhabitants, wasting with heat, toiled languidly in the desert.
But no temperature made the melancholy mad elephants more
mad or more sane. Their wearisome heads went up and down
at the same rate, in hot weather and cold, wet weather and
dry, fair weather and foul. The measured motion of their
shadows on the walls, was the substitute Coketown had to
show for the shadows of rustling woods; while, for the summer
hum of insects, it could offer, all the year round, from the
dawn of Monday to the night of Saturday, the whirr of shafts
and wheels.

Drowsily they whirred all through this sunny day, making
the passenger more sleepy and more hot as he passed the
humming walls of the mills. Sun-blinds, and sprinklings of
water, a little cooled the main streets and the shops; but the
mills, and the courts and alleys, baked at a fierce heat. Down
upon the river that was black and thick with dye, some Coketown boys who were at large—a rare sight there—rowed a
crazy boat, which made a spumous track upon the water as it
jogged along, while every dip of an oar stirred up vile smells.
But the sun itself, however beneficent generally, was less kind
to Coketown than hard frost, and rarely looked intently into
any of its closer regions without engendering more death than
life. So does the eye of Heaven itself become an evil eye,
when incapable or sordid hands are interposed between it and
the things it looks upon to bless.

Mrs. Sparsit sat in her afternoon apartment at the Bank, on
the shadier side of the frying street. Office-hours were over;
and at that period of the day, in warm weather, she usually
embellished with her genteel presence, a managerial board-
room over the public office. Her own private sitting-room
was a story higher, at the window of which post of observation
she was ready, every morning, to greet Mr. Bounderby, as he
came across the road, with the sympathising recognition
appropriate to a Victim. He had been married now a year;
and Mrs. Sparsit had never released him from her determined
pity for a moment.

The Bank offered no violence to the wholesome monotony of the town. It was another red brick house, with black outside shutters, green inside blinds, a black street-door up two white steps, a brazen door-plate, and a brazen door-handle full stop. It was a size larger than Mr. Bounderby's house, as other houses were from a size to half-a-dozen sizes smaller; in all other particulars, it was strictly according to pattern.

Mrs. Sparsit was conscious that by coming in the evening-tide among the desks and writing implements, she shed a feminine, not to say also aristocratic, grace upon the office. Seated, with her needlework or netting apparatus, at the window, she had a self-laudatory sense of correcting, by her lady-like deportment, the rude business aspect of the place. With this impression of her interesting character upon her, Mrs. Sparsit considered herself, in some sort, the Bank Fairy. The townspeople who, in their passing and repassing, saw her there, regarded her as the Bank Dragon keeping watch over the treasures of the mine.

What those treasures were, Mrs. Sparsit knew as little as they did. Gold and silver coin, precious paper, secrets that if divulged would bring vague destruction upon vague persons (generally, however, people whom she disliked,) were the chief items in her ideal catalogue thereof. For the rest, she knew that after office-hours, she reigned supreme over all the office furniture, and over a locked-up iron room with three locks, against the door of which strong chamber the night porter laid his head every night, on a truckle bed, that disappeared at cockcrow. Further, she was lady paramount over certain vaults in the basement, sharply spiked off from communication with the predatory world; and over the relics of the current day's work, consisting of blots of ink, worn-out pens, fragments of wafers, and scraps of paper torn so small, that nothing interesting could ever be deciphered on them when Mrs. Sparsit tried. Lastly, she was guardian over a little armoury of cutlasses and carbines, arrayed in vengeful order above one of the official chimney-pieces; and over that respectable tradition never to be separated from a place of business claiming to be wealthy—a row of fire-buckets—vessels calculated to be of no physical utility on any occasion, but observed to exercise a fine moral influence, almost equal to bullion, on most beholders.

A deaf serving-woman and a light porter completed Mrs. Sparsit's empire. The deaf serving-woman was rumoured to be wealthy; and a saying had for years gone about among the lower orders of Coketown, that she would be murdered some night when the Bank was shut, for the sake of her money. It was generally considered, indeed, that she had been due some time, and ought to have fallen long ago; but she had kept her life and her situation, with an ill-conditioned tenacity that occasioned much offence and disappointment.

Mrs. Sparsit's tea was just set for her on a pert little table, with its tripod of legs in an attitude, which she insinuated after office hours, into the company of the stern, leathern-topped, long board-table that bestrode the middle of the room. The light porter placed the tea-tray on it, knuckling his forehead as a form of homage.

"Thank you, Bitzer," said Mrs. Sparsit.

"Thank *you*, ma'am," returned the light porter. He was a very light porter indeed; as light as in the days when he blinkingly defined a horse, for girl number twenty.

"All is shut up, Bitzer?" said Mrs. Sparsit.

"All is shut up, ma'am."

"And what," said Mrs. Sparsit, pouring out her tea, "is the news of the day? Anything?"

"Well, ma'am, I can't say that I have heard anything particular. Our people are a bad lot, ma'am; but that is no news, unfortunately."

"What are the restless wretches doing now?" asked Mrs. Sparsit.

"Merely going on in the old way, ma'am. Uniting, and leaguing, and engaging to stand by one another."

"It is much to be regretted," said Mrs. Sparsit, making her nose more Roman and her eyebrows more Coriolanian in the strength of her severity, "that the united masters allow of any such class-combinations."

"Yes, ma'am," said Bitzer.

"Being united themselves, they ought one and all to set their faces against employing any man who is united with any other man," said Mrs. Sparsit.

"They have done that, ma'am," returned Bitzer; "but it rather fell through, ma'am."

"I do not pretend to understand these things," said Mrs. Sparsit, with dignity, "my lot having been signally cast in a widely different sphere; and Mr. Sparsit, as a Powler, being also quite out of the pale of any such dissensions. I only know that these people must be conquered, and that it's high time it was done, once and for all."

"Yes, ma'am," returned Bitzer, with a demonstration of great respect for Mrs. Sparsit's oracular authority. "You couldn't put it clearer, I am sure, ma'am."

As this was his usual hour for having a little confidential chat with Mrs. Sparsit, and as he had already caught her eye and seen that she was going to ask him something, he made a pretence of arranging the rulers, inkstands, and so forth, while the lady went on with her tea, glancing through the open window down into the street.

"Has it been a busy day, Bitzer?" asked Mrs. Sparsit.

"Not a very busy day, my lady. About an average day."
He now and then slided into my lady, instead of ma'am, as an
involuntary acknowledgment of Mrs. Sparsit's personal dignity and claims to reverence.

"The clerks," said Mrs. Sparsit, carefully brushing an
imperceptible crumb of bread and butter from her left hand
mitten, "are trustworthy, punctual, and industrious, of
course?"

"Yes, ma'am, pretty fair, ma'am. With the usual exception."

He held the respectable office of general spy and informer in
the establishment, for which volunteer service he received a
present at Christmas, over and above his weekly wage. He
had grown into an extremely clear-headed, cautious, prudent
young man, who was safe to rise in the world. His mind was
so exactly regulated, that he had no affections or passions.
All his proceedings were the result of the nicest and coldest
calculation; and it was not without cause that Mrs. Sparsit
habitually observed of him, that he was a young man of the
steadiest principle she had ever known. Having satisfied himself, on his father's death, that his mother had a right of settlement in Coketown, this excellent young economist had
asserted that right for her with such a steadfast adherence to
the principle of the case, that she had been shut up in the
workhouse ever since. It must be admitted that he allowed
her half a pound of tea a year, which was weak in him: first,
because all gifts have an inevitable tendency to pauperise the
recipient, and secondly, because his only reasonable trans-
action in that commodity would have been to buy it for as
little as he could possibly give, and sell it for as much as he
could possibly get; it having been clearly ascertained by philosophers that in this is comprised the whole duty of man—not
a part of man's duty, but the whole.

"Pretty fair, ma'am. With the usual exception, ma'am,"
repeated Bitzer.

"Ah—h!" said Mrs. Sparsit, shaking her head over her tea-
cup, and taking a long gulp.

"Mr. Thomas, ma'am, I doubt Mr. Thomas very much,
ma'am, I don't like his ways at all."

"Bitzer," said Mrs. Sparsit, in a very impressive manner,
"do you recollect my having said anything to you respecting
names?"

"I beg your pardon, ma'am. It's quite true that you did
object to names being used, and they're always best avoided."

"Please to remember that I have a charge here," said Mrs.
Sparsit, with her air of state. "I hold a trust here, Bitzer,
under Mr. Bounderby. However improbable both Mr.
Bounderby and myself might have deemed it years ago, that
he would ever become my patron, making me an annual
compliment, I cannot but regard him in that light. From

Mr. Bounderby I have received every acknowledgment of my social station, and every recognition of my family descent, that I could possibly expect. More, far more. Therefore, to my patron I would be scrupulously true. And I do not consider, I will not consider, I cannot consider," said Mrs. Sparsit, with a most extensive stock on hand of honour and morality, "that I *should* be scrupulously true, if I allowed names to be mentioned under this roof, that are unfortunately —most unfortunately—no doubt of that—connected with his."

Bitzer knuckled his forehead again, and again begged pardon.

"No, Bitzer," continued Mrs. Sparsit, "say an individual, and I will hear you; say Mr. Thomas, and you must excuse me."

"With the usual exception, ma'am," said Bitzer, trying back, "of an individual."

"Ah—h!" Mrs. Sparsit repeated the ejaculation, the shake of the head over her tea-cup, and the long gulp, as taking up the conversation again at the point where it had been interrupted.

"An individual, ma'am," said Bitzer, "has never been what he ought to have been, since he first came into the place. He is a dissipated, extravagant idler. He is not worth his salt, ma'am. He wouldn't get it either, if he hadn't a friend and relation at court, ma'am!"

"Ah—h!" said Mrs. Sparsit, with another melancholy shake of her head.

"I only hope, ma'am," pursued Bitzer, "that his friend and relation may not supply him with the means of carrying on. Otherwise, ma'am, we know out of whose pocket *that* money comes."

"Ah—h!" sighed Mrs. Sparsit again, with another melancholy shake of her head.

"He is to be pitied, ma'am. The last party I have alluded to, is to be pitied, ma'am," said Bitzer.

"Yes, Bitzer," said Mrs. Sparsit. "I have always pitied the delusion, always."

"As to an individual, ma'am," said Bitzer, dropping his voice and drawing nearer, "he is as improvident as any of the people in this town. And you know what *their* improvidence is, ma'am. No one could wish to know better than a lady of your eminence does."

"They would do well," returned Mrs. Sparsit, "to take example by you, Bitzer."

"Thank you, ma'am. But, since you do refer to me, now look at me, ma'am. I have put by a little ma'am, already. That gratuity which I receive at Christmas, ma'am: I never touch it. I don't even go the length of my wages, though they're not high, ma'am. Why can't they do as I have done, ma'am? What one person can do, another can do."

This, again, was among the fictions of Coketown. Any capitalist there, who had made sixty thousand pounds out of sixpence, always professed to wonder why the sixty thousand nearest Hands didn't each make sixty thousand pounds out of sixpence, and more or less reproached them every one for not accomplishing the little feat. What I did you can do. Why don't you go and do it?

"As to their wanting recreations, ma'am," said Bitzer, "it's stuff and nonsense. I don't want recreations. I never did, and I never shall: I don't like 'em. As to their combining together; there are many of them, I have no doubt, that by watching and informing upon one another could earn a trifle now and then, whether in money or goodwill, and improve their livelihood. Then, why don't they improve it, ma'am! It's the first consideration of a rational creature, and it's what they pretend to want."

"Pretend indeed!" said Mrs. Sparsit.

"I am sure we are constantly hearing, ma'am, till it becomes quite nauseous, concerning their wives and families," said Bitzer. "Why look at me, ma'am! I don't want a wife and family. Why should they?"

"Because they are improvident," said Mrs. Sparsit.

"Yes, ma'am," returned Bitzer, "that's where it is. If they were more provident and less perverse, ma'am, what would they do? They would say, 'While my hat covers my family,' or 'while my bonnet covers my family,'—as the case might be, ma'am—'I have only one to feed, and that's the person I most like to feed.'"

"To be sure," assented Mrs. Sparsit, eating muffin.

"Thank you, ma'am," said Bitzer, knuckling his forehead again, in return for the favour of Mrs. Sparsit's improving conversation. "Would you wish a little more hot water, ma'am, or is there anything else I could fetch you?"

"Nothing just now, Bitzer."

"Thank you, ma'am. I shouldn't wish to disturb you at your meals, ma'am, particularly tea, knowing your partiality for it," said Bitzer, craning a little to look over into the street from where he stood; "but there's a gentleman been looking up here for a minute or so, ma'am, and he has come across as if he was going to knock. That is his knock, ma'am, no doubt."

He stepped to the window; and looking out, and drawing in his head again, confirmed himself with, "Yes, ma'am. Would you wish the gentleman to be shown in, ma'am?"

"I don't know who it can be," said Mrs. Sparsit, wiping her mouth and arranging her mittens.

"A stranger, ma'am, evidently."

"What a stranger can want at the Bank at this time of the evening unless he comes upon some business for which he is too late, I don't know," said Mrs. Sparsit, "but I hold a charge in this establishment from Mr. Bounderby, and I will never shrink from it. If to see him is any part of the duty I have accepted, I will see him. Use your own discretion, Bitzer."

Here the visitor, all unconscious of Mrs. Sparsit's magnanimous words, repeated his knock so loudly that the light porter hastened down to open the door; while Mrs. Sparsit, took the precaution of concealing her little table, with all its appliances upon it, in a cupboard and then decamped upstairs, that she might appear, if needful, with the greater dignity.

"If you please, ma'am, the gentleman would wish to see you," said Bitzer, with his light eye at Mrs. Sparsit's keyhole. So, Mrs. Sparsit, who had improved the interval by touching up her cap, took her classical features downstairs again, and entered the board-room in the manner of a Roman matron going outside the city walls to treat with an invading general.

The visitor having strolled to the window, and being then engaged in looking carelessly out, was as unmoved by this impressive entry as man could possibly be. He stood whistling to himself with all imaginable coolness, with his hat still on, and a certain air of exhaustion upon him, in part arising from excessive summer, and in part from excessive gentility. For it was to be seen with half an eye that he was a thorough gentleman, made to the model of the time; weary of everything, and putting no more faith in anything than Lucifer.

"I believe, sir," quoth Mrs. Sparsit, "you wished to see me."

"I beg your pardon," he said, turning and removing his hat; "pray excuse me."

"Humph!" thought Mrs. Sparsit, as she made a stately bend. "Five-and-thirty, good-looking, good figure, good teeth, good voice, good breeding, well-dressed, dark hair, bold eyes." All which Mrs. Sparsit observed in her womanly way —like the Sultan who put his head in the pail of water— merely in dipping down and coming up again.

"Please to be seated, sir," said Mrs. Sparsit.

"Thank you. Allow me." He placed a chair for her, but remained himself carelessly lounging against the table. "I left my servant at the railway looking after the luggage—very heavy train and vast quantity of it in the van—and strolled on, looking about me. Exceedingly odd place. Will you allow me to ask you if it's *always* as black as this?"

"In general much blacker," returned Mrs. Sparsit, in her uncompromising way.

"Is it possible! Excuse me: you are not a native, I think?"

"No, sir," returned Mrs. Sparsit. "It was once my good or ill fortune as it may be—before I became a widow—to move in a very different sphere. My husband was a Powler."

"Beg your pardon, really!" said the stranger. "Was——?"
Mrs. Sparsit repeated, "A Powler."

"Powler Family," said the stranger, after reflecting a few moments. Mrs. Sparsit signified assent. The stranger seemed a little more fatigued than before.

"You must be very much bored here?" was the inference he drew from the communication.

"I am the servant of circumstances, sir," said Mrs. Sparsit, "and I have long adapted myself to the governing power of my life."

"Very philosophical," returned the stranger, "and very exemplary and laudable, and——" It seemed to be scarcely worth his while to finish the sentence, so he played with his watch-chain wearily.

"May I be permitted to ask, sir," said Mrs. Sparsit, "to what I am indebted for the favour of——"

"Assuredly," said the stranger. "Much obliged to you for reminding me. I am the bearer of a letter of introduction to Mr. Bounderby the banker. Walking through this extraordinary black town, while they were getting dinner ready at the hotel, I asked a fellow whom I met; one of the working-people; who appeared to have been taking a shower-bath of something fluffy, which I assume to be the raw material——"

Mrs. Sparsit inclined her head.

"——Raw material—where Mr. Bounderby, the banker, might reside. Upon which, misled no doubt by the word Banker, he directed me to the Bank.—Fact being, I presume, that Mr. Bounderby the Banker, does *not* reside in the edifice in which I have the honour of offering this explanation?"

"No, sir," returned Mrs. Sparsit, "he does not."

"Thank you. I had no intention of delivering my letter at the present moment, nor have I. But strolling on to the Bank to kill time, and having the good fortune to observe at the window," towards which he languidly waved his hand, then slightly bowed, "a lady of a very superior and agreeable appearance, I considered that I could not do better than take the liberty of asking that lady where Mr. Bounderby the Banker *does* live. Which I accordingly venture, with all suitable apologies, to do."

The inattention and indolence of his manner were sufficiently relieved, to Mrs. Sparsit's thinking, by a certain gallantry at ease, which offered her homage too. Here he was, for instance, at this moment, all but sitting on the table, and yet lazily bending over her, as if he acknowledged an attraction in her that made her charming—in her way.

"Banks, I know, are always suspicious, and officially must be," said the stranger, whose lightness and smoothness of speech were pleasant likewise; suggesting matter far more sensible and humorous than it ever contained—which was perhaps a shrewd device of the founder of this numerous sect, whosoever may have been that great man: "therefore I may observe that my letter—here it is—is from the member for this place—Gradgrind—whom I have had the pleasure of knowing in London."

Mrs. Sparsit recognised the hand, intimated that such confirmation was quite unnecessary, and gave Mr. Bounderby's address, with all needful clues and directions in aid.

"Thousand thanks," said the stranger. "Of course you know the Banker well?"

"Yes, sir," rejoined Mrs. Sparsit. "In my dependent relation towards him, I have known him ten years."

"Quite an eternity! I think he married Gradgrind's daughter?"

"Yes," said Mrs. Sparsit, suddenly compressing her mouth, "he had that—honour."

"The lady is quite a philosopher, I am told?"

"Indeed, sir," said Mrs. Sparsit. "*Is* she?"

"Excuse my impertinent curiosity," pursued the stranger, fluttering over Mrs. Sparsit's eyebrows, with a propitiatory air, "but you know the family, and know the world. I am about to know the family, and may have much to do with them. Is the lady so very alarming? Her father gives her such a portentously hard-headed reputation, that I have a burning desire to know. Is she absolutely unapproachable? Repellently and stunningly clever? I see, by your meaning smile, you think not. You have poured balm into my anxious soul. As to age, now, Forty! Five-and-thirty?"

Mrs. Sparsit laughed outright. "A chit," said she. "Not twenty when she was married."

"I give you my honour, Mrs. Powler," returned the stranger, detaching himself from the table, "that I never was so astonished in my life!"

It really did seem to impress him, to the utmost extent of his capacity of being impressed. He looked at his informant for a full quarter of a minute, and appeared to have the surprise in his mind all the time. "I assure you, Mrs. Powler," he then said, much exhausted, "that the father's manner prepared me for a grim and stony maturity. I am obliged to you, of all things, for correcting so absurd a mistake. Pray excuse my intrusion. Many thanks. Good day!"

He bowed himself out; and Mrs. Sparsit, hiding in the window curtain, saw him languishing down the street on the shady side of the way, observed of all the town.

"What do you think of the gentleman, Bitzer?" she asked the light porter, when he came to take away.

"Spends a deal of money on his dress, ma'am."

"It must be admitted," said Mrs. Sparsit, "that it's very tasteful."

"Yes, ma'am," returned Bitzer, "if that's worth the money."

"Besides which, ma'am," resumed Bitzer, while he was polishing the table, "he looks to me as if he gamed."

"It's immoral to game," said Mrs. Sparsit.

"It's ridiculous, ma'am," said Bitzer, "because the chances are against the players."

Whether it was that the heat prevented Mrs. Sparsit from working, or whether it was that her hand was out, she did no work that night. She sat at the window, when the sun began to sink behind the smoke; she sat there, when the smoke was burning red, when the colour faded from it, when darkness seemed to rise slowly out of the ground, and creep upward, upward, up to the house-tops, up the church steeple, up to the summits of the factory chimneys, up to the sky. Without a candle in the room, Mrs. Sparsit sat at the window, with her hands before her, not thinking much of the sounds of evening; the whooping of boys, the barking of dogs, the rumbling of wheels, the steps and voices of passengers, the shrill street cries, the clogs upon the pavement when it was their hour for going by, the shutting-up of shop-shutters. Not until the light porter announced that her nocturnal sweetbread was ready, did Mrs. Sparsit arouse herself from her reverie, and convey her dense black eyebrows—by that time creased with meditation, as if they needed ironing out—upstairs.

"O, you Fool!" said Mrs. Sparsit, when she was alone at her supper. Whom she meant, she did not say; but she could scarcely have meant the sweetbread.

CHAPTER II: *Mr. James Harthouse*

THE Gradgrind party wanted assistance in cutting the throats of the Graces. They went about recruiting; and where could they enlist recruits more hopefully, than among the fine gentlemen who, having found out everything to be worth nothing, were equally ready for anything?

Moreover, the healthy spirits who had mounted to this sublime height were attractive to many of the Gradgrind school. They liked fine gentlemen; they pretended that they did not, but they did. They became exhausted in imitation of them; and they yaw-yawed in their speech like them; and they served out, with an enervated air, the little mouldy rations of political economy, on which they regaled their disciples. There never before was seen on earth such a wonderful hybrid race as was thus produced.

Among the fine gentlemen not regularly belonging to the Gradgrind school, there was one of a good family and a better appearance, with a happy turn of humour which had told immensely with the House of Commons on the occasion of his entertaining it with his (and the Board of Directors') view of a railway accident, in which the most careful officers ever known, employed by the most liberal managers ever heard of, assisted by the finest mechanical contrivances ever devised, the whole in action on the best line ever constructed, had killed five people and wounded thirty-two, by a casualty without which the excellence of the whole system would have been positively incomplete. Among the slain was a cow, and among the scattered articles unowned, a widow's cap. And the honourable member had so tickled the House (which has a delicate sense of humour) by putting the cap on the cow, that it became impatient of any serious reference to the Coroner's Inquest, and brought the railway off with Cheers and Laughter.

Now, this gentleman had a younger brother of still better appearance than himself, who had tried life as a Cornet of Dragoons, and found it a bore; and had afterwards tried it in the train of an English minister abroad, and found it a bore; and had then strolled to Jerusalem, and got bored there; and had then gone yachting about the world, and got bored everywhere. To whom this honourable and jocular member fraternally said one day, "Jem, there's a good opening among the hard Fact fellows, and they want men. I wonder you don't go in for statistics." Jem, rather taken by the novelty of the idea, and very hard up for a change, was as ready to "go in" for statistics as for anything else. So, he went in. He coached himself up with a blue book or two; and his brother put it about among the hard Fact fellows, and said, "If you want to bring in, for any place, a handsome dog who can make you a devilish good speech, look after my brother Jem, for he's your man." After a few dashes in the public meeting way, Mr. Gradgrind and a council of political sages approved of Jem, and it was resolved to send him down to Coketown, to become known there and in the neighbourhood. Hence the letter Jem had last night shown to Mrs. Sparsit, which Mr. Bounderby now held in his hand; superscribed, "Josiah Bounderby, Esquire, Banker, Coketown. Specially to introduce James Harthouse, Esquire. Thomas Gradgrind."

Within an hour of the receipt of this despatch and Mr. James Harthouse's card, Mr. Bounderby put on his hat and went down to the Hotel. There he found Mr. James Harthouse looking out of window, in a state of mind so disconsolate, that he was already half disposed to "go in" for something else.

"My name, sir," said his visitor, "is Josiah Bounderby, of Coketown."

Mr. James Harthouse was very happy indeed (though he scarcely looked so), to have a pleasure he had long expected.

"Coketown, sir," said Bounderby, obstinately taking a chair, "is not the kind of place you have been accustomed

MR. HARTHOUSE DINES AT THE BOUNDERBYS'.

to. Therefore, if you will allow me—or whether you will or not, for I am a plain man—I'll tell you something about it before we go any further."

Mr. Harthouse would be charmed.

"Don't be too sure of that," said Bounderby. "I don't promise it. First of all, you see our smoke. That's meat and drink to us. It's the healthiest thing in the world in all respects, and particularly for the lungs. If you are one of those who want us to consume it, I differ from you. We are not going to wear the bottoms of our boilers out any faster than we wear 'em out now, for all the humbugging sentiment in Great Britain and Ireland."

By way of "going in" to the fullest extent, Mr. Harthouse rejoined, "Mr. Bounderby, I assure you I am entirely and completely of your way of thinking. On conviction."

"I am glad to hear it," said Bounderby. "Now, you have heard a lot of talk about the work in our mills, no doubt. You have? Very good. I'll state the fact of it to you. It's the pleasantest work there is, and it's the lightest work there is, and it's the best paid work there is. More than that, we couldn't improve the mills themselves, unless we laid down Turkey carpets on the floors. Which we're not going to do."

"Mr. Bounderby, perfectly right."

"Lastly," said Bounderby, "as to our Hands. There's not a Hand in this town, sir, man, woman, or child, but has one ultimate object in life. That object is, to be fed on turtle soup and venison with a gold spoon. Now, they're not a going —none of 'em—ever to be fed on turtle soup and venison with a gold spoon. And now you know the place."

Mr. Harthouse professed himself in the highest degree instructed and refreshed, by this condensed epitome of the whole Coketown question.

"Why, you see," replied Mr. Bounderby, "it suits my disposition to have a full understanding with a man, particularly with a public man, when I make his acquaintance. I have only one thing more to say to you, Mr. Harthouse, before assuring you of the pleasure with which I shall respond, to the utmost of my poor ability, to my friend Tom Gradgrind's letter of introduction. You are a man of family. Don't you deceive yourself by supposing for a moment that I am a man of family. I am a bit of dirty riff-raff, and a genuine scrap of tag, rag, and bobtail."

If anything could have exalted Jem's interest in Mr. Bounderby, it would have been this very circumstance. Or, so he told him.

"So now," said Bounderby, "we may shake hands on equal terms. I say, equal terms, because although I know what I am, and the exact depth of the gutter I have lifted myself out of, better than any man does, I am as proud as you are. I am just as proud as you are. Having now asserted my independence in a proper manner, I may come to how do you find yourself, and I hope you're pretty well."

The better, Mr. Harthouse gave him to understand as they shook hands, for the salubrious air of Coketown. Mr. Bounderby received the answer with favour.

"Perhaps you know," said he, "or perhaps you don't know, I married Tom Gradgrind's daughter. If you have nothing better to do than to walk up-town with me, I shall be glad to introduce you to Tom Gradgrind's daughter."

"Mr. Bounderby," said Jem, "you anticipate my dearest wishes."

They went out without further discourse; and Mr. Bounderby piloted the new acquaintance who so strongly contrasted with him, to the private red brick dwelling, with the black outside shutters, the green inside blinds, and the black street door up the two white steps. In the drawing-room of which mansion, there presently entered to them the most remarkable girl Mr. James Harthouse had ever seen. She was so constrained, and yet so careless; so reserved, and yet so watchful; so cold and proud, and yet so sensitively ashamed of her husband's braggart humility—from which she shrunk as if every example of it were a cut or a blow; that it was quite a new sensation to observe her. In face she was no less remarkable than in manner. Her features were handsome, but their natural play was so locked up, that it seemed impossible to guess at their genuine expression. Utterly indifferent, perfectly self-reliant, never at a loss, and yet never at her ease, with her figure in company with them there, and her mind apparently quite alone—it was of no use "going in" yet awhile to comprehend this girl, for she baffled all penetration.

From the mistress of the house, the visitor glanced to the house itself. There was no mute sign of a woman in the room. No graceful little adornment, no fanciful little device, however trivial, anywhere expressed her influence. Cheerless and comfortless, boastfully and doggedly rich, there the room stared at its present occupants, unsoftened and unrelieved by the least trace of any womanly occupation. As Mr. Bounderby stood in the midst of his household gods, so those unrelenting divinities occupied their places around Mr. Bounderby, and they were worthy of one another, and well matched.

"This, sir," said Bounderby, "is my wife, Mrs. Bounderby: Tom Gradgrind's eldest daughter. Loo, Mr. James Harthouse. Mr. Harthouse has joined your father's muster-roll. If he is not Tom Gradgrind's colleague before long, I believe we shall at least hear of him in connection with one of our neighbouring towns. You observe, Mr. Harthouse, that my wife is my junior. I don't know what she saw in me to marry me, but she saw something in me, I suppose, or she wouldn't have married me.

She has lots of expensive knowledge, sir, political and otherwise. If you want to cram for anything, I should be troubled to recommend you to a better adviser than Loo Bounderby."

To a more agreeable adviser, or one from whom he would be more likely to learn, Mr. Harthouse could never be recommended.

"Come!" said his host. "If you're in the complimentary line, you'll get on here, for you'll meet with no competition. I have never been in the way of learning compliments myself, and I don't profess to understand the art of paying 'em. In fact, despise 'em. But, your bringing-up was different from mine; mine was a real thing, by George! You're a gentleman, and I don't pretend to be one. I am Josiah Bounderby of Coketown, and that's enough for me. However, though I am not influenced by manners and station, Loo Bounderby may be. She hadn't my advantages—disadvantages you would call 'em, but I call 'em advantages—so you'll not waste your power, I dare say."

"Mr. Bounderby," said Jem, turning with a smile to Louisa, "is a noble animal in a comparatively natural state, quite free from the harness in which a conventional hack like myself works."

"You respect Mr. Bounderby very much," she quietly returned. "It is natural that you should."

He was disgracefully thrown out, for a gentleman who had seen so much of the world, and thought, "Now, how am I to take this?"

"You are going to devote yourself, as I gather from what Mr. Bounderby has said, to the service of your country. You have made up your mind," said Louisa, still standing before him where she had first stopped—in all the singular contrariety of her self-possession, and her being obviously very ill at ease—"to show the nation the way out of all its difficulties."

"Mrs. Bounderby," he returned, laughing, "upon my honour, no. I will make no such pretence to you. I have seen a little, here and there, up and down; I have found it all to be very worthless, as everybody has, and as some confess they have, and some do not; and I am going in for your respected father's opinions—really because I have no choice of opinions, and may as well back them as anything else."

"Have you none of your own?" asked Louisa.

"I have not so much as the slightest predilection left. I assure you I attach not the least importance to any opinions. The result of the varieties of boredom I have undergone is a conviction (unless conviction is too industrious a word for the lazy sentiment I entertain on the subject), that any set of ideas will do just as much good as any other set, and just as much harm as any other set. There's an English family with a charming Italian motto. What will be, will be. It's the only truth going!"

This vicious assumption of honesty in dishonesty—a vice so dangerous, so deadly, and so common—seemed, he observed, a little to impress her in his favour. He followed up the advantage, by saying in his pleasantest manner: a manner to which she might attach as much or as little meaning as she pleased: "The side that can prove anything in a line of units, tens, hundreds, and thousands, Mrs. Bounderby, seems to me to afford the most fun, and to give a man the best chance. I am quite as much attached to it as if I believed it. I am quite ready to go in for it, to the same extent as if I believed it. And what more could I possibly do, if I did believe it!"

"You are a singular politician," said Louisa.

"Pardon me; I have not even that merit. We are the largest party in the state, I assure you, Mrs. Bounderby, if we fell out of our adopted ranks and were reviewed together."

Mr. Bounderby, who had been in danger of bursting in silence, interposed here with a project for postponing the family dinner till half-past six, and taking Mr. James Harthouse in the meantime on a round of visits to the voting and interesting notabilities of Coketown and its vicinity. The round of visits was made; and Mr. James Harthouse, with a discreet use of his blue coaching, came off triumphantly, though with a considerable accession of boredom.

In the evening, he found the dinner-table laid for four, but they sat down only three. It was an appropriate occasion for Mr. Bounderby to discuss the flavour of the hap'orth of stewed eels he had purchased in the streets at eight years old; and also of the inferior water, specially used for laying the dust, with which he had washed down that repast. He likewise entertained his guest over the soup and fish, with the calculation that he (Bounderby) had eaten in his youth at least three horses under the guise of polonies and saveloys. These recitals, Jem, in a languid manner, received with "charming!" every now and then; and they probably would have decided him to "go in" for Jerusalem again to-morrow morning, had he been less curious respecting Louisa.

"Is there nothing," he thought, glancing at her as she sat at the head of the table, where her youthful figure, small and slight, but very graceful, looked as pretty as it looked misplaced; " is there nothing that will move that face?"

Yes! By Jupiter, there was something, and here it was, in an unexpected shape. Tom appeared. She changed as the door opened, and broke into a beaming smile.

A beautiful smile. Mr. James Harthouse might not have thought so much of it, but that he had wondered so long at her impassive face. She put out her hand—a pretty little soft hand; and her fingers closed upon her brother's, as if she would have carried them to her lips.

"Ay, ay!" thought the visitor. "This whelp is the only creature she cares for. So, so!"

The whelp was presented, and took his chair. The appellation was not flattering, but not unmerited.

"When I was your age, young Tom," said Bounderby, "I was punctual, or I got no dinner!"

"When you were my age," returned Tom, "you hadn't a wrong balance to get right, and hadn't to dress afterwards."

"Never mind that now," said Bounderby.

"Well, then," grumbled Tom. "Don't begin with me."

"Mrs. Bounderby," said Harthouse, perfectly hearing this understrain as it went on; "your brother's face is quite familiar to me. Can I have seen him abroad? Or at some public school, perhaps?"

"No," she returned, quite interested, "he has never been abroad yet, and was educated here, at home. Tom, love, I am telling Mr. Harthouse that he never saw you abroad."

"No such luck, sir," said Tom.

There was little enough in him to brighten her face, for he was a sullen young fellow, and ungracious in his manner even to her. So much the greater must have been the solitude of her heart, and her need of some one on whom to bestow it. "So much the more is this whelp the only creature she has ever cared for," thought Mr. James Harthouse, turning it over and over. "So much the more. So much the more."

Both in his sister's presence, and after she had left the room, the whelp took no pains to hide his contempt for Mr. Bounderby, whenever he could indulge it without the observation of that independent man, by making wry faces, or shutting one eye. Without responding to these telegraphic communications, Mr. Harthouse encouraged him much in the course of the evening, and showed an unusual liking for him. At last, when he rose to return to his hotel, and was a little doubtful whether he knew the way by night, the whelp immediately proffered his services as guide, and turned out with him to escort him thither.

CHAPTER III: *The Whelp*

IT was very remarkable that a young gentleman who had been brought up under one continuous system of unnatural restraint, should be a hypocrite; but it was certainly the case with Tom. It was very strange that a young gentleman who had never been left to his own guidance for five consecutive minutes, should be incapable at last of governing himself; but so it was with Tom. It was altogether unaccountable that a young gentleman whose imagination had been strangled in his cradle, should be still inconvenienced by its ghost in the form of grovelling sensualities; but such a monster, beyond all doubt, was Tom.

"Do you smoke?" asked Mr. James Harthouse, when they came to the hotel.

"I believe you!" said Tom.

He could do no less than ask Tom up; and Tom could do no less than go up. What with a cooling drink adapted to the weather, but not so weak as cool; and what with a rarer tobacco than was to be bought in those parts; Tom was soon in a highly free and easy state at his end of the sofa, and more than ever disposed to admire his new friend at the other end.

Tom blew his smoke aside, after he had been smoking a little while, and took an observation of his friend. "He don't seem to care about his dress," thought Tom, "and yet how capitally he does it. What an easy swell he is!"

Mr. James Harthouse, happening to catch Tom's eye, remarked that he drank nothing, and filled his glass with his own negligent hand.

"Thank'ee," said Tom. "Thank'ee. Well, Mr. Harthouse, I hope you have had about a dose of old Bounderby to-night." Tom said this with one eye shut up again, and looking over his glass knowingly, at his entertainer.

"A very good fellow indeed!" returned Mr. James Harthouse.

"You think so, don't you?" said Tom. And shut up his eye again.

Mr. James Harthouse smiled; and rising from his end of the sofa, and lounging with his back against the chimney-piece, so that he stood before the empty fire-grate as he smoked, in front of Tom and looking down at him, observed:

"What a comical brother-in-law you are!"

"What a comical brother-in-law old Bounderby is, I think you mean," said Tom.

"You are a piece of caustic, Tom," retorted Mr. James Harthouse.

There was something so very agreeable in being so intimate with such a waistcoat; in being called Tom, in such an intimate way, by such a voice; in being on such off-hand terms so soon, with such a pair of whiskers; that Tom was uncommonly pleased with himself.

"Oh! I don't care for old Bounderby," said he, "if you mean that. I have always called old Bounderby by the same name when I have talked about him, and I have always thought of him in the same way. I am not going to begin to be polite now, about old Bounderby. It would be rather late in the day."

"Don't mind me," returned James; "but take care when his wife is by, you know."

"His wife?" said Tom. "My sister Loo? O yes!" And he laughed and took a little more of the cooling drink.

James Harthouse continued to lounge in the same place and attitude, smoking his cigar in his own easy way, and looking pleasantly at the whelp, as if he knew himself to be a kind of agreeable demon who had only to hover over him, and he must give up his whole soul if required. It certainly did seem that the whelp yielded to this influence. He looked at his companion sneakingly, he looked at him admiringly, he looked at him boldly, and put up one leg on the sofa.

"My sister Loo?" said Tom. "*She* never cared for old Bounderby."

"That's the past tense, Tom," returned Mr. James Harthouse, striking the ash from his cigar with his little finger. "We are in the present tense, now."

"Verb neuter, not to care. Indicative mood, present tense. First person singular, I do not care; second person singular, thou dost not care; third person singular, she does not care," returned Tom.

"Good! Very quaint!" said his friend. "Though you don't mean it."

"But I *do* mean it," cried Tom. "Upon my honour! Why, you won't tell me, Mr. Harthouse, that you really supposed my sister Loo does care for old Bounderby."

"My dear fellow," returned the other, "what am I bound to suppose, when I find two married people living in harmony and happiness?"

Tom had by this time got both his legs on the sofa. If his second leg had not been already there when he was called a dear fellow, he would have put it up at that great stage of the conversation. Feeling it necessary to do something then, he stretched himself out at greater length, and, reclining with the back of his head on the end of the sofa, and smoking with an infinite assumption of negligence, turned his common face, and not yet too sober eyes, towards the face looking down upon him so carelessly yet so potently.

"You know our governor, Mr. Harthouse," said Tom, "and therefore you needn't be surprised that Loo married old Bounderby. She never had a lover, and the governor proposed old Bounderby, and she took him."

"Very dutiful in your interesting sister," said Mr. James Harthouse.

"Yes, but she wouldn't have been as dutiful, and it would not have come off as easily," returned the whelp, "if it hadn't been for me."

The tempter merely lifted his eyebrows; but the whelp was obliged to go on.

"*I* persuaded her," he said, with an edifying air of superiority. "I was stuck into old Bounderby's bank (where I never wanted to be), and I knew I should get into scrapes there, if she put old Bounderby's pipe out; so I told her my wishes, and she came into them. She would do anything for me. It was very game of her, wasn't it?"

"It was charming, Tom!"

"Not that it was altogether so important to her as it was to me," continued Tom coolly, "because my liberty and comfort, and perhaps my getting on, depended on it; and she had no other lover, and staying at home was like staying in jail—especially when I was gone. It wasn't as if she gave up another lover for old Bounderby; but still it was a good thing in her."

"Perfectly delightful. And she gets on so placidly."

"Oh," returned Tom, with contemptuous patronage, "she's a regular girl. A girl can get on anywhere. She has settled down to the life, and *she* don't mind. It does just as well as another. Besides, though Loo is a girl, she's not a common sort of girl. She can shut herself up within herself, and think—as I have often known her sit and watch the fire—for an hour at a stretch."

"Ay, ay? Has resources of her own," said Harthouse, smoking quietly.

"Not so much of that as you may suppose," returned Tom; "for our governor had her crammed with all sorts of dry bones and saw-dust. It's his system."

"Formed his daughter on his own model?" suggested Harthouse.

"His daughter? Ah! and everybody else. Why he formed Me that way," said Tom.

"Impossible!"

"He did, though," said Tom, shaking his head. "I mean to say, Mr. Harthouse, that when I first left home and went to old Bounderby's, I was as flat as a warming-pan, and knew no more about life, than any oyster does."

"Come, Tom! I can hardly believe that. A joke's a joke."

"Upon my soul!" said the whelp. "I am serious; I am indeed!" He smoked with great gravity and dignity for a little while, and then added, in a highly complacent tone, "Oh! I have picked up a little since. I don't deny that. But I have done it myself; no thanks to the governor."

"And your intelligent sister?"

"My intelligent sister is about where she was. She used to complain to me that she had nothing to fall back upon, that girls usually fall back upon; and I don't see how she is to have got over that since. But *she* don't mind," he sagaciously added, puffing at his cigar again. "Girls can always get on, somehow."

"Calling at the Bank yesterday evening, for Mr. Bounderby's address, I found an ancient lady there, who seems to entertain great admiration for your sister," observed Mr. James Harthouse, throwing away the last small remnant of the cigar he had now smoked out.

"Mother Sparsit!" said Tom. "What! you have seen her already, have you?"

His friend nodded. Tom took his cigar out of his mouth, to shut up his eye (which had grown rather unmanageable) with the greater expression, and to tap his nose several times with his finger.

"Mother Sparsit's feeling for Loo is more than admiration, I should think," said Tom. "Say affection and devotion. Mother Sparsit never set her cap at Bounderby when he was a bachelor. Oh no!"

These were the last words spoken by the whelp, before a giddy drowsiness came upon him, followed by complete oblivion. He was roused from the latter state by an uneasy dream of being stirred up with a boot, and also of a voice saying: "Come, it's late. Be off!"

"Well!" he said, scrambling from the sofa. "I must take my leave of you though. I say. Yours is very good tobacco. But it's too mild."

"Yes, it's too mild," returned his entertainer.

"It's—it's ridiculously mild," said Tom. "Where's the door! Good night!"

He had another odd dream of being taken by a waiter through a mist, which, after giving him some trouble and difficulty, resolved itself into the main street, in which he stood alone. He then walked home pretty easily, though not yet free from an impression of the presence and influence of his new friend—as if he were lounging somewhere in the air, in the same negligent attitude, regarding him with the same look.

The whelp went home, and went to bed. If he had had any sense of what he had done that night, and had been less of a whelp and more of a brother, he might have turned short on the road, might have gone down to the ill-smelling river that was dyed black, might have gone to bed in it for good and all, and have curtained his head for ever with its filthy waters.

CHAPTER IV: *Men and Brothers*

"Oh my friends, the down-trodden operatives of Coketown! Oh my friends and fellow-countrymen, the slaves of an iron-handed and a grinding despotism! Oh my friends and fellow-sufferers, and fellow-workmen, and fellow-men! I tell you that the hour is come, when we must rally round one another as One united power, and crumble into dust the oppressors that too long have battened upon the plunder of our families, upon the sweat of our brows, upon the labour of our hands, upon the strength of our sinews, upon the God-created glorious rights of Humanity, and upon the holy and eternal privileges of Brotherhood!"

"Good!" "Hear, hear, hear!" "Hurrah!" and other cries, arose in many voices from various parts of the densely crowded and suffocatingly close Hall, in which the orator, perched on a stage, delivered himself of this and what other froth and fume he had in him. He had declaimed himself into a violent heat, and was as hoarse as he was hot. By dint of roaring at the top of his voice under a flaring gas-light, clenching his fists, knitting his brows, setting his teeth, and pounding with his arms, he had taken so much out of himself by this time, that he was brought to a stop, and called for a glass of water.

As he stood there, trying to quench his fiery face with his drink of water, the comparison between the orator and the crowd of attentive faces turned towards him, was extremely to his disadvantage. Judging him by Nature's evidence, he was above the mass in very little but the stage on which he stood. In many great respects he was essentially below them. He was not so honest, he was not so manly, he was not so good-humoured; he substituted cunning for their simplicity, and passion for their safe solid sense. An ill-made, high-shouldered man, with lowering brows, and his features crushed into an habitually sour expression, he contrasted most unfavourably, even in his mongrel dress, with the great body of his hearers in their plain working clothes. Strange as it always is to consider any assembly in the act of submissively resigning itself to the dreariness of some complacent person, lord or commoner, whom three-fourths of it could, by no human means, raise out of the slough of inanity to their own intellectual level, it was particularly strange, and it was even particularly affecting, to see this crowd of earnest faces, whose honesty in the main no competent observer free from bias could doubt, so agitated by such a leader.

Good! Hear, hear! Hurrah! The eagerness both of attention and intention, exhibited in all the countenances, made them a most impressive sight. There was no carelessness, no languor, no idle curiosity; none of the many shades of indifference to be seen in all other assemblies, visible for one moment there. That every man felt his condition to be, somehow or other, worse than it might be; that every man considered it incumbent on him to join the rest, towards the making of it better; that every man felt his only hope to be in his allying himself to the comrades by whom he was surrounded; and that in this belief, right or wrong (unhappily wrong then), the whole of that crowd were gravely, deeply, faithfully in earnest; must have been as plain to any one who chose to see what was there, as the bare beams of the roof and the whitened brick walls. Nor could any such spectator fail to know in his own breast, that these men, through their very delusions, showed great qualities, susceptible of being turned to the happiest and best account; and that to pretend (on the strength of sweeping axioms, howsoever cut and dried) that they went astray wholly without cause, and of their own irrational wills, was to pretend that there could be smoke without fire, death without birth, harvest without seed, anything or everything produced from nothing.

The orator having refreshed himself, wiped his corrugated forehead from left to right several times with his handkerchief folded into a pad, and concentrated all his revived forces, in a sneer of great disdain and bitterness.

"But, oh my friends and brothers! Oh men and Englishmen, the down-trodden operatives of Coketown! What shall we say of that man—that working-man, that I should find it necessary so to libel the glorious name—who, being practically and well acquainted with the grievances and wrongs of you, the injured pith and marrow of this land, and having heard you, with a noble and majestic unanimity that will make Tyrants tremble, resolve for to subscribe to the funds of the United Aggregate Tribunal, and to abide by the injunctions issued by that body for your benefit, whatever they may be— what, I ask you, will you say of that working-man, since such I must acknowledge him to be, who, at such a time, deserts his post, and sells his flag; who, at such a time, turns a traitor and a craven and a recreant; who, at such a time, is not ashamed to make to you the dastardly and humiliating avowal that he will hold himself aloof, and will *not* be one of those associated in the gallant stand for Freedom and for Right?"

The assembly was divided at this point. There were some groans and hisses, but the general sense of honour was much too strong for the condemnation of a man unheard. "Be sure you're right, Slackbridge!" "Put him up!" "Let's hear him!" Such things were said on many sides. Finally, one strong voice called out "Is the man heer? If the man's heer, Slackbridge, let's hear the man himseln, 'stead o' yo." Which was received with a round of applause.

Slackbridge, the orator, looked about him with a withering smile; and, holding out his right hand at arm's length (as the manner of all Slackbridges is), to still the thundering sea, waited until there was profound silence.

"Oh my friends and fellow-men!" said Slackbridge then, shaking his head with violent scorn, "I do not wonder that you, the prostrate sons of labour, are incredulous of the existence of such a man. But he who sold his birthright for a mess of pottage existed, and Judas Iscariot existed, and Castlereagh existed, and this man exists!"

Here, a brief press and confusion near the stage, ended in

the man himself standing at the orator's side before the concourse. He was pale and a little moved in the face—his lips
especially showed it; but he stood quiet, with his left hand
at his chin, waiting to be heard. There was a chairman to
regulate the proceedings, and this functionary now took the
case into his own hands.

"My friends," said he, "by virtue o' my office as your president, I ashes o' our friend Slackbridge, who may be a little over
hetter in this business, to take his seat, whiles this man
Stephen Blackpool is heern. You all know this man Stephen
Blackpool. You know him awlung o' his misfort'ns, and his
good name."

With that, the chairman shook him frankly by the hand,
and sat down again. Slackbridge likewise sat down, wiping
his hot forehead—always from left to right, and never the
reverse way.

"My friends," Stephen began, in the midst of a dead calm;
"I ha' hed what's been spok'n o' me, and 'tis lickly that I
shan't mend it. But I'd liefer you'd learn the truth concern-
in' myseln fro my lips than fro onny other man's, though I
never cud'n speak after so monny, wi'out bein moydert and
muddled."

Slackbridge shook his head as if he would shake it off, in his
bitterness.

"I'm th' one single Hand in Bounderby's mill, o' a' the men
theer, as don't coom in wi' th' proposed reg'lations. I canna'
coom in wi' 'em. My friends, I doubt their doin' yo onny
good. Licker they'll do yo hurt."

Slackbridge laughed, folded his arms, and frowned sar-
castically.

"But 't an't sommuch for that as I stands out. If that were
aw, I'd coom in wi' th' rest. But I ha' my reasons—mine,
you see—for being hindered; not on'y now, but awlus—awlus
—life long!"

Slackbridge jumped up and stood beside him, gnashing and
tearing. "Oh my friends, what but this did I tell you? Oh
my fellow-countrymen, what warning but this did I give you?
And how shows this recreant conduct in a man on whom
unequal laws are known to have fallen heavy? Oh you Englishmen, I ask you how does this subornation show in one of yourselves, who is thus consenting to his own undoing and to yours,
and to your children's and your children's children's?"

There was some applause, and some crying of Shame upon
the man; but the greater part of the audience were quiet.
They looked at Stephen's worn face, rendered more pathetic
by the homely emotions it evinced; and, in the kindness of
their nature, they were more sorry than indignant.

"'Tis this Delegate's trade for t' speak," said Stephen, "an'
he's paid for't, 'an he knows his work. Let him keep to 't.

Let him give no heed to what I ha had'n to bear. That's not
for him. That's not for nobbody but me."

There was a propriety, not to say a dignity in these words,
that made the hearers yet more quiet and attentive. The
same strong voice called out, "Slackbridge, let the man be
heern, and howd thee tongue!" Then the place was wonderfully still.

"My brothers," said Stephen, whose low voice was distinctly heard, "and my fellow-workmen—for that yo are to
me, though not, as I knows on, to this delegate here—I ha'
but a word to sen, and I could sen nommore if I was to speak
till Strike o' day. I know weel, aw what's afore me. I know
weel that yo aw resolve to ha nommore ado wi' a man who is
not wi' yo in this matther. I know weel that if I was a lyin
parisht i' th' road, yo'd feel it right to pass me by, as a
forrenner and stranger. What I ha' getn, I mun mak th'
best on."

"Stephen Blackpool," said the chairman, rising, "think
on't agen. Think on't once agen, lad, afore thour't shunned
by aw owd friends."

There was an universal murmur to the same effect, though
no man articulated a word. Every eye was fixed on Stephen's
face. To repent of his determination, would be to take a load
from all their minds. He looked around him, and knew that
it was so. Not a grain of anger with them was in his heart;
he knew them, far below their surface weaknesses and mis-
conceptions, as no one but their fellow-labourer could.

"I ha' thowt on't, above a bit, sir. I simply canna coom in.
I mun go th' way as lays afore me. I mun tak leave o' aw
heer."

He made a sort of reverence to them by holding up his arms,
and stood for the moment in that attitude: not speaking until
they slowly dropped at his sides.

"Monny's the pleasant word as soom heer has spok'n wi'
me; monny's the face I see heer, as I first seen when I were
yoong and lighter heart'n than now. I ha' never had no
fratch afore, sin ever I were born, wi' any o' my like; Gonnows
I ha' none now that's o' my makin'. Yo'll ca' me traitor and
that—yo I mean t' say," addressing Slackbridge, "but 'tis
easier to ca' than mak' out. So let be."

He had moved away a pace or two to come down from the
platform, when he remembered something he had not said,
and returned again.

"Haply," he said, turning his furrowed face slowly about,
that he might as it were individually address the whole audience, those both near and distant; "haply, when this question
has been tak'n up and discoosed, there'll be a threat to turn
out if I'm let to work among yo. I hope I shall die ere ever
such a time cooms, and I shall work solitary among yo unless

it cooms—truly, I mun do't, my friends; not to brave yo, but to live. I ha' nobbut work to live by; and wheerever can I go, I who ha' worked sin I were no heighth at aw, in Coketown heer? I mak' no complaints o' bein turned to the wa', o' being outcasten and overlooken fro this time forrard, but I hope I shall be let to work. If there is any right for me at aw, my friends, I think 'tis that.''

Not a word was spoken. Not a sound was audible in the building, but the slight rustle of men moving a little apart, all along the centre of the room, to open a means of passing out, to the man with whom they had all bound themselves to renounce companionship. Looking at no one, and going his way with a lowly steadiness upon him that asserted nothing and sought nothing, Old Stephen, with all his troubles on his head, left the scene.

Then Slackbridge, who had kept his oratorical arm extended during the going out, as if he were representing with infinite solicitude and by a wonderful moral power the vehement passions of the multitude, applied himself to raising their spirits. Had not the Roman Brutus, oh my British country-men, condemned his son to death; and had not the Spartan mothers, oh my soon to be victorious friends, driven their flying children on the points of their enemies' swords? Then was it not the sacred duty of the men of Coketown, with forefathers before them, an admiring world in company with them, and a posterity to come after them, to hurl out traitors from the tents they had pitched in a sacred and a Godlike cause? The winds of heaven answered Yes; and bore Yes, east, west, north, and south. And consequently three cheers for the United Aggregate Tribunal!

Slackbridge acted as fugleman, and gave the time. The multitude of doubtful faces (a little conscience-stricken) brightened at the sound, and took it up. Private feeling must yield to the common cause. Hurrah! The roof yet vibrated with the cheering, when the assembly dispersed.

Thus easily did Stephen Blackpool fall into the loneliest of lives, the life of solitude among a familiar crowd. The stranger in the land who looks into ten thousand faces for some answer-ing look and never finds it, is in cheering society as compared with him who passes ten averted faces daily, that were once the countenances of friends. Such experience was to be Stephen's now, in every waking moment of his life; at his work, on his way to it and from it, at his door, at his window, everywhere. By general consent, they even avoided that side of the street on which he habitually walked; and left it, of all the working-men, to him only.

He had been for many years a quiet, silent man, associating but little with other men, and used to companionship with his own thoughts. He had never known before the strength of the want in his heart for the frequent recognition of a nod, a look, a word; or the immense amount of relief that had been poured into it by drops through such small means. It was even harder than he could have believed possible, to separate in his own conscience his abandonment by all his fellows from a baseless sense of shame and disgrace.

The first four days of his endurance were days so long and heavy, that he began to be appalled by the prospect before him. Not only did he see no Rachael all the time, but he avoided every chance of seeing her; for, although he knew that the prohibition did not yet formally extend to the women working in the factories, he found that some of them with whom he was acquainted were changed to him, and he feared to try others, and dreaded that Rachael might be even singled out from the rest if she were seen in his company. So, he had been quite alone during the four days, and had spoken to no one, when, as he was leaving his work at night, a young man of a very light complexion accosted him in the street.

"Your name's Blackpool, ain't it?" said the young man.

Stephen coloured to find himself with his hat in his hand, in his gratitude for being spoken to, or in the suddenness of it, or both. He made a feint of adjusting the lining, and said, "Yes."

"You are the Hand they have sent to Coventry, I mean?" said Bitzer, the very light young man in question.

Stephen answered "Yes," again.

"I supposed so, from their all appearing to keep away from you. Mr. Bounderby wants to speak to you. You know his house, don't you?"

Stephen said "Yes," again.

"Then go straight up there, will you?" said Bitzer. "You're expected, and have only to tell the servant it's you. I belong to the Bank; so, if you go straight up without me (I was sent to fetch you), you'll save me a walk."

Stephen, whose way had been in the contrary direction, turned about, and betook himself, as in duty bound, to the red brick castle of the giant Bounderby.

CHAPTER V : *Men and Masters*

"WELL, Stephen," said Bounderby, in his windy manner, "what's this I hear? What have these pests of the earth been doing to *you*? Come in, and speak up."

It was into the drawing-room that he was thus bidden. A tea-table was set out; and Mr. Bounderby's young wife, and her brother, and a great gentleman from London, were present. To whom Stephen made his obeisance, closing the door and standing near it, with his hat in his hand.

"This is the man I was telling you about, Harthouse," said

Mr. Bounderby. The gentleman he addressed, who was talking to Mrs. Bounderby on the sofa, got up, saying in an indolent way, "Oh really?" and dawdled to the hearth-rug where Mr. Bounderby stood.

"Now," said Bounderby, "speak up!"

After the four days he had passed, this address fell rudely and discordantly on Stephen's ear. Besides being a rough handling of his wounded mind, it seemed to assume that he really was the self-interested deserter he had been called.

"What were it, sir," said Stephen, "as yo were pleased to want wi' me?"

"Why, I have told you," returned Bounderby. "Speak up like a man, since you are a man, and tell us about yourself and this Combination."

"Wi' yor pardon, sir," said Stephen Blackpool, "I ha' nowt to sen about it."

Mr. Bounderby, who was always more or less like a Wind, finding something in his way here, began to blow at it directly.

"Now, look here, Harthouse," said he, "here's a specimen of 'em. When this man was here once before, I warned this man against the mischievous strangers who are always about —and who ought to be hanged wherever they are found—and I told this man that he was going in the wrong direction. Now, would you believe it, that although they have put this mark upon him, he is such a slave to them still, that he's afraid to open his lips about them?"

"I sed as I had nowt to sen, sir; not as I was fearfo' o' openin' my lips."

"You said. Ah! *I* know what you said; more than that, I know what you mean, you see. Not always the same thing, by the Lord Harry! Quite different things. You had better tell us at once, that that fellow Slackbridge is not in the town, stirring up the people to mutiny; and that he is not a regular qualified leader of the people: that is, a most confounded scoundrel. You had better tell us so at once; you can't deceive me. You want to tell us so. Why don't you?"

"I'm as sooary as yo, sir, when the people's leaders is bad," said Stephen, shaking his head. "They taks such as offers. Haply 'tis na' the sma'est o' their misfortuns when they can get no better."

The wind began to get boisterous.

"Now, you'll think this pretty well, Harthouse," said Mr. Bounderby. "You'll think this tolerably strong. You'll say, upon my soul this is a tidy specimen of what my friends have to deal with; but this is nothing, sir! You shall hear me ask this man a question. Pray, Mr. Blackpool"—wind springing up very fast—"may I take the liberty of asking you how it happens that you refused to be in this Combination?"

"How't happens?"

"Ah!" said Mr. Bounderby, with his thumbs in the arms of his coat, and jerking his head and shutting his eyes in confidence with the opposite wall: "how it happens."

"I'd leefer not coom to't, sir; but sin you put th' question—an not want'n t' be ill-manner'n—I'll answer. I ha' passed a promess."

"Not to me, you know," said Bounderby. (Gusty weather with deceitful calms. One now prevailing.)

"O no, sir. Not to yo."

"As for me, any consideration for me has had just nothing at all to do with it," said Bounderby, still in confidence with the wall. "If only Josiah Bounderby of Coketown had been in question, you would have joined and made no bones about it?"

"Why yes, sir. 'Tis true."

"Though he knows," said Mr. Bounderby, now blowing a gale, "that there are a set of rascals and rebels whom transportation is too good for! Now, Mr. Harthouse, you have been knocking about in the world some time. Did you ever meet with anything like that man out of this blessed country?" And Mr. Bounderby pointed him out for inspection, with an angry finger.

"Nay, ma'am," said Stephen Blackpool, staunchly protesting against the words that had been used, and instinctively addressing himself to Louisa, after glancing at her face. "Not rebels, nor yet rascals. Nowt o' th' kind, ma'am, nowt o' th' kind. They've not doon me a kindness, ma'am, as I know and feel. But there's not a dozen men amoong 'em, ma'am—a dozen? Not six—but what believes as he has doon his duty by the rest and by himseln. God forbid as I, that ha' known, and had'n experience o' these men aw my life—I, that ha' ett'n an droonken wi' 'em, an seet'n wi' 'em, and toil'n wi' 'em, and lov'n 'em, should fail fur to stan' by 'em wi' the truth, let 'em ha' doon to me what they may!"

He spoke with the rugged earnestness of his place and character—deepened perhaps by a proud consciousness that he was faithful to his class under all their mistrust; but he fully remembered where he was, and did not even raise his voice.

"No, ma'am, no. They're true to one another, faithfo' to one another, fectionate to one another, e'en to death. Be poor amoong 'em, be sick amoong 'em, grieve amoong 'em for onny o' th' monny causes that carries grieve to the poor man's door, and they'll be tender wi' yo, gentle wi' yo, comfortable wi' yo, Chrisen wi' yo. Be sure o' that, ma'am. They'd be riven to bits, ere ever they'd be different."

"In short," said Mr. Bounderby, "it's because they are so full of virtues that they have turned you adrift. Go through with it while you are about it. Out with it."

"How 'tis, ma'am," resumed Stephen, appearing still to find his natural refuge in Louisa's face, "that what is best in us fok, seems to turn us most to trouble an misfort'n an mistake, I dunno. But 'tis so. I know 'tis, as I know the heavens is over me ahint the smoke. We're patient too, an wants in general to do right. An' I canna think the fawt is aw wi' us."

"Now, my friend," said Mr. Bounderby, whom he could not have exasperated more, quite unconscious of it though he was, than by seeming to appeal to any one else, "if you will favour me with your attention for half a minute, I should like to have a word or two with you. You said just now, that you had nothing to tell us about this business. You are quite sure of that before we go any further."

"Sir, I am sure on't."

"Here's a gentleman from London present," Mr. Bounderby made a backhanded point at Mr. James Harthouse with his thumb, "a Parliament gentleman. I should like him to hear a short bit of dialogue between you and me, instead of taking the substance of it—for I know precious well, beforehand, what it will be; nobody knows better than I do, take notice!—instead of receiving it on trust from my mouth."

Stephen bent his head to the gentleman from London, and showed a rather more troubled mind than usual. He turned his eyes involuntarily to his former refuge, but at a look from that quarter (expressive though instantaneous) he settled them on Mr. Bounderby's face.

"Now, what do you complain of?" asked Mr. Bounderby.

"I ha' not coom here, sir," Stephen reminded him, "to complain. I coom for that I were sent for."

"What," repeated Mr. Bounderby, folding his arms, "do you people, in a general way, complain of?"

Stephen looked at him with some little irresolution for a moment, and then seemed to make up his mind.

"Sir, I were never good at showing o't, though I ha' had'n my share in feeling o't. 'Deed we are in a muddle, sir. Look round town—so rich as 'tis—and see the numbers o' people as has been broughten into bein heer, fur to weave, an to card, an to piece out a livin', aw the same one way, somehows, twixt their cradles and their graves. Look how we live, and wheer we live, an in what numbers, an by what chances, and wi' what sameness; and look how the mills is awlus a goin, and how they never works us no nigher to ony dis'ant object—ceptin awlus, Death. Look how you considers of us, and writes of us, and talks of us, and goes up wi' yor deputations to Secretaries o' State 'bout us, and how yo are awlus right, and how we are awlus wrong, and never had'n no reason in us sin ever we were born. Look how this ha' growen an growen, sir, bigger an bigger, broader an broader, harder an harder, fro year to year, fro generation unto generation. Who can look on 't, sir, and fairly tell a man 'tis not a muddle?"

"Of course," said Mr. Bounderby. "Now perhaps you'll let the gentleman know, how you would set this muddle (as you're so fond of calling it) to rights."

"I donno, sir. I canna be expecten to 't. 'Tis not me as should be looken to for that, sir. 'Tis them as is put ower me, and ower aw the rest of us. What do they tak upon themseln, sir, if not to do 't?"

"I'll tell you something towards it, at any rate," returned Mr. Bounderby. "We will make an example of half-a-dozen Slackbridges. We'll indict the blackguards for felony, and get 'em shipped off to penal settlements."

Stephen gravely shook his head.

"Don't tell me we won't, man," said Mr. Bounderby, by this time blowing a hurricane, "because we will, I tell you!"

"Sir," returned Stephen, with the quiet confidence of absolute certainty, "if yo was t' tak a hundred Slackbridges—aw as there is, and aw the number ten times towd—an' was t' sew 'em up in separate sacks, an sink 'em in the deepest ocean as were made ere ever dry land coom to be, yo'd leave the muddle just wheer 'tis. Mischeevous strangers!" said Stephen, with an anxious smile; "when ha' we not heern, I am sure, sin ever we can call to mind, o' th' mischeevous strangers! 'Tis not by *them* the trouble's made, sir. 'Tis not wi' *them* 't commences. I ha' no favour for 'em—I ha' no reason to favour 'em—but 'tis hopeless and useless to dream o' takin them fro their trade, 'stead o' takin their trade fro them! Aw that's now about me in this room were heer afore I coom, an will be heer when I am gone. Put that clock aboard a ship an pack it off to Norfolk Island, an the time will go on just the same. So 'tis wi' Slackbridge every bit."

Reverting for a moment to his former refuge, he observed a cautionary movement of her eyes towards the door. Stepping back, he put his hand upon the lock. But he had not spoken out of his own will and desire; and he felt it in his heart a noble return for his late injurious treatment to be faithful to the last to those who had repudiated him. He stayed to finish what was in his mind.

"Sir, I canna, wi' my little learning an my common way, tell the genelman what will better aw this—though some working-men o' this town could, above my powers—but I can tell him what I know will never do 't. The strong hand will never do 't. Vict'ry and triumph will never do 't. Agreeing fur to mak one side unnat'rally awlus and for ever right, and toother side unnat'rally awlus and for ever wrong, will never, never do 't. Nor yet lettin alone will never do 't. Let thousands upon thousands alone, aw leading the like lives and aw faw'en into the like muddle, and they will be as one, and yo will be as anoother, wi' a black unpassable world betwixt yo, just as long or short a time as sitch-like misery can last. Not drawin nigh to fok, wi' kindness and patience an cheery ways, that so draws nigh to one another in their monny troubles, and so cherishes one another in their distresses wi' what they need themseln—like, I humbly believe, as no people the genelman ha seen in aw his travels can beat—will never do 't till th' Sun turns t' ice. Most o' aw, rating 'em as so much Power, and reg'latin 'em as if they was figures in a soom, or machines: wi'out loves and likens, wi'out memories and inclinations, wi'out souls to weary and souls to hope—when aw goes quiet, draggin on wi' 'em as if they'd nowt o' th' kind, and when aw goes onquiet, reproachin 'em for their want o' sitch humanly feelins in their dealins wi' yo—this will never do 't, sir, till God's work is onmade."

Stephen stood with the open door in his hand, waiting to know if anything more were expected of him.

"Just stop a moment," said Mr. Bounderby, excessively red in the face. "I told you, the last time you were here with a grievance, that you had better turn about and come out of that. And I also told you, if you remember, that I was up to the gold spoon lookout."

"I were not up to 't myseln, sir; I do assure yo."

"Now it's clear to me," said Mr. Bounderby, "that you are one of those chaps who have always got a grievance. And you go about, sowing it and raising crops. That's the business of *your* life, my friend."

Stephen shook his head, mutely protesting that indeed he had other business to do for his life.

"You are such a waspish, raspish, ill-conditioned chap, you see," said Mr. Bounderby, "that even your own Union, the men who know you best, will have nothing to do with you. I never thought those fellows could be right in anything; but I tell you what! I so far go along with them for a novelty, that I'll have nothing to do with you either."

Stephen raised his eyes quickly to his face.

"You can finish off what you're at," said Mr. Bounderby, with a meaning nod, "and then go elsewhere."

"Sir, yo know weel," said Stephen expressively, "that if I canna get work wi' yo, I canna get it elsewheer."

The reply was, "What I know, I know; and what you know, you know. I have no more to say about it."

Stephen glanced at Louisa again, but her eyes were raised to his no more; therefore, with a sigh, and saying, barely above his breath, "Heaven help us aw in this world!" he departed.

CHAPTER VI : *Fading Away*

IT was falling dark when Stephen came out of Mr. Bounderby's house. The shadows of night had gathered so fast, that he did not look about him when he closed the door, but plodded straight along the street. Nothing was further from his thoughts than the curious old woman he had encountered on his previous visit to the same house, when he heard a step behind him that he knew, and turning, saw her in Rachael's company.

He saw Rachael first, as he had heard her only.

"Ah, Rachael, my dear! Missus, thou wi' her!"

"Well, and now you are surprised to be sure, and with reason I must say," the old woman returned. "Here I am again, you see."

"But how wi' Rachael?" said Stephen, falling into their step, walking between them, and looking from the one to the other.

"Why, I come to be with this good lass pretty much as I came to be with you," said the old woman, cheerfully, taking the reply upon herself. "My visiting time is later this year than usual, for I have been rather troubled with shortness of breath, and so put it off till the weather was fine and warm. For the same reason I don't make all my journey in one day, but divide it into two days, and get a bed to-night at the Travellers' Coffee House down by the railroad (a nice clean house) and go back Parliamentary, at six in the morning. Well, but what has this to do with this good lass, says you? I'm going to tell you. I have heard of Mr. Bounderby being married. I read it in the paper, where it looked grand—oh, it looked fine!" the old woman dwelt on it with strange enthusiasm: "and I want to see his wife. I have never seen her yet. Now if you'll believe me, she hasn't come out of that house since noon to-day. So not to give her up too easily, I was waiting about, a little last bit more, when I passed close to this good lass two or three times; and her face being so friendly I spoke to her, and she spoke to me. There!" said the old woman to Stephen, "you can make all the rest out for yourself now, a deal shorter than I can, I dare say!"

Once again, Stephen had to conquer an instinctive propensity to dislike this old woman, though her manner was as honest and simple as a manner possibly could be. With a gentleness that was as natural to him as he knew it to be to Rachael, he pursued the subject that interested her in her old age.

"Well, missus," said he, "I ha' seen the lady, and she were young and hansom. Wi' fine dark thinkin eyes, and a still way, Rachael, as I ha' never seen the like on."

"Young and handsome. Yes!" cried the old woman, quite delighted. "As bonny as a rose! And what a happy wife!"

"Aye, missus, I suppose she be," said Stephen. But with a doubtful glance at Rachael.

"Suppose she be? She must be. She's your master's wife," returned the old woman.

Stephen nodded assent. "Though as to master," said he, glancing again at Rachael, "not master onny more. That's aw enden twixt him and me."

"Have you left his work, Stephen?" asked Rachael, anxiously and quickly.

"Why, Rachael," he replied, "whether I ha' lef'n his work, or whether his work ha' lef'n me, cooms t' th' same. His work and me are parted. 'Tis as weel so—better, I were thinkin when yo coom up wi' me. It would ha' brought'n trouble upon trouble if I had stayed theer. Haply 'tis a kindness to monny that I go; haply 'tis a kindness to myseln; anyways it mun be done. I mun turn my face fro Coketown fur th' time, and seek a fort'n, dear, by beginnin fresh."

"Where will you go, Stephen?"

"I donno t'night," said he, lifting off his hat, and smoothing his thin hair with the flat of his hand. "But I'm not goin t'night, Rachael, nor yet t'morrow. Tan't easy overmuch, t' know wheer t' turn, but a good heart will coom to me."

Herein, too, the sense of even thinking unselfishly aided him. Before he had so much as closed Mr. Bounderby's door, he had reflected that at least his being obliged to go away was good for her, as it would save her from the chance of being brought into question for not withdrawing from him. Though it would cost him a hard pang to leave her, and though he could think of no similar place in which his condemnation would not pursue him, perhaps it was almost a relief to be forced away from the endurance of the last four days, even to unknown difficulties and distresses.

So he said, with truth, "I'm more leetsome, Rachael, under 't, than I could ha' believed." It was not her part to make his burden heavier. She answered with her comforting smile, and the three walked on together.

Age, especially when it strives to be self-reliant and cheerful, finds much consideration among the poor. The old woman was so decent and contented, and made so light of her infirmities, though they had increased upon her since her former interview with Stephen, that they both took an interest in her. She was too sprightly to allow of their walking at a slow pace on her account, but she was very grateful to be talked to, and very willing to talk to any extent: so, when they came to their part of the town, she was more brisk and vivacious than ever.

"Coom to my poor place, missus," said Stephen, "and tak a coop o' tea. Rachael will coom then; and arterwards I'll see thee safe t' thy Travellers' lodgin. 'T may be long, Rachael, ere ever I ha' th' chance o' thy coompany agen."

They complied, and the three went on to the house where he lodged. When they turned into a narrow street, Stephen glanced at his window with a dread that always haunted his desolate home; but it was open, as he had left it, and no one was there. The evil spirit of his life had flitted away again, months ago, and he had heard no more of her since. The only evidence of her last return now, were the scantier movables in his room, and the greyer hair upon his head.

He lighted a candle, set out his little tea-board, got hot water from below, and brought in small portions of tea and sugar, a loaf, and some butter from the nearest shop. The bread was new and crusty, the butter fresh, and the sugar lump, of course—in fulfilment of the standard testimony of the Coketown magnates, that these people lived like princes, sir. Rachael made the tea (so large a party necessitated the borrowing of a cup), and the visitor enjoyed it mightily. It was the first glimpse of sociality the host had had for many days. He too, with the world a wide heath before him, enjoyed the meal—again in corroboration of the magnates, as exemplifying the utter want of calculation on the part of these people, sir.

"I ha' never thowt yet, missus," said Stephen, "o' askin thy name."

The old lady announced herself as "Mrs. Pegler."

"A widder, I think?" said Stephen.

"Oh, many long years!" Mrs. Pegler's husband (one of the best on record) was already dead, by Mrs. Pegler's calculation, when Stephen was born.

"'Twere a bad job, too, to lose so good a one," said Stephen. "Onny children?"

Mrs. Pegler's cup, rattling against her saucer as she held it, denoted some nervousness on her part. "No," she said. "Not now, not now."

"Dead, Stephen," Rachael softly hinted.

"I'm sooary I ha' spok'n on 't," said Stephen. "I ought t' hadn in my mind as I might touch a sore place. I—I blame myseln."

While he excused himself, the old lady's cup rattled more and more. "I had a son," she said, curiously distressed, and not by any of the usual appearances of sorrow; "and he did well, wonderfully well. But he is not to be spoken of, if you please. He is—" Putting down her cup, she moved her hands as if she would have added, by her action, "dead!" Then she said aloud, "I have lost him."

Stephen had not yet got the better of his having given the old lady pain, when his landlady came stumbling up the narrow stairs, and calling him to the door, whispered in his ear. Mrs. Pegler was by no means deaf, for she caught a word as it was uttered.

"Bounderby!" she cried, in a suppressed voice, starting up from the table. "Oh hide me! Don't let me be seen for the world. Don't let him come up till I've got away. Pray, pray!" She trembled, and was excessively agitated; getting behind Rachael, when Rachael tried to reassure her, and not seeming to know what she was about.

"But hearken, missus, hearken," said Stephen, astonished. "'Tisn't Mr. Bounderby; 'tis his wife. Yor not fearfo' o' her. Yo was hey-go-mad about her, but an hour sin."

"But are you sure it's the lady, and not the gentleman?" she asked, still trembling.

"Certain sure!"

"Well then, pray don't speak to me, nor yet take any notice of me," said the old woman. "Let me be quiet to myself in this corner."

Stephen nodded; looking to Rachael for an explanation, which she was quite unable to give him; took the candle, went downstairs, and in a few moments returned, lighting Louisa into the room. She was followed by the whelp.

Rachael had risen, and stood apart with her shawl and bonnet in her hand, when Stephen, himself profoundly astonished by this visit, put the candle on the table. Then he too stood, with his doubled hand upon the table near it, waiting to be addressed.

For the first time in her life Louisa had come into one of the dwellings of the Coketown Hands; for the first time in her life she was face to face with anything like individuality in connection with them. She knew of their existence by hundreds and by thousands. She knew what results in work a given number of them would produce in a given space of time. She knew them in crowds passing to and from their nests, like ants or beetles. But she knew from her reading infinitely more of the ways of toiling insects than of these toiling men and women.

Something to be worked so much and paid so much, and there ended; something to be infallibly settled by laws of supply and demand; something that blundered against those laws, and floundered into difficulty; something that was a little pinched when wheat was dear, and over-ate itself when wheat was cheap; something that increased at such a rate of percentage, and yielded such another percentage of crime, and such another percentage of pauperism; something wholesale, of which vast fortunes were made; something that occasionally rose like a sea, and did some harm and waste (chiefly to itself), and fell again; this she knew the Coketown Hands to be. But, she had scarcely thought more of separating them into units, than of separating the sea itself into its component drops.

She stood for some moments looking round the room. From the few chairs, the few books, the common prints, and the bed, she glanced to the two women, and to Stephen.

"I have come to speak to you, in consequence of what passed just now. I should like to be serviceable to you, if you will let me. Is this your wife?"

Rachael raised her eyes, and they sufficiently answered no, and dropped again.

"I remember," said Louisa, reddening at her mistake; "I recollect, now, to have heard your domestic misfortunes spoken of, though I was not attending to the particulars at the time. It was not my meaning to ask a question that would give pain to any one here. If I should ask any other question that may happen to have that result, give me credit, if you please, for being in ignorance how to speak to you as I ought."

As Stephen had but a little while ago instinctively addressed himself to her, so she now instinctively addressed herself to Rachael. Her manner was short and abrupt, yet faltering and timid.

"He has told you what has passed between himself and my husband? You would be his first resource, I think."

"I have heard the end of it, young lady," said Rachael.

"Did I understand, that, being rejected by one employer, he would probably be rejected by all? I thought he said as much?"

"The chances are very small, young lady—next to nothing—for a man who gets a bad name among them."

"What shall I understand that you mean by a bad name?"

"The name of being troublesome."

"Then, by the prejudices of his own class, and by the prejudices of the other, he is sacrificed alike? Are the two so deeply separated in this town, that there is no place whatever, for an honest workman between them?"

Rachael shook her head in silence.

"He fell into suspicion," said Louisa, "with his fellow-weavers, because he had made a promise not to be one of them. I think it must have been to you that he made that promise. Might I ask you why he made it?"

Rachael burst into tears. "I didn't seek it of him, poor lad. I prayed him to avoid trouble for his own good, little thinking he'd come to it through me. But I know he'd die a hundred deaths, ere ever he'd break his word. I know that of him well."

Stephen had remained quietly attentive, in his usual thoughtful attitude, with his hand at his chin. He now spoke in a voice rather less steady than usual.

"No one, excepting myseln, can ever know what honour, an what love, an a respect, I bear to Rachael, or wi' what cause. When I passed that promess, I towd her true, she were th' Angel o' my life. 'Twere a solemn promess. 'Tis gone fro' me, for ever."

Louisa turned her head to him, and bent it with a deference that was new in her. She looked from him to Rachael, and her features softened. "What will you do?" she asked him. And her voice had softened too.

"Weel, ma'am," said Stephen, making the best of it, with a smile; "when I ha' finished off, I mun quit this part, and try another. Fortnet or misfortnet, a man can but try; there's nowt to be done wi'out tryin'—'cept laying down and dying."

"How will you travel?"

"Afoot, my kind ledy, afoot."

Louisa coloured, and a purse appeared in her hand. The rustling of a bank-note was audible, as she unfolded one and laid it on the table.

"Rachael, will you tell him—for you know how, without offence—that this is freely his, to help him on his way? Will you entreat him to take it?"

"I canna do that, young lady," she answered, turning her head aside; "bless you for thinking o' the poor lad wi' such tenderness. But 'tis for him to know his heart, and what is right according to it."

Louisa looked, in part incredulous, in part frightened, in part overcome with quick sympathy, when this man of so much self-command, who had been so plain and steady through the late interview, lost his composure in a moment, and now stood with his hand before his face. She stretched out hers, as if she would have touched him; then checked herself, and remained still.

"Not e'en Rachael," said Stephen, when he stood again with his face uncovered, "could mak sitch a kind offerin, by onny words, kinder. T' show that I'm not a man wi'out reason and gratitude, I'll tak two pound. I'll borrow 't for t' pay 't back. 'Twill be the sweetest work as ever I ha' done, that puts it in my power t' acknowledge once more my lastin thankfulness for this present action."

She was fain to take up the note again, and to substitute the much smaller sum he had named. He was neither courtly, nor handsome, nor picturesque, in any respect; and yet his manner of accepting it, and of expressing his thanks without more words, had a grace in it that Lord Chesterfield could not have taught his son in a century.

Tom had sat upon the bed, swinging one leg and sucking his walking-stick with sufficient unconcern, until the visit had attained this stage. Seeing his sister ready to depart, he got up, rather hurriedly, and put in a word.

"Just wait a moment, Loo! Before we go, I should like to speak to him a moment. Something comes into my head. If you'll step out on the stairs, Blackpool, I'll mention it. Never mind a light, man!" Tom was remarkably impatient of his moving towards the cupboard, to get one. "It don't want a light."

Stephen followed him out, and Tom closed the room door, and held the lock in his hand.

"I say!" he whispered. "I think I can do you a good turn.

Don't ask me what it is, because it may not come to anything. But there's no harm in my trying."

His breath fell like a flame of fire on Stephen's ear, it was so hot.

"That was our light porter at the Bank," said Tom, "who brought you the message to-night. I call him our light porter, because I belong to the Bank too."

Stephen thought, "What a hurry he is in!" He spoke so confusedly.

"Well!" said Tom. "Now look here! When are you off?"

"'T' day's Monday," replied Stephen, considering. "Why, sir, Friday or Saturday, nigh 'bout."

"Friday or Saturday," said Tom. "Now, look here! I am not sure that I can do you the good turn I want to do you—that's my sister, you know, in your room—but I may be able to, and if I should not be able to, there's no harm done. So I tell you what. You'll know our light porter again?"

"Yes, sure," said Stephen.

"Very well," returned Tom. "When you leave work of a night, between this and your going away, just hang about the Bank an hour or so, will you? Don't take on, as if you meant anything, if he should see you hanging about there; because I shan't put him up to speak to you, unless I find I can do you the service I want to do you. In that case he'll have a note or a message for you, but not else. Now look here! You are sure you understand."

He had wormed a finger, in the darkness, through a button-hole of Stephen's coat, and was screwing that corner of the garment tight up round and round, in an extraordinary manner.

"I understand, sir," said Stephen.

"Now look here!" repeated Tom. "Be sure you don't make any mistake then, and don't forget. I shall tell my sister as we go home, what I have in view, and she'll approve, I know. Now look here! You're all right, are you? You understand all about it? Very well then. Come along, Loo!"

He pushed the door open as he called to her, but did not return into the room, or wait to be lighted down the narrow stairs. He was at the bottom when she began to descend, and was in the street before she could take his arm.

Mrs. Pegler remained in her corner until the brother and sister were gone, and until Stephen came back with the candle in his hand. She was in a state of inexpressible admiration of Mrs. Bounderby, and, like an unaccountable old woman, wept, "because she was such a pretty dear." Yet Mrs. Pegler was so flurried lest the object of her admiration should return by chance, or anybody else should come, that her cheerfulness was ended for that night. It was late too, to people who rose early and worked hard; therefore the party broke up; and

Stephen and Rachael escorted their mysterious acquaintance to the door of the Travellers' Coffee House, where they parted from her.

They walked back together to the corner of the street where Rachael lived, and as they drew nearer and nearer to it, silence crept upon them. When they came to the dark corner where their unfrequent meetings always ended, they stopped, still silent, as if both were afraid to speak.

"I shall strive t' see thee agen, Rachael, afore I go, but if not——"

"Thou wilt not, Stephen, I know. 'Tis better that we make up our minds to be open wi' one another."

"Thou'rt awlus right. 'Tis bolder and better. I ha' been thinkin then, Rachael, that as 'tis but a day or two that remains, 'twere better for thee, my dear, not t' be seen wi' me. 'T might bring thee into trouble, fur no good."

"'Tis not for that, Stephen, that I mind. But thou know'st our old agreement. 'Tis for that."

"Well, well," said he. "'Tis better, onnyways."

"Thou'lt write to me, and tell me all that happens, Stephen?"

"Yes. What can I say now, but Heaven be wi' thee, Heaven bless thee, Heaven thank thee and reward thee!"

"May it bless thee, Stephen, too, in all thy wanderings, and send thee peace and rest at last!"

"I towd thee, my dear," said Stephen Blackpool—"that night—that I would never see or think o' onnything that angered me, but thou, so much better than me, should'st be beside it. Thou'rt beside it now. Thou mak'st me see it wi' a better eye. Bless thee. Good night. Good-bye!"

It was but a hurried parting in a common street, yet it was a sacred remembrance to these two common people. Utilitarian economists, skeletons of schoolmasters, Commissioners of Fact, genteel and used-up infidels, gabblers of many little dog's-eared creeds, the poor you will have always with you. Cultivate in them, while there is yet time, the utmost graces of the fancies and affections, to adorn their lives so much in need of ornament; or, in the day of your triumph, when romance is utterly driven out of their souls, and they and a bare existence stand face to face, Reality will take a wolfish turn, and make an end of you.

Stephen worked the next day, and the next, uncheered by a word from any one, and shunned in all his comings and goings as before. At the end of the second day, he saw land; at the end of the third, his loom stood empty.

He had overstayed his hour in the street outside the Bank, on each of the two first evenings; and nothing had happened there, good or bad. That he might not be remiss in his part of the engagement, he resolved to wait two hours, on this third and last night.

There was the lady who had once kept Mr. Bounderby's house, sitting at the first floor window as he had seen her before; and there was the light porter, sometimes talking with her there, and sometimes looking over the blind below which had BANK upon it, and sometimes coming to the door and standing on the steps for a breath of air. When he first came out, Stephen thought he might be looking for him, and passed near; but the light porter only cast his winking eyes upon him slightly, and said nothing.

Two hours were a long stretch of lounging about, after a long day's labour. Stephen sat upon the step of a door, leaned against a wall under an archway, strolled up and down, listened for the church clock, stopped and watched children playing in the street. Some purpose or other is so natural to every one, that a mere loiterer always looks and feels remarkable. When the first hour was out, Stephen even began to have an uncomfortable sensation upon him of being for the time the disreputable character.

Then came the lamplighter, and two lengthening lines of light all down the long perspective of the street, until they were blended and lost in the distance. Mrs. Sparsit closed the first floor window, drew down the blind, and went upstairs. Presently, a light went upstairs after her, passing first the fanlight of the door, and afterwards the two staircase windows, on its way up. By-and-bye, one corner of the second floor blind was disturbed, as if Mrs. Sparsit's eye were there; also the other corner, as if the light porter's eye were on that side. Still, no communication was made to Stephen. Much relieved when the two hours were at last accomplished, he went away at a quick pace, as a recompense for so much loitering.

He had only to take leave of his landlady, and lie down on his temporary bed upon the floor; for his bundle was made up for to-morrow, and all was arranged for his departure. He meant to be clear of the town very early; before the Hands were in the streets.

It was barely daybreak, when, with a parting look round his room, mournfully wondering whether he should ever see it again, he went out. The town was as entirely deserted as if the inhabitants had abandoned it, rather than hold communication with him. Everything looked wan at that hour. Even the coming sun made but a pale waste in the sky, like a sad sea.

By the place where Rachael lived, though it was not in his way; by the red brick streets; by the great silent factories, not trembling yet; by the railway, where the danger-lights were waning in the strengthening day; by the railway's crazy neighbourhood, half pulled down and half built up; by scattered red brick villas, where the besmoked evergreens were sprinkled with a dirty powder, like untidy snuff-takers; by coal-dust paths and many varieties of ugliness, Stephen got to the top of the hill, and looked back.

Day was shining radiantly upon the town then, and the bells were going for the morning work. Domestic fires were not yet lighted, and the high chimneys had the sky to themselves. Puffing out their poisonous volumes, they would not be long in hiding it; but, for half an hour, some of the many windows were golden, which showed the Coketown people a sun eternally in eclipse, through a medium of smoked glass.

So strange to turn from the chimneys to the birds. So strange to have the road-dust on his feet instead of the coal-grit. So strange to have lived to his time of life, and yet to be beginning like a boy this summer morning! With these musings in his mind, and his bundle under his arm, Stephen took his attentive face along the high road. And the trees arched over him, whispering that he had left a true and loving heart behind.

CHAPTER VII : *Gunpowder*

MR. JAMES HARTHOUSE, "going in" for his adopted party, soon began to score. With the aid of a little more coaching for the political sages, a little more genteel listlessness for the general society, and a tolerable management of the assumed honesty in dishonesty, most effective and most patronised of the polite deadly sins, he speedily came to be considered of much promise. The not being troubled with earnestness was a grand point in his favour, enabling him to take to the hard Fact fellows with as good a grace as if he had been born one of the tribe, and to throw all other tribes overboard, as conscious hypocrites.

"Whom none of us believe, my dear Mrs. Bounderby, and who do not believe themselves. The only difference between us and the professors of virtue or benevolence, or philanthropy —never mind the name—is, that we know it is all meaningless, and say so; while they know it equally and will never say so."

Why should she be shocked or warned by this reiteration? It was not so unlike her father's principles, and her early training, that it need startle her. Where was the great difference between the two schools, when each chained her down to material realities, and inspired her with no faith in anything else? What was there in her soul for James Harthouse to destroy, which Thomas Gradgrind had nurtured there in its state of innocence!

It was even the worse for her at this pass, that in her mind— implanted there before her eminently practical father began to form it—a struggling disposition to believe in a wider and nobler humanity than she had ever heard of constantly strove with doubts and resentments. With doubts, because the aspiration had been so laid waste in her youth. With resentments, because of the wrong that had been done her, if it were indeed a whisper of the truth. Upon a nature long accustomed to self-suppression, thus torn and divided, the Harthouse philosophy came as a relief and justification. Everything being hollow and worthless, she had missed nothing and sacrificed nothing. What did it matter, she had said to her father, when he proposed her husband. What did it matter, she said still. With a scornful self-reliance, she asked herself, What did anything matter—and went on.

Towards what? Step by step, onward and downward, towards some end, yet so gradually, that she believed herself to remain motionless. As to Mr. Harthouse, whither *he* tended, he neither considered nor cared. He had no particular design or plan before him: no energetic wickedness ruffled his lassitude. He was as much amused and interested, at present, as it became so fine a gentleman to be; perhaps even more than it would have been consistent with his reputation to confess. Soon after his arrival he languidly wrote to his brother, the honourable and jocular member, that the Bounderbys were "great fun"; and further, that the female Bounderby, instead of being the Gorgon he had expected, was young, and remarkably pretty. After that, he wrote no more about them, and devoted his leisure chiefly to their house. He was very often in their house, in his flittings and visitings about the Coketown district; and was much encouraged by Mr. Bounderby. It was quite in Mr. Bounderby's gusty way to boast to all his world that *he* didn't care about your highly connected people, but that if his wife Tom Gradgrind's daughter did, she was welcome to their company.

Mr. James Harthouse began to think it would be a new sensation, if the face which changed so beautifully for the whelp, would change for him.

He was quick enough to observe; he had a good memory, and did not forget a word of the brother's revelations. He interwove them with everything he saw of the sister, and he began to understand her. To be sure, the better and profounder part of her character was not within his scope of perception; for in natures, as in seas, depth answers unto depth; but he soon began to read the rest with a student's eye.

Mr. Bounderby had taken possession of a house and grounds, about fifteen miles from the town, and accessible within a mile or two, by a railway striding on many arches over a wild country, undermined by deserted coal-shafts, and spotted at night by fires and black shapes of stationary engines at pits' mouths. This country, gradually softening towards the neighbourhood of Mr. Bounderby's retreat, there mellowed into a rustic landscape, golden with heath, and snowy with hawthorn in the spring of the year, and tremulous with leaves and their shadows all the summer time. The bank had fore-closed a mortgage effected on the property thus pleasantly situated, by one of the Coketown magnates, who, in his de-termination to make a shorter cut than usual to an enormous fortune, over-speculated himself by about two hundred thousand pounds. These accidents did sometimes happen in the best regulated families of Coketown, but the bankrupts had no connection whatever with the improvident classes.

It afforded Mr. Bounderby supreme satisfaction to install himself in this snug little estate, and with demonstrative humility to grow cabbages in the flower-garden. He delighted to live, barrack-fashion, among the elegant furniture, and he bullied the very pictures with his origin. "Why, sir," he would say to a visitor, "I am told that Nickits," the late owner, "gave seven hundred pound for that Seabeach. Now, to be plain with you, if I ever, in the whole course of my life, take seven looks at it, at a hundred pound a look, it will be as much as I shall do. No, by George! I don't forget that I am Josiah Bounderby of Coketown. For years upon years, the only pictures in my possession, or that I could have got into my possession, by any means, unless I stole 'em, were the engrav-ings of a man shaving himself in a boot, on the blacking bottles that I was overjoyed to use in cleaning boots with, and that I sold when they were empty for a farthing apiece, and glad to get it!"

Then he would address Mr. Harthouse in the same style.

"Harthouse, you have a couple of horses down here. Bring half a dozen more if you like, and we'll find room for 'em. There's stabling in this place for a dozen horses; and unless Nickits is belied, he kept the full number. A round dozen of 'em, sir. When that man was a boy, he went to Westminster School. Went to Westminster School as a King's Scholar, when I was principally living on garbage, and sleeping in market baskets. Why, if I wanted to keep a dozen horses— which I don't, for one's enough for me—I couldn't bear to see 'em in their stalls here, and think what my own lodging used to be. I couldn't look at 'em, sir, and not order 'em out. Yet so things come round. You see this place; you know what sort of a place it is; you are aware that there's not a completer place of its size in this kingdom or elsewhere—I don't care where—and here, got into the middle of it, like a maggot in a nut, is Josiah Bounderby. While Nickits (as a man came into my office and told me yesterday), Nickits, who used to act in Latin, in the Westminster School plays, with the chief-justices and nobility of this country applauding him till they were black in the face, is drivelling at this minute—drivelling, sir!—in a fifth floor, up a narrow dark back street in Antwerp."

It was among the leafy shadows of this retirement, in the

long sultry summer days, that Mr. Harthouse began to prove the face which had set him wondering when he first saw it, and to try if it would change for him.

"Mrs. Bounderby, I esteem it a most fortunate accident that I should find you alone here. I have for some time had a particular wish to speak to you."

It was not by any wonderful accident that he found her, the time of day being that at which she was always alone, and the place being her favourite resort. It was an opening in a dark wood, where some felled trees lay, and where she would sit watching the fallen leaves of last year, as she had watched the falling ashes at home.

He sat down beside her, with a glance at her face.

"Your brother. My young friend Tom——"

Her colour brightened, and she turned to him with a look of interest. "I never in my life," he thought, "saw anything so remarkable and so captivating as the lighting of those features!" His face betrayed his thoughts—perhaps without betraying him, for it might have been according to its instructions so to do.

"Pardon me. The expression of your sisterly interest is so beautiful—Tom should be so proud of it—I know this is inexcusable, but I am so compelled to admire."

"Being so impulsive," she said composedly.

"Mrs. Bounderby, no: you know I make no pretence with you. You know I am a sordid piece of human nature, ready to sell myself at any time for any reasonable sum, and altogether incapable of any Arcadian proceeding whatever."

"I am waiting," she returned, "for your further reference to my brother."

"You are rigid with me, and I deserve it. I am as worthless a dog as you will find, except that I am not false—not false. But you surprised and started me from my subject, which was your brother. I have an interest in him."

"Have you an interest in anything, Mr. Harthouse?" she asked, half incredulously and half gratefully.

"If you had asked me when I first came here, I should have said no. I must say now—even at the hazard of appearing to make a pretence, and of justly awakening your incredulity —yes."

She made a slight movement, as if she were trying to speak, but could not find voice; at length she said, "Mr. Harthouse, I give you credit for being interested in my brother."

"Thank you. I claim to deserve it. You know how little I do claim, but I will go that length. You have done so much for him, you are so fond of him; your whole life, Mrs. Bounderby, expresses such charming self-forgetfulness on his account— pardon me again—I am running wide of the subject. I am interested in him for his own sake."

She had made the slightest action possible, as if she would have risen in a hurry and gone away. He had turned the course of what he said at that instant, and she remained.

"Mrs. Bounderby," he resumed, in a lighter manner, and yet with a show of effort in assuming it, which was even more expressive than the manner he dismissed; "it is no irrevocable offence in a young fellow of your brother's years, if he is heedless, inconsiderate, and expensive—a little dissipated, in the common phrase. Is he?"

"Yes."

"Allow me to be frank. Do you think he games at all?"

"I think he makes bets." Mr. Harthouse waiting, as if that were not her whole answer, she added, "I know he does."

"Of course he loses?"

"Yes."

"Everybody does lose who bets. May I hint at the probability of your sometimes supplying him with money for these purposes?"

She sat, looking down; but, at this question, raised her eyes searchingly and a little resentfully.

"Acquit me of impertinent curiosity, my dear Mrs. Bounderby. I think Tom may be gradually falling into trouble, and I wish to stretch out a helping hand to him from the depths of my wicked experience.—Shall I say again, for his sake? Is that necessary?"

She seemed to try to answer, but nothing came of it.

"Candidly to confess everything that has occurred to me," said James Harthouse, again gliding with the same appearance of effort into his more airy manner; "I will confide to you my doubt whether he has had many advantages. Whether—forgive my plainness—whether any great amount of confidence is likely to have been established between himself and his most worthy father."

"I do not," said Louisa, flushing with her own great remembrance in that wise, "think it likely."

"Or, between himself, and—I may trust to your perfect understanding of my meaning, I am sure—and his highly esteemed brother-in-law."

She flushed deeper and deeper, and was burning red when she replied in a fainter voice, "I do not think that likely, either."

"Mrs. Bounderby," said Harthouse, after a short silence, "may there be a better confidence between yourself and me? Tom has borrowed a considerable sum of you?"

"You will understand, Mr. Harthouse," she returned, after some indecision: she had been more or less uncertain, and troubled throughout the conversation, and yet had in the main preserved her self-contained manner; "you will understand that if I tell you what you press to know, it is not by way of complaint or regret. I would never complain of anything, and what I have done I do not in the least regret."

"So spirited, too!" thought James Harthouse.

"When I married, I found that my brother was even at that time heavily in debt. Heavily for him, I mean. Heavily enough to oblige me to sell some trinkets. They were no sacrifice. I sold them very willingly. I attached no value to them. They were quite worthless to me."

Either she saw in his face that he knew, or she only feared in her conscience that he knew, that she spoke of some of her husband's gifts. She stopped, and reddened again. If he had not known it before, he would have known it then, though he had been a much duller man than he was.

"Since then, I have given my brother, at various times, what money I could spare: in short, what money I have had. Confiding in you at all, on the faith of the interest you profess for him, I will not do so by halves. Since you have been in the habit of visiting here, he has wanted in one sum as much as a hundred pounds. I have not been able to give it to him. I have felt uneasy for the consequences of his being so involved, but I have kept these secrets until now, when I trust them to your honour. I have held no confidence with any one, because—you anticipated my reason just now." She abruptly broke off.

He was a ready man, and he saw, and seized, an opportunity here of presenting her own image to her, slightly disguised as her brother.

"Mrs. Bounderby, though a graceless person, of the world worldly, I feel the utmost interest, I assure you, in what you tell me. I cannot possibly be hard upon your brother. I understand and share the wise consideration with which you regard his errors. With all possible respect both for Mr. Gradgrind and for Mr. Bounderby, I think I perceive that he has not been fortunate in his training. Bred at a disadvantage towards the society in which he has his part to play, he rushes into these extremes for himself, from opposite extremes that have long been forced—with the very best intentions we have no doubt—upon him. Mr. Bounderby's fine bluff English independence, though a most charming characteristic, does not—as we have agreed—invite confidence. If I might venture to remark that it is the least in the world deficient in that delicacy to which a youth mistaken, a character misconceived, and abilities misdirected, would turn for relief and guidance, I should express what it presents to my own view."

As she sat looking straight before her, across the changing lights upon the grass into the darkness of the wood beyond, he saw in her face her application of his very distinctly uttered words.

"All allowance," he continued, "must be made. I have one

great fault to find with Tom, however, which I cannot forgive, and for which I take him heavily to account."

Louisa turned her eyes to his face, and asked him what fault was that?

"Perhaps," he returned, "I have said enough. Perhaps it would have been better, on the whole, if no allusion to it had escaped me."

"You alarm me, Mr. Harthouse. Pray let me know it."

"To relieve you from needless apprehension—and as this confidence regarding your brother, which I prize I am sure above all possible things, has been established between us— I obey. I cannot forgive him for not being more sensible in every word, look, and act of his life, of the affection of his best friend; of the devotion of his best friend; of her unselfishness; of her sacrifice. The return he makes her, within my observation, is a very poor one. What she has done for him demands his constant love and gratitude, not his ill-humour and caprice. Careless fellow as I am, I am not so indifferent, Mrs. Bounderby, as to be regardless of this vice in your brother, or inclined to consider it a venial offence."

The wood floated before her, for her eyes were suffused with tears. They rose from a deep well, long concealed, and her heart was filled with acute pain that found no relief in them.

"In a word, it is to correct your brother in this, Mrs. Bounderby, that I must aspire. My better knowledge of his circumstances, and my direction and advice in extricating them—rather valuable, I hope, as coming from a scapegrace on a much larger scale—will give me some influence over him, and all I gain I shall certainly use towards this end. I have said enough, and more than enough. I seem to be protesting that I am a sort of good fellow, when, upon my honour, I have not the least intention to make any protestation to that effect, and openly announce that I am nothing of the sort. Yonder, among the trees," he added, having lifted up his eyes and looked about; for he had watched her closely until now; "is your brother himself; no doubt, just come down. As he seems to be loitering in this direction, it may be as well, perhaps, to walk towards him, and throw ourselves in his way. He has been very silent and doleful of late. Perhaps his brotherly conscience is touched—if there are such things as consciences. Though, upon my honour, I hear of them much too often to believe in them."

He assisted her to rise, and she took his arm, and they advanced to meet the whelp. He was idly beating the branches as he lounged along: or he stooped viciously to rip the moss from the trees with his stick. He was startled when they came upon him while he was engaged in this latter pastime, and his colour changed.

"Halloa!" he stammered; "I didn't know you were here."

"Whose name, Tom," said Mr. Harthouse, putting his hand upon his shoulder and turning him, so that they all three walked towards the house together, "have you been carving on the trees?"

"Whose name?" returned Tom. "Oh! You mean what girl's name?"

"You have a suspicious appearance of inscribing some fair creature's on the bark, Tom."

"Not much of that, Mr. Harthouse, unless some fair creature with a slashing fortune at her own disposal would take a fancy to me. Or she might be as ugly as she was rich, without any fear of losing me. I'd carve her name as often as she liked."

"I am afraid you are mercenary, Tom."

"Mercenary," repeated Tom. "Who is not mercenary? Ask my sister."

"Have you so proved it to be a failing of mine, Tom?" said Louisa, showing no other sense of his discontent and ill-nature.

"You know whether the cap fits you, Loo," returned her brother, sulkily. "If it does, you can wear it."

"Tom is misanthropical to-day, as all bored people are now and then," said Mr. Harthouse. "Don't believe him, Mrs. Bounderby. He knows much better. I shall disclose some of his opinions of you, privately expressed to me, unless he relents a little."

"At all events, Mr. Harthouse," said Tom, softening in his administration of his patron, but shaking his head sullenly too, "you can't tell her that I ever praised her for being mercenary. I may have praised her for being the contrary, and I should do it again, if I had as good reason. However, never mind this now; it's not very interesting to you, and I am sick of the subject."

They walked on to the house, where Louisa quitted her visitor's arm and went in. He stood looking after her, as she ascended the steps, and passed into the shadow of the door; then put his hand upon her brother's shoulder again, and invited him with a confidential nod to a walk in the garden.

"Tom, my fine fellow, I want to have a word with you."

They had stopped among a disorder of roses—it was part of Mr. Bounderby's humility to keep Nickit's roses on a reduced scale—and Tom sat down on a terrace-parapet, plucking buds and picking them to pieces; while his powerful Familiar stood over him, with a foot upon the parapet, and his figure easily resting on the arm supported by that knee. They were just visible from her window. Perhaps she saw them.

"Tom, what's the matter?"

"Oh! Mr. Harthouse," said Tom with a groan "I am hard up, and bothered out of my life."

"My good fellow, so am I."

"You!" returned Tom. "You are the picture of independence. Mr. Harthouse, I am in a horrible mess. You have no idea what a state I have got myself into—what a state my sister might have got me out of, if she would only have done it."

He took to biting the rose-buds now, and tearing them away from his teeth with a hand that trembled like an infirm old man's. After one exceedingly observant look at him, his companion relapsed into his lightest air.

"Tom, you are inconsiderate: you expect too much of your sister. You have had money of her, you dog, you know you have."

"Well, Mr. Harthouse, I know I have. How else was I to get it? Here's old Bounderby always boasting that at my age he lived upon twopence a month, or something of that sort. Here's my father drawing what he calls a line, and tying me down to it from a baby, neck and heels. Here's my mother who never has anything of her own, except her complaints. What *is* a fellow to do for money, and where *am* I to look for it, if not to my sister?"

He was almost crying, and scattered the buds about by dozens. Mr. Harthouse took him persuasively by the coat.

"But, my dear Tom, if your sister has not got it——"

"Not got it, Mr. Harthouse? I don't say she has got it. I may have wanted more than she was likely to have got. But then she ought to get it. She could get it. It's of no use pretending to make a secret of matters now, after what I have told you already; you know she didn't marry old Bounderby for her own sake, or for his sake, but for my sake. Then why doesn't she get what I want, out of him, for my sake? She is not obliged to say what she is going to do with it; she is sharp enough; she could manage to coax it out of him, if she chose. Then why doesn't she choose, when I tell her of what consequence it is? But no. There she sits in his company like a stone, instead of making herself agreeable and getting it easily. I don't know what you may call this, but *I* call it unnatural conduct."

There was a piece of ornamental water immediately below the parapet, on the other side, into which Mr. James Harthouse had a very strong inclination to pitch Mr. Thomas Gradgrind, Junior, as the injured men of Coketown threatened to pitch their property into the Atlantic. But he preserved his easy attitude; and nothing more solid went over the stone balustrades than the accumulated rosebuds now floating about, a little surface-island.

"My dear Tom," said Harthouse, "let me try to be your banker."

"For God's sake," replied Tom, suddenly, "don't talk about

bankers!" And very white he looked, in contrast with the roses. Very white.

Mr. Harthouse, as a thoroughly well-bred man, accustomed to the best society, was not to be surprised—he could as soon have been affected—but he raised his eyelids a little more, as if they were lifted by a feeble touch of wonder. Albeit it was as much against the precepts of his school to wonder, as it was against the doctrines of the Gradgrind College.

"What is the present need, Tom? Three figures? Out with them. Say what they are."

"Mr. Harthouse," returned Tom, now actually crying; and his tears were better than his injuries, however pitiful a figure he made; "it's too late; the money is of no use to me at present. I should have had it before to be of use to me. But I am very much obliged to you; you're a true friend."

A true friend! "Whelp, whelp!" thought Mr. Harthouse, lazily; "what an Ass you are!"

"And I take your offer as a great kindness," said Tom, grasping his hand. "As a great kindness, Mr. Harthouse."

"Well," returned the other, "it may be of more use by-and-by. And, my good fellow, if you will open your bedevilments to me when they come thick upon you, I may show you better ways out of them than you can find for yourself."

"Thank you," said Tom, shaking his head dismally, and chewing rose-buds. "I wish I had known you sooner, Mr. Harthouse."

"Now, you see, Tom," said Mr. Harthouse in conclusion, himself tossing over a rose or two, as a contribution to the island, which was always drifting to the wall as if it wanted to become a part of the mainland: "every man is selfish in everything he does, and I am exactly like the rest of my fellow-creatures. I am desperately intent;" the languor of his desperation being quite tropical; "on your softening towards your sister—which you ought to do; and on your being a more loving and agreeable sort of brother—which you ought to be."

"I will be, Mr. Harthouse."

"No time like the present, Tom. Begin at once."

"Certainly I will. And my sister Loo shall say so."

"Having made which bargain, Tom," said Harthouse, clapping him on the shoulder again, with an air which left him at liberty to infer—as he did, poor fool—that this condition was imposed upon him in mere careless good-nature to lessen his sense of obligation, "we will tear ourselves asunder until dinner-time."

When Tom appeared before dinner, though his mind seemed heavy enough, his body was on the alert; and he appeared before Mr. Bounderby came in. "I didn't mean to be cross, Loo," he said, giving her his hand, and kissing her. "I know you are fond of me, and you know I am fond of you."

After this, there was a smile upon Louisa's face that day, for some one else. Alas, for some one else!

"So much the less is the whelp the only creature that she cares for," thought James Harthouse, reversing the reflection of his first day's knowledge of her pretty face. "So much the less, so much the less."

CHAPTER VIII: *Explosion*

THE next morning was too bright a morning for sleep, and James Harthouse rose early, and sat in the pleasant bay window of his dressing-room, smoking the rare tobacco that had had so wholesome an influence on his young friend. Reposing in the sunlight, with the fragrance of his eastern pipe about him, and the dreamy smoke vanishing into the air, so rich and soft with summer odours, he reckoned up his advantages as an idle winner might count his gains. He was not at all bored for the time, and could give his mind to it.

He had established a confidence with her, from which her husband was excluded. He had established a confidence with her, that absolutely turned upon her indifference towards her husband, and the absence, now and at all times, of any congeniality between them. He had artfully, but plainly assured her, that he knew her heart in its last most delicate recesses; he had come so near to her through its tenderest sentiment; he had associated himself with that feeling; and the barrier behind which she lived, had melted away. All very odd, and very satisfactory!

And yet he had not, even now, any earnest wickedness of purpose in him. Publicly and privately, it were much better for the age in which he lived, that he and the legion of whom he was one were designedly bad, than indifferent and purposeless. It is the drifting icebergs setting with any current anywhere, that wreck the ships.

When the Devil goeth about like a roaring lion, he goeth about in a shape by which few but savages and hunters are attracted. But, when he is trimmed, smoothed, and varnished according to the mode: when he is aweary of vice, and aweary of virtue, used up as to brimstone, and used up as to bliss; then, whether he take to the serving out of red tape, or to the kindling of red fire, he is the very Devil.

So, James Harthouse reclined in the window, indolently smoking, and reckoning up the steps he had taken on the road by which he happened to be travelling. The end to which it led was before him, pretty plainly; but he troubled himself with no calculations about it. What will be, will be.

As he had rather a long ride to take that day—for there was a public occasion "to do" at some distance, which afforded a tolerable opportunity of going in for the Gradgrind men—he dressed early, and went down to breakfast. He was anxious to see if she had relapsed since the previous evening. No. He resumed where he had left off. There was a look of interest for him again.

He got through the day as much (or as little) to his own satisfaction, as was to be expected under the fatiguing circumstances; and came riding back at six o'clock. There was a sweep of some half mile between the lodge and the house, and he was riding along at a footpace over the smooth gravel, once Nickits's, when Mr. Bounderby burst out of the shrubbery, with such violence as to make his horse shy across the road.

"Harthouse!" cried Mr. Bounderby. "Have you heard?"

"Heard what?" said Harthouse, soothing his horse, and inwardly favouring Mr. Bounderby with no good wishes.

"Then you *haven't* heard!"

"I have heard you, and so has this brute. I have heard nothing else."

Mr. Bounderby, red and hot, planted himself in the centre of the path before the horse's head, to explode his bombshell with more effect.

"The Bank's robbed!"

"You don't mean it!"

"Robbed last night, sir. Robbed in an extraordinary manner. Robbed with a false key."

"Of much?"

Mr. Bounderby, in his desire to make the most of it, really seemed mortified by being obliged to reply, "Why, no; not of very much. But it might have been."

"Of how much?"

"Oh! as a sum—if you stick to a sum—of not more than a hundred and fifty pound," said Bounderby, with impatience. "But it's not the sum; it's the fact. It's the fact of the Bank being robbed, that's the important circumstance. I am surprised you don't see it."

"My dear Bounderby," said James, dismounting, and giving his bridle to his servant, "I *do* see it; and am as overcome as you can possibly desire me to be, by the spectacle afforded to my mental view. Nevertheless, I may be allowed, I hope, to congratulate you—which I do with all my soul, I assure you—on your not having sustained a greater loss."

"Thank'ee," replied Bounderby, in a short, ungracious manner. "But I tell you what. It might have been twenty thousand pound."

"I suppose it might."

"Suppose it might! By the Lord, you *may* suppose so. By George!" said Mr. Bounderby, with sundry menacing nods and shakes of his head. "It might have been twice twenty. There's no knowing what it would have been, or wouldn't have been, as it was, but for the fellows' being disturbed."

Louisa had come up now, and Mrs. Sparsit, and Bitzer.

"Here's Tom Gradgrind's daughter knows pretty well what it might have been, if you don't," blustered Bounderby. "Dropped, sir, as if she were shot when I told her! Never knew her to do such a thing before. Does her credit, under the circumstances, in my opinion!"

She still looked faint and pale. James Harthouse begged her to take his arm; and as they moved on very slowly, asked her how the robbery had been committed.

"Why, I am going to tell you," said Bounderby, irritably giving his arm to Mrs. Sparsit. "If you hadn't been so mighty particular about the sum, I should have begun to tell you before. You know this lady (for she *is* a lady), Mrs. Sparsit?"

"I have already had the honour——"

"Very well. And this young man, Bitzer, you saw him too on the same occasion?" Mr Harthouse inclined his head in assent, and Bitzer knuckled his forehead.

"Very well. They live at the Bank. You know they live at the Bank, perhaps? Very well. Yesterday afternoon, at the close of business hours, everything was put away as usual. In the iron room that this young fellow sleeps outside of, there was never mind how much. In the little safe in young Tom's closet, the safe used for petty purposes, there was a hundred and fifty odd pound."

"A hundred and fifty-four, seven, one," said Bitzer.

"Come!" retorted Bounderby, stopping to wheel round upon him, "let's have none of *your* interruptions. It's enough to be robbed while you're snoring because you're too comfortable, without being put right with *your* four seven ones. I didn't snore, myself, when I was your age, let me tell you. I hadn't victuals enough to snore. And I didn't four seven one. Not if I knew it."

Bitzer knuckled his forehead again, in a sneaking manner, and seemed at once particularly impressed and depressed by the instance last given of Mr. Bounderby's moral abstinence.

"A hundred and fifty odd pound," resumed Mr. Bounderby. "That sum of money, young Tom locked in his safe, not a very strong safe, but that's no matter now. Everything was left, all right. Some time in the night, while this young fellow snored—Mrs. Sparsit, ma'am, you say you have heard him snore?"

"Sir," returned Mrs. Sparsit, "I cannot say that I have heard him precisely snore, and therefore must not make that statement. But on winter evenings, when he has fallen asleep at his table, I have heard him, what I should prefer to describe as partially choke. I have heard him on such occasions produce sounds of a nature similar to what may be sometimes heard in Dutch clocks. Not," said Mrs. Sparsit, with a lofty sense of giving strict evidence, "that I would convey any imputation on his moral character. Far from it. I have always considered Bitzer a young man of the most upright principle; and to that I beg to bear my testimony."

"Well!" said the exasperated Bounderby, "while he was snoring, or choking, or Dutch-clocking, or something or other —being asleep—some fellows, somehow, whether previously concealed in the house or not remains to be seen, got to young Tom's safe, forced it, and abstracted the contents. Being then disturbed, they made off; letting themselves out at the main door, and double-locking it again (it was double-locked, and the key under Mrs. Sparsit's pillow) with a false key, which was picked up in the street near the Bank, about twelve o'clock to-day. No alarm takes place till this chap, Bitzer, turns out this morning, and begins to open and prepare the offices for business. Then, looking at Tom's safe, he sees the door ajar, and finds the lock forced, and the money gone."

"Where is Tom, by-the-bye?" asked Harthouse, glancing round.

"He has been helping the police," said Bounderby, "and stays behind at the Bank. I wish these fellows had tried to rob me when I was at his time of life. They would have been out of pocket if they had invested eighteen-pence in the job; I can tell 'em that."

"Is anybody suspected?"

"Suspected? I should think there was somebody suspected. Egod!" said Bounderby, relinquishing Mrs. Sparsit's arm to wipe his heated head. "Josiah Bounderby of Coketown is not to be plundered and nobody suspected. No, thank you!"

Might Mr. Harthouse inquire Who was suspected?

"Well," said Bounderby, stopping and facing about to confront them all, "I'll tell you. It's not to be mentioned everywhere; it's not to be mentioned anywhere: in order that the scoundrels concerned (there's a gang of 'em) may be thrown off their guard. So take this in confidence. Now wait a bit." Mr. Bounderby wiped his head again. "What should you say to;" here he violently exploded; "to a Hand being in it?"

"I hope," said Harthouse, lazily, "not our friend Blackpot?"

"Say Pool instead of Pot, sir," returned Bounderby, "and that's the man."

Louisa faintly uttered some word of incredulity and surprise.

"O yes! I know!" said Bounderby, immediately catching at the sound. "I know! I am used to that. I know all about it. They are the finest people in the world, these fellows are. They have got the gift of the gab, they have. They only want to have their rights explained to them, they do. But I tell you what. Show me a dissatisfied Hand, and I'll show you a man that's fit for anything bad, I don't care what it is."

Another of the popular fictions of Coketown, which some

pains had been taken to disseminate—and which some people really believed.

"But I am acquainted with these chaps," said Bounderby. "I can read 'em off, like books. Mrs. Sparsit, ma'am, I appeal to you. What warning did I give that fellow, the first time he set foot in the house, when the express object of his visit was to know how he could knock Religion over, and floor the Established Church? Mrs. Sparsit, in point of high connections, you are on a level with the aristocracy,—did I say, or did I not say, to that fellow, 'you can't hide the truth from me: you are not the kind of fellow I like; you'll come to no good'?"

"Assuredly, sir," returned Mrs. Sparsit, "you did, in a highly impressive manner, give him such an admonition."

"When he shocked you, ma'am," said Bounderby; "when he shocked your feelings?"

"Yes, sir," returned Mrs. Sparsit, with a meek shake of her head, "he certainly did so. Though I do not mean to say but that my feelings may be weaker on such points—more foolish if the term is preferred—than they might have been, if I had always occupied my present position."

Mr. Bounderby stared with a bursting pride at Mr. Harthouse, as much as to say, "I am the proprietor of this female, and she's worth your attention, I think." Then, resumed his discourse.

"You can recall for yourself, Harthouse, what I said to him when you saw him. I didn't mince the matter with him. I am never mealy with 'em. I KNOW 'em. Very well, sir. Three days after that, he bolted. Went off, nobody knows where: as my mother did in my infancy—only with this difference, that he is a worse subject than my mother, if possible. What did he do before he went? What do you say;" Mr. Bounderby, with his hat in his hand, gave a beat upon the crown at every little division of his sentences, as if it were a tambourine; "to his being seen—night after night—watching the Bank?—to his lurking about there—after dark?—To its striking Mrs. Sparsit—that he could be lurking for no good—To her calling Bitzer's attention to him, and their both taking notice of him—And to its appearing on inquiry to-day—that he was also noticed by the neighbours?" Having come to the climax, Mr. Bounderby, like an oriental dancer, put his tambourine on his head.

"Suspicious," said James Harthouse, "certainly."

"I think so, sir," said Bounderby, with a defiant nod. "I think so. But there are more of 'em in it. There's an old woman. One never hears of these things till the mischief's done; all sorts of defects are found out in the stable door after the horse is stolen; there's an old woman turns up now. An old woman who seems to have been flying into town on a broomstick, every now and then. *She* watches the place a whole day

MR. HARTHOUSE AND TOM GRADGRIND IN THE GARDEN.

before this fellow begins, and on the night when you saw him, she steals away with him, and holds a council with him—I suppose, to make her report on going off duty, and be damned to her."

There was such a person in the room that night, and she shrunk from observation, thought Louisa.

"This is not all of 'em, even as we already know 'em," said Bounderby, with many nods of hidden meaning. "But I have said enough for the present. You'll have the goodness to keep it quiet, and mention it to no one. It may take time, but we shall have 'em. It's policy to give 'em line enough, and there's no objection to that."

"Of course, they will be punished with the utmost rigour of the law, as notice-boards observe," replied James Harthouse, "and serve them right. Fellows who go in for Banks must take the consequences. If there were no consequences, we should all go in for Banks." He had gently taken Louisa's parasol from her hand, and had put it up for her; and she walked under its shade, though the sun did not shine there.

"For the present, Loo Bounderby," said her husband, "here's Mrs. Sparsit to look after. Mrs. Sparsit's nerves have been acted upon by this business, and she'll stay here a day or two. So, make her comfortable."

"Thank you very much, sir," that discreet lady observed, "but pray do not let My comfort be a consideration. Anything will do for Me."

It soon appeared that if Mrs. Sparsit had a failing in her association with that domestic establishment, it was that she was so excessively regardless of herself and regardful of others, as to be a nuisance. On being shown her chamber, she was so dreadfully sensible of its comforts as to suggest the inference that she would have preferred to pass the night on the mangle in the laundry. True, the Powlers and the Scadgerses were accustomed to splendour, "but it is my duty to remember," Mrs. Sparsit was fond of observing with a lofty grace: particularly when any of the domestics were present, "that what I was, I am no longer. Indeed," said she, "if I could altogether cancel the remembrance that Mr. Sparsit was a Powler, or that I myself am related to the Scadgers family; or if I could even revoke the fact, and make myself a person of common descent and ordinary connections; I would gladly do so. I should think it, under existing circumstances, right to do so." The same Hermitical state of mind led to her renunciation of made dishes and wines at dinner, until fairly commanded by Mr. Bounderby to take them; when she said, "Indeed you are very good, sir;" and departed from a resolution of which she had made rather formal and public announcement, to "wait for the simple mutton." She was likewise deeply apologetic for wanting the salt; and, feeling amiably bound to bear out Mr. Bounderby to the fullest extent in the testimony he had borne to her nerves, occasionally sat back in her chair and silently wept; at which periods a tear of large dimensions, like a crystal earring, might be observed (or rather, must be, for it insisted on public notice) sliding down her Roman nose.

But Mrs. Sparsit's greatest point, first and last, was her determination to pity Mr. Bounderby. There were occasions when in looking at him she was involuntarily moved to shake her head, as who would say, "Alas, poor Yorick!" After allowing herself to be betrayed into these evidences of emotion, she would force a lambent brightness, and would be fitfully cheerful, and would say, "You have still good spirits, sir, I am thankful to find;" and would appear to hail it as a blessed dispensation that Mr. Bounderby bore up as he did. One idiosyncrasy for which she often apologised, she found it excessively difficult to conquer. She had a curious propensity to call Mrs. Bounderby "Miss Gradgrind," and yielded to it some three or four score times in the course of the evening. Her repetition of this mistake covered Mrs. Sparsit with modest confusion; but indeed, she said, it seemed so natural to say Miss Gradgrind: whereas, to persuade herself that the young lady whom she had had the happiness of knowing from a child could be really and truly Mrs. Bounderby, she found almost impossible. It was a further singularity of this remarkable case that the more she thought about it, the more impossible it appeared; "the differences," she observed, "being such."

In the drawing-room after dinner, Mr. Bounderby tried the case of the robbery, examined the witnesses, made notes of the evidence, found the suspected persons guilty, and sentenced them to the extreme punishment of the law. That done, Bitzer was dismissed to town with instructions to recommend Tom to come home by the mail-train.

When candles were brought, Mrs. Sparsit murmured, "Don't be low, sir. Pray let me see you cheerful, sir, as I used to do." Mr. Bounderby, upon whom these consolations had begun to produce the effect of making him, in a bull-headed blundering way, sentimental, sighed like some large sea-animal. "I cannot bear to see you so, sir," said Mrs. Sparsit. "Try a hand at backgammon, sir, as you used to do when I had the honour of living under your roof." "I haven't played backgammon, ma'am," said Mr. Bounderby, "since that time." "No, sir," said Mrs. Sparsit, soothingly, "I am aware that you have not. I remember that Miss Gradgrind takes no interest in the game. But I shall be happy, sir, if you will condescend."

They played near a window, opening on the garden. It was a fine night: not moonlight, but sultry and fragrant. Louisa and Mr. Harthouse strolled out into the garden, where their voices could be heard in the stillness, though not what they said. Mrs. Sparsit, from her place at the backgammon board, was constantly straining her eyes to pierce the shadows without. "What's the matter, ma'am?" said Mr. Bounderby; "you don't see a Fire, do you?" "Oh dear no, sir," returned Mrs. Sparsit, "I was thinking of the dew." "What have you got to do with the dew, ma'am?" said Mr. Bounderby. "It's not myself, sir," returned Mrs. Sparsit, "I am fearful of Miss Gradgrind's taking cold." "She never takes cold," said Mr. Bounderby. "Really, sir?" said Mrs. Sparsit. And was affected with a cough in her throat.

When the time drew near for retiring, Mr. Bounderby took a glass of water. "Oh, sir?" said Mrs. Sparsit. "Not your sherry warm, with lemon-peel and nutmeg?" "Why I have got out of the habit of taking it now, ma'am," said Mr. Bounderby. "The more's the pity, sir," returned Mrs. Sparsit; "you are losing all your good old habits. Cheer up, sir! If Miss Gradgrind will permit me, I will offer to make it for you, as I have often done."

Miss Gradgrind readily permitting Mrs. Sparsit to do anything she pleased, that considerate lady made the beverage, and handed it to Mr. Bounderby. "It will do you good, sir. It will warm your heart. It is the sort of thing you want, and ought to take, sir." And when Mr. Bounderby said, "Your health, ma'am!" she answered with great feeling. "Thank you, sir. The same to you, and happiness also." Finally, she wished him good night, with great pathos; and Mr. Bounderby went to bed, with a maudlin persuasion that he had been crossed in something tender, though he could not, for his life, have mentioned what it was.

Long after Louisa had undressed and lain down, she watched and waited for her brother's coming home. That could hardly be, she knew, until an hour past midnight; but in the country silence, which did anything but calm the trouble of her thoughts, time lagged wearily. At last, when the darkness and stillness had seemed for hours to thicken one another, she heard the bell at the gate. She felt as though she would have been glad that it rang on until daylight; but it ceased, and the circles of its last sound spread out fainter and wider in the air, and all was dead again.

She waited yet some quarter of an hour, as she judged. Then she arose, put on a loose robe, and went out of her room in the dark, and up the staircase to her brother's room. His door being shut, she softly opened it and spoke to him, approaching his bed with noiseless step.

She kneeled down beside it, passed her arm over his neck, and drew his face to hers. She knew that he only feigned to be asleep, but she said nothing to him.

He started by-and-by as if he were just then awakened, and asked who that was, and what was the matter?

"Tom, have you anything to tell me? If ever you loved

me in your life, and have anything concealed from every one besides, tell it to me."

"I don't know what you mean, Loo. You have been dreaming."

"My dear brother:" she laid her head down on his pillow, and her hair flowed over him as if she would hide him from every one but herself: "is there nothing that you have to tell me? Is there nothing you can tell me if you will? You can tell me nothing that will change me. O Tom, tell me the truth!"

"I don't know what you mean, Loo!"

"As you lie here alone, my dear, in the melancholy night, so you must lie somewhere one night, when even I, if I am living then, shall have left you. As I am here beside you, barefoot, unclothed, undistinguishable in darkness, so must I lie through all the night of my decay, until I am dust. In the name of that time, Tom, tell me the truth now!"

"What is it you want to know?"

"You may be certain;" in the energy of her love she took him to her bosom as if he were a child; "that I will not reproach you. You may be certain that I will be compassionate and true to you. You may be certain that I will save you at whatever cost. O Tom, have you nothing to tell me? Whisper very softly. Say only 'yes,' and I shall understand you!"

She turned her ear to his lips, but he remained doggedly silent.

"Not a word, Tom?"

"How can I say Yes, or how can I say No, when I don't know what you mean? Loo, you are a brave, kind girl, worthy I begin to think of a better brother than I am. But I have nothing more to say. Go to bed, go to bed."

"You are tired," she whispered presently, more in her usual way.

"Yes, I am quite tired out."

"You have been so hurried and disturbed to-day. Have any fresh discoveries been made?"

"Only those you have heard of, from—him."

"Tom, have you said to any one that we made a visit to those people, and that we saw those three together?"

"No. Didn't you yourself particularly ask me to keep it quiet when you asked me to go there with you?"

"Yes. But I did not know then what was going to happen'."

"Nor I neither. How could I?"

He was very quick upon her with this retort.

"Ought I to say, after what has happened," said his sister, standing by the bed—she had gradually withdrawn herself and risen, "that I made that visit? Should I say so? Must I say so?"

"Good Heavens, Loo," returned her brother, "you are not in the habit of asking my advice. Say what you like. If you keep it to yourself, I shall keep it to *myself*. If you disclose it, there's an end of it."

It was too dark for either to see the other's face; but each seemed very attentive, and to consider before speaking.

"Tom, do you believe the man I gave the money to, is really implicated in this crime?"

"I don't know. I don't see why he shouldn't be."

"He seemed to me an honest man."

"Another person may seem to you dishonest, and yet not be so."

There was a pause, for he had hesitated and stopped.

"In short," resumed Tom, as if he had made up his mind, "if you come to that, perhaps I was so far from being altogether in his favour, that I took him outside the door to tell him quietly, that I thought he might consider himself very well off to get such a windfall as he had got from my sister, and that I hoped he would make good use of it. You remember whether I took him out or not. I say nothing against the man; he may be a very good fellow, for anything I know; I hope he is."

"Was he offended by what you said?"

"No, he took it pretty well; he was civil enough. Where are you, Loo?" He sat up in bed and kissed her. "Good night, my dear, good night!"

"You have nothing more to tell me?"

"No. What should I have? You wouldn't have me tell you a lie!"

"I wouldn't have you do that to-night, Tom, of all the nights in your life; many and much happier as I hope they will be."

"Thank you, my dear Loo. I am so tired, that I am sure I wonder I don't say anything to get to sleep. Go to bed, go to bed."

Kissing her again, he turned round, drew the coverlet over his head, and lay as still as if that time had come by which she had adjured him. She stood for some time at the bedside before she slowly moved away. She stopped at the door, looked back when she had opened it, and asked him if he had called her? But he lay still, and she softly closed the door and returned to her room.

Then the wretched boy looked cautiously up and found her gone, crept out of bed, fastened his door, and threw himself upon his pillow again: tearing his hair, morosely crying, grudgingly loving her, hatefully but impenitently spurning himself, and no less hatefully and unprofitably spurning all the good in the world.

CHAPTER IX: *Hearing the Last of It*

MRS. SPARSIT, lying by to recover the tone of her nerves in Mr. Bounderby's retreat, kept such a sharp look-out, night and day, under her Coriolanian eyebrows, that her eyes, like a couple of lighthouses on an iron-bound coast, might have warned all prudent mariners from that bold rock her Roman nose and the dark and craggy region in its neighbourhood, but for the placidity of her manner. Although it was hard to believe that her retiring for the night could be anything but a form, so severely wide awake were those classical eyes of hers, and so impossible did it seem that her rigid nose could yield to any relaxing influence, yet her manner of sitting, smoothing her uncomfortable, not to say, gritty mittens (they were constructed of a cool fabric like a meat-safe), or of ambling to unknown places of destination with her foot in her cotton stirrup, was so perfectly serene, that most observers would have been constrained to suppose her a dove embodied by some freak of nature, in the earthly tabernacle of a bird of the hooked-beaked order.

She was a most wonderful woman for prowling about the house. How she got from story to story was a mystery beyond solution. A lady so decorous in herself, and so highly connected, was not to be suspected of dropping over the banisters or sliding down them, yet her extraordinary facility of locomotion suggested the wild idea. Another noticeable circumstance in Mrs. Sparsit was that she was never hurried. She would shoot with consummate velocity from the roof to the hall, yet would be in full possession of her breath and dignity on the moment of her arrival there. Neither was she ever seen by human vision to go at a great pace.

She took very kindly to Mr. Harthouse, and had some pleasant conversation with him soon after her arrival. She made him her stately curtsey in the garden, one morning before breakfast.

"It appears but yesterday, sir," said Mrs. Sparsit, "that I had the honour of receiving you at the Bank, when you were so good as to wish to be made acquainted with Mr. Bounderby's address."

"An occasion, I am sure, not to be forgotten by myself in the course of Ages," said Mr. Harthouse, inclining his head to Mrs. Sparsit with the most indolent of all possible airs.

"We live in a singular world, sir," said Mrs. Sparsit.

"I have had the honour, by a coincidence of which I am proud, to have made a remark, similar in effect, though not so epigrammatically expressed."

"A singular world, I would say, sir," pursued Mrs. Sparsit;

after acknowledging the compliment with a drooping of her dark eyebrows, not altogether so mild in its expression as her voice was in its dulcet tones; "as regards the intimacies we form at one time, with individuals we were quite ignorant of, at another. I recall, sir, that on that occasion you went so far as to say you were actually apprehensive of Miss Gradgrind."

"Your memory does me more honour than my insignificance deserves. I availed myself of your obliging hints to correct my timidity, and it is unnecessary to add that they were perfectly accurate. Mrs. Sparsit's talent for—in fact for anything requiring accuracy—with a combination of strength of mind—and Family—is too habitually developed to admit of any question." He was almost falling asleep over this compliment; it took him so long to get through, and his mind wandered so much in the course of its execution.

"You found Miss Gradgrind—I really cannot call her Mrs. Bounderby; it's very absurd of me—as youthful as I described her?" asked Mrs. Sparsit, sweetly.

"You drew her portrait perfectly," said Mr. Harthouse. "Presented her dead image."

"Very engaging, sir," said Mrs. Sparsit, causing her mittens slowly to revolve over one another.

"Highly so."

"It used to be considered," said Mrs. Sparsit, "that Miss Gradgrind was wanting in animation, but I confess she appears to me considerably and strikingly improved in that respect. Ay, and indeed here *is* Mr. Bounderby!" cried Mrs. Sparsit, nodding her head a great many times, as if she had been talking and thinking of no one else. "How do you find yourself this morning, sir? Pray let us see you cheerful, sir."

Now, these persistent assuagements of his misery, and lightenings of his load, had by this time begun to have the effect of making Mr. Bounderby softer than usual towards Mrs. Sparsit, and harder than usual to most other people from his wife downward. So, when Mrs. Sparsit said with forced lightness of heart, "you want your breakfast, sir, but I dare say Miss Gradgrind will soon be here to preside at the table," Mr. Bounderby replied, "If I waited to be taken care of by my wife, ma'am, I believe you know pretty well I should wait till Doomsday, so I'll trouble *you* to take charge of the teapot." Mrs. Sparsit complied, and assumed her old position at table.

This again made the excellent woman vastly sentimental. She was so humble withal, that when Louisa appeared, she rose, protesting she never could think of sitting in that place under existing circumstances, often as she had had the honour of making Mr. Bounderby's breakfast, before Mrs. Gradgrind—she begged pardon, she meant to say Miss Bounderby—she hoped to be excused, but she really could not get it right yet,

though she trusted to become familiar with it by-and-by—
had assumed her present position. It was only (she observed)
because Miss Gradgrind happened to be a little late, and
Mr. Bounderby's time was so very precious, and she knew
it of old to be so essential that he should breakfast to the
moment, that she had taken the liberty of complying with his
request; long as his will had been a law to her.

"There! Stop where you are, ma'am," said Mr. Bounderby,
"stop where you are! Mrs. Bounderby will be very glad to
be relieved of the trouble, I believe."

"Don't say that, sir," returned Mrs. Sparsit, almost with
severity, "because that is very unkind to Mrs. Bounderby.
And to be unkind is not to be you, sir."

"You may set your mind at rest, ma'am.—You can take it
very quietly, can't you, Loo?" said Mr. Bounderby, in a
blustering way to his wife.

"Of course. It is of no moment. Why should it be of
any importance to me?"

"Why should it be of any importance to any one, Mrs.
Sparsit, ma'am?" said Mr. Bounderby, swelling with a sense
of slight. "You attach too much importance to these things,
ma'am. By George, you'll be corrupted in some of your
notions here. You are old-fashioned, ma'am. You are
behind Tom Gradgrind's children's time."

"What is the matter with you?" asked Louisa, coldly
surprised. "What has given you offence?"

"Offence!" repeated Bounderby. "Do you suppose if there
was any offence given me, I shouldn't name it, and request
to have it corrected? I am a straightforward man, I believe.
I don't go beating about for side-winds."

"I suppose no one ever had occasion to think you too
diffident, or too delicate," Louisa answered him composedly:
"I have never made that objection to you, either as a child
or as a woman. I don't understand what you would have."

"Have?" returned Mr. Bounderby. "Nothing. Otherwise,
don't you, Loo Bounderby, know thoroughly well that I,
Josiah Bounderby of Coketown, would have it?"

She looked at him, as he struck the table and made the
teacups ring, with a proud colour in her face that was a new
change, Mr. Harthouse thought. "You are incomprehensible
this morning," said Louisa. "Pray take no further trouble
to explain yourself. I am not curious to know your meaning.
What does it matter?"

Nothing more was said on this theme, and Mr. Harthouse
was soon idly gay on indifferent subjects. But from this day, the
Sparsit action upon Mr. Bounderby threw Louisa and James
Harthouse more together, and strengthened the dangerous
alienation from her husband and confidence against him with
another, into which she had fallen by degrees so fine that she

could not retrace them if she tried. But whether she ever tried or no, lay hidden in her own closed heart.

Mrs. Sparsit was so much affected on this particular occasion, that, assisting Mr. Bounderby to his hat after breakfast, and being then alone with him in the hall, she imprinted a chaste kiss upon his hand, murmured "My benefactor!" and retired, overwhelmed with grief. Yet it is an indubitable fact, within the cognizance of this history, that five minutes after he had left the house in the self-same hat, the same descendant of the Scadgerses and connection by matrimony of the Powlers, shook her right-hand mitten at his portrait, made a contemptuous grimace at that work of art, and said "Serve you right, you Noodle, and I am glad of it."

Mr. Bounderby had not been long gone, when Bitzer appeared. Bitzer had come down by train, shrieking and rattling over the long line of arches that bestrode the wild country of past and present coal-pits, with an express from Stone Lodge. It was a hasty note to inform Louisa, that Mrs. Gradgrind lay very ill. She had never been well within her daughter's knowledge; but, she had declined within the last few days, had continued sinking all through the night, and was now as nearly dead, as her limited capacity of being in any state that implied the ghost of an intention to get out of it allowed.

Accompanied by the lightest of porters, fit colourless servitor at Death's door when Mrs. Gradgrind knocked, Louisa rumbled to Coketown, over the coalpits past and present, and was whirled into its smoky jaws. She dismissed the messenger to his own devices, and rode away to her old home.

She had seldom been there since her marriage. Her father was usually sifting and sifting at his parliamentary cinder-heap in London (without being observed to turn up many precious articles among the rubbish), and was still hard at it in the national dust-yard. Her mother had taken it rather as a disturbance than otherwise, to be visited, as she reclined upon her sofa; young people, Louisa felt herself all unfit for; Sissy she had never softened to again, since the night when the stroller's child had raised her eyes to look at Mr. Bounderby's intended wife. She had no inducements to go back, and had rarely gone.

Neither, as she approached her old home now, did any of the best influences of old home descend upon her. The dreams of childhood—its airy fables; its graceful, beautiful, humane, impossible adornments of the world beyond: so good to be believed in once, so good to be remembered when outgrown, for then the least among them rises to the stature of a great Charity in the heart, suffering little children to come into the midst of it, and to keep with their pure hands a garden in the stony ways of this world, wherein it were better for all the children of Adam that they should oftener sun themselves, simple and trustful, and not worldly-wise—what had she to do with these? Remembrances of how she had journeyed to the little that she knew, by the enchanted roads of what she and millions of innocent creatures had hoped and imagined; of how, first coming upon Reason through the tender light of Fancy, she had seen it a beneficent god, deferring to gods as great as itself: not a grim Idol, cruel and cold, with its victims bound hand to foot, and its big dumb shape set up with a sightless stare, never to be moved by anything but so many calculated tons of leverage—what had she to do with these? Her remembrances of home and childhood were remembrances of the drying up of every spring and fountain in her young heart as it gushed out. The golden waters were not there. They were flowing for the fertilisation of the land where grapes are gathered from thorns, and figs from thistles.

She went, with a heavy, hardened kind of sorrow upon her, into the house and into her mother's room. Since the time of her leaving home, Sissy had lived with the rest of the family on equal terms. Sissy was at her mother's side; and Jane, her sister, now ten or twelve years old, was in the room.

There was great trouble before it could be made known to Mrs. Gradgrind that her eldest child was there. She reclined, propped up, from mere habit, on a couch: as nearly in her old usual attitude, as anything so helpless could be kept in. She had positively refused to take to her bed; on the ground that if she did, she would never hear the last of it.

Her feeble voice sounded so far away in her bundle of shawls, and the sound of another voice addressing her seemed to take such a long time in getting down to her ears, that she might have been lying at the bottom of a well. The poor lady was nearer Truth than she ever had been: which had much to do with it.

On being told that Mr. Bounderby was there, she replied, at cross-purposes, that she had never called him by that name since he married Louisa; that pending her choice of an objectionable name, she had called him J; and that she could not at present depart from that regulation, not being yet provided with a permanent substitute. Louisa had sat by her for some minutes, and had spoken to her often, before she arrived at a clear understanding who it was. She then seemed to come to it all at once.

"Well, my dear," said Mrs. Gradgrind, "and I hope you are going on satisfactorily to yourself. It was all your father's doing. He set his heart upon it. And he ought to know."

"I want to hear of you, mother; not of myself."

"You want to hear of me, my dear? That's something

new, I am sure, when anybody wants to hear of me. Not at all well, Louisa. Very faint and giddy."

"Are you in pain, dear mother?"

"I think there's a pain somewhere in the room," said Mrs. Gradgrind, "but I couldn't positively say that I have got it."

After this strange speech, she lay silent for some time. Louisa, holding her hand, could feel no pulse; but kissing it, could see a slight thin thread of life in fluttering motion.

"You very seldom see your sister," said Mrs. Gradgrind. "She grows like you. I wish you would look at her. Sissy, bring her here."

She was brought, and stood with her hand in her sister's. Louisa had observed her with her arm round Sissy's neck, and she felt the difference of this approach.

"Do you see the likeness, Louisa?"

"Yes, mother. I should think her like me. But——"

"Eh! Yes, I always say so," Mrs. Gradgrind cried, with unexpected quickness. "And that reminds me. I—I want to speak to you, my dear. Sissy, my good girl, leave us alone a minute."

Louisa had relinquished the hand: had thought that her sister's was a better and brighter face than hers had ever been: had seen in it, not without a rising feeling of resentment, even in that place and at that time, something of the gentleness of the other face in the room; the sweet face with the trusting eyes, made paler than watching and sympathy made it, by the rich dark hair.

Left alone with her mother, Louisa saw her lying with an awful lull upon her face, like one who was floating away upon some great water, all resistance over, content to be carried down the stream. She put the shadow of a hand to her lips again, and recalled her.

"You were going to speak to me, mother."

"Eh? Yes, to be sure, my dear. You know your father is almost always away now, and therefore I must write to him about it."

"About what, mother? Don't be troubled. About what?"

"You must remember, my dear, that whenever I have said anything, on any subject, I have never heard the last of it: and consequently, that I have long left off saying anything."

"I can hear you, mother." But, it was only by dint of bending down to her ear, and at the same time attentively watching the lips as they moved, that she could link such faint and broken sounds into any chain of connection.

"You learnt a great deal, Louisa, and so did your brother. Ologies of all kinds from morning to night. If there is any Ology left, of any description, that has not been worn to rags in this house, all I can say is, I hope I shall never hear its name."

"I can hear you, mother, when you have strength to go on."
This, to keep her from floating away.

"But there is something—not an Ology at all—that your
father has missed, or forgotten, Louisa. I don't know what
it is. I have often sat with Sissy near me, and thought about
it. I shall never get its name now. But your father may.
It makes me restless. I want to write to him, to find out for
God's sake, what it is. Give me a pen, give me a pen."

Even the power of restlessness was gone, except from the
poor head, which could just turn from side to side.

She fancied, however, that her request had been complied
with, and that the pen she could not have held was in her hand.
It matters little what figures of wonderful no-meaning she
began to trace upon her wrappers. The hand soon stopped
in the midst of them; the light that had always been feeble
and dim behind the weak transparency, went out; and even
Mrs. Gradgrind, emerged from the shadow in which man
walketh and disquieteth himself in vain, took upon her the
dread solemnity of the sages and patriarchs.

CHAPTER X: *Mrs. Sparsit's Staircase*

MRS. SPARSIT's nerves being slow to recover their tone, the
worthy woman made a stay of some weeks in duration at Mr.
Bounderby's retreat, where, notwithstanding her anchorite
turn of mind based upon her becoming consciousness of her
altered station, she resigned herself with noble fortitude to
lodging, as one may say, in clover, and feeding on the fat of
the land. During the whole term of this recess from the
guardianship of the Bank, Mrs. Sparsit was a pattern of con-
sistency; continuing to take such pity on Mr. Bounderby to
his face, as is rarely taken on man, and to call his portrait a
Noodle to *its* face, with the greatest acrimony and contempt.

Mr. Bounderby, having got it into his explosive composition
that Mrs. Sparsit was a highly superior woman to perceive
that he had that general cross upon him in his deserts (for
he had not yet settled what it was), and further that Louisa
would have objected to her as a frequent visitor if it had
comported with his greatness that she should object to anything he chose to do, resolved not to lose sight of Mrs. Sparsit
easily. So when her nerves were strung up to the pitch of
again consuming sweetbreads in solitude, he said to her at
the dinner-table, on the day before her departure, "I tell you
what, ma'am; you shall come down here of a Saturday,
while the fine weather lasts, and stay till Monday." To
which Mrs. Sparsit returned, in effect, though not of the
Mahomedan persuasion: "To hear is to obey."

Now, Mrs. Sparsit was not a poetical woman; but she
took an idea in the nature of an allegorical fancy, into her

head. Much watching of Louisa, and much consequent observation of her impenetrable demeanour, which keenly whetted and sharpened Mrs. Sparsit's edge, must have given her as it were a lift, in the way of inspiration. She erected in her mind a mighty Staircase, with a dark pit of shame and ruin at the bottom; and down those stairs, from day to day and hour to hour, she saw Louisa coming.

It became the business of Mrs. Sparsit's life, to look up at her staircase, and to watch Louisa coming down. Sometimes slowly, sometimes quickly, sometimes several steps at one bout, sometimes stopping, never turning back. If she had once turned back, it might have been the death of Mrs. Sparsit in spleen and grief.

She had been descending steadily, to the day, and on the day, when Mr. Bounderby issued the weekly invitation recorded above. Mrs. Sparsit was in good spirits, and inclined to be conversational.

"And pray, sir," said she, "if I may venture to ask a question appertaining to any subject on which you show reserve—which is indeed hardy in me, for I well know you have a reason for everything you do—have you received intelligence respecting the robbery?"

"Why, ma'am, no; not yet. Under the circumstances, I didn't expect it yet. Rome wasn't built in a day, ma'am."

"Very true, sir," said Mrs. Sparsit, shaking her head.

"Nor yet in a week, ma'am."

"No, indeed, sir," returned Mrs. Sparsit, with a gentle melancholy upon her.

"In a similar manner, ma'am," said Bounderby, "I can wait, you know. If Romulus and Remus could wait, Josiah Bounderby can wait. They were better off in their youth than I was, however. They had a she-wolf for a nurse; I had only a she-wolf for a grandmother. She didn't give any milk, ma'am; she gave bruises. She was a regular Alderney at that."

"Ah!" Mrs. Sparsit sighed and shuddered.

"No, ma'am," continued Bounderby, "I have not heard anything more about it. It's in hand, though; and young Tom, who rather sticks to business at present—something new for him; he hadn't the schooling I had—is helping. My injunction is, Keep it quiet, and let it seem to blow over. Do what you like under the rose, but don't give a sign of what you're about; or half a hundred of 'em will combine together and get this fellow who has bolted, out of reach for good. Keep it quiet, and the thieves will grow in confidence by little and little, and we shall have 'em."

"Very sagacious indeed, sir," said Mrs. Sparsit. "Very interesting. The old woman you mentioned, sir——"

"The old woman I mentioned, ma'am," said Bounderby,

cutting the matter short, as it was nothing to boast about, "is not laid hold of; but, she may take her oath she will be, if that is any satisfaction to her villainous old mind. In the meantime, ma'am, I am of opinion, if you ask me my opinion, that the less she is talked about, the better."

That same evening, Mrs. Sparsit, in her chamber window, resting from her packing operations, looked towards her great staircase and saw Louisa still descending.

She sat by Mr. Harthouse, in an alcove in the garden, talking very low; he stood leaning over her, as they whispered together, and his face almost touched her hair. "If not quite!" said Mrs. Sparsit, straining her hawk's eyes to the utmost. Mrs. Sparsit was too distant to hear a word of their discourse, or even to know that they were speaking softly, otherwise than from the expression of their figures; but what they said was this:

"You recollect the man, Mr. Harthouse?"

"Oh, perfectly!"

"His face, and his manner, and what he said?"

"Perfectly. And an infinitely dreary person he appeared to me to be. Lengthy and prosy in the extreme. It was knowing to hold forth, in the humble-virtue school of eloquence; but, I assure you I thought at the time, 'My good fellow, you are overdoing this!'"

"It has been very difficult to me to think ill of that man."

"My dear Louisa—as Tom says." Which he never did say. "You know no good of the fellow?"

"No, certainly."

"Nor of any other such person?"

"How can I," she returned, with more of her first manner on her than he had lately seen, "when I know nothing of them, men or women?"

"My dear Louisa, then consent to receive the submissive representation of your devoted friend, who knows something of several varieties of his excellent fellow-creatures—for excellent they are, I am quite ready to believe, in spite of such little foibles as always helping themselves to what they can get hold of. This fellow talks. Well; every fellow talks. He professes morality. Well; all sorts of humbugs profess morality. From the House of Commons to the House of Correction, there is a general profession of morality, except among our people; it really is that exception which makes our people quite reviving. You saw and heard the case. Here was one of the fluffy classes pulled up extremely short by my esteemed friend Mr. Bounderby—who, as we know, is not possessed of that delicacy which would soften so tight a hand. The member of the fluffy classes was injured, exasperated, left the house grumbling, met somebody who proposed to him to go in for some share in this Bank business, went in, put something in his pocket which had nothing in it before, and relieved his mind extremely. Really he would have been an uncommon, instead of a common, fellow, if he had not availed himself of such an opportunity. Or he may have originated it altogether, if he had the cleverness."

"I almost feel as though it must be bad in me," returned Louisa, after sitting thoughtful awhile, "to be so ready to agree with you, and to be so lightened in my heart by what you say."

"I only say what is reasonable; nothing worse. I have talked it over with my friend Tom more than once—of course I remain on terms of perfect confidence with Tom—and he is quite of my opinion, and I am quite of his. Will you walk?"

They strolled away, among the lanes beginning to be indistinct in the twilight—she leaning on his arm—and she little thought how she was going down, down, down, Mrs. Sparsit's staircase.

Night and day, Mrs. Sparsit kept it standing. When Louisa had arrived at the bottom and disappeared in the gulf, it might fall in upon her if it would; but, until then, there it was to be, a Building, before Mrs. Sparsit's eyes. And there Louisa always was, upon it. And always gliding down, down, down!

Mrs. Sparsit saw James Harthouse come and go; she heard of him here and there; she saw the changes of the face he had studied; she, too, remarked to a nicety how and when it clouded, how and when it cleared; she kept her black eyes wide open, with no touch of pity, with no touch of compunction, all absorbed in interest. In the interest of seeing her, ever drawing, with no hand to stay her, nearer and nearer to the bottom of this New Giant's Staircase.

With all her deference for Mr. Bounderby as contradistinguished from his portrait, Mrs. Sparsit had not the smallest intention of interrupting the descent. Eager to see it accomplished, and yet patient, she waited for the last fall, as for the ripeness and fulness of the harvest of her hopes. Hushed in expectancy, she kept her wary gaze upon the stairs; and seldom so much as darkly shook her right mitten (with her fist in it), at the figure coming down.

CHAPTER XI : *Lower and Lower*

THE figure descended the great stairs, steadily, steadily; always verging, like a weight in deep water, to the black gulf at the bottom.

Mr. Gradgrind, apprised of his wife's decease, made an expedition from London, and buried her in a business-like manner. He then returned with promptitude to the national cinder-heap, and resumed his sifting for the odds and ends he wanted, and his throwing of the dust about into the eyes of other people who wanted other odds and ends—in fact resumed his parliamentary duties.

In the meantime, Mrs. Sparsit kept unwinking watch and ward. Separated from her staircase, all the week, by the length of iron road dividing Coketown from the country-house, she yet maintained her cat-like observation of Louisa, through her husband, through her brother, through James Harthouse, through the outsides of letters and packets, through everything animate and inanimate that at any time went near the stairs. "Your foot on the last step, my lady," said Mrs. Sparsit, apostrophising the descending figure, with the aid of her threatening mitten, "and all your art shall never blind me."

Art or nature though, the original stock of Louisa's character or the graft of circumstances upon it,—her curious reserve did baffle, while it stimulated, one as sagacious as Mrs. Sparsit. There were times when Mr. James Harthouse was not sure of her. There were times when he could not read the face he had studied so long; and when this lonely girl was a greater mystery to him, than any woman of the world with a ring of satellites to help her.

So the time went on; until it happened that Mr. Bounderby was called away from home by business which required his presence elsewhere, for three or four days. It was on a Friday that he intimated this to Mrs. Sparsit at the Bank, adding: "But you'll go down to-morrow, all the same. You'll go down just as if I was there. It will make no difference to you."

"Pray, sir," returned Mrs. Sparsit, reproachfully, "let me beg you not to say that. Your absence will make a vast difference to me, sir, as I think you very well know."

"Well, ma'am, then you must get on in my absence as well as you can," said Bounderby, not displeased.

"Mr Bounderby," retorted Mrs. Sparsit, "your will is to me a law, sir; otherwise, it might be my inclination to dispute your kind commands, not feeling sure that it will be quite so agreeable to Miss Gradgrind to receive me, as it ever is to your own munificent hospitality. But you shall say no more, sir. I will go, upon your invitation."

"Why, when I invite you to my house, ma'am," said Bounderby, opening his eyes, "I should hope you want no other invitation."

"No, indeed, sir," returned Mrs. Sparsit, "I should hope not. Say no more, sir. I would, sir, I could see you gay again."

"What do you mean, ma'am?" blustered Bounderby.

"Sir," rejoined Mrs. Sparsit, "there was wont to be an elasticity in you which I sadly miss. Be buoyant, sir!"

Mr. Bounderby, under the influence of this difficult adjuration, backed up by her compassionate eye, could only scratch his head in a feeble and ridiculous manner, and afterwards assert himself at a distance, by being heard to bully the small fry of business all the morning.

"Bitzer," said Mrs. Sparsit that afternoon, when her patron was gone on his journey, and the Bank was closing, "present my compliments to young Mr. Thomas, and ask him if he would step up and partake of a lamb chop and walnut ketchup, with a glass of India ale?" Young Mr. Thomas being usually ready for anything in that way, returned a gracious answer, and followed on its heels. "Mr. Thomas," said Mrs. Sparsit, "these plain viands being on table, I thought you might be tempted."

"Thank'ee, Mrs. Sparsit," said the whelp. And gloomily fell to.

"How is Mr. Harthouse, Mr. Tom?" asked Mrs. Sparsit.

"Oh, he's all right," said Tom.

"Where may he be at present?" Mrs. Sparsit asked in a light conversational manner, after mentally devoting the whelp to the Furies for being so uncommunicative.

"He is shooting in Yorkshire," said Tom. "Sent Loo a basket half as big as a church, yesterday."

"The kind of gentleman, now," said Mrs. Sparsit, sweetly, "whom one might wager to be a good shot!"

"Crack," said Tom.

He had long been a down-looking young fellow, but this characteristic had so increased of late, that he never raised his eyes to any face for three seconds together. Mrs. Sparsit consequently had ample means of watching his looks, if she were so inclined.

"Mr. Harthouse is a great favourite of mine," said Mrs. Sparsit, "as indeed he is of most people. May we expect to see him again shortly, Mr. Tom?"

"Why, I expect to see him to-morrow," returned the whelp.

"Good news!" cried Mrs. Sparsit, blandly.

"I have got an appointment with him to meet him in the evening at the station here," said Tom, "and I am going to dine with him afterwards, I believe. He is not coming down to the country house for a week or so, being due somewhere else. At least, he says so; but I shouldn't wonder if he was to stop here over Sunday, and stray that way."

"Which reminds me!" said Mrs. Sparsit. "Would you remember a message to your sister, Mr. Tom, if I was to charge you with one?"

"Well? I'll try," returned the reluctant whelp, "if it isn't a long un."

"It is merely my respectful compliments," said Mrs. Sparsit, "and I fear I may not trouble her with my society this week; being still a little nervous, and better perhaps by my poor self."

"Oh! If that's all," observed Tom, "it wouldn't much

matter, even if I was to forget it, for Loo's not likely to think
of you unless she sees you."

Having paid for his entertainment with this agreeable
compliment, he relapsed into a hangdog silence until there was
no more India ale left, when he said, "Well, Mrs. Sparsit, I
must be off!" and went off.

Next day, Saturday, Mrs. Sparsit sat at her window all day
long looking at the customers coming in and out, watching the
postmen, keeping an eye on the general traffic of the street,
revolving many things in her mind, but, above all, keeping her
attention on her staircase. The evening come, she put on her
bonnet and shawl, and went quietly out: having her reasons
for hovering in a furtive way about the station by which a
passenger would arrive from Yorkshire, and for preferring to
peep into its round pillars and corners, and out of ladies'
waiting-room windows, to appearing in its precincts openly.

Tom was in attendance, and loitered about until the expected train came in. It brought no Mr. Harthouse. Tom
waited until the crowd had dispersed, and the bustle was over;
and then referred to a posted list of trains, and took counsel
with porters. That done, he strolled away idly, stopping in
the street and looking up it and down it, and lifting his hat off
and putting it on again, and yawning and stretching himself,
and exhibiting all the symptoms of mortal weariness to be
expected in one who had still to wait until the next train should
come in, an hour and forty minutes hence.

"This is a device to keep him out of the way," said Mrs.
Sparsit, starting from the dull office window whence she had
watched him last. "Harthouse is with his sister now!"

It was the conception of an inspired moment, and she shot
off with her utmost swiftness to work it out. The station for
the country house was at the opposite end of the town, the
time was short, the road was not easy; but she was so quick in
pouncing on a disengaged coach, so quick in darting out of it,
producing her money, seizing her ticket, and diving into the
train, that she was borne along the arches spanning the land of
coalpits past and present, as if she had been caught up in a
cloud and whirled away.

All the journey, immovable in the air though never left
behind; plain to the dark eyes of her mind, as the electric
wires which ruled a colossal strip of music paper out of the
evening sky, were plain to the dark eyes of her body; Mrs.
Sparsit saw her staircase, with the figure coming down. Very
near the bottom now. Upon the brink of the abyss.

An overcast September evening, just at nightfall, saw
beneath its drooping eyelid Mrs. Sparsit glide out of her
carriage, pass down the wooden steps of the little station into
a stony road, cross it into a green lane, and become hidden in
a summer growth of leaves and branches. One or two late

birds sleepily chirping in their nests, and a bat heavily crossing and recrossing her, and the reek of her own tread in the thick dust that felt like velvet, were all Mrs. Sparsit heard or saw until she very softly closed a gate.

She went up to the house, keeping within the shrubbery, and went round it, peeping between the leaves at the lower windows. Most of them were open, as they usually were in such warm weather, but there were no lights yet, and all was silent. She tried the garden with no better effect. She thought of the wood, and stole towards it, heedless of long grass and briers: of worms, snails, and slugs, and all the creeping things that be. With her dark eyes and her hook nose warily in advance of her, Mrs. Sparsit softly crushed her way through the thick undergrowth, so intent upon her object that she probably would have done no less, if the wood had been a wood full of adders.

Hark!

The smaller birds might have tumbled out of their nests, fascinated by the glittering of Mrs. Sparsit's eyes in the gloom, as she stopped and listened.

Low voices close at hand. His voice and hers. The appointment *was* a device to keep the brother away! There they were yonder, by the felled tree.

Bending low among the dewy grass, Mrs. Sparsit advanced closer to them. She drew herself up and stood behind a tree, like Robinson Crusoe in his ambuscade against the savages; so near to them that at a spring, and that no great one, she could have touched them both. He was there secretly, and had not shown himself at the house. He had come on horseback, and must have passed through the neighbouring fields; for his horse was tied to the meadow side of the fence, within a few paces.

"My dearest love," said he, "what could I do? Knowing you were alone, was it possible that I could stay away?"

"You may hang your head to make yourself the more attractive; *I* don't know what they see in you when you hold it up," thought Mrs. Sparsit; "but you little think, my dearest love, whose eyes are on you!"

That she hung her head, was certain. She urged him to go away, she commanded him to go away; but she neither turned her face to him, nor raised it. Yet it was remarkable that she sat as still as ever the amiable woman in ambuscade had seen her sit, at any period in her life. Her hands rested in one another like the hands of a statue; and even her manner of speaking was not hurried.

"My dear child," said Harthouse; Mrs. Sparsit saw with delight that his arm embraced her; "will you not bear with my society for a little while?"

"Not here."

"Where, Louisa?"

"Not here."

"But we have so little time to make so much of, and I have come so far, and am altogether so devoted, and distracted. There never was a slave at once so devoted and ill-used by his mistress. To look for your sunny welcome that has warmed me into life, and to be received in your frozen manner, is heart-rending."

"Am I to say again, that I must be left to myself here?"

"But we must meet, my dear Louisa. Where shall we meet?"

They both started. The listener started, guiltily, too; for she thought there was another listener among the trees. It was only rain, beginning to fall fast, in heavy drops.

"Shall I ride up to the house a few minutes hence, innocently supposing that its master is at home and will be charmed to receive me?"

"No!"

"Your cruel commands are implicitly to be obeyed; though I am the most unfortunate fellow in the world, I believe, to have been insensible to all other women, and to have fallen prostrate at last under the foot of the most beautiful, and the most engaging, and the most imperious. My dearest Louisa, I cannot go myself, or let you go, in this hard abuse of your power."

Mrs. Sparsit saw him detain her with his encircling arm, and heard him then and there, within her (Mrs. Sparsit's) greedy hearing, tell her how he loved her, and how she was the stake for which he ardently desired to play away all that he had in life. The objects he had lately pursued, turned worthless beside her; such success as was almost in his grasp, he flung away from him like the dirt it was, compared with her. Its pursuit, nevertheless, if it kept him near her, or its renunciation if it took him from her, or flight if she shared it, or secrecy if she commanded it, or any fate, or every fate, all were alike to him, so that she was true to him,—the man who had seen how cast away she was, whom she inspired at their first meeting with an admiration, an interest, of which he had thought himself incapable, whom she had received into her confidence, who was devoted to her and adored her. All this, and more, in his hurry, and in hers, in the whirl of her own gratified malice, in the dread of being discovered, in the rapidly increasing noise of heavy rain among the leaves, and a thunderstorm rolling up—Mrs. Sparsit received into her mind, set off with such an unavoidable halo of confusion and indistinctness, that when at length he climbed the fence and led his horse away, she was not sure where they were to meet, or when, except that they had said it was to be that night.

But one of them yet remained in the darkness before her;

and while she tracked that one she must be right. "Oh, my dearest love," thought Mrs. Sparsit, "you little think how well attended you are!"

Mrs. Sparsit saw her out of the wood, and saw her enter the house. What to do next? It rained now, in a sheet of water. Mrs. Sparsit's white stockings were of many colours, green predominating; prickly things were in her shoes; caterpillars slung themselves, in hammocks of their own making, from various parts of her dress; rills ran from her bonnet, and her Roman nose. In such condition, Mrs. Sparsit stood hidden in the density of the shrubbery, considering what next?

Lo, Louisa coming out of the house! Hastily cloaked and muffled, and stealing away. She elopes! She falls from the lowermost stair, and is swallowed up in the gulf.

Indifferent to the rain, and moving with a quick determined step, she struck into a side-path parallel with the ride. Mrs. Sparsit followed in the shadow of the trees, at but a short distance, for it was not easy to keep a figure in view going quickly through the umbrageous darkness.

When she stopped to close the side-gate without noise, Mrs. Sparsit stopped. When she went on, Mrs. Sparsit went on. She went by the way Mrs. Sparsit had come, emerged from the green lane, crossed the stony road, and ascended the wooden steps to the railroad. A train for Coketown would come through presently, Mrs. Sparsit knew; so she understood Coketown to be her first place of destination.

In Mrs. Sparsit's limp and streaming state, no extensive precautions were necessary to change her usual appearance; but, she stopped under the lee of the station wall, tumbled her shawl into a new shape, and put it on over her bonnet. So disguised she had no fear of being recognised when she followed up the railroad steps, and paid her money in the small office. Louisa sat waiting in a corner. Mrs. Sparsit sat waiting in another corner. Both listened to the thunder, which was loud, and to the rain, as it washed off the roof, and pattered on the parapets of the arches. Two or three lamps were rained out and blown out; so both saw the lightning to advantage as it quivered and zigzagged on the iron tracks.

The seizure of the station with a fit of trembling, gradually deepening to a complaint of the heart, announced the train. Fire and steam, and smoke, and red light; a hiss, a crash, a bell and a shriek; Louisa put into one carriage, Mrs. Sparsit put into another: the little station a desert in the thunderstorm.

Though her teeth chattered in her head from wet and cold, Mrs. Sparsit exulted hugely. The figure had plunged down the precipice, and she felt herself, as it were, attending on the body. Could she, who had been so active in the getting up of the funeral triumph, do less than exult? "She will be at

Coketown long before him," thought Mrs. Sparsit, "though his horse is never so good. Where will she wait for him? And where will they go together? Patience. We shall see."

The tremendous rain occasioned infinite confusion, when the train stopped at its destination. Gutters and pipes had burst, drains had overflowed, and streets were under water. In the first instant of alighting, Mrs. Sparsit turned her distracted eyes towards the waiting coaches, which were in great request. "She will get into one," she considered, "and be away before I can follow in another. At all risks of being run over, I must see the number, and hear the order given to the coachman."

But Mrs. Sparsit was wrong in her calculation. Louisa got into no coach, and was already gone. The black eyes kept upon the railroad carriage in which she had travelled, settled upon it a moment too late. The door not being opened after several minutes, Mrs. Sparsit passed it and repassed it, saw nothing, looked in, and found it empty. Wet through and through: with her feet squelching in her shoes whenever she moved; with a rash of rain upon her classical visage; with a bonnet like an over-ripe fig; with all her clothes spoiled; with damp impressions of every button, string, and hook-and-eye she wore, printed off upon her highly connected back; with a stagnant verdure on her general exterior, such as accumulates on an old park fence in a mouldy lane; Mrs. Sparsit had no resource but to burst into tears of bitterness and say, "I have lost her!"

CHAPTER XII: *Down*

THE national dustmen, after entertaining one another with a great many noisy little fights among themselves, had dispersed for the present, and Mr. Gradgrind was at home for the vacation.

He sat writing in the room, with the deadly statistical clock, proving something no doubt—probably, in the main, that the Good Samaritan was a Bad Economist. The noise of the rain did not disturb him much; but it attracted his attention sufficiently to make him raise his head sometimes, as if he were rather remonstrating with the elements. When it thundered very loudly, he glanced towards Coketown, having it in his mind that some of the tall chimneys might be struck by lightning.

The thunder was rolling into distance, and the rain was pouring down like a deluge, when the door of his room opened. He looked round the lamp upon his table, and saw with amazement, his eldest daughter.

"Louisa!"

"Father, I want to speak to you."

"What is the matter? How strange you look! And good

Heaven," said Mr. Gradgrind, wondering more and more, "have you come here exposed to this storm?"

She put her hands to her dress, as if she hardly knew. "Yes." Then she uncovered her head, and letting her cloak and hood fall where they might, stood looking at him: so colourless, so dishevelled, so defiant and despairing, that he was afraid of her.

"What is it? I conjure you, Louisa, tell me what is the matter."

She dropped into a chair before him, and put her cold hand on his arm.

"Father, you have trained me from my cradle?"

"Yes, Louisa."

"I curse the hour in which I was born to such a destiny."

He looked at her in doubt and dread, vacantly repeating: "Curse the hour? Curse the hour?"

"How could you give me life, and take from me all the inappreciable things that raise it from the state of conscious death? Where are the graces of my soul? Where are the sentiments of my heart? What have you done, O father, what have you done, with the garden that should have bloomed once, in this great wilderness here!"

She struck herself with both her hands upon her bosom.

"If it had ever been here, its ashes alone would save me from the void in which my whole life sinks. I did not mean to say this; but, father, you remember the last time we conversed in this room?"

He had been so wholly unprepared for what he heard now, that it was with difficulty he answered "Yes, Louisa."

"What has risen to my lips now, would have risen to my lips then, if you had given me a moment's help. I don't reproach you, father. What you have never nurtured in me, you have never nurtured in yourself; but O! if you had only done so long ago, or if you had only neglected me, what a much better and much happier creature I should have been this day!"

On hearing this, after all his care, he bowed his head upon his hand and groaned aloud.

"Father, if you had known, when we were last together here, what even I feared while I strove against it—as it has been my task from infancy to strive against every natural prompting that has arisen in my heart; if you had known that there lingered in my breast, sensibilities, affections, weaknesses capable of being cherished into strength, defying all the calculations ever made by man, and no more known to his arithmetic than his Creator is,—would you have given me to the husband whom I am now sure that I hate?"

He said, "No. No, my poor child."

"Would you have doomed me, at any time, to the frost and blight that have hardened and spoiled me? Would you have

robbed me—for no one's enrichment—only for the greater
desolation of this world—of the immaterial part of my life,
the spring and summer of my belief, my refuge from
what is sordid and bad in the real things around me, my
school in which I should have learned to be more humble and
more trusting with them, and to hope in my little sphere to
make them better?"

"O no, no. No, Louisa."

"Yet, father, if I had been stone blind; if I had groped my
way by my sense of touch, and had been free, while I knew
the shapes and surfaces of things, to exercise my fancy
somewhat, in regard to them; I should have been a million
times wiser, happier, more loving, more contented, more
innocent and human in all good respects, than I am with the
eyes I have. Now, hear what I have come to say."

He moved, to support her with his arm. She rising as he
did so, they stood close together: she, with a hand upon his
shoulder, looking fixedly in his face.

"With a hunger and thirst upon me, father, which have
never been for a moment appeased; with an ardent impulse
towards some region where rules, and figures, and definitions
were not quite absolute; I have grown up, battling every inch
of my way."

"I never knew you were unhappy, my child."

"Father, I always knew it. In this strife I have almost
repulsed and crushed my better angel into a demon. What
I have learned has left me doubting, misbelieving, despising,
regretting, what I have not learned; and my dismal resource
has been to think that life would soon go by, and that nothing
in it could be worth the pain and trouble of a contest."

"And you so young, Louisa!" he said with pity.

"And I so young. In this condition, father—for I show
you now, without fear or favour, the ordinary deadened state
of my mind as I know it—you proposed my husband to me.
I took him. I never made a pretence to him or you that I
loved him. I knew, and, father, you knew, and he knew,
that I never did. I was not wholly indifferent, for I had a
hope of being pleasant and useful to Tom. I made that wild
escape into something visionary, and have slowly found out
how wild it was. But Tom had been the subject of all the
little tenderness of my life; perhaps he became so because I
knew so well how to pity him. It matters little now, except
as it may dispose you to think more leniently of his errors."

As her father held her in his arms, she put her other hand
upon his other shoulder, and still looking fixedly in his face,
went on.

"When I was irrevocably married, there rose up into
rebellion against the tie, the old strife, made fiercer by all
those causes of disparity which arise out of our two individual

natures, and which no general laws shall ever rule or state for me, father, until they shall be able to direct the anatomist where to strike his knife into the secrets of my soul."

"Louisa!" he said, and said imploringly; for he well remembered what had passed between them in their former interview.

"I do not reproach you, father, I make no complaint. I am here with another object."

"What can I do, child? Ask me what you will."

"I am coming to it. Father, chance then threw into my way a new acquaintance; a man such as I had had no experience of; used to the world; light, polished, easy; making no pretences; avowing the low estimate of everything, that I was half afraid to form in secret; conveying to me almost immediately, though I don't know how or by what degrees, that he understood me, and read my thoughts. I could not find that he was worse than I. There seemed to be a near affinity between us. I only wondered it should be worth his while, who cared for nothing else, to care so much for me."

"For you, Louisa!"

Her father might instinctively have loosened his hold, but that he felt her strength departing from her, and saw a wild dilating fire in the eyes steadfastly regarding him.

"I say nothing of his plea for claiming my confidence. It matters very little how he gained it. Father, he did gain it. What you know of the story of my marriage, he soon knew, just as well."

Her father's face was ashy white, and he held her in both his arms.

"I have done no worse, I have not disgraced you. But if you ask me whether I have loved him, or do love him, I tell you plainly, father, that it may be so. I don't know."

She took her hands suddenly from his shoulders, and pressed them both upon her side; while in her face, not like itself—and in her figure, drawn up, resolute to finish by a last effort what she had to say—the feelings long suppressed broke loose.

"This night, my husband being away, he has been with me, declaring himself my lover. This minute he expects me, for I could release myself of his presence by no other means. I do not know that I am sorry, I do not know that I am ashamed, I do not know that I am degraded in my own esteem. All that I know is, your philosophy and your teaching will not save me. Now, father, you have brought me to this. Save me by some other means!"

He tightened his hold in time to prevent her sinking on the floor, but she cried out in a terrible voice, "I shall die if you hold me! Let me fall upon the ground!" And he laid her down there, and saw the pride of his heart and the triumph of his system, lying, an insensible heap, at his feet.

[END OF THE SECOND BOOK

BOOK THE THIRD: GARNERING

CHAPTER I: *Another Thing Needful*

LOUISA awoke from a torpor, and her eyes languidly opened on her old bed at home, and her old room. It seemed, at first, as if all that had happened since the days when these objects were familiar to her were the shadows of a dream; but gradually, as the objects became more real to her sight, the events became more real to her mind.

She could scarcely move her head for pain and heaviness, her eyes were strained and sore, and she was very weak. A curious passive inattention had such possession of her, that the presence of her little sister in the room did not attract her notice for some time. Even when their eyes had met, and her sister had approached the bed, Louisa lay for minutes looking at her in silence, and suffering her timidly to hold her passive hand, before she asked:

"When was I brought to this room?"

"Last night, Louisa."

"Who brought me here?"

"Sissy, I believe."

"Why do you believe so?"

"Because I found her here this morning. She didn't come to my bedside to wake me, as she always does; and I went to look for her. She was not in her own room either; and I went looking for her all over the house, until I found her here taking care of you and cooling your head. Will you see father? Sissy said I was to tell him when you woke."

"What a beaming face you have, Jane!" said Louisa, as her young sister—timidly still—bent down to kiss her.

"Have I? I am very glad you think so. I am sure it must be Sissy's doing."

The arm Louisa had begun to twine about her neck, unbent itself. "You can tell father if you will." Then, staying her a moment, she said, "It was you who made my room so cheerful, and gave it this look of welcome?"

"Oh no, Louisa, it was done before I came. It was——"

Louisa turned upon her pillow, and heard no more. When her sister had withdrawn, she turned her head back again, and lay with her face towards the door, until it opened and her father entered.

He had a jaded anxious look upon him, and his hand, usually

steady, trembled in hers.   He sat down at the side of the bed, tenderly asking how she was, and dwelling on the necessity of her keeping very quiet after her agitation and exposure to the weather last night.   He spoke in a subdued and troubled voice, very different from his usual dictatorial manner; and was often at a loss for words.

"My dear Louisa. My poor daughter." He was so much at a loss at that place, that he stopped altogether. He tried again.

"My unfortunate child." The place was so difficult to get over, that he tried again.

"It would be hopeless for me, Louisa, to endeavour to tell you how overwhelmed I have been, and still am, by what broke upon me last night. The ground on which I stand has ceased to be solid under my feet. The only support on which I leaned, and the strength of which it seemed and still does seem, impossible to question, has given way in an instant. I am stunned by these discoveries. I have no selfish meaning in what I say; but I find the shock of what broke upon me last night, to be very heavy indeed."

She could give him no comfort herein. She had suffered the wreck of her whole life upon the rock.

"I will not say, Louisa, that if you had by any happy chance undeceived me some time ago, it would have been better for us both; better for your peace, and better for mine. For I am sensible that it may not have been a part of my system to invite any confidence of that kind. I have proved my—my system to myself, and I have rigidly administered it; and I must bear the responsibility of its failures. I only entreat you to believe, my favourite child, that I have meant to do right."

He said it earnestly, and to do him justice he had. In gauging fathomless deeps with his little mean excise-rod, and in staggering over the universe with his rusty stiff-legged compasses, he had meant to do great things. Within the limits of his short tether he had tumbled about, annihilating the flowers of existence with greater singleness of purpose than many of the blatant personages whose company he kept.

"I am well assured of what you say, father. I know I have been your favourite child. I know you have intended to make me happy. I have never blamed you, and I never shall."

He took her outstretched hand, and retained it in his.

"My dear, I have remained all night at my table, pondering again and again on what has so painfully passed between us. When I consider your character; when I consider that what has been known to me for hours, has been concealed by you for years; when I consider under what immediate pressure it has been forced from you at last; I come to the conclusion that I cannot but mistrust myself."

He might have added more than all, when he saw the face now looking at him. He did add it in effect, perhaps, as he

softly moved her scattered hair from her forehead with his
hand. Such little actions, slight in another man, were very
noticeable in him; and his daughter received them as if they
had been words of contrition.

"But," said Mr. Gradgrind, slowly, and with hesitation, as
well as with a wretched sense of helplessness, "if I see reason
to mistrust myself for the past, Louisa, I should also mistrust
myself for the present and the future. To speak unreservedly
to you, I do. I am far from feeling convinced now, however
differently I might have felt only this time yesterday, that I am
fit for the trust you repose in me; that I know how to respond
to the appeal you have come home to make to me; that I have
the right instinct—supposing it for the moment to be some
quality of that nature—how to help you, and to set you right,
my child."

She had turned upon her pillow, and lay with her face upon
her arm, so that he could not see it. All her wildness and
passion had subsided; but, though softened, she was not in
tears. Her father was changed in nothing so much as in the
respect that he would have been glad to see her in tears.

"Some persons hold," he pursued, still hesitating, "that
there is a wisdom of the Head, and that there is a wisdom of
the Heart. I have not supposed so; but, as I have said, I
mistrust myself now. I have supposed the head to be all-
sufficient; how can I venture this morning to say it is! If that
other kind of wisdom should be what I have neglected, and
should be the instinct that is wanted, Louisa——"

He suggested it very doubtfully, as if he were half unwilling
to admit it even now. She made him no answer, lying before
him on the bed, still half dressed, much as he had seen her
lying on the floor of his room last night.

"Louisa," and his hand rested on her hair again, "I have
been absent from here, my dear, a good deal of late; and though
your sister's training has been pursued according to—the
system," he appeared to come to that word with great reluctance always, "it has necessarily been modified by daily
associations begun, in her case, at an early age. I ask you—
ignorantly and humbly, my daughter—for the better, do you
think?"

"Father," she replied, without stirring, "if any harmony has
been awakened in her young breast that was mute in mine
until it turned to discord, let her thank Heaven for it, and go
upon her happier way, taking it as her greatest blessing that
she has avoided my way."

"O my child, my child!" he said, in a forlorn manner, "I
am an unhappy man to see you thus! What avails it to me
that you do not reproach me, if I so bitterly reproach myself!"
He bent his head, and spoke low to her. "Louisa, I have a
misgiving that some change may have been slowly working

about me in this house, by mere love and gratitude: that what the Head had left undone and could not do, the Heart may have been doing silently. Can it be so?"

She made him no reply.

"I am not too proud to believe it, Louisa. How could I be arrogant, and you before me! Can it be so? Is it so, my dear?"

He looked upon her once more, lying cast away there; and without another word went out of the room. He had not been long gone, when she heard a light tread near the door, and knew that some one stood beside her.

She did not raise her head. A dull anger that she should be seen in her distress, and that the involuntary look she had so resented should come to this fulfilment, smouldered within her like an unwholesome fire. All closely imprisoned forces rend and destroy. The air that would be healthful to the earth, the water that would enrich it, the heat that would ripen it, tear it when caged up. So in her bosom even now; the strongest qualities she possessed, long turned upon themselves, became a heap of obduracy, that rose against a friend.

It was well that soft touch came upon her neck, and that she understood herself to be supposed to have fallen asleep. The sympathetic hand did not claim her resentment. Let it lie there, let it lie.

It lay there, warming into life a crowd of gentler thoughts; and she rested. As she softened with the quiet, and the consciousness of being so watched, some tears made their way into her eyes. The face touched hers, and she knew that there were tears upon it too, and she the cause of them.

As Louisa feigned to rouse herself, and sat up, Sissy retired, so that she stood placidly near the bedside.

"I hope I have not disturbed you. I have come to ask if you would let me stay with you?"

"Why should you stay with me? My sister will miss you. You are everything to her."

"Am I?" returned Sissy, shaking her head. "I would be something to you, if I might."

"What?" said Louisa, almost sternly.

"Whatever you want most, if I could be that. At all events, I would like to try to be as near it as I can. And however far off that may be, I will never tire of trying. Will you let me?"

"My father sent you to ask me."

"No indeed," replied Sissy. "He told me that I might come in now, but he sent me away from the room this morning —or at least—" She hesitated and stopped.

"At least, what?" said Louisa, with her searching eyes upon her.

"I thought it best myself that I should be sent away, for I felt very uncertain whether you would like to find me here."

"Have I always hated you so much?"

"I hope not, for I have always loved you, and have always wished that you should know it. But you changed to me a little, shortly before you left home. Not that I wondered at it. You knew so much, and I knew so little, and it was so natural in many ways, going as you were among other friends, that I had nothing to complain of, and was not at all hurt."

Her colour rose as she said it modestly and hurriedly. Louisa understood the loving pretence, and her heart smote her.

"May I try?" said Sissy, emboldened to raise her hand to the neck that was insensibly drooping towards her.

Louisa, taking down the hand that would have embraced her in another moment, held it in one of hers, and answered:

"First, Sissy, do you know what I am? I am so proud and so hardened, so confused and troubled, so resentful and unjust to every one and to myself, that everything is stormy, dark, and wicked to me. Does not that repel you?"

"No!"

"I am so unhappy, and all that should have made me otherwise is so laid waste, that if I had been bereft of sense to this hour, and instead of being as learned as you think me, had to begin to acquire the simplest truths, I could not want a guide to peace, contentment, honour, all the good of which I am quite devoid, more abjectly than I do. Does not that repel you?"

"No!"

In the innocence of her brave affection, and brimming up of her old devoted spirit, the once deserted girl shone like a beautiful light upon the darkness of the other.

Louisa raised the hand that it might clasp her neck and join its fellow there. She fell upon her knees, and clinging to this stroller's child looked up at her almost with veneration.

"Forgive me, pity me, help me! Have compassion on my great need, and let me lay this head of mine upon a loving heart?"

"O lay it here!" cried Sissy. "Lay it here, my dear."

CHAPTER II : *Very Ridiculous*

MR. JAMES HARTHOUSE passed a whole night and a day in a state of so much hurry, that the World, with its best glass in its eye, would scarcely have recognised him during that insane interval, as the brother Jem of the honourable and jocular member. He was positively agitated. He several times spoke with an emphasis, similar to the vulgar manner. He went in and went out in an unaccountable way, like a man without an object. He rode like a highwayman. In a word, he was so horribly bored by existing circumstances, that he forgot to go in for boredom in the manner prescribed by the authorities.

After putting his horse at Coketown through the storm, as if it were a leap, he waited up all night: from time to time ringing his bell with the greatest fury, charging the porter who kept watch with delinquency in withholding letters or messages that could not fail to have been entrusted to him, and demanding restitution on the spot. The dawn coming, the morning coming, and the day coming, and neither message nor letter coming with either, he went down to the country-house. There, the report was, Mr. Bounderby away, and Mrs. Bounderby in town. Left for town suddenly last evening. Not even known to be gone until receipt of message, importing that her return was not to be expected for the present.

In these circumstances he had nothing to do but to follow her to town. He went to the house in town. Mrs. Bounderby was not there. He looked in at the Bank. Mr. Bounderby away and Mrs. Sparsit away. Mrs. Sparsit away? Who could have been reduced to sudden extremity for the company of that griffin!

"Well! I don't know," said Tom, who had his own reasons for being uneasy about it. "She was off somewhere at day-break this morning. She's always full of mystery; I hate her. So I do that white chap; he's always got his blinking eyes upon a fellow."

"Where were you last night, Tom?"

"Where was I last night!" said Tom. "Come! I like that. I was waiting for you, Mr. Harthouse, till it came down as I never saw it come down before. Where was I too! Where were you, you mean."

"I was prevented from coming—detained."

"Detained!" murmured Tom. "Two of us were detained. I was detained looking for you, till I lost every train but the mail. It would have been a pleasant job to go down by that on such a night, and have to walk home through a pond. I was obliged to sleep in town after all."

"Where?"

"Where? Why in my own bed at Bounderby's."

"Did you see your sister?"

"How the deuce," returned Tom, staring, "could I see my sister when she was fifteen miles off?"

Cursing these quick retorts of the young gentleman to whom he was so true a friend, Mr. Harthouse disembarrassed himself of that interview with the smallest conceivable amount of ceremony, and debated for the hundredth time what all this could mean? He made only one thing clear. It was, that whether she was in the town or out of town, whether he had been premature with her who was so hard to comprehend, or she had lost courage, or they were discovered, or some mischance or mistake, at present incomprehensible, had occurred, he must remain to confront his fortune, whatever it was. The hotel where he was known to live when condemned to that region of blackness, was the stake to which he was tied. As to all the rest—What will be, will be.

"So, whether I am waiting for a hostile message, or an assignation, or a penitent remonstrance, or an impromptu wrestle with my friend Bounderby in the Lancashire manner—which would seem as likely as anything else in the present state of affairs—I'll dine," said Mr. James Harthouse. "Bounderby has the advantage in point of weight; and if anything of a British nature is to come off between us, it may be as well to be in training."

Therefore he rang the bell, and tossing himself negligently on a sofa, ordered "Some dinner at six—with a beefsteak in it," and got through the intervening time as well as he could. That was not particularly well; for he remained in the greatest perplexity, and, as the hours went on, and no kind of explanation offered itself, his perplexity augmented at compound interest.

However, he took affairs as coolly as it was in human nature to do, and entertained himself with the facetious idea of training more than once. "It wouldn't be bad," he yawned at one time, "to give the waiter five shillings, and throw him." At another time it occurred to him, "Or a fellow of about thirteen or fourteen stone might be hired by the hour." But these jests did not tell materially on the afternoon, or his suspense; and, sooth to say, they both lagged fearfully.

It was impossible, even before dinner, to avoid often walking about in the pattern of the carpet, looking out of the window, listening at the door for footsteps, and occasionally becoming rather hot when any steps approached that room. But, after dinner, when the day turned to twilight, and the twilight turned to night, and still no communication was made to him, it began to be, as he expressed it, "like the Holy Office and slow torture." However, still true to his conviction that indifference was the genuine high-breeding (the only conviction he had), he seized this crisis as the opportunity for ordering candles and a newspaper.

He had been trying in vain, for half an hour, to read this newspaper, when the waiter appeared and said, at once mysteriously and apologetically:

"Beg your pardon, sir. You are wanted, sir, if you please."

A general recollection that this was the kind of thing the Police said to the swell mob, caused Mr. Harthouse to ask the waiter in return, with bristling indignation, what the Devil he meant by "wanted"?

"Beg your pardon, sir. Young lady outside, sir, wishes to see you."

"Outside? Where?"

"Outside this door, sir."

Giving the waiter to the personage before mentioned, as a blockhead duly qualified for that consignment, Mr. Harthouse hurried into the gallery. A young woman whom he had never seen stood there. Plainly dressed, very quiet, very pretty. As he conducted her into the room and placed a chair for her, he observed, by the light of the candles, that she was even prettier than he had at first believed. Her face was innocent and youthful, and its expression remarkably pleasant. She was not afraid of him, or in any way disconcerted; she seemed to have her mind entirely preoccupied with the occasion of her visit, and to have substituted that consideration for herself.

"I speak to Mr. Harthouse?" she said, when they were alone.

"To Mr. Harthouse." He added in his mind, "And you speak to him with the most confiding eyes I ever saw, and the most earnest voice (though so quiet) I ever heard."

"If I do not understand—and I do not, sir"—said Sissy, "what your honour as a gentleman binds you to, in other matters:" the blood really rose in his face as she began in these words: "I am sure I may rely upon it to keep my visit secret, and to keep secret what I am going to say. I will rely upon it, if you will tell me I may so far trust——"

"You may, I assure you."

"I am young, as you see; I am alone, as you see. In coming to you, sir, I have no advice or encouragement beyond my own hope."

He thought "But that is very strong," as he followed the momentary upward glance of her eyes. He thought besides, "This is a very odd beginning. I don't see where we are going."

"I think," said Sissy, "you have already guessed whom I left just now!"

"I have been in the greatest concern and uneasiness during the last four-and-twenty hours (which have appeared as many years)," he returned, "on a lady's account. The hopes I have been encouraged to form that you come from that lady, do not deceive me, I trust."

"I left her within an hour."

"At——!"

"At her father's."

Mr. Harthouse's face lengthened in spite of his coolness, and his perplexity increased. "Then I certainly," he thought, "do *not* see where we are going."

"She hurried there last night. She arrived there in great agitation, and was insensible all through the night. I live at her father's, and was with her. You may be sure, sir, you will never see her again as long as you live."

Mr. Harthouse drew a long breath; and, if ever man found

himself in the position of not knowing what to say, made the discovery beyond all question that he was so circumstanced. The childlike ingenuousness with which his visitor spoke, her modest fearlessness, her truthfulness which put all artifice aside, her entire forgetfulness of herself in her earnest quiet holding to the object with which she had come; all this, together with her reliance on his easily given promise—which in itself shamed him—presented something in which he was so inexperienced, and against which he knew any of his usual weapons would fall so powerless, that not a word could he rally to his relief.

At last he said:

"So startling an announcement, so confidently made, and by such lips, is really disconcerting in the last degree. May I be permitted to inquire, if you are charged to convey that information to me in those hopeless words, by the lady of whom we speak?"

"I have no charge from her."

"The drowning man catches at the straw. With no disrespect for your judgment, and with no doubt of your sincerity, excuse my saying that I cling to the belief that there is yet hope that I am not condemned to perpetual exile from that lady's presence."

"There is not the least hope. The first object of my coming here, sir, is to assure you that you must believe that there is no more hope of your ever speaking with her again, than there would be if she had died when she came home last night."

"Must believe? But if I can't—or if I should, by infirmity of nature, be obstinate—and won't——"

"It is still true. There is no hope."

James Harthouse looked at her with an incredulous smile upon his lips; but her mind looked over and beyond him, and the smile was quite thrown away.

He bit his lip, and took a little time for consideration.

"Well! If it should unhappily appear," he said, "after due pains and duty on my part, that I am brought to a position so desolate as this banishment, I shall not become the lady's persecutor. But you said you had no commission from her?"

"I have only the commission of my love for her, and her love for me. I have no other trust, than that I have been with her since she came home, and that she has given me her confidence. I have no further trust, than that I know something of her character and her marriage. Oh, Mr. Harthouse, I think you had that trust too!"

He was touched in the cavity where his heart should have been—in that nest of addled eggs, where the birds of heaven would have lived if they had not been whistled away—by the fervour of this reproach.

"I am not a moral sort of fellow," he said, "and I never make any pretensions to the character of a moral sort of fellow. I am as immoral as need be. At the same time, in bringing any distress upon the lady who is the subject of the present conversation, or in unfortunately compromising her in any way, or in committing myself by any expression of sentiments towards her, not perfectly reconcilable with—in fact with—the domestic hearth; or in taking any advantage of her father's being a machine, or of her brother's being a whelp, or of her husband's being a bear; I beg to be allowed to assure you that I have had no particularly evil intentions, but have glided on from one step to another with a smoothness so perfectly diabolical, that I had not the slightest idea the catalogue was half so long until I began to turn it over. Whereas I find," said Mr. James Harthouse, in conclusion, "that it is really in several volumes."

Though he said all this in his frivolous way, the way seemed, for that once, a conscious polishing of but an ugly surface. He was silent for a moment; and then proceeded with a more self-possessed air, though with traces of vexation and disappointment that would not be polished out.

"After what has been just now represented to me, in a manner I find it impossible to doubt—I know of hardly any other source from which I could have accepted it so readily—I feel bound to say to you, in whom the confidence you have mentioned has been reposed, that I cannot refuse to contemplate the possibility (however unexpected) of my seeing the lady no more. I am solely to blame for the thing having come to this—and—and, I cannot say," he added, rather hard up for a general peroration, "that I have any sanguine expectation of ever becoming a moral sort of fellow, or that I have any belief in any moral sort of fellow whatever."

Sissy's face sufficiently showed that her appeal to him was not finished.

"You spoke," he resumed, as she raised her eyes to him again, "of your first object. I may assume that there is a second to be mentioned?"

"Yes."

"Will you oblige me by confiding it?"

"Mr. Harthouse," returned Sissy, with a blending of gentleness and steadiness that quite defeated him, and with a simple confidence in his being bound to do what she required, that held him at a singular disadvantage, "the only reparation that remains with you, is to leave here immediately and finally. I am quite sure that you can mitigate in no other way the wrong and harm you have done. I am quite sure that it is the only compensation you have left it in your power to make. I do not say that it is much, or that it is enough; but it is something, and it is necessary. Therefore, though without any other author-

ity than I have given you, and even without the knowledge of
any other person than yourself and myself, I ask you to depart
from this place to-night, under an obligation never to return
to it."

If she had asserted any influence over him beyond her plain
faith in the truth and right of what she said; if she had concealed the least doubt or irresolution, or had harboured for the
best purpose any reserve or pretence; if she had shown, or felt,
the lightest trace of any sensitiveness to his ridicule or his astonishment, or any remonstrance he might offer; he would have
carried it against her at this point. But he could as easily
have changed a clear sky by looking at it in surprise, as affect
her.

"But do you know," he asked, quite at a loss, "the extent
of what you ask? You probably are not aware that I am here
on a public kind of business, preposterous enough in itself, but
which I have gone in for, and sworn by, and am supposed to be
devoted to in quite a desperate manner? You probably are
not aware of that, but I assure you it's the fact."

It had no effect on Sissy, fact or no fact.

"Besides which," said Mr. Harthouse, taking a turn or two
across the room, dubiously, "it's so alarmingly absurd. It
would make a man so ridiculous, after going in for these fellows,
to back out in such an incomprehensible way."

"I am quite sure," repeated Sissy, "that it is the only
reparation in your power, sir. I am quite sure, or I would not
have come here."

He glanced at her face, and walked about again. "Upon my
soul, I don't know what to say. So immensely absurd!"

It fell to his lot, now, to stipulate for secrecy.

"If I were to do such a very ridiculous thing," he said,
stopping again presently, and leaning against the chimney-
piece, "it could only be in the most inviolable confidence."

"I will trust to you, sir," returned Sissy, "and you will
trust to me."

His leaning against the chimney-piece reminded him of the
night with the whelp. It was the self-same chimney-piece,
and somehow he felt as if *he* were the whelp to-night. He
could make no way at all.

"I suppose a man never was placed in a more ridiculous
position," he said, after looking down, and looking up, and
laughing, and frowning, and walking off, and walking back
again. "But I see no way out of it. What will be, will be.
This will be, I suppose. I must take off myself, I imagine—in
short, I engage to do it."

Sissy rose. She was not surprised by the result, but she was
happy in it, and her face beamed brightly.

"You will permit me to say," continued Mr. James Harthouse, "that I doubt if any other ambassador, or ambas-

sadress, could have addressed me with the same success. I must not only regard myself as being in a very ridiculous position, but as being vanquished at all points. Will you allow me the privilege of remembering my enemy's name?"

"*My* name?" said the ambassadress.

"The only name I could possibly care to know, to-night."

"Sissy Jupe."

"Pardon my curiosity at parting. Related to the family?"

"I am only a poor girl," returned Sissy. "I was separated from my father—he was only a stroller—and taken pity on by Mr. Gradgrind. I have lived in the house ever since."

"It wanted this to complete the defeat," said Mr. James Harthouse, sinking, with a resigned air, on the sofa, after standing transfixed a little while. "The defeat may now be considered perfectly accomplished. Only a poor girl—only a stroller—only James Harthouse made nothing of—only James Harthouse a Great Pyramid of failure."

The Great Pyramid put it into his head to go up the Nile. He took a pen upon the instant, and wrote the following note (in appropriate hieroglyphics) to his brother:

"DEAR JACK,—All up at Coketown. Bored out of the place, and going in for camels.—Affectionately, JEM."

He rang the bell.

"Send my fellow here."

"Gone to bed, sir."

"Tell him to get up, and pack up."

He wrote two more notes. One to Mr. Bounderby, announcing his retirement from that part of the country, and showing where he would be found for the next fortnight. The other, similar in effect, to Mr. Gradgrind. Almost as soon as the ink was dry upon their superscriptions, he had left the tall chimneys of Coketown behind, and was in a railway carriage, tearing and glaring over the dark landscape.

The moral sort of fellows might suppose that Mr. James Harthouse derived some comfortable reflections afterwards, from this prompt retreat, as one of his few actions that made any amends for anything, and as a token to himself that he had escaped the climax of a very bad business. But it was not so, at all. A secret sense of having failed and been ridiculous—a dread of what other fellows who went in for similar sorts of things, would say at his expense if they knew it—so oppressed him, that what was about the very best passage in his life was the one of all others he would not have owned to on any account, and the only one that made him ashamed of himself.

CHAPTER III: *Very Decided*

THE indefatigable Mrs. Sparsit, with a violent cold upon her, her voice reduced to a whisper, and her stately frame so racked by continual sneezes that it seemed in danger of dismemberment, gave chase to her patron until she found him in the metropolis; and there, majestically sweeping in upon him at his hotel in St. James's Street, exploded the combustibles with which she was charged, and blew up. Having executed her mission with infinite relish, this high-minded woman then fainted away on Mr. Bounderby's coat collar.

Mr. Bounderby's first procedure was to shake Mrs. Sparsit off, and leave her to progress as she might through various stages of suffering on the floor. He next had recourse to the administration of potent restoratives, such as screwing the patient's thumbs, smiting her hands, abundantly watering her face, and inserting salt in her mouth. When these attentions had recovered her (which they speedily did), he hustled her into a fast train without offering any other refreshment, and carried her back to Coketown more dead than alive.

Regarded as a classical ruin, Mrs. Sparsit was an interesting spectacle on her arrival at her journey's end; but considered in any other light, the amount of damage she had by that time sustained was excessive, and impaired her claims to admiration. Utterly heedless of the wear and tear of her clothes and constitution, and adamant to her pathetic sneezes, Mr. Bounderby immediately crammed her into a coach, and bore her off to Stone Lodge.

"Now, Tom Gradgrind," said Bounderby, bursting into his father-in-law's room late at night; "here's a lady here—Mrs. Sparsit—you know Mrs. Sparsit—who has something to say to you that will strike you dumb."

"You have missed my letter!" exclaimed Mr. Gradgrind, surprised by the apparition.

"Missed your letter, sir!" bawled Bounderby. "The present time is no time for letters. No man shall talk to Josiah Bounderby of Coketown about letters, with his mind in the state it's in now."

"Bounderby," said Mr. Gradgrind, in a tone of temperate remonstrance, "I speak of a very special letter I have written to you, in reference to Louisa."

"Tom Gradgrind," replied Bounderby, knocking the flat of his hand several times with great vehemence on the table, "I speak of a very special messenger that has come to me, in reference to Louisa. Mrs. Sparsit, ma'am, stand forward!"

That unfortunate lady hereupon essaying to offer testimony, without any voice and with painful gestures expressive of an inflamed throat, became so aggravating and underwent so many facial contortions, that Mr. Bounderby, unable to bear it, seized her by the arm and shook her.

"If you can't get it out, ma'am," said Bounderby, "leave me to get it out. This is not a time for a lady, however highly connected, to be totally inaudible, and seemingly swallowing marbles. Tom Gradgrind, Mrs. Sparsit latterly found herself, by accident, in a situation to overhear a conversation out of doors between your daughter and your precious gentleman friend, Mr. James Harthouse."

"Indeed!" said Mr. Gradgrind.

"Ah! Indeed!" cried Bounderby. "And in that conversation——"

"It is not necessary to repeat its tenor, Bounderby. I know what passed."

"You do? Perhaps," said Bounderby, starting with all his might at his so quiet and assuasive father-in-law, "you know where your daughter is at the present time!"

"Undoubtedly. She is here."

"Here?"

"My dear Bounderby, let me beg you to restrain these loud outbreaks, on all accounts. Louisa is here. The moment she could detach herself from that interview with the person of whom you speak, and whom I deeply regret to have been the means of introducing to you, Louisa hurried here, for protection. I myself had not been at home many hours, when I received her—here, in this room. She hurried by the train to town, she ran from town to this house through a raging storm, and presented herself before me in a state of distraction. Of course, she has remained here ever since. Let me entreat you, for your own sake and for hers, to be more quiet."

Mr. Bounderby silently gazed about him for some moments, in every direction except Mrs. Sparsit's direction; and then, abruptly turning upon the niece of Lady Scadgers, said to that wretched woman:

"Now, ma'am! We shall be happy to hear any little apology you may think proper to offer, for going about the country at express pace, with no other luggage than a Cock-and-a-Bull, ma'am!"

"Sir," whispered Mrs. Sparsit, "my nerves are at present too much shaken, and my health is at present too much impaired, in your service, to admit of my doing more than taking refuge in tears."

(Which she did.)

"Well, ma'am," said Bounderby, "without making any observation to you that may not be made with propriety to a woman of good family, what I have got to add to that, is that there is something else in which it appears to me you may take refuge, namely, a coach. And the coach in which we came here, being at the door, you'll allow me to hand you down to it, and pack you home to the Bank: where the best course for you to pursue, will be to put your feet into the hottest water you can bear, and take a glass of scalding rum and butter after you get into bed." With these words, Mr. Bounderby extended his right hand to the weeping lady, and escorted her to the conveyance in question, shedding many plaintive sneezes by the way. He soon returned alone.

"Now, as you showed me in your face, Tom Gradgrind, that you wanted to speak to me," he resumed, "here I am. But, I am not in a very agreeable state, I tell you plainly: not relishing this business, even as it is, and not considering that I am at any time as dutifully and submissively treated by your daughter, as Josiah Bounderby of Coketown ought to be treated by his wife. You have your opinion, I dare say; and I have mine, I know. If you mean to say anything to me to-night, that goes against this candid remark, you had better let it alone."

Mr. Gradgrind, it will be observed, being much softened, Mr. Bounderby took particular pains to harden himself at all points. It was his amiable nature.

"My dear Bounderby," Mr. Gradgrind began in reply.

"Now, you'll excuse me," said Bounderby, "but I don't want to be too dear. That, to start with. When I begin to be dear to a man, I generally find that his intention is to come over me. I am not speaking to you politely; but, as you are aware, I am *not* polite. If you like politeness, you know where to get it. You have your gentleman friends you know, and they'll serve you with as much of the article as you want. I don't keep it myself."

"Bounderby," urged Mr. Gradgrind, "we are all liable to mistakes——"

"I thought you couldn't make 'em," interrupted Bounderby.

"Perhaps I thought so. But, I say we are all liable to mistakes; and I should feel sensible of your delicacy, and grateful for it, if you would spare me these references to Harthouse. I shall not associate him in our conversation with your intimacy and encouragement; pray do not persist in connecting him with mine."

"I never mentioned his name!" said Bounderby.

"Well, well!" returned Mr. Gradgrind, with a patient, even a submissive, air. And he sat for a little while pondering. "Bounderby, I see reason to doubt whether we have ever quite understood Louisa."

"Who do you mean by We?"

"Let me say I, then," he returned, in answer to the coarsely blurted question: "I doubt whether I have understood

Louisa. I doubt whether I have been quite right in the manner of her education."

"There you hit it," returned Bounderby. "There I agree with you. You have found it out at last, have you? Education! I'll tell you what education is—To be tumbled out of doors, neck and crop, and put upon the shortest allowance of everything except blows. That's what *I* call education."

"I think your good sense will perceive," Mr. Gradgrind remonstrated in all humility, "that whatever the merits of such a system may be, it would be difficult of general application to girls."

"I don't see it at all, sir," returned the obstinate Bounderby.

"Well," sighed Mr. Gradgrind, "we will not enter into the question. I assure you I have no desire to be controversial. I seek to repair what is amiss, if I possibly can; and I hope you will assist me in a good spirit, Bounderby, for I have been very much distressed."

"I don't understand you yet," said Bounderby, with determined obstinacy, "and therefore I won't make any promises."

"In the course of a few hours, my dear Bounderby," Mr. Gradgrind proceeded, in the same depressed and propitiatory manner, "I appear to myself to have become better informed as to Louisa's character, than in previous years. The enlightenment has been painfully forced upon me, and the discovery is not mine. I think there are—Bounderby, you will be surprised to hear me say this—I think there are qualities in Louisa, which—which have been harshly neglected, and—and a little perverted. And—and I would suggest to you, that—that if you would kindly meet me in a timely endeavour to leave her to her better nature for a while—and to encourage it to develop itself by tenderness and considera- tion—it—it would be the better for the happiness of all of us. Louisa," said Mr. Gradgrind, shading his face with his hand, "has always been my favourite child."

The blustrous Bounderby crimsoned and swelled to such an extent on hearing these words, that he seemed to be, and probably was, on the brink of a fit. With his very ears a bright purple shot with crimson, he pent up his indignation, however, and said:

"You'd like to keep her here for a time?"

"I—I had intended to recommend, my dear Bounderby, that you should allow Louisa to remain here on a visit, and be attended by Sissy (I mean of course Cecilia Jupe), who understands her, and in whom she trusts."

"I gather from all this, Tom Gradgrind," said Bounderby, standing up with his hands in his pockets, "that you are of opinion that there's what people call some incompatibility between Loo Bounderby and myself."

"I fear there is at present a general incompatibility between Louisa, and—and—and almost all the relations in which I have placed her," was her father's sorrowful reply.

"Now, look you here, Tom Gradgrind," said Bounderby the flushed, confronting him with his legs wide apart, his hands deeper in his pockets, and his hair like a hayfield wherein his windy anger was boisterous. "You have said your say; I am going to say mine. I am a Coketown man. I am Josiah Bounderby of Coketown. I know the bricks of this town, and I know the works of this town, and I know the chimneys of this town, and I know the smoke of this town, and I know the Hands of this town. I know 'em all pretty well. They're real. When a man tells me anything about imaginative qualities, I always tell that man, whoever he is, that I know what he means. He means turtle-soup and venison, with a gold spoon, and that he wants to be set up with a coach and six. That's what your daughter wants. Since you are of opinion that she ought to have what she wants, I recommend you to provide it for her. Because, Tom Gradgrind, she will never have it from me."

"Bounderby," said Mr. Gradgrind, "I hoped, after my entreaty, you would have taken a different tone."

"Just wait a bit," retorted Bounderby, "you have said your say, I believe. I heard you out; hear me out, if you please. Don't make yourself a spectacle of unfairness as well as inconsistency, because, although I am sorry to see Tom Gradgrind reduced to his present position, I should be doubly sorry to see him brought so low as that. Now, there's an incompatibility of some sort or another, I am given to understand by you, between your daughter and me. I'll give *you* to understand, in reply to that, that there unquestionably is an incompatibility of the first magnitude—to be summed up in this—that your daughter don't properly know her husband's merits, and is not impressed with such a sense as would become her, by George! of the honour of his alliance. That's plain speaking, I hope."

"Bounderby," urged Mr. Gradgrind, "this is unreasonable."

"Is it?" said Bounderby. "I am glad to hear you say so. Because when Tom Gradgrind with his new lights, tells me that what I say is unreasonable, I am convinced at once it must be devilish sensible. With your permission I am going on. You know my origin; and you know that for a good many years of my life I didn't want a shoeing-horn, in consequence of not having a shoe. Yet you may believe or not, as you think proper, that there are ladies—born ladies—belonging to families—Families!—who next to worship the ground I walk on."

He discharged this like a Rocket, at his father-in-law's head.

"Whereas your daughter," proceeded Bounderby, "is far from being a born lady. That you know, yourself. Not that I care a pinch of candle-snuff about such things, for you are very well aware I don't; but that such is the fact, and you, Tom Gradgrind, can't change it. Why do I say this?"

"Not, I fear," observed Mr. Gradgrind, in a low voice, "to spare me."

"Hear me out," said Bounderby, "and refrain from cutting in till your turn comes round. I say this, because highly connected females have been astonished to see the way in which your daughter has conducted herself, and to witness her insensibility. They have wondered how I have suffered it. And I wonder myself now, and I won't suffer it."

"Bounderby," returned Mr. Gradgrind, rising, "the less we say to-night the better, I think."

"On the contrary, Tom Gradgrind, the more we say to-night, the better, I think. That is," the consideration checked him, "till I have said all I mean to say, and then I don't care how soon we stop. I come to a question that may shorten the business. What do you mean by the proposal you made just now?"

"What do I mean, Bounderby?"

"By your visiting proposition," said Bounderby, with an inflexible jerk of the hayfield.

"I mean that I hope you may be induced to arrange in a friendly manner, for allowing Louisa a period of repose and reflection here, which may tend to a gradual alteration for the better in many respects."

"To a softening down of your ideas of the incompatibility?" said Bounderby.

"If you put it in those terms."

"What made you think of this?" said Bounderby.

"I have already said, I fear Louisa has not been understood. Is it asking too much, Bounderby, that you, so far her elder, should aid in trying to set her right? You have accepted a great charge of her; for better for worse, for——"

Mr. Bounderby may have been annoyed by the repetition of his own words to Stephen Blackpool, but he cut the quotation short with an angry start.

"Come!" said he, "I don't want to be told about that. I know what I took her for, as well as you do. Never you mind what I took her for; that's my look-out."

"I was merely going on to remark, Bounderby, that we may all be more or less in the wrong, not even excepting you; and that some yielding on your part, remembering the trust you have accepted, may not only be an act of true kindness, but perhaps a debt incurred towards Louisa."

"I think differently," blustered Bounderby. "I am going to finish this business according to my own opinions. Now,

I don't want to make a quarrel of it with you, Tom Gradgrind. To tell you the truth, I don't think it would be worthy of my reputation to quarrel on such a subject. As to your gentleman friend, he may take himself off, wherever he likes best. If he falls in my way, I shall tell him my mind; if he don't fall in my way, I shan't, for it won't be worth my while to do it. As to your daughter, whom I made Loo Bounderby, and might have done better by leaving Loo Gradgrind, if she don't come home to-morrow, by twelve o'clock at noon, I shall understand that she prefers to stay away, and I shall send her wearing apparel and so forth over here, and you'll take charge of her for the future. What I shall say to people in general, of the incompatibility that led to my so laying down the law, will be this. I am Josiah Bounderby, and I had my bringing up; she's the daughter of Tom Gradgrind, and she had her bringing up; and the two horses wouldn't pull together. I am pretty well known to be rather an uncommon man, I believe; and most people will understand fast enough that it must be a woman rather out of the common, also, who, in the long run, would come up to my mark."

"Let me seriously entreat you to reconsider this, Bounderby," urged Mr. Gradgrind, "before you commit yourself to such a decision."

"I always come to a decision," said Bounderby, tossing his hat on: "and whatever I do, I do at once. I should be surprised at Tom Gradgrind's addressing such a remark to Josiah Bounderby of Coketown, knowing what he knows of him, if I could be surprised by anything Tom Gradgrind did, after his making himself a party to sentimental humbug. I have given you my decision, and I have got no more to say. Good night!"

So Mr. Bounderby went home to his town house to bed. At five minutes past twelve o'clock next day, he directed Mrs. Bounderby's property to be carefully packed up and sent to Tom Gradgrind's; advertised his country retreat for sale by private contract; and resumed a bachelor life.

CHAPTER IV: *Lost*

THE robbery at the Bank had not languished before, and did not cease to occupy a front place in the attention of the principal of that establishment now. In boastful proof of his promptitude and activity, as a remarkable man, and a self-made man, and a commercial wonder more admirable than Venus, who had risen out of the mud instead of the sea, he liked to show how little his domestic affairs abated his business ardour. Consequently, in the first few weeks of his resumed bachelorhood, he even advanced upon his usual display of bustle, and every day made such a route in renewing his investigations into the robbery, that the officers who had it in hand almost wished it had never been committed.

They were at fault too, and off the scent. Although they had been so quiet since the first outbreak of the matter, that most people really did suppose it to have been abandoned as hopeless, nothing new occurred. No implicated man or woman took untimely courage, or made a self-betraying step. More remarkable yet, Stephen Blackpool could not be heard of, and the mysterious old woman remained a mystery.

Things having come to this pass, and showing no latent signs of stirring beyond it, the upshot of Mr. Bounderby's investigations was, that he resolved to hazard a bold burst. He drew up a placard, offering Twenty Pounds reward for the apprehension of Stephen Blackpool, suspected of complicity in the robbery of the Coketown Bank on such a night; he described the said Stephen Blackpool by dress, complexion, estimated height, and manner, as minutely as he could; he recited how he had left the town, and in what direction he had been last seen going; he had the whole printed in great black letters on a staring broadsheet; and he caused the walls to be posted with it in the dead of night, so that it should strike upon the sight of the whole population at one blow.

The factory-bells had need to ring their loudest that morning to disperse the group of workers who stood in the tardy daybreak, collected round the placards, devouring them with eager eyes. Not the least eager of the eyes assembled, were the eyes of those who could not read. These people, as they listened to the friendly voice that read aloud—there was always some such ready to help them—stared at the characters which meant so much with a vague awe and respect that would have been half ludicrous, if any aspect of public ignorance could ever be otherwise than threatening and full of evil. Many ears and eyes were busy with a vision of the matter of these placards, among turning spindles, rattling looms, and whirring wheels, for hours afterwards; and when the Hands cleared out again into the streets, there were still as many readers as before.

Slackbridge, the delegate, had to address his audience too that night; and Slackbridge had obtained a clean bill from the printer, and had brought it in his pocket. O my friends and fellow countrymen, the down-trodden operatives of Coketown, oh my fellow brothers and fellow workmen and fellow citizens and fellow men, what a to-do was there, when Slackbridge unfolded what he called "that damning document," and held it up to the gaze, and for the execration of the working-man community! "Oh my fellow men, behold of what a traitor in the camp of those great spirits who are enrolled upon the holy scroll of Justice and of Union, is appropriately capable! Oh my prostrate friends, with the galling yoke of tyrants on your necks and the iron foot of despotism treading down your fallen forms into the dust of the earth, upon which right glad would your oppressors be to see you creeping on your bellies all the days of your lives, like the serpent in the garden—oh my brothers, and shall I as a man not add, my sisters too, what do you say, *now*, of Stephen Blackpool, with a slight stoop in his shoulders and about five foot seven in height, as set forth in this degrading and disgusting document, this blighting bill, this pernicious placard, this abominable advertisement; and with what majesty of denouncement will you crush the viper, who would bring this stain and shame upon the God-like race that happily has cast him out for ever! Yes, my compatriots, happily cast him out and sent him forth! For you remember how he stood here before you on this platform; you remember how, face to face and foot to foot, I pursued him through all his intricate windings; you remember how he sneaked and slunk, and sidled, and splitted of straws, until, with not an inch of ground to which to cling, I hurled him out from amongst us: an object for the undying finger of scorn to point at, and for the avenging fire of every free and thinking mind to scorch and sear! And now, my friends—my labouring friends, for I rejoice and triumph in that stigma—my friends whose hard but honest beds are made in toil, and whose scanty but independent pots are boiled in hardship; and, now I say, my friends, what appellation has that dastard craven taken to himself, when, with the mask torn from his features, he stands before us in all his native deformity, a What? A thief! A plunderer! A proscribed fugitive, with a price upon his head; a fester and a wound upon the noble character of the Coketown operative! Therefore, my band of brothers in a sacred bond, to which your children and your children's children yet unborn have set their infant hands and seals, I propose to you on the part of the United Aggregate Tribunal, ever watchful for your welfare, ever zealous for your benefit, that this meeting does Resolve: That Stephen Blackpool, weaver, referred to in this placard, having been already solemnly disowned by the community of Coketown Hands, the same are free from the shame of his misdeeds, and cannot as a class be reproached with his dishonest actions!"

Thus Slackbridge; gnashing and perspiring after a prodigious sort. A few stern voices called out "No!" and a score or two hailed, with assenting cries of "Hear, hear!" the caution from one man, "Slackbridge, y' or over hetter int; y' or a goen too fast!" But these were pigmies against an army; the general assemblage subscribed to the gospel according to Slackbridge, and gave three cheers for him, as he sat demonstratively panting at them.

These men and women were yet in the streets, passing quietly to their homes, when Sissy, who had been called away from Louisa some minutes before, returned.

"Who is it?" asked Louisa.

"It is Mr. Bounderby," said Sissy, timid of the name, "and your brother Mr. Tom, and a young woman who says her name is Rachael, and that you know her."

"What do they want, Sissy dear?"

"They want to see you. Rachael has been crying, and seems angry."

"Father," said Louisa, for he was present, "I cannot refuse to see them, for a reason that will explain itself. Shall they come in here?"

As he answered in the affirmative, Sissy went away to bring them. She reappeared with them directly. Tom was last; and remained standing in the obscurest part of the room, near the door.

"Mrs. Bounderby," said her husband, entering with a cool nod, "I don't disturb you, I hope. This is an unseasonable hour, but here is a young woman who has been making statements which render my visit necessary. Tom Gradgrind, as your son, young Tom, refuses for some obstinate reason or other to say anything at all about those statements, good or bad, I am obliged to confront her with your daughter."

"You have seen me once before, young lady," said Rachael, standing in front of Louisa.

Tom coughed.

"You have seen me, young lady," repeated Rachael, as she did not answer, "once before."

Tom coughed again.

"I have."

Rachael cast her eyes proudly towards Mr. Bounderby, and said, "Will you make it known, young lady, where, and who was there?"

"I went to the house where Stephen Blackpool lodged, on the night of his discharge from his work, and I saw you there. He was there too; and an old woman who did not speak, and whom I could scarcely see, stood in a dark corner. My brother was with me."

"Why couldn't you say so, young Tom?" demanded Bounderby.

"I promised my sister I wouldn't." Which Louisa hastily confirmed. "And besides," said the whelp bitterly, "she tells her own story so precious well—and so full—that what business had I to take it out of her mouth!"

"Say, young lady, if you please," pursued Rachael, "why in an evil hour, you ever came to Stephen's that night."

"I felt compassion for him," said Louisa, her colour deepening, "and I wished to know what he was going to do, and wished to offer him assistance."

"Thank you, ma'am," said Bounderby. "Much flattered and obliged."

"Did you offer him," asked Rachael, "a bank-note?"

"Yes; but he refused it, and would only take two pounds in gold."

Rachael cast her eyes towards Mr. Bounderby again.

"Oh certainly!" said Bounderby. "If you put the question whether your ridiculous and improbable account was true or not, I am bound to say it's confirmed."

"Young lady," said Rachael, "Stephen Blackpool is now named as a thief in public print all over this town, and where else! There have been a meeting to-night where he have been spoken of in the same shameful way. Stephen! The honest lad, the truest lad, the best!" Her indignation failed her, and she broke off sobbing.

"I am very, very sorry," said Louisa.

"O young lady, young lady," returned Rachael, "I hope you may be, but I don't know! I can't say what you may ha' done! The like of you don't know us, don't care for us, don't belong to us. I am not sure why you may ha' come that night. I can't tell but what you may ha' come wi' some aim of your own, not mindin so what trouble you brought such as the poor lad. I said then, Bless you for coming; and I said it of my heart, you seemed to take so pitifully to him; but I don't know now, I don't know!"

Louisa could not reproach her for her unjust suspicions; she was so faithful to her idea of the man, and so afflicted.

"And when I think," said Rachael through her sobs, "that the poor lad was so grateful, thinkin you so good to him—when I mind that he put his hand over his hard-worken face to hide the tears that you brought up there—O, I hope you may be sorry, and ha' no bad cause to be it; but I don't know, I don't know!"

"You're a pretty article," growled the whelp, moving uneasily in his dark corner, "to come here with these precious imputations! You ought to be bundled out for not knowing how to behave yourself, and you would be by rights."

She said nothing in reply; and her low weeping was the only sound that was heard, until Mr. Bounderby spoke.

"Come!" said he, "you know what you have engaged to do. You had better give your mind to that; not this."

"'Deed, I am loath," returned Rachael, drying her eyes, "that any here should see me like this; but I won't be seen so again. Young lady, when I had read what's put in print of Stephen—and what had just as much truth in it as if it had been put in print of you—I went straight to the Bank to say I knew where Stephen was, and to give a sure and certain promise that he should be here in two days. I couldn't meet wi' Mr. Bounderby then, and your brother sent me away, and

I tried to find you, but you was not to be found, and I went back to work. Soon as I come out of the Mill to-night, I hastened to hear what was said of Stephen—for I know wi' pride he will come back to shame it!—and then I went again to seek Mr. Bounderby, and I found him, and I told him every word I knew; and he believed no word I said, and brought me here."

"So far, that's true enough," assented Mr. Bounderby, with his hands in his pockets and his hat on. "But I have known you people before to-day, you'll observe, and I know you never die for want of talking. Now, I recommend you not so much to mind talking just now, as doing. You have undertaken to do something; all I remark upon that at present is, do it!"

"I have written to Stephen by the post that went out this afternoon, as I have written to him once before sin' he went away," said Rachael; "and he will be here, at furthest, in two days."

"Then, I'll tell you something. You are not aware, perhaps," retorted Mr. Bounderby, "that you yourself have been looked after now and then, not being considered quite free from suspicion in this business, on account of most people being judged according to the company they keep. The post-office hasn't been forgotten either. What I'll tell you is, that no letter to Stephen Blackpool has ever got into it. Therefore, what has become of yours, I leave you to guess. Perhaps you're mistaken, and never wrote any."

"He hadn't been gone from here, young lady," said Rachael, turning appealingly to Louisa, "as much as a week, when he sent me the only letter I have had from him, saying that he was forced to seek work in another name."

"Oh, by George!" cried Bounderby, shaking his head, with a whistle, "he changes his name, does he! That's rather unlucky, too, for such an immaculate chap. It's considered a little suspicious in Courts of Justice, I believe, when an Innocent happens to have many names."

"What," said Rachael, with the tears in her eyes again, "what, young lady, in the name of Mercy, was left the poor lad to do! The masters against him on one hand, the men against him on the other, he only wantin to work hard in peace, and do what he felt right. Can a man have no soul of his own, no mind of his own? Must he go wrong all through wi' this side, or must he go wrong all through wi' that, or else be hunted like a hare?"

"Indeed, indeed, I pity him from my heart," returned Louisa; "and I hope that he will clear himself."

"You need have no fear of that, young lady. He is sure!"

"All the surer, I suppose," said Mr. Bounderby, "for your refusing to tell where he is? Eh?"

"He shall not, through any act of mine, come back wi' the unmerited reproach of being brought back. He shall come back of his own accord to clear himself, and put all those that have injured his good character, and he not here for its defence, to shame. I have told him what has been done against him," said Rachael, throwing off all distrust as a rock throws off the sea, "and he will be here, at furthest, in two days."

"Notwithstanding which," added Mr. Bounderby, "if he can be laid hold of any sooner, he shall have an earlier opportunity of clearing himself. As to you, I have nothing against you; what you came and told me turns out to be true, and I have given you the means of proving it to be true, and there's an end of it. I wish you good night all! I must be off to look a little further into this."

Tom came out of his corner when Mr. Bounderby moved, moved with him, kept close to him, and went away with him. The only parting salutation of which he delivered himself was a sulky "Good night, father!" With a brief speech, and a scowl at his sister, he left the house.

Since his sheet-anchor had come home, Mr. Gradgrind had been sparing of speech. He still sat silent, when Louisa mildly said:

"Rachael, you will not mistrust me one day, when you know me better."

"It goes against me," Rachael answered, in a gentler manner, "to mistrust any one; but when I am so mistrusted—when we all are—I cannot keep such things quite out of my mind. I ask your pardon for having done you an injury. I don't think what I said now. Yet I might come to think it again, wi' the poor lad so wronged."

"Did you tell him in your letter," inquired Sissy, "that suspicion seemed to have fallen upon him, because he had been seen about the Bank at night? He would then know what he would have to explain on coming back, and would be ready."

"Yes, dear," she returned; "but I can't guess what can have ever taken him there. He never used to go there. It was never in his way. His way was the same as mine, and not near it."

Sissy had already been at her side asking her where she lived, and whether she might come to-morrow night, to inquire if there were news of him.

"I doubt," said Rachael, "if he can be here till next day."

"Then I will come next night too," said Sissy.

When Rachael, assenting to this, was gone, Mr. Gradgrind lifted up his head, and said to his daughter:

"Louisa, my dear, I have never, that I know of, seen this man. Do you believe him to be implicated?"

"I think I have believed it, father, though with great difficulty. I do not believe it now."

"That is to say, you once persuaded yourself to believe it, from knowing him to be suspected. His appearance and manner; are they so honest?"

"Very honest."

"And her confidence not to be shaken! I ask myself," said Mr. Gradgrind, musing, "does the real culprit know of these accusations? Where is he? Who is he?"

His hair had latterly began to change its colour. As he leaned upon his hand again, looking grey and old, Louisa, with a face of fear and pity, hurriedly went over to him, and sat close at his side. Her eyes by accident met Sissy's at the moment. Sissy flushed and started, and Louisa put her finger on her lip.

Next night, when Sissy returned home and told Louisa that Stephen was not come, she told it in a whisper. Next night again, when she came home with the same account, and added that he had not been heard of, she spoke in the same low frightened tone. From the moment of that interchange of looks, they never uttered his name, or any reference to him, aloud; nor ever pursued the subject of the robbery, when Mr. Gradgrind spoke of it.

The two appointed days ran out, three days and nights ran out, and Stephen Blackpool was not come, and remained unheard of. On the fourth day, Rachael, with unabated confidence, but considering her despatch to have miscarried, went up to the Bank, and showed her letter from him with his address, at a working colony, one of many, not upon the main road, sixty miles away. Messengers were sent to that place, and the whole town looked for Stephen to be brought in next day.

During this whole time the whelp moved about with Mr. Bounderby like his shadow, assisting in all the proceedings. He was greatly excited, horribly fevered, bit his nails down to the quick, spoke in a hard rattling voice, and with lips that were black and burnt up. At the hour when the suspected man was looked for, the whelp was at the station; offering to wager that he had made off before the arrival of those who were sent in quest of him, and that he would not appear.

The whelp was right. The messengers returned alone. Rachael's letter had gone, Rachael's letter had been delivered, Stephen Blackpool had decamped in that same hour; and no soul knew more of him. The only doubt in Coketown was, whether Rachael had written in good faith, believing that he really would come back, or warning him to fly. On this point opinion was divided.

Six days, seven days, far on into another week. The wretched whelp plucked up a ghastly courage, and began to grow defiant. "*Was* the suspected fellow the thief? A pretty question! If not, where was the man, and why did he not come back?"

Where was the man, and why did he not come back? In the dead of night the echoes of his own words, which had rolled Heaven knows how far away in the daytime, came back instead, and abided by him until morning.

CHAPTER V : *Found*

DAY and night again, day and night again. No Stephen Blackpool. Where was the man, and why did he not come back?

Every night, Sissy went to Rachael's lodging, and sat with her in her small neat room. All day, Rachael toiled as such people must toil, whatever their anxieties. The smoke-serpents were indifferent who was lost or found, who turned out bad or good; the melancholy mad elephants, like the Hard Fact men, abated nothing of their set routine, whatever happened. Day and night again, day and night again. The monotony was unbroken. Even Stephen Blackpool's disappearance was falling into the general way, and becoming as monotonous a wonder as any piece of machinery in Coketown.

"I misdoubt," said Rachael, "if there is as many as twenty left in all this place, who have any trust in the poor dear lad now."

She said it to Sissy, as they sat in her lodging, lighted only by the lamp at the street corner. Sissy had come there when it was already dark, to wait her return from work; and they had since sat at the window where Rachael had found her, wanting no brighter light to shine on their sorrowful talk.

"If it hadn't been mercifully brought about, that I was to have you to speak to," pursued Rachael, "times are, when I think my mind would not have kept right. But I get hope and strength through you; and you believe that though appearances may rise against him, he will be proved clear?"

"I do believe so," returned Sissy, "with all my heart. I feel so certain, Rachael, that the confidence you hold in yours against all discouragement, is not like to be wrong, that I have no more doubt of him than if I had known him through as many years of trial as you have."

"And I, my dear," said Rachael, with a tremble in her voice, "have known him through them all, to be, according to his quiet ways, so faithful to everything honest and good, that if he was never to be heard of more, and I was to live to be a hundred years old, I could say with my last breath, God knows my heart. I have never once left trusting Stephen Blackpool!"

"We all believe, up at the Lodge, Rachael, that he will be freed from suspicion, sooner or later."

"The better I know it to be so believed there, my dear,"

said Rachael, "and the kinder I feel it that you come away from there, purposely to comfort me, and keep me company, and be seen wi' me when I am not yet free from all suspicion myself, the more grieved I am that I should ever have spoken those mistrusting words to the young lady. And yet——"

"You don't mistrust her now, Rachael?"

"Now that you have brought us more together, no. But I can't at all times keep out of my mind——"

Her voice so sunk into a low and slow communing with herself, that Sissy, sitting by her side, was obliged to listen with attention.

"I can't at all times keep out of my mind, mistrustings of some one. I can't think who 'tis, I can't think how or why it may be done, but I mistrust that some one has put Stephen out of the way. I mistrust that by his coming back of his own accord, and showing himself innocent before them all, some one would be confounded, who—to prevent that—has stopped him, and put him out of the way."

"That is a dreadful thought," said Sissy, turning pale.

"It *is* a dreadful thought to think he may be murdered."

Sissy shuddered, and turned paler yet.

"When it makes its way into my mind, dear," said Rachael, "and it will come sometimes, though I do all I can to keep it out, wi' counting on to high numbers as I work, and saying over and over again pieces that I knew when I were a child—I fall into such a wild, hot hurry, that, however tired I am, I want to walk fast, miles and miles. I must get the better of this before bedtime. I'll walk home wi' you."

"He might fall ill upon the journey back," said Sissy, faintly offering a worn-out scrap of hope; "and in such a case, there are many places on the road where he might stop."

"But he is in none of them. He has been sought for in all, and he's not there."

"True," was Sissy's reluctant admission.

"He'd walk the journey in two days. If he was footsore and couldn't walk, I sent him, in the letter he got, the money to ride, lest he should have none of his own to spare."

"Let us hope that to-morrow will bring something better, Rachael. Come into the air!"

Her gentle hand adjusted Rachael's shawl upon her shining black hair in the usual manner of her wearing it, and they went out. The night being fine, little knots of Hands were here and there lingering at street corners; but it was supper-time with the greater part of them, and there were but few people in the streets.

"You're not so hurried now, Rachael, and your hand is cooler."

"I get better, dear, if I can only walk, and breathe a little fresh. Times when I can't, I turn weak and confused."

"But you must not begin to fail, Rachael, for you may be wanted at any time to stand by Stephen. To-morrow is Saturday. If no news comes to-morrow, let us walk in the country on Sunday morning, and strengthen you for another week. Will you go?"

"Yes, dear."

They were by this time in the street where Mr. Bounderby's house stood. The way to Sissy's destination led them past the door, and they were going straight towards it. Some train had newly arrived in Coketown, which had put a number of vehicles in motion, and scattered a considerable bustle about the town. Several coaches were rattling before them and behind them as they approached Mr. Bounderby's, and one of the latter drew up with such briskness as they were in the act of passing the house, that they looked round involuntarily. The bright gaslight over Mr. Bounderby's steps showed them Mrs. Sparsit in the coach, in an ecstasy of excitement, struggling to open the door; Mrs. Sparsit seeing them at the same moment, called to them to stop.

"It's a coincidence," exclaimed Mrs. Sparsit, as she was released by the coachman. "It's a Povidence! Come out, ma'am!" then said Mrs. Sparsit, to some one inside, "come out, or we'll have you dragged out!"

Hereupon, no other than the mysterious old woman descended. Whom Mrs. Sparsit incontinently collared.

"Leave her alone, everybody!" cried Mrs. Sparsit, with great energy. "Let nobody touch her. She belongs to me. Come in, ma'am!" then said Mrs. Sparsit, reversing her former word of command. "Come in, ma'am, or we'll have you dragged in!"

The spectacle of a matron of classical deportment, seizing an ancient woman by the throat, and haling her into a dwelling-house, would have been, under any circumstances, sufficient temptation to all true English stragglers so blest as to witness it, to force a way into that dwelling-house and see the matter out. But when the phenomenon was enhanced by the notoriety and mystery by this time associated all over the town, with the Bank robbery, it would have lured the stragglers in, with an irresistible attraction, though the roof had been expected to fall upon their heads. Accordingly, the chance witnesses on the ground, consisting of the busiest of the neighbours to the number of some five-and-twenty, closed in after Sissy and Rachael, as they closed in after Mrs. Sparsit and her prize; and the whole body made a disorderly irruption into Mr. Bounderby's dining-room, where the people behind lost not a moment's time in mounting on the chairs, to get the better of the people in front.

"Fetch Mr. Bounderby down!" cried Mrs. Sparsit. "Rachael, young woman; you know who this is?"

"It's Mrs. Pegler," said Rachael.

"I should think it is!" cried Mrs. Sparsit, exulting. "Fetch Mr. Bounderby. Stand away, everybody!" Here old Mrs. Pegler, muffling herself up, and shrinking from observation, whispered a word of entreaty. "Don't tell me," said Mrs. Sparsit, aloud, "I have told you twenty times, coming along, that I will *not* leave you till I have handed you over to him myself."

Mr. Bounderby now appeared, accompánied by Mr. Gradgrind and the whelp, with whom he had been holding conference upstairs. Mr. Bounderby looked more astonished than hospitable, at sight of this uninvited party in his dining-room.

"Why, what's the matter now!" said he. "Mrs. Sparsit, ma'am?"

"Sir," explained that worthy woman, "I trust it is my good fortune to produce a person you have much desired to find. Stimulated by my wish to relieve your mind, sir, and connecting together such imperfect clues to the part of the country in which that person might be supposed to reside, as have been afforded by the young woman, Rachael, fortunately now present to identify, I have had the happiness to succeed, and to bring that person with me—I need not say most unwillingly on her part. It has not been, sir, without some trouble that I have effected this; but trouble in your service is to me a pleasure, and hunger, thirst, and cold a real gratification."

Here Mrs. Sparsit ceased; for Mr. Bounderby's visage exhibited an extraordinary combination of all possible colours and expressions of discomfiture, as old Mrs. Pegler was disclosed to his view.

"Why, what do you mean by this?" was his highly unexpected demand, in great warmth. "I ask you, what do you mean by this, Mrs. Sparsit, ma'am?"

"Sir!" exclaimed Mrs. Sparsit, faintly.

"Why don't you mind your own business, ma'am?" roared Bounderby. "How dare you go and poke your officious nose into my family affairs?"

This allusion to her favourite feature overpowered Mrs. Sparsit. She sat down stiffly in a chair, as if she were frozen; and with a fixed stare at Mr. Bounderby, slowly grated her mittens against one another, as if they were frozen too.

"My dear Josiah!" cried Mrs. Pegler, trembling. "My darling boy! I am not to blame. It's not my fault, Josiah. I told this lady over and over again, that I knew she was doing what would not be agreeable to you, but she would do it."

"What did you let her bring you for? Couldn't you knock her cap off, or her tooth out, or scratch her, or do something or other to her?" asked Bounderby.

"My own boy! She threatened me that if I resisted her, I

should be brought by constables, and it was better to come quietly than make that stir in such a"—Mrs. Pegler glanced timidly but proudly round the walls—"such a fine house as this. Indeed, indeed, it is not my fault! My dear, noble, stately boy! I have always lived quiet and secret, Josiah, my dear. I have never broken the condition once. I have never said I was your mother. I have admired you at a distance; and if I have come to town sometimes, with long times between, to take a proud peep at you, I have done it unbeknown, my love, and gone away again."

Mr. Bounderby, with his hands in his pockets, walked in impatient mortification up and down at the side of the long dining-table, while the spectators greedily took in every syllable of Mrs. Pegler's appeal, and at each succeeding syllable became more and more round-eyed. Mr. Bounderby still walking up and down when Mrs. Pegler had done, Mr. Gradgrind addressed that maligned old lady:

"I am surprised, ma'am," he observed with severity, "that in your old age you have the face to claim Mr. Bounderby for your son, after your unnatural and inhuman treatment of him."

"*Me* unnatural!" cried poor old Mrs. Pegler. "*Me* inhuman! To my dear boy?"

"Dear!" repeated Mr. Gradgrind. "Yes; dear in his self-made prosperity, madam, I dare say. Not very dear, however, when you deserted him in his infancy, and left him to the brutality of a drunken grandmother."

"*I* deserted my Josiah!" cried Mrs. Pegler, clasping her hands. "Now, Lord forgive you, sir, for your wicked imaginations, and for your scandal against the memory of my poor mother, who died in my arms before Josiah was born. May you repent of it, sir, and live to know better!"

She was so very earnest and injured, that Mr. Gradgrind, shocked by the possibility which dawned upon him, said in a gentler tone:

"Do you deny, then, madam, that you left your son to—to be brought up in the gutter?"

"Josiah in the gutter!" exclaimed Mrs. Pegler. "No such a thing, sir. Never! For shame on you! My dear boy knows, and will give *you* to know, that though he come of humble parents, he come of parents that loved him as dear as the best could, and never thought it hardship on themselves to pinch a bit that he might write and cipher beautiful, and I've his books at home to show it! Aye, have I!" said Mrs. Pegler, with indignant pride. "And my dear boy knows, and will give *you* to know, sir, that after his beloved father died, when he was eight years old, his mother, too, could pinch a bit, as it was her duty and her pleasure and her pride to do it, to help him out in life, and put him 'prentice. And a steady lad he was, and a kind master he had to lend him a hand, and well he worked his own way forward to be rich and thriving. And I'll give you to know, sir—for this my dear boy won't—that though his mother kept but a little village shop, he never forgot her, but pensioned me on thirty pound a year—more than I want, for I put by out of it—only making the condition that I was to keep down in my own part, and make no boast about him, and not trouble him. And I never have, except with looking at him once a year, when he has never knowed it. And it's right," said poor old Mrs. Pegler, in affectionate championship, "that I *should* keep down in my own part, and I have no doubts that if I was here I should do a many unbefitting things, and I am well contented, and I can keep my pride in my Josiah to myself, and I can love for love's own sake! And I am ashamed of you sir," said Mrs. Pegler, lastly, "for your slanders and suspicions. And I never stood here before, nor never wanted to stand here when my dear son said no. And I shouldn't be here now, if it hadn't been for being brought here. And for shame upon you, O for shame, to accuse me of being a bad mother to my son, with my son standing here to tell you so different!"

The bystanders, on and off the dining-room chairs, raised a murmur of sympathy with Mrs. Pegler, and Mr. Gradgrind felt himself innocently placed in a very distressing predicament, when Mr. Bounderby, who had never ceased walking up and down, and had every moment swelled larger and larger, and grown redder and redder, stopped short.

"I don't exactly know," said Mr. Bounderby, "how I come to be favoured with the attendance of the present company, but I don't inquire. When they're quite satisfied, perhaps they'll be so good as to disperse; whether they're satisfied or not, perhaps they'll be so good as to disperse. I'm not bound to deliver a lecture on my family affairs, I have not undertaken to do it, and I'm not a going to do it. Therefore those who expect any explanation whatever upon that branch of the subject, will be disappointed—particularly Tom Gradgrind, and he can't know it too soon. In reference to the Bank robbery, there has been a mistake made, concerning my mother. If there hadn't been over-officiousness it wouldn't have been made, and I hate over-officiousness at all times, whether or no. Good evening!"

Although Mr. Bounderby carried it off in these terms, holding the door open for the company to depart, there was a blustering sheepishness upon him, at once extremely crestfallen and superlatively absurd. Detected as the Bully of humility, who had built his windy reputation upon lies, and in his boastfulness had put the honest truth as far away from him as if he had advanced the mean claim (there is no meaner) to tack himself on to a pedigree, he cut a most ridiculous figure. With the people filing off at the door he held, who he knew would carry what had passed to the whole town, to be given to the four winds, he could not have looked a Bully more shorn and forlorn, if he had had his ears cropped. Even that unlucky female, Mrs. Sparsit, fallen from her pinnacle of exultation into the Slough of Despond, was not in so bad a plight as that remarkable man and self-made Humbug, Josiah Bounderby of Coketown.

Rachael and Sissy, leaving Mrs. Pegler to occupy a bed at her son's for that night, walked together to the gate of Stone Lodge and there parted. Mr. Gradgrind joined them before they had gone very far, and spoke with much interest of Stephen Blackpool; for whom he thought this signal failure of the suspicions against Mrs. Pegler was likely to work well.

As to the whelp; throughout this scene as on all other late occasions, he had stuck close to Bounderby. He seemed to feel that as long as Bounderby could make no discovery without his knowledge, he was so far safe. He never visited his sister, and had only seen her once since she went home: that is to say on the night when he still stuck close to Bounderby, as already related.

There was one dim unformed fear lingering about his sister's mind, to which she never gave utterance, which surrounded the graceless and ungrateful boy with a dreadful mystery. The same dark possibility had presented itself in the same shapeless guise, this very day, to Sissy, when Rachael spoke of some one who would be confounded by Stephen's return, having put him out of the way. Louisa had never spoken of harbouring any suspicion of her brother in connection with the robbery, she and Sissy had held no confidence of the subject, save in that one interchange of looks when the unconscious father rested his grey head on his hand; but it was understood between them, and they both knew it. This other fear was so awful, that it hovered about each of them like a ghostly shadow; neither daring to think of its being near herself, far less of its being near the other.

And still the forced spirit which the whelp had plucked up, throve with him. If Stephen Blackpool was not the thief, let him show himself. Why didn't he?

Another night. Another day and night. No Stephen Blackpool. Where was the man, and why did he not come back?

CHAPTER VI : *The Starlight*

THE Sunday was a bright Sunday in autumn, clear and cool, when early in the morning Sissy and Rachael met, to walk in the country.

As Coketown cast ashes not only on its own head but on the neighbourhood's too—after the manner of those pious persons who do penance for their own sins by putting other people into sackcloth—it was customary for those who now and then thirsted for a draught of pure air, which is not absolutely the most wicked among the vanities of life, to get a few miles away by the railroad, and then begin their walk, or their lounge, in the fields. Sissy and Rachael helped themselves out of the smoke by the usual means, and were put down at a station about midway between the town and Mr. Bounderby's retreat.

Though the green landscape was blotted here and there with heaps of coal, it was green elsewhere, and there were trees to see, and there were larks singing (though it was Sunday), and there were pleasant scents in the air, and all was overarched by a bright blue sky. In the distance one way, Coketown showed as a black mist; in another distance hills began to rise; in a third, there was a faint change in the light of the horizon where it shone upon the far-off sea. Under their feet, the grass was fresh; beautiful shadows of branches flickered upon it, and speckled it; hedgerows were luxuriant; everything was at peace. Engines at pits' mouths, and lean old horses that had worn the circle of their daily labour into the ground, were alike quiet; wheels had ceased for a short space to turn; and the great wheel of earth seemed to revolve without the shocks and noises of another time.

They walked on across the fields and down the shady lanes, sometimes getting over a fragment of a fence so rotten that it dropped at a touch of the foot, sometimes passing near a wreck of bricks and beams overgrown with grass, marking the site of deserted works. They followed paths and tracks, however slight. Mounds where the grass was rank and high, and where brambles, dock-weed, and suchlike vegetation, were confusedly heaped together, they always avoided; for dismal stories were told in that country of the old pits hidden beneath such indications.

The sun was high when they sat down to rest. They had seen no one, near or distant, for a long time; and the solitude remained unbroken. "It is so still here, Rachael, and the way is so untrodden, that I think we must be the first who have been here all the summer."

As Sissy said it, her eyes were attracted by another of those rotten fragments of fence upon the ground. She got up to look at it. "And yet I don't know. This has not been broken very long. The wood is quite fresh where it gave way. Here are footsteps too.—O Rachael!"

She ran back, and caught her round the neck. Rachael had already started up.

"What is the matter?"

"I don't know. There is a hat lying in the grass."

They went forward together. Rachael took it up, shaking from head to foot. She broke into a passion of tears and lamentations: Stephen Blackpool was written in his own hand on the inside.

"O the poor lad, the poor lad! He has been made away with. He is lying murdered here!"

"Is there—has the hat any blood upon it?" Sissy faltered.

They were afraid to look; but they did examine it, and found no mark of violence, inside or out. It had been lying there some days, for rain and dew had stained it, and the mark of its shape was on the grass where it had fallen. They looked fearfully about them, without moving, but could see nothing more. "Rachael," Sissy whispered, "I will go on a little by myself."

She had unclasped her hand, and was in the act of stepping forward, when Rachael caught her in both arms with a scream that resounded over the wide landscape. Before them, at their very feet, was the brink of a black ragged chasm hidden by the thick grass. They sprang back, and fell upon their knees, each hiding her face upon the other's neck.

"O, my good Lord! He's down there! Down there!" At first this, and her terrific screams, were all that could be got from Rachael, by any tears, by any prayers, by any representations, by any means. It was impossible to hush her; and it was deadly necessary to hold her, or she would have flung herself down the shaft.

"Rachael, dear Rachael, good Rachael, for the love of Heaven, not these dreadful cries! Think of Stephen, think of Stephen, think of Stephen!"

By an earnest repetition of this entreaty, poured out in all the agony of such a moment, Sissy at last brought her to be silent, and to look at her with a tearless face of stone.

"Rachael, Stephen may be living. You wouldn't leave him lying maimed at the bottom of this dreadful place, a moment, if you could bring help to him?"

"No, no, no!"

"Don't stir from here, for his sake! Let me go and listen."

She shuddered to approach the pit; but she crept towards it on her hands and knees, and called to him as loud as she could call. She listened, but no sound replied. She called again and listened; still no answering sound. She did this, twenty, thirty times. She took a little clod of earth from the broken ground where he had stumbled, and threw it in. She could not hear it fall.

The wide prospect, so beautiful in its stillness but a few minutes ago, almost carried despair to her brave heart, as she rose and looked all round her, seeing no help. "Rachael, we must lose not a moment. We must go in different directions, seeking aid. You shall go by the way we have come, and I will go forward by the path. Tell any one you see, and every one what has happened. Think of Stephen, think of Stephen!"

She knew by Rachael's face that she might trust her now. And after standing for a moment to see her running, wringing her hands as she ran, she turned and went upon her own search; she stopped at the hedge to tie her shawl there as a guide to the place, then threw her bonnet aside, and ran as she had never run before.

Run, Sissy, run, in Heaven's name! Don't stop for breath. Run, run! Quickening herself by carrying such entreaties in her thought, she ran from field to field, and lane to lane, and place to place, as she had never run before; until she came to a shed by an engine-house, where two men lay in the shade, asleep on straw.

First to wake them, and next to tell them, all so wild and breathless as she was, what had brought her there, were difficulties; but they no sooner understood her than their spirits were on fire like hers. One of the men was in a drunken slumber, but on his comrade's shouting to him that a man had fallen down the Old Hell Shaft, he started out to a pool of dirty water, put his head in it, and came back sober.

With these two men she ran to another half a mile further, and with that one to another, while they ran elsewhere. Then a horse was found; and she got another man to ride for life or death to the railroad, and send a message to Louisa, which she wrote and gave him. By this time a whole village was up; and windlasses, ropes, poles, candles, lanterns, all things necessary, were fast collecting and being brought into one place, to be carried to the Old Hell Shaft.

It seemed now hours and hours since she had left the lost man lying in the grave where he had been buried alive. She could not bear to remain away from it any longer—it was like deserting him—and she hurried swiftly back, accompanied by half a dozen labourers, including the drunken man whom the news had sobered, and who was the best man of all. When they came to the Old Hell Shaft, they found it as lonely as she had left it. The men called and listened as she had done, and examined the edge of the chasm, and settled how it had happened, and then sat down to wait until the implements they wanted should come up.

Every sound of insects in the air, every stirring of the leaves, every whisper among these men, made Sissy tremble, for she thought it was a cry at the bottom of the pit. But the wind blew idly over it, and no sound arose to the surface, and they sat upon the grass, waiting and waiting. After they had waited some time, straggling people who had heard of the accident began to come up; then the real help of implements began to arrive. In the midst of this Rachael returned; and with her party there was a surgeon, who brought some wine and medicines. But, the expectation among the people that the man would be found alive, was very slight indeed.

There being now people enough present to impede the work, the sobered man put himself at the head of the rest, or was put there by the general consent, and made a large ring round the Old Hell Shaft, and appointed men to keep it. Besides such volunteers as were accepted to work, only Sissy and Rachael were at first permitted within this ring; but, later in the day, when the message brought an express from Coketown, Mr. Gradgrind and Louisa, and Mr. Bounderby, and the whelp, were also there.

The sun was four hours lower than when Sissy and Rachael had first sat down upon the grass, before a means of enabling two men to descend securely was rigged with poles and ropes. Difficulties had arisen in the construction of this machine, simple as it was; requisites had been found wanting, and messages had had to go and return. It was five o'clock in the afternoon of the bright autumnal Sunday, before a candle was sent down to try the air, while three or four rough faces stood crowded close together, attentively watching it: the men at the windlass lowering as they were told. The candle was brought up again, feebly burning, and then some water was cast in. Then the bucket was hooked on; and the sobered man and another got in with lights, giving the word "Lower away!"

As the rope went out, tight and strained, and the windlass creaked, there was not a breath among the one or two hundred men and women looking on, that came as it was wont to come. The signal was given and the windlass stopped, with abundant rope to spare. Apparently so long an interval ensued with the men at the windlass standing idle, that some woman shrieked that another accident had happened! But the surgeon who held the watch, declared five minutes not to have elapsed yet, and sternly admonished them to keep silence. He had not well done speaking, when the windlass was reversed and worked again. Practised eyes knew that it did not go as heavily as it would if both workmen had been coming up, and that only one was returning.

The rope came in tight and strained; and ring after ring was coiled upon the barrel of the windlass, and all eyes were fastened on the pit. The sobered man was brought up and leaped out briskly on the grass. There was an universal cry of "Alive or dead?" and then a deep, profound hush.

When he said "Alive!" a great shout arose and many eyes had tears in them.

"But he's hurt very bad," he added, as soon as he could

STEPHEN BLACKPOOL RECOVERED FROM THE OLD
HELL SHAFT.

make himself heard again. "Where's doctor? He's hurt so very bad, sir, that we donno how to get him up."

They all consulted together, and looked anxiously at the surgeon, as he asked some questions, and shook his head on receiving the replies. The sun was setting now; and the red light in the evening sky touched every face there, and caused it to be distinctly seen in all its wrapt suspense.

The consultation ended in the men returning to the windlass, and the pitman going down again, carrying the wine and some other small matters with him. Then the other man came up. In the meantime, under the surgeon's directions, some men brought a hurdle, on which others made a thick bed of spare clothes covered with loose straw, while he himself contrived some bandages and slings from shawls and handkerchiefs. As these were made, they were hung upon an arm of the pitman who had last come up, with instructions how to use them: and as he stood, shown by the light he carried, leaning his powerful loose hand upon one of the poles, and sometimes glancing down the pit, and sometimes glancing round upon the people, he was not the least conspicuous figure in the scene. It was dark now, and torches were kindled.

It appeared from the little this man said to those about him, which was quickly repeated all over the circle, that the lost man had fallen upon a mass of crumbled rubbish with which the pit was half choked up, and that his fall had been further broken by some jagged earth at the side. He lay upon his back with one arm doubled under him, and according to his own belief had hardly stirred since he fell, except that he had moved his free hand to a side pocket, in which he remembered to have some bread and meat (of which he had swallowed crumbs), and had likewise scooped up a little water in it now and then. He had come straight away from his work, on being written to, and had walked the whole journey; and was on his way to Mr. Bounderby's country house after dark, when he fell. He was crossing that dangerous country at such a dangerous time, because he was innocent of what was laid to his charge, and couldn't rest from coming the nearest way to deliver himself up. The Old Hell Shaft, the pitman said, with a curse upon it, was worthy of its bad name to the last; for though Stephen could speak now, he believed it would soon be found to have mangled the life out of him.

When all was ready, this man, still taking his last hurried charges from his comrades and the surgeon after the windlass had begun to lower him, disappeared into the pit. The rope went out as before, the signal was made as before, and the windlass stopped. No man removed his hand from it now. Every one waited with his grasp set, and his body bent down to the work, ready to reverse and wind in. At length the signal was given, and all the ring leaned forward.

For, now, the rope came in, tightened and strained to its utmost as it appeared, and the men turned heavily, and the windlass complained. It was scarcely endurable to look at the rope, and think of its giving way. But, ring after ring was coiled upon the barrel of the windlass safely, and the connecting chains appeared, and finally the bucket with the two men holding on at the sides—a sight to make the head swim, and oppress the heart—and tenderly supporting between them, slung and tied within, the figure of a poor, crushed, human creature.

A low murmur of pity went round the throng, and the women wept aloud, as this form, almost without form, was moved very slowly from its iron deliverance, and laid upon the bed of straw. At first, none but the surgeon went close to it. He did what he could in its adjustment on the couch, but the best that he could do was to cover it. That gently done, he called to him Rachael and Sissy. And at that time the pale, worn, patient face was seen looking up at the sky, with the broken right hand lying bare on the outside of the covering garments, as if waiting to be taken by another hand.

They gave him drink, moistened his face with water, and administered some drops of cordial and wine. Though he lay quite motionless looking up at the sky, he smiled and said, "Rachael."

She stooped down on the grass at his side, and bent over him until her eyes were between his and the sky, for he could not so much as turn them to look at her.

"Rachael, my dear."

She took his hand. He smiled again and said, "Don't let 't go."

"Thou'rt in great pain, my own dear Stephen?"

"I ha' been, but not now. I ha' been—dreadful, and dree, and long, my dear—but 'tis ower now. Ah, Rachael, aw a muddle! Fro' first to last, a muddle!"

The spectre of his old look seemed to pass as he said the word.

"I ha' fell into th' pit, my dear, as have cost wi'in the knowledge o' old fok now livin, hundreds and hundreds o' men's lives —fathers, sons, brothers, dear to thousands an thousands, an keeping 'em fro' want and hunger. I ha' fell into a pit that ha' been wi' th' Firedamp crueller than battle. I ha' read on 't in the public petition, as onny one may read, fro' the men that works in pits, in which they ha' pray'n and pray'n the lawmakers for Christ's sake not to let their work be murder to 'em, but to spare 'em for th' wives and children that they loves as well as gentlefok loves theirs. When it were in work, it killed wi'out need; when 'tis let alone, it kills wi'out need. See how we die an no need, one way an another —in a muddle—every day!"

He faintly said it, without any anger against any one. Merely as the truth.

"Thy little sister, Rachael, thou hast not forgot her. Thou'rt not like to forget her now, and me so nigh her. Thou know'st—poor, patient, suff'rin, dear—how thou didst work for her, seet'n all day long in her little chair at thy winder, and how she died, young and misshapen, awlung o' sickly air as had'n no need to be, an awlung o' working people's miserable homes. A muddle! Aw a muddle!"

Louisa approached him; but he could not see her, lying with his face turned up to the night sky.

"If aw th' things that tooches us, my dear, was not so muddled, I should'n ha' had'n need to coom heer. If we was not in a muddle among ourseln, I should'n ha' been, by my own fellow weavers and workin' brothers, so mistook. If Mr. Bounderby had ever know'd me right—if he'd ever know'd me at aw—he would'n ha' took'n offence wi' me. He would'n ha' suspect'n me. But look up yonder, Rachael! Look aboove!"

Following his eyes, she saw that he was gazing at a star.

"It ha' shined upon me," he said reverently, "in my pain and trouble down below. It ha' shined into my mind. I ha' look'n at 't and thowt o' thee, Rachael, till the muddle in my mind have cleared awa, above a bit, I hope. If soom ha' been wantin' in unnerstan'in me better, I, too, ha' been wantin' in unnerstan'in them better. When I got thy letter, I easily believen that what the yoong ledy sen and done to me, and what her brother sen and done to me, was one, and that there were a wicked plot betwixt 'em. When I fell, I were in anger wi' her, an hurryin' on t' be as onjust t' her as oothers was t' me. But in our judgments, like as in our doins, we mun bear and forbear. In my pain an trouble, lookin up yonder,—wi' it shinin' on me—I ha' seen more clear, and ha' made it my dyin prayer that aw th' world may on'y coom toogether more, an get a better unnerstan'in o' one another, than when I were in't my own weak seln."

Louisa hearing what he said, bent over him on the opposite side to Rachael, so that he could see her.

"You ha' heard?" he said, after a few moments' silence. "I ha' not forgot you, ledy."

"Yes, Stephen, I have heard you. And your Prayer is mine."

"You ha' a father. Will yo' tak' a message to him?"

"He is here," said Louisa, with dread. "Shall I bring him to you?"

"If yo please."

Louisa returned with her father. Standing hand in hand, they both looked down upon the solemn countenance.

"Sir, yo will clear me an mak my name good wi' aw men. This I leave to yo."

Mr. Gradgrind was troubled and asked how?

"Sir," was the reply: "yor son will tell yo how. Ask him. I mak no charges: I leave none ahint me: not a single word. I ha' seen an spok'n wi' yor son, one night. I ask no more o' yo than that yo clear me—an I trust to yo to do 't."

The bearers being now ready to carry him away, and the surgeon being anxious for his removal, those who had torches or lanterns, prepared to go in front of the litter. Before it was raised, and while they were arranging how to go, he said to Rachael, looking upward at the star:

"Often as I coom to myseln, and found it shinin on me down there in my trouble, I thowt it were the star as guided to Our Saviour's home. I awmust think it be the very star!"

They lifted him up, and he was overjoyed to find that they were about to take him in the direction whither the star seemed to him to lead.

"Rachael, beloved lass! Don't let go my hand. We may walk together t'night, my dear!"

"I will hold thy hand, and keep beside thee, Stephen, all the way."

"Bless thee! Will soombody be pleased to coover my face!"

They carried him very gently along the fields, and down the lanes, and over the wide landscape; Rachael always holding the hand in hers. Very few whispers broke the mournful silence. It was soon a funeral procession. The star had shown him where to find the God of the poor; and through humility, and sorrow, and forgiveness, he had gone to his Redeemer's rest.

CHAPTER VII : *Whelp-hunting*

BEFORE the ring formed round the Old Hell Shaft was broken, one figure had disappeared from within it. Mr. Bounderby and his shadow had not stood near Louisa, who held her father's arm, but in a retired place by themselves. When Mr. Gradgrind was summoned to the couch, Sissy, attentive to all that happened, slipped behind that wicked shadow—a sight in the horror of his face, if there had been eyes there for any sight but one—and whispered in his ear. Without turning his head, he conferred with her a few moments, and vanished. Thus the whelp had gone out of the circle before the people moved.

When the father reached home, he sent a message to Mr. Bounderby's, desiring his son to come to him directly. The reply was, that Mr. Bounderby having missed him in the crowd, and seeing nothing of him since, had supposed him to be at Stone Lodge.

"I believe, father," said Louisa, "he will not come back to town to-night." Mr. Gradgrind turned away, and said no more.

In the morning, he went down to the Bank himself as soon

as it was opened, and seeing his son's place empty (he had not the courage to look in at first) went back along the street to meet Mr. Bounderby on his way there. To whom he said that, for reasons he would soon explain, but entreated not then to be asked for, he had found it necessary to employ his son at a distance for a little while. Also, that he was charged with the duty of vindicating Stephen Blackpool's memory, and declaring the thief. Mr. Bounderby, quite confounded, stood stock-still in the street after his father-in-law had left him, swelling like an immense soap-bubble, without its beauty.

Mr. Gradgrind went home, locked himself in his room, and kept it all that day. When Sissy and Louisa tapped at his door, he said, without opening it, "Not now, my dears; in the evening." On their return in the evening, he said, "I am not able yet—to-morrow." He ate nothing all day, and had no candle after dark; and they heard him walking to and fro late at night.

But, in the morning he appeared at breakfast at the usual hour, and took his usual place at the table. Aged and bent he looked, and quite bowed down; and yet he looked a wiser man, and a better man, than in the days when in this life he wanted nothing but Facts. Before he left the room, he appointed a time for them to come to him; and so, with his grey head drooping, went away.

"Dear father," said Louisa, when they kept their appointment, "you have three young children left. They will be different, *I* will be different yet, with Heaven's help."

She gave her hand to Sissy, as if she meant with her help too.

"Your wretched brother," said Mr. Gradgrind. "Do you think he had planned this robbery, when he went with you to the lodging?"

"I fear so, father. I know he had wanted money very much, and had spent a great deal."

"The poor man being about to leave town, it came into his evil brain to cast suspicion on him?"

"I think it must have flashed upon him while he sat there, father. For, I asked him to go there with me. The visit did not originate with him."

"He had some conversation with the poor man. Did he take him aside?"

"He took him out of the room. I asked him afterwards, why he had done so, and he made a plausible excuse; but since last night, father, and when I remember the circumstances by its light, I am afraid I can imagine too truly what passed between them."

"Let me know," said her father, "if your thoughts present your guilty brother in the same dark view as mine."

"I fear, father," hesitated Louisa, "that he must have made

some representation to Stephen Blackpool—perhaps in my name, perhaps in his own—which induced him to do in good faith and honesty, what he had never done before, and to wait about the Bank those two or three nights before he left the town."

"Too plain!" returned the father. "Too plain!"

He shaded his face, and remained silent for some moments. Recovering himself, he said:

"And now, how is he to be found? How is he to be saved from justice? In the few hours that I can possibly allow to elapse before I publish the truth, how is he to be found by us, and only by us? Ten thousand pounds could not effect it."

"Sissy has effected it, father."

He raised his eyes to where she stood, like a good fairy in his house, and said in a tone of softened gratitude and grateful kindness, "It is always you, my child!"

"We had our fears," Sissy explained, glancing at Louisa, "before yesterday; and when I saw you brought to the side of the litter last night, and heard what passed (being close to Rachael all the time), I went to him when no one saw, and said to him, 'Don't look at me. See where your father is. Escape at once, for his sake and your own!' He was in a tremble before I whispered to him, and he started and trembled more then, and said, 'Where can I go? I have very little money, and I don't know who will hide me!' I thought of father's old circus. I have not forgotten where Mr. Sleary goes at this time of year, and I read of him in a paper only the other day. I told him to hurry there, and tell his name, and ask Mr. Sleary to hide him till I came. 'I'll get to him before the morning,' he said. And I saw him shrink away among the people."

"Thank Heaven!" exclaimed his father. "He may be got abroad yet."

It was the more hopeful as the town to which Sissy had directed him was within three hours' journey of Liverpool, whence he could be swiftly despatched to any part of the world. But, caution being necessary in communicating with him—for there was a greater danger every moment of his being suspected now, and nobody could be sure at heart but that Mr. Bounderby himself, in a bullying vein of public zeal, might play a Roman part—it was consented that Sissy and Louisa should repair to the place in question, by a circuitous course, alone; and that the unhappy father, setting forth in an opposite direction, should get round to the same bourne by another and wider route. It was further agreed that he should not present himself to Mr. Sleary, lest his intentions should be mistrusted, or the intelligence of his arrival should cause his son to take flight anew; but, that the communication should be left to Sissy and Louisa to open; and that they should inform the cause of so much misery and disgrace, of his father's being at hand and of the purpose for which they had come. When these arrangements had been well considered and were fully understood by all three, it was time to begin to carry them into execution. Early in the afternoon, Mr. Gradgrind walked direct from his own house into the country, to be taken up on the line by which he was to travel; and at night the remaining two set forth upon their different course, encouraged by not seeing any face they knew.

The two travelled all night, except when they were left, for odd numbers of minutes, at branch-places, up illimitable flights of steps, or down wells—which was the only variety of those branches—and, early in the morning, were turned out on a swamp, a mile or two from the town they sought. From this dismal spot they were rescued by a savage old postilion, who happened to be up early, kicking a horse in a fly: and so were smuggled into the town by all the back lanes where the pigs lived: which, although not a magnificent or even savoury approach, was, as is usual in such cases, the legitimate highway.

The first thing they saw on entering the town was the skeleton of Sleary's Circus. The company had departed for another town more than twenty miles off, and had opened there last night. The connection between the two places was by a hilly turn-pike road, and the travelling on that road was very slow. Though they took but a hasty breakfast, and no rest (which it would have been in vain to seek under such anxious circumstances), in was noon before they began to find the bills of Sleary's Horseriding on barns and walls, and one o'clock when they stopped in the market-place.

A Grand Morning Performance by the Riders, commencing at that very hour, was in course of announcement by the bellman as they set their feet upon the stones of the street. Sissy recommended that, to avoid making inquiries and attracting attention in the town, they should present themselves to pay at the door. If Mr. Sleary were taking the money, he would be sure to know her, and would proceed with discretion. If he were not he would be sure to see them inside; and, knowing what he had done with the fugitive, would proceed with discretion still.

Therefore, they repaired, with fluttering hearts, to the well-remembered booth. The flag with the inscription SLEARY'S HORSERIDING, was there; and the Gothic niche was there; but Mr. Sleary was not there. Master Kidderminster, grown too maturely turfy to be received by the wildest credulity as Cupid any more, had yielded to the invincible force of circumstances (and his beard), and, in the capacity of a man who made himself generally useful, presided on this occasion over the exchequer—having also a drum in reserve, on which to expend his leisure moments and superfluous forces. In the extreme sharpness of his look-out for base coin, Mr. Kidderminster, as at present situated, never saw anything but money; so Sissy passed him unrecognised, and they went in.

The Emperor of Japan, on a steady old white horse stencilled with black spots, was twirling five wash-hand basins at once, as it is the favourite recreation of that monarch to do. Sissy, though well acquainted with his Royal line, had no personal knowledge of the present Emperor, and his reign was peaceful. Miss Josephine Sleary, in her celebrated graceful Equestrian Tyrolean Flower-Act, was then announced by a new clown (who humorously said Cauliflower Act), and Mr. Sleary appeared, leading her in.

Mr. Sleary had only made one cut at the Clown with his long whip-lash, and the Clown had only said, "If you do it again, I'll throw the horse at you!" when Sissy was recognised both by father and daughter. But they both got through the Act with great self-possession; and Mr. Sleary, saving for the first instant, conveyed no more expression into his locomotive eye than into his fixed one. The performance seemed a little long to Sissy and Louisa, particularly when it stopped to afford the Clown an opportunity of telling Mr. Sleary (who said "Indeed, sir!" to all his observations in the calmest way, and with his eye on the house) about two legs sitting on three legs looking at one leg, when in came four legs, and laid hold of one leg, and up got two legs, caught hold of three legs, and threw 'em at four legs, who ran away with one leg. For, although an ingenious Allegory relating to a butcher, a three-legged stool, a dog, and a leg of mutton, this narrative consumed time; and they were in great suspense. At last, however, little fair-haired Josephine made her curtsey amid great applause; and the Clown, left alone in the ring, had just warmed himself, and said, "Now, *I'*ll have a turn!" when Sissy was touched on the shoulder, and beckoned out.

She took Louisa with her; and they were received by Mr. Sleary in a very little private apartment, with canvas sides, a grass floor, and a wooden ceiling all aslant, on which the box company stamped their approbation, as if they were coming through. "Thethilia," said Mr. Sleary, who had brandy and water at hand, "it doth me good to thee you. You wath alwayth a favourite with uth, and you've done uth credith thinth the old timeth I'm thure. You mutht thee our people, my dear, afore we thpeak of bithnith, or they'll break their hearth—ethpethially the women. Here'th Jothphine hath been and got married to E. W. B. Childerth, and thee hath got a boy, and though he'th only three yearth old, he thtickth on to any pony you can bring againtht him. He'th named The Little Wonder of Thcolathtic Equitation; and if you don't hear of that boy at Athley'th, you'll hear of him at Parith. And you recollect Kidderminthter, that wath thought to be rather thweet upon yourthelf? Well. He'th married too. Married a widder. Old enough to be hith mother. Thee wath Tight-rope, thee wath, and now thee'th nothing—on accounth of fat. They've got two children, tho we're thtrong in the Fairy bithnith and the Nurthery dodge. If you wath to thee our Children in the Wood, with their father and mother both a dyin' on a horthe—their uncle a rethieving of 'em ath hith wardth, upon a horthe—themthelvth both a goin' a black-berryin' on a horthe—and the Robinth a coming in to cover 'em with leavth, upon a horthe—you'd thay it wath the com-pletetht thing ath ever you thet your eyeth on! And you remember Emma Gordon, my dear, ath wath a'moth a mother to you? Of courthe you do; I needn't athk. Well! Emma, thee lotht her huthband. He wath throw'd a heavy backfall off a Elephant in a thort of a Pagoda thing ath the Thultan of Indieth, and he never got the better of it; and thee married a thecond time—married a Cheethemonger ath fell in love with her from the front—and he'th a Overtheer and makin' a fortun."

These various changes, Mr. Sleary, very short of breath now, related with great heartiness, and with a wonderful kind of innocence, considering what a bleary and brandy-and-watery old veteran he was. Afterwards he brought in Josephine, and E. W. B. Childers (rather deeply lined in the jaws by daylight), and the Little Wonder of Scholastic Equitation, and in a word, all the company. Amazing creatures they were in Louisa'a eyes, so white and pink of complexion, so scant of dress, and so demonstrative of leg; but it was very agreeable to see them crowding about Sissy, and very natural in Sissy to be unable to refrain from tears.

"There! Now Thethilia hath kithd all the children, and hugged all the women, thaken handth all round with all the men, clear, every one of you, and ring in the band for the thecond part!"

As soon as they were gone, he continued in a low tone. "Now, Thethilia, I don't athk to know any thecreth, but I thuppothe I may conthider thith to be Mith Thquire."

"This is his sister. Yes."

"And t'other on'th daughter. That'h what I mean. Hope I thee you well, mith. And I hope the Thquire'th well?"

"My father will be here soon," said Louisa, anxious to bring him to the point. "Is my brother safe?"

"Thafe and thound," he replied. "I want you jutht to take a peep at the Ring, mith, through here. Thethilia, you know the dodgeth; find a thpy-hole for yourthelf."

They each looked though a chink in the boards.

"That'th Jack the Giant Killer—piethe of comic infant bithnith," said Sleary. "There'th a property-houthe, you thee. for Jack to hide in; there'th my Clown with a thauthepan-lid and a thpit, for Jack'th thervant; there'th little Jack himthelf in a thplendid thoot of armour; there'th two comic black thervanth twithe ath big ath the houthe, to thand by it and to bring it in and clear it; and the Giant (a very ecthpenthive bathket one), he an't on yet. Now, do you thee 'em all?"

"Yes," they both said.

"Look at 'em again," said Sleary, "look at 'em well. You thee 'em all? Very good. Now, mith;" he put a form for them to sit on; "I have my opinionth, and the Thquire your father hath hith. I don't want to know what your brother'th been up to; ith better for me not to know. All I thay ith, the Thquire hath thtood by Thethilia, and I'll thtand by the Thquire. Your brother ith one o' them black thervanth."

Louisa uttered an exclamation, partly of distress, partly of satisfaction.

"Ith a fact," said Sleary, "and even knowin' it, you couldn't put your finger on him. Let the Thquire come. I shall keep your brother here after the performanth. I than't undreth him, nor yet wath hith paint off. Let the Thquire come here after the performanth, or come here yourthelf after the performanth, and you thall find your brother, and have the whole plathe to talk to him in. Never mind the lookth of him, ath long ath he'th well hid."

Louisa, with many thanks and with a lightened load, detained Mr. Sleary no longer then. She left her love for her brother, with her eyes full of tears; and she and Sissy went away until later in the afternoon.

Mr. Gradgrind arrived within an hour afterwards. He too had encountered no one whom he knew; and was now sanguine with Sleary's assistance of getting his disgraced son to Liverpool in the night. As neither of the three could be his companion without almost identifying him under any disguise, he prepared a letter to a correspondent whom he could trust, beseeching him to ship the bearer off at any cost, to North or South America, or any distant part of the world to which he could be the most speedily and privately despatched.

This done, they walked about, waiting for the Circus to be quite vacated; not only by the audience, but by the company and by the horses. After watching it a long time, they saw Mr. Sleary bring out a chair and sit down by the side-door, smoking; as if that were his signal that they might approach.

"Your thervant, Thquire," was his cautious salutation as they passed in. "If you want me you'll find me here. You muthn't mind your thon having a comic livery on."

They all three went in; and Mr. Gradgrind sat down forlorn, on the Clown's performing chair in the middle of the ring.

On one of the back benches, remote in the subdued light and the strangeness of the place, sat the villainous whelp, sulky to the last, whom he had the misery to call his son.

In a preposterous coat, like a beadle's, with cuffs and flaps exaggerated to an unspeakable extent; in an immense waistcoat, knee-breeches, buckled shoes, and a mad cocked hat; with nothing fitting him, and everything of coarse material, moth-eaten and full of holes; with seams in his black face, where fear and heat had started through the greasy composition daubed all over it; anything so grimly, detestably, ridiculously shameful as the whelp in his comic livery, Mr. Gradgrind never could by any other means have believed in, weighable and measurable fact though it was. And one of his model children had come to this!

At first the whelp would not draw any nearer, but persisted in remaining up there by himself. Yielding at length, if any consession so suddenly made can be called yielding, to the entreaties of Sissy—for Louisa he disowned altogether—he came down, bench by bench, until he stood in the sawdust, on the verge of the circle, as far as possible, within its limits from where his father sat.

"How was this done?" asked the father.

"How was what done?" moodily answered the son.

"This robbery," said the father, raising his voice upon the word.

"I forced the safe myself over night, and shut it up ajar before I went away. I had had the key that was found, made long before. I dropped it that morning, that it might be supposed to have been used. I didn't take the money all at once. I pretended to put my balance away every night, but I didn't. Now you know all about it."

"If a thunderbolt had fallen on me," said the father, "it would have shocked me less than this!"

"I don't see why," grumbled the son. "So many people are employed in situations of trust; so many people, out of so many, will be dishonest. I have heard you talk, a hundred times, of its being a law. How can *I* help laws? You have comforted others with such things, father. Comfort yourself!"

The father buried his face in his hands, and the son stood in his disgraceful grotesqueness, biting straw: his hands, with the black partly worn away inside, looking like the hands of a monkey. The evening was fast closing in; and from time to time, he turned the whites of his eyes restlessly and impatiently towards his father. They were the only parts of his face that showed any life or expression, the pigment upon it was so thick.

"You must be got to Liverpool, and sent abroad."

"I suppose I must. I can't be more miserable anywhere,"

whimpered the whelp, "than I have been here, ever since I can remember. That's one thing."

Mr. Gradgrind went to the door, and returned with Sleary, to whom he submitted the question, How to get this deplorable object away?

"Why, I've been thinking of it, Thquire. There'th not muth time to lothe, tho you muth thay yeth or no. Ith over twenty mileth to the rail. There'th a coath in half an hour, that goeth to the rail, 'purpothe to cath the mail train. That train will take him right to Liverpool."

"But look at him," groaned Mr. Gradgrind. "Will any coach——"

"I don't mean that he thould go in comic livery," said Sleary. "Thay the word, and I'll make a Jothkin of him, out of the wardrobe, in five minutes."

"I don't understand," said Mr. Gradgrind.

"A Jothkin—a Carter. Make up your mind quick, Thquire. There'll be beer to feth. I've never met with nothing but beer ath'll ever clean a comic blackamoor."

Mr. Gradgrind rapidly assented; Mr. Sleary rapidly turned out from a box, a small frock, a felt hat, and other essentials; the whelp rapidly changed clothes behind a screen of baize; Mr. Sleary rapidly brought beer, and washed him white again.

"Now," said Sleary, "come along to the coath, and jump up behind; I'll go with you there, and they'll thuppothe you one of my people. Thay farewell to your family, and tharp'th the word." With which he delicately retired.

"Here is your letter," said Mr. Gradgrind. "All necessary means will be provided for you. Atone, by repentance and better conduct, for the shocking action you have committed, and the dreadful consequences to which it has led. Give me your hand, my poor boy, and may God forgive you as I do!"

The culprit was moved to a few abject tears by these words and their pathetic tone. But, when Louisa opened her arms, he repulsed her afresh.

"Not you. I don't want to have anything to say to you!"

"O Tom, Tom, do we end so, after all my love!"

"After all your love!" he returned, obdurately. "Pretty love! Leaving old Bounderby to himself, and packing my best friend Mr. Harthouse off, and going home just when I was in the greatest danger. Pretty love that! Coming out with every word about our having gone to that place, when you saw the net was gathering round me. Pretty love that! You have regularly given me up. You never cared for me."

"Tharp'th the word!" said Sleary, at the door.

They all confusedly went out: Louisa crying to him that she forgave him, and loved him still, and that he would one day be sorry to have left her so, and glad to think of these her last words, far away: when some one ran against them.

Mr. Gradgrind and Sissy, who were both before him while his sister yet clung to his shoulder, stopped and recoiled.

For, there was Bitzer, out of breath, his thin lips parted, his thin nostrils distended, his white eyelashes quivering, his colourless face more colourless than ever, as if he ran himself into a white heat, when other people ran themselves into a glow. There he stood, panting and heaving, as if he had never stopped since the night, now long ago, when he had run them down before.

"I'm sorry to interfere with your plans," said Bitzer, shaking his head, "but I can't allow myself to be done by horseriders. I must have young Mr. Tom; he mustn't be got away by horseriders; here he is in a smock frock, and I must have him!"

By the collar, too, it seemed. For, so he took possession of him.

CHAPTER VIII: *Philosophical*

THEY went back into the booth, Sleary shutting the door to keep intruders out. Bitzer, still holding the paralysed culprit by the collar, stood in the Ring, blinking at his old patron through the darkness of the twilight.

"Bitzer," said Mr. Gradgrind, broken down, and miserably submissive to him, "have you a heart?"

"The circulation, sir," returned Bitzer, smiling at the oddity of the question, "couldn't be carried on without one. No man, sir, acquainted with the facts established by Harvey relating to the circulation of the blood, can doubt that I have a heart."

"Is it accessible," cried Mr. Gradgrind, "to any compassionate influence?"

"It is accessible to Reason, sir," returned the excellent young man. "And to nothing else."

They stood looking at each other; Mr. Gradgrind's face as white as the pursuer's.

"What motive—even what motive in reason—can you have for preventing the escape of this wretched youth," said Mr. Gradgrind, "and crushing his miserable father? See his sister here. Pity us!"

"Sir," returned Bitzer, in a very business-like and logical manner, "since you ask me what motive I have in reason, for taking young Mr. Tom back to Coketown, it is only reasonable to let you know. I have suspected young Mr. Tom of this bank robbery from the first. I had had my eye upon him before that time, for I knew his ways. I have kept my observations to myself, but I have made them; and I have got ample proofs against him now, besides his running away, and besides his own confession, which I was just in time to overhear. I had the pleasure of watching your house yesterday morning, and following you here. I am going to take young Mr. Tom back to Coketown, in order to deliver him over to Mr. Bounderby. Sir, I have no doubt whatever that Mr. Bounderby will then promote me to young Mr. Tom's situation. And I wish to have his situation, sir, for it will be a rise to me, and will do me good."

"If this is solely a question of self-interest with you"— Mr. Gradgrind began.

"I beg your pardon for interrupting you, sir," returned Bitzer; "but I am sure you know that the whole social system is a question of self-interest. What you must always appeal to, is a person's self-interest. It's your only hold. We are so constituted. I was brought up in that catechism when I was very young, sir, as you are aware."

"What sum of money," said Mr. Gradgrind, "will you set against your expected promotion?"

"Thank you, sir," returned Bitzer, "for hinting at the proposal; but I will not set any sum against it. Knowing that your clear head would propose that alternative, I have gone over the calculations in my mind; and I find that to compound a felony, even on very high terms indeed, would not be as safe and good for me as my improved prospects in the Bank."

"Bitzer," said Mr. Gradgrind, stretching out his hands as though he would have said, See how miserable I am! "Bitzer, I have but one chance left to soften you. You were many years at my school. If, in remembrance of the pains bestowed upon you there, you can persuade yourself in any degree to disregard your present interest and release my son, I entreat and pray you to give him the benefit of that remembrance."

"I really wonder, sir," rejoined the old pupil in an argumentative manner, "to find you taking a position so untenable. My schooling was paid for; it was a bargain; and when I came away, the bargain ended."

It was a fundamental principle of the Gradgrind philosophy that everything was to be paid for. Nobody was ever on any account to give anybody anything, or render anybody help without purchase. Gratitude was to be abolished, and the virtues springing from it were not to be. Every inch of the existence of mankind, from birth to death, was to be a bargain across the counter. And if we didn't get to Heaven that way, it was not a politico-economical place, and we had no business there.

"I don't deny," added Bitzer, "that my schooling was cheap. But that comes right, sir. I was made in the cheapest market, and have to dispose of myself in the dearest."

He was a little troubled here, by Louisa and Sissy crying.

"Pray don't do that," said he, "it's of no use doing that: it only worries. You seem to think that I have some animosity against young Mr. Tom; whereas I have none at all. I am only going, on the reasonable grounds I have mentioned, to take him back to Coketown. If he was to resist, I should set up the cry of Stop Thief! But, he won't resist, you may depend upon it."

Mr. Sleary, who with his mouth open and his rolling eye as immovably jammed in his head as his fixed one, had listened to these doctrines with profound attention, here stepped forward.

"Thquire, you know perfectly well, and your daughter knowth perfectly well (better than you, becauthe I thed it to her), that I didn't know what your thon had done, and that I didn't want to know—I thed it wath better not, though I only thought, then, it wath thome thkylarking. However, thith young man having made it known to be a robbery of a bank, why, that'th a theriouth thing; muth too theriouth a thing for me to compound, ath thith young man hath very properly called it. Conthequently, Thquire, you muthn't quarrel with me if I take thith young man'th thide, and thay he'th right and there'th no help for it. But I tell you what I'll do, Thquire; I'll drive your thon and thith young man over to the rail, and prevent expothure here. I can't conthent to do more, but I'll do that."

Fresh lamentations from Louisa, and deeper affliction on Mr. Gradgrind's part, followed this desertion of them by their last friend. But Sissy glanced at him with great attention; nor did she in her own breast misunderstand him. As they were all going out again, he favoured her with one slight roll of his movable eye, desiring her to linger behind. As he locked the door, he said excitedly:

"The Thquire thtood by you, Thethilia, and I'll thtand by the Thquire. More than that: thith ith a prethiouth rathcal, and belongth to that bluthtering Cove that my people nearly pitht out o' winder. It'll be a dark night; I've got a horthe that'll do anything but thpeak; I've got a pony that'll go fifteen mile an hour with Childerth driving of him; I've got a dog that'll keep a man to one plathe four-and-twenty hourth. Get a word with the young Thquire. Tell him, when he theeth our horthe begin to danthe, not to be afraid of being thpilt, but to look out for a pony-gig coming up. Tell him, when he theeth that gig clothe by, to jump down, and it'll take him off at a rattling pathe. If my dog leth thith young man thtir a peg on foot, I give him leave to go. And if my horthe ever thtirth from that thpot where he beginth a danthing, till the morning—I don't know him?—Tharp'th the word!"

The word was so sharp, that in ten minutes Mr. Childers,

sauntering about the market-place in a pair of slippers, had his cue, and Mr. Sleary's equipage was ready. It was a fine sight, to behold the learned dog barking round it, and Mr. Sleary instructing him, with his one practicable eye, that Bitzer was the object of his particular attentions. Soon after dark they all three got in and started; the learned dog (a formidable creature) already pinning Bitzer with his eye, and sticking close to the wheel on his side, that he might be ready for him in the event of his showing the slightest disposition to alight.

The other three set up at the inn all night in great suspense. At eight o'clock in the morning Mr. Sleary and the dog reappeared: both in high spirits.

"All right, Thquire!" said Mr. Sleary, "your thon may be aboard-a-thip by thith time. Childerth took him off, an hour and a half after we left here latht night. The horthe danthed the polka till he wath dead beat (he would have walthed if he hadn't been in harneth), and then I gave him the word and he went to thleep comfortable. When that prethiouth young Rathcal thed he'd go for'ard afoot, the dog hung on to hith neck-hankercher with all four legth in the air and pulled him down and rolled him over. Tho he come back into the drag, and there he that, 'till I turned the horthe'th head, at half-patht thixth thith morning."

Mr. Gradgrind overwhelmed him with thanks, of course; and hinted as delicately as he could, at a handsome remuneration in money.

"I don't want money mythelf, Thquire; but Childerth ith a family man, and if you wath to like to offer him a five-pound note, it mightn't be unactheptable. Likewithe if you wath to thtand a collar for the dog, or a thet of bellth for the horthe, I thould be very glad to take 'em. Brandy and water I alwayth take." He had already called for a glass, and now called for another. "If you wouldn't think it going to far, Thquire, to make a little thpread for the company at about three and thixth a head, not reckoning Luth, it would make 'em happy."

All these little tokens of his gratitude, Mr. Gradgrind very willingly undertook to render. Though he thought them far too slight, he said, for such a service.

"Very well, Thquire; then, if you'll only give a Hortheriding a bethpeak, whenever you can, you'll more than balanthe the account. Now, Thquire, if your daughter will ethcuthe me, I thould like one parting word with you."

Louisa and Sissy withdrew into an adjoining room; Mr. Sleary, stirring and drinking his brandy and water as he stood, went on:

"Thquire, you don't need to be told that dogth ith wonderful animalth."

"Their instinct," said Mr. Gradgrind, "is surprising."

"Whatever you call it—and I'm bleth if *I* know what to call it"—said Sleary, "it ith athtonithing. The way in whith a dog'll find you—the dithtanthe he'll come!"

"His scent," said Mr. Gradgrind, "being so fine."

"I'm bleth if I know what to call it," repeated Sleary, shaking his head, "but I have had dogth find me, Thquire, in a way that made me think whether that dog hadn't gone to another dog, and thed, 'You don't happen to know a perthon of the name of Thleary, do you? Perthon of the name of Thleary, in the Horthe-Riding way—thtout man—game eye?' And whether that dog mightn't have thed, 'Well, I can't thay I know him mythelf, but I know a dog that I think would be likely to be acquainted with him.' And whether that dog mightn't have thought it over, and thed, 'Thleary, Thleary! O yeth, to be sure! A friend of mine menthioned him to me at one time. I can get you hith addreth directly.' In conthequenth of my being afore the public, and going about tho muth, you thee, there mutht be a number of dogth acquainted with me, Thquire, that *I* don't know!"

Mr. Gradgrind seemed to be quite confounded by this speculation.

"Anyway," said Sleary, after putting his lips to his brandy and water, "ith fourteen months ago, Thquire, thinthe we wath at Chethter. We wath getting up our Children in the Wood one morning, when there cometh into our Ring, by the thtage door, a dog. He had travelled a long way, he wath in very bad condithon, he wath lame, and pretty well blind. He went round to our children, one after another, as if he wath a-theeking for a child he know'd; and then he come to me, and throwd hithelf up behind, and thtood on hith two forelegth, weak ath he wath, and then he wagged hith tail and died. Thquire, that dog wath Merrylegth."

"Sissy's father's dog!"

"Thethilia'th father'th old dog. Now, Thquire, I can take my oath, from my knowledge of that dog, that that man wath dead—and buried—afore that dog come back to me. Joth'-phine and Childerth and me talked it over for a long time, whether I thould write or not. But we agreed, 'No. There'th nothing comfortable to tell; why unthettle her mind, and make her unhappy?' Tho, whether her father bathely detherted her; or whether he broke hith own heart alone, rather than pull her down along with him; never will be known, now, Thquire, till—no, not till we know how the dogth findth uth out!"

"She keeps the bottle that he sent her for, to this hour; and she will believe in his affection to the last moment of her life," said Mr. Gradgrind.

"It theemth to prethent two thingth to a perthon, don't it. Thquire?" said Mr. Sleary, musing as he looked down into the depths of his brandy and water: "one, that there ith a love in the world, not all Thelf-interetht after all, but thomething very different; t'other, that it hath a way of ith own of calculating or not calculating, whith thomehow or another ith at leatht ath hard to give a name to, ath the wayth of the dogth ith!"

Mr. Gradgrind looked out of the window, and made no reply. Mr. Sleary emptied his glass and recalled the ladies.

"Thethilia, my dear, kith me and good-bye! Mith Thquire, to thee you treating of her like a thithter, and a thithter that you trutht and honour with all your heart and more, ith a very pretty thight to me. I hope your brother may live to be better detherving of you, and a greater comfort to you. Thquire, thake handth, firtht and latht! Don't be croth with uth poor vagabondth. People mutht be amuthed. They can't be alwayth a learning, nor yet they can't be alwayth a working, they an't made for it. You *mutht* have uth, Thquire. Do the withe thing and the kind thing too, and make the betht of uth; not the wurtht!"

"And I never thought before," said Mr. Sleary, putting his head in at the door again to say it, "that I wath tho muth of a Cackler!"

CHAPTER IX : *Final*

IT is a dangerous thing to see anything in the sphere of a vain blusterer, before the vain blusterer sees it himself. Mr. Bounderby felt that Mrs. Sparsit had audaciously anticipated him, and presumed to be wiser than he. Inappeasably indignant with her for her triumphant discovery of Mrs. Pegler, he turned this presumption, on the part of a woman in her dependent position, over and over in his mind, until it accumulated with turning like a great snowball. At last he made the discovery that to discharge this highly connected female—to have it in his power to say, "She was a woman of family, and wanted to stick to me, but I wouldn't have it, and got rid of her"—would be to get the utmost possible amount of crowning glory out of the connection, and at the same time to punish Mrs. Sparsit according to her deserts.

Filled fuller than ever with this great idea, Mr. Bounderby came in to lunch, and sat himself down in the dining-room of former days, where his portrait was. Mrs. Sparsit sat by the fire, with her foot in her cotton stirrup, little thinking whither she was posting.

Since the Pegler affair, this gentlewoman had covered her pity for Mr. Bounderby, with a veil of quiet melancholy and contrition. In virtue thereof, it had become her habit to assume a woful look, which woful look she now bestowed upon her patron.

"What's the matter now, ma'am?" said Mr. Bounderby, in a very short, rough way.

"Pray, sir," returned Mrs. Sparsit, "do not bite my nose off."

"Bite your nose off, ma'am?" repeated Mr. Bounderby. "*Your* nose!" meaning, as Mrs. Sparsit conceived, that it was too developed a nose for the purpose. After which offensive implication, he cut himself a crust of bread, and threw the knife down with a noise.

Mrs. Sparsit took her foot out of her stirrup, and said, "Mr. Bounderby, sir!"

"Well, ma'am?" retorted Mr. Bounderby. "What are you staring at?"

"May I ask, sir," said Mrs. Sparsit, "have you been ruffled this morning?"

"Yes, ma'am."

"May I inquire, sir," pursued the injured woman, "whether *I* am the unfortunate cause of your having lost your temper?"

"Now, I'll tell you what, ma'am," said Bounderby, "I am not come here to be bullied. A female may be highly connected, but she can't be permitted to bother and badger a man in my position, and I am not going to put up with it." (Mr. Bounderby felt it necessary to get on: foreseeing that if he allowed of details, he would be beaten.)

Mrs. Sparsit first elevated, then knitted, her Coriolanian eyebrows; gathered up her work into its proper basket; and rose.

"Sir," said she, majestically. "It is apparent to me that I am in your way at present. I will retire to my own apartment."

"Allow me to open the door, ma'am."

"Thank you, sir; I can do it for myself."

"You had better allow me, ma'am," said Bounderby, passing her, and getting his hand upon the lock; "because I can take the opportunity of saying a word to you, before you go. Mrs. Sparsit, ma'am, I rather think you are cramped here, do you know? It appears to me that, under my humble roof, there's hardly opening enough for a lady of your genius in other people's affairs."

Mrs. Sparsit gave him a look of the darkest scorn, and said with great politeness, "Really, sir?"

"I have been thinking it over, you see, since the late affairs have happened, ma'am," said Bounderby; "and it appears to my poor judgment——"

"Oh! Pray, sir," Mrs. Sparsit interposed, with sprightly cheerfulness, "don't disparage your judgment. Everybody knows how unerring Mr. Bounderby's judgment is. Everybody has had proofs of it. It must be the theme of general conversation. Disparage anything in yourself but your judgment, sir," said Mrs. Sparsit, laughing.

Mr. Bounderby, very red and uncomfortable, resumed:

"It appears to me, ma'am, I say, that a different sort of establishment altogether would bring out a lady of *your* powers. Such an establishment as your relation, Lady Scadgers's, now. Don't you think you might find some affairs there, ma'am, to interfere with?"

"It never occurred to me before, sir," returned Mrs. Sparsit; "but now you mention it, I should think it highly probable."

"Then suppose you try, ma'am," said Bounderby, laying an envelope with a cheque in it in her little basket. "You can take your own time for going, ma'am; but perhaps in the meanwhile, it will be more agreeable to a lady of your powers of mind, to eat her meals by herself, and not to be intruded upon. I really ought to apologise to you—being only Josiah Bounderby of Coketown—for having stood in your light so long."

"Pray don't name it, sir," returned Mrs. Sparsit. "If that portrait could speak, sir—but it has the advantage over the original of not possessing the power of committing itself and disgusting others,—it would testify, that a long period has elapsed since I first habitually addressed it as the picture of a Noodle. Nothing that a Noodle does, can awaken surprise or indignation; the proceedings of a Noodle can only inspire contempt."

Thus saying, Mrs. Sparsit, with her Roman features like a medal struck to commemorate her scorn of Mr. Bounderby, surveyed him fixedly from head to foot, swept disdainfully past him, and ascended the staircase. Mr. Bounderby closed the door, and stood before the fire; projecting himself after his old explosive manner into his portrait—and into futurity.

Into how much of futurity? He saw Mrs. Sparsit fighting out a daily fight at the points of all the weapons in the female armoury, with the grudging, smarting, peevish, tormenting Lady Scadgers, still laid up in bed with her mysterious leg, and gobbling her insufficient income down by about the middle of every quarter, in a mean little airless lodging, a mere closet for one, a mere crib for two; but did he see more? Did he catch any glimpse of himself making a show of Bitzer to strangers, as the rising young man, so devoted to his master's great merits, who had won young Tom's place, and had almost captured young Tom himself, in the times when by various rascals he was spirited away? Did he see any faint reflection of his own image making a vainglorious will, whereby five-and-twenty Humbugs, past five-and-fifty years of age, each taking upon himself the name, Josiah Bounderby of Coketown, should for ever dine in Bounderby Hall, for ever lodge in Bounderby Buildings, for ever attend a Bounderby chapel, for ever go to sleep under a Bounderby chaplain, for ever be supported out of a Bounderby estate, and for ever nauseate all healthy stomachs, with a vast amount of Bounderby balderdash and bluster? Had he any prescience of the day, five years to come, when Josiah Bounderby of Coketown was to die of a fit in the Coketown street, and this same precious will was to begin its long career of quibble, plunder, false pretences, vile example, little service and much law? Probably not. Yet the portrait was to see it all out.

Here was Mr. Gradgrind on the same day, and in the same hour, sitting thoughtful in his own room. How much futurity did *he* see? Did he see himself, a white-haired decrepit man, bending his hitherto inflexible theories to appointed circumstances; making his facts and figures subservient to Faith, Hope, and Charity; and no longer trying to grind that Heavenly trio in his dusty little mills? Did he catch sight of himself, therefore, much despised by his late political associates? Did he see them, in the era of its being quite settled that the national dustmen have only to do with one another, and owe no duty to an abstraction called a People, "taunting the honourable gentleman" with this and with that and with what not, five nights a week, until the small hours of the morning? Probably he had that much foreknowledge, knowing his men.

Here was Louisa on the night of the same day, watching the fire as in days of yore, though with a gentler and a humbler face. How much of the future might arise before *her* vision? Broadsides in the streets, signed with her father's name, exonerating the late Stephen Blackpool, weaver, from misplaced suspicion, and publishing the guilt of his own son, with such extenuation as his years and temptation (he could not bring himself to add, his education) might beseech; were of the Present. So, Stephen Blackpool's tombstone, with her father's record of his death, was almost of the Present, for she knew it was to be. These things she could plainly see. But, how much of the Future?

A working woman, christened Rachael, after a long illness once again appearing at the ringing of the Factory bell, and passing to and fro at the set hours, among the Coketown Hands; a woman of pensive beauty, always dressed in black, but sweet-tempered and serene, and even cheerful; who, of all the people in the place, alone appeared to have compassion on a degraded, drunken wretch of her own sex, who was sometimes seen in the town secretly begging of her, and crying to her; a woman working, ever working, but content to do it, and preferring to do it as her natural lot, until she should be too old to labour any more? Did Louisa see this? Such a thing was to be.

A lonely brother, many thousands of miles away, writing, on

paper blotted with tears, that her words had too soon come true, and that all the treasures in the world would be cheaply bartered for a sight of her dear face? At length this brother coming nearer home, with hope of seeing her, and being delayed by illness; and then a letter, in a strange hand, saying "he died in hospital, of fever, such a day, and died in penitence and love of you: his last word being your name"? Did Louisa see these things? Such things were to be.

Herself again a wife—a mother—lovingly watchful of her children, ever careful that they should have a childhood of the mind no less than a childhood of the body, as knowing it to be even a more beautiful thing, and a possession, any hoarded scrap of which, is a blessing and happiness to the wisest? Did Louisa see this? Such a thing was never to be.

But, happy Sissy's happy children loving her; all children loving her; she, grown learned in childish lore; thinking no innocent and pretty fancy ever to be despised; trying hard to know her humbler fellow creatures, and to beautify their lives of machinery and reality with those imaginative graces and delights, without which the heart of infancy will wither up, the sturdiest physical manhood will be morally stark death, and the plainest national prosperity figures can show, will be the Writing on the Wall,—she holding this course as part of no fantastic vow, or bond, or brotherhood, or sisterhood, or pledge, or covenant, or fancy dress, or fancy fair; but simply as a duty to be done,—did Louisa see these things of herself? These things were to be.

Dear reader! It rests with you and me, whether, in our two fields of action, similar things shall be or not. Let them be! We shall sit with lighter bosoms on the hearth, to see the ashes of our fires turn grey and cold.

THE END OF HARD TIMES

NO THOROUGHFARE

THE OVERTURE

DAY of the month and year, November the thirtieth, one thousand eight hundred and thirty-five. London Time by the great clock of Saint Paul's, ten at night. All the lesser London churches strain their metallic throats. Some, flippantly begin before the heavy bell of the great cathedral; some, tardily begin three, four, half a dozen, strokes behind it; all are insufficiently near accord, to leave a resonance in the air, as if the winged father who devours his children, had made a sounding sweep with his gigantic scythe in flying over the city.

What is this clock lower than most of the rest, and nearer to the ear, that lags so far behind to-night as to strike into the vibration alone? This is the clock of the Hospital for Foundling Children. Time was, when the Foundlings were received without question in a cradle at the gate. Time is, when inquiries are made respecting them, and they are taken as by favour from the mothers who relinquish all natural knowledge of them and claim to them for evermore.

The moon is at the full, and the night is fair with light clouds. The day has been otherwise than fair, for slush and mud, thickened with the droppings of heavy fog, lie black in the streets. The veiled lady who flutters up and down near the postern-gate of the Hospital for Foundling Children has need to be well shod to-night.

She flutters to and fro, avoiding the stand of hackney-coaches, and often pausing in the shadow of the western end of the great quadrangle wall, with her face turned towards the gate. As above her there is the purity of the moonlit sky, and below her there are the defilements of the pavements, so may she, haply, be divided in her mind between two vistas of reflection or experience? As her foot-prints crossing and recrossing one another have made a labyrinth in the mire, so may her track in life have involved itself in an intricate and unravellable tangle?

The postern-gate of the Hospital for Foundling Children opens, and a young woman comes out. The lady stands aside, observes closely, sees that the gate is quietly closed again from within, and follows the young woman.

Two or three streets have been traversed in silence before she, following close behind the object of her attention, stretches out her hand and touches her. Then the young woman stops and looks round, startled.

"You touched me last night, and, when I turned my head, you would not speak. Why do you follow me like a silent ghost?"

"It was not," returned the lady, in a low voice, "that I would not speak, but that I could not when I tried."

"What do you want of me? I have never done you any harm?"

"Never."

"Do I know you?"

"No."

"Then what can you want of me?"

"Here are two guineas in this paper. Take my poor little present, and I will tell you."

Into the young woman's face, which is honest and comely, comes a flush as she replies: "There is neither grown person nor child in all the large establishment that I belong to who hasn't a good word for Sally. I am Sally. Could I be so well thought of, if I was to be bought?"

"I do not mean to buy you; I mean only to reward you very slightly."

Sally firmly, but not urgently, closes and puts back the offering hand. "If there is anything that I can do for you, ma'am, that I will not do for its own sake, you are much mistaken in me if you think that I will do it for money. What is it you want?"

"You are one of the nurses or attendants at the Hospital; I saw you leave to-night and last night."

"Yes, I am. I am Sally."

"There is a pleasant patience in your face which makes me believe that very young children would take readily to you."

"God bless 'em! So they do."

The lady lifts her veil, and shows a face no older than the nurse's. A face far more refined and capable than hers, but wild and worn with sorrow.

"I am the miserable mother of a baby lately received under your care. I have a prayer to make to you."

Instinctively respecting the confidence which has drawn aside the veil, Sally—whose ways are all ways of simplicity and spontaneity—replaces it, and begins to cry.

"You will listen to my prayer?" the lady urges. "You will not be deaf to the agonised entreaty of such a broken suppliant as I am?"

"Oh, dear, dear, dear!" cries Sally. "What shall I say, or can I say! Don't talk of prayers. Prayers are to be put up to the Good Father of All, and not to nurses and such. And there! I am only to hold my place for half a year longer, till another young woman can be trained up to it. I am going to be married. I shouldn't have been out last night, and I shouldn't have been out to-night, but that my Dick (he is the young man I am going to be married to) lies ill, and I help his mother and sister to watch him. Don't take on so, don't take on so!"

"O good Sally, dear Sally," moans the lady, catching at her dress entreatingly. "As you are hopeful and I am hopeless; as a fair way in life is before you, which can never, never, be before me; as you can aspire to become a respected wife, and as you can aspire to become a proud mother; as you are a living, loving woman, and must die; for GOD's sake hear my distracted petition!"

"Deary, deary, deary ME!" cries Sally, her desperation culminating in the pronoun, "what am I ever to do? And there! See how you turn my own words back upon me. I tell you I am going to be married, on purpose to make it clearer to you that I am going to leave, and therefore couldn't help you if I would, Poor Thing, and you make it seem to my own self as if I was cruel in going to be married and not helping you. It ain't kind. Now, is it kind, Poor Thing?"

"Sally! Hear me, my dear. My entreaty is for no help in the future. It applies to what is past. It is only to be told in two words."

"There! This is worse and worse," cries Sally, "supposing that I understand what two words you mean."

"You do understand. What are the names they have given my poor baby? I ask no more than that. I have read of the customs of the place. He has been christened in the chapel, and registered by some surname in the book. He was received last Monday evening. What have they called him?"

Down upon her knees in the foul mud of the by-way into which they have strayed—an empty street without a thoroughfare, giving on the dark gardens of the Hospital—the lady would drop in her passionate entreaty, but that Sally prevents her.

"Don't! Don't! You make me feel as if I was setting myself up to be good. Let me look in your pretty face again. Put your two hands in mine. Now, promise. You will never ask me anything more than the two words?"

"Never! Never!"

"You will never put them to a bad use, if I say them!"

"Never! Never!"

"Walter Wilding."

The lady lays her face upon the nurse's breast, draws her close in her embrace with both arms, murmurs a blessing and the words, "Kiss him for me!" and is gone.

Day of the month and year, the first Sunday in October, one thousand eight hundred and forty-seven. London Time by the great clock of Saint Paul's, half-past one in the afternoon. The clock of the Hospital for Foundling Children is well up with the Cathedral to-day. Service in the chapel is over, and the Foundling Children are at dinner.

There are numerous lookers-on at the dinner, as the custom is. There are two or three governors, whole families from the congregation, smaller groups of both sexes, individual stragglers of various degrees. The bright autumnal sun strikes freshly into the wards; and the heavy-framed windows through which it shines, and the panelled walls on which it strikes, are such windows and such walls as pervade Hogarth's pictures. The girls' refectory (including that of the younger children) is the principal attraction. Neat attendants silently glide about the orderly and silent tables; the lookers-on move or stop as the fancy takes them; comments in whispers on face such a number from such a window are not unfrequent; many of the faces are of a character to fix attention. Some of the visitors from the outside public are accustomed visitors. They have established a speaking acquaintance with the occupants of particular seats at the tables, and halt at those points to bend down and say a word or two. It is no disparagement to their kindness that those points are generally points where personal attractions are. The monotony of long spacious rooms and the double lines of faces is agreeably relieved by these incidents, although so slight.

A veiled lady, who has no companion, goes among the company. It would seem that curiosity and opportunity have never brought her there before. She has the air of being a little troubled by the sight, and, as she goes the length of the tables, it is with a hesitating step and an uneasy manner. At length she comes to the refectory of the boys. They are so much less popular than the girls that it is bare of visitors when she looks in at the doorway.

But just within the doorway chances to stand, inspecting, an elderly female attendant: some order of matron or housekeeper. To whom the lady addresses natural questions: As, how many boys? At what age are they usually put out in life? Do they often take a fancy to the sea? So, lower and lower in tone until the lady puts the question: "Which is Walter Wilding?"

Attendant's head shaken. Against the rules.

"You know which is Walter Wilding?"

So keenly does the attendant feel the closeness with which the lady's eyes examine her face, that she keeps her own eyes fast upon the floor, lest by wandering in the right direction they should betray her.

"I know which is Walter Wilding, but it is not my place, ma'am, to tell names to visitors."

"But you can show me without telling me."

The lady's hand moves quietly to the attendant's hand.

Pause and silence.

"I am going to pass round the tables," says the lady's interlocutor, without seeming to address her. "Follow me with your eyes. The boy that I stop and speak to, will not matter to you. But the boy that I touch, will be Walter Wilding. Say nothing more to me, and move a little away."

Quickly acting on the hint, the lady passes on into the room, and looks about her. After a few moments, the attendant, in a staid official way, walks down outside the line of tables commencing on her left hand. She goes the whole length of the line, turns, and comes back on the inside. Very slightly glancing in the lady's direction, she stoops, bends forward, and speaks. The boy whom she addresses, lifts his head and replies. Good-humouredly and easily, as she listens to what he says, she lays her hand upon the shoulder of the next boy on his right. That the action may be well noted, she keeps her hand on the shoulder while speaking in return, and pats it twice or thrice before moving away. She completes her tour of the tables, touching no one else, and passes out by a door at the opposite end of the long room.

Dinner is done, and the lady, too, walks down outside the line of tables commencing on her left hand, goes the whole length of the line, turns, and comes back on the inside. Other people have strolled in, fortunately for her, and stand sprinkled about. She lifts her veil, and, stopping at the touched boy, asks how old he is?

"I am twelve, ma'am," he answers, with his bright eyes fixed on hers.

"Are you well and happy?"

"Yes, ma'am."

"May you take these sweetmeats from my hand?"

"If you please to give them to me."

In stooping low for the purpose, the lady touches the boy's face with her forehead and with her hair. Then, lowering her veil again, she passes on, and passes out without looking back.

ACT I : *The Curtain Rises*

IN a courtyard in the City of London, which was No Thoroughfare either for vehicles or foot-passengers; a courtyard diverging from a steep, a slippery, and a winding street connecting Tower-street with the Middlesex shore of the Thames; stood the place of business of Wilding and Co., Wine Merchants. Probably as a jocose acknowledgment of the obstructive character of this main approach, the point nearest to its base

at which one could take the river (if so inodorously minded)
bore the appellation Break-Neck-Stairs. The courtyard itself had likewise been descriptively entitled in old time,
Cripple Corner.

Years before the year one thousand eight hundred and sixty-
one, people had left off taking boat at Break-Neck-Stairs, and
watermen had ceased to ply there. The slimy little causeway
had dropped into the river by a slow process of suicide, and
two or three stumps of piles and a rusty iron mooring-ring
were all that remained of the departed Break-Neck glories.
Sometimes, indeed, a laden coal barge would bump itself into
the place, and certain laborious heavers, seemingly mud-en-
gendered, would arise, deliver the cargo in the neighbourhood,
shove off, and vanish; but at most times the only commerce of
Break-Neck-Stairs arose out of the conveyance of casks and
bottles, both full and empty, both to and from the cellars of
Wilding and Co., Wine Merchants. Even that commerce was
but occasional, and through three-fourths of its rising tides the
dirty indecorous drab of a river would come solitarily oozing
and lapping at the rusty ring, as if it had heard of the Doge
and the Adriatic, and wanted to be married to the great con-
server of its filthiness, the Right Honourable the Lord Mayor.

Some two hundred and fifty yards on the right, up the opposite hill (approaching it from the low ground of Break-Neck-
Stairs) was Cripple Corner. There was a pump in Cripple
Corner, there was a tree in Cripple Corner. All Cripple Corner
belonged to Wilding and Co., Wine Merchants. Their cellars
burrowed under it, their mansion towered over it. It really
had been a mansion in the days when merchants inhabited the
City, and had a ceremonious shelter to the doorway without
visible support, like the sounding-board over an old pulpit. It
had also a number of long narrow strips of window, so disposed
in its grave brick front as to render it symmetrically ugly. It
had also, on its roof, a cupola with a bell in it.

"When a man at five-and-twenty can put his hat on, and
can say 'this hat covers the owner of this property and of the
business which is transacted on this property,' I consider, Mr.
Bintrey, that, without being boastful, he may be allowed to be
deeply thankful. I don't know how it may appear to you, but
so it appears to me."

Thus Mr. Walter Wilding to his man of law, in his own
counting-house; taking his hat down from its peg to suit the
action to the word, and hanging it up again when he had done
so, not to overstep the modesty of nature.

An innocent, open-speaking, unused-looking man, Mr.
Walter Wilding, with a remarkably pink and white complexion,
and a figure much too bulky for so young a man, though of a
good stature. With crispy curling brown hair, and amiable
bright blue eyes. An extremely communicative man: a man

with whom loquacity was the irrestrainable outpouring of contentment and gratitude. Mr. Bintrey, on the other hand, a cautious man with twinkling beads of eyes in a large over-hanging bald head, who inwardly but intensely enjoyed the comicality of openness of speech, or hand, or heart.

"Yes," said Mr. Bintrey. "Yes. Ha, ha!"

A decanter, two wine-glasses, and a plate of biscuits, stood on the desk.

"You like this forty-five year old port wine?" said Mr. Wilding.

"Like it?" repeated Mr. Bintrey. "Rather, sir!"

"It's from the best corner of our best forty-five year old bin," said Mr. Wilding.

"Thank you, sir," said Mr. Bintrey. "It's most excellent."

He laughed again, as he held up his glass and ogled it, at the highly ludicrous idea of giving away such wine.

"And now," said Wilding, with a childish enjoyment in the discussion of affairs, "I think we have got everything straight, Mr. Bintrey."

"Everything straight," said Bintrey.

"A partner secured——"

"Partner secured," said Bintrey.

"A housekeeper advertised for——"

"Housekeeper advertised for," said Bintrey, "'apply per-sonally at Cripple Corner, Great Tower-street, from ten to twelve'—to-morrow, by the bye."

"My late dear mother's affairs wound up——"

"Wound up," said Bintrey.

"And all charges paid."

"And all charges paid," said Bintrey, with a chuckle: probably occasioned by the droll circumstance that they had been paid without a haggle.

"The mention of my late dear mother," Mr. Wilding con-tinued, his eyes filling with tears and his pocket-handkerchief drying them, "unmans me still, Mr. Bintrey. You know how I loved her; you (her lawyer) know how she loved me. The utmost love of mother and child was cherished between us, and we never experienced one moment's division or unhappi-ness from the time when she took me under her care. Thir-teen years in all! Thirteen years under my late dear mother's care, Mr. Bintrey, and eight of them her confidentially ac-knowledged son! You know the story, Mr. Bintrey, who but you, sir!" Mr. Wilding sobbed and dried his eyes, without attempt at concealment, during these remarks.

Mr. Bintrey enjoyed his comical port, and said, after rolling it in his mouth: "I know the story."

"My late dear mother, Mr. Bintrey," pursued the wine-merchant, "had been deeply deceived, and had cruelly suffered. But on that subject my late dear mother's lips were for ever sealed. By whom deceived, or under what circumstances, Heaven only knows. My late dear mother never betrayed her betrayer."

"She had made up her mind," said Mr. Bintrey, again turning his wine on his palate, "and she could hold her peace." An amused twinkle in his eyes pretty plainly added—"A devilish deal better than *you* ever will!"

"'Honour,'" said Mr. Wilding, sobbing as he quoted from the Commandments, "'thy father and thy mother, that thy days may be long in the land.' When I was in the Foundling, Mr. Bintrey, I was at such a loss how to do it, that I apprehended my days would be short in the land. But I afterwards came to honour my mother deeply, profoundly. And I honour and revere her memory. For seven happy years, Mr. Bintrey," pursued Wilding, still with the same innocent catching in his breath, and the same unabashed tears, "did my excellent mother article me to my predecessors in this business, Pebbleson Nephew. Her affectionate forethought likewise apprenticed me to the Vintners' Company, and made me in time a Free Vintner, and—and—everything else that the best of mothers could desire. When I came of age, she bestowed her inherited share in this business upon me; it was her money that afterwards bought out Pebbleson Nephew, and painted in Wilding and Co.; it was she who left me everything she possessed, but the mourning ring you wear. And yet, Mr. Bintrey," with a fresh burst of honest affection, "she is no more. It is a little over half a year since she came into the Corner to read on that door-post with her own eyes, WILDING AND CO., WINE MERCHANTS. And yet she is no more!"

"Sad. But the common lot, Mr. Wilding," observed Bintrey. "At some time or other we must all be no more." He placed the forty-five year old port wine in the universal condition, with a relishing sigh.

"So now, Mr. Bintrey," pursued Wilding, putting away his pocket-handkerchief, and smoothing his eyelids with his fingers, "now that I can no longer show my love and honour for the dear parent to whom my heart was mysteriously turned by Nature when she first spoke to me, a strange lady, I sitting at our Sunday dinner-table in the Foundling, I can at least show that I am not ashamed of having been a Foundling, and that I, who never knew a father of my own, wish to be a father to all in my employment. Therefore," continued Wilding, becoming enthusiastic in his loquacity, "therefore, I want a thoroughly good housekeeper to undertake this dwelling-house of Wilding and Co., Wine Merchants, Cripple Corner, so that I may restore in it some of the old relations betwixt employer and employed! So that I may live in it on the spot where my money is made! So that I may daily sit at the head of the table at which the people in my employment eat together, and may eat of the same roast and boiled, and drink of the same beer! So that the people in my employment may lodge under the same roof with me! So that we may one and all—I beg your pardon, Mr. Bintrey, but that old singing in my head has suddenly come on, and I shall feel obliged if you will lead me to the pump."

Alarmed by the excessive pinkness of his client, Mr. Bintrey lost not a moment in leading him forth into the courtyard. It was easily done, for the counting-house in which they talked together opened on to it, at one side of the dwelling-house. There, the attorney pumped with a will, obedient to a sign from the client, and the client laved his head and face with both hands, and took a hearty drink. After these remedies, he declared himself much better.

"Don't let your good feelings excite you," said Bintrey, as they returned to the counting-house, and Mr. Wilding dried himself on a jack-towel behind an inner door.

"No, no. I won't," he returned, looking out of the towel. "I won't. I have not been confused, have I?"

"Not at all. Perfectly clear."

"Where did I leave off, Mr. Bintrey?"

"Well, you left off—but I wouldn't excite myself, if I was you, by taking it up again just yet."

"I'll take care. I'll take care. The singing in my head came on at where, Mr. Bintrey?"

"At roast, and boiled, and beer," answered the lawyer, prompting—"lodging under the same roof—and one and all——"

"Ah! And one and all singing in the head together——"

"Do you know I really *would not* let my good feelings excite me, if I was you," hinted the lawyer again, anxiously. "Try some more pump."

"No occasion, no occasion. All right, Mr. Bintrey. And one and all forming a kind of family! You see, Mr. Bintrey, I was not used in my childhood to that sort of individual existence which most individuals have led, more or less, in their childhood. After that time I became absorbed in my late dear mother. Having lost her, I find that I am more fit for being one of a body than one by myself one. To be that, and at the same time to do my duty to those dependent on me, and attach them to me, has a patriarchal and pleasant air about it. I don't know how it may appear to you, Mr. Bintrey, but so it appears to me."

"It is not I who am all-important in the case, but you," returned Bintrey. "Consequently, how it may appear to me, is of very small importance."

"It appears to *me*," said Mr. Wilding, in a glow, "hopeful, useful, de-lightful!"

"Do you know," hinted the lawyer again, "I really would not ex——"

"I am not going to. Then there's Handel."

"There's who?" asked Bintrey.

"Handel, Mozart, Haydn, Kent, Purcell, Doctor Arne, Greene, Mendelssohn. I know the choruses to those anthems by heart. Foundling Chapel Collection. Why shouldn't we learn them together!"

"Who learn them together?" asked the lawyer, rather shortly.

"Employer and employed."

"Ay, ay!" returned Bintrey, mollified; as if he had half expected the answer to be, Lawyer and client. "That's another thing."

"Not another thing, Mr. Bintrey! The same thing. A part of the bond among us. We will form a Choir in some quiet church near the Corner here, and, having sung together of a Sunday with a relish, we will come home and take an early dinner together with a relish. The object that I have at heart now, is to get this system well in action without delay, so that my new partner may find it founded when he enters on his partnership."

"All good be with it!" exclaimed Bintrey, rising. "May it prosper! Is Joey Ladle to take a share in Handel, Mozart, Haydn, Kent, Purcell, Doctor Arne, Greene, and Mendelssohn?"

"I hope so."

"I wish them all well out of it," returned Bintrey, with much heartiness. "Good-bye, sir."

They shook hands and parted. Then (first knocking with his knuckles for leave) entered to Mr. Wilding, from a door of communication between his private counting-house and that in which his clerks sat, the Head Cellarman of the cellars of Wilding and Co., Wine Merchants, and erst Head Cellarman of the cellars of Pebbleson Nephew. The Joey Ladle in question. A slow and ponderous man, of the drayman order of human architecture, dressed in a corrugated suit and bibbed apron, apparently a composite of door-mat and rhinoceros-hide.

"Respecting this same boarding and lodging, Young Master Wilding," said he.

"Yes, Joey?"

"Speaking for myself, Young Master Wilding—and I never did speak and I never do speak for no one else—I don't want no boarding nor yet no lodging. But if you wish to board me and to lodge me, take me. I can peck as well as most men. Where I peck, ain't so high a object with me as What I peck. Nor even so high a object with me as How Much I peck. Is all to live in the house, Young Master Wilding? The two other cellarmen, the three porters, the two 'prentices, and the odd men?"

"Yes. I hope we shall all be an united family, Joey."

"Ah!" said Joey. "I hope they may be."

"They? Rather say we, Joey."

Joey Ladle shook his head. "Don't look to me to make we on it, Young Master Wilding, not at my time of life and under the circumstances which has formed my disposition. I have said to Pebbleson Nephew many a time, when they have said to me, 'Put a livelier face upon it, Joey'—I have said to them, 'Gentlemen, it is all wery well for you that has been accustomed to take your wine into your systems by the conwivial channel of your throttles, to put a lively face upon it; but,' I says, 'I have been accustomed to take *my* wine in at the pores of the skin, and, took that way, it acts different. It acts depressing. It's one thing, gentlemen,' I says to Pebbleson Nephew, 'to charge your glasses in a dining-room with a Hip Hurrah and a Jolly Companions Every One, and it's another thing to be charged yourself, through the pores, in a low dark cellar and a mouldy atmosphere. It makes all the difference betwixt bubbles and wapours,' I tells Pebbleson Nephew. And so it do. I've been a cellarman my life through, with my mind fully given to the business. What's the consequence? I'm as muddled a man as lives—you won't find a muddleder man than me—nor yet you won't find my equal in molloncolly. Sing of Filling the bumper fair, Every drop you sprinkle, O'er the brow of care, Smooths away a wrinkle? Yes. P'raps so. But try filling yourself through the pores, underground, when you don't want to it!"

"I am sorry to hear this, Joey. I had even thought that you might join a singing-class in the house."

"Me, sir? No, no, Young Master Wilding, you won't catch Joey Ladle muddling the Armory. A pecking-machine, sir, is all that I am capable of proving myself, out of my cellars; but that you're welcome to, if you think it's worth your while to keep such a thing on your premises."

"I do, Joey."

"Say no more, sir. The Business's word is my law. And you're a going to take Young Master George Vendale partner into the old Business?"

"I am, Joey."

"More changes, you see! But don't change the name of the Firm again. Don't do it, Young Master Wilding. It was bad luck enough to make it Yourself and Co. Better by far have left it Pebbleson Nephew that good luck always stuck to. You should never change luck when its good, sir."

"At all events, I have no intention of changing the name of the House again, Joey."

"Glad to hear it, and wish you good day, Young Master

Wilding. But you had better by half," muttered Joey Ladle, inaudibly, as he closed the door and shook his head, "have let the name alone from the first. You had better by half have followed the luck instead of crossing it."

Enter the Housekeeper]

The wine-merchant sat in his dining-room next morning, to receive the personal applicants for the vacant post in his establishment. It was an old-fashioned wainscoted room; the panels ornamented with festoons of flowers carved in wood; with an oaken floor, a well-worn Turkey carpet, and dark mahogany furniture, all of which had seen service and polish under Pebbleson Nephew. The great sideboard had assisted at many business-dinners given by Pebbleson Nephew to their connection, on the principle of throwing sprats overboard to catch whales; and Pebbleson Nephew's comprehensive three-sided plate-warmer, made to fit the whole front of the large fire-place, kept watch beneath it over a sarcophagus-shaped cellaret that had in its time held many a dozen of Pebbleson Nephew's wine. But the little rubicund old bachelor with a pigtail, whose portrait was over the sideboard (and who could easily be identified as decidedly Pebbleson and decidedly not Nephew), had retired into another sarcophagus, and the plate-warmer had grown as cold as he. So, the golden and black griffins that supported the candelabra, with black balls in their mouths at the end of gilded chains, looked as if in their old age they had lost all heart for playing at ball, and were dolefully exhibiting their chains in the missionary line of inquiry, whether they had not earned emancipation by this time, and were not griffins and brothers?

Such a Columbus of a morning was the summer morning, that it discovered Cripple Corner. The light and warmth pierced in at the open windows, and irradiated the picture of a lady hanging over the chimney-piece, the only other decoration of the walls.

"My mother at five-and-twenty," said Mr. Wilding to himself, as his eyes enthusiastically followed the light to the portrait's face, "I hang up here, in order that visitors may admire my mother in the bloom of her youth and beauty. My mother at fifty I hang in the seclusion of my own chamber, as a remembrance sacred to me. Oh! It's you, Jarvis!"

These latter words he addressed to a clerk who had tapped at the door, and now looked in.

"Yes, sir. I merely wish to mention that it's gone ten, sir, and that there are several females in the Counting-House."

"Dear me!" said the wine-merchant, deepening in the pink of his complexion and whitening in the white, "are there several? So many as several? I had better begin before there are more. I'll see them one by one, Jarvis, in the order of their arrival."

Hastily entrenching himself in his easy-chair at the table behind a great inkstand, having first placed a chair on the other side of the table opposite his own seat, Mr. Wilding entered on his task with considerable trepidation.

He ran the gauntlet that must be run on any such occasion. There were the usual species of profoundly unsympathetic women, and the usual species of much too sympathetic women. There were the buccaneering widows who came to seize him, and who gripped umbrellas under their arms, as if each umbrella were he, and each griper had got him. There were towering maiden ladies who had seen better days, and who came armed with clerical testimonials to their theology, as if he were Saint Peter with his keys. There were gentle maiden ladies who came to marry him. There were professional housekeepers, like non-commissioned officers, who put him through his domestic exercise, instead of submitting themselves to catechism. There were languid invalids to whom salary was not so much an object as the comforts of a private hospital. There were sensitive creatures who burst into tears on being addressed, and had to be restored with glasses of cold water. There were some respondents who came two together, a highly promising one and a wholly unpromising one: of whom the promising one answered all questions charmingly, until it would at last appear that she was not a candidate at all, but only the friend of the unpromising one, who had glowered in absolute silence and apparent injury.

At last, when the good wine-merchant's simple heart was failing him, there entered an applicant quite different from all the rest. A woman, perhaps fifty, but looking younger, with a face remarkable for placid cheerfulness, and a manner no less remarkable for its quiet expression of equability of temper. Nothing in her dress could have been changed to her advantage. Nothing in the noiseless self-possession of her manner could have been changed to her advantage. Nothing could have been in better unison with both, than her voice when she answered the question: "What name shall I have the pleasure of noting down?" with the words, "My name is Sarah Goldstraw. Mrs. Goldstraw. My husband has been dead many years, and we had no family."

Half a dozen questions had scarcely extracted as much to the purpose from any one else. The voice dwelt so agreeably on Mr. Wilding's ear as he made his note, that he was rather long about it. When he looked up again, Mrs. Goldstraw's glance had naturally gone round the room, and now returned to him from the chimney-piece. Its expression was one of frank readiness to be questioned, and to answer straight.

"You will excuse my asking you a few questions?" said the modest wine-merchant.

"Oh, surely, sir. Or I should have no business here."

"Have you filled the station of housekeeper before?"

"Only once. I have lived with the same widow lady for twelve years. Ever since I lost my husband. She was an invalid, and is lately dead: which is the occasion of my now wearing black."

"I do not doubt that she has left you the best credentials?" said Mr. Wilding.

"I hope I may say, the very best. I thought it would save trouble, sir, if I wrote down the name and address of her representatives, and brought it with me." Laying a card on the table.

"You singularly remind me, Mrs. Goldstraw," said Wilding, taking the card beside him, "of a manner and tone of voice that I was once acquainted with. Not of an individual—I feel sure of that, though I cannot recall what it is I have in my mind—but of a general bearing. I ought to add, it was a kind and pleasant one."

She smiled, as she rejoined: "At least, I am very glad of that, sir."

"Yes," said the wine-merchant, thoughtfully repeating his last phrase, with a momentary glance at his future housekeeper, "it was a kind and pleasant one. But that is the most I can make of it. Memory is sometimes like a half-forgotten dream. I don't know how it may appear to you, Mrs. Goldstraw, but so it appears to me."

Probably it appeared to Mrs. Goldstraw in a similar light, for she quickly assented to the proposition. Mr. Wilding then offered to put himself at once in communication with the gentleman named upon the card: a firm of proctors in Doctors' Commons. To this, Mrs. Goldstraw thankfully assented. Doctors' Commons not being far off, Mr. Wilding suggested the feasibility of Mrs. Goldstraw's looking in again, say in three hours' time. Mrs. Goldstraw readily undertook to do so. In fine, the result of Mr. Wilding's inquiries being eminently satisfactory, Mrs. Goldstraw was that afternoon engaged (on her own perfectly fair terms) to come to-morrow and set up her rest as housekeeper in Cripple Corner.

The Housekeeper Speaks]

On the next day Mrs. Goldstraw arrived, to enter on her domestic duties.

Having settled herself in her own room, without troubling the servants, and without wasting time, the new housekeeper announced herself as waiting to be favoured with any instructions which her master might wish to give her. The wine-merchant received Mrs. Goldstraw in the dining-room, in which he had seen her on the previous day; and, the usual preliminary civilities having passed on either side, the two sat down to take counsel together on the affairs of the house.

"About the meals, sir?" said Mrs. Goldstraw. "Have I a large, or a small, number to provide for?"

"If I can carry out a certain old-fashioned plan of mine," replied Mr. Wilding "you will have a large number to provide for. I am a lonely single man, Mrs. Goldstraw; and I hope to live with all the persons in my employment as if they were members of my family. Until that time comes, you will only have me, and the new partner whom I expect immediately, to provide for. What my partner's habits may be, I cannot yet say. But I may describe myself as a man of regular hours, with an invariable appetite that you may depend upon to an ounce."

"About breakfast, sir?" asked Mrs. Goldstraw. "Is there anything particular——?"

She hesitated, and left the sentence unfinished. Her eyes turned slowly away from her master, and looked towards the chimney-piece. If she had been a less excellent and experienced housekeeper, Mr. Wilding might have fancied that her attention was beginning to wander at the very outset of the interview.

"Eight o'clock is my breakfast-hour," he resumed. "It is one of my virtues to be never tired of broiled bacon, and it is one of my vices to be habitually suspicious of the freshness of eggs." Mrs. Goldstraw looked back at him, still a little divided between her master's chimney-piece and her master. "I take tea," Mr. Wilding went on; "and I am perhaps rather nervous and fidgety about drinking it, within a certain time after it is made. If my tea stands too long——"

He hesitated, on his side, and left the sentence unfinished. If he had not been engaged in discussing a subject of such paramount interest to himself as his breakfast, Mrs. Goldstraw might have fancied that *his* attention was beginning to wander at the very outset of the interview.

"If your tea stands too long, sir——?" said the housekeeper, politely taking up her master's lost thread.

"If my tea stands too long," repeated the wine-merchant, mechanically, his mind getting further and further away from his breakfast, and his eyes fixing themselves more and more inquiringly on his housekeeper's face. "If my tea—— Dear, dear me, Mrs. Goldstraw! what *is* the manner and tone of voice that you remind me of? It strikes me even more strongly to-day, than it did when I saw you yesterday. What can it be?"

"What can it be?" repeated Mrs. Goldstraw.

She said the words, evidently thinking while she spoke them of something else. The wine-merchant, still looking at her inquiringly, observed that her eyes wandered towards the chimney-piece once more. They fixed on the portrait of his mother, which hung there, and looked at it with that slight contraction of the brow which accompanies a scarcely conscious effort of memory. Mr. Wilding remarked:

"My late dear mother, when she was five-and-twenty."

Mrs. Goldstraw thanked him with a movement of the head for being at the pains to explain the picture, and said, with a cleared brow, that it was the portrait of a very beautiful lady.

Mr. Wilding, falling back into his former perplexity, tried once more to recover that lost recollection, associated so closely, and yet so undiscoverably, with his new housekeeper's voice and manner.

"Excuse my asking you a question which has nothing to do with me or my breakfast," he said. "May I inquire if you have ever occupied any other situation than the situation of housekeeper?"

"Oh yes, sir. I began life as one of the nurses at the Foundling."

"Why, that's it!" cried the wine-merchant, pushing back his chair. "By Heaven! Their manner is the manner you remind me of!"

In an astonished look at him, Mrs. Goldstraw changed colour, checked herself, turned her eyes upon the ground, and sat still and silent.

"What is the matter?" asked Mr. Wilding.

"Do I understand that you were in the Foundling, sir?"

"Certainly. I am not ashamed to own it."

"Under the name you now bear?"

"Under the name of Walter Wilding."

"And the lady—?" Mrs. Goldstraw stopped short, with a look at the portrait which was now unmistakably a look of alarm.

"You mean my mother," interrupted Mr. Wilding.

"Your—mother," repeated the housekeeper, a little constrainedly, "removed you from the Foundling? At what age, sir?"

"At between eleven and twelve years old. It's quite a romantic adventure, Mrs. Goldstraw."

He told the story of the lady having spoken to him, while he sat at dinner with the other boys in the Foundling, and of all that had followed, in his innocently communicative way. "My poor mother could never have discovered me," he added, "if she had not met with one of the matrons who pitied her. The matron consented to touch the boy whose name was 'Walter Wilding' as she went round the dinner-tables—and so my mother discovered me again, after having parted from me as an infant at the Foundling doors."

At those words Mrs. Goldstraw's hand, resting on the table, dropped helplessly into her lap. She sat, looking at her new master, with a face that had turned deadly pale, and with eyes that expressed an unutterable dismay.

"What does this mean?" asked the wine-merchant. "Stop!" he cried. "Is there something else in the past time which I ought to associate with you? I remember, my mother telling me of another person at the Foundling, to whose kindness she owed a debt of gratitude. When she first parted with me, as an infant, one of the nurses informed her of the name that had been given to me in the institution. You were that nurse?"

"God forgive me, sir—I was that nurse!"

"God forgive you?"

"We had better get back, sir (if I may make so bold as to say so), to my duties in the house," said Mrs. Goldstraw. "Your breakfast hour is eight. Do you lunch, or dine, in the middle of the day?"

The excessive pinkness which Mr. Bintrey had noticed in his client's face began to appear there once more. Mr. Wilding put his hand to his head, and mastered some momentary confusion in that quarter, before he spoke again.

"Mrs. Goldstraw," he said, "you are concealing something from me!"

The housekeeper obstinately repeated, "Please to favour me, sir, by saying whether you lunch, or dine, in the middle of the day?"

"I don't know what I do in the middle of the day. I can't enter into my household affairs, Mrs. Goldstraw, till I know why you regret an act of kindness to my mother, which she always spoke of gratefully to the end of her life. You are not doing me a service by your silence. You are agitating me, you are alarming me, you are bringing on the singing in my head."

His hand went up to his head again, and the pink in his face deepened by a shade or two.

"It's hard, sir, on just entering your service," said the housekeeper, "to say what may cost me the loss of your good will. Please to remember, end how it may, that I only speak because you have insisted on my speaking, and because I see that I am alarming you by my silence. When I told the poor lady, whose portrait you have got there, the name by which her infant was christened in the Foundling, I allowed myself to forget my duty, and dreadful consequences, I am afraid, have followed from it. I'll tell you the truth, as plainly as I can. A few months from the time when I had informed the lady of her baby's name, there came to our institution in the country another lady (a stranger), whose object was to adopt one of our children. She brought the needful permission with her, and after looking at a great many of the children, without being able to make up her mind, she took a sudden fancy to one of the babies—a boy—under my care. Try, pray try, to compose yourself, sir! It's no use disguising it any longer. The child the stranger took away was the child of that lady whose portrait hangs there!"

Mr. Wilding started to his feet. "Impossible!" he cried out, vehemently. "What are you talking about? What absurd story are you telling me now? There's her portrait! Haven't I told you so already? The portrait of my mother!"

"When that unhappy lady removed you from the Foundling in after years," said Mrs. Goldstraw, gently, "she was the victim, and you were the victim, sir, of a dreadful mistake."

He dropped back into his chair. "The room goes round with me," he said. "My head! my head!" The housekeeper rose in alarm, and opened the windows. Before she could get to the door to call for help, a sudden burst of tears relieved the oppression which had at first almost appeared to threaten his life. He signed entreatingly to Mrs. Goldstraw not to leave him. She waited until the paroxysm of weeping had worn itself out. He raised his head as he recovered himself, and looked at her with the angry unreasoning suspicion of a weak man.

"Mistake?" he said, wildly repeating her last words. "How do I know you are not mistaken yourself?"

"There is no hope that I am mistaken, sir. I will tell you why, when you are better fit to hear it."

"Now! now!"

The tone in which he spoke warned Mrs. Goldstraw that it would be cruel kindness to let him comfort himself a moment longer with the vain hope that she might be wrong. A few words more would end it—and those few words she determined to speak.

"I have told you," she said, "that the child of the lady whose portrait hangs there, was adopted in its infancy, and taken away by a stranger. I am as certain of what I say as that I am now sitting here, obliged to distress you, sir, sorely against my will. Please to carry your mind on, now, to about three months after that time. I was then at the Foundling, in London, waiting to take some children to our institution in the country. There was a question that day about naming an infant—a boy—who had just been received. We generally named them out of the Directory. On this occasion, one of the gentlemen who managed the Hospital happened to be looking over the Register. He noticed that the name of the baby who had been adopted ('Walter Wilding') was scratched out—for the reason, of course, that the child had been removed for good from our care. 'Here's a name to let,' he said. 'Give it to the new Foundling who has been received to-day.' The name was given, and the child was christened. You, sir, were that child!"

The wine-merchant's head dropped on his breast. "I was

that child!" he said to himself, trying helplessly to fix the idea in his mind. "I was that child!"

"Not very long after you had been received into the Institution, sir," pursued Mrs. Goldstraw, "I left my situation there, to be married. If you will remember that, and if you can give your mind to it, you will see for yourself how the mistake happened. Between eleven and twelve years passed before the lady, whom you have believed to be your mother, returned to the Foundling, to find her son, and to remove him to her own home. The lady only knew that her infant had been called 'Walter Wilding.' The matron who took pity on her, could but point out the only 'Walter Wilding' known in the Institution. I, who might have set the matter right, was far away from the Foundling and all that belonged to it. There was nothing—there was really nothing that could prevent this terrible mistake from taking place. I feel for you—I do indeed, sir! You must think—and with reason—that it was in an evil hour that I came here (innocently enough, I'm sure), to apply for your housekeeper's place. I feel as if I was to blame—I feel as if I ought to have had more self-command. If I had only been able to keep my face from showing you, what that portrait and what your own words put into my mind—you need never, to your dying day, have known what you know now."

Mr. Wilding looked up suddenly. The inbred honesty of the man rose in protest against the housekeeper's last words. His mind seemed to steady itself, for the moment, under the shock that had fallen on it.

"Do you mean to say that you would have concealed this from me if you could?" he exclaimed.

"I hope I should always tell the truth, sir, if I was asked," said Mrs. Goldstraw. "And I know it is better for *me* that I should not have a secret of this sort weighing on my mind. But is it better for *you?* What use can it serve now——?"

"What use? Why, good Lord! if your story is true——"

"Should I have told it, sir, as I am now situated, if it had not been true?"

"I beg your pardon," said the wine-merchant. "You must make allowance for me. This dreadful discovery is something I can't realise even yet. We loved each other so dearly—I felt so fondly that I was her son. She died, Mrs. Goldstraw, in my arms—she died blessing me as only a mother *could* have blessed me. And now, after all these years, to be told she was *not* my mother! O me, O me! I don't know what I am saying!" he cried, as the impulse of self control under which he had spoken a moment since, flickered, and died out. "It was not this dreadful grief—it was something else that I had it in my mind to speak of. Yes, yes. You surprised me—you wounded me just now.

You talked as if you would have hidden this from me, if you could. Don't talk in that way again. It would have been a crime to have hidden it. You mean well, I know. I don't want to distress you—you are a kind-hearted woman. But you don't remember what my position is. She left me all that I possess, in the firm persuasion that I was her son. I am not her son. I have taken the place, I have innocently got the inheritance of another man. He must be found! How do I know he is not at this moment in misery, without bread to eat? He must be found! My only hope of bearing up against the shock that has fallen on me, is the hope of doing something which *she* would have approved. You must know more, Mrs. Goldstraw, than you have told me yet. Who was the stranger who adopted the child? You must have heard the lady's name?"

"I never heard it, sir. I have never seen her, or heard of her, since."

"Did she say nothing when she took the child away? Search your memory. She must have said something."

"Only one thing, sir, that I can remember. It was a miserably bad season, that year; and many of the children were suffering from it. When she took the baby away, the lady said to me, laughing, 'Don't be alarmed about his health. He will be brought up in a better climate than this—I am going to take him to Switzerland.'"

"To Switzerland? What part of Switzerland?"

"She didn't say, sir."

"Only that faint clue!" said Mr. Wilding. "And a quarter of a century has passed since the child was taken away! What am I to do?"

"I hope you won't take offence at my freedom, sir," said Mrs. Goldstraw; "but why should you distress yourself about what is to be done? He may not be alive now, for anything you know. And, if he is alive, it's not likely he can be in any distress. The lady who adopted him was a bred and born lady—it was easy to see that. And she must have satisfied them at the Foundling that she could provide for the child, or they would never have let her take him away. If I was in your place, sir—please to excuse my saying so—I should comfort myself with remembering that I had loved that poor lady whose portrait you have got there—truly loved her as my mother, and that she had truly loved me as her son. All she gave to you, she gave for the sake of that love. It never altered while she lived; and it won't alter, I'm sure, as long as *you* live. How can you have a better right, sir, to keep what you have got than that?"

Mr. Wilding's immovable honesty saw the fallacy in his housekeeper's point of view at a glance.

"You don't understand me," he said. "It's *because I*

loved her that I feel it a duty—a sacred duty—to do justice to her son. If he is a living man, I must find him: for my own sake, as well as for his. I shall break down under this dreadful trial, unless I employ myself—actively, instantly employ myself—in doing what my conscience tells me ought to be done. I must speak to my lawyer; I must set my lawyer at work before I sleep to-night." He approached a tube in the wall of the room, and called down through it to the office below. "Leave me for a little, Mrs. Goldstraw," he resumed; "I shall be more composed, I shall be better able to speak to you later in the day. We shall get on well —I hope we shall get on well together—in spite of what has happened. It isn't your fault; I know it isn't your fault. There! there! shake hands; and—and do the best you can in the house—I can't talk about it now."

The door opened as Mrs. Goldstraw advanced towards it; and Mr. Jarvis appeared.

"Send for Mr. Bintrey," said the wine-merchant. "Say I want to see him directly."

The clerk unconsciously suspended the execution of the order, by announcing "Mr. Vendale," and showing in the new partner in the firm of Wilding and Co.

"Pray excuse me for one moment, George Vendale," said Wilding. "I have a word to say to Jarvis. Send for Mr. Bintrey," he repeated—"send at once."

Mr. Jarvis laid a letter on the table before he left the room.

"From our correspondents at Neuchâtel, I think, sir. The letter has got the Swiss postmark."

New Characters on the Scene]

The words, "The Swiss Postmark," following so soon upon the housekeeper's reference to Switzerland, wrought Mr. Wilding's agitation to such a remarkable height, that his new partner could not decently make a pretence of letting it pass unnoticed.

"Wilding," he asked hurriedly, and yet stopping short and glancing around as if for some visible cause of his state of mind: "what is the matter?"

"My good George Vendale," returned the wine-merchant, giving his hand with an appealing look, rather as if he wanted help to get over some obstacle, than as if he gave it in welcome or salutation: "my good George Vendale, so much is the matter, that I shall never be myself again. It is impossible that I can ever be myself again. For, in fact, I am not myself."

The new partner, a brown-cheeked handsome fellow, of about his own age, with a quick determined eye and an impulsive manner, retorted with natural astonishment: "Not yourself?"

"Not what I supposed myself to be," said Wilding.

"What, in the name of wonder, *did* you suppose yourself to be that you are not?" was the rejoinder, delivered with a cheerful frankness, inviting confidence from a more reticent man. "I may ask without impertinence, now that we are partners."

"There again!" cried Wilding, leaning back in his chair, with a lost look at the other. "Partners! I had no right to come into this business. It was never meant for me. My mother never meant it should be mine. I mean, his mother meant it should be his—if I mean anything—or if I am anybody."

"Come, come," urged his partner, after a moment's pause, and taking possession of him with that calm confidence which inspires a strong nature when it honestly desires to aid a weak one. "Whatever has gone wrong, has gone wrong through no fault of yours, I am very sure. I was not in this counting-house with you under the old *régime*, for three years, to doubt you, Wilding. We were not younger men than we are, together, for that. Let me begin our partnership by being a serviceable partner, and setting right whatever is wrong. Has that letter anything to do with it?"

"Hah!" said Wilding, with his hand to his temple. "There again! My head! I was forgetting the coincidence. The Swiss postmark."

"At a second glance I see that the letter is unopened, so it is not very likely to have much to do with the matter," said Vendale, with comforting composure. "Is it for you, or for us?"

"For us," said Wilding.

"Suppose I open it and read it aloud, to get it out of our way?"

"Thank you, thank you."

"The letter is only from our champagne-making friends, the House at Neuchâtel. 'Dear Sir. We are in receipt of yours of the 28th ult., informing us that you have taken your Mr. Vendale into partnership, whereon we beg you to receive the assurance of our felicitations. Permit us to embrace the occasion of specially commending to you, M. Jules Obenreizer.' Impossible!"

Wilding looked up in quick apprehension, and cried, "Eh?"

"Impossible sort of name," returned his partner, slightly —"Obenreizer. '—Of specially commending to you M. Jules Obenreizer, of Soho-square, London (north side), henceforth fully accredited as our agent, and who has already had the honour of making the acquaintance of your Mr. Vendale, in his (said M. Obenreizer's) native country, Switzerland.' To be sure: pooh, pooh, what have I been thinking of! I remember now; 'when travelling with his niece.'"

"With his—?" Vendale had so slurred the last word, that Wilding had not heard it.

"When travelling with his Niece. Obenreizer's Niece," said Vendale, in a somewhat superfluously lucid manner. "Niece of Obenreizer. (I met them in my first Swiss tour, travelled a little with them, and lost them for two years; met them again, my Swiss tour before last, and have lost them ever since.) Obenreizer. Niece of Obenreizer. To be sure! Possible sort of name, after all. 'M. Obenreizer is in possession of our absolute confidence, and we do not doubt you will esteem his merits.' Duly signed by the House, 'Defresnier et Cie.' Very well. I undertake to see M. Obenreizer presently, and clear him out of the way. That clears the Swiss postmark out of the way. So now, my dear Wilding, tell me what I can clear out of *your* way, and I'll find a way to clear it."

More than ready and grateful to be thus taken charge of, the honest wine-merchant wrung his partner's hand, and, beginning his tale by pathetically declaring himself an Imposter, told it.

"It was on this matter, no doubt, that you were sending for Bintrey, when I came in?" said his partner, after reflecting.

"It was."

"He has experience and a shrewd head; I shall be anxious to know his opinion. It is bold and hazardous in me to give you mine before I know his, but I am not good at holding back. Plainly, then, I do not see these circumstances as you see them. I do not see your position as you see it. As to your being an Imposter, my dear Wilding, that is simply absurd, because no man can be that without being a consenting party to an imposition. Clearly you never were so. As to your enrichment by the lady who believed you to be her son, and whom you were forced to believe, on her own showing, to be your mother, consider whether that did not arise out of the personal relations between you. You gradually became much attached to her; she gradually became much attached to you. It was on you, personally you, as I see the case, that she conferred these wordly advantages; it was from her, personally her, that you took them."

"She supposed me," objected Wilding, shaking his head, "to have a natural claim upon her, which I had not."

"I must admit that," replied his partner, "to be true. But if she had made the discovery that you have made, six months before she died, do you think it would have cancelled the years you were together, and the tenderness that each of you had conceived for the other, each on increasing knowledge of the other?"

"What I think," said Wilding, simply but stoutly holding to the bare fact, "can no more change the truth than it can bring down the sky. The truth is that I stand possessed of what was meant for another man."

"He may be dead," said Vendale.

"He may be alive," said Wilding. "And if he is alive, have I not—innocently, I grant you innocently—robbed him of enough? Have I not robbed him of all the happy time that I enjoyed in his stead? Have I not robbed him of the exquisite delight that filled my soul when that dear lady," stretching his hand towards the picture, "told me she was my mother? Have I not robbed him of all the care she lavished on me? Have I not even robbed him of all the devotion and duty that I so proudly gave to her? Therefore it is that I ask myself, George Vendale, and I ask you, where is he? What has become of him?"

"Who can tell!"

"I must try to find out who can tell. I must institute inquiries. I must never desist from prosecuting inquiries. I will live upon the interest of my share—I ought to say his share—in this business, and will lay up the rest for him. When I find him, I may perhaps throw myself upon his generosity; but I will yield up all to him. I will, I swear. As I loved and honoured her," said Wilding, reverently kissing his hand towards the picture, and then covering his eyes with it. "As I loved and honoured her, and have a world of reasons to be grateful to her!" And so broke down again.

His partner rose from the chair he had occupied, and stood beside him with a hand softly laid upon his shoulder. "Walter, I knew you before to-day to be an upright man, with a pure conscience and a fine heart. It is very fortunate for me that I have the privilege to travel on in life so near to so trustworthy a man. I am thankful for it. Use me as your right hand, and rely upon me to the death. Don't think the worse of me if I protest to you that my uppermost feeling at present is a confused, you may call it an unreasonable one. I feel far more pity for the lady and for you, because you did not stand in your supposed relations, than I can feel for the unknown man (if he ever became a man), because he was unconsciously displaced. You have done well in sending for Mr. Bintrey. What I think will be a part of his advice, I know is the whole of mine. Do not move a step in this serious matter precipitately. The secret must be kept among us with great strictness, for to part with it lightly would be to invite fraudulent claims, to encourage a host of knaves, to let loose a flood of perjury and plotting. I have no more to say now, Walter, than to remind you that you sold me a share in your business, expressly to save yourself from more work than your present health is fit for, and that I bought it expressly to do work, and mean to do it."

With these words, and a parting grip of his partner's shoulder that gave them the best emphasis they could have had, George Vendale betook himself presently to the counting-house, and presently afterwards to the address of M. Jules Obenreizer.

As he turned into Soho-square, and directed his steps towards its north side, a deepened colour shot across his sun-browned face, which Wilding, if he had been a better observer, or had been less occupied with his own trouble, might have noticed when his partner read aloud a certain passage in their Swiss correspondent's letter, which he had not read so distinctly as the rest.

A curious colony of mountaineers has long been enclosed within that small flat London district of Soho. Swiss watch-makers, Swiss silver-chasers, Swiss jewellers, Swiss importers of Swiss musical boxes and Swiss toys of various kinds, draw close together there. Swiss professors of music, painting, and languages; Swiss artificers in steady work; Swiss couriers, and other Swiss servants chronically out of place; industrious Swiss laundresses and clear-starchers; mysteriously existing Swiss of both sexes; Swiss creditable and Swiss discreditable; Swiss to be trusted by all means, and Swiss to be trusted by no means; these diverse Swiss particles are attracted to a centre in the district of Soho. Shabby Swiss eating-houses, coffee-houses, and lodging-houses, Swiss drinks and dishes, Swiss service for Sundays, and Swiss schools for week-days, are all to be found there. Even the native-born English taverns drive a sort of broken-English trade; announcing in their windows Swiss whets and drams, and sheltering in their bars Swiss skirmishes of love and animosity on most nights in the year.

When the new partner in Wilding and Co. rang the bell of a door bearing the blunt inscription OBENREIZER on a brass plate—the inner door of a substantial house, whose ground story was devoted to the sale of Swiss clocks—he passed at once into domestic Switzerland. A white-tiled stove for winter-time filled the fireplace of the room into which he was shown, the room's bare floor was laid together in a neat pattern of several ordinary woods, the room had a prevalent air of surface bareness and much scrubbing; and the little square of flowery carpet by the sofa, and the velvet chimney-board with its capacious clock and vases of artificial flowers, contended with that tone, as if, in bringing out the whole effect, a Parisian had adapted a dairy to domestic purposes.

Mimic water was dropping off a mill-wheel under the clock. The visitor had not stood before it, following it with his eyes, a minute, when M. Obenreizer, at his elbow, startled

him by saying, in very good English, very slightly clipped:
"How do you do? So glad!"

"I beg your pardon. I didn't hear you come in."

"Not at all! Sit, please."

Releasing his visitor's two arms, which he had lightly
pinioned at the elbows by way of embrace, M. Obenreizer
also sat, remarking, with a smile: "You are well? So glad!"
and touching his elbows again.

"I don't know," said Vendale, after exchange of salutations,
"whether you may yet have heard of me from your house at
Neuchâtel?"

"Ah, yes!"

"In connection with Wilding and Co.?"

"Ah, surely!"

"Is it not odd that I should come to you, in London here,
as one of the Firm of Wilding and Co., to pay the Firm's
respects?"

"Not at all! What did I always observe when we were
on the mountains? We call them vast; but the world is so
little. So little is the world, that one cannot keep away
from persons. There are so few persons in the world, that
they continually cross and recross. So very little is the
world, that one cannot get rid of a person. Not," touching
his elbows again, with an ingratiatory smile, "that one would
desire to get rid of you."

"I hope not, M. Obenreizer."

"Please call me, in your country, Mr. I call myself so,
for I love your country. If I *could* be English! But I am
born. And you? Though descended from so fine a family,
you have had the condescension to come into trade? Stop
though. Wines? Is it trade in England or profession?
Not fine art?"

"Mr. Obenreizer," returned Vendale, somewhat out of
countenance, "I was but a silly young fellow, just of age,
when I first had the pleasure of travelling with you, and
when you and I and Mademoiselle your niece—who is
well?"

"Thank you. Who is well."

"—Shared some slight glacier dangers together. If, with
a boy's vanity, I rather vaunted my family, I hope I did so
as a kind of introduction of myself. It was very weak, and
in very bad taste; but perhaps you know our English proverb,
'Live and learn.'"

"You make too much of it," returned the Swiss. "And
what the devil! After all, yours *was* a fine family."

George Vendale's laugh betrayed a little vexation as he
rejoined: "Well! I was strongly attached to my parents,
and when we first travelled together, Mr. Obenreizer, I was
in the first flush of coming into what my father and mother

left me. So I hope it may have been, after all, more youthful openness of speech and heart than boastfulness."

"All openness of speech and heart! No boastfulness!" cried Obenreizer. "You tax yourself too heavily. You tax yourself, my faith! as if you was your Government taxing you! Besides, it commenced with me. I remember, that evening in the boat upon the lake, floating among the reflections of the mountains and valleys, the crags and pine woods, which were my earliest remembrance, I drew a word-picture of my sordid childhood. Of our poor hut, by the waterfall which my mother showed to travellers; of the cowshed where I slept with the cow; of my idiot half-brother always sitting at the door, or limping down the Pass to beg; of my half-sister always spinning, and resting her enormous goitre on a great stone; of my being a famished naked little wretch of two or three years, when they were men and women with hard hands to beat me, I, the only child of my father's second marriage—if it even was a marriage. What more natural than for you to compare notes with me, and say, ' We are as one by age; at that same time I sat upon my mother's lap in my father's carriage, rolling through the rich English streets, all luxury surrounding me, all squalid poverty kept far from me. Such is *my* earliest remembrance as opposed to yours!'"

Mr. Obenreizer was a black-haired young man of a dark complexion, through whose swarthy skin no red glow ever shone. When colour would have come into another cheek, a hardly discernible beat would come into his, as if the machinery for bringing up the ardent blood were there, but the machinery were dry. He was robustly made, well proportioned, and had handsome features. Many would have perceived that some surface change in him would have set them more at their ease with him, without being able to define what change. If his lips could have been made much thicker, and his neck much thinner, they would have found their want supplied.

But the great Obenreizer peculiarity was, that a certain nameless film would come over his eyes—apparently by the action of his own will—which would impenetrably veil, not only from those tellers of tales, but from his face at large, every expression save one of attention. It by no means followed that his attention should be wholly given to the person with whom he spoke, or even wholly bestowed on present sounds and objects. Rather, it was a comprehensive watchfulness of everything he had in his own mind, and everything that he knew to be, or suspected to be, in the minds of other men.

At this stage of the conversation, Mr. Obenreizer's film came over him.

"The object of my present visit," said Vendale, "is, I need hardly say, to assure you of the friendliness of Wilding and Co., and of the goodness of your credit with us, and of our desire to be of service to you. We hope shortly to offer you our hospitality. Things are not quite in train with us yet, for my partner, Mr. Wilding, is reorganising the domestic part of our establishment, and is interrupted by some private affairs. You don't know Mr. Wilding, I believe?"

Mr. Obenreizer did not.

"You must come together soon. He will be glad to have made your acquaintance, and I think I may predict that you will be glad to have made his. You have not been long established in London, I suppose, Mr. Obenreizer?"

"It is only now that I have undertaken this agency."

"Mademoiselle your niece—is—not married?"

"Not married."

George Vendale glanced about him, as if for any tokens of her.

"She has been in London?"

"She *is* in London."

"When, and where, might I have the honour of recalling myself to her remembrance?"

Mr. Obenreizer, discarding his film and touching his visitor's elbows as before, said lightly: "Come up-stairs."

Fluttered enough by the suddenness with which the interview he had sought was coming upon him after all, George Vendale followed up-stairs. In a room over the chamber he had just quitted—a room also Swiss-appointed—a young lady sat near one of three windows, working at an embroidery-frame; and an older lady sat with her face turned close to another white-tiled stove (though it was summer, and the stove was not lighted), cleaning gloves. The young lady wore an unusual quantity of fair bright hair, very prettily braided about a rather rounder white forehead than the average English type, and so her face might have been a shade—or say a light—rounder than the average English face, and her figure slightly rounder than the figure of the average English girl at nineteen. A remarkable indication of freedom and grace of limb, in her quiet attitude, and a wonderful purity and freshness of colour in her dimpled face and bright grey eyes, seemed fraught with mountain air. Switzerland, too, though the general fashion of her dress was English, peeped out of the fanciful bodice she wore, and lurked in the curious clocked red stocking, and in its little silver-buckled shoe. As to the elder lady, sitting with her feet apart upon the lower brass ledge of the stove, supporting a lapful of gloves while she cleaned one stretched on her left hand, she was a true Swiss impersonation of another kind; from the breadth of her cushion-like back, and the ponderosity

of her respectable legs (if the word be admissible), to the black velvet band tied tightly round her throat for the repression of a rising tendency to goitre; or, higher still, to her great copper-coloured gold earrings; or, higher still, to her head-dress of black gauze stretched on wire.

"Miss Marguerite," said Obenreizer to the young lady, "do you recollect this gentleman?"

"I think," she answered, rising from her seat, surprised and a little confused: "it is Mr. Vendale?"

"I think it is," said Obenreizer, dryly. "Permit me, Mr. Vendale. Madame Dor."

The elder lady by the stove, with the glove stretched on her left hand, like a glover's sign, half got up, half looked over her broad shoulder, and wholly plumped down again and rubbed away.

"Madame Dor," said Obenreizer, smiling, "is so kind as to keep me free from stain or tear. Madame Dor humours my weakness for being always neat, and devotes her time to removing every one of my specks and spots."

Madame Dor, with the stretched glove in the air, and her eyes closely scrutinising its palm, discovered a tough spot in Mr. Obenreizer at that instant, and rubbed hard at him. George Vendale took his seat by the embroidery-frame (having first taken the fair right hand that his entrance had checked), and glanced at the gold cross that dipped into the bodice, with something of the devotion of a pilgrim who had reached his shrine at last. Obenreizer stood in the middle of the room with his thumbs in his waistcoat-pockets, and became filmy.

"He was saying down-stairs, Miss Obenreizer," observed Vendale, "that the world is so small a place, that people cannot escape one another. I have found it much too large for me since I saw you last."

"Have you travelled so far, then?" she inquired.

"Not so far, for I have only gone back to Switzerland each year; but I could have wished—and indeed I have wished very often—that the little world did not afford such opportunities for long escapes as it does. If it had been less, I might have found my fellow-travellers sooner, you know."

The pretty Marguerite coloured, and very slightly glanced in the direction of Madame Dor.

"You find us at length, Mr. Vendale. Perhaps you may lose us again."

"I trust not. The curious coincidence that has enabled me to find you, encourages me to hope not."

"What is that coincidence, sir, if you please?" A dainty little native touch in this turn of speech, and in its tone, made it perfectly captivating, thought George Vendale, when again he noticed an instantaneous glance towards Madame Dor. A

caution seemed to be conveyed in it, rapid flash though it was; so he quietly took heed of Madame Dor from that time forth.

"It is that I happen to have become a partner in a house of business in London, to which Mr. Obenreizer happens this very day to be expressly recommended: and that, too, by another house of business in Switzerland, in which (as it turns out) we both have a commercial interest. He has not told you?"

"Ah!" cried Obenreizer, striking in, filmless. "No. I had not told Miss Marguerite. The world is so small and so monotonous that a surprise is worth having in such a little jog-trot place. It is as he tells you, Miss Marguerite. He, of so fine a family, and so proudly bred, has condescended to trade. To trade! Like us poor peasants who have risen from ditches!"

A cloud crept over the fair brow, and she cast down her eyes.

"Why, it is good for trade!" pursued Obenreizer, enthusiastically. "It ennobles trade! It is the misfortune of trade, it is its vulgarity, that any low people—for example, we poor peasants—may take to it, and climb by it. See you, my dear Vendale!" He spoke with great energy. "The father of Miss Marguerite, my eldest half-brother, more than two times your age or mine, if living now, wandered without shoes, almost without rags, from that wretched Pass—wandered—wandered—got to be fed with the mules and dogs at an Inn in the main valley far away—got to be Boy there—got to be Ostler—got to be Waiter—got to be Cook—got to be Landlord. As Landlord, he took me (could he take the idiot beggar his brother, or the spinning monstrosity his sister?) to put as pupil to the famous watchmaker, his neighbour and friend. His wife dies when Miss Marguerite is born. What is his will, and what are his words, to me, when *he* dies, she being between girl and woman? 'All for Marguerite, except so much by the year for you. You are young, but I make her your ward, for you were of the obscurest and the poorest peasantry, and so was I, and so was her mother; we were abject peasants all, and you will remember it.' The thing is equally true of most of my countrymen, now in trade in this your London quarter of Soho. Peasants once; low-born drudging Swiss peasants. Then how good and great for trade:" here, from having been warm, he became playfully jubilant, and touched the young wine-merchant's elbows again with his light embrace: "to be exalted by gentlemen!"

"I do not think so," said Marguerite, with a flushed cheek, and a look away from the visitor, that was almost defiant. "I think it is as much exalted by us peasants."

"Fie, fie, Miss Marguerite," said Obenreizer. "You speak in proud England."

"I speak in proud earnest," she answered, quietly resuming her work, "and I am not English, but a Swiss peasant's daughter."

There was a dismissal of the subject in her words, which Vendale could not contend against. He only said in an earnest manner, "I most heartily agree with you, Miss Obenreizer, and I have already said so, as Mr. Obenreizer will bear witness," which he by no means did, "in this house."

Now, Vendale's eyes were quick eyes, and sharply watching Madame Dor by times, noted something in the broad back view of that lady. There was considerable pantomimic expression in her glove-cleaning. It had been very softly done when he spoke with Marguerite, or it had altogether stopped, like the action of a listener. When Obenreizer's peasant-speech came to an end, she rubbed most vigorously, as if applauding it. And once or twice, as the glove (which she always held before her, a little above her face) turned in the air, or as this finger went down, or that went up, he even fancied that it made some telegraphic communication to Obenreizer: whose back was certainly never turned upon it, though he did not seem at all to heed it.

Vendale observed, too, that in Marguerite's dismissal of the subject twice forced upon him to his misrepresentation, there was an indignant treatment of her guardian which she tried to check: as though she would have flamed out against him, but for the influence of fear. He also observed—though this was not much—that he never advanced within the distance of her at which he first placed himself: as though there were limits fixed between them. Neither had he ever spoken of her without the prefix "Miss," though whenever he uttered it, it was with the faintest trace of an air of mockery. And now it occurred to Vendale for the first time that something curious in the man which he had never before been able to define, was definable as a certain subtle essence of mockery that eluded touch or analysis. He felt convinced that Marguerite was in some sort a prisoner as to her free will—though she held her own against those two combined, by the force of her character, which was nevertheless inadequate to her release. To feel convinced of this, was not to feel less disposed to love her than he had always been. In a word, he was desperately in love with her, and thoroughly determined to pursue the opportunity which had opened at last.

For the present, he merely touched upon the pleasure that Wilding and Co. would soon have in entreating Miss Obenreizer to honour their establishment with her presence —a curious old place, though a bachelor house withal—and so did not protract his visit beyond such a visit's ordinary length. Going down-stairs, conducted by his host, he found the Obenreizer counting-house at the back of the entrance-hall, and several shabby men in outlandish garments, hanging about, whom Obenreizer put aside that he might pass, with a few words in *patois*.

"Countrymen," he explained, as he attended Vendale to the door. "Poor compatriots. Grateful and attached, like dogs! Good-bye. To meet again. So glad!"

Two more light touches on his elbows dismissed him into the street.

Sweet Marguerite at her frame, and Madame Dor's broad back at her telegraph, floated before him to Cripple Corner. On his arrival there, Wilding was closeted with Bintrey. The cellar doors happening to be open, Vendale lighted a candle in a cleft stick, and went down for a cellarous stroll. Graceful Marguerite floated before him faithfully, but Madame Dor's broad back remained outside.

The vaults were very spacious, and very old. There had been a stone crypt down there, when bygones were not bygones; some said, part of a monkish refectory; some said, of a chapel; some said, of a Pagan temple. It was all one now. Let who would, make what he liked of a crumbled pillar and a broken arch or so. Old time had made what *he* liked of it, and was quite indifferent to contradiction.

The close air, the musty smell, and the thunderous rumbling in the streets above, as being out of the routine of ordinary life, went well enough with the picture of pretty Marguerite holding her own against those two. So Vendale went on until, at a turning in the vaults, he saw a light like the light he carried.

"Oh! You are here, are you, Joey?"

"Oughtn't it rather to go, 'Oh! *You're* here, are you, Master George?' For it's my business to be here. But it ain't yourn."

"Don't grumble, Joey."

"Oh! *I* don't grumble," returned the Cellarman. "If anything grumbles, it's what I've took in through the pores; it ain't me. Have a care as something in *you* don't begin a-grumbling, Master George. Stop here long enough for the wapours to work, and they'll be at it."

His present occupation consisted of poking his head into the bins, making measurements and mental calculations, and entering them in a rhinoceros-hide-looking note-book, like a piece of himself.

"They'll be at it," he resumed, laying the wooden rod that he measured with, across two casks, entering his last calculation, and straightening his back, "trust 'em! And so you've regularly come into the business, Master George?"

"Regularly. I hope you don't object, Joey?"

"*I* don't, bless you. But Wapours objects that you're too young. You're both on you too young."

"We shall get over that objection day by day, Joey."

"Ay, Master George; but I shall day by day get over the objection that I'm too old, and so I shan't be capable of seeing much improvement in you."

The retort so tickled Joey Ladle that he grunted forth a laugh and delivered it again, grunting forth another laugh after the second edition of "improvement in you."

"But what's no laughing matter, Master George," he resumed, straightening his back once more, "is, that Young Master Wilding has gone and changed the luck. Mark my words. He has changed the luck, and he'll find it out. *I* ain't been down here all my life for nothing! *I* know, by what *I* notices down here, when it's a going to rain, when it's a going to hold up, when it's a going to blow, when it's a going to be calm. *I* know, by what *I* notices down here, when the luck's changed, quite as well."

"Has this growth on the roof anything to do with your divination!" asked Vendale, holding his light towards a gloomy ragged growth of dark fungus, pendent from the arches with a very disagreeable and repellent effect. "We are famous for this growth in this vault, aren't we?"

"We are, Master George," replied Joey Ladle, moving a step or two away, "and if you'll be advised by me, you'll let it alone."

Taking up the rod just now laid across the two casks, and faintly moving the languid fungus with it, Vendale asked, "Ay, indeed? Why so?"

"Why, not so much because it rises from the casks of wine, and may leave you to judge what sort of stuff a Cellarman takes into himself when he walks in the same all the days of his life, nor yet so much because at a stage of its growth it's maggots, and you'll fetch 'em down upon you," returned Joey Ladle, still keeping away, "as for another reason, Master George."

"What other reason?"

"(I wouldn't keep on touchin' it, if I was you, sir.) I'll tell you if you'll come out of the place. First, take a look at its colour, Master George."

"I am doing so."

"Done, sir. Now, come out of the place."

He moved away with his light, and Vendale followed with his. When Vendale came up with him, and they were going back together, Vendale, eyeing him as they walked through the arches, said: "Well, Joey? The colour."

"Is it like clotted blood, Master George?"

"Like enough, perhaps."

"More than enough, I think," muttered Joey Ladle, shaking his head solemnly.

"Well, say it is like; say it is exactly like.   What then?"

"Master George, they do say——"

"Who?"

"How should I know who?" rejoined the Cellarman, apparently much exasperated by the unreasonable nature of the question.   "Them!   Them as says pretty well everything, you know.   How should I know who They are, if you don't?"

"True.   Go on."

"They do say that the man that gets by any accident a piece of that dark growth right upon his breast, will, for sure and certain, die by Murder."

As Vendale laughingly stopped to meet the Cellarman's eyes, which he had fastened on his light while dreamily saying those words, he suddenly became conscious of being struck upon his own breast by a heavy hand.   Instantly following with his eyes the action of the hand that struck him—which was his companion's—he saw that it had beaten off his breast a web or clot of the fungus, even then floating to the ground.

For a moment he turned upon the Cellarman almost as scared a look as the Cellarman turned upon him.   But in another moment they had reached the daylight at the foot of the cellar-steps, and before he cheerfully sprang up them, he blew out his candle and the superstition together.

Exit Wilding]

On the morning of the next day, Wilding went out alone, after leaving a message with his clerk.   "If Mr. Vendale should ask for me," he said, "or if Mr. Bintrey should call, tell them I am gone to the Foundling."   All that his partner had said to him, all that his lawyer, following on the same side, could urge, had left him persisting unshaken in his own point of view.   To find the lost man, whose place he had usurped, was now the paramount interest of his life, and to inquire at the Foundling was plainly to take the first step in the direction of discovery.   To the Foundling, accordingly, the wine-merchant now went.

The once familiar aspect of the building was altered to him, as the look of the portrait over the chimney-piece was altered to him.   His one dearest association with the place which had sheltered his childhood had been broken away from it for ever.   A strange reluctance possessed him, when he stated his business at the door.   His heart ached as he sat alone in the waiting-room while the Treasurer of the institution was being sent for to see him.   When the interview began it was only by a painful effort that he could compose himself sufficiently to mention the nature of his errand.

The Treasurer listened with a face which promised all needful attention, and promised nothing more.

"We are obliged to be cautious," he said, when it came to his turn to speak, "about all inquiries which are made by strangers."

"You can hardly consider me a stranger," answered Wilding, simply. "I was one of your poor lost children here, in the bygone time."

The Treasurer politely rejoined that this circumstance inspired him with a special interest in his visitor. But he pressed, nevertheless, for that visitor's motive in making his inquiry. Without further preface, Wilding told him his motive, suppressing nothing.

The Treasurer rose, and led the way into the room in which the registers of the institution were kept. "All the information which our books can give is heartily at your service," he said. "After the time that has elapsed, I am afraid it is the only information we have to offer you."

The books were consulted, and the entry was found, expressed as follows:

"3d March, 1836. Adopted, and removed from the Foundling Hospital, a male infant, named Walter Wilding. Name and condition of the person adopting the child—Mrs. Jane Ann Miller, widow. Address—Lime-Tree Lodge, Groombridge Wells. References—the Reverend John Harker, Groombridge Wells; and Messrs. Giles, Jeremie, and Giles, bankers, Lombard-street."

"Is that all?" asked the wine-merchant. "Had you no after-communication with Mrs. Miller?"

"None—or some reference to it must have appeared in this book."

"May I take a copy of the entry?"

"Certainly! You are a little agitated. Let me make the copy for you."

"My only chance, I suppose," said Wilding, looking sadly at the copy, "is to inquire at Mrs. Miller's residence, and to try if her references can help me?"

"That is the only chance I see at present," answered the Treasurer. "I heartily wish I could have been of some further assistance to you."

With those farewell words to comfort him, Wilding set forth on the journey of investigation which began from the Foundling doors. The first stage to make for, was plainly the house of business of the bankers in Lombard-street. Two of the partners in the firm were inaccessible to chance-visitors when he asked for them. The third, after raising certain inevitable difficulties, consented to let a clerk examine the Ledger marked with the initial letter "M." The account of Mrs. Miller, widow, of Groombridge Wells, was found.

Two long lines, in faded ink, were drawn across it; and at the bottom of the page there appeared this note: "Account closed, September 30th, 1837."

So the first stage of the journey was reached—and so it ended in No Thoroughfare! After sending a note to Cripple Corner to inform his partner that his absence might be prolonged for some hours, Wilding took his place in the train, and started for the second stage on the journey—Mrs. Miller's residence at Groombridge Wells.

Mothers and children travelled with him; mothers and children met each other at the station; mothers and children were in the shops when he entered them to inquire for Lime-Tree Lodge. Everywhere, the nearest and dearest of human relations showed itself happily in the happy light of day. Everywhere, he was reminded of the treasured delusion from which he had been awakened so cruelly—of the lost memory which had passed from him like a reflection from a glass.

Inquiring here, inquiring there, he could hear of no such place as Lime-Tree Lodge. Passing a house-agent's office, he went in wearily, and put the question for the last time. The house-agent pointed across the street to a dreary mansion of many windows, which might have been a manufactory, but which was an hotel. "That's where Lime-Tree Lodge stood, sir," said the man, "ten years ago."

The second stage reached, and No Thoroughfare again!

But one chance was left. The clerical reference, Mr. Harker, still remained to be found. Customers coming in at the moment to occupy the house-agent's attention, Wilding went down the street, and, entering a bookseller's shop, asked if he could be informed of the Reverend John Harker's present address.

The bookseller looked unaffectedly shocked and astonished, and made no answer.

Wilding repeated his question.

The bookseller took up from his counter a prim little volume in a binding of sober grey. He handed it to his visitor, open at the title-page. Wilding read:

"The martyrdom of the Reverend John Harker in New Zealand. Related by a former member of his flock."

Wilding put the book down on the counter. "I beg your pardon," he said, thinking a little, perhaps, of his own present martyrdom while he spoke. The silent bookseller acknowledged the apology by a bow. Wilding went out.

Third and last stage, and No Thoroughfare for the third and last time.

There was nothing more to be done; there was absolutely no choice but to go back to London, defeated at all points. From time to time on the return journey, the wine-merchant looked at his copy of the entry in the Foundling Register. There is one among the many forms of despair—perhaps the most pitiable of all—which persists in disguising itself as Hope. Wilding checked himself in the act of throwing the useless morsel of paper out of the carriage window. "It may lead to something yet," he thought. "While I live, I won't part with it. When I die, my executors shall find it sealed up with my will."

Now, the mention of his will set the good wine-merchant on a new track of thought, without diverting his mind from its engrossing subject. He must make his will immediately.

The application of the phrase, No Thoroughfare, to the case had originated with Mr. Bintrey. In their first long conference following the discovery, that sagacious personage had a hundred times repeated, with an obstructive shake of the head, "No Thoroughfare, sir, No Thoroughfare. My belief is that there is no way out of this at this time of day, and my advice is, make yourself comfortable where you are."

In the course of the protracted consultation, a magnum of the forty-five year old port wine had been produced for the wetting of Mr. Bintrey's legal whistle; but the more clearly he saw his way through the wine, the more emphatically he did not see his way through the case; repeating as often as he set his glass down empty, "Mr. Wilding, No Thoroughfare. Rest and be thankful."

It is certain that the honest wine-merchant's anxiety to make a will originated in profound conscientiousness; though it is possible (and quite consistent with his rectitude) that he may unconsciously have derived some feeling of relief from the prospect of delegating his own difficulty to two other men who were to come after him. Be that as it may, he pursued his new tract of thought with great ardour, and lost no time in begging George Vendale and Mr. Bintrey to meet him in Cripple Corner and share his confidence.

"Being all three assembled with closed doors," said Mr. Bintrey, addressing the new partner on the occasion, "I wish to observe, before our friend (and my client) entrusts us with his further views, that I have endorsed what I understand from him to have been your advice, Mr. Vendale, and what would be the advice of every sensible man. I have told him that he positively must keep his secret. I have spoken with Mrs. Goldstraw, both in his presence and in his absence; and if anybody is to be trusted (which is a very large IF), I think she is to be trusted to that extent. I have pointed out to our friend (and my client), that to set on foot random inquiries would not only be to raise the Devil, in the likeness of all the swindlers in the kingdom, but would also be to waste the estate. Now, you see, Mr. Vendale, our friend (and my client) does not desire to waste the estate, but, on the contrary, desires to husband it for what he considers—but I can't say I do—the rightful owner, if such rightful owner should ever be found. I am very much mistaken if he ever will be, but never mind that. Mr. Wilding and I are, at least, agreed that the estate is not to be wasted. Now, I have yielded to Mr. Wilding's desire to keep an advertisement at intervals flowing through the newspapers, cautiously inviting any person who may know anything about that adopted infant, taken from the Foundling Hospital, to come to my office; and I have pledged myself that such advertisement shall regularly appear. I have gathered from our friend (and my client) that I meet you here to-day to take his instructions, not to give him advice. I am prepared to receive his instructions, and to respect his wishes; but you will please observe that this does not imply my approval of either as a matter of professional opinion."

Thus Mr. Bintrey; talking quite as much *at* Wilding as *to* Vendale. And yet, in spite of his care for his client, he was so amused by his client's Quixotic conduct, as to eye him from time to time with twinkling eyes, in the light of a highly comical curiosity.

"Nothing," observed Wilding, "can be clearer. I only wish my head were as clear as yours, Mr. Bintrey."

"If you feel that singing in it coming on," hinted the lawyer, with an alarmed glance, "put it off,—I mean the interview."

"Not at all, I thank you," said Wilding. "What was I going to——"

"Don't excite yourself, Mr. Wilding," urged the lawyer.

"No; I *wasn't* going to," said the wine-merchant. "Mr. Bintrey and George Vendale, would you have any hesitation or objection to become my joint trustees and executors, or can you at once consent?"

"*I* consent," replied George Vendale, readily.

"*I* consent," said Bintrey, not so readily.

"Thank you both. Mr. Bintrey, my instructions for my last will and testament are short and plain. Perhaps you will now have the goodness to take them down. I leave the whole of my real and personal estate, without any exception or reservation whatsoever, to you two, my joint trustees and executors, in trust to pay over the whole to the true Walter Wilding, if he shall be found and identified within two years after the day of my death. Failing that, in trust to you two to pay over the whole as a benefaction and legacy to the Foundling Hospital."

"Those are all your instructions, are they, Mr. Wilding?" demanded Bintrey, after a blank silence, during which nobody had looked at anybody.

"The whole."

"And as to those instructions, you have absolutely made up your mind, Mr. Wilding?"

"Absolutely, decidedly, finally."

"It only remains," said the lawyer, with one shrug of his shoulders, "to get them into technical and binding form, and to execute and attest. Now, does that press? Is there any hurry about it? You are not going to die yet, sir."

"Mr. Bintrey," answered Wilding, gravely, "when I am going to die is within other knowledge than yours or mine. I shall be glad to have this matter off my mind, if you please."

"We are lawyer and client again," rejoined Bintrey, who, for the nonce, had become almost sympathetic. "If this day week—here, at the same hour—will suit Mr. Vendale and yourself, I will enter in my Diary that I attend you accordingly."

The appointment was made, and in due sequence kept. The will was formally signed, sealed, delivered, and witnessed, and was carried off by Mr. Bintrey for safe storage among the papers of his clients, ranged in their respective iron boxes, with their respective owners' names outside, on iron tiers in his consulting-room, as if that legal sanctuary were a condensed Family Vault of Clients.

With more heart than he had lately had for former subjects of interest, Wilding then set about completing his patriarchal establishment, being much assisted not only by Mrs. Goldstraw but by Vendale too: who, perhaps, had in his mind the giving of an Obenreizer dinner as soon as possible. Anyhow, the establishment being reported in sound working order, the Obenreizers, Guardian and Ward, were asked to dinner, and Madame Dor was included in the invitation. If Vendale had been over head and ears in love before—a phrase not to be taken as implying the faintest doubt about it—this dinner plunged him down in love ten thousand fathoms deep. Yet, for the life of him, he could not get one word alone with charming Marguerite. So surely as a blessed moment seemed to come, Obenreizer, in his filmy state, would stand at Vendale's elbow, or the broad back of Madame Dor would appear before his eyes. That speechless matron was never seen in a front view, from the moment of her arrival to that of her departure—except at dinner. And from the instant of her retirement to the drawing-room, after a hearty participation in that meal, she turned her face to the wall again.

Yet, through four or five delightful though distracting hours, Marguerite was to be seen, Marguerite was to be heard, Marguerite was to be occasionally touched. When they made the round of the old dark cellars, Vendale led her by the hand; when she sang to him in the lighted room at night, Vendale, standing by her, held her relinquished gloves, and would have bartered against them every drop of the forty-five year old, though it had been forty-five times forty-five years old, and its net price forty-five times forty-five pounds per dozen. And still, when she was gone, and a great gap of an extinguisher was clapped on Cripple Corner, he tormented himself by wondering, Did she think she adored her! Did she think that he adored her! Did she suspect that she had won him, heart and soul! Did she care to think at all about it! And so, Did she and Didn't she, up and down the gamut, and above the line and below the line, dear, dear! Poor restless heart of humanity! To think that the men who were mummies thousands of years ago, did the same, and ever found the secret how to be quiet after it!

"What do you think, George," Wilding asked him next day, "of Mr. Obenreizer? (I won't ask you what you think of Miss Obenreizer.)"

"I don't know," said Vendale, "and I never did know, what to think of him."

"He is well informed and clever," said Wilding.

"Certainly clever."

"A good musician." (He had played very well, and sung very well, overnight.)

"Unquestionably a good musician."

"And talks well."

"Yes," said George Vendale, ruminating, "and talks well. Do you know, Wilding, it oddly occurs to me, as I think about him, that he doesn't keep silence well!"

"How do you mean? He is not obtrusively talkative."

"No, and I don't mean that. But when he is silent, you can hardly help vaguely, though perhaps most unjustly, mistrusting him. Take people whom you know and like. Take any one you know and like."

"Soon done, my good fellow," said Wilding. "I take you."

"I didn't bargain for that, or foresee it," returned Vendale, laughing. "However, take me. Reflect for a moment. Is your approving knowledge of my interesting face mainly founded (however various the momentary expressions it may include) on my face when I am silent?"

"I think it is," said Wilding.

"I think so too. Now, you see, when Obenreizer speaks— in other words, when he is allowed to explain himself away— he comes out right enough; but when he has not the opportunity of explaining himself away, he comes out rather wrong. Therefore it is, that I say he does not keep silence well. And passing hastily in review such faces as I know, and don't trust, I am inclined to think, now I give my mind to it, that none of them keep silence well."

This proposition in Physiognomy being new to Wilding, he was at first slow to admit it, until asking himself the question whether Mrs. Goldstraw kept silence well, and remembering that her face in repose decidedly invited trustfulness, he was as glad as men usually are to believe what they desire to believe.

But, as he was very slow to regain his spirits or his health, his partner, as another means of setting him up—and perhaps also with contingent Obenreizer views—reminded him of those musical schemes of his in connection with his family, and how a singing-class was to be formed in the house, and a Choir in a neighbouring church. The class was established speedily, and two or three of the people having already some musical knowledge, and singing tolerably, the Choir soon followed. The latter was led and chiefly taught, by Wilding himself: who had hopes of converting his dependents into so many Foundlings, in respect of their capacity to sing sacred choruses.

Now, the Obenreizers being skilled musicians it was easily brought to pass that they should be asked to join these musical unions. Guardian and Ward consenting, or Guardian consenting for both, it was necessarily brought to pass that Vendale's life became a life of absolute thraldom and enchantment. For, in the mouldy Christopher-Wren church on Sundays, with its dearly beloved brethren assembled and met together, five-and-twenty strong, was not that Her voice that shot like light into the darkest places, thrilling the walls and pillars as though they were pieces of his heart! What time, too, Madame Dor in a corner of the high pew, turning her back upon everybody and everything, could not fail to be Ritualistically right at some moment of the service; like the man whom the doctors recommended to get drunk once a month, and who, that he might not overlook it, got drunk every day.

But, even those seraphic Sundays were surpassed by the Wednesday concerts established for the patriarchal family. At those concerts she would sit down to the piano and sing them, in her own tongue, songs of her own land, songs calling from the mountain-tops to Vendale, "Rise above the grovelling level country; come far away from the crowd; pursue me as I mount higher, higher, higher, melting into the azure distance; rise to my supremest height of all, and love me here!" Then would the pretty bodice, the clocked stocking, and the silver-buckled shoe be, like the broad forehead and the bright eyes, fraught with the spring of a very chamois, until the strain was over.

Not even over Vendale himself did these songs of hers cast a more potent spell than over Joey Ladle in his different way. Steadily refusing to muddle the harmony by taking any share in it, and evincing the supremest contempt for scales and such like rudiments of music—which, indeed, seldom captivate mere listeners—Joey did at first give up the whole business for a bad job, and the whole of the performers for a set of howling Dervishes. But, descrying traces of un-muddled harmony in a part-song one day, he gave his two under-cellarmen faint hopes of getting on towards something in course of time. An anthem of Handel's led to further encouragement from him: though he objected that that great musician must have been down in some of them foreign cellars pretty much, for to go and say the same thing so many times over; which, took it in how you might, he con-sidered a certain sign of your having took it in somehow. On a third occasion, the public appearance of Mr. Jarvis with a flute, and of an odd man with a violin, and the performance of a duet by the two, did so astonish him that, solely of his own impulse and motion, he became inspired with the words, "Ann Koar!" repeatedly pronouncing them as if calling in a familiar manner for some lady who had distinguished her-self in the orchestra. But this was his final testimony to the merits of his mates, for, the instrumental duet being performed at the first Wednesday concert, and being presently followed by the voice of Marguerite Obenreizer, he sat with his mouth wide open, entranced, until she had finished; when, rising in his place with much solemnity, and prefacing what he was about to say with a bow that specially included Mr. Wilding in it, he delivered himself of the gratifying sentiment: "Arter that, ye may all on ye get to bed!" And ever after-wards declined to render homage in any other words to the musical powers of the family.

Thus began a separate personal acquaintance between Marguerite Obenreizer and Joey Ladle. She laughed so heartily at his compliment, and yet was so abashed by it, that Joey made bold to say to her, after the concert was over, he hoped he wasn't so muddled in his head as to have took a liberty? She made him a gracious reply, and Joey ducked in return.

"You'll change the luck time about, Miss," said Joey, ducking again. "It's such as you in the place that can bring round the luck of the place."

"Can I? Round the luck?" she answered, in her pretty English, and with a pretty wonder. "I fear I do not under-stand. I am so stupid."

"Young Master Wilding, Miss," Joey explained confiden-tially, though not much to her enlightenment, "changed the luck, afore he took in young Master George. So I say, and so they'll find. Lord! Only come into the place and sing over the luck a few times, Miss, and it won't be able to help itself!"

With this, and with a whole brood of ducks, Joey backed out of the presence. But Joey being a privileged person, and even an involuntary conquest being pleasant to youth and beauty, Marguerite merrily looked out for him next time.

"Where is my Mr. Joey, please?" she asked of Vendale.

So Joey was produced and shaken hands with, and that became an Institution.

Another Institution arose in this wise. Joey was a little hard of hearing. He himself said it was "Wapours," and perhaps it might have been; but whatever the cause of the effect, there the effect was, upon him. On the first occasion he had been seen to sidle along the wall, with his left hand to his left ear, until he had sidled himself into a seat pretty near the singer, in which place and position he had remained, until addressing to his friends the amateurs the compliment before mentioned. It was observed on the following Wednesday that Joey's action as a Pecking Machine was impaired at dinner, and it was rumoured about the table that this was explainable by his high-strung expectations of Miss Obenreizer's singing, and his fears of not getting a place where he could hear every note and syllable. The rumour reaching Wilding's ears, he in his good nature called Joey to the front at night before Marguerite began. Thus the Institution came into being that on succeeding nights, Marguerite, running her hands over the keys before singing, always said to Vendale, "Where is my Mr. Joey, please?" and that Vendale always brought him forth, and stationed him near by. That he should then, when all eyes were upon him, express in his face the utmost contempt for the exertions of his friends and confidence in Marguerite alone, whom he would stand contemplating, not unlike the rhinoceros out of the spelling-book, tamed and on his hind legs, was a part of the Institution. Also that when he remained after the singing in his most ecstatic state, some bold spirit from the back should say, "What do you think of it, Joey?" and he should be goaded to reply, as having that instant conceived the retort, "Arter that ye may all on ye get to bed!" These were other parts of the Institution.

But the simple pleasures and small jests of Cripple Corner were not destined to have a long life. Underlying them from the first was a serious matter, which every member of the patriarchal family knew of, but which, by tacit agreement, all forbore to speak of. Mr. Wilding's health was in a bad way.

He might have overcome the shock he had sustained in the one great affection of his life, or he might have overcome his consciousness of being in the enjoyment of another man's property; but the two together were too much for him. A man haunted by twin ghosts, he became deeply depressed. The inseparable spectres sat at the board with him, ate from his platter, drank from his cup, and stood by his bedside at night. When he recalled his supposed mother's love, he felt as though he had stolen it. When he rallied a little under the respect and attachment of his dependants, he felt as though he were even fraudulent in making them happy, for that should have been the unknown man's duty and gratification.

Gradually, under the pressure of his brooding mind, his body stooped, his step lost its elasticity, his eyes were seldom lifted from the ground. He knew he could not help the deplorable mistake that had been made, but he knew he could not mend it; for the days and weeks went by, and no one claimed his name or his possessions. And now there began to creep over him a cloudy consciousness of often recurring confusion in his head. He would unaccountably lose, sometimes whole hours, sometimes a whole day and night. Once, his remembrance stopped as he sat at the head of the dinner-table, and was blank until daybreak. Another time, it stopped as he was beating time to their singing, and went on again when he and his partner were walking in the courtyard by the light of the moon, half the night later. He asked Vendale (always full of consideration, work, and help) how this was? Vendale only replied, "You have not been quite well; that's all." He looked for explanation into the faces of his people. But they would put it off with, "Glad to see you looking so much better, sir;" or "Hope you're doing nicely now, sir;" in which was no information at all.

At length, when the partnership was but five months old, Walter Wilding took to his bed, and his housekeeper became his nurse.

"Lying here, perhaps you will not mind my calling you Sally, Mrs. Goldstraw?" said the poor wine-merchant.

"It sounds more natural to me, sir, than any other name, and I like it better."

"Thank you, Sally. I think, Sally, I must of late have been subject to fits. Is that so, Sally? Don't mind telling me now."

"It has happened, sir."

"Ah! That is the explanation!" he quietly remarked. "Mr. Obenreizer, Sally, talks of the world being so small that it is not strange how often the same people come together, and come together, at various places, and in various stages of life. But it does seem strange, Sally, that I should, as I may say, come round to the Foundling to die."

He extended his hand to her, and she gently took it.

"You are not going to die, dear Mr. Wilding."

"So Mr. Bintrey said, but I think he was wrong. The old child-feeling is coming back to me, Sally. The old hush and rest, as I used to fall asleep."

After an interval he said, in a placid voice, "Please kiss me,

Nurse," and, it was evident, believed himself to be lying in the old Dormitory.

As she had been used to bend over the fatherless and motherless children, Sally bent over the fatherless and motherless man, and put her lips to his forehead, murmuring:

"God bless you!"

"God bless you!" he replied, in the same tone.

After another interval, he opened his eyes in his own character, and said: "Don't move me, Sally, because of what I am going to say; I lie quite easily. I think my time is come. I don't know how it may appear to you, Sally, but——"

Insensibility fell upon him for a few minutes; he emerged from it once more.

"—I don't know how it may appear to you, Sally, but so it appears to me."

When he had thus conscientiously finished his favourite sentence, his time came, and he died.

ACT II: *Vendale makes Love*

THE summer and the autumn had passed. Christmas and the New Year were at hand.

As executors honestly bent on performing their duty towards the dead, Vendale and Bintrey had held more than one anxious consultation on the subject of Wilding's will. The lawyer had declared, from the first, that it was simply impossible to take any useful action in the matter at all. The only obvious inquiries to make, in relation to the lost man, had been made already by Wilding himself; with this result, that time and death together had not left a trace of him discoverable. To advertise for the claimant to the property, it would be necessary to mention particulars—a course of proceeding which would invite half the impostors in England to present themselves in the character of the true Walter Wilding. "If we find a chance of tracing the lost man, we will take it. If we don't, let us meet for another consultation on the first anniversary of Wilding's death." So Bintrey advised. And so, with the most earnest desire to fulfil his dead friend's wishes, Vendale was fain to let the matter rest for the present.

Turning from his interest in the past to his interest in the future, Vendale still found himself confronting a doubtful prospect. Months on months had passed since his first visit to Soho-square—and through all that time, the one language in which he had told Marguerite that he loved her was the language of the eyes, assisted, at convenient opportunities, by the language of the hand.

What was the obstacle in his way? The one immovable obstacle which had been in his way from the first. No matter how fairly the opportunities looked. Vendale's efforts to speak with Marguerite alone, ended invariably in one and the same result. Under the most accidental circumstances, in the most innocent manner possible, Obenreizer was always in the way.

With the last days of the old year came an unexpected chance of spending an evening with Marguerite, which Vendale resolved should be a chance of speaking privately to her as well. A cordial note from Obenreizer invited him, on New Year's Day, to a little family dinner in Soho-square. "We shall be only four," the note said. "We shall be only two," Vendale determined, "before the evening is out!"

New Year's Day among the English, is associated with the giving and receiving of dinners, and with nothing more. New Year's Day, among the foreigners, is the grand opportunity of the year for the giving and receiving of presents. It is occasionally possible to acclimatise a foreign custom. In this instance Vendale felt no hesitation about making the attempt. His one difficulty was to decide what his New Year's gift to Marguerite should be. The defensive pride of the peasant's daughter—morbidly sensitive to the inequality between her social position and his—would be secretly roused against him if he ventured on a rich offering. A gift, which a poor man's purse might purchase, was the one gift that could be trusted to find its way to her heart, for the giver's sake. Stoutly resisting temptation, in the form of diamonds and rubies, Vendale bought a brooch of the filigree-work of Genoa—the simplest and most unpretending ornament that he could find in the jeweller's shop.

He slipped his gift into Marguerite's hand as she held it out to welcome him on the day of the dinner.

"This is your first New Year's Day in England," he said. "Will you let me help to make it like a New Year's Day at home?"

She thanked him, a little constrainedly, as she looked at the jeweller's box, uncertain what it might contain. Opening the box, and discovering the studiously simple form under which Vendale's little keepsake offered itself to her, she penetrated his motive on the spot. Her face turned on him brightly, with a look which said, "I own you have pleased and flattered me." Never had she been so charming, in Vendale's eyes, as she was at that moment. Her winter dress—a petticoat of dark silk, with a bodice of black velvet rising to her neck, and enclosing it softly in a little circle of swansdown—heightened, by all the force of contrast, the dazzling fairness of her hair and her complexion. It was only when she turned aside from him to the glass, and, taking out the brooch that she wore, put his New Year's gift in its place, that Vendale's attention wandered far enough away from her to discover the presence of other persons in the room. He now became conscious that the hands of Obenreizer were affectionately in possession of his elbows. He now heard the voice of Obenreizer thanking him for his attention to Marguerite, with the faintest possible ring of mockery in its tone. ("Such a simple present, dear sir! and showing such nice tact!") He now discovered, for the first time, that there was one other guest, and but one, beside himself, whom Obenreizer presented as a compatriot and friend. The friend's face was mouldy, and the friend's figure was fat. His age was suggestive of the autumnal period of human life. In the course of the evening he developed two extraordinary capacities. One was a capacity for silence; the other was a capacity for emptying bottles.

Madame Dor was not in the room. Neither was there any visible place reserved for her when they sat down to table. Obenreizer explained that it was "the good Dor's simple habit to dine always in the middle of the day. She would make her excuses later in the evening." Vendale wondered whether the good Dor had, on this occasion, varied her domestic employment from cleaning Obenreizer's gloves to cooking Obenreizer's dinner. This at least was certain—the dishes served were, one and all, as achievements in cookery, high above the reach of the rude elementary art of England. The dinner was unobtrusively perfect. As for the wine, the eyes of the speechless friend rolled over it, as in solemn ecstasy. Sometimes he said "Good!" when a bottle came in full; and sometimes he said "Ah!" when a bottle went out empty— and there his contributions to the gaiety of the evening ended.

Silence is occasionally infectious. Oppressed by private anxieties of their own, Marguerite and Vendale appeared to feel the influence of the speechless friend. The whole responsibility of keeping the talk going rested on Obenreizer's shoulders, and manfully did Obenreizer sustain it. He opened his heart in the character of an enlightened foreigner, and sang the praises of England. When other topics ran dry, he returned to this inexhaustible source, and always set the stream running again as copiously as ever. Obenreizer would have given an arm, an eye, or a leg to have been born an Englishman. Out of England there was no such institution as a home, no such thing as a fire-side, no such object as a beautiful woman. His dear Miss Marguerite would excuse him, if he accounted for *her* attractions on the theory that English blood must have mixed at some former time with their obscure and unknown ancestry. Survey this English nation, and behold a tall, clean, plump, and solid people! Look at their cities! What magnificence in their public buildings! What admirable order and propriety in their streets! Admire their laws, combining the eternal principle of justice with the other

eternal principle of pounds, shillings, and pence; and applying
the product to all civil injuries, from an injury to a man's
honour, to an injury to a man's nose! You have ruined my
daughter—pounds, shillings, and pence! You have knocked
me down with a blow in my face—pounds, shillings, and
pence! Where was the material prosperity of such a country
as *that* to stop? Obenreizer, projecting himself into the
future, failed to see the end of it. Obenreizer's enthusiasm
entreated permission to exhale itself, English fashion, in a
toast. Here is our modest little dinner over, here is our frugal
dessert on the table, and here is the admirer of England con-
forming to national customs, and making a speech! A toast
to your white cliffs of Albion, Mr. Vendale! to your national
virtues, your charming climate, and your fascinating women!
to your Hearths, to your Homes, to your Habeas Corpus, and
to all your other institutions! In one word—to England!
Heep-heep-heep! hooray!

Obenreizer's voice had barely chanted the last note of the
English cheer, the speechless friend had barely drained the
last drop out of his glass, when the festive proceedings were
interrupted by a modest tap at the door. A woman-servant
came in, and approached her master with a little note in her
hand. Obenreizer opened the note with a frown; and, after
reading it with an expression of genuine annoyance, passed
it on to his compatriot and friend. Vendale's spirits rose as
he watched these proceedings. Had he found an ally in the
annoying little note? Was the long-looked-for chance
actually coming at last?

"I am afraid there is no help for it?" said Obenreizer,
addressing his fellow-countryman. "I am afraid we must
go."

The speechless friend handed back the letter, shrugged his
heavy shoulders, and poured himself out a last glass of wine.
His fat fingers lingered fondly round the neck of the bottle.
They pressed it with a little amatory squeeze at parting. His
globular eyes looked dimly, as through an intervening haze, at
Vendale and Marguerite. His heavy articulation laboured,
and brought forth a whole sentence at a birth. "I think," he
said, "I should have liked a little more wine." His breath
failed him after that effort; he gasped, and walked to the door.

Obenreizer addressed himself to Vendale with an appearance
of the deepest distress.

"I am so shocked, so confused, so distressed," he began.
"A misfortune has happened to one of my compatriots. He
is alone, he is ignorant of your language—I and my good
friend, here, have no choice but to go and help him. What can
I say in my excuse? How can I describe my affliction at
depriving myself in this way of the honour of your company?"

He paused, evidently expecting to see Vendale take up his

hat and retire. Discerning his opportunity at last, Vendale determined to do nothing of the kind. He met Obenreizer dexterously, with Obenreizer's own weapons.

"Pray don't distress yourself," he said. "I'll wait here with the greatest pleasure till you come back."

Marguerite blushed deeply, and turned away to her embroidery-frame in a corner by the window. The film showed itself in Obenreizer's eyes, and the smile came something sourly to Obenreizer's lips. To have told Vendale that there was no reasonable prospect of his coming back in good time would have been to risk offending a man whose favourable opinion was of solid commercial importance to him. Accepting his defeat with the best possible grace, he declared himself to be equally honoured and delighted by Vendale's proposal. "So frank, so friendly, so English!" He bustled about, apparently looking for something he wanted, disappeared for a moment through the folding-doors communicating with the next room, came back with his hat and coat, and protesting that he would return at the earliest possible moment, embraced Vendale's elbows, and vanished from the scene in company with the speechless friend.

Vendale turned to the corner by the window, in which Marguerite had placed herself with her work. There, as if she had dropped from the ceiling, or come up through the floor—there, in the old attitude, with her face to the stove—sat an Obstacle that had not been foreseen, in the person of Madame Dor! She half got up, half looked over her broad shoulder at Vendale, and plumped down again. Was she at work? Yes. Cleaning Obenreizer's gloves, as before? No; darning Obenreizer's stockings.

The case was now desperate. Two serious considerations presented themselves to Vendale. Was it possible to put Madame Dor into the stove? The stove wouldn't hold her. Was it possible to treat Madame Dor, not as a living woman but as an article of furniture? Could the mind be brought to contemplate this respectable matron purely in the light of a chest of drawers, with a black gauze head-dress accidentally left on the top of it? Yes, the mind could be brought to do that. With a comparatively trifling effort, Vendale's mind did it. As he took his place on the old-fashioned window-seat, close by Marguerite and her embroidery, a slight movement appeared in the chest of drawers, but no remark issued from it. Let it be remembered that solid furniture is not easy to move, and that it has this advantage in consequence—there is no fear of upsetting it.

Unusually silent and unusually constrained—with the bright colour fast fading from her face, with a feverish energy possessing her fingers—the pretty Marguerite bent over her embroidery, and worked as if her life depended on it. Hardly less agitated himself, Vendale felt the importance of leading her very gently to the avowal which he was eager to make—to the other sweeter avowal still, which he was longing to hear. A woman's love is never to be taken by storm; it yields insensibly to a system of gradual approach. It ventures by the round-about way, and listens to the low voice. Vendale led her memory back to their past meetings when they were travelling together in Switzerland. They revived the impressions, they recalled the events, of the happy bygone time. Little by little, Marguerite's constraint vanished. She smiled, she was interested, she looked at Vendale, she grew idle with her needle, she made false stitches in her work. Their voices sank lower and lower; their faces bent nearer and nearer to each other as they spoke. And Madame Dor? Madame Dor behaved like an angel. She never looked round; she never said a word; she went on with Obenreizer's stockings. Pulling each stocking up tight over her left arm, and holding that arm aloft from time to time, to catch the light on her work, there were moments, delicate and indescribable moments, when Madame Dor appeared to be sitting upside down, and con-templating one of her own respectable legs elevated in the air. As the minutes wore on, these elevations followed each other at longer and longer intervals. Now and again, the black gauze head-dress nodded, dropped forward, recovered itself. A little heap of stockings slid softly from Madame Dor's lap, and remained unnoticed on the floor. A prodigious ball of worsted followed the stockings, and rolled lazily under the table. The black gauze head-dress nodded, dropped forward, recovered itself, nodded again, dropped forward again, and recovered itself no more. A composite sound, partly as of the purring of an immense cat, partly as of the planing of a soft board, rose over the hushed voices of the lovers, and hummed at regular intervals through the room. Nature and Madame Dor had combined together in Vendale's interests. The best of women was asleep.

Marguerite rose to stop—not the snoring—let us say, the audible repose of Madame Dor. Vendale laid his hand on her arm, and pressed her back gently into her chair.

"Don't disturb her," he whispered. "I have been waiting to tell you a secret. Let me tell it now."

Marguerite resumed her seat. She tried to resume her needle. It was useless; her eyes failed her; her hand failed her; she could find nothing.

"We have been talking," said Vendale, "of the happy time when we first met, and first travelled together. I have a confession to make. I have been concealing something. When we spoke of my first visit to Switzerland, I told you of all the impressions I had brought back with me to England—except one. Can you guess what that one is?"

Her eyes looked steadfastly at the embroidery, and her face turned a little away from him. Signs of disturbance began to appear in her neat velvet bodice, round the region of the brooch. She made no reply. Vendale pressed the question without mercy.

"Can you guess what the one Swiss impression is, which I have not told you yet?"

Her face turned back towards him, and a faint smile trembled on her lips.

"An impression of the mountains, perhaps?" she said, slily.

"No; a much more precious impression than that."

"Of the lakes?"

"No. The lakes have not grown dearer and dearer in remembrance to me every day. The lakes are not associated with my happiness in the present, and my hopes in the future. Marguerite! all that makes life worth having hangs, for me, on a word from your lips. Marguerite! I love you!"

Her head dropped as he took her hand. He drew her to him, and looked at her. The tears escaped from her downcast eyes, and fell slowly over her cheeks.

"Oh, Mr. Vendale," she said, sadly, "it would have been kinder to have kept your secret. Have you forgotten the distance between us? It can never, never, be!"

"There can be but one distance between us, Marguerite— a distance of your making. My love, my darling, there is no higher rank in goodness, there is no higher rank in beauty, than yours! Come! whisper the one little word which tells me you will be my wife!"

She sighed bitterly. "Think of your family," she murmured; "and think of mine!"

Vendale drew her a little nearer to him.

"If you dwell on such an obstacle as that," he said, "I shall think but one thought—I shall think I have offended you."

She started, and looked up. "Oh, no!" she exclaimed, innocently. The instant the words passed her lips, she saw the construction that might be placed on them. Her confession had escaped her in spite of herself. A lovely flush of colour overspread her face. She made a momentary effort to disengage herself from her lover's embrace. She looked up at him entreatingly. She tried to speak. The words died on her lips in the kiss that Vendale pressed on them. "Let me go, Mr. Vendale!" she said, faintly.

"Call me George."

She laid her head on his bosom. All her heart went out to him at last. "George!" she whispered.

"Say you love me!"

Her arms twined themselves gently round his neck. Her lips, timidly touching his cheek, murmured the delicious words—"I love you!"

In the moment of silence that followed, the sound of the opening and closing of the house-door came clear to them through the wintry stillness of the street.

Marguerite started to her feet.

"Let me go!" she said. "He has come back!"

She hurried from the room, and touched Madame Dor's shoulder in passing. Madame Dor woke up with a loud snort, looked first over one shoulder and then over the other, peered down into her lap, and discovered neither stockings, worsted, nor darning-needle in it. At the same moment, footsteps became audible ascending the stairs. "Mon Dieu!" said Madame Dor, addressing herself to the stove, and trembling violently. Vendale picked up the stockings and the ball, and huddled them all back in a heap over her shoulder. "Mon Dieu!" said Madame Dor, the second time, as the avalanche of worsted poured into her capacious lap.

The door opened, and Obenreizer came in. His first glance round the room showed him that Marguerite was absent.

"What!" he exclaimed, "my niece is away? My niece is not here to entertain you in my absence? This is unpardonable. I shall bring her back instantly."

Vendale stopped him.

"I beg you will not disturb Miss Obenreizer," he said. "You have returned, I see, without your friend?"

"My friend remains, and consoles our afflicted compatriot. A heart-rending scene, Mr. Vendale! The household gods at the pawn-broker's—the family immersed in tears. We all embraced in silence. My admirable friend alone possessed his composure. He sent out, on the spot, for a bottle of wine."

"Can I say a word to you in private, Mr. Obenreizer?"

Assuredly." He turned to Madame Dor. "My good creature, you are sinking for want of repose. Mr. Vendale will excuse you."

Madame Dor rose, and set forth sideways on her journey from the stove to bed. She dropped a stocking. Vendale picked it up for her, and opened one of the folding-doors. She advanced a step, and dropped three more stockings. Vendale, stooping to recover them as before, Obenreizer interfered with profuse apologies, and with a warning look at Madame Dor. Madame Dor acknowledged the look by dropping the whole of the stockings in a heap, and then shuffling away panic-stricken from the scene of disaster. Obenreizer swept up the complete collection fiercely in both hands. "Go!" he cried, giving his prodigious handful a preparatory swing in the air. Madame Dor said, "Mon Dieu," and vanished into the next room, pursued by a shower of stockings.

"What must you think, Mr. Vendale," said Obenreizer, closing the door, "of this deplorable intrusion of domestic details? For myself, I blush at it. We are beginning the New Year as badly as possible; everything has gone wrong to-night. Be seated, pray—and say, what may I offer you? Shall we pay our best respects to another of your noble English institutions? It is my study to be what you call, jolly. I propose a grog."

Vendale declined the grog with all needful respect for that noble institution.

"I wish to speak to you on a subject in which I am deeply interested," he said. "You must have observed, Mr. Obenreizer, that I have, from the first, felt no ordinary admiration for your charming niece?"

"You are very good. In my niece's name, I thank you."

"Perhaps you may have noticed, latterly, that my admiration for Miss Obenreizer has grown into a tenderer and deeper feeling——?"

"Shall we say friendship, Mr. Vendale?"

"Say love—and we shall be nearer to the truth."

Obenreizer started out of his chair. The faintly discernible beat, which was his nearest approach to a change of colour, showed itself suddenly in his cheeks.

"You are Miss Obenreizer's guardian," pursued Vendale. "I ask you to confer upon me the greatest of all favours—I ask you to give me her hand in marriage."

Obenreizer dropped back into his chair. "Mr. Vendale," he said, "you petrify me."

"I will wait," rejoined Vendale, "until you have recovered yourself."

"One word before I recover myself. You have said nothing about this to my niece?"

"I have opened my whole heart to you niece. And I have reason to hope——"

"What!" interposed Obenreizer. "You have made a proposal to my niece, without first asking for my authority to pay your addresses to her?" He struck his hand or the table, and lost his hold over himself for the first time in Vendale's experience of him. "Sir!" he exclaimed, indignantly, "what sort of conduct is this? As a man of honour, speaking to a man of honour, how can you justify it?"

"I can only justify it as one of our English institutions," said Vendale, quietly. "You admire our English institutions. I can't honestly tell you, Mr. Obenreizer, that I regret what I have done. I can only assure you that I have not acted in the matter with any intentional disrespect towards yourself. This said, may I ask you to tell me plainly what objection you see to favouring my suit?"

"I see this immense objection," answered Obenreizer,

"that my niece and you are not on a social equality together. My niece is the daughter of a poor peasant; and you are the son of a gentleman. You do us an honour," he added, lowering himself again gradually to his customary polite level, "which deserves, and has, our most grateful acknowledgments. But the inequality is too glaring; the sacrifice is too great. You English are a proud people, Mr. Vendale. I have observed enough of this country to see that such a marriage as you propose would be a scandal here. Not a hand would be held out to your peasant-wife; and all your best friends would desert you."

"One moment," said Vendale, interposing on his side. "I may claim, without any great arrogance, to know more of my country-people in general, and of my own friends in particular, than you do. In the estimation of everybody whose opinion is worth having, my wife herself would be the one sufficient justification of my marriage. If I did not feel certain—observe, I say certain—that I am offering her a position which she can accept without so much as the shadow of a humiliation—I would never (cost me what it might) have asked her to be my wife. Is there any other obstacle that you see? Have you any personal objection to me?"

Obenreizer spread out both his hands in courteous protest. "Personal objection!" he exclaimed. "Dear sir, the bare question is painful to me."

"We are both men of business," pursued Vendale, "and you naturally expect me to satisy you that I have the means of supporting a wife. I can explain my pecuniary position in two words. I inherit from my parents a fortune of twenty thousand pounds. In half of that sum I have only a life-interest, to which, if I die, leaving a widow, my widow succeeds. If I die, leaving children, the money itself is divided among them, as they come of age. The other half of my fortune is at my own disposal, and is invested in the wine-business. I see my way to greatly improving that business. As it stands at present, I cannot state my return from my capital embarked at more than twelve hundred a year. Add the yearly value of my life-interest—and the total reaches a present annual income of fifteen hundred pounds. I have the fairest prospect of soon making it more. In the meantime, do you object to me on pecuniary grounds?"

Driven back to his last entrenchment, Obenreizer rose, and took a turn backwards and forwards in the room. For the moment, he was plainly at a loss what to say or do next.

"Before I answer that last question," he said, after a little close consideration with himself, "I beg leave to revert for a moment to Miss Marguerite. You said something just now which seemed to imply that she returns the sentiment with which you are pleased to regard her?"

"I have the inestimable happiness," said Vendale, "of knowing that she loves me."

Obenreizer stood silent for a moment, with the film over his eyes, and the faintly perceptible beat becoming visible again in his cheeks.

"If you will excuse me for a few minutes," he said, with ceremonious politeness, "I should like to have the opportunity of speaking to my niece." With those words, he bowed, and quitted the room.

Left by himself, Vendale's thoughts (as a necessary result of the interview, thus far) turned instinctively to the consideration of Obenreizer's motives. He had put obstacles in the way of the courtship; he was now putting obstacles in the way of the marriage—a marriage offering advantages which even his ingenuity could not dispute. On the face of it, his conduct was incomprehensible. What did it mean?

Seeking, under the surface, for the answer to that question—and remembering that Obenreizer was a man of about his own age; also, that Marguerite was, strictly speaking, his half-niece only—Vendale asked himself, with a lover's ready jealousy, whether he had a rival to fear, as well as a guardian to conciliate. The thought just crossed his mind, and no more. The sense of Marguerite's kiss still lingering on his cheek reminded him gently that even the jealousy of a moment was now a treason to *her*.

On reflection, it seemed most likely that a personal motive of another kind might suggest the true explanation of Obenreizer's conduct. Marguerite's grace and beauty were precious ornaments in that little household. They gave it a special social attraction and a special social importance. They armed Obenreizer with a certain influence in reserve, which he could always depend upon to make his house attractive, and which he might always bring more or less to bear on the forwarding of his own private ends. Was he the sort of man to resign such advantages as were here implied, without obtaining the fullest possible compensation for the loss. A connection by marriage with Vendale offered him solid advantages, beyond all doubt. But there were hundreds of men in London with far greater power and far wider influence than Vendale possessed. Was it possible that this man's ambition secretly looked higher than the highest prospects that could be offered to him by the alliance now proposed for his niece? As the question passed through Vendale's mind, the man himself reappeared to answer it, or not to answer it, as the event might prove.

A marked change was visible in Obenreizer when he resumed his place. His manner was less assured, and there were plain traces about his mouth of recent agitation which had not been successfully composed. Had he said something, referring either to Vendale or to himself, which had roused Marguerite's spirit, and which had placed him, for the first time, face to face with a resolute assertion of his niece's will? It might or might not be. This only was certain—he looked like a man who had met with a repulse.

"I have spoken to my niece," he began. "I find, Mr. Vendale, that even your influence has not entirely blinded her to the social objections to your proposal."

"May I ask," returned Vendale, "if that is the only result of your interview with Miss Obenreizer?"

A momentary flash leapt out through the Obenreizer film.

"You are master of the situation," he answered, in a tone of sardonic submission. "If you insist on my admitting it, I do admit it in those words. My niece's will and mine used to be one, Mr. Vendale. You have come between us, and her will is now yours. In my country, we know when we are beaten, and we submit with our best grace. I submit, with my best grace, on certain conditions. Let us revert to the statement of your pecuniary position. I have an objection to you, my dear sir—a most amazing, a most audacious objection, from a man in my position to a man in yours."

"What is it?"

"You have honoured me by making a proposal for my niece's hand. For the present (with best thanks and respects), I beg to decline it."

"Why?"

"Because you are not rich enough."

The objection, as the speaker had foreseen, took Vendale completely by surprise. For the moment he was speechless.

"Your income is fifteen hundred a year," pursued Obenreizer. "In my miserable country I should fall on my knees before your income, and say, 'What a princely fortune!' In wealthy England, I sit as I am, and say, 'A modest independence, dear sir; nothing more. Enough, perhaps, for a wife in your own rank of life, who had no social prejudices to conquer. Not more than half enough for a wife who is a meanly born foreigner, and who has all your social prejudices against her.' Sir! if my niece is ever to marry you, she will have what you call uphill work of it in taking her place at starting. Yes, yes; this is not your view, but it remains, immovably remains, my view for all that. For my niece's sake, I claim that this uphill work shall be made as smooth as possible. Whatever material advantages she can have to help her, ought, in common justice, to be hers. Now, tell me, Mr. Vendale, on your fifteen hundred a year can your wife have a house in a fashionable quarter, a footman to open her door, a butler to wait at her table, and a carriage and horses to drive about in? I see the answer in your face—your face says, No. Very good. Tell me one more thing, and I have done. Take the mass of your educated, accomplished, and lovely countrywomen, is it, or is it not, the fact that a lady who has a house in a fashionable quarter, a footman to open her door, a butler to wait at her table, and a carriage and horses to drive about in, is a lady who has gained four steps, in female estimation, at starting? Yes? or No?"

"Come to the point," said Vendale. "You view this question as a question of terms. What are your terms?"

"The lowest terms, dear sir, on which you can provide your wife with those four steps at starting. Double your present income—the most rigid economy cannot do it in England on less. You said just now that you expected greatly to increase the value of your business. To work—and increase it! I am a good devil after all! On the day when you satisfy me, by plain proofs, that your income has risen to three thousand a year, ask me for my niece's hand, and it is yours."

"May I inquire if you have mentioned this arrangement to Miss Obenreizer?"

"Certainly. She has a last little morsel of regard still left for me, Mr. Vendale, which is not yours yet; and she accepts my terms. In other words, she submits to be guided by her guardian's regard for her welfare, and by her guardian's superior knowledge of the world." He threw himself back in his chair, in firm reliance on his position, and in full possession of his excellent temper.

Any open assertion of his own interests, in the situation in which Vendale was now placed, seemed to be (for the present at least) hopeless. He found himself literally left with no ground to stand on. Whether Obenreizer's objections were the genuine product of Obenreizer's own view of the case, or whether he was simply delaying the marriage in the hope of ultimately breaking it off altogether—in either of these events, any present resistance on Vendale's part would be equally useless. There was no help for it but to yield, making the best terms that he could on his own side.

"I protest against the conditions you impose on me," he began.

"Naturally," said Obenreizer; "I dare say I should protest, myself, in your place."

"Say, however," pursued Vendale, "that I accept your terms. In that case, I must be permitted to make two stipulations on my part. In the first place, I shall expect to be allowed to see your niece."

"Aha! to see my niece? and to make her in as great a hurry to be married as you are yourself? Suppose I say, No? you would see her perhaps without my permission?"

"Decidedly!"

"How delightfully frank! How exquisitely English! You shall see her, Mr. Vendale, on certain days, which we will appoint together. What next?"

"Your objection to my income," proceeded Vendale, "has taken me completely by surprise. I wish to be assured against any repetition of that surprise. Your present views of my qualification for marriage require me to have an income of three thousand a year. Can I be certain, in the future, as your experience of England enlarges, that your estimate will rise no higher?"

"In plain English," said Obenreizer, "you doubt my word?"

"Do you purpose to take *my* word for it when I inform you that I have doubled my income?" said Vendale. "If my memory does not deceive me, you stipulated, a minute since, for plain proofs?"

"Well played, Mr. Vendale! You combine the foreign quickness with the English solidity. Accept my best congratulations. Accept, also, my written guarantee."

He rose; seated himself at a writing-desk at a side-table, wrote a few lines, and presented them to Vendale with a low bow. The engagement was perfectly explicit, and was signed and dated with scrupulous care.

"Are you satisfied with your guarantee?"

"I am satisfied."

"Charmed to hear it, I am sure. We have had our little skirmish—we have really been wonderfully clever on both sides. For the present our affairs are settled. I bear no malice. You bear no malice. Come, Mr. Vendale, a good English shake hands."

Vendale gave his hand, a little bewildered by Obenreizer's sudden transitions from one humour to another.

"When may I expect to see Miss Obenreizer again?" he asked, as he rose to go.

"Honour me with a visit to-morrow," said Obenreizer, "and we will settle it then. Do have a grog before you go! No? Well! well! we will reserve the grog till you have your three thousand a year, and are ready to be married. Aha! When will that be?"

"I made an estimate, some months since, of the capacities of my business," said Vendale. "If that estimate is correct, I shall double my present income——"

"And be married!" added Obenreizer.

"And be married," repeated Vendale, "within a year from this time. Good night."

Vendale makes Mischief]

When Vendale entered his office the next morning, the dull commercial routine at Cripple Corner met him with a new face. Marguerite had an interest in it now! The whole machinery which Wilding's death had set in motion, to realise the value of the business—the balancing of ledgers, the estimating of debts, the taking of stock, and the rest of it—was now transformed into machinery which indicated the chances for and against a speedy marriage. After looking over results, as presented by his accountant, and checking additions and subtractions, as rendered by the clerks, Vendale turned his attention to the stock-taking department next, and sent a message to the cellars, desiring to see the report.

The Cellarman's appearance, the moment he put his head in at the door of his master's private room, suggested that something very extraordinary must have happened that morning. There was an approach to alacrity in Joey Ladle's movements! There was something which actually simulated cheerfulness in Joey Ladle's face!

"What's the matter?" asked Vendale. "Anything wrong?"

"I should wish to mention one thing," answered Joey. "Young Mr. Vendale, I have never set myself up for a prophet."

"Who ever said you did?"

"No prophet, as far as I've heard tell of that profession," proceeded Joey, "ever lived principally underground. No prophet, whatever else he might take in at the pores, ever took in wine from morning to night, for a number of years together. When I said to Young Master Wilding, respecting his changing the name of the firm, that one of these days he might find he'd changed the luck of the firm—did I put myself forward as a prophet? No, I didn't. Has what I said to him come true? Yes, it has. In the time of Pebbleson Nephew, Young Mr. Vendale, no such thing was ever known as a mistake made in a consignment delivered at these doors. There's a mistake been made now. Please to remark that it happened before Miss Margaret came here. For which reason it don't go against what I've said respecting Miss Margaret singing round the luck. Read that, sir," concluded Joey, pointing attention to a special passage in the report, with a forefinger which appeared to be in process of taking in through the pores nothing more remarkable than dirt. "It's foreign to my nature to crow over the house I serve, but I feel it _ kind of a solemn duty to ask you to read that."

Vendale read as follows: "Note, respecting the Swiss champagne. An irregularity has been discovered in the last consignment received from the firm of Defresnier and Co." Vendale stopped, and referred to a memorandum-book by his side. "That was in Mr. Wilding's time," he said. "The vintage was a particularly good one, and he took the whole of it. The Swiss champagne has done very well, hasn't it?"

"I don't say it's done badly," answered the Cellarman. "It may have got sick in our customers' bins, or it may have bust in our customers' hands. But I don't say it's done badly with _us._"

Vendale resumed the reading of the note: "We find the

number of the cases to be quite correct by the books. But six of them, which present a slight difference from the rest in the brand, have been opened, and have been found to contain a red wine instead of champagne. The similarity in the brands, we suppose, caused a mistake to be made in sending the consignment from Neuchâtel. The error has not been found to extend beyond six cases."

"Is that all!" exclaimed Vendale, tossing the note away from him.

Joey Ladle's eye followed the flying morsel of paper drearily.

"I'm glad to see you take it easy, sir," he said. "Whatever happens, it will be always a comfort to you to remember that you took it easy at first. Sometimes one mistake leads to another. A man drops a bit of orange-peel on the pavement by mistake, and another man treads on it by mistake, and there's a job at the hospital, and a party crippled for life. I'm glad you take it easy, sir. In Pebbleson Nephew's time we shouldn't have taken it easy till we had seen the end of it. Without desiring to crow over the house, Young Mr. Vendale, I wish you well through it. No offence, sir," said the Cellarman, opening the door to go out, and looking in again ominously before he shut it. "I'm muddled and molloncolly, I grant you. But I'm an old servant of Pebbleson Nephew, and I wish you well through them six cases of red wine."

Left by himself, Vendale laughed, and took up his pen. "I may as well send a line to Defresnier and Company," he thought, "before I forget it." He wrote at once in these terms:

"DEAR SIRS,—We are taking stock, and a trifling mistake has been discovered in the last consignment of champagne sent by your house to ours. Six of the cases contain red wine—which we hereby return to you. The matter can easily be set right, either by your sending us six cases of champagne, if they can be produced, or, if not, by your crediting us with the value of six cases on the amount last paid (five hundred pounds) by our firm to yours. Your faithful servants,

"WILDING AND CO."

This letter despatched to the post, the subject dropped at once out of Vendale's mind. He had other and far more interesting matters to think of. Later in the day he paid the visit to Obenreizer which had been agreed on between them. Certain evenings in the week were set apart which he was privileged to spend with Marguerite — always, however, in the presence of a third person. On this stipulation Obenreizer politely but positively insisted. The one concession he made was to give Vendale his choice of who the third person should be. Confiding in past experience, his choice fell unhesitatingly upon the excellent woman who mended Obenreizer's stockings. On hearing of the responsibility entrusted to her, Madame Dor's intellectual nature burst suddenly into a new stage of development. She waited till Obenreizer's eye was off her—and then she looked at Vendale and dimly winked.

The time passed—the happy evenings with Marguerite came and went. It was the tenth morning since Vendale had written to the Swiss firm, when the answer appeared on his desk, with the other letters of the day:

"DEAR SIRS,—We beg to offer our excuses for the little mistake which has happened. At the same time, we regret to add that the statement of our error, with which you have favoured us, has led to a very unexpected discovery. The affair is a most serious one for you and for us. The particulars are as follows:

"Having no more champagne of the vintage last sent to you, we made arrangements to credit your firm with the value of the six cases, as suggested by yourself. On taking this step, certain forms observed in our mode of doing business necessitated a reference to our bankers' book, as well as to our ledger. The result is a moral certainty that no such remittance as you mention can have reached our house, and a literal certainty that no such remittance has been paid to our account at the bank.

"It is needless, at this stage of the proceedings, to trouble you with details. The money has unquestionably been stolen in the course of its transit from you to us. Certain peculiarities which we observe, relating to the manner in which the fraud has been perpetrated, lead us to conclude that the thief may have calculated on being able to pay the missing sum to our bankers, before an inevitable discovery followed the annual striking of our balance. This would not have happened, in the usual course, for another three months. During that period, but for your letter, we might have remained perfectly unconscious of the robbery that has been committed.

"We mention this last circumstance, as it may help to show you that we have to do, in this case, with no ordinary thief. Thus far we have not even a suspicion of who that thief is. But we believe you will assist us in making some advance towards discovery, by examining the receipt (forged, of course) which has no doubt purported to come to you from our house. Be pleased to look and see whether it is a receipt entirely in manuscript, or whether it is a numbered and printed form which merely requires the filling in of the amount. The settlement of this apparently trivial question is, we assure you, a matter of vital importance. Anxiously awaiting your reply, we remain, with high esteem and consideration,

DEFRESNIER & Cie"

Vendale laid the letter on his desk, and waited a moment to steady his mind under the shock that had fallen on it. At the time of all others when it was most important to him to increase the value of his business, that business was threatened with a loss of five hundred pounds. He thought of Marguerite, as he took the key from his pocket and opened the iron chamber in the wall in which the books and papers of the firm were kept.

He was still in the chamber, searching for the forged receipt, when he was startled by a voice speaking close behind him.

"A thousand pardons," said the voice; "I am afraid I disturb you."

He turned, and found himself face to face with Marguerite's guardian.

"I have called," pursued Obenreizer, "to know if I can be of any use. Business of my own takes me away for some days to Manchester and Liverpool. Can I combine any business of yours with it? I am entirely at your disposal, in the character of commercial traveller for the firm of Wilding and Co."

"Excuse me for one moment," said Vendale; "I will speak to you directly." He turned round again, and continued his search among the papers. "You come at a time when friendly offers are more than usually precious to me," he resumed. "I have had very bad news this morning from Neuchâtel."

"Bad news!" exclaimed Obenreizer. "From Defresnier and Company?"

"Yes. A remittance we sent to them has been stolen. I am threatened with a loss of five hundred pounds. What's that?"

Turning sharply, and looking into the room for the second time, Vendale discovered his envelope-case overthrown on the floor, and Obenreizer on his knees picking up the contents.

"All my awkwardness!" said Obenreizer. "This dreadful news of yours startled me; I stepped back—" He became too deeply interested in collecting the scattered envelopes to finish the sentence.

"Don't trouble yourself," said Vendale. "The clerk will pick the things up."

"This dreadful news!" repeated Obenreizer, persisting in collecting the envelopes. "This dreadful news!"

"If you will read the letter," said Vendale, "you will find I have exaggerated nothing. There it is, open on my desk."

He resumed his search, and in a moment more discovered the forged receipt. It was on the numbered and printed form, described by the Swiss firm. Vendale made a memorandum of the number and the date. Having replaced the receipt and locked up the iron chamber, he had leisure to notice Obenreizer, reading the letter in the recess of a window at the far end of the room.

"Come to the fire," said Vendale. "You look perished with the cold out there. I will ring for some more coals."

Obenreizer rose, and came slowly back to the desk. "Marguerite will be as sorry to hear of this as I am," he said, kindly. "What do you mean to do?"

"I am in the hands of Defresnier and Company," answered Vendale. "In my total ignorance of the circumstances, I can only do what they recommend. The receipt which I have just found, turns out to be the numbered and printed form. They seem to attach some special importance to its discovery. You have had experience, when you were in the Swiss house, of their way of doing business. Can you guess what object they have in view?"

Obenreizer offered a suggestion.

"Suppose I examine the receipt?" he said.

"Are you ill?" asked Vendale, startled by the change in his face, which now showed itself plainly for the first time. "Pray go to the fire. You seem to be shivering—I hope you are not going to be ill?"

"Not I!" said Obenreizer. "Perhaps I have caught cold. Your English climate might have spared an admirer of your English institutions. Let me look at the receipt."

Vendale opened the iron chamber. Obenreizer took a chair, and drew it close to the fire. He held both hands over the flames. "Let me look at the receipt," he repeated, eagerly, as Vendale reappeared with the paper in his hand. At the same moment a porter entered the room with a fresh supply of coals. Vendale told him to make a good fire. The man obeyed the order with a disastrous alacrity. As he stepped forward and raised the scuttle, his foot caught in a fold of the rug, and he discharged his entire cargo of coals into the grate. The result was an instant smothering of the flame, and the production of a stream of yellow smoke, without a visible morsel of fire to account for it.

"Imbecile!" whispered Obenreizer to himself, with a look at the man which the man remembered for many a long day afterwards.

"Will you come into the clerks' room?" asked Vendale. "They have a stove there."

"No, no. No matter."

Vendale handed him the receipt. Obenreizer's interest in examining it appeared to have been quenched as suddenly and as effectually as the fire itself. He just glanced over the document, and said, "No; I don't understand it! I am sorry to be of no use."

"I will write to Neuchâtel by to-night's post," said Vendale, putting away the receipt for the second time. "We must wait, and see what comes of it."

"By to-night's post," repeated Obenreizer. "Let me see.

You will get the answer in eight or nine days' time. I shall be back before that. If I can be of any service, as commercial traveller, perhaps you will let me know between this and then. You will send me written instructions? My best thanks. I shall be most anxious for your answer from Neuchâtel. Who knows? It may be a mistake, my dear friend, after all. Courage! courage! courage!" He had entered the room with no appearance of being pressed for time. He now snatched up his hat, and took his leave with the air of a man who had not another moment to lose.

Left by himself, Vendale took a turn thoughtfully in the room.

His previous impression of Obenreizer was shaken by what he had heard and seen at the interview which had just taken place. He was disposed, for the first time, to doubt whether, in this case, he had not been a little hasty and hard in his judgment on another man. Obenreizer's surprise and regret, on hearing the news from Neuchâtel, bore the plainest marks of being honestly felt—not politely assumed for the occasion. With troubles of his own to encounter, suffering, to all appearance, from the first insidious attack of a serious illness, he had looked and spoken like a man who really deplored the disaster that had fallen on his friend. Hitherto, Vendale had tried vainly to alter his first opinion of Marguerite's guardian, for Marguerite's sake. All the generous instincts in his nature now combined together and shook the evidence which had seemed unanswerable up to this time. "Who knows?" he thought, "I may have read that man's face wrongly, after all."

The time passed—the happy evenings with Marguerite came and went. It was again the tenth morning since Vendale had written to the Swiss firm: and again the answer appeared on his desk with the other letters of the day.

"DEAR SIR,—My senior partner, M. Defresnier, has been called away, by urgent business, to Milan. In his absence (and with his full concurrence and authority), I now write you again on the subject of the missing five hundred pounds.

"Your discovery that the forged receipt is executed upon one of our numbered and printed forms has caused inexpressible surprise and distress to my partner and to myself. At the time when your remittance was stolen, but three keys were in existence opening the strong box in which our receipt-forms are invariably kept. My partner had one key; I had the other. The third was in the possession of a gentleman who, at that period, occupied a position of trust in our house. We should as soon have thought of suspecting one of ourselves as of suspecting this person. Suspicion now points at him, nevertheless. I cannot prevail on myself to inform you who the person is, so long as there is the shadow of a chance that he may come innocently out of the inquiry which must now be instituted. Forgive my silence; the motive of it is good.

"The form our investigation must now take is simple enough. The handwriting on your receipt must be compared, by competent persons whom we have at our disposal, with certain specimens of handwriting in our possession. I cannot send you the specimens, for business reasons, which, when you hear them, you are sure to approve. I must beg you to send me the receipt to Neuchâtel—and, in making this request, I must accompany it by a word of necessary warning.

"If the person, at whom suspicion now points, really proves to be the person who has committed this forgery and theft, I have reason to fear that circumstances may have already put him on his guard. The only evidence against him is the evidence in your hands, and he will move heaven and earth to obtain and destroy it. I strongly urge you not to trust the receipt to the post. Send it to me, without loss of time, by a private hand, and choose nobody for your messenger but a person long established in your own employment, accustomed to travelling, capable of speaking French; a man of courage, a man of honesty, and, above all things, a man who can be trusted to let no stranger scrape acquaintance with him on the route. Tell no one—absolutely no one—but your messenger of the turn this matter has now taken. The safe transit of the receipt may depend on your interpreting *literally* the advice which I give you at the end of this letter.

"I have only to add that every possible saving of time is now of the last importance. More than one of our receipt-forms is missing—and it is impossible to say what new frauds may not be committed, if we fail to lay our hands on the thief. Your faithful servant,

"ROLLAND
"(Signing for Defresnier & Cie)."

Who was the suspected man? In Vendale's position, it seemed useless to inquire.

Who was to be sent to Neuchâtel with the receipt? Men of courage and men of honesty were to be had at Cripple Corner for the asking. But where was the man who was accustomed to foreign travelling, who could speak the French language, and who could be really relied on to let no stranger scrape acquaintance with him on his route? There was but one man at hand who combined all those requisites in his own person, and that man was Vendale himself.

It was a sacrifice to leave his business; it was a greater sacrifice to leave Marguerite. But a matter of five hundred pounds was involved in the pending inquiry; and a literal interpretation of M. Rolland's advice was insisted on in terms which there was no trifling with. The more Vendale thought of it, the more plainly the necessity faced him, and said, "Go!"

As he locked up the letter with the receipt, the association of ideas reminded him of Obenreizer. A guess at the identity of the suspected man looked more possible now. Obenreizer might know.

The thought had barely passed through his mind, when the door opened, and Obenreizer entered the room.

"They told me at Soho-square you were expected back last night," said Vendale, greeting him. "Have you done well in the country? Are you better?"

A thousand thanks. Obenreizer had done admirably well; Obenreizer was infinitely better. And now, what news? Any letter from Neuchâtel?

"A very strange letter," answered Vendale. "The matter has taken a new turn, and the letter insists—without excepting anybody—on my keeping our next proceedings a profound secret."

"Without excepting anybody?" repeated Obenreizer. As he said the words, he walked away again, thoughtfully, to the window at the other end of the room, looked out for a moment, and suddenly came back to Vendale. "Surely they must have forgotten?" he resumed, "or they would have excepted *me?*"

"It is Monsieur Rolland who writes," said Vendale. "And, as you say, he must certainly have forgotten. That view of the matter quite escaped me. I was just wishing I had you to consult, when you came into the room. And here I am tied by a formal prohibition, which cannot possibly have been intended to include you. How very annoying!"

Obenreizer's filmy eyes fixed on Vendale attentively.

"Perhaps it is more than annoying!" he said. "I came this morning not only to hear the news, but to offer myself as messenger, negotiator—what you will. Would you believe it? I have letters which oblige me to go to Switzerland immediately. Messages, documents, anything—I could have taken them all to Defresnier and Rolland for you."

"You are the very man I wanted," returned Vendale. "I had decided, most unwillingly, on going to Neuchâtel myself, not five minutes since, because I could find no one here capable of taking my place. Let me look at the letter again."

He opened the strong-room to get at the letter. Obenreizer, after first glancing round him to make sure that they were alone, followed a step or two and waited, measuring Vendale with his eye. Vendale was the tallest man, and unmistakably the strongest man also of the two. Obenreizer turned away, and warmed himself at the fire.

Meanwhile, Vendale read the last paragraph in the letter for the third time. There was the plain warning—there was the closing sentence, which insisted on a literal interpretation of it. The hand, which was leading Vendale in the dark, led

him on that condition only. A large sum was at stake: a terrible suspicion remained to be verified. If he acted on his own responsibility, and if anything happened to defeat the object in view, who would be blamed? As a man of business, Vendale had but one course to follow. He locked the letter up again.

"It is most annoying," he said to Obenreizer—"it is a piece of forgetfulness on Monsieur Rolland's part which puts me to serious inconvenience, and places me in an absurdly false position towards you. What am I to do? I am acting in a very serious matter, and acting entirely in the dark. I have no choice but to be guided, not by the spirit, but the letter of my instructions. You understand me, I am sure? You know, if I had not been fettered in this way, how gladly I should have accepted your services?"

"Say no more!" returned Obenreizer. "In your place I should have done the same. My good friend, I take no offence. I thank you for your compliment. We shall be travelling companions, at any rate," added Obenreizer. "You go, as I go, at once?"

"At once. I must speak to Marguerite first, of course!"

"Surely! surely. Speak to her this evening. Come, and pick me up on the way to the station. We go together by the mail train to-night?"

"By the mail train to-night."

It was later than Vendale had anticipated when he drove up to the house in Soho-square. Business difficulties, occasioned by his sudden departure, had presented themselves by dozens. A cruelly large share of the time which he had hoped to devote to Marguerite had been claimed by duties at his office which it was impossible to neglect.

To his surprise and delight, she was alone in the drawing-room when he entered it.

"We have only a few minutes, George," she said. "But Madame Dor has been good to me—and we can have those few minutes alone." She threw her arms round his neck, and whispered eagerly, "Have you done anything to offend Mr. Obenreizer?"

"I!" exclaimed Vendale, in amazement.

"Hush!" she said, "I want to whisper it. You know the little photograph I have got of you. This afternoon it happened to be on the chimney-piece. He took it up and looked at it—and I saw his face in the glass. I know you have offended him! He is merciless; he is revengeful; he is as secret as the grave. Don't go with him, George—don't go with him!"

"My own love," returned Vendale, "you are letting your fancy frighten you! Obenreizer and I were never better friends than we are at this moment."

Before a word more could be said, the sudden movement of some ponderous body shook the floor of the next room. The shock was followed by the appearance of Madame Dor. "Obenreizer!" exclaimed this excellent person in a whisper, and plumped down instantly in her regular place by the stove.

Obenreizer came in with a courier's bag strapped over his shoulder.

"Are you ready?" he asked, addressing Vendale. "Can I take anything for you? You have no travelling-bag. I have got one. Here is the compartment for papers, open at your service."

"Thank you," said Vendale. "I have only one paper of importance with me; and that paper I am bound to take charge of myself. Here it is," he added, touching the breast-pocket of his coat, "and here it must remain till we get to Neuchâtel."

As he said those words, Marguerite's hand caught his, and pressed it significantly. She was looking towards Obenreizer. Before Vendale could look, in his turn, Obenreizer had wheeled round, and was taking leave of Madame Dor.

"Adieu, my charming niece!" he said, turning to Marguerite next. "En route, my friend, for Neuchâtel!" He tapped Vendale lightly over the breast-pocket of his coat, and led the way to the door.

Vendale's last look was for Marguerite. Marguerite's last words to him were, "Don't go!"

ACT III : *In the Valley*

IT was about the middle of the month of February when Vendale and Obenreizer set forth on their expedition. The winter being a hard one, the time was bad for travellers. So bad was it that these two travellers, coming to Strasbourg, found its great inns almost empty. And even the few people they did encounter in that city, who had started from England or from Paris on business journeys towards the interior of Switzerland, were turning back.

Many of the railroads in Switzerland that tourists pass easily enough now, were almost or quite impracticable then. Some were not begun; more were not completed. On such as were open, there were still large gaps of old road where communication in the winter season was often stopped; on others, there were weak points where the new road was not safe, either under conditions of severe frost, or of rapid thaw. The running of trains on this last class was not to be counted on in the worst time of the year, was contingent upon weather, or was wholly abandoned through the months considered the most dangerous.

At Strasbourg there were more travellers' stories afloat, respecting the difficulties of the way further on, than there were travellers to relate them. Many of these tales were as wild as usual; but the more modestly marvellous did derive some colour from the circumstance that people were indisputably turning back. However, as the road to Basle was open, Vendale's resolution to push on was in no wise disturbed. Obenreizer's resolution was necessarily Vendale's, seeing that he stood at bay thus desperately:—He must be ruined, or must destroy the evidence that Vendale carried about him, even if he destroyed Vendale with it.

The state of mind of each of these two fellow-travellers towards the other was this. Obenreizer, encircled by impending ruin through Vendale's quickness of action, and seeing the circle narrowed every hour by Vendale's energy, hated him with the animosity of a fierce cunning lower animal. He had always had instinctive movements in his breast against him; perhaps, because of the openness of his nature; perhaps, because of his better looks; perhaps, because of his success with Marguerite; perhaps, on all those grounds, the two last not the least. And now he saw in him, besides, the hunter who was tracking him down. Vendale, on the other hand, always contending generously against his first vague mistrust, now felt bound to contend against it more than ever: reminding himself, "He is Marguerite's guardian. We are on perfectly friendly terms; he is my companion of his own proposal, and can have no interested motive in sharing this undesirable journey." To which pleas in behalf of Obenreizer, chance added one consideration more, when they came to Basle, after a journey of more than twice the average duration.

They had had a late dinner, and were alone in an inn room there, overhanging the Rhine: at that place rapid and deep, swollen and loud. Vendale lounged upon a couch, and Obenreizer walked to and fro: now, stopping at the window looking at the crooked reflections of the town lights in the dark water (and peradventure thinking, "If I could fling him into it!"); now, resuming his walk with his eyes upon the floor.

"Where shall I rob him, if I can? Where shall I murder him, if I must?" So, as he paced the room, ran the river, ran the river, ran the river.

The burden seemed to him at last, to be growing so plain that he stopped; thinking it as well to suggest another burden to his companion.

"The Rhine sounds to-night," he said with a smile, "like the old waterfall at home. That waterfall which my mother showed to travellers (I told you of it once). The sound of it changed with the weather, as does the sound of all falling waters and flowing waters. When I was a pupil of the watch-maker, I remembered it as sometimes saying to me for whole days, 'Who are you, my little wretch? Who are you, my little wretch?' I remembered it as saying, other times, when its sound was hollow, and storm was coming up the Pass: 'Boom, boom, boom. Beat him, beat him, beat him.' Like my mother enraged—if she was my mother."

"If she was?" said Vendale, gradually changing his attitude to a sitting one. "If she was? Why do you say 'if'?"

"What do I know?" replied the other negligently, throwing up his hands and letting them fall as they would. "What would you have? I am so obscurely born, that how can I say? I was very young, and all the rest of the family were men and women, and my so-called parents were old. Anything is possible in a case like that?"

"Did you ever doubt——?"

"I told you once, I doubt the marriage of those two," he replied, throwing up his hands again, as if he were throwing the unprofitable subject away. "But here I am in Creation. *I* come of no fine family. What does it matter?"

"At least you are Swiss," said Vendale, after following him with his eyes to and fro.

"How do I know?" he retorted abruptly, and stopping to look back over his shoulder. "I say to you, at least you are English. How do you know?"

"By what I have been told from infancy."

"Ah! I know of myself that way."

"And," added Vendale, pursuing the thought that he could not drive back, "by my earliest recollections."

"I also. I know of myself that way—if that way satisfies."

"Does it not satisfy you?"

"It must. There is nothing like 'it must' in this little world. It must. Two short words those, but stronger than long proof or reasoning."

"You and poor Wilding were born in the same year. You were nearly of an age," said Vendale, again thoughtfully looking after him as he resumed his pacing up and down.

"Yes. Very nearly."

Could Obenreizer be the missing man? In the unknown association of things, was there a subtler meaning than he himself thought, in that theory so often on his lips about the smallness of the world? Had the Swiss letter presenting him, followed so close on Mrs. Goldstraw's revelation concerning the infant who had been taken away to Switzerland, because he was that infant grown a man? In a world where so many depths lie unsounded, it might be. The chances, or the laws—call them either—that had wrought out the revival of Vendale's own acquaintance with Obenreizer, and had ripened it into intimacy, and had brought them here together this present winter night, were hardly less curious; while read by such a light, they were seen to cohere towards the further-ance of a continuous and an intelligible purpose. Vendale's awakened thoughts ran high while his eyes musingly followed Obenreizer pacing up and down the room, the river ever running to the tune: "Where shall I rob him, if I can? Where shall I murder him, if I must?" The secret of his dead friend was in no hazard from Vendale's lips; but just as his friend had died of its weight, so did he in his lighter succession feel the burden of the trust, and the obligation to follow any clue, however obscure. He rapidly asked himself, would he like this man to be the real Wilding? No. Argue down his mistrust as he might, he was unwilling to put such a substitute in the place of his late guileless, outspoken, childlike partner. He rapidly asked himself, would he like this man to be rich? No. He had more power than enough over Marguerite as it was, and wealth might invest him with more. Would he like this man to be Marguerite's guardian, and yet proved to stand in no degree of relationship towards her, however disconnected and distant? No. But these were not considerations to come between him and fidelty to the dead. Let him see to it that they passed him with no other notice than the knowledge that they *had* passed him, and left him bent on the discharge of a solemn duty. And he did see to it, so soon that he followed his companion with ungrudging eyes, while he still paced the room; that companion, whom he supposed to be moodily reflecting on his own birth, and not on another man's—least of all what man's—violent Death.

The road in advance from Basle to Neuchâtel was better than had been represented. The latest weather had done it good. Drivers, both of horses and mules, had come in that evening after dark, and had reported nothing more difficult to be overcome than trials of patience, harness, wheels, axles, and whipcord. A bargain was soon struck for a carriage and horses, to take them on in the morning, and to start before daylight.

"Do you lock your door at night when travelling?" asked Obenreizer, standing warming his hands by the wood fire in Vendale's chamber, before going to his own.

"Not I. I sleep too soundly."

"You are so sound a sleeper?" he retorted, with an admiring look. "What a blessing!"

"Anything but a blessing to the rest of the house," rejoined Vendale, "if I had to be knocked up in the morning from the outside of my bedroom door."

"I, too," said Obenreizer, "leave open my room. But let me advise you, as a Swiss, who knows: always, when you travel in my country, put your papers—and, of course your money—under your pillow. Always the same place."

"You are not complimentary to your countrymen," laughed Vendale.

"My countrymen," said Obenreizer, with that light touch of his friend's elbows by way of Good Night and benediction,

"I suppose, are like the majority of men. And the majority of men will take what they can get. Adieu! At four in the morning."

"Adieu! At four."

Left to himself, Vendale raked the logs together, sprinkled over them the white wood-ashes lying on the hearth, and sat down to compose his thoughts. But they still ran high on their latest theme, and the running of the river tended to agitate rather than to quiet them. As he sat thinking, what little disposition he had had to sleep departed. He felt it hopeless to lie down yet, and sat dressed by the fire. Marguerite, Wilding, Obenreizer, the business he was then upon, and a thousand hopes and doubts that had nothing to do with it, occupied his mind at once. Everything seemed to have power over him, but slumber. The departed disposition to sleep kept far away.

He sat for a long time thinking, on the hearth, when his candle burned down, and its light went out. It was of little moment; there was light enough in the fire. He changed his attitude, and, leaning his arm on the chairback, and his chin upon that hand, sat thinking still.

But he sat between the fire and the bed, and, as the fire flickered in the play of air from the fast-flowing river, his enlarged shadow fluttered on the white wall by the bedside. His attitude gave it an air, half of mourning, and half of bending over the bed imploring. His eyes were observant of it, when he became troubled by the disagreeable fancy that it was like Wilding's shadow, and not his own.

A slight change of place would cause it to disappear. He made the change, and the apparition of his disturbed fancy vanished. He now sat in the shade of a little nook beside the fire, and the door of the room was before him.

It had a long cumbrous iron latch. He saw the latch slowly and softly rise. The door opened a very little, and came to again: as though only the air had moved it. But he saw that the latch was out of the hasp.

The door opened again very slowly, until it opened wide enough to admit some one. It afterwards remained still for a while, as though cautiously held open on the other side. The figure of a man then entered, with its face turned towards the bed, and stood quiet just within the door. Until it said, in a low half-whisper, at the same time taking one step forward: "Vendale!"

"What now?" he answered, springing from his seat; "who is it?"

It was Obenreizer, and he uttered a cry of surprise as Vendale came upon him from that unexpected direction. "Not in bed?" he said, catching him by both shoulders with an instinctive tendency to a struggle, "Then something *is* wrong!"

"What do you mean?" said Vendale, releasing himself.

"First tell me; you are not ill?"

"Ill? No."

"I have had a bad dream about you. How is it that I see you up and dressed?"

"My good fellow, I may as well ask you how is it that I see *you* up and undressed?"

"I have told you why. I have had a bad dream about you. I tried to rest after it, but it was impossible. I could not make up my mind to stay where I was, without knowing you were safe; and yet I could not make up my mind to come in here. I have been minutes hesitating at the door. It is so easy to laugh at a dream that you have not dreamed. Where is your candle?"

"Burnt out."

"I have a whole one in my room. Shall I fetch it?"

"Do so."

His room was very near, and he was absent for but a few seconds. Coming back with the candle in his hand, he kneeled down on the hearth and lighted it. As he blew with his breath a charred billet into flame for the purpose, Vendale, looking down at him, saw that his lips were white and not easy of control.

"Yes!" said Obenreizer, setting the lighted candle on the table, "it was a bad dream. Only look at me!"

His feet were bare; his red-flannel shirt was thrown back at the throat, and its sleeves were rolled above the elbows; his only other garment, a pair of under pantaloons or drawers, reaching to the ankles, fitted him close and tight. A certain lithe and savage appearance was on his figure, and his eyes were very bright.

"If there had been a wrestle with a robber, as I dreamed," said Obenreizer, "you see, I was stripped for it."

"And armed, too," said Vendale, glancing at his girdle.

"A traveller's dagger, that I always carry on the road," he answered carelessly, half drawing it from its sheath with his left hand, and putting it back again. "Do you carry no such thing?"

"Nothing of the kind."

"No pistols?" said Obenreizer, glancing at the table, and from it to the untouched pillow.

"Nothing of the sort."

"You Englishmen are so confident! You wish to sleep?"

"I have wished to sleep this long time, but I can't do it."

"I neither, after the bad dream. My fire has gone the way of your candle. May I come and sit by yours? Two o'clock! It will so soon be four, that it is not worth the trouble to go to bed again."

"I shall not take the trouble to go to bed at all, now," said Vendale; "sit here and keep me company, and welcome."

Going back to his room to arrange his dress, Obenreizer soon returned in a loose cloak and slippers, and they sat down on opposite sides of the hearth. In the interval, Vendale had replenished the fire from the wood-basket in his room, and Obenreizer had put upon the table a flask and cup from his.

"Common cabaret brandy, I am afraid," he said, pouring out; "bought upon the road, and not like yours from Cripple Corner. But yours is exhausted; so much the worse. A cold night, a cold time of night, a cold country, and a cold house. This may be better than nothing; try it."

Vendale took the cup, and did so.

"How do you find it?"

"It has a coarse after-flavour," said Vendale, giving back the cup with a slight shudder, "and I don't like it."

"You are right," said Obenreizer, tasting, and smacking his lips; "it *has* a coarse after-flavour, and *I* don't like it. Booh! it burns, though!" He had flung what remained in the cup, upon the fire.

Each of them leaned an elbow on the table, reclining his head upon his hand, and sat looking at the flaring logs. Obenreizer remained watchful and still; but Vendale, after certain nervous twitches and starts, in one of which he rose to his feet and looked wildly about him, fell into the strangest confusion of dreams. He carried his papers in a leather case or pocket-book, in an inner breast-pocket of his buttoned travelling coat; and whatever he dreamed of, in the lethargy that got possession of him, something importunate in these papers called him out of that dream, though he could not wake from it. He was belated on the steppes of Russia (some shadowy person gave that name to the place) with Marguerite; and yet the sensation of a hand at his breast, softly feeling the outline of the pocket-book as he lay asleep before the fire, was present to him. He was shipwrecked in an open boat at sea, and having lost his clothes, had no other covering than an old sail; and yet a creeping hand, tracing outside all the other pockets of the dress he actually wore, for papers, and finding none answer its touch, warned him to rouse himself. He was in the ancient vault at Cripple Corner, to which was transferred the very bed substantial and present in that very room at Basle; and Wilding (not dead, as he had supposed, and yet he did not wonder much) shook him, and whispered, "Look at that man! Don't you see he has risen, and is turning the pillow? Why should he turn the pillow, if not to seek those papers that are in your breast? Awake!" And yet he slept, and wandered off into other dreams.

Watchful and still, with his elbow on the table and his head upon that hand, his companion at length said: "Vendale!

We are called. Past four!" Then, opening his eyes, he saw, turned sideways on him, the filmy face of Obenreizer.

"You have been in a heavy sleep," he said. "The fatigue of constant travelling and the cold!"

"I am broad awake now," cried Vendale, springing up, but with an unsteady footing. "Haven't you slept at all?"

"I may have dozed, but I seem to have been patiently looking at the fire. Whether or no, we must wash, and break-fast, and turn out. Past four, Vendale; past four!"

It was said in a tone to rouse him, for already he was half asleep again. In his preparation for the day, too, and at his breakfast, he was often virtually asleep while in mechanical action. It was not until the cold dark day was closing in, that he had any distincter impressions of the ride than jingling bells, bitter weather, slipping horses, frowning hillsides, bleak woods, and a stoppage at some wayside house of entertain-ment, where they had passed through a cowhouse to reach the travellers' room above. He had been conscious of little more, except of Obenreizer sitting thoughtful at his side all day, and eyeing him much.

But when he shook off his stupor, Obenreizer was not at his side. The carriage was stopping to bait at another way-side house; and a line of long narrow carts, laden with casks of wine, and drawn by horses with a quantity of blue collar and head-gear, were baiting too. These came from the direction in which the travellers were going, and Obenreizer (not thoughtful now, but cheerful and alert) was talking with the foremost driver. As Vendale stretched his limbs, circulated his blood, and cleared off the lees of his lethargy, with a sharp run to and fro in the bracing air, the line of carts moved on: the drivers all saluting Obenreizer as they passed him.

"Who are those?" asked Vendale.

"They are our carriers—Defresnier and Company's," replied Obenreizer. "Those are our casks of wine." He was singing to himself, and lighting a cigar.

"I have been drearily dull company to-day," said Vendale, "I don't know what has been the matter with me."

"You had no sleep last night; and a kind of brain-congestion frequently comes, at first, of such cold," said Obenreizer. "I have seen it often. After all, we shall have our journey for nothing, it seems."

"How for nothing?"

"The House is at Milan. You know, we are a Wine House at Neuchâtel, and a Silk House at Milan? Well, Silk hap-pening to press of a sudden, more than Wine, Defresnier was summoned to Milan. Rolland, the other partner, has been taken ill since his departure, and the doctors will allow him to see no one. A letter awaits you at Neuchâtel to tell you so. I have it from our chief carrier whom you saw me talking with.

He was surprised to see me, and said he had that word for you if he met you. What do you do? Go back?"

"Go on," said Vendale.

"On?"

"On? Yes. Across the Alps, and down to Milan."

Obenreizer stopped in his smoking to look at Vendale, and then smoked heavily, looked up the road, looked down the road, looked down at the stones in the road at his feet.

"I have a very serious matter in charge," said Vendale, "more of these missing forms may be turned to as bad account, or worse; I am urged to lose no time in helping the House to take the thief; and nothing shall turn me back."

"No?" cried Obenreizer, taking out his cigar to smile, and giving his hand to his fellow-traveller. "Then nothing shall turn me back. Ho, driver! Despatch. Quick there! Let us push on!"

They travelled through the night. There had been snow, and there was a partial thaw, and they mostly travelled at a foot-pace, and always with many stoppages to breathe the splashed and floundering horses. After an hour's broad daylight, they drew rein at the inn-door at Neuchâtel, having been some eight-and-twenty hours in conquering some eighty English miles.

When they had hurriedly refreshed and changed, they went together to the house of business of Defresnier and Company. There they found the letter which the wine-carrier had described, enclosing the tests and comparisons of hand-writing essential to the discovery of the Forger. Vendale's determination to press forward, without resting, being already taken, the only question to delay them was by what Pass could they cross the Alps? Respecting the state of the two Passes of the St. Gothard and the Simplon, the guides and mule-drivers differed greatly; and both Passes were still far enough off, to prevent the travellers from having the benefit of any recent experience of either. Besides which, they well knew that a fall of snow might altogether change the described conditions in a single hour, even if they were correctly stated. But, on the whole, the Simplon appearing to be the hopefuller route, Vendale decided to take it. Obenreizer bore little or no part in the discussion, and scarcely spoke.

To Geneva, to Lusanne, along the level margin of the lake to Vevay, so into the winding valley between the spurs of the mountains, and into the valley of the Rhone. The sound of the carriage-wheels, as they rattled on, through the day, through the night, became as the wheels of a great clock, recording the hours. No change of weather varied the journey, after it had hardened into a sullen frost. In a sombre-yellow sky, they saw the Alpine ranges; and they saw enough of snow on nearer and much lower hill-tops, and hill-sides, to sully, by contrast, the purity of lake, torrent, and waterfall, and make the villages look discoloured and dirty. But no snow fell, nor was there any snow-drift on the road. The stalking along the valley of more or less of white mist, changing on their hair and dress into icicles, was the only variety between them and the gloomy sky. And still by day, and still by night, the wheels. And still they rolled, in the hearing of one of them, to the burden, altered from the burden of the Rhine: "The time is gone for robbing him alive, and I must murder him."

They came, at length, to the poor little town of Brieg, at the foot of the Simplon. They came there after dark, but yet could see how dwarfed men's work and men became with the immense mountains towering over them. Here they must lie for the night; and here was warmth of fire, and lamp, and dinner, and wine, and after-conference resounding, with guides and drivers. No human creature had come across the Pass for four days. The snow above the snow-line was too soft for wheeled carriage, and not hard enough for sledge. There was snow in the sky. There had been snow in the sky for days past, and the marvel was that it had not fallen, and the certainty was that it must fall. No vehicle could cross. The journey might be tried on mules, or it might be tried on foot; but the best guides must be paid danger-price in either case, and that, too, whether they succeeded in taking the two travellers across, or turned for safety and brought them back.

In this discussion, Obenreizer bore no part whatever. He sat silently smoking by the fire until the room was cleared and Vendale referred to him.

"Bah! I am weary of these poor devils and their trade," he said, in reply. "Always the same story. It is the story of their trade to-day, as it was the story of their trade when I was a ragged boy. What do you and I want? We want a knapsack each, and a mountain-staff each. We want no guide; we should guide him; he would not guide us. We leave our portmanteaus here, and we cross together. We have been on the mountains together before now, and I am mountain-born, and I know this Pass—Pass!—rather High Road!—by heart. We will leave these poor devils, in pity, to trade with others; but they must not delay us to make a pretence of earning money. Which is all they mean."

Vendale, glad to be quit of the dispute, and to cut the knot: active, adventurous, bent on getting forward, and therefore very susceptible to the last hint: readily assented. Within two hours, they had purchased what they wanted for the expedition, had packed their knapsacks, and lay down to sleep.

At break of day, they found half the town collected in the narrow street to see them depart. The people talked together in groups; the guides and drivers whispered apart, and looked up at the sky; no one wished them a good journey.

As they began the ascent, a gleam of sun shone from the otherwise unaltered sky, and for a moment turned the tin spires of the town to silver.

"A good omen!" said Vendale (though it died out while he spoke). "Perhaps our example will open the Pass on this side."

"No; we shall not be followed," returned Obenreizer, looking up at the sky and back at the valley. "We shall be alone up yonder."

On the Mountain]

The road was fair enough for stout walkers, and the air grew lighter and easier to breathe as the two ascended. But the settled gloom remained as it had remained for days back. Nature seemed to have come to a pause. The sense of hearing, no less than the sense of sight, was troubled by having to wait so long for the change, whatever it might be, that impended. The silence was as palpable and heavy as the lowering clouds— or rather cloud, for there seemed to be but one in all the sky, and that one covering the whole of it.

Although the light was thus dismally shrouded, the prospect was not obscured. Down in the valley of the Rhone behind them, the stream could be traced through all its many windings, oppressively sombre and solemn in its one leaden hue, a colourless waste. Far and high above them, glaciers and suspended avalanches overhung the spots where they must pass by-and-by; deep and dark below them, on their right, were awful precipice and roaring torrent; tremendous mountains arose in every vista. The gigantic landscape, uncheered by a touch of changing light or a solitary ray of sun, was yet terribly distinct in its ferocity. The hearts of two lonely men might shrink a little, if they had to win their way for miles and hours among a legion of silent and motionless men—mere men like themselves—all looking at them with fixed and frowning front. But how much more, when the legion is of Nature's mightiest works, and the frown may turn to fury in an instant!

As they ascended, the road became gradually more rugged and difficult. But the spirits of Vendale rose as they mounted higher, leaving so much more of the road behind them conquered. Obenreizer spoke little, and held on with a determined purpose. Both, in respect of agility and endurance, were well qualified for the expedition. Whatever the born mountaineer read in the weather-tokens, that was illegible to the other, he kept to himself.

"Shall we get across to-day?" asked Vendale.

"No," replied the other. "You see how much deeper the

snow lies here than it lay half a league lower. The higher we mount, the deeper the snow will lie. Walking is half wading even now. And the days are so short! If we get as high as the fifth Refuge, and lie to-night at the Hospice, we shall do well."

"Is there no danger of the weather rising in the night," asked Vendale, anxiously, "and snowing us up?"

"There is danger enough about us," said Obenreizer, with a cautious glance onward and upward, "to render silence our best policy. You have heard of the Bridge of the Ganther?"

"I have crossed it once."

"In the summer?"

"Yes; in the travelling season."

"Yes; but it is another thing at this season;" with a sneer, as though he were out of temper. "This is not a time of year, or a state of things, on an Alpine Pass, that you gentlemen holiday-travellers know much about."

"You are my Guide," said Vendale, good-humouredly. "I trust to you."

"I am your Guide," said Obenreizer, "and I will guide you to your journey's end. There is the Bridge before us."

They had made a turn into a desolate and dismal ravine, where the snow lay deep below them, deep above them, deep on every side. While speaking, Obenreizer stood pointing at the Bridge, and observing Vendale's face with a very singular expression on his own.

"If I, as Guide, had sent you over there, in advance, and encouraged you to give a shout or two, you might have brought down upon yourself tons and tons and tons of snow, that would not only have struck you dead, but buried you deep, at a blow."

"No doubt," said Vendale.

"No doubt. But that is not what I have to do, as Guide. So pass silently. Or, going as we go, our indiscretion might else crush and bury *me*. Let us go on!"

There was a great accumulation of snow on the Bridge; and such enormous accumulations of snow overhung them from projecting masses of rock, that they might have been making their way through a stormy sky of white clouds. Using his staff skilfully, sounding as he went, and looking upward, with bent shoulders, as if it were to resist the mere idea of a fall from above, Obenreizer softly led. Vendale closely followed. They were yet in the midst of their dangerous way, when there came a mighty rush, followed by a sound as of thunder. Obenreizer clapped his hand on Vendale's mouth and pointed to the track behind them. Its aspect had been wholly changed in a moment. An avalanche had swept over it, and plunged into the torrent at the bottom of the gulf below.

Their appearance at the solitary Inn not far beyond this

terrible Bridge, elicited many expressions of astonishment from the people shut up in the house. "We stay but to rest," said Obenreizer, shaking the snow from his dress at the fire. "This gentleman has very pressing occasion to get across;—tell them, Vendale."

"Assuredly, I have very pressing occasion. I must cross."

"You hear, all of you. My friend has very pressing occasion to get across, and we want no advice and no help. I am as good a guide, my fellow-countrymen, as any of you. Now, give us to eat and drink."

In exactly the same way, and in nearly the same words, when it was coming on dark and they had struggled through the greatly increased difficulties of the road, and had at last reached their destination for the night, Obenreizer said to the astonished people of the Hospice, gathering about them at the fire, while they were yet in the act of getting their wet shoes off, and shaking the snow from their clothes:

"It is well to understand one another, friends all. This gentleman——"

"—Has," said Vendale, readily taking him up with a smile, "very pressing occasion to get across. Must cross."

"You hear?—has very pressing occasion to get across, must cross. We want no advice and no help. I am mountain-born, and act as Guide. Do not worry us by talking about it, but let us have supper, and wine, and bed."

All through the intense cold of the night, the same awful stillness. Again at sunrise, no sunny tinge to gild or redden the snow. The same interminable waste of deathly white; the same immovable air; the same monotonous gloom in the sky.

"Travellers!" a friendly voice called to them from the door, after they were afoot, knapsack on back and staff in hand, as yesterday: "recollect! There are five places of shelter, near together, on the dangerous road before you; and there is the wooden cross, and there is the next Hospice. Do not stray from the track. If the *Tourmente* comes on, take shelter instantly!"

"The trade of these poor devils!" said Obenreizer to his friend, with a contemptuous backward wave of his hand towards the voice. "How they stick to their trade! You Englishmen say we Swiss are mercenary. Truly, it does look like it."

They had divided between the two knapsacks, such refreshments as they had been able to obtain that morning, and as they deemed it prudent to take. Obenreizer carried the wine as his share of the burden; Vendale, the bread and meat and cheese, and the flask of brandy.

They had for some time laboured upward and onward

through the snow—which was now above their knees in the track, and of unknown depth elsewhere—and they were still labouring upward and onward through the most frightful part of that tremendous desolation, when snow began to fall. At first, but a few flakes descended slowly and steadily. After a little while the fall grew much denser, and suddenly it began without apparent cause to whirl itself into spiral shapes. Instantly ensuing upon this last change, an icy blast came roaring at them, and every sound and force imprisoned until now was let loose.

One of the dismal galleries through which the road is carried at that perilous point, a cave eked out by arches of great strength, was near at hand. They struggled into it, and the storm raged wildly. The noise of the wind, the noise of the water, the thundering down of displaced masses of rock and snow, the awful voices with which not only that gorge but every other gorge in the whole monstrous range seemed to be suddenly endowed, the darkness as of night, the violent revolving of the snow which beat and broke it into spray and blinded them, the madness of everything around insatiate for destruction, the rapid substitution of furious violence for un-natural calm, and hosts of appalling sounds for silence: these were things, on the edge of a deep abyss, to chill the blood, though the fierce wind, made actually solid by ice and snow, had failed to chill it.

Obenreizer, walking to and fro in the gallery without ceasing, signed to Vendale to help him unbuckle his knapsack. They could see each other, but could not have heard each other speak. Vendale complying, Obenreizer produced his bottle of wine, and poured some out, motioning Vendale to take that for warmth's sake, and not brandy. Vendale again complying, Obenreizer seemed to drink after him, and the two walked backwards and forwards side by side; both well knowing that to rest or sleep would be to die.

The snow came driving heavily into the gallery by the upper end at which they would pass out of it, if they ever passed out; for greater dangers lay on the road behind them than before. The snow soon began to choke the arch. An hour more, and it lay so high as to block out half of the returning daylight. But it froze hard now, as it fell, and could be clambered through or over. The violence of the mountain storm was gradually yielding to a steady snowfall. The wind still raged at intervals, but not incessantly; and when it paused, the snow fell in heavy flakes.

They might have been two hours in their frightful prison, when Obenreizer, now crunching into the mound, now creeping over it with his head bowed down and his body touching the top of the arch, made his way out. Vendale followed close upon him, but followed without clear motive or calculation.

For the lethargy of Basle was creeping over him again, and mastering his senses.

How far he had followed out of the gallery, or with what obstacles he had since contended, he knew not. He became roused to the knowledge that Obenreizer had set upon him, and that they were struggling desperately in the snow. He became roused to the remembrance of what his assailant carried in a girdle. He felt for it, drew it, struck at him, struggled again, struck at him again, cast him off, and stood face to face with him.

"I promised to guide you to your journey's end," said Obenreizer, "and I have kept my promise. The journey of your life ends here. Nothing can prolong it. You are sleeping as you stand."

"You are a villain. What have you done to me?"

"You are a fool. I have drugged you. You are doubly a fool, for I drugged you once before upon the journey, to try you. You are trebly a fool, for I am the thief and forger, and in a few moments I shall take those proofs against the thief and forger from your insensible body."

The entrapped man tried to throw off the lethargy, but its fatal hold upon him was so sure that, even while he heard those words, he stupidly wondered which of them had been wounded, and whose blood it was that he saw sprinkled on the snow.

"What have I done to you," he asked, heavily and thickly, "that you should be—so base—a murderer?"

"Done to me? You would have destroyed me, but that you have come to your journey's end. Your cursed activity interposed between me, and the time I had counted on in which I might have replaced the money. Done to me? You have come in my way—not once, not twice, but again and again and again. Did I try to shake you off in the beginning, or no? You were not to be shaken off. Therefore you die here."

Vendale tried to think coherently, tried to speak coherently, tried to pick up the iron-shod staff he had let fall; failing to touch it, tried to stagger on without its aid. All in vain, all in vain! He stumbled, and fell heavily forward on the brink of the deep chasm.

Stupefied, dozing, unable to stand upon his feet, a veil before his eyes, his sense of hearing deadened, he made such a vigorous rally that, supporting himself on his hands, he saw his enemy standing calmly over him, and heard him speak.

"You call me murderer," said Obenreizer, with a grim laugh. "The name matters very little. But at least I have set my life against yours, for I am surrounded by dangers, and may never make my way out of this place. The *Tourmente* is rising again. The snow is now on the whirl. I must have the papers now. Every moment has my life in it."

"Stop!" cried Vendale, in a terrible voice, staggering up with a last flash of fire breaking out of him, and clutching the thievish hands at his breast, in both of his. "Stop! Stand away from me! God bless my Marguerite! Happily she will never know how I died. Stand off from me, and let me look at your murderous face. Let it remind me—of something—left to say."

The sight of him fighting so hard for his senses, and the doubt whether he might not for the instant be possessed by the strength of a dozen men, kept his opponent still. Wildly glaring at him, Vendale faltered out the broken words:

"It shall not be—the trust—of the dead—betrayed by me—reputed parents—misinherited fortune—see to it!"

As his head dropped on his breast, and he stumbled on the brink of the chasm as before, the thievish hands went once more, quick and busy, to his breast. He made a convulsive attempt to cry "No!" desperately rolled himself over into the gulf; and sank away from his enemy's touch, like a phantom in a dreadful dream.

The mountain storm raged again, and passed again. The awful mountain-voices died away, the moon rose, and the soft and silent snow fell.

Two men and two large dogs came out at the door of the Hospice. The men looked carefully around them, and up at the sky. The dogs rolled in the snow, and took it into their mouths, and cast it up with their paws.

One of the men said to the other: "We may venture now. We may find them in one of the five Refuges." Each fastened on his back, a basket; each took in his hand, a strong spiked pole; each girded under his arms, a looped end of a stout rope, so that they were tied together.

Suddenly the dogs desisted from their gambols in the snow, stood looking down the ascent, put their noses up, put their noses down, became greatly excited, and broke into a deep loud bay together.

The two men looked in the faces of the two dogs. The two dogs looked, with at least equal intelligence, in the faces of the two men.

"Au secours, then! Help! To the rescue!" cried the two men. The two dogs, with a glad, deep, generous bark, bounded away.

"Two more mad ones!" said the men, stricken motionless, and looking away into the moonlight. "Is it possible in such weather! And one of them a woman!"

Each of the dogs had the corner of a woman's dress in its mouth and drew her along. She fondled their heads as she came up, and she came up through the snow with an accustomed tread. Not so the large man with her, who was spent and winded.

"Dear guides, dear friends of travellers! I am of your country. We seek two gentlemen crossing the Pass, who should have reached the Hospice this evening."

"They have reached it, ma'amselle."

"Thank Heaven! O thank Heaven!"

"But, unhappily, they have gone on again. We are setting forth to seek them even now. We had to wait until the *Tourmente* passed. It has been fearful up here."

"Dear guides, dear friends of travellers! Let me go with you. Let me go with you, for the love of GOD! One of those gentlemen is to be my husband. I love him, oh, so dearly. O so dearly! You see I am not faint, you see I am not tired. I am born a peasant girl. I will show you that I know well how to fasten myself to your ropes. I will do it with my own hands. I will swear to be brave and good. But let me go with you! If any mischance should have befallen him, my love would find him, when nothing else could. On my knees, dear friends of travellers! By the love your dear mothers had for your fathers!"

The good rough fellows were moved. "After all," they murmured to one another, "she speaks but the truth. She knows the ways of the mountains. See how marvellously she has come here! But as to Monsieur there, ma'amselle?"

"Dear Mr. Joey," said Marguerite, addressing him in his own tongue, "you will remain at the house, and wait for me; will you not?"

"If I know'd which o' you two men with great indignation, "I'd fight you for sixpence, and give you half-a-crown towards your expenses. No, Miss. I'll stick by you as long as there's any sticking left in me, and I'll die for you when I can't do better."

The state of the moon rendering it highly important that no time should be lost, and the dogs showing signs of great uneasiness, the two men quickly took their resolution. The rope that yoked them together was exchanged for a longer one; the party were secured, Marguerite second, and the Cellarman last; and they set out for the Refuges. The actual distance of those places was nothing; the whole five and the next Hospice to boot, being within two miles; but the ghastly way was whitened out and sheeted over.

They made no miss in reaching the Gallery where the two had taken shelter. The second storm of wind and snow had so wildly swept over it since, that their tracks were gone. But the dogs went to and fro with their noses down, and were confident. The party stopping, however, at the further arch, where the second storm had been especially furious, and where the drift was deep, the dogs became troubled, and went about and about, in quest of a lost purpose.

The great abyss being known to lie on the right, they wandered too much to the left, and had to regain the way with infinite labour through a deep field of snow. The leader of the line had stopped it, and was taking note of the landmarks, when one of the dogs fell to tearing up the snow a little before them. Advancing and stooping to look at it, thinking that some one might be overwhelmed there, they saw that it was stained, and that the stain was red.

The other dog was now seen to look over the brink of the gulf, with his fore legs straightened out, lest he should fall into it, and to tremble in every limb. Then the dog who had found the stained snow joined him, and then they ran to and fro, distressed and whining. Finally, they both stopped on the brink together, and setting up their heads, howled dolefully.

"There is some one lying below," said Marguerite.

"I think so," said the foremost man. "Stand well inward, the two last, and let us look over."

The last man kindled two torches from his basket, and handed them forward. The leader taking one, and Marguerite the other, they looked down: now shading the torches, now moving them to the right or left, now raising them, now depressing them, as moonlight far below contended with black shadows. A piercing cry from Marguerite broke a long silence.

"My God! On a projecting point, where a wall of ice stretches forward over the torrent, I see a human form!"

"Where, ma'amselle, where?"

"See, there! On the shelf of ice below the dogs!"

The leader, with a sickened aspect, drew inward, and they were all silent. But they were not all inactive, for Marguerite, with swift and skilful fingers, had detached both herself and him from the rope in a few seconds.

"Show me the baskets. These two are the only ropes?"

"The only ropes here, ma'amselle; but at the Hospice——"

"If he is alive—I know it is my lover—he will be dead before you can return. Dear Guides! Blessed friends of travellers! Look at me! Watch my hands. If they falter or go wrong, make me your prisoner by force. If they are steady and go right, help me to save him!"

She girded herself with a cord under the breast and arms, she formed it into a kind of jacket, she drew it into knots, she laid its end side by side with the end of the other cord, she twisted and twined the two together, she knotted them together, she set her foot upon the knots, she strained them, she held them for the two men to strain at.

"She is inspired," they said to one another.

"By the Almighty's mercy!" she exclaimed. "You both know that I am by far the lightest here. Give me the brandy and the wine, and lower me down to him. Then go for assistance and a stronger rope. You see that when it is lowered to me—look at this about me now—I can make it fast and safe to his body. Alive or dead, I will bring him up, or die with him. I love him passionately. Can I say more?"

They turned to her companion, but he was lying senseless on the snow.

"Lower me down to him," she said, taking two little kegs they had brought, and hanging them about her, "or I will dash myself to pieces! I am a peasant, and I know no giddiness or fear; and this is nothing to me, and I passionately love him. Lower me down!"

"Ma'amselle, ma'amselle, he must be dying or dead."

"Dying or dead, my husband's head shall lie upon my breast, or I will dash myself to pieces."

They yielded, overborne. With such precautions as their skill and the circumstances admitted, they let her slip from the summit, guiding herself down the precipitous icy wall with her hand, and they lowered down, and lowered down, and lowered down, until the cry came up: "Enough!"

"Is it really he, and is he dead?" they called down, looking over.

The cry came up: "He is insensible; but his heart beats. It beats against mine."

"How does he lie?"

The cry came up: "Upon a ledge of ice. It has thawed beneath him, and it will thaw beneath me. Hasten. If we die, I am content."

One of the two men hurried off with the dogs at such topmost speed as he could make; the other set up the lighted torches in the snow, and applied himself to recovering the Englishman. Much snow-chafing and some brandy got him on his legs, but delirious and quite unconscious where he was.

The watch remained upon the brink, and his cry went down continually: "Courage! They will soon be here. How goes it?" And the cry came up: "His heart still beats against mine. I warm him in my arms. I have cast off the rope, for the ice melts under us, and the rope would separate me from him; but I am not afraid."

The moon went down behind the mountain tops, and all the abyss lay in darkness. The cry went down: "How goes it?" The cry came up: "We are sinking lower, but his heart still beats against mine."

At length, the eager barking of the dogs, and a flare of light upon the snow, proclaimed that help was coming on. Twenty or thirty men, lamps, torches, litters, ropes, blankets, wood to kindle a great fire, restoratives and stimulants, came in fast. The dogs ran from one man to another, and from this thing to that, and ran to the edge of the abyss, dumbly entreating Speed, speed, speed!

The cry went down: "Thanks to God, all is ready. How goes it?"

The cry came up: "We are sinking still, and we are deadly cold. His heart no longer beats against mine. Let no one come down to add to our weight. Lower the rope only."

The fire was kindled high, a great glare of torches lighted the sides of the precipice, lamps were lowered, a strong rope was lowered. She could be seen passing it round him, and making it secure.

The cry came up into a deathly silence: "Raise! Softly!" They could see her diminished figure shrink, as he was swung into the air.

They gave no shout when some of them laid him on a litter, and others lowered another strong rope. The cry again came up into a deathly silence: "Raise! Softly!" But when they caught her at the brink, then they shouted, then they wept, then they gave thanks to Heaven, then they kissed her feet, then they kissed her dress, then the dogs caressed her, licked her icy hands, and with their honest faces warmed her frozen bosom!

She broke from them all, and sank over him on his litter, with both her loving hands upon the heart that stood still.

ACT IV: *The Clock-lock*

THE pleasant scene was Neuchâtel; the pleasant month was April; the pleasant place was a notary's office; the pleasant person in it was the notary: a rosy, hearty, handsome old man, chief notary of Neuchâtel, known far and wide in the canton as Maître Voigt. Professionally and personally, the notary was a popular citizen. His innumerable kindnesses and his innumerable oddities had for years made him one of the recognised public characters of the pleasant Swiss town. His long brown frock-coat and his black skull-cap were among the institutions of the place; and he carried a snuff-box which, in point of size, was popularly believed to be without a parallel in Europe.

There was another person in the notary's office, not so pleasant as the notary. This was Obenreizer.

An oddly pastoral kind of office it was, and one that would never have answered in England. It stood in a neat back-yard, fenced off from a pretty flower-garden. Goats browsed in the doorway, and a cow was within half a dozen feet of keeping company with the clerk. Maître Voigt's room was a bright and varnished little room, with panelled walls, like a toy-chamber. According to the seasons of the year, roses, sunflowers, hollyhocks, peeped in at the windows. Maître Voigt's bees hummed through the office all the summer, in at this window and out at that, taking it frequently in their day's work, as if honey were to be made from Maître Voigt's sweet disposition. A large musical-box on the chimmy-piece often trilled away at the Overture to Fra Diavolo, or a Selection from William Tell, with a chirruping liveliness that had to be stopped by force on the entrance of a client, and irrepressibly broke out again the moment his back was turned.

"Courage, courage, my good fellow!" said Maître Voigt, patting Obenreizer on the knee, in a fatherly and comforting way. "You will begin a new life to-morrow morning in my office here."

Obenreizer—dressed in mourning, and subdued in manner—lifted his hand, with a white handkerchief in it, to the region of his heart. "The gratitude is here," he said. "But the words to express it are not here."

"Ta-ta-ta! Don't talk to me about gratitude!" said Maître Voigt. "I hate to see a man oppressed. I see you oppressed, and I hold out my hand to you by instinct. Besides, I am not too old yet, to remember my young days. Your father sent me my first client. (It was on a question of half an acre of vineyard that seldom bore any grapes.) Do I owe nothing to your father's son? I owe him a debt of friendly obligation, and I pay it to you. That's rather neatly expressed, I think," added Maître Voigt, in high good humour with himself. "Permit me to reward my own merit with a pinch of snuff!"

Obenreizer dropped his eyes to the ground, as though he were not even worthy to see the notary take snuff.

"Do me one last favour, sir," he said, when he raised his eyes. "Do not act on impulse. Thus far, you have only a general knowledge of my position. Hear the case for and against me, in its details, before you take me into your office. Let my claim on your benevolence be recognised by your sound reason as well as by your excellent heart. In *that* case, I may hold up my head against the bitterest of my enemies, and build myself a new reputation on the ruins of the character I have lost."

"As you will," said Maître Voigt. "You speak well, my son. You will be a fine lawyer one of these days."

"The details are not many," pursued Obenreizer. "My troubles begin with the accidental death of my late travelling companion, my lost dear friend, Mr. Vendale."

"Mr. Vendale," repeated the notary. "Just so. I have heard and read of the name, several times within these two months. The name of the unfortunate English gentleman who was killed on the Simplon. When you got that scar upon your cheek and neck."

"—From my own knife," said Obenreizer, touching what must have been an ugly gash at the time of its infliction.

"From your own knife," assented the notary, "and in trying to save him. Good, good, good. That was very good. Vendale. Yes. I have several times, lately, thought it droll that I should once have had a client of that name."

"But the world, sir," returned Obenreizer, "is *so* small!" Nevertheless he made a mental note that the notary had once had a client of that name.

"As I was saying, sir, the death of that dear travelling comrade begins my troubles. What follows? I save myself. I go down to Milan. I am received with coldness by Defresnier and Company. Shortly afterwards, I am discharged by Defresnier and Company. Why? They give no reason why. I ask, do they assail my honour? No answer. I ask, what is the imputation against me? No answer. I ask, where are their proofs against me? No answer. I ask, what am I to think? The reply is, 'M. Obenreizer is free to think what he will. What M. Obenreizer thinks, is of no importance to Defresnier and Company.' And that is all."

"Perfectly. That is all," assented the notary, taking a large pinch of snuff.

"But is that enough, sir?"

"That is not enough," said Maître Voigt. "The House of Defresnier are my fellow-townsmen—much respected, much esteemed—but the House of Defresnier must not silently destroy a man's character. You can rebut assertion. But how can you rebut silence?"

"Your sense of justice, my dear patron," answered Obenreizer, "states in a word the cruelty of the case. Does it stop there? No. For, what follows upon that?"

"True, my poor boy," said the notary, with a comforting nod or two; "your ward rebels upon that."

"Rebels is too soft a word," retorted Obenreizer "My ward revolts from me with horror. My ward defies me: My ward withdraws herself from my authority, and takes shelter (Madame Dor with her) in the house of that English lawyer, Mr. Bintrey, who replies to your summons to her to submit herself to my authority, that she will not do so."

"—And who afterwards writes," said the notary, moving his large snuff-box to look among the papers underneath it for the letter, "that he is coming to confer with me."

"Indeed?" replied Obenreizer, rather checked. "Well, sir. Have I no legal rights?"

"Assuredly, my poor boy," returned the notary. "All but felons have their legal rights."

"And who calls me felon?" said Obenreizer, fiercely.

"No one. Be calm under your wrongs. If the House of Defresnier would call you felon, indeed, we should know how to deal with them."

While saying these words, he had handed Bintrey's very short letter to Obenreizer, who now read it and gave it back.

"In saying," observed Obenreizer with recovered composure, "that he is coming to confer with you, this English lawyer means that he is coming to deny my authority over my ward."

"You think so?"

"I am sure of it. I know him. He is obstinate and contentious. You will tell me, my dear sir, whether my authority is unassailable, until my ward is of age?"

"Absolutely unassailable."

"I will enforce it. I will make her submit herself to it. For," said Obenreizer, changing his angry tone to one of grateful submission, "I owe it to you, sir; to you, who have so confidingly taken an injured man under your protection, and into your employment."

"Make your mind easy," said Maître Voigt. "No more of this now, and no thanks! Be here to-morrow morning, before the other clerk comes—between seven and eight. You will find me in this room; and I will myself initiate you in your work. Go away! go away! I have letters to write. I won't hear a word more."

Dismissed with this generous abruptness, and satisfied with the favourable impression he had left on the old man's mind, Obenreizer was at leisure to revert to the mental note he had made that Maître Voigt once had a client whose name was Vendale.

"I ought to know England well enough by this time;" so his meditations ran, as he sat on a bench in the yard; "and it is not a name I ever encountered there, except"—he looked involuntarily over his shoulder—"as *his* name. Is the world so small that I cannot get away from him, even now when he is dead? He confessed at the last that he had betrayed the trust of the dead, and misinherited a fortune. And I was to see to it. And I was to stand off, that my face might remind him of it. Why *my* face, unless it concerned *me*? I am sure of his words, for they have been in my ears ever since. Can there be anything bearing on them, in the keeping of this old idiot? Anything to repair my fortunes, and blacken his memory? He dwelt upon my earliest remembrances, that night at Basle. Why, unless he had a purpose in it?"

Maître Voigt's two largest he-goats were butting at him to butt him out of the place, as if for that disrespectful mention of their master. So he got up and left the place. But he

walked alone for a long time on the border of the lake, with his head drooped in deep thought.

Between seven and eight next morning, he presented himself again at the office. He found the notary ready for him, at work on some papers which had come in on the previous evening. In a few clear words, Maître Voigt explained the routine of the office, and the duties Obenreizer would be expected to perform. It still wanted five minutes to eight when the preliminary instructions were declared to be complete.

"I will show you over the house and the offices," said Maître Voigt, "but I must put away these papers first. They come from the municipal authorities and they must be taken special care of."

Obenreizer saw his chance here of finding out the repository in which his employer's private papers were kept.

"Can't I save you the trouble, sir?" he asked. "Can't I put those documents away under your directions?"

Maître Voigt laughed softly to himself; closed the portfolio in which the papers had been sent to him; handed it to Obenreizer.

"Suppose you try," he said. "All my papers of importance are kept yonder."

He pointed to a heavy oaken door, thickly studded with nails, at the lower end of the room. Approaching the door, with the portfolio, Obenreizer discovered, to his astonishment, that there were no means whatever of opening it from the outside. There was no handle, no bolt, no key, and (climax of passive obstruction!) no keyhole.

"There is a second door to this room?" said Obenreizer, appealing to the notary.

"No," said Maître Voigt. "Guess again."

"There is a window?"

"Nothing of the sort. The window has been bricked up. The only way in, is the way by that door. Do you give it up?" cried Maître Voigt in high triumph. "Listen, my good fellow, and tell me if you hear nothing inside?"

Obenreizer listened for a moment, and started back from the door.

"I know!" he exclaimed. "I heard of this when I was apprenticed here at the watch-maker's. Perrin Brothers have finished their famous clock-lock at last—and you have got it?"

"Bravo!" said Maître Voigt. "The clock-lock it is! There, my son! There you have one more of what the good people of this town call 'Daddy Voigt's follies.' With all my heart! Let those laugh who win. No thief can steal *my* keys. No burglar can pick *my* lock. No power on earth, short of a battering-ram or a barrel of gunpowder, can move

that door, till my little sentinel inside—my worthy friend who goes 'Tick, Tick,' as I tell him—says, 'Open!' The big door obeys the little Tick, Tick, and the little Tick, Tick obeys *me*. That!'' cried Daddy Voigt, snapping his fingers, "for all the thieves in Christendom!"

"May I see it in action?" asked Obenreizer. "Pardon my curiosity, dear sir! You know that I was once a tolerable worker in the clock trade."

"Certainly you shall see it in action," said Maître Voigt. "What is the time now? One minute to eight. Watch, and in one minute you will see the door open of itself."

In one minute, smoothly and slowly and silently, as if invisible hands had set it free, the heavy door opened inward, and disclosed a dark chamber beyond. On three sides, shelves filled the walls, from floor to ceiling. Arranged on the shelves, were rows upon rows of boxes made in the pretty inlaid woodwork of Switzerland, and bearing inscribed on their fronts (for the most part in fanciful coloured letters) the names of the notary's clients.

Maître Voigt lighted a taper, and led the way into the room.

"You shall see the clock," he said, proudly. "I possess the greatest curiosity in Europe. It is only a privileged few whose eyes can look at it. I give the privilege to your good father's son—you shall be one of the favoured few who enter the room with me. See! here it is, on the right-hand wall at the side of the door."

"An ordinary clock," exclaimed Obenreizer. "No! Not an ordinary clock. It has only one hand."

"Aha!" said Maître Voigt. "Not an ordinary clock, my friend. No, no. That one hand goes round the dial. As I put it, so it regulates the hour at which the door shall open. See! The hand points to eight. At eight the door opened, as you saw for yourself."

"Does it open more than once in the four-and-twenty hours?" asked Obenreizer.

"More than once?" repeated the notary, with great scorn. "You don't know my good friend, Tick, Tick! He will open the door as often as I ask him. All he wants, is his directions, and he gets them here. Look below the dial. Here is a half-circle of steel let into the wall, and here is a hand (called the regulator) that travels round it, just as *my* hand chooses. Notice, if you please, that there are figures to guide me on the half-circle of steel. Figure I. means: Open once in the four-and-twenty hours. Figure II. means: Open twice; and so on to the end. I set the regulator every morning, after I have read my letters, and when I know what my day's work is to be. Would you like to see me set it now? What is to-day?

Wednesday. Good! This is the day of our rifle-club; there is little business to do; I grant a half-holiday. No work here to-day, after three o'clock. Let us first put away this portfolio of municipal papers. There! No need to trouble Tick, Tick to open the door until eight to-morrow. Good! I leave the dial-hand at eight; I put back the regulator to 'I.'; I close the door; and closed the door remains, past all opening by anybody, till to-morrow morning at eight."

Obenreizer's quickness instantly saw the means by which he might make the clock-lock betray its master's confidence, and place its master's papers at his disposal.

"Stop, sir!" he cried, at the moment when the notary was closing the door. "Don't I see something moving among the boxes—on the floor there?"

(Maître Voigt turned his back for a moment to look. In that moment, Obenreizer's ready hand put the regulator on from the figure "I." to the figure "II." Unless the notary looked again at the half-circle of steel, the door would open at eight that evening, as well as at eight next morning, and nobody but Obenreizer would know it.)

"There is nothing!" said Maître Voigt. "Your troubles have shaken your nerves, my son. Some shadow thrown by my taper; or some poor little beetle, who lives among the old lawyer's secrets, running away from the light. Hark! I hear your fellow-clerk in the office. To work! to work! and build to-day the first step that leads to your new fortunes!"

He good humouredly pushed Obenreizer out before him; extinguished the taper, with a last fond glance at his clock which passed harmlessly over the regulator beneath; and closed the oaken door.

At three the office was shut up. The notary and everybody in the notary's employment, with one exception, went to see the rifle-shooting. Obenreizer had pleaded that he was not in spirits for a public festival. Nobody knew what had become of him. It was believed that he had slipped away for a solitary walk.

The house and offices had been closed but a few minutes, when the door of a shining wardrobe, in the notary's shining room, opened, and Obenreizer stepped out. He walked to a window, unclosed the shutters, satisfied himself that he could escape unseen by way of the garden, turned back into the room, and took his place in the notary's easy-chair. He was locked up in the house, and there were five hours to wait before eight o'clock came. He wore his way through the five hours: sometimes reading the books and newspapers that lay on the table: sometimes thinking: sometimes walking to and fro. Sunset came on. He closed the window-shutters before he kindled a light. The candle lighted, and the time drawing nearer and nearer, he sat, watch in hand, with his eyes on the oaken door.

At eight, smoothly and softly and silently the door opened.

One after another, he read the names on the outer rows of boxes. No such name as Vendale! He removed the outer row, and looked at the row behind. These were older boxes, and shabbier boxes. The four first that he examined were inscribed with French and German names. The fifth bore a name which was almost illegible. He brought it out into the room, and examined it closely. There, covered thickly with time-stains and dust, was the name: "Vendale."

The key hung to the box by a string. He unlocked the box, took out four loose papers that were in it, spread them open on the table, and began to read them. He had not so occupied a minute, when his face fell from its expression of eagerness and avidity, to one of haggard astonishment and disappointment. But, after a little consideration, he copied the papers. He then replaced the papers, replaced the box, closed the door, extinguished the candle, and stole away.

As his murderous and thievish footfall passed out of the garden, the steps of the notary and someone accompanying him stopped at the front door of the house. The lamps were lighted in the little street, and the notary had his door-key in his hand.

"Pray do not pass my house, Mr. Bintrey," he said. "Do me the honour to come in. It is one of our town half-holidays —our Tir—but my people will be back directly. It is droll that you should ask your way to the Hotel of me. Let us eat and drink before you go there.

"Thank you; not to-night," said Bintrey. "Shall I come to you at ten to-morrow?"

"I shall be enchanted, sir, to take so early an opportunity of redressing the wrongs of my injured client," returned the good notary.

"Yes," retorted Bintrey; "your injured client is all very well—but—a word in your ear."

He whispered to the notary, and walked off. When the notary's housekeeper came home, she found him standing at his door motionless, with the key still in his hand, and the door unopened.

Obenreizer's Victory]

The scene shifts again—to the foot of the Simplon, on the Swiss side.

In one of the dreary rooms of the dreary little Inn at Brieg, Mr. Bintrey and Maître Voigt sat together at a professional council of two. Mr. Bintrey was searching in his despatch-box.

Maître Voigt was looking towards a closed door, painted brown to imitate mahogany, and communicating with an inner room.

"Isn't it time he was here?" asked the notary, shifting his position, and glancing at a second door at the other end of the room, painted yellow to imitate deal.

"He *is* here," answered Bintrey, after listening for a moment.

The yellow door was opened by a waiter, and Obenreizer walked in.

After greeting Maître Voigt with a cordiality which apeared to cause the notary no little embarrassment, Obenreizer bowed with grave and distant politeness to Bintrey. "For what reason have I been brought from Neuchâtel to the foot of the mountain?" he inquired, taking the seat which the English lawyer had indicated to him.

"You shall be quite satisfied on that head before our interview is over," returned Bintrey. "For the present, permit me to suggest proceeding at once to business. There has been a correspondence, Mr. Obenreizer, between you and your niece. I am here to represent your niece."

"In other words, you, a lawyer, are here to represent an infraction of the law."

"Admirably put!" said Bintrey. "If all the people I have to deal with were only like you, what an easy profession mine would be! I am here to represent an infraction of the law— that is your point of view. I am here to make a compromise between you and your niece—that is my point of view."

"There must be two parties to a compromise," rejoined Obenreizer. "I decline, in this case, to be one of them. The law gives me authority to control my niece's actions, until she comes of age. She is not yet of age; and I claim my authority."

At this point Maître Voigt attempted to speak. Bintrey silenced him with a compassionate indulgence of tone and manner, as if he was silencing a favourite child.

"No, my worthy friend, not a word. Don't excite yourself unnecessarily; leave it to me." He turned, and addressed himself again to Obenreizer. "I can think of nothing comparable to you, Mr. Obenreizer, but granite—and even that wears out in course of time. In the interests of peace and quietness—for the sake of your own dignity—relax a little. If you will only delegate your authority to another person whom I know of, that person may be trusted never to lose sight of your niece, night or day!"

"You are wasting your time and mine," returned Obenreizer. "If my niece is not rendered up to my authority within one week from this day, I invoke the law. If you resist the law, I take her by force."

He rose to his feet as he said the last word. Maître Voigt looked round again towards the brown door which led into the inner room.

"Have some pity on the poor girl," pleaded Bintrey. "Remember how lately she lost her lover by a dreadful death! Will nothing move you?"

"Nothing."

Bintrey, in his turn, rose to his feet, and looked at Maître Voigt. Maître Voigt's hand, resting on the table, began to tremble. Maître Voigt's eyes remained fixed, as if by irresistible fascination, on the brown door. Obenreizer, suspiciously observing him, looked that way, too.

"There is somebody listening in there!" he exclaimed, with a sharp backward glance at Bintrey.

"There are two people listening," answered Bintrey.

"Who are they?"

"You shall see."

With that answer, he raised his voice and spoke the next words—the two common words which are on everybody's lips, at every hour of the day: "Come in!"

The brown door opened. Supported on Marguerite's arm —his sunburnt colour gone, his right arm bandaged and slung over his breast—Vendale stood before the murderer, a man risen from the dead.

In the moment of silence that followed, the singing of a caged bird in the courtyard outside was the one sound stirring in the room. Maître Voigt touched Bintrey, and pointed to Obenreizer. "Look at him!" said the notary, in a whisper.

The shock had paralysed every movement in the villain's body, but the movement of the blood. His face was like the face of a corpse. The one vestige of colour left in it was a livid purple streak which marked the course of the scar, where his victim had wounded him on the cheek and neck. Speechless, breathless, motionless alike in eye and limb, it seemed as if, at the sight of Vendale, the death to which he had doomed Vendale had struck him where he stood.

"Somebody ought to speak to him," said Maître Voigt. "Shall I?"

Even at that moment, Bintrey persisted in silencing the notary, and in keeping the lead in the proceedings to himself. Checking Maître Voigt by a gesture, he dismissed Marguerite and Vendale in these words:—"The object of your appearance here is answered," he said. "If you will withdraw for the present, it may help Mr. Obenreizer to recover himself."

It did help him. As the two passed through the door, and closed it behind them, he drew a deep breath of relief. He looked round him for the chair from which he had risen, and dropped into it.

"Give him time!" pleaded Maître Voigt.

"No," said Bintrey. "I don't know what use he may make of it, if I do." He turned once more to Obenreizer, and went on. "I owe it to myself," he said—"I don't admit, mind, that I owe it to *you*—to account for my appearance in these proceedings, and to state what has been done under my advice, and on my sole responsibility. Can you listen to me?"

"I can listen to you."

"Recall the time when you started for Switzerland with Mr. Vendale," Bintrey began. "You had not left England four-and-twenty hours, before your niece committed an act of imprudence which not even your penetration could foresee. She followed her promised husband on his journey, without asking anybody's advice or permission, and without any better companion to protect her than a Cellarman in Mr. Vendale's employment."

"Why did she follow me on the journey? and how came the Cellarman to be the person who accompanied her?"

"She followed you on the journey," answered Bintrey, "because she suspected there had been some serious collision between you and Mr. Vendale, which had been kept secret from her; and because she rightly believed you to be capable of serving your interests, or of satisfying your enmity, at the price of a crime. As for the Cellarman, he was one, among the other people in Mr. Vendale's establishment, to whom she had applied (the moment your back was turned) to know if anything had happened between their master and you. The Cellarman alone had something to tell her. A senseless superstition, and a common accident which had happened to his master, in his master's cellar, had connected Mr. Vendale in this man's mind with the idea of danger by murder. Your niece surprised him into a confession, which aggravated tenfold the terrors that possessed her. Aroused to a sense of the mischief he had done, the man, of his own accord, made the one atonement in his power. 'If my master is in danger, Miss,' he said, 'it's my duty to follow him, too; and it's more than my duty to take care of *you*.' The two set forth together—and, for once, a superstition has had its use. It decided your niece on taking the journey; and it led the way to saving a man's life's. Do you understand me, so far?"

"I understand you, so far."

"My first knowledge of the crime that you had committed," pursued Bintrey, "came to me in the form of a letter from your niece. All you need know is that her love and her courage recovered the body of your victim, and aided the after-efforts which brought him back to life. While he lay helpless at Brieg, under her care, she wrote to me to come out to him. Before starting, I informed Madame Dor that I knew Miss Obenreizer to be safe, and knew where she was. Madame Dor informed me, in return, that a letter had come for your niece, which she knew to be in your handwriting. I took possession of it, and arranged for the forwarding of any other letters which might follow. Arrived at Brieg, I found Mr. Vendale out of danger, and at once devoted myself to hastening the day of reckoning with you. Defresnier and Company turned you off on suspicion; acting on information privately supplied by me. Having stripped you of your false character, the next thing to do was to strip you of your authority over your niece. To reach this end, I not only had no scruple in digging the pitfall under your feet in the dark—I felt a certain professional pleasure in fighting you with your own weapons. By my advice, the truth has been carefully concealed from you, up to this day. By my advice, the trap into which you have walked was set for you (you know why, now, as well as I do) in this place. There was but one certain way of shaking the devilish self-control which has hitherto made you a formidable man. That way has been tried, and (look at me as you may) that way has succeeded. The last thing that remains to be done," concluded Bintrey, producing two little slips of manuscript from his despatch-box, "is to set your niece free. You have attempted murder, and you have committed forgery and theft. We have the evidence ready against you in both cases. If you are convicted as a felon, you know as well as I do what becomes of your authority over your niece. Personally, I should have preferred taking that way out of it. But considerations are pressed on me which I am not able to resist, and this interview must end, as I have told you already, in a compromise. Sign those lines, resigning all authority over Miss Obenreizer, and pledging yourself never to be seen in England or in Switzerland again; and I will sign an indemnity which secures you against further proceedings on our part."

Obenreizer took the pen, in silence, and signed his niece's release. In receiving the indemnity in return, he rose, but made no movement to leave the room. He stood looking at Maître Voigt with a strange smile gathering at his lips, and a strange light flashing in his filmy eyes.

"What are you waiting for?" asked Bintrey.

Obenreizer pointed to the brown door. "Call them back," he answered. "I have something to say in their presence before I go."

"Say it in my presence," retorted Bintrey. "I decline to call them back."

Obenreizer turned to Maître Voigt. "Do you remember telling me that you once had an English client named Vendale?" he asked.

"Well," answered the notary. "And what of that?"

"Maître Voigt, your clock-lock has betrayed you."

"What do you mean?"

"I have read the letters and certificates in your client's box. I have taken copies of them. I have got the copies here. Is there, or is there not, a reason for calling them back?"

For a moment the notary looked to and fro, between Obenreizer and Bintrey, in helpless astonishment. Recovering himself, he drew his brother-lawyer aside, and hurriedly spoke a few words close at his ear. The face of Bintrey—after first faithfully reflecting the astonishment on the face of Maître Voigt—suddenly altered its expression. He sprang, with the activity of a young man, to the door of the inner room, entered it, remained inside for a minute, and returned followed by Marguerite and Vendale. "Now, Mr. Obenreizer," said Bintrey, "the last move in the game is yours. Play it."

"Before I resign my position as that young lady's guardian," said Obenreizer, "I have a secret to reveal in which she is interested. In making my disclosure, I am not claiming her attention for a narrative which she, or any other person present, is expected to take on trust. I am possessed of written proofs, copies of originals, the authenticity of which Maître Voigt himself can attest. Bear that in mind, and permit me to refer you, at starting, to a date long past—the month of February, in the year one thousand eight hundred and thirty-six."

"Mark the date, Mr. Vendale," said Bintrey.

"My first proof," said Obenreizer, taking a paper from his pocket-book. "Copy of a letter, written by an English lady (married) to her sister, a widow. The name of the person writing the letter I shall keep suppressed until I have done. The name of the person to whom the letter is written I am willing to reveal. It is addressed to 'Mrs. Jane Ann Miller, of Groombrige Wells, England.'"

Vendale started, and opened his lips to speak. Bintrey instantly stopped him, as he had stopped Maître Voigt. "No," said the pertinacious lawyer. "Leave it to me."

Obenreizer went on.

"It is needless to trouble you with the first half of the letter," he said. "I can give the substance of it in two words. The writer's position at the time is this. She has been long living in Switzerland with her husband—obliged to live there for the sake of her husband's health. They are about to move to a new residence on the Lake of Neuchâtel in a week, and they will be ready to receive Mrs. Miller as visitor in a fortnight from that time. This said, the writer next enters into an important domestic detail. She has been childless for years—she and her husband have now no hope of children; they are lonely; they want an interest in life; they have decided on adopting a child. Here the important part of the letter begins; and here, therefore, I read it to you word for word." He folded back the first page of the letter and read as follows:

"* * * Will you help us, my dear sister, to realise our new project? As English people, we wish to adopt an English child. This may be done, I believe, at the Foundling: my husband's lawyers in London will tell you how. I leave the choice to you, with only these conditions attached to it— that the child is to be an infant under a year old, and is to be a boy. Will you pardon the trouble I am giving you, for my sake; and will you bring our adopted child to us, with your own children, when you come to Neuchâtel?

"I must add a word to my husband's wishes in this matter. He is resolved to spare the child whom we make our own, any future mortification and loss of self-respect which might be caused by a discovery of his true origin. He will bear my husband's name, and he will be brought up in the belief that he is really our son. His inheritance of what we have to leave will be secured to him—not only according to the laws of England in such cases, but according to the laws of Switzerland also; for we have lived so long in this country that there is a doubt whether we may not be considered as 'domiciled' in Switzerland. The one precaution left to take is to prevent any after-discovery at the Foundling. Now, our name is a very uncommon one; and if we appear on the Register of the Institution, as the persons adopting the child, there is just a chance that something might result from it. Your name, my dear, is the name of thousands of other people; and if *you* will consent to appear on that Register, there need be no fear of any discoveries in that quarter. We are moving, by the doctor's orders, to a part of Switzerland in which our circumstances are quite unknown; and you, as I understand, are about to engage a new nurse for the journey when you come to see us. Under these circumstances, the child may appear as my child, brought back to me under my sister's care. The only servant we take with us from our old home is my own maid, who can be safely trusted. As for the lawyers in England and in Switzerland, it is their profession to keep secrets—and we may feel quite easy in that direction. So there you have our harmless little conspiracy! Write by return of post, my love, and tell me you will join it."

"Do you still conceal the name of the writer of that letter?" asked Vendale.

"I keep the name of the writer till the last," answered Obenreizer, "and I proceed to my second proof—a mere slip of paper, this time, as you see. Memorandum given to the Swiss lawyer, who drew the documents referred to in the letter I have just read, expressed as follows;—'Adopted from the Foundling Hospital of England, 3rd March 1836, a male infant, called, in the Institution, Walter Wilding. Person appearing on the register, as adopting the child, Mrs. Jane Ann Miller, widow, acting in this matter for her married sister, domiciled in Switzerland.' Patience!" resumed Obenreizer, as Vendale, breaking loose from Bintrey, started to his feet. "I shall not keep the name concealed much longer. Two more little slips of paper, and I have done. Third proof! Certificate of Doctor Ganz, still living in practice at Neuchâtel, dated July 1838. The doctor certifies (you shall read it for yourselves directly), first, that he attended the adopted child in its infant maladies; second, that, three months before the date of the certificate, the gentleman adopting the child as his son died; third, that on the date of the certificate, his widow and her maid, taking the adopted child with them, left Neuchâtel on their return to England. One more link now added to this, and my chain of evidence is complete. The maid remained with her mistress till her mistress's death, only a few years since. The maid can swear to the identity of the adopted infant, from his childhood to his youth—from his youth to his manhood, as he is now. There is her address in England—and there, Mr. Vendale, is the fourth, and final proof!"

"Why do you address yourself to *me*?" said Vendale, as Obenreizer threw the written address on the table.

Obenreizer turned on him, in a sudden frenzy of triumph.

"*Because you are the man!* If my niece marries you, she marries a bastard, brought up by public charity. If my niece marries you, she marries an impostor, without name or lineage, disguised in the character of a gentleman of rank and family!"

"Bravo!" cried Bintrey. "Admirably put, Mr. Obenreizer! It only wants one word more to complete it. She marries—thanks entirely to your exertions—a man who inherits a handsome fortune, and a man whose origin will make him prouder than ever of his peasant-wife. George Vendale, as brother-executors, let us congratulate each other! Our dear dead friend's last wish on earth is accomplished. We have found the lost Walter Wilding. As Mr. Obenreizer said just now—you are the man!"

The words passed by Vendale unheeded. For the moment

he was conscious of but one sensation; he heard but one voice. Marguerite's hand was clasping his. Marguerite's voice was whispering to him: "I never loved you, George, as I love you now!"

The Curtain Falls]

May Day. There is merry-making in Cripple Corner, the chimneys smoke, the patriarchal dining-hall is hung with garlands, and Mrs. Goldstraw, the respected housekeeper, is very busy. For, on this bright morning the young master of Cripple Corner is married to its young mistress, far away; to wit, in the little town of Brieg, in Switzerland, lying at the foot of the Simplon Pass where she saved his life.

The bells ring gaily in the little town of Brieg, and flags are stretched across the street, and rifle-shots are heard, and sounding music from brass instruments. Streamer-decorated casks of wine have been rolled out under a gay awning in the public way before the Inn, and there will be free feasting and revelry. What with bells and banners, draperies hanging from windows, explosion of gunpowder, and reverberation of brass music, the little town of Brieg is all in a flutter, like the hearts of its simple people.

It was a stormy night last night, and the mountains are covered with snow. But the sun is bright to-day, the sweet air is fresh, the tin spires of the little town of Brieg are burnished silver, and the Alps are ranges of far-off white cloud in a deep blue sky.

The primitive people of the little town of Brieg have built a greenwood arch across the street, under which the newly married pair shall pass in triumph from the church. It is inscribed, on that side, "HONOUR AND LOVE TO MARGUERITE VENDALE!" for the people are proud of her to enthusiasm. This greeting of the bride under her new name is affectionately meant as a surprise, and therefore the arrangement has been made that she, unconscious why, shall be taken to the church by a tortuous back way. A scheme not difficult to carry into execution in the crooked little town of Brieg.

So, all things are in readiness, and they are to go and come on foot. Assembled in the Inn's best chamber, festively adorned, are the bride and bridegroom, the Neuchâtel notary, the London lawyer, Madame Dor, and a certain large mysterious Englishman, popularly known as Monsieur Zhoé-Ladelle. And behold Madame Dor, arrayed in a spotless pair of gloves of her own, with no hand in the air, but both hands clasped round the neck of the bride; to embrace whom Madame Dor has turned her broad back on the company, consistent to the last.

"Forgive me, my beautiful," pleads Madame Dor, "for that I ever was his she-cat!"

"She-cat, Madame Dor?"

"Engaged to sit watching my so charming mouse," are the explanatory words of Madame Dor, delivered with a penitential sob.

"Why, you were our best friend! George, dearest, tell Madame Dor. Was she not our best friend?"

"Undoubtedly, darling. What should we have done without her?"

"You are both so generous," cries Madame Dor, accepting consolation, and immediately relapsing. "But I commenced as a she-cat."

"Ah! But like the cat in the fairy-story, good Madame Dor," says Vendale, saluting her cheek, "you were a true woman. And, being a true woman, the sympathy of your heart was with true love."

"I don't wish to deprive Madame Dor of her share in the embraces that are going on," Mr. Bintrey puts in, watch in hand, "and I don't presume to offer any objection to your having got yourselves mixed together, in the corner there, like the three Graces. I merely remark that I think it's time we were moving. What are *your* sentiments on that subject, Mr. Ladle?"

"Clear, sir," replies Joey, with a gracious grin. "I'm clearer altogether, sir, for having lived so many weeks upon the surface. I never was half so long upon the surface afore, and it's done me a power of good. At Cripple Corner, I was too much below it. Atop of the Simpleton, I was a deal too high above it. I've found the medium here, sir. And if ever I take it in convivial, in all the rest of my days, I mean to do it this day, to the toast of 'Bless 'em both.'"

"I, too!" says Bintrey. "And now, Monsieur Voigt, let you and me be two men of Marseilles, and allons, marchons, arm-in-arm!"

They go down to the door, where others are waiting for them, and they go quietly to the church, and the happy marriage takes place. While the ceremony is yet in progress, the notary is called out. When it is finished, he has returned, is standing behind Vendale, and touches him on the shoulder.

"Go to the side door, one moment, Monsieur Vendale. Alone. Leave Madame to me."

At the side door of the church, are the same two men from the Hospice. They are snow-stained and travel-worn. They wish him joy, and then each lays his broad hand upon Vendale's breast, and one says in a low voice, while the other steadfastly regards him:

"It is here, monsieur. Your litter. The very same."

"My litter is here? Why?"

"Hush! For the sake of Madame. Your companion of that day——"

"What of him?"

The man looks at his comrade, and his comrade takes him up. Each keeps his hand laid earnestly on Vendale's breast.

"He had been living at the first Refuge, monsieur, for some days. The weather was now good, now bad."

"Yes?"

"He arrived at our Hospice the day before yesterday, and, having refreshed himself with sleep on the floor before the fire, wrapped in his cloak, was resolute to go on, before dark, to the next Hospice. He had a great fear of that part of the way, and thought it would be worse to-morrow."

"Yes?"

"He went on alone. He had passed the gallery, when an avalanche—like that which fell behind you near the Bridge of the Ganther——"

"Killed him?"

"We dug him out, suffocated and broken all to pieces! But, monsieur, as to Madame. We have brought him here on the litter to be buried. We must ascend the street outside. Madame must not see. It would be an accursed thing to bring the litter through the arch across the street, until Madame has passed through. As you descend, we who accompany the litter will set it down on the stones of the street the second to the right, and will stand before it. But do not let Madame turn her head towards the street the second to the right. There is no time to lose. Madame will be alarmed by your absence. Adieu!"

Vendale returns to his bride, and draws her hand through his unmaimed arm. A pretty procession awaits them at the main door of the church. They take their station in it, and descend the street amidst the ringing of the bells, the firing of the guns, the waving of the flags, the playing of the music, the shouts, the smiles, and tears, of the excited town. Heads are uncovered as she passes, hands are kissed to her, all the people bless her. "Heaven's benediction on the dear girl! See where she goes in her youth and beauty; she who so nobly saved his life!"

Near the corner of the street the second to the right, he speaks to her, and calls her attention to the windows on the opposite side. The corner well passed, he says: "Do not look round, my darling, for a reason that I have," and turns his head. Then, looking back along the street, he sees the litter and its bearers passing up alone under the arch, as he and she and their marriage train go down towards the shining valley.

MADE AND PRINTED BY THE GREYCAINE BOOK MANU-
FACTURING COMPANY LIMITED, WATFORD, HERTS.